Detroit Monographs in Musicology/Studies in Music, No. 28

Editor
J. Bunker Clark
University of Kansas

Music in the Theater, Church, and Villa

*Essays in Honor of
Robert Lamar Weaver and Norma Wright Weaver*

―――――――――――――――

EDITED BY

Susan Parisi

WITH COLLABORATION OF

Ernest Harriss II and Calvin M. Bower

―――――――――――――――

HARMONIE PARK PRESS • MICHIGAN • 2000

frontispiece:
Portrait of Robert Lamar Weaver and Norma Wright Weaver

Copyright 2000 by Harmonie Park Press

Printed and bound in the United States of America
Published by
Harmonie Park Press
23630 Pinewood
Warren, Michigan 48091

Production Manager, Elaine Gorzelski
Editor, J. Bunker Clark
Book design, Colleen McRorie
Typesetting, Colleen McRorie
Music typesetting, Ernest Harriss

Library of Congress Cataloging-in-Publication Data

Music in the theater, church, and villa : essays in honor of Robert Lamar Weaver and
Norma Wright Weaver / edited by Susan Parisi with collaboration of Ernest Harriss II and
Calvin M. Bower.
      p. cm. — (Detroit monographs in musicology/Studies in music ; no. 28)
  Includes bibliographical references and index.
  ISBN 0-89990-092-5
    1. Music—History and criticism. I. Weaver, Robert Lamar. II. Weaver, Norma Wright.
III. Parisi, Susan Helen. IV. Harriss, Ernest Charles II. V. Bower, Calvin M.
VI. Series.
ML55.W27 2000
780'.9—dc21   00-031977

Contents

List of Illustrations   vii

List of Music Examples   ix

List of Tables   xi

Preface   xiii

Tributes to Robert Lamar Weaver and Norma Wright Weaver   xv
  James Haar, Ernest Harriss II, Calvin M. Bower,
  Gerhard Herz, Marian Green, Susan Parisi

1	Alleluia, Confitemini Domino, Quoniam Bonus—An *Alleluia, Versus, Sequentia,* and Five *Prosae* Recorded in Aquitanian Sources Calvin M. Bower	3
2	The Tao of Singing: On the Schola Hungarica's Interpretation of the Nonantolan Sequences Lance W. Brunner	33
3	A Didactic Musical Treatise from the Late Middle Ages: Ebstorf, Klosterarchiv, Ms. V,3 Karl-Werner Gümpel	51
4	Some Sixteenth-Century "Thematic" Madrigal Anthologies James Haar	65
5	An Organ Building Project of the Sixteenth Century: The Large Organ of St. Vitus Cathedral in Prague Lilian P. Pruett	81
6	The Unknown Letters of Marco da Gagliano Edmond Strainchamps	89
7	The "Staging" of Genres Other Than Opera in Baroque Italy Carolyn Gianturco	113

8	Oil and Opera Don't Mix: The Biography of S. Aponal, a Seventeenth-Century Venetian Opera Theater JONATHAN E. GLIXON AND BETH L. GLIXON	131
9	The Influence of Architect and Playwright Sir John Vanbrugh and His Musical Taste on the London Stage, 1696-1711 CAROLINE S. FRUCHTMAN	145
10	The Correspondence of the Impresario Luca Casimiro degli Albizzi: An Index WILLIAM C. HOLMES	159
11	Johann Mattheson: The Enlightenment, *L'Éclaircissement*, or *Die Aufklärung* ERNEST HARRISS II	187
12	Mozart's Milanese Theatrical Works KATHLEEN KUZMICK HANSELL	195
13	Violence, Pathos, and Comedy in Salieri's *La finta scema* JOHN A. RICE	213
14	Alfieri and the Revitalization of Opera Seria MARITA PETZOLDT MCCLYMONDS	227
15	*Le finte pazzie* of Ferdinando Rutini: A Rediscovered Florentine Opera Buffa of the Late Eighteenth Century SUSAN PARISI	233
16	The Magical Moment in Mozart's *Zauberflöte*, and a Note on the Production of the Opera at the Teatro di S. Maria in Florence in 1818 MARCELLO DE ANGELIS	259
17	Historicism in Nineteenth-Century German Oratorio HOWARD E. SMITHER	263
18	Wanda Landowska and the Revival of the Harpsichord ALICE HUDNALL CASH	277
19	Stravinsky's *Scènes de Ballet* and Billy Rose's *The Seven Lively Arts*: The Abravanel Account JOHN SCHUSTER-CRAIG	285
20	Henry Wolking's Ballet *Forever Yesterday* JEANNE MARIE BELFY	291

Appendix
    Publications of Robert Lamar Weaver   307
    COMPILED BY RICHARD GRISCOM

Index   311

Contributors   325

List of Illustrations

Figures

2.1	*Congaudent angelorum chori*, Munich, Bayerische Staatsbibliothek, Ms. Clm 14083	36
2.2	*Congaudent angelorum chori*, Bamberg, Staatsbibliothek, Ms. lit. 5	37
2.3	*Victimae paschali laudes*, Einsiedeln, Stiftsbibliothek, Ms. 366, p. 17	38
2.4	*Sequentia* from St. Gall, Stiftsbibliothek, Ms. 484, pp. 274-75	39
2.5	Portion of the *Prosarium* and portion of the *Sequentiarium*, Paris, Bibliothèque Nationale, Ms. lat. 1121	40
2.6	*Ecce vicit*, Rome, Biblioteca Casanatense Ms. 1741	43
3.1	Pen-and-ink drawing of the Manus Guidonica in Ebstorf, Klosterarchiv Ms. V,3	55
3.2	Pen-and-ink drawing of the tonal system in Ebstorf, Klosterarchiv Ms. V,3	57
6.1	Letter of Marco da Gagliano to Ferdinando Gonzaga, 19 August 1608	92
6.2	Letter of Marco da Gagliano to Ferdinando Gonzaga, 9 November 1613	94
6.3	Letter of Marco da Gagliano to Ferdinando Gonzaga, 16 April 1610	97
6.4	Letter of Marco da Gagliano to Ferdinando Gonzaga, 4 January 1621/22	99
7.1	Catafalque for the funeral of Sig. Don Antonio Miraballo, Naples, 1695	121
7.2	Catafalque for the funeral of Philip V of Spain, Naples, 1746	122
7.3	Fireworks structure for the pregnancy of Empress Elizabeth of Austria, Naples, 1723	123
7.4	Fireworks structure for the coronation of King Charles of Sicily, Palermo, 1736	124
7.5	Stage set for Metastasio's *Componimento sacro per la festività dell SS. Natale* set to music by Giovanni Battista Costanza, Palazzo Ottoboni, Rome, 1727	125
7.6	Stage set for *Scherno festivo tra le ninfe di Partenope*, set to music by Domenico Sarro, Palazzo Reale, Naples, 1720	126
7.7	Stage set for Ranieri de' Calzabigi's *Il sogno d'Olimpia*, set to music by Giuseppe de Majo, Palazzo Reale, Naples, 1748	127
7.8	Stage set for Ranieri de' Calzabigi's *Il sogno d'Olimpia*, set to music by Giuseppe de Majo, Teatro San Carlo, Naples, 1748	128

Figures

7.9	Stanza d'Apollo, Villa Aldobrandini, Frascati (Rome) site of Giovan Filippo Apolloni's *La Circe*, set to music by Alessandro Stradella in 1668	129
12.1	From the autograph score of Mozart's *Lucio Silla* (at Cracow), act 2, f. 43v	202
12.2a	From a copy of the score of *Lucio Silla* (at Paris), act 2, f. 47r	203
12.2b	From the autograph score of *Lucio Silla* (at Cracow), act 2, f. 41v	203
12.3	From a copy of the score of *Lucio Silla* (at Turin), act 3, no. 21, aria "Pupille amate"	204
12.4	A detail from the painting by Pietro Domenico Olivero of a performance at Turin's Teatro Regio in 1740, showing the principal cello and double bass players flanking the first harpsichord	211
13.1	Box office receipts from the premiere of Salieri's *La finta scema*	214
15.1	Title page of manuscript containing Ferdinando Rutini's *Domine Deus*	236
15.2	Title page of manuscript score of Rutini's *Le finte pazzie*	238
15.3	Title page of the libretto of *Le finte pazzie*	239
15.4	Obbligato recitative "Numi che sento ecco tuona," from *Le finte pazzie*	247
15.5	Cavatina "Ombra tremenda, e cara del sopradetto Nino," from *Le finte pazzie*	248-49
15.6	Aria "Superba di me stessa," meas. 46-64, from *Le finte pazzie*	252
15.7	Aria "Superba di me stessa," meas. 91-102, from *Le finte pazzie*	253

List of Music Examples

Examples

1.1	Synoptic transcription of *Alleluia, Confitemini ... bonus* (Schlager, no. 354), with *sequentia*	5-8
1.2	Synoptic transcription of *prosae* for *sequentia Confitemini ... bonus*	15-18
1.3	*Sequentia cum prosa: Iubilate deo omnis arva*	25
1.4	*Sequentia cum prosa: Omnes iubilate*	26
1.5	*Sequentia cum prosa: Iam turma caelica*	27
1.6	*Sequentia cum prosa: Hoc pium recitat*	28
1.7	*Sequentia cum prosa: Pangamus carmina*	29
2.1	*Ecce vicit* (excerpt)	44
2.2	*Dic nobis* (excerpt)	44
2.3	*Summi triumphum* (excerpt)	45
2.4	*Stans a longe* (excerpt)	45
2.5	*Laeta mente*, with Alleluia *Exultate Deo*	46
2.6	*Sanctae crucis celebremus* (excerpt)	47
3.1	Ebstorf, Klosterarchiv, V,3, f. 201v, exercise	58
3.2	Ebstorf, Klosterarchiv, V,3, f. 202, exercise	59
3.3a	Ebstorf, Klosterarchiv, V,3, ff. 202v-203, exercise	59-60
3.3b	Ebstorf, Klosterarchiv, V,3, f. 203, exercise	61
13.1	Salieri, *La finta scema*, act 1, "Questa gamba è all'Ercolina," meas. 2-10	216
13.2	Salieri, *La finta scema*, act 1, "Quando ascolto il dolce moto," meas. 25-49	217
13.3	Salieri, *La finta scema*, act 1, "nonagenaria caratteristica sinfonia" accompanying Ortensia's entrance, meas. 1-16	218
13.4	Salieri, *La finta scema*, act 1, "Questa è un'aria d'Egiziello," meas. 5-141	220
13.5	Salieri, *La finta scema*, "Questa è un'aria d'Egiziello," meas. 97-120	221
13.6	Salieri, *La finta scema*, act 2, "Questo fioco urlo dolente," meas. 14-31	221

Examples

17.1	Friedrich Schneider, *Das Weltgericht*, ending	270
17.2	Schneider, *Das Weltgericht*, beginning of no. 9, "Sein Wort ist Wahrheit"	270
17.3	Liszt, *Christus*, beginning of no. 3, "Stabat mater speciosa"	272
17.4	Mendelssohn, *St. Paul*, chorale "Wir glauben all' an einen Gott"	273-74
17.5	Liszt, *Die Legende von der heiligen Elisabeth*:	275
	a. Antiphon for the feast of St. Elizabeth, as given by Liszt in the appendix	275
	b. From the "Einleitung"	275
	c. From no. 1, scene A	275
	d. From no. 2, scene D	275
20.1	Wolking, *Forever Yesterday*, flute 1, meas. 5-7	297
20.2	Wolking, *Forever Yesterday*, clarinet, meas. 67-70	297
20.3	Wolking, *Forever Yesterday*, horn, meas. 82-94	298
20.4	Wolking, *Forever Yesterday*, various winds, meas. 140-52	299
20.5	Wolking, *Forever Yesterday*, Interlude, "Flowing Water/Running Water," horn, meas. 1	299
20.6	Wolking, *Forever Yesterday*, horn, meas. 239-40	300
20.7	Wolking, *Forever Yesterday*, trumpet, meas. 242-46	300
20.8	Wolking, *Forever Yesterday*, bassoon, meas. 265-69	301
20.9	Wolking, *Forever Yesterday*, Interlude, "The Wind Is Wandering," soprano, meas. 1-4	301
20.10	Wolking, *Forever Yesterday*, clarinet, meas. 373-76	303
20.11	Wolking, *Forever Yesterday*, clarinet, meas. 396-97	303

List of Tables

Tables

2.1	Sequences from Nonantolan Repertory recorded by Schola Hungarica [Quint 903084]	42
12.1	Mozart's Early Dramatic Works	196
12.2	Mozart's Milanese Casts	201
12.3	*Liaison des scènes* in Mozart's *Mitridate*	206
12.4	*Liaison des scènes* in Mozart's *Ascanio in Alba*	207
12.5	*Liaison des scènes* in Mozart's *Lucio Silla*	208
12.6	Disposition of Opera Orchestras at Turin, Milan, Rome, and Naples, 1737-1845	210
15.1	Inventory of Scenes in Rutini's *Le finte pazzie o sia la pupilla bizzarra*	242-43
15.2	Structural Outline of Lindora's aria "Superba di me stessa" (act 1, scene 8) in *Le finte pazzie*	250-51
15.3	Structural Outline of the Act 1 Finale of *Le finte pazzie*	254-55
15.4	Structural Outline of the Act 2 Finale of *Le finte pazzie*	257

Preface

The plan of producing this volume took shape a little over two years ago in conversations with Calvin Bower, James Haar, and Ernest Harriss. At that time, as Robert Weaver's colleague at the University of Louisville, I had been thinking about how his friends, colleagues, and former students might pay tribute to his and Norma Weaver's life-long commitment to the pursuit of musicological research and publication, and give recognition to the many contributions they have made to academia over the course of careers spanning more than forty years. After considering the various possibilities—book, conference, lecture, library acquisition—it seemed to us that the most fitting and enduring testimonial would be a volume of essays. We broached the idea of producing such a collection for the occasion of Robert Weaver's seventy-fifth birthday with Elaine Gorzelski, president of Harmonie Park Press, and J. Bunker Clark, the press's music editor, and, since Harmonie Park Press is the publisher of the Weavers' two-volume *A Chronology of Music in the Florentine Theater*, we were especially pleased that our formal proposal was accepted. The musical interests of Robert Weaver and Norma Weaver are decidedly wide-ranging, as are the subjects of the dissertations Bob has guided and the many reviews he has written. Hence it was decided the essays in the present collection would not be confined to music of the Baroque and Classic eras, the focus of much of Bob's and Norma's distinguished published work, but rather would reflect the divergent interests and perspectives of the contributors.

This volume could not have been completed without the assistance of a number of individuals, whom I would like to thank here. Ernest Harriss, always generous in his support, spent countless hours preparing camera-ready copy of all of the musical examples and contributed to the portrait of Robert Weaver as mentor in the Introduction. Calvin Bower gave freely of his time to consider many other details of the production of the volume. He and James Haar, who provided equally valuable advice, both offer special words of tribute to the Weavers. Gerhard Herz and Marian Green also contributed importantly to the Introduction, sharing personal recollections of their relationships with the Weavers. Richard Griscom compiled the bibliography of their publications.

Warm thanks are owed to the staff of the Music Library of the University of Louisville, and in particular to Joy Stephens, who provided assistance with eighteenth-century materials in the library's special collection. Marina Karem of the Department of Art History, University of Louisville, provided a fine and much appreciated translation of one essay in the volume. I am indebted to Shirley Marie Watts, music librarian at Vanderbilt University, who also kindly supplied important information. And it is a pleasure to express my very sincere thanks to the University of Illinois Research Board and its Graduate College Scholars Program, for support of this project in its final stages.

I wish to convey my deep appreciation to the staff of Harmonie Park Press: in particular to Elaine Gorzelski for her backing of the volume and her constructive assistance through the months of its gestation, and J. Bunker Clark for his careful attention to detail and editorial rigor, from which the essays in the volume benefited. Lastly, I would like also to acknowledge Colleen McRorie, typographer, and the production staff for their valuable assistance in seeing the volume into print.

Susan Parisi

Urbana, 1998

Tributes to Robert Lamar Weaver and Norma Wright Weaver

This collection of essays honors Robert Lamar Weaver and Norma Wright Weaver in the year of their seventy-fifth birthdays. It is offered as a token of affection and esteem from a number of their many friends, colleagues, and former students who admire their scholarship and treasure their friendship.

Born in Dahlonega, Georgia, and raised in Ducktown, Tennessee, Robert Weaver attended Emory University until the outbreak of the Second World War. From 1942 to 1946 he was stationed in Europe with the United States Army Signal Corps Intelligence where his job was "to make sense of"—as he lightly puts it—German radio emissions sent in code. While in Paris toward the end of the war, he studied harpsichord with Marcelle Delacour and harmony at the Conservatoire. At Columbia University after the war, he completed a Bachelor of Arts degree *cum laude* in 1948, followed in 1952 by a Master of Arts degree in musicology under Paul Henry Lang, with a thesis on operatic instrumental ensembles before and after Monteverdi's *Orfeo*. During the Columbia years he also studied musicology with Erich Hertzmann, composition with Otto Luening and Elliot Carter, and organ with Carl Weinrich. Bob and Norma met in New York in the mid-1940s as members of the King's Chapel Choir. A native New Yorker, Norma graduated from Hunter College with a Bachelor's degree in music and English in 1943, and took a Master of Arts degree in music and music education at Columbia University the following year. They were married in King's Chapel in 1948. In 1950 Norma received tenure at Passaic Junior High School in Passaic, New Jersey.

Bob went on to doctoral work under William Newman and Glen Haydon at the University of North Carolina, earning the Ph.D. degree in 1958 with a dissertation on Florentine comic operas of the seventeenth century. A fellow graduate student was Jim Haar, who reminisces below about those years. Bob and Norma spent 1952-53 in Florence, Bob having been awarded a Fulbright scholarship. His teaching career began at Catawba College in Salisbury, North Carolina, in 1955, the year before their son was born. He then taught at George Peabody College for Teachers, Nashville, Tennessee from 1960 until 1975, except for the year 1966-67 spent in Vienna on a Fulbright Research Fellowship. Among his doctoral students were Edward Barrett (d. 1997), and Calvin Bower and Ernest Harriss, who also share their memories below. In these years Norma worked as an editor at the Vanderbilt University Press, and in various administrative positions. Due to typical Weaver modesty, it is not widely known that the South-Central Chapter of the American Musicological Society owes its existence to Robert Lamar Weaver, who founded it in 1963.

In 1975, the Weavers moved to the University of Louisville School of Music, where Bob joined Gerhard Herz, a member of the Music History faculty since 1938, and Karl-Werner Gümpel, who had arrived in 1969. Norma served as a staff accompanist in the School. Reminiscences by Gerhard Herz about their friendship will be found later in this section. Under Bob's chairmanship, Louisville enrolled the first students in a cooperative doctoral program in musicology with the University of Kentucky. Essays by three graduates of this program, Jeanne Belfy, Alice Cash, and John Schuster-Craig, appear in this volume. The Louisville years were productive ones: volume 1 of *A Chronology of Music in the Florentine Theater 1590-1750*, written in collaboration with Norma, was published in 1978. 1981 saw the publication of a Festschrift for Gerhard Herz. Among other distinctions, the Weavers received a three-year NEH Research Resources Grant, and Bob received a Gladys Krieble Delmas Foundation Grant, in support of research for volume 2 of the Florentine

Theater chronology, 1751-1800, subsequently published in 1993. Bob was a visiting professor at the University of North Carolina in spring 1980, and won the President's Award for Outstanding Research and Creativity, University of Louisville, in 1987. Though not one to actually retire, in 1989 he nominally retired from teaching to devote more time to research.

Robert Weaver's major scholarly writings have dealt with Italian music, with particular emphasis on the history, sources, and performance of Florentine opera from the late sixteenth to the end of the eighteenth century. For over forty-five years he has engaged in archival research on that subject, undoubtedly the most ambitious and sustained effort in the field of early opera. The results, disseminated in articles in the principal journals and in two books, have made an invaluable contribution to our understanding of Florentine culture and society, and have fundamentally changed our view of the development and patronage of opera in Italy. The two volumes on the Florentine theater written with Norma Weaver present a new interpretation of the historical order of the Florentine dramaturgical academies (vol. 1) and a clearer definition of the Leopoldine School of Tuscan music (vol. 2). His contributions to *New Grove Opera*, including articles on composers, performers, and librettists of the Leopoldine School provide a considerably expanded view of the place and era.

One of Robert Weaver's most significant achievements has been the discovery and acquisition for the University of Louisville of the Ricasoli Collection, the largest collection of Florentine music of the eighteenth and early nineteenth centuries outside of Florence itself. This library, which he saved from dispersal, had belonged to the prominent Ricasoli family of Florence, and comprises over 450 manuscripts and early prints of music, dating between 1738 and 1820. Among the composers represented are Johann Christian Bach, Beethoven, Cherubini, Cimarosa, Clementi, Handel, Haydn, Mayr, Mozart, Paer, Paisiello, Pergolesi, Pleyel, Rossini, as well as the principal Florentine composers of the time, including Felici, Giuliani, Moneta, Rutini, and Sborgi. In 1989, to mark the arrival of this treasure in the United States, Bob hosted an international festival-conference in Louisville. Marian Green was teaching at the University of Louisville then; in the section of tributes that follows, she remembers Bob's panache and leadership in that endeavor.

It does not appear that Bob and Norma will be retiring from scholarly projects any time soon, though they do have other passions—grandchildren, tennis, and the Louisville Bach Society Chorus, to name but three. In the last few years Bob has overseen the preparation of the Ricasoli Conference proceedings, and the cataloging of that collection. His detective work has revealed the location of most of the items previously thought lost; the collection is now 93% complete. And through his intercessions—in the form of "development" of support, and persistent investigatory research across two continents—the University of Louisville Music Library has continued to acquire other rare music manuscripts and prints of the seventeenth and eighteenth centuries.

*   *   *   *   *

The research of Robert and Norma Weaver is impeccable, and I have long admired it. I also admire Bob's unfailing sense of decency and hold in highest regard his advocacy of respect for collegiality and due process within the academy. And I value deeply his and Norma's friendship. It is thus the greatest pleasure for me to join all those here represented in offering to Bob and Norma this volume of tribute, and in this small way celebrating all their contributions, which have changed the face of Italian studies.

SUSAN PARISI

I first met Bob and Norma Weaver in September 1950, in Chapel Hill, where we had arrived to begin graduate work. I was fresh out of college, shy and awkward in a way that I don't think twenty-one year-olds are any more. I needed friends but wasn't very good at making them. People in Chapel Hill were in general open and welcoming, but this was my first experience of living in the South, and it was in strong contrast with my undergraduate experience in an urban New England milieu (for which I nonetheless was homesick). The first-year students sort of hung together, and I slowly began to feel less strange. Most of the other new students seemed to be acclimating themselves faster than I.

But nobody could equal the Weavers, who in short order seemed to get to know not only all of us, but all the older students as well, and even people from other departments. It was as if they had been living in Chapel Hill for years.

Bob was of course a Southerner, though not a North Carolinian, and most recently a New Yorker. He and Norma were a bit older, with initial stages of graduate work already behind them. But this didn't explain it. Bob was in fact a bit shy himself, and Norma let it be known that nothing in the Southern Part of Heaven could match her native New York, either her Staten Island childhood or the Upper East Side of her college years. What did it was the Bob-and-Norma combination, a uniquely successful blend—did it then and does it now. I saw more of Bob as a matter of course, but soon came to know Norma as well as I knew him. There were other married graduate students, but one met the spouses only once in a while. Not so with the Weavers: always the welcoming of hosts, they often invited me and many others to their apartment for their trademark cocktail hour. How many glasses of Weaver sherry, how many mouthfuls of Weaver chips-and-dip I consumed, how many rubbers of Weaver bridge I played during my two student years in Chapel Hill I blush to think. Of course we talked a lot as well, of musicology and musicologists, or of cabbages and kings. Bob's gentle irony and Norma's vigorous forthrightness combined to draw me out of my shell, and in their presence everyone seemed more open, more genuinely sociable. Their companionship was a big part of what being a student at Carolina came to be—more fun than I could have imagined.

After I left Chapel Hill in 1954 we saw much less of each other, and for a while it was just Christmas cards and an occasional get-together at an AMS meeting. But we never lost touch. Bob and Norma were such naturally good friends, and so inimitably themselves, that we simply picked up where we had left off. However long the interval might have been since we had last seen one another, the first chip-and-dip erased it. After I returned to Chapel Hill in 1978 (Bob, after years at Peabody in Nashville, was now at the University of Louisville), we began to see one another more often. And there was a memorable term in the early 80s when they were back in Chapel Hill. Of late we have been meeting at their charming wintering spot in Gulf Coast Florida.

I admire and respect Bob's intelligence and sensitivity, evident in all his scholarly work, whether the subject be sixteenth-century orchestration, Schoenberg, or his special field, Italian opera of the seventeenth and eighteenth centuries. But wait: the biggest Weaver achievement, the monumental study of opera in Florence from 1590 to 1800, is a joint Bob-and-Norma undertaking, the product of years of patient collaborative work. It is a great pleasure to salute them together as scholars, even as I treasure a friendship of what is now approaching fifty years' duration.

Jim Haar

Upon returning to academe in the fall of 1963 after my second stint in the U.S. Army, I remember how eager I felt to become a part of the intellectual atmosphere. Little did I know my life would be changed—profoundly and forever—by events that were to occur at Peabody College during the next six years. Had it come up at the time, I would have laughed at the thought that a musicologist on the faculty would be a key agent in those events. Changing universities had taken me from the certainty of a large state university's focused curriculum, designed to prepare future band directors, to the unpredictability of Peabody's more interdisciplinary curriculum, and to its more intimate environment. At Peabody I soon found my values and career plans challenged, and it became clear that teaching public school children the rudiments of music was not the particular challenge with which I wanted to deal for the next thirty or more years. The field of musicology, on the other hand, intrigued me. With the encouragement—more than anyone else—of Robert Lamar Weaver, I began taking those courses that would prepare me for the life of the "scholar-teacher." Professor Weaver's devotion to his work and to his students convinced me, slowly and almost imperceptibly, that I would find life much more interesting as a musicologist. And about that he was dead right of course. Bob Weaver's continuous support of my work and of my aspirations during those years, made this decision easy. Without his steadfast support, though, I could never have stayed the course. It is thus the greatest pleasure for me now, thirty-five years later, as a colleague, and as a friend of Bob and Norma, to thank him for the invaluable model he has given me, and has given the many others over the years who, like me, have been inspired by his guidance and his scholarship.

Ernie Harriss

I am here to contribute in some small way to the celebration of the scholarly careers of Robert Lamar Weaver and Norma Wright Weaver. I hear some talk about retirement. But as a student of Bob Weaver, I believe little of such hear-say; rather I'll try to bring the components of these rumors into some critical perspective.

When I was asked to participate in this celebration, I first thought I should appear with a book of imposing size, powdered with stage dust, walk to the podium, and get my first response from you as I blew the dust off the book. I would then proceed to read to you an ancient Florentine comic opera libretto about a young Roberto from the southern provinces, a tenor, who moved north to the big city, met, fell in love with, and married the energetic and dynamic Norma, a mezzo soprano, and then we would follow the many adventures of this pair as they contrived to wit their way through a variety of intrigues, musical and scholarly of course, in such complex societies as Nashville, Louisville, and even Italy. The end of the first act, which is about where I think we are now, would end with a duet for these two to a text something like:

> So much done,
> Wasn't it fun,
> So let's begin
> all over again!

But then I realized that this approach to tribute would be one that I first experienced as a graduate student in Nashville, an act that Bob Weaver put on to prepare that sophisticated audience for a performance of excerpts from a Melani opera we—the Collegium Musicum—were to present at Peabody College. As you can see, even attempts by a loyal student to pay some light-hearted tribute to his professor are, inevitably, shaped by the rhetoric and humor of the professor himself.

So as I realized that I could not possibly approach Bob Weaver in wit, I decided to celebrate three aspects of his career that have shaped his own work as well as that of his students, aspects which are particularly important to call to mind on this particular occasion. Following the Weaver tradition I shall be brief, hoping that focus rather than prolixity will leave you with the sharper image.

The first aspect of Bob's work and character I would present is his ceaseless critical, questioning approach to both scholarly and pedagogical problems. It was through the experience of having Bob Weaver as major professor and dissertation advisor that I first experienced this well-honed side, or should I say "edge," of his character. No amount of enthusiasm or sheer weight of research can distract him from the central problem of an argument or thesis. And he has always been able to cut through any distraction or elaboration to that center, and to confront the person or problem with the probing question—a question usually leaving one speechless for a moment. If you happen to be the student or advisee, these moments are always accomplished with a twinkle in the eye, but never with the personal put-down so characteristic of much graduate instruction. I feel the intensity and character of Bob's critical edge is perhaps his greatest legacy to his students and colleagues.

The second aspect of this career I would celebrate here is the role played by Norma Wright Weaver. No one who has spent much time with Bob and Norma can fail to recognize the intellectual and professional partnership which had added grace to an already beautiful marriage. Norma and Bob studied at Columbia together under Paul Henry Lang. Norma is a professional musicologist in her own right, and she has always been an active practicing musician as well as a scholarly partner and critic of her husband. (She has even been known to voice criticism in matters other than the scholarly.) The social evenings with the Weavers enjoyed by students and colleagues, many memorable occasions of making music and lively conversations about our discipline, the renewals of friendships and critical discussions shared at annual meetings, all are important to those of us who have worked under and with Bob. And Norma's presence has been a vital part of this Weaver tradition. Her influence in our discipline goes well beyond the not-insignificant role she played as co-author with Bob of the monumental two-volume *A Chronology of Music in the Florentine Theater, 1590-1800*.

And Florence leads me to the third aspect of the Weaver career that should be celebrated, particularly at the University of Louisville: that is, the central role Italy has played in all of his work. Interest in Italian dramatic music manifested itself in Bob's master's thesis, continued in his dissertation, and has been the central theme of most of his publications. Our friend and colleague James Haar often speaks of the northern Renaissance musicians changing their character after having been "kissed by the Mediterranean sun," and I like to think Bob Weaver's work has been affected by the best of Italy just as he has shaped our appreciation of some of the most notable of Italian music. Had Italian culture not been the center of Bob's interest he would never have discovered those few notable scores in the bookshop of Florence, and the Ricasoli Collection would never have come to the University of Louisville. The discovery and rescue of this musical monument must be considered one of the most distinguishing achievements of Bob Weaver's career, and it has brought a unique distinction to the University of Louisville which it would otherwise never have achieved.

Critical insight, Norma, a love of the study of Italian musical culture—these three always come to mind when I think of Bob Weaver. I think these three are particularly important to keep in mind as we hear these rumors of retirement, for these three transcend any particular job or even any particular profession. All of us who know and admire Bob know these aspects of his vocation will remain with him, and thus with us. I ask you to celebrate with me these riches we all share. Perhaps that Italian libretto I first considered is not such a bad idea. It seems as if I do hear some tunes coming from these two, not only about how good it has been, but about how much remains to be done. We all look forward to celebrating that work as well.

CALVIN BOWER

Born in the year Gustav Mahler died and Richard Strauss conducted the world premiere of his *Rosenkavalier*, I have now reached the almost biblical age of eighty-seven. It is my state of health that no longer allows me to contribute an article to the Festschrift for Robert L. and Norma Weaver.

As colleagues who specialized in investigating music of the Baroque era, we became friends when Bob founded the South-Central Chapter of the American Musicological Society. From 1963 onward we met at the Society's annual conferences and were stimulated by the findings and discoveries we presented in the papers of these meetings. It was the respect that these papers and their subsequent publications earned which led to our mutual friendship. This was demonstrated in 1975 when I was able to invite Bob Weaver to join the faculty of the Music History Department at the University of Louisville. When I retired three years later it was only logical that Bob, whose organizational capabilities had always been outstanding, would take over the chairmanship of the department.

One of Bob Weaver's greatest contributions to the University of Louisville during these years was, without doubt, his acquisition of the Ricasoli Collection for the School of Music. This eighteenth- and nineteenth-century music library of the Florentine Ricasoli family is now the prized possession of the Music Library.

Since I am unable to contribute an article to his Festschrift, I recently gave Bob a taped copy of the Distinguished Lecture "The Changing Image of Bach (Four Decades of New Findings)" I was chosen to present in 1978. This was the first time that Music History, a sine-qua-non subject in the Humanities Division since 1946, had been selected for the award by the University's College of Arts and Sciences. I would like to share this tribute with my friend Bob Weaver, without whose contribution this honor would not have been bestowed on our field of specialization.

GERHARD HERZ

My association with Robert Weaver began in 1980, shortly after my arrival in Louisville, where my husband had accepted a teaching position at the University. I knew of Bob through his work, but we had never met. In an effort to establish some professional contact in an unfamiliar city, I telephoned the Department of Music and made an appointment to speak with Bob, who was then serving as chairman. I shall always be grateful for his cordiality on that occasion and later for his efforts to include me in the life of the department by appointing me an adjunct assistant professor. He and Norma were also gracious hosts at lively parties in their home, where we became acquainted with the Louisvillian worlds of music and academe.

When I founded the *Journal of Musicology* in 1981, Bob agreed to join the editorial board and was strongly supportive in *JM*'s early years. I have vivid memories of Norma and Bob reading proof with me for the first issue of the journal in late fall 1981.

Realizing how basic to the strength of a musicology department was the quality of its library, Bob succeeded in significantly expanding the library's holdings. In this regard, surely his most impressive accomplishment was his acquisition for the School of Music of the large music collection (some 450 items) formerly belonging to a noble Florentine family, the Ricasoli, who still occupy a Renaissance palace in via Maggio in Florence where the music library lay in a cabinet forgotten for almost two centuries. The Ricasoli had served the Grand Dukes of Tuscany long before the last Medici, Gian Gastone, died in 1737. But the bulk of the collection dates from the reigns of Francesco I of Lorraine (1737-65), Pietro Leopoldo of Austria (1765-90), and Ferdinando III of Hapsburg-Lorraine (1790-1824). The musical items reflect the Florentine tradition, as well as connections with Napoleonic France.

Only through Bob's talents as a musicological sleuth was the collection retained intact. It had been divided into lots that were being advertised and sold separately by a Florentine bookseller, when Bob came to realize that they were all part of one library. Then (with the ever-present help of Norma) he raised funds to buy the collection and then spent great effort and ingenuity in convincing Italian officials to release for export these important documents of their cultural heritage.

To celebrate the arrival in Louisville of this rich array of primary source material, Bob organized an interdisciplinary inaugural conference entitled, "Patrons, Politics, and Art in Italy, 1738-1859." The conference took place in March of 1989, and over a five-day period presented papers by ten American and eight Italian scholars, on topics relating in various ways to material in the Ricasoli Collection. In addition, four concerts of music from the collection were performed by faculty and students from the School of Music. Several plenary sessions focused on the challenges of making available to researchers music and other primary source material still in private hands.

Owing to Bob's consummate planning, diplomacy, and charm, strengthened always by Norma's inimitable ability for organization, her unflagging energy, and impeccable common sense, the conference was a great success. A volume containing the eighteen individual papers will be published shortly by Harmonie Park Press. The collection itself, now catalogued and available to researchers worldwide, will stand as a significant legacy from Robert Weaver to the musicological discipline, and testimony to his abiding love for Florentine music and culture.

MARIAN GREEN

Music in the Theater, Church, and Villa

Essays in Honor of
Robert Lamar Weaver and Norma Wright Weaver

1

Alleluia, Confitemini Domino, Quoniam Bonus—
An *Alleluia, Versus, Sequentia*, and Five *Prosae* Recorded in Aquitanian Sources

CALVIN M. BOWER

Few moments in medieval liturgy are comparable in dramatic intensity to the return of the *alleluia*—banished from its position before the Gospel by the severe *tractus* since Septuagesima Sunday. For nine weeks, a period extending over the three Sundays of pre-Lent plus the forty ferial days and six Sundays of Lent, no *alleluia* has been said or sung, then it unfolds as the first and final symbol of the Easter mystery, sung with the verse "Confitemini Domino, quoniam bonus" the first and final verse of Psalm 117, the psalm from which the Easter gradual, "Haec dies" and its verses will be taken throughout Easter week.[1] To paraphrase some of the texts that will be examined in this study, this *alleluia* and the musical entities associated with it "thunder" the arrival of Easter.

The present study will examine the *alleluia* of the Paschal Vigil and its *versus*, along with a *sequentia* and five *prosae*, as recorded in eight Aquitanian sources from the late tenth and eleventh centuries.[2] The basic melodies and texts have appeared in previous publications.[3] Moreover, the sequence melody has been examined and analyzed

---

[1] The most thorough and enlightened discussion of this venerable *Alleluia* is James W. McKinnon, *The Advent Project*, chapter 10, "The Alleluia," subsection entitled "The Easter Vigil Alleluia" (forthcoming). McKinnon considers "Confitemini Domino, quoniam bonus" one of the most ancient of alleluias, and points out (n. 31) its affinity with the tonality of the fourth-century Sanctus discussed by Kenneth Levy in "The Byzantine Sanctus and its Modal Tradition in East and West," *Annales musicologiques* 6 (1958/63): 7-67. The association of this melody with the ancient tone of the Roman mass was first noted by Peter Wagner, *Gregorianische Formenlehre, Einführung in die gregorianischen Melodien* (Leipzig, 1921), part 3, pp. 397-98, n. 2.

[2] The codices are listed below, along with the abbreviations that will be used. The dates and probable centers of origin are given in David Hiley, *Western Plainchant: A Handbook* (Oxford: Oxford University Press, 1993). For complete bibliographic citations, see the appendix at the end of this study.

Paris, Bibliothèque nationale, lat. 1118	abbr: **Pa1118**	late 10th	Auch?
Paris, Bibliothèque nationale, lat. 1084	abbr: **Pa1084**	late 10th	?
London, British Library, Harley 4951	abbr: **LoHar4951**	mid-11th	Toulouse
Paris, Bibliothèque nationale, lat. 1121	abbr: **Pa1121**	ca. 1000	Saint-Martial
Paris, Bibliothèque nationale, lat. 1138 and	abbr: **Pa1138**	early 11th	Limoges
Paris, Bibliothèque nationale, lat. 1338	abbr: **Pa1338**	early 11th	Limoges
(these two codices considered a single source)			
Paris, Bibliothèque nationale, lat. 903	abbr: **Pa903**;	11th, first half	Saint-Yrieix
Paris, Bibliothèque nationale, lat. 776	abbr: **Pa776**	late 11th	Gaillac (Albi)
Paris, Bibliothèque nationale, nouv. acq. lat. 1871	abbr: **Pa/na1871**	late 11th	Aurillac?

For further discussion and description of these sources, see Dreves, *AH7*, 1889, pp. 4-10; Crocker, "Proses at Saint Martial" (diss.), 1957; Crocker, "Repertoire of Proses," 1958; Chailley, "Tropaires," 1957; Chailley, *L'École de Saint Martial*, 1960; Steiner, "Prosulae . . . Pa1118," 1969; and Planchart and Fuller, "St Martial" in *NG*, 1980. Concerning Pa/na1871 see Daux, *Pa/na1871*, 1901, and cf. Bannister, "Pa/na1871," 1903.

[3] The melody of the *sequentia* with the text *Lux de luce* was first discussed [by Herbert] in Paléographie musicale, 14 (*Le Codex 10673 de la Bibliothèque Vaticane fond latin (XIe siècle): Graduel Bénéventain*, Solesmes, 1931), pp. 437-39; in these pages the relation of the melody with a verse of the offertory *Gressus meos* is also mentioned, as is the Beneventan *prosula* for the Offertory melisma (cf. p. 214, n. 4). Husmann, "Alleluia,..."

both as a *sequentia* and a wandering melisma,[4] nevertheless, the editions that contain the five *prosae* central to this study are less than satisfactory, and no edition of the five *prosae* set to the sequence melody has been published. Furthermore, I hold that new insights into the complex of melody and texts as a whole can be gained by bringing together the various manifestations of these entities as they appeared in a rather unified geographic area and temporal period. The inflection of the sequence melody by the prose texts may lead to a fresh awareness of the musical structure and character of the melody, and the texts themselves may in turn shed light on the nature of the liturgical moment that this entire complex celebrates.

I: The Alleluia, Verse, and Sequence

In most liturgical books that contain musical elements for the Mass, the melodies we call sequences and their texts are found in fascicles (or books) separated from the traditional contents of the Graduale (i.e., introit, gradual, alleluia, offertory, communion).[5] In three Aquitanian graduals, however, all dating from the eleventh century, an extended melisma is found following the alleluia and verse "Confitemini Domino, quoniam bonus."[6] While the third member of this complex—the extended melisma—is not labeled in any way,[7] it obviously fits the description of the *sequentia*[8] written by Amalarius in the early ninth century.[9] Moreover, the same melody is found in four *sequentiaria* approximately contemporary with the three graduals. Example 1.1 presents the *alleluia, versus*, and *sequentia* recorded in these codices, and the melodies and texts transcribed and analyzed in this example will serve as the basis for the following discussion.[10]

1956 (pp. 21-22) discussed the Aquitanian tradition, pointed out the occurrence of the *sequentia* in Pa776 and Pa903, and briefly discussed the five *prosae* that are central to this study. De Goede, *Utrecht Prosarium,* 1965 (pp. xxi-xxii) prints the Italian *Lux de luce,* and compares it with the *sequentia* as it appears in Pa903 and the setting of *Iubilate deo omnis arva* from Pa1084. He also mentions the *prosula Iniustitia longe sit a terra* for the offertory verse from *Gressus meos*. Schlager, *Alleluia-Melodien,* 1968 (pp. 83-84) presents an edition of *Alleluia, Confitemini Domino* with the *sequentia* from Pa903. Steiner, "Prosulae . . . Pa1118," 1969 (pp. 384-86) carefully examines the *prosulae* of *Gressus meos* as found in Pa1118, and she offers editions of both *Iniusticia longe sit a terra* and *Iniusticia gehenna vicina*. Levy, "*Lux de luce,*" 1971 thoroughly discusses the Italian tradition of the melody and its relation to the offertory verse and its *prosula*. Finally Kohrs, *Die aparallelen Sequenzen,* 1978 (p. 158) prints an edition of *Lux de luce* after two Beneventan manuscripts (Bibl. cap. VI. 34 and VI. 40). The above survey shows that the Beneventan tradition has received considerably more attention than the Aquitanian.

[4] See the comparative analysis of two versions of *Lux de luce,* the *sequentia* from LoHar4851, Pa776, Pa903, Pa/na1871, the Offertory *prosula,* and the *prosae Iubilate Deo omnis arva, Pangamus carmina,* and *Hoc pium recita* in Levy, "*Lux de luce,*" 1971, p. 46. See also the thorough, insightful analysis of the *prosulae* for this melody in Björkwall and Haug, "Texting Melismas," 1993, an article that is essential reading in conjunction with the present study.

[5] See Schlager, "Beobachtungen," 1984, for a description of eastern and western sources from the same period as the sources used in this study.

[6] Two alleluia verses begin with the word "Confitemini": "Confitemini Domino et invocate," and "Confitemini Domino quoniam bonus." Karl-Heinz Schlager's *Thematischer Katalog der ältesten Alleluia-Melodien aus Handschriften des 10. und 11. Jahrhunderts, ausgenommen das ambrosianische, alt-römische und alt-spanische Repertoire*, Erlanger Arbeiten zur Musikwissenschaft, Band 2 (Munich, 1965) records "Confitemini Domino et invocate" as melody no. 58; Schlager's *Katalog* records two melodies that contain the verse "Confitemini Domino quoniam bonus": nos. 254 and 277. Melody no. 254 is the subject of this study; and when I subsequently refer to "Confitemini . . . bonus" in this study, melody no. 254 is implied.

[7] The rubric "unde supra" is found in Pa776, and the melisma begins a new line. In Pa903 and LoHar4159, the extended melisma follows the verse (marked with the traditional V) on the same line.

[8] I shall use the Latin term *sequentia* to refer to the extended, untexted melisma, the term *prosa* to designate the text set to a *sequentia*.

[9] Amalarius, *Liber officialis* III,16,3 (*Amalarii episcopi Opera liturgica omnia*, ed. Hanssens, Studi e Testi 139 [Citta del Vaticano, 1948], vol. 2, p. 304).

[10] Neumatic groupings are indicated with slurs in my transcriptions, although it is often difficult to determine neumatic groups in Aquitanian notation. The liquescent forms, the *quilisma,* and the *pressus* are indicated with comparable symbols.

Example 1.1. Synoptic transcription of *Alleluia, Confitemini . . . bonus* (Schlager no. 354).

Alleluia:

Pa903:76v — Al-le - lu - ia. all-b
Pa776:67v — Al-le - lu - ia. all-b
LoHar4159:214r — Al-le - lu - ia. all-b

Versus:

Pa903 — Con-fi-te-mi-ni do - mi - no, quo - ni-am bo - nus,
Pa776 — Con-fi-te-mi-ni do - mi - no, quo - ni-am bo - nus,
LoHar4159 — Con-fi-te-mi-ni do - mi - no, quo - ni-am bo - nus,

Pa903 — quo - ni-am in se-cu - lum mi - se-ricor - di - a e - ius.
Pa776 — quo - ni-am in se-cu - lum mi - se-ricor - di - a e - ius.
LoHar4159 — quo - ni-am in se-cu - lum mi - se-ricor - di - a e - ius.

Continued

Example 1.1.—*Continued*

Sequentia:

Example 1.1.—*Continued*

A. *Alleluia*

The melody of the *alleluia* found in our three sources is remarkably stable. While the G[11] that follows the opening gesture varies in number of repercussions, the pitch sequence of the three sources is identical. The *alleluia* divides itself into two commas,[12] which I have labeled "**all-a**" and "**all-b**." The opening comma rises from **D** to **G**, then elaborates the **G** with pitches **a** and **b**. The only melodic skip after the opening gesture is that from **b** returning to **G**; one begins to hear **G** as the final (tonic), and to sense that **b** desires to rise to **c**. The opening comma (**all-a**) closes with an "open" gesture—the rise to **a**. The opening gesture of **all-b** complements **all-a** in two ways: 1) it opens up the musical ambitus to the **C**—approached by a skip in the opening two pitches—thus completing the fourth required to resolve the **b**; 2) it reiterates the **a** that closed **all-a**, then finally resolves it to the final. This comma makes it clear that the functions outlined by the tetrachord **G-a-b-c** are the principal pitches in what has been heard and in what is about to unfold. The opening **D** remains somewhat unresolved in the memory, for the pitches that fill out the fourth between **D** and **G** have not sounded.

The basic tonal content of the second comma of the *alleluia* will play a crucial function throughout the three parts of this complex. It forms the final comma of the *versus* in one source (Pa903), probably in a second source (Pa776, see below), and it is implied in **a2**, **b2**, and **d2** of the *sequentia*. Moreover, the cadential gesture of **all-b**—the reiterated **a**, approached after a high **c**, resolving to the final—appears as the basic cadence in three commas in the *versus* (**vs-1b**, **vs-2b**, and **vs-2d´´**).

B. *Versus*

The transmission of the *versus* is likewise stable—at least until the closing comma. The period that forms the verse is created from two major distinctions, each defined by textual clauses, and each unfolding in four commas (or two colons—marked by ticks on the staves following **vs-1b** and **vs-2b**), again shaped by the content of the text. The pitch content of the **vs-1a** is identical with that of the *alleluia*, while **vs-1b** ascends to **d**, which is essentially used to elaborate **c** in this comma. In **vs-1c** and **vs-1d** the **d** becomes structural, for it is itself elaborated in **vs-1d**, and the tetrachord of the *alleluia* becomes expanded to a pentachord (**G-a-b-c-d**). The initial colons of each distinction close with almost identical cadences (cf. **vs-1b** and **vs-2b**), thereby giving these two opening phrases a clearly discernible symmetry. The first distinction cadences on **b** (end of **vs-1d**) with a gesture reminiscent of the cadence in **all-b**, but here with the feel of an "open" cadence. The second distinction returns to **G**, the final, but the variants of that return in the three sources offer crucial insight into a melodic process at work within *alleluia, versus,* and *sequentia*.

The verse of an alleluia often closes with all or part of the closing phrase of the alleluia.[13] This process is evident in the melodic tradition of "Confitemini . . . bonus" transmitted in Pa903, for **vs-2d´** repeats the last seven pitches of **all-a**, and **vs-2d´´** offers a literal repetition of **all-b**. While this version from Pa903 reveals effective symmetry with the close of the alleluia and gives a remarkable degree of aesthetic satisfaction to the singer and listener, it is by no means the usual ending of this *versus*. It seems to be, in fact, a unique version of the final phrase.[14] The most common ending of the verse in Aquitanian manuscripts is that found in Pa776. Here **vs-2d** closes with a five-note elaboration of **C**[15] (an elaboration omitted in Pa903), and one assumes that the cantor may conclude the verse as he

---

[11] For clarity and consistency in this study, I shall use boldface type to indicate pitches and sections of the chant being discussed. Italic, boldface type is reserved to indicate repetitions within the chant. I will use the Guidonian forms of letters to give pitches, with upper case for the lower octave, lower case for the high octave.

[12] I will use vocabulary from medieval theory in describing melodies and their constituent parts. The basic hierarchy of melodic parts will be: comma, colon, distinction, and period. See Bower, "Grammatical Model," 1989.

[13] This statement is such a given that it hardly needs documentation; see, e.g., Husmann, "Alleluia . . .," 1956, pp. 32-33. The closing phrase of the *alleluia* has been called the *iubilus* by most modern chant scholars, but McKinnon's corrective study concerning this question leads me to avoid that word in this context (see McKinnon, "Patristic Iubilus," 1990).

[14] See Schlager, *Alleluia-Melodien,* 1987, pp. 635-36.

[15] See, for example, the exact same reading in Pa1121, f. 112r; Pa1135, f. 107v; Pa1136, f. 78r and f. 81v; and Pa1137, f. 112r.

sees fit. In written traditions outside of the Aquitanian realm, the custom seems to have been to conclude with a repetition of **all-b**, as recorded in brackets in the transcription.[16] Thus it seems that some degree of symmetry with the *alleluia* was preserved in most performances of the final comma of the verse.

A second unique version of the close of the verse is found in LoHar4159, but here the complexity of interrelationships becomes compounded. The closing notes of **vs-2d** (those omitted by Pa903) are similar to the more common version recorded in Pa776, but in this source the second syllable of "e-ius" is placed on the reiterated **c** following the falling fourth of **vs-2d**, and the **d** that follows seems to imply something of an open cadence, for it does not resolve back to the **c** as in the most common rendering of the melody. The following section (**vs-2d´**) moves smoothly by thirds to **G**, which pitch is then elaborated with an upper and lower conjunct tone, and the verse concludes with a slightly modified version of **all-b** (and **vs-2d´´** as in Pa903) in which **a** replaces the opening **G**. The listener does not become aware of the import of the closing gestures in LoHar4159 until the close of the *sequentia*, for the final two melodic elements of the *sequentia* (**s-d1** and **s-d2**) repeat this cadence almost verbatim—only the approach is different.

Just as a *versus* often closes with some reference to the end of the *alleluia*, so a *sequentia* sometimes concludes with some reference to this same gesture.[17] But in the "Confitemini . . . bonus" complex the relationship is perplexing, for the variant of the closing of the verse found in LoHar4159 proves to be identical with the closing of the *sequentia*, not the *alleluia*. The last four notes of **vs-2d´** and all of **vs-2d´´** as found in LoHar4159 correspond exactly with **s-d1** and **s-d2** of all sources recording the *sequentia*. Did the cantor whose version LoHar4159 records confuse the endings, or did a cantor have the freedom to unify the end of the verse with the closing of the sequence? It is important to recall that the most common written close of verse (that found in Pa776) left the final gesture to the memory—or the liberty—of the cantor.

I find it significant that variants in the closing of the verse "Confitemini . . . bonus" are rather unusual in the Aquitanian tradition,[18] and that the only occasions in which these variants occur are found in sources in which *alleluia*, *versus*, and *sequentia* are written together as a three-part whole. Could the variants in this context imply that cantors exercised more freedom in these genres during the decades before they were neatly separated into different sections of manuscripts and "frozen" in notation? The kinds of variants that occur in these seven versions of the *sequentia* would seem to evoke an affirmative answer.

C. *Sequentia*

The question of articulation of parts in an extended, untexted melody forms one of the most fundamental problems facing the musician approaching a *sequentia*. Where do phrases occur? Where should a *mora* or *morula vocis*[19] be performed? These questions are crucial to projecting these ancient melodies into the material of sound. We shall see that comparison of different texts set to a sequence melodies offers invaluable evidence in forming answers to these questions. Nevertheless, four musical criteria may aid in defining basic distinctions within a *sequentia*: First, the repetition of patterns of pitches reveals symmetry, and we can assume that these repetitions may have been articulated with some lengthening of the final pitch in the series. Second, melodic resonances (similar, but not exact repetition) within *alleluia*, *versus*, and *sequentia* may help define a melodic member to be articulated with a lengthening. Third, recurrence of similar cadential patterns within the complex as a whole may define commas and distinctions. Finally, important functional pitches—e.g., the final, the highest pitch, the lowest pitch, pitches used for interior cadences in associated *alleluia* and *versus*—may serve to indicate possible places of melodic repose. When several of these criteria occur concurrently, the evidence for articulation of a phrase is all the stronger.

---

[16] Schlager, *Alleluia-Melodien*, 1987, pp. 635-36.

[17] Husmann, "Alleluia . . .," 1956, p. 42-43.

[18] See above, n. 14.

[19] These words (*mora* and *morula*) represent the language used in *Musica enchiriadis* for articulation of musical distinctions; see, e.g., pp. 87-89 in *Musica et Scolica Enchiriadis una cum aliquibus tractatulis adiunctis*, ed. Hans Schmid, Veröffentlichungen der Musikhistorischen Komission, Bayerische Akademie der Wissenschaften, Bd. 5 (Munich, 1981).

The structure of the opening of the *sequentia* offers few difficulties. Previous scholars have recognized and discussed the parallel structure I have identified in my layered edition.[20] The melody of the sequence opens with an exact restatement of the first member of the *alleluia* (**s-a1**=**all-a**), followed by a comma (**s-a2**) that forms a melodic resonance with the second member of the *alleluia* (**all-b**). Pitch **b** (present in **all-b**) is notably absent in **s-a2**, leaving an apparent gap in the tetrachord and giving the comma a distinctively pentatonic quality. Segment **s-a2** is repeated in six of the seven sources,[21] yet the absence of the repetition of Pa903 foreshadows a degree of the freedom with which this melody unfolds in its second distinction.

The second distinction of the *sequentia* is formed from two commas, both of which are defined by their repetition. The two melodic members are complementary in several respects: **s-b1** begins with a leap from **G** to **b**, then moves conjunctly to elaborate **G**, but the final is elaborated here with the degree below (i.e., **F**) as well as that above, and thus the tonal content of the tetrachord defined by the initial leap from **D** begins to unfold; **s-b2** begins with a repetition of the opening gesture of the alleluia, the leap from **D** to **G** (as in both **all-a** and **a1**), then repeats the disjunct set that formed **s-a2**. The conjunct, diatonic character of **s-b1** is complemented by the disjunct, pentatonic character of **s-b2**; the **b** of **s-b1** opens into the **c** of **s-b2** (similar to the tonal unfolding of the *alleluia*), and the gaps of **s-b2** are implicitly filled in by the tonal content of **s-b1**.

The role of **s-b2** in the structure of the whole is typical of the *sequentia* as a genre. The early *sequentia*, since it is fundamentally a genre without text, is comparable to instrumental music, and thus structured elements that are musical in nature must be employed to give unity to the unfolding series of abstract pitches. Hence repetition functions as one of the—if not *the*—crucial compositional strategies in the genre.[22] Repetition, on the other hand, serves as a tactic for prolongation and articulation of musical time and space; it functions, on the other hand, as a method for unification within a distinction—or over several distinctions. The musical form as a whole, however, requires overall unity in addition to unity within proximity. Various procedures are used in the genre to achieve overall unity,[23] and the **s-b2** functions as the strategic unifying member in this "composition." The repetition of **s-b1** and **s-b2** within this distinction obviously offers proximate unity. Yet **s-b2** also functions to unify the *sequentia* as a whole, indeed to unify the three-movement complex. The relation between **s-b2** and **s-a2** is undeniable, for the opening **D** forms the only difference between them in every source. Thus this comma serves to unify the first two distinctions of the *sequentia*. Yet this melodic entity also resonates with the second comma of the *alleluia*, both by virtue of its position (immediately following **all-a** and **s-a1**) and through its pitch content and melodic contour. Despite the ascent through a tone and minor third rather than a fourth, despite the absence of the **b** in **s-b2**, the related set of pitches and the same cadence demonstrate that **s-a1** and **s-b2** are variations of **all-b**. Moreover, this comma unifies not only the *alleluia* and *sequentia*, for some form of this melodic set appears at the close of the *versus* (**vs-2d´´**), and thus the second movement of this complex resonates with the outer two. Finally, the closing comma of the *sequentia* (**s-d2**) is a further variation of **all-a**, and resonates with **s-a1** and **s-b2** all the more because of the opening leap of a minor third. Thus **s-b2** and its related manifestations (**all-b**, **vs-2d´´**, **s-a2**, and **s-d2**) perform the double role of unifying the sequence melody and lending unity to the multi-movement complex of *alleluia*, *versus*, and *sequentia*.

Yet despite the undeniably pivotal function of **s-b2**, the variations in the order and number of its iterations with **s-b1** offer the greatest number of variants in the transmission of the melody, and each variation yields a distinct musical effect. No less than four different patterns of transmission unfold in the seven sources:

---

[20] See discussions in Husmann, "Alleluia . . .," 1956, p. 44; Stäblein, "Sequenz," 1965, col. 539; Levy, "Lux de luce," 1971, p. 46; I have marked the members with **s** (for *sequentia*) plus lower-case letters and numbers, and have repeated the same in italics to indicate melodic repetitions.

[21] Repetitions in Pa/na1871 are indicated by **δ**, a repetition sign in effect.

[22] For a most perceptive discussion of the role of repetition in the early sequence, see chapter XXI of Crocker, *The Early Medieval Sequence*, 1977, especially pp. 274-76. I obviously emphasize the purely musical aspect of the early sequence more than Crocker, and perceive the earlier history of the genre as exisiting melodies being given texts—being "set to text," as it were—rather than a compositional process in which text and melody play more or less equal roles. While I have basically come to this conclusion through my own work with the early sources, I have been particularly influenced by Haug, "Textdokument," 1991; Hiley, "Chartres," 1992; Hiley, "Cluny," 1993; Hiley, "Winchester," 1995; and Kruckenberg, "Sequence from 1050-1150," 1997.

[23] Reichert, "Strukturprobleme," 1949, offers eloquent analysis and evidence to document structural elements that determine proximate and large-scale unity within this form.

Pattern 1:	b1	b2	*b1*	*b2*		Pa1118, Pa1121, Pa/na1871
Pattern 2:	b1	b2	*b1*	*b2*	*b2+*	Pa903
Pattern 3:	b1	b2		*b2*		Pa776, Pa1084
Pattern 4:	b1	*b1*	b2	*b2*		LoHar4159

(**s-** omitted before each signifier in this summary)

The first pattern—appearing in three sources—treats **s-b1** and **s-b2** as an antecedent and consequent, repeats them as the whole, and thereby most clearly defines the distinction. The second pattern—appearing in only one source—is identical to the first, but repeats **s-b2** yet again following repetition of antecedent and consequent, thereby giving more emphasis to **s-b2** and lessening the perception that **s-b2** invariably belongs with **s-b1**. The third pattern—appearing in two sources—maintains the antecedent and consequent order of **s-b1** and **s-b2**, but repeats only **s-b2**, thereby lessening the apparent unity of **s-b1** and **s-b2** and heightening the proximate importance of **s-b2**. The fourth pattern treats each of the commas as distinct entities, first repeating **s-b1** and then repeating **s-b2**, thereby giving the impression that they are merely sequential and negating the perception that they form a unified distinction. One might hear this last pattern, without reference to the first three patterns, simply as **s-b** and **s-c** rather than **s-b1** and **s-b2**.

The treatment of this melodic segment in the Aquitanian sources is obviously similar to the treatment of the close of the *versus*—in fact, that close involves one of the melodic segments related to **s-b2**. Richard Crocker has stressed the role of the individual artist in shaping the formal manifestations of individual sequences, but he has always done so at the moment when text was added to the melody, or, in Crocker's terms, when the poet-musician brought text and melody together as a creative process.[24] In this example, I hold that we can indeed see records of individual artists—the cantors—at work unfolding the remembered elements that formed this melody, but the creative impulse here is independent of texts; indeed it seems to be purely melodic. In the discussion of the sequence *Laudes deo* found in Chartre, Bibliothèque municipale, Ms. 47, David Hiley refers to an "impression of a fluid mixture of ideas, which can be poured into any mold of the redactor's choice."[25] Hiley's language is clearly appropriate to the four different redactions of the "Confitemini . . . bonus" complex. We shall see this same fluidity in the second distinctions of the melody when we consider the texted manifestations of the *sequentia*.

The first problem of discussing the remainder of this *sequentia* concerns dividing the remaining string of notes into commas and distinctions, for following the second distinction no further repetitions occur, and thus repetition no longer serves as a principle for definition of distinctions.

An extended, descending melodic sequence follows the crisp symmetrical articulation marked by **s-b1** and **s-b2**. The basic melodic motive of this segment—the three note descending figure—is strongly reminiscent of **s-b1**, and, since the actual descent of three-note figures begins from the pitch **b**—like **s-b1**—before it continues to descend into the lower tetrachord, the distinction may be heard as an extension of (or a "development" of) **s-b1**. The musical space between the low **D** and the final had remained essentially undefined since the opening melodic gesture of the *alleluia*—the space was only broached when **F** occurred in the previous distinction of the *sequentia*. Now the pitches unfold in their entirety, pushing downward to the **D**, pushing even further to the **C**, although one is not certain that **C** is the goal until the second, more direct descent from **b** (**s-c3**), and then the low **C** may even be heard as the goal of the distinction as well as a resolution of the **b** that sounded as the fourth pitch in the distinction.

The arrival at low **C** thus represents the most obvious signal for definition of the distinction I have identified as "**s-c**"; for this arrival not only signals the lowest pitch of the entire complex, but the cadence at this point is strongly reminiscent of that found in the *alleluia* (**all-b**), the *versus* (**vs-1b, vs-2b, vs-2d´´**), and earlier in the *sequence* (**s-a2, s-b2**). Moreover, the segments which follow this arrival resonate with earlier commas of the complex.

The distinction defined by the cadence on the low **C** represents one of the most stable phrases of the piece. The only minor variants are found in the opening **D** of Pa1121 and in the reiteration of the penultimate pitch of the cadence. The principal difficulty of this distinction lies in its garrulous length and the question of subdivision, or of articulation and phrasing. The return to **G** following the descent and ascent represents one obvious possibility

---

[24] See Crocker, *The Early Medieval Sequence*, 1977, esp. pp. 398-401.

[25] Hiley, "Chartres," 1992, p. 115.

for a *mora vocis*. The facts that this juncture marks a return to the final and that the arrival marks the end of an extended conjunct sequence of pitches—followed then by a leap—support the judgment that the **G** may function as the last note of a comma. The return to **b** by a leap, followed by a more direct descent ending in the characteristic cadence on **C**, also defines the final segment of the distinction as a comma. Thus I have identified the first and longer division of this distinction as "**s-c1**," and have named the final, shorter comma "**s-c3**."

While **s-c1** can be sung in one breath, it remains a very long series of unarticulated notes if no subdivision into commas occurs—even if (or perhaps because) the phrase represents a descending melodic sequence. But no purely musical principle defines a comma here, and consequently I have placed a letter and number (**s-c2**) signifying possible subdivision in parentheses, thereby indicating its uncertain placement. When texts are added to the phrase, one may better identify possible positions for this minor articulation.

The third distinction may be considered the musical climax of the *sequentia*: it is the longest, taxing the performer's and listener's ability to perceive and make sense of the extended series of pitches. It unfolds the largest ambitus of any phrase, from **b** to **C**; it represents the melodic and tonal resolution of a leap that had occurred twice before, that from **D** to **G** which began the *alleluia* and the *sequentia*; and it is the only phrase that establishes a co-final, namely the low **C**. Following these dramatic extensions, an additional distinction is required to reestablish a more regular length for melodic parts and reestablish the final.

I have identified the two commas within the final distinction as "**s-d1**" and "**s-d2**"; they differentiate themselves from **s-c** and its parts by their length, their compass, and their tonal character. The comma **s-d1** returns to **G**—the final—and elaborates that pitch with upper and lower neighbors reminiscent of the close of **s-b1**. The second of these segments is defined by its resonance with the figure that unifies the complex as a whole (**all-b**, **a2**, and **s-b2**). The transmission of the final distinction is quite stable in the Aquitanian sources, for only one minor variant occurs: three sources rise to the **G** by skip from the **C**, defined as a co-final in the previous distinction, while most sources begin the final distinction on the final itself. Both **s-d1** and **s-d2** are similar in length to **s-a2** and **s-b2**, and thus a more regular length of phrase is reestablished. The final comma not only returns to the final with the predominant cadence of the complex as a whole, it reaffirms the unity of the whole by sounding the figure resonant with **all-b**, **vs-2d´´**, **s-a2**, and **s-b2**.

II: The *Prosae*

One of the most perplexing problems in the early history of the sequence revolves around the question of memory, recall, and recorded iterations of a given extended, wordless melody. In the first section of this study we have observed a limited reflection of this process at work: one melody recorded in four different versions from seven different manuscripts. The most persuasive way to account for these "different versions," in my view, would posit them as individual recordings of a vigorous performance tradition that was not dependent on notation. Some degree of freedom is obviously present in the formal unfolding of these four iterations. While notation becomes a means of recall, it also becomes a fixed record, and it inevitably tempers the spontaneity of a tradition based on aural recall during performance.

A second means of remembering an extended, wordless melody is the addition of text. This was the method advocated by Notker in the preface to his *Liber ymnorum*. The *melodiae longissimae* could be fixed in his memory through the added *versus*. I find it significant that Notker makes no reference to musical notation; he refers only to the remembered melodies, the difficulty of their recall, and the aid of the added text in "fastening" them in his memory.[26]

Recent studies of *prosulae* have demonstrated that a text added to a melisma offers evidence concerning the performance of a melody beyond that offered in neumatic notation—adiastematic or diastematic.[27] Words that are

---

[26] See *Prooemium* to *Liber ymnorum* (von den Steinen, *Notker der Dichter*, Bern, 1948, Editionsband p. 8). Notker's word that I translate as "fasten" is *colligo, colligare*.

[27] See Schlager, "Lebenslauf eines Melismas," 1983; Schlager, "Beobachtungen," 1984; Björkwall and Haug, "Texting Melismas," 1993 is particularly relevant to this study, for it discusses the same melody, although in its manifestation as a texted offertory melisma rather than a sequence. Atkinson, "*Dulcis est cantica*," 1993, is important in that he discusses the role of text in memory as well as in articulating melodic parts and distinctions.

set to a preexisting melisma may aid in indicating where commas and distinctions are found; they may indicate melodic sections than cannot be perceived in the rather abstract unfolding of neumes, or they may reinforce sections defined by musical criteria alone. Multiple *prosae* for a single *sequentia* offer even more evidence concerning the parts of a melody; for with multiple texts set under one melody, no word is likely to overlap what is perceived to be a melodic segment by more than one singer-poet. Moreover, where word breaks consistently occur in various textings, at those places some kind of musical section may be being defined. Syntax and meaning add a further dimension, for where textual phrases and clauses occur, an articulation may be implied in the melody. When phrases and clauses consistently occur at a given point in more than one text, evidence becomes rather convincing that a significant structural moment in the melody is being defined. In short, the texts—at the same time—analyze and articulate the bare melody.

Five different *prosae* are extant in Aquitanian sources set to the *sequentia* of the "Confitemini . . . bonus" complex. The ten occurrences of these texts are documented in ex. 1.2, which offers a diplomatic transcription of the five *prosae* from four different manuscripts (considering Pa1138 and Pa1338 a single source), recording melodies and texts with spelling and capitalization as found in the Aquitanian codices. In the following pages I shall a) discuss the *sequentia* as articulated by these texts, then b) discuss each text and melody individually.

A. The *sequentia* articulated by *prosae*

The *prosae* generally articulate the melody in such a manner that the distinctions and commas outlined in the analysis of the *sequentia* are confirmed. Only the first *prosa* replaces the opening word "alleluia" with text, and in this version "alleluia" is replaced syllable-for-syllable with "Iubilate." Thus the remainder of the melody (**a2** through **d2**[28]) will offer the most fruitful material for study.

All of the texts divide the melody into two distinct parts, for a major syntactical break occurs between **b2** and **c1** in each *prosa*,[29] and this break dramatically punctuates the division between the first "half" of the melody with its symmetrical repetitions and the second "half" with its absence of repetition and continuous flow. The overall form revealed by the *prosae* can thus be discussed following these two broad divisions.

Following the melodically identical opening phrase (**a1**), the second comma (**a2**) is treated syllabically in four of the five *prosae*, each parsing out six syllables for six notes.[30] Melodies 1, 2, and 4 repeat **a2**, and thus these versions are consistent with those of the untexted melody in all sources except Pa903 (see ex. 1.1). Melodies 3 and 5 omit the repetition, and thus follow the pattern established in Pa903.

The unfolding of **b1** and **b2** revealed four different patterns in the untexted *sequentia* (see above), and two of those patterns recur in the texted versions. *Prosae* 1, 2, and 4 repeat **b1** and **b2** in order—as found in pattern 1 of the *sequentia*. Yet in the repeat of **b1**, *prosa* 1 and one version of *prosa* 4 (Pa1338) add a note at the beginning of the distinction. The rationale for this addition is difficult to find; it is present in melody 1, clearly the oldest *prosa*, and it is indeed organic to the text (i.e., "quievit," a three-syllable word, begins the distinction rather than an optional monosyllable such as "et"). Could this added syllable signify an optional performance practice of lengthening the first note of a repetition? No indication of this lengthening is found in the untexted versions.[31] Melodies 3 and 5— following pattern 3 of the *sequentia*—repeat only **b2**.

The second major division of the melody has already been described as difficult to subdivide, for one of the principal criteria for determining commas and distinctions is notably absent, namely repetition. Thus, in the discussion of the third distinction of the *sequentia*, the placement of **s-c2** in ex. 1.1 was left indeterminate. The texts found in ex. 1.2 prove helpful in dividing the third distinction into parts, although two different moments emerge for the

---

[28] Insofar as the prose articulation of the sequence melody forms the principal discussion in this section, the **s-** prefix used in the previous sections is dropped in analysis and labeling of parts.

[29] The syntactical break is marked by periods and semicolons in the editions given below, and can be read in the translations.

[30] Comma **a2** in *Iubilate Deo* represents a special case, and will be discussed below.

[31] Similar expansions of the opening of a repetition can be found in other melodies: see, e.g., the fourth distinction of *Quid tu virgo* (Notker) and *Haec est sancta solemnitas*, in Crocker, *The Early Medieval Sequence*, 1978, pp. 118 and 132; and the melody IUSTUS UT PALMA MINOR (with Notker's *Dilecte deo Galle*), fifth distinction, ibid., p. 264.

Example. 1.2. Synoptic transcription of *prosae* for *sequentia Confitemini . . . bonus.*

1: Iubilate Deo

2: Omnes iubilate

3: Iam turma

4: Hoc pium

5: Pangamus

Continued

Example. 1.2.—*Continued*

Example. 1.2.—*Continued*

1:
- Pa1118: Mu-li-e-res ↑o-ci-us↑ per-gen-tes cum a-ro-ma-ta pul-cra cer-nunt il-lic ad-es-se an-ge-lo-rum cu-sto-di-a
- Pa1084: Mu-li-e-res per-gen-tes cum a-ro-ma-ta pul-cra cer-nunt il-lic ad-es-se an-ge-lo-rum cu-sto-di-a
- Pa/na1871: mu-li-e-res o-ci-us per-gen-tes cum a-ro-ma-ta pul-cra cer-nunt il-lic ad-es-se an-ge-lo-rum cu-sto-di-a
- Pa1138: mu-li-e-res o-ci-us per-gen-tes cum a-ro-ma-ta pul-cra cer-nunt il-lic ad-es-se an-ge-lo-rum cu-sto-di-a

2:
- Pa/na1871: Sed mu-li-e-res o-ci-us per-gen-tes cum a-ro-ma-ta pul-cra cer-nunt il-lic ad-es-se an-ge-lo-rum cu-sto-di-a

3:
- Pa1138: Ve-xil-la re-por-tat qui post tar-tar-e-a spo-li-a no-stra ca-nat tur-ma so-ci-a-ta su-per a-stra tin-nu-la
- Pa1338: Ve-xil-la re-por-tat qui post tar-thar-e-a spo-li-a no-stra ca-nat tur-ma so-ci-a-ta su-per a-stra tin-nu-la

4:
- Pa/na1871: Tu con-tra re-na-ta ex a-qua iu-bi-la do-mi-no can-ti-ca in-cli-ta ti-bi vi-ta re-sti-tu-ta nunc per-pe-tu-a
- Pa1338: Tu con-tra re-na-ta ex a-qua iu-bi-lat do-mi-no can-ti-ca in-cli-ta ti-bi vi-ta re-sti-tu-ta nunc per-pe-tu-a

5:
- Pa/na1871: Lin-gua-rum di-vi-sa lo-quen-tes ta-li-a mi-sti-ca vo-ce to-nat sum-ma de-co-ra-ta ka-ris-ma-ta gra-ti-a su-per-na

Example. 1.2.—*Continued*

placement of this minor point of articulation. In *prosae* 1 and 2 (the latter a revision of 1), a slight pause might occur on the last syllable of "pulcra," on the **C**, for the verb "cernunt" introduces a new syntactical element and the dramatic appearance of angels. Given the flow of words and meaning before this point, no other subdivision seems possible. The **C** thus may receive a minor *mora vocis* at this point, anticipating the major cadence on **C** at the end of the distinction.

Prosae 3, 4, and 5 offer a different point of articulation. *Prosa* 3 clearly exemplifies this division on two grounds: 1) the word "canat" spans the pitches **C** and **D**, which marked the point of division in *prosae* 1 and 2, and a division is not likely to occur in the middle of a word; 2) a major syntactical unit ends on the word "spolia," and a fresh and contrasting idea begins on "nostra."

> c1 [The king] carries back banners following the spoils of hell;
> c2 let our choir sing in unison [with that] above the ringing heavens . . .[32]

This "recording" of the melody thus stresses the **D** rather than the **C**, and the **C** functions largely to elaborate the **D** in anticipation of the push beyond **D** to **C** at the close of **c3**.

A similar version of the third distinction is found in *prosa* 4, for "cantica inclita" marks the accusative of the clause following the dative "Domino," and "cantica inclita," spanning pitches **C** and **D**, form a distinct grammatical unit. Grammatical coherence is difficult to determine in *prosa* 5, but one can affirm that **c2** cannot fall at the point of articulation in *prosae* 1 and 2; the word "tonat" spans pitches **C** and **D** at this point, similar to "cantat" in *prosa* 2. I thus assume a division between "mystica" and "voce," and this division affects my translation of the text.[33]

More minor variants are discovered in the final comma of the third distinction (**c3**) than in any other comma of the *prosae*. Three manuscripts recording *prosa* 1 offer a slightly different reading (Pa1138 follows Pa1118), yet all push downward to cadence on **C**. The variants seem to record different realizations of the cadence, although Pa1084 seems most intent on setting one syllable on each note (a trend that will be continued in the final distinction). The most notable variant is found in *Omnes iubilate* (*Prosa* 2), for here the arrival on **C** is replaced by a cadence on **D**, and the arrival of **C** is delayed until the beginning of the final distinction. The indecisiveness concerning the functions of **D** and **C** recalls the variants in the articulation of **c2** within this same distinction.

The principal variant in the transmission of the final distinction of the *sequentia* lies in the very opening of the phrase, i.e., the presence or absence of an opening **C**. The *prosae* pose the same question, for three (1, 2, and 4) begin with the anacrusis, while two (3 and 5) begin on the **G**. This ambiguity is also noted in the version of *prosa* 1 found in Pa1084.

The central question raised in the final distinction relates to its two-part structure, for two sources offer a text that clearly negates that division. While three sources that transmit *prosa* 1 (Pa1118, Pa/na1871, and Pa1138) offer the possibility of a *mora vocis* on the final at the sixth note, Pa1084 negates the division by setting the word "vivere" over the possible cadence. The exceptional source (Pa1084) offers a version of the distinction that is most syllabic (consistent with its version of the previous phrase), and thus may represent a "refinement" of this rather archaic prose in which consistent syllabic setting is not an overriding principle. The use of the unusual word "affantur"— set dramatically to **d2** with its resonances with earlier melodic gestures—strongly suggests a minor division in the final distinction. This division is similarly implied by the textual settings and syntactical structure of *prosae* 3, 4, and 5. Only *prosa* 2—similar to the version of *prosa* 1 in Pa1084—sets a text that spans the moment of articulation with a word (i.e., "resurrexisse").

B. The individual *prosae*

When one tries to make sense of the Latin texts of these *prosae* published by Dreves and Daux, one quickly becomes aware of the difficulties of the texts themselves as well as the inadequate punctuation, faulty division, and possible mistakes in the printed editions. Texts for sequences are always better served *qua* text if they are carefully

---

[32] Cf. edition and translation of *Iam turma caelica* below.

[33] See discussion of *Pangamus carmina* below.

coordinated with their musical precursor, and ideally the *prosae* should be published with their melody—hence the final section of this study.

The principal obstacle to reading these texts in the Dreves' edition lies in his failure to recognize elements of melodic symmetry in the opening distinctions of the sequence melody. This melody has been consistently categorized as one of the more ancient, "aparallel" sequences, one of those that went out of style following the rise of the sequence with predictably paired repetitions.[34] While this *sequentia* is indeed of venerable age, to describe it as "aparallel" is, at best, misleading. Yet Dreves repeatedly notes the absence of parallelism as he offers three of these texts, and his failure to see the relation between text and melody leads him into nonsensical division and punctuation of the texts.[35] Moreover, two of the texts published by Dreves are also found in Pa/na1871, a manuscript not available to Dreves in 1889. While Daux's editions of the *prosae* from Pa/na1871 somewhat reflect the parallel structure of the melody, they are little more than uncritical transcriptions of Pa/na1871, and require more critical examination. Thus, an edition with translation will be given for each *prosa*, an edition that is keyed to the musical structure of the *sequentia*; an edition of each *prose* with the melody will be offered in exx. 1.3-7 at the end of the article.

1. Iubilate Deo omnis arva

a1	Iubilate	Shout for joy
a2	deo	to God,
a2	omnis arva,	all you lands,
b1	Quia hodie rex heros,	For today the hero king,
b2	conditus antro,	buried in the cave,
b1	Quievit in sepulcri aula	spelt in the chamber of the sepulcher
b2	porta obtrusa;	with the door sealed;
c1	Mulieres ocius pergentes cum aromata pulcra	The women proceeding quickly with precious balm
c2	cernunt illic adesse	discern there present
c3	angelorum custodia,	a company of angels,
d1	Qui Iesum vivere	Who proclaim
d2	affantur	that Jesus lives!

Notes on text:
Pa1084, f. 305r; Pa1118, f. 170v; Pa1138, f. 75v; Pa/na1871, f. 88v.
See Dreves, *AH 7*, 1889, no. 41, p. 56.
The word "ocius" is omitted in both Pa1084 and Pa1118. The word is added above the line—without neumes—in Pa1118. The melody clearly demands three syllables in this position, thus one might assume that the source shared by the two codices omitted the word as well. With the exception of this omission, the transmission of the text is remarkably consistent in all four sources.

Notes on music:
Example 1.3 (p. 25) represents a transcription of Pa1118, a version which is repeated identically in Pa1138.
Cadences are altered with a *pressus* in *a2* and *b2* in Pa1084; the altered cadence of *a2* required an adjustment in placement of the second syllable of "arva."
Pa1084 presents a syllabic descent in c3; Pa/na1871 adds an anticipatory C before arrival at the final note.
Pa1084 is at odds with all other sources in **d1** and **d2**: the text and melody seem adjusted so as to make the final distinction as syllabic as possible.

Iubilate Deo omnis arva opens with the words of Psalm 65:1 (*Iubilate Deo omnis terra*), but the word "terra" is conspicuously changed to "arva." This change, clearly recognizable to any Christian of the Middle Ages, signals the tone of the *prosa*, for the elevated character of its language distinguishes it from ordinary liturgical diction, and from the other *prosae* set to this *sequentia*. Vocabulary such as "rex heros," "conditus," "aula sepulchri," and "affantur"

---

[34] See, e.g., in Kohrs, *Die aparallelen Sequenzen*, 1978.

[35] See Dreves, *AH 7*, pp. 56-57: by *Iubilate Deo*, "Die Melodie läßt die Abwesenheit jeden Parallelismus erkennen"; by *Iam turma caelica*, "Sequenz ohne Parallelismus"; by *Hoc pium recitat*, "Sequenz nach Ausweis der Melodie ohne Parallelismus." Kohrs, *Die aparallelen Sequenzen*, 1978, categorizes this melody among his "aparallel" sequences and makes no mention of the obvious parallel structures in the opening distinctions (see especially pp. 66-67).

reflects a degree of learning and sophistication somewhat above that of ordinary liturgical diction. The tone of the text seems to represent an attempt to elevate the moment to an almost epic level, a level appropriate to the event celebrated by the return of the *alleluia*.

The most striking aspect of *Iubilate Deo omnis arva* lies in the relation of word and syllable to melodic gesture. In the opening comma (**a1**), *Iubilate* replaces *Alleluia* syllable-for-syllable, and one can perceive the rationale behind the texting. But in the second comma and its repetition, *Deo* is spread over six notes, then *omnis arva* is parsed over the same pitches. No systematic attempt to match a note with a syllable is evident. Again, at the cadences of **b2** and its repetition (*b2*), the final syllables of *antro* and *obtrusa* are given to two pitches. The third distinction (**c1**) begins with the second syllable of *mulieres* spread over two notes, and the final comma of this distinction (**c3**) exhibits four different divisions of notes and syllables in the four different sources—only one of which assigns one syllable per note (Pa1084). The final distinction of the piece remains consistent with the whole, for *affantur* is spread over seven notes in three of the four sources.

Might the inconsistency of syllabic setting in this *prose* testify to its antiquity? Notker's earliest efforts seem to have imitated similar models, and his master Iso encouraged him to follow the rule of one syllable per melodic movement.[36] Of the *prosae* set to this *sequentia*, *Iubilate Deo* is clearly the most ancient, and the relation of syllable to text as well as its elevated diction may bespeak an age that predates the sources by at least a century.

The four versions of this unusual text demonstrate the ability of text to "fasten" a melody in the memory. So long as the text remains syllabic with respect to the melody, the transmission of the sources remains remarkably consistent; variants arise precisely when the correspondence of one syllable to one note disappears—see **a2**, *b2*, **d1**, and **d2**.[37]

2. OMNES IUBILATE

a1	Alleluia.	Alleluia.
a2	Omnes iubilate	Let all shout for joy,
a2	Cordaque laetate,	Indeed with happy hearts!
b1	Quia hodie rex heros,	For today the hero king,
b2	pro salute humana,	for the salvation of humankind,
b1	Mansit in sepulchri aula	Remained in the enclosure of the sepulcer
b2	sub custodum munia.	under the watch of guards.
c1	Sed mulieres ocius pergentes cum aromata pulcra	But the women proceeding quickly with precious balm
c2	cernunt illic adesse	discern there present
c3	angelorum custodia,	a company of angels,
d1	Qui eum a morte re—	Who assert that
d2	surrexisse aaffirmant.	he has risen.

NOTES ON TEXT:
Pa/na1871, f. 115v
Daux, *Pa/na1871*, 1901, p. 113
The relation of this text to *Iubilate Deo omnis arva* is evident throughout; *Omnes iubilate* is a contrafactum ("revision") of the earlier text.
The "sed" of c1, added to make the distinction consistently syllabic, appears to be corrected from "ses"; Daux read the word as "set."
In the context of revising an earlier text, I find the word "atra" for "aula" in **c1** of Pa/na1871 suspicious. I find no evidence for a Latin noun "atra, atrae," and thus suspect that "atra" may represent a scribal error. While "sepulchri aula" reflects the elevated diction of the earlier text—a diction that is consistently lowered in this revision—I have nevertheless emended the text to sepulchri aula," as found in *Iubilate Deo*.

NOTES ON MUSIC:
Ex. 1.4 (p. 26) follows the only source, Pa/na1871.

---

[36] See *Prooemium* to *Liber ymnorum*—von den Steinen, *Notker der Dichter*, Bern, 1948, Editionsband, pp. 8-9: "Singulae motus cantilenae singulas syllabas debent habere."

[37] The cantor whom Pa1084 records seems to be trying to reformulate the final commas in order to achieve a more syllabic version.

Two principles seem to lie behind this revision of *Iubilate Deo omnis arva*: 1) strict syllabic correspondence and 2) rhyme and assonance of words ending in *-a*. The opening rhyme of "iubilate" and "laetate" sets the tone for the whole, and revisions such as "pro salute humana" for "contidus antro" in **b2** both make the syllables correspond to individual pitches and create more *a*-assonance; the change of "porta obtrusa" into "sub costodum munia" in **b2** achieves the same goals. The substitution of "mansit" for "quievit" at the opening of *b1* makes the repeat of **b1** exactly parallel, and the addition of the anacrusis "sed" at the beginning of **c1** enables the distinction to unfold strictly syllabically.

The cadence on **D** at the end of **c3** makes this *prosa* a unique articulation of the *sequentia*, for all other melodies stress the **C** as a co-final. Moreover, the elevation of **D** to co-final is not the result of syllabic correspondence within **c3**, for the move to **C** was clearly possible within the syllabic principle. Perhaps the cantor/poet wanted to stress **D**, or perhaps he chose to shove the **C** into the next distinction in order to more easily force that distinction into syllabic correspondence. The text for the final distinction—*qui eum a morte resurexisse affirmant*—is indeed "wordy," and one extra note was required to make the text fit. In comparison with the other *prosae* at the juncture between **c3** and **d1**, I find *Omnes iubilate* musically rather unconvincing.

3. Iam turma caelica

a1	Alleluia!	Alleluia!
a2	Iam turma caelica	Now the celestial choir—
a3		
b1	Laeta reboans iubilat	loudly rejoicing—shouts
b2	Nova melodemata	the new, triumphant melodies
b1		
b2	Regi triumphalia,	to the king—
c1	Vexilla reportat qui post tartarea spolia;	Who carries back banners following the spoils of hell;
c2	nostra canat turma sociata	let our choir sing in unison [with that]
c3	super astra tinnula	above the ringing heavens,
d1	quis voce tonans	thundering to them with [pure] voice
d2	perenne Alleluia!	an eternal Alleluia

Notes on text:
Pa1138, f. 76r; Pa1338, f. 58v.
Dreves, *AH7*, 1889, no. 42, p. 56.
Pa1138 has "turma" in **a2**, Pa1338 "turba." Pa1338 offers "quas" for "quis" in **d1**.

Notes on music:
Example 1.5 (p. 27) is based on both Pa1138 and 1338, which are musically identical.

The overriding image that emerges from *Iam turma caelica* is the allegorical relationship between the earthly choir singing its Easter *alleluia* and the eternal *alleluia* sung by the heavenly choir. This image frames that of Christ returning from the harrowing of hell with banners following the procession, perhaps an illusion to banners in the gospel procession taking place as the *prosa* was being sung. *Iam turma caelica* carries assonance of words ending in *-a* to the extreme, for every comma and every distinction ends with an *a*-vowel, and considerable *a*-assonance is found within individual lines—especially in **c1**, **c2**, and **c3**. Correspondence between syllable and note is applied consistently in this *prosa*, with the exception of the cadence on **C** that closes **c3**.

The "quis" that begins the last distinction must be for "quibus," a learned usage that may have confused other readers besides the present author.[38] The use of the word "vox" in **d1** may imply "musical pitch" rather than "sung words," for "vox" is used in medieval theory to represent "phthongos," or abstract pitch. The reference thus may be to a *sequentia* without text that sounds the eternal, wordless *alleluia*—hence the editorial "[pure] voice" in the translation.

---

[38] I wish to acknowledge the insight and learning Professor Daniel J. Sheerin shared with me in reading these texts. Many of my readings and revisions reflect his suggestions, yet none of my blunders should be attributed to any weakness in his advice and guidance.

4. Hoc pium recitat

a1	Alleluia!	Alleluia!
a2	Hoc pium recitat	The people newly joyful proclaim
a2	plebs nova nunc laeta,	this sacred word:
b1	Quia resonant trophea	For the victories of Christ resound abroad
b2	Christi iam pretiosa,	—victories won at great cost.
b1	Et nox instat in qua tartara	And the night is at hand in which hell,
b2	lugent evacuata.	now left empty, wails its lament.
c1	Tu contra renata ex aqua	You people, to the contrary, reborn of water,
	iubila domino	shout glorious songs to the Lord,
c2	cantica inclita tibi vita	for at this moment life without end
c3	restituta nunc perpetua,	has been restored to you,
d1	Ut reiterata	So that life renewed
d2	se solvat peccamina.	might be set free from sins.

NOTES ON TEXT:
Pa1338, f. 34v; Pa/na1871, f. 88v.
Dreves, *AH7*, 1889, no. 43, p. 57 (according to Pa1338); Daux, *Pa/na1871*, 1901, p. 113 (according to Pa/na1871).
The imperative and indicative are easily confused in this text, as evidenced in the two sources. Pa1338 offers "recitat" in **a2**, while Pa/na1871 gives "recita"; the clause requires the indicative "recitat." On the other hand, Pa/na1871 offers "iubila" in **c1**, while Pa1338 gives "iubilat"; in this context the singular imperative "iubila" (with *tu*) is required.
The "et" of **b1** is omitted in Pa/na1871.
The word "caterva" of Dreves's edition is not found in the manuscript, nor is the Amen that he appends at the end of the text.

NOTES ON MUSIC:
Example 1.6 (p. 28) is based on Pa1338, the source which preserves the extra note (and syllable) that begins "b1." The additional G is preserved here because of the precedence of *Iubilate Deo omnis arva*. No other discrepancy between the two melodies is present.

Hoc pium recitat presents a prose text that is rich in *a*-assonance, symmetry, and imagery. Like *Iam turma*, every comma and every distinction ends in *-a*, indeed only the indicative verb of the opening distinction adds a consonant following the vowel. The "a" of *alleluia* resonates at every hand in this text. *Hoc pium recitat* introduces the harrowing of hell in a symmetrical repetition (**b1** and **b2**), while the second, asymmetrical half of the prose introduces the image of baptism—an event to occur at a later moment in the Paschal Vigil—and associates redemption and life freed from sins with the Paschal drama. The imagery, symmetry, assonance, and grammatical clarity of this prose make it perhaps the most elegant of the texts associated with "Confitemini . . . bonus."

The Paschal season lasts from the Easter Vigil to Pentecost, and a vigil mass occurs on the eve of Pentecost that frames the season symmetrically. At the vigil of Pentecost the "Alleluia, Confitemini . . . bonus" is repeated, thereby giving Pentecost a clear resonance with the Easter Vigil.[39] The last *prosa* associated with the *sequentia* was composed for the Vigil of Pentecost.

Of all texts associated with the "Confitemini . . . bonus" complex, "Pangamus carmina" is the most difficult. While the *prosa* offers a minimus of repetition (only *b2*), it seems overly laden with words ending in *-a*, thereby making it quite difficult to determine which words are linked grammatically. The problem is compounded by three present participles (*resultans*, *loquentes*, and *regnans*), the translations of which offer no easy solutions. The presence of the participles mixed in with words of Greek derivation (*dogma*, *karismata*, *Theos*), further combined with ambiguous agreements of nouns and adjectives, lead me to suspect that the author is perhaps playing with the conceit of Pentecost, that is, offering a linguistic construction that might be construed as "speaking in tongues." My translation is offered in the same spirit. Thus I combine *carmina* with *pia*, thereby framing the first two distinctions, and leaving *sancta* to be paired with *agmina*, thereby forming a frame of *resultans* within the larger frame. The precise grammatical function of

---

[39] See, e.g., Pa903, f. 91v, (*PM* 13, p. 182) where the pieces of the liturgy for the Vigil of Pentecost are listed, and the *All. Confitemini* is specifically mentioned (line 3).

5. Pangamus carmina

a1	Alleluia!	Alleluia!
a2	Pangamus carmina,	Let us sing songs:
a2		
b1	Sancta resultans agmina,	Pious [songs of]
b2	sancti spiritus dogma	the dogma of the Holy Spirit,
b1		echoing the sacred hosts
b2	Apostolorum pia.	of the apostles.
c1	Linguarum divisa loquentes,	Speaking in a voice divided in languages
	talia mistica	they thunder forth
c2	voce tonant summa decorata	these great mystical gifts
c3	karismata gratia superna,	adorned with heavenly grace:
d1	Regnans, O Theos,	You are the one who reigns, O God,
d2	per secula cuncta.	throughout all ages.

NOTES ON TEXT:
Pa/na1871, f. 88v.
Daux, *Pa/na1871*, 1901, p. 146.
Difficulties are present in every distinction of this text. The third distinction seems impossible to read with the singular verb ("tonat") found in the manuscript; I have thus emended "tonat" to "tonant," and have attempted a reading assuming the plural subject implied in the text.

NOTES ON MUSIC:
Example 1.7 (p. 29) follows Pa/na1871 with no alterations.

resultans remains a mystery. The apostles must be those speaking in tongues and thundering gifts, hence the necessity for a plural verb in the third distinction. Agreement of noun with adjective and participle again offers difficulty in this distinction, and other translations are clearly possible. Finally, I can only read the final distinction as a vocative outcry, an enthusiastic, final Paschal *laudes* to the Eternal King.

* * * * *

The ecstatic character of the long melodies known as *sequentiae* is evident in their wordless exultation and in their function of raising expectations before the reading of the Gospel. The liturgical moment represents the climax of the synaxis. Ecstasy demands spontaneity, creativity, and the early history of the genre fulfilled those expectations. The relatively late history of the "Confitemini . . . bonus" complex followed in this study repeatedly demonstrates a creative freedom at work as different "performances" of the work were recorded in the Aquitanian sources. The mnemonic devices of neumatic notation and syllabic texting were capable of fixing the musical forms of a given time and place, but freedom remains evident at every stage in the transmission of the Aquitanian "Confitemini . . . bonus." The ecstatic spontaneity of the wordless melodies may have been compromised by the formal limitations of texts, but the character of the texts, determined both by their content and assonant sensuality, maintains the ecstatic spirit of both the melodic precursor and the liturgical moment.

Example 1.3. *Sequentia cum prosa: Iubilate deo omnis arva.*

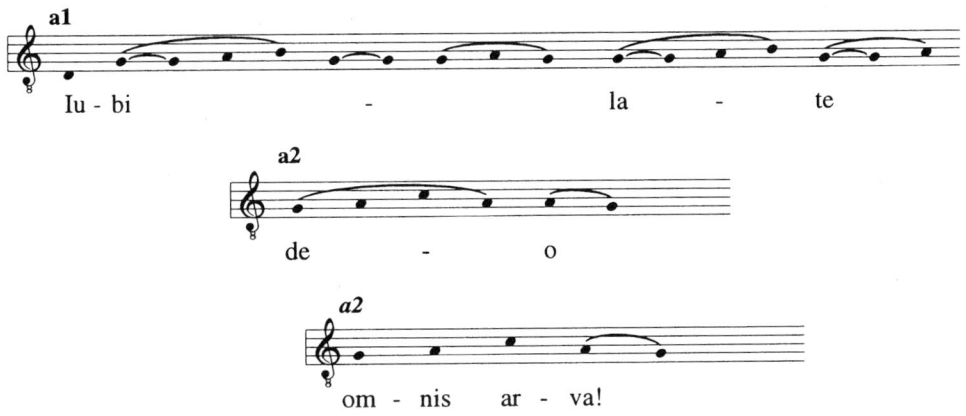

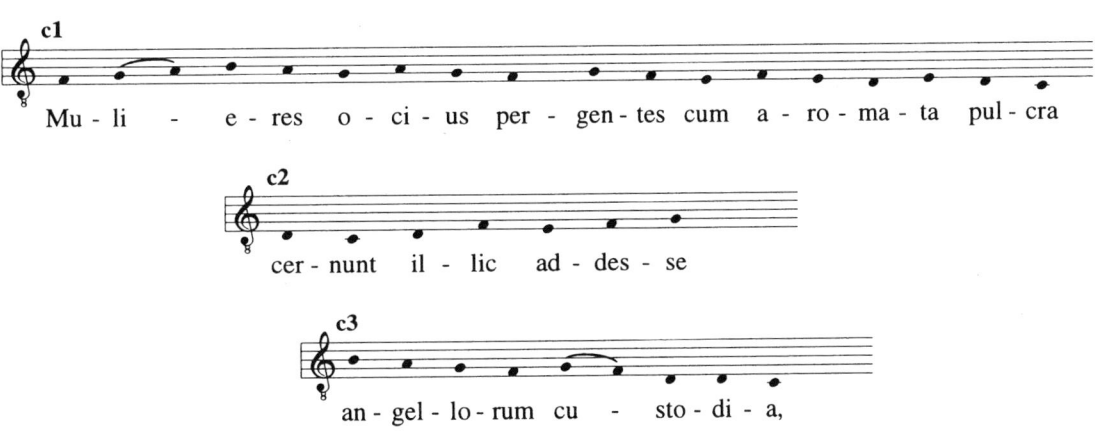
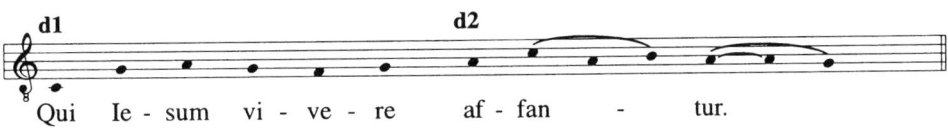

Example 1.4. *Sequentia cum prosa: Omnes iubilate.*

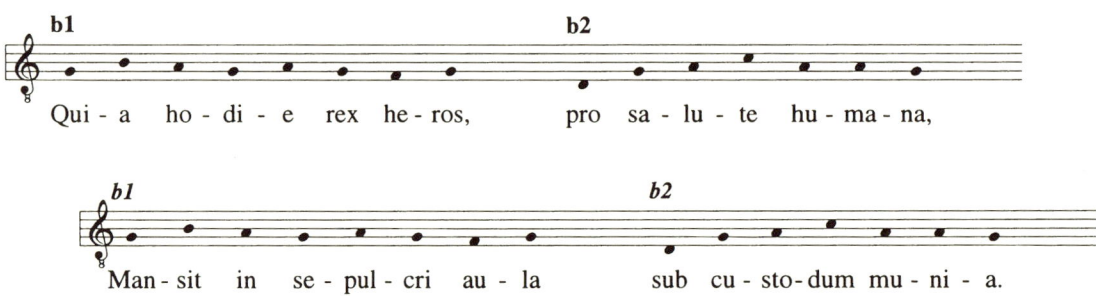

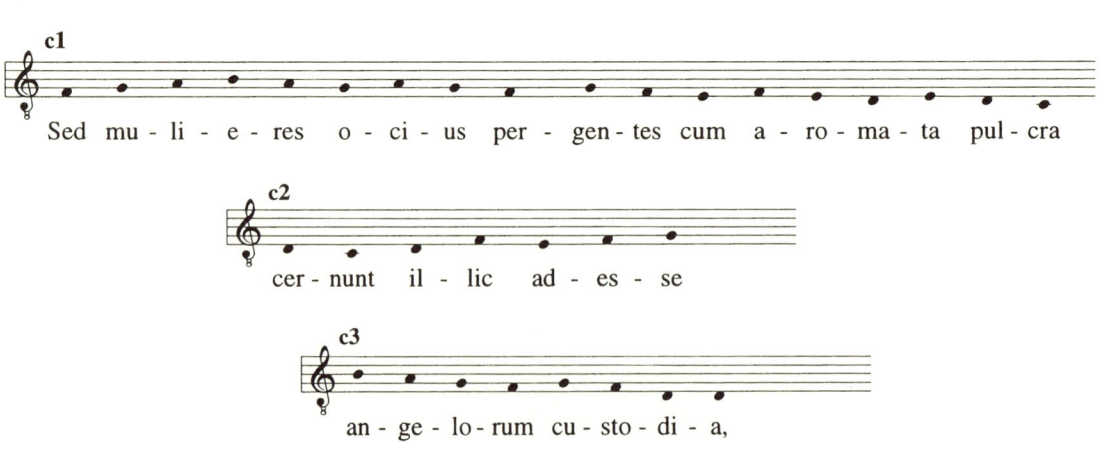

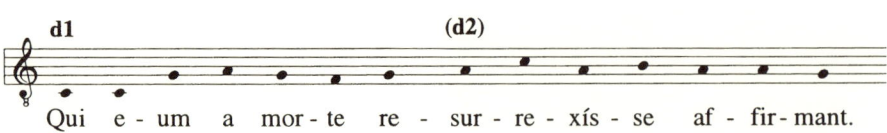

Example 1.5. *Sequentia cum prosa: Iam turma caelica.*

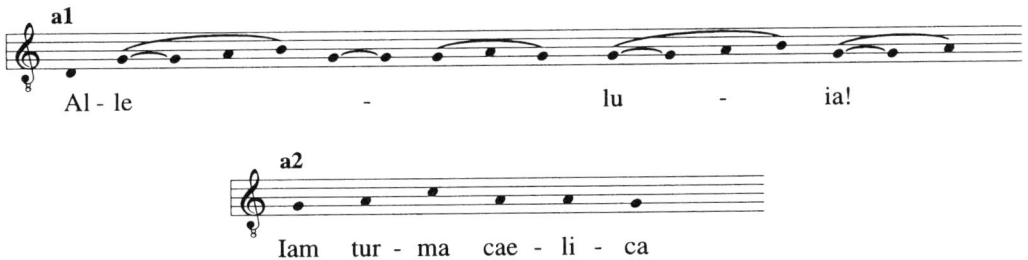

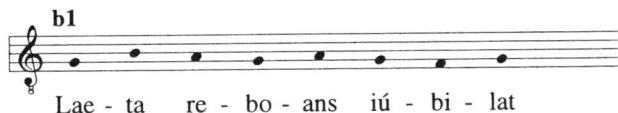

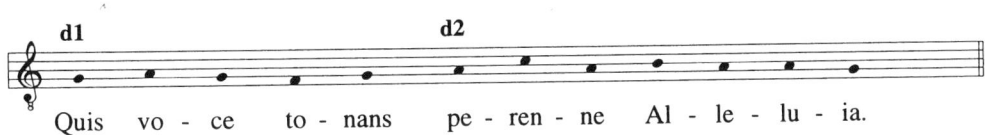

Example 1.6. *Sequentia cum prosa: Hoc pium recitat.*

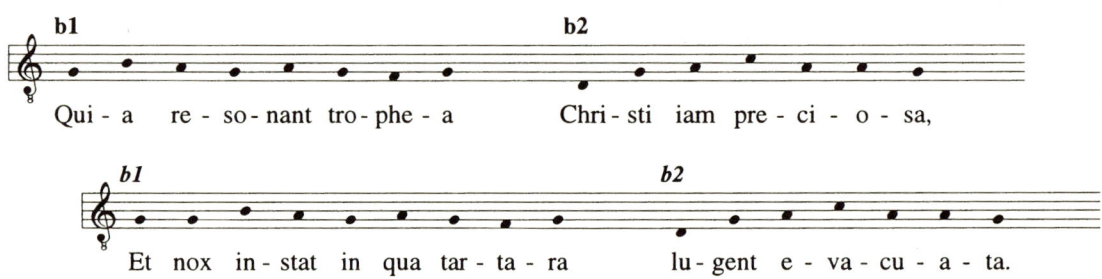

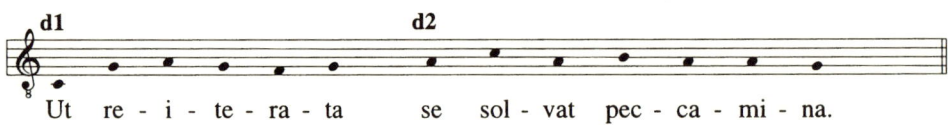

Example 1.7. *Sequentia cum prosa: Pangamus carmina.*

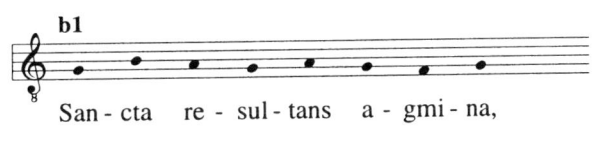
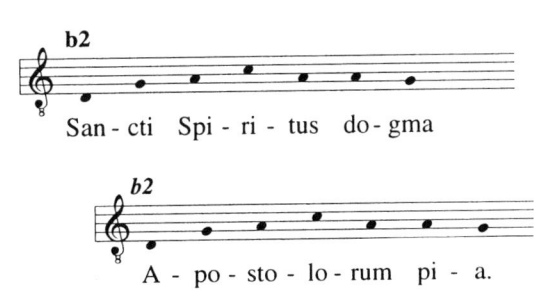

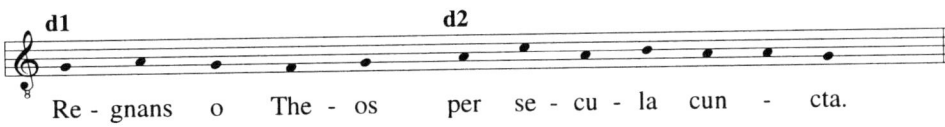

APPENDIX

PM 13
    Le Codex 903 de la Bibliothèque nationale de Paris (XIe siècle): Graduel de Saint-Yrieix. Paléographie musicale, 13. Tournai: Desclée, 1925.

PM 14
    Le Codex 10673 de la Bibliothèque Vaticane fond latin (XIe siècle): Graduel Bénéventain. Paléographie musicale, 14. Tournai: Desclée, 1931.

Atkinson, "*Dulcis est cantica*," 1993.
    Charles M. Atkinson. "Text, Music, and the Persistence of Memory in *Dulcis est cantica*." In *Recherches nouvelles sur les tropes liturgiques*, ed. Wulf Arlt and Gunilla Björkvall, 95-117. Stockholm: Almqvist & Wiksel International, 1993.

Bannister, "Pa/na1871," 1903.
    Henry Marriot Bannister. "Un tropaire–prosier de Moissac." *Revue d'histoire et de littérature religieuse* 8 (1903): 554-81.

Björkval and Haug, "Texting Melismas," 1993.
    Gunilla Björkvall and Andreas Haug. "Texting Melismas: Criteria for and Problems in Analyzing Melogene Tropes." *Rivista de Musicología* 16 (1993): 805-31.

Bower, "Grammatical Model," 1989.
    Calvin M. Bower. "The Grammatical Model of Musical Understanding in the Middle Ages." In *Hermeneutics and Medieval Culture*, ed. Patrick J. Gallacher and Helen Damico, 133-45. Albany: State University of New York Press, 1989.

Chailley, "Tropaires," 1957.
    Jacques Chailley. "Les anciens tropaires et séquentiaires de l'École de Saint Martial de Limoges (X^e-XIe siècles)." *Études Grégoriennes* 2 (1957): 163-88.

Chailley, *L'École de Saint Martial*, 1960.
    Jacques Chailley. *L'École de Saint Martial de Limoges jusqu'à la fin du XIe siècle.* Paris: Les Livres essentiels, 1960.

Crocker, "Proses at Saint Martial" (diss.), 1957.
    Richard Crocker. "The Repertoire of Proses at Saint Martial de Limoges (Tenth and Eleventh Centuries)." Ph.D. diss., Yale University, 1957.

Crocker, "Repertoire of Proses," 1958.
    Richard L. Crocker. "The Repertory of Proses at Saint Martial de Limoges in the 10th Century." *Journal of the American Musicological Society* 11 (1958): 149-64.

Crocker, *The Early Medieval Sequence*, 1977.
    Richard L. Crocker. *The Early Medieval Sequence.* Berkeley: University of California Press, 1977.

Daux, *Pa/na1871*, 1901.
    Camille Daux. *Tropaire-Prosier de l'abbe Saint-Martin de Montauriol publié d'après le manuscrit original (XIe-XIIIe siècles).* Bibliothèque Liturgique 9, ed. Ulysse Chevalier. Paris: A. Picard, 1901.

Dreves, *AH 7*, 1889.
    Guido Maria Dreves, ed. *Prosarium Lemovicense: Die Prosen der Abtei St. Martial zu Limoges, aus Troparien des 10., 11., und 12. Jahrhunderts.* Analecta Hymnica medii aevi, 7. Leipzig: Fues Verlag, 1889.

de Goede, *Utrecht Prosarium*, 1965.
> Nicholas de Goede. *The Utrecht Prosarium.* Monumenta musica Nederlandica, 6. Amsterdam: Vereniging voor Nederlandse Muziekgeschiedenis, 1965.

Haug, "Textdocument," 1991.
> Andreas Haug. "Ein neues Textdocument zur Entstehungsgeschichte der Sequenz." In *Festschrift Ulrich Siegele zum 60. Geburtstag*, ed. Rudolf Faber, et al., 9-19. Kassel, 1991.

Hiley, "Chartres," 1992.
> David Hiley. "The Sequentiary of Chartres, Bibliothèque Municipale, Ms. 47." In *La Sequenza medievale: Atti del Convegno Internazionale Milano, 7-8 aprile 1984*, ed. Agostino Ziino, 105-17. Lucca: Libreria Musicale Italiana, 1992.

Hiley, "Cluny," 1993.
> David Hiley. "The Sequence Melodies Sung at Cluny and Elsewhere." In *De Musica et Cantu: Studien zur Geschichte der Kirchenmusik und der Oper. Helmut Hucke zum 60. Geburtstag*, ed. Peter Cahn and Ann-Katrin Heimer, 131-55. Hildesheim, Zürich, New York: G. Olms, 1993.

Hiley, "Winchester," 1995.
> David Hiley. "The Repertory of Sequences at Winchester." In *Essays on Medieval Music in Honor of David G. Hughes*, ed. Graeme M. Boone, 153-93. Cambridge: Harvard University Department of Music, 1995.

Hiley, *Handbook*, 1993.
> David Hiley. *Western Plainchant: A Handbook.* Oxford: Oxford University Press, 1993.

Husmann, "Alleluia . . .," 1956.
> Heinrich Husmann. "Alleluia, Vers und Sequenz." *Annales musicologiques* 4 (1956): 19-53.

Kohrs, *Die aparallelen Sequenzen*, 1978.
> Klaus Heinrich Kohrs. *Die aparallelen Sequenzen: Repertoire, liturgische Ordnung, musikalischer Stil.* Beiträge zur Musikforschung, 6, ed. Reinhold Hammerstein and Wilhelm Seidel. Munich-Salzburg: Musikverlag Emil Katzbicher, 1978.

Kruckenberg, "The Sequence from 1050-1150," 1997.
> Lori A. Kruckenberg-Goldenstein. "The Sequence from 1050-1150: Study of a Genre in Change." Ph.D. diss., University of Iowa, 1997.

Levy, "*Lux de luce*," 1971.
> Kenneth Levy. "*Lux de luce*: The Origin of an Italian Sequence." *Musical Quarterly* 57 (1971): 40-61.

McKinnon, "Patristic Jubilus," 1990.
> James W. McKinnon. "The Patristic Jubilus and the Alleluia of the Mass." In *International Musicological Society, Study Group CANTUS PLANUS, Papers Read at the Third Meeting, Tihany, Hungary, 19-24 September 1998*, ed. L. Dobszay, et al., 61-70. Budapest: Hungarian Academy of Sciences Institute for Musicology, 1990.

Planchart and Fuller, "St Martial."
> *The New Grove Dictionary of Music and Musicians* (1980). S.v. "St Martial," by Alejandro Enrique Planchart and Sarah Fuller.

Reichert, "Struktureprobleme," 1949.
> G. Reichert. "Strukturprobleme der ältern Sequenz." *Deutsche Vierteljahrschrift für Literaturgeschichte* 23 (1949): 227-51.

RISM B/V/1
> Heinrich Husmann. *Tropen- und Sequenzenhandschriften.* RISM B/V/1, München-Duisberg: G. Henle, 1964.

Schlager, *Alleluia-Melodien*, 1968.
 Karl-Heinz Schlager. *Alleluia-Melodien I, bis 1100*. Monumenta monodica medii aevi, 7. Kassel: Bärenreiter, 1968.

Schlager, "Lebenslauf eines Melismas," 1983.
 Karl-Heinz Schlager. "Tropen als Forschungsbereich der Musikwissenschaft: Vom Lebenslauf eines Melismas." In *Research on Tropes: Proceedings of a Symposium Organized by the Royal Academy of Literature, History and Antiquities and the Corpus Troporum, Stockholm, June 1-3, 1981*, ed. Gunilla Iversen, 17-28. Stockholm: Almqvist & Wiksell International, 1983.

Schlager, "Beobachtungen," 1984.
 Karl-Heinz Schlager. "Beobachtungen zur frühen Sequenz in ost- und westfränkischer Überlieferung." In *Gordon Athol Anderson (1929-1981): In memoriam*, ed. Luther Dittmer, 531-43. Henryville, Pa.: Institute of Medieval Music, 1984.

Stäblein, "Sequence."
 Die Musik in Geschichte und Gegenwart (1965). S.v. "Sequenz," by Bruno Stäblein.

Steiner, "Prosulae . . . Pa1118," 1969.
 Ruth Steiner. "The Prosulae of the MS Paris BN lat. 1118." *Journal of the American Musicological Society* 22 (1969): 367-93.

2

The Tao of Singing:
On the Schola Hungarica's Interpretation of the Nonantolan Sequences

LANCE W. BRUNNER

Khing, the master carver, on the Prince of Lu's command, made a bell stand of such beauty and power that those who saw it considered it the work of the spirits. When the Prince asked his secret, Khing replied that he was only a workman with no secret, just a straightforward method:

> When I began to think about the work you commanded
> I guarded my spirit, did not expend it
> On trifles, that were not to the point.
> I fasted in order to set
> My heart at rest.
> After three days fasting,
> I had forgotten gain and success.
> After five days
> I had forgotten praise or criticism.
> After seven days
> I had forgotten my body
> With all its limbs.
>
> By this time all thought of your Highness
> And of the court had faded away.
> All that might distract me from the work
> Had vanished.
> I was collected in the single thought
> of the bell stand.
>
> Then I went to the forest
> To see the trees in their own natural state.
> When the right tree appeared before my eyes,
> The bell stand also appeared in it, clearly, beyond doubt.
> All I had to do was to put forth my hand
> And begin.
>
> If I had not met this particular tree
> There would have been
> No bell stand at all.
> What happened?

A version of this essay was presented at the meeting of the International Musicological Society study group Cantus Planus, in Sopron, Hungary, 8 September 1995.

> My own collected thought
> Encountered the hidden potential in the wood;
> From this live encounter came the work
> Which you ascribe to the spirits.[1]

Rereading this little allegory by Chuang-tzu, the Taoist master writing in the fourth century, B.C.E., caused me to reflect late one night on my experience as a consultant to a recording of medieval sequences made by the Schola Hungarica in Budapest in 1992.[2] The allegory is about, among other things, the practice of *wu wei*, often translated as "non-doing" or "inaction." But these words are misleading, since *wu wei* is not passive, but a special kind of action, what we might call "right action," action that is not egocentric and is aligned more with a natural unfolding of things. Quaker writer Parker Palmer refers to it as "a form of action that is at once more disciplined and more liberating than the frenzy that we in the West often equate with active life."[3]

Observing the recording process, I was struck by how, through the singers of the Schola, Láslzó Dobszay and Janka Szendrei's "live encounter" with each piece allowed its hidden potential to emerge into the magic of sound. I would like to share some observations and reflections about the Schola Hungarica's recorded performances, and the disciplined musical intelligence that informs their singing, and also about how I can make a case, unlikely as it may seem to them, that they are modern counterparts to the Taoist masters of yore.

To be sure, any convincing act of recreating music in performance from a notated source or the recesses of memory, however recent or remote, as spirit is breathed back into a dormant vertige of sound, has analogies to this little story of Khing the woodcarver. Great performances allow the form hidden in the notation, or one's memory, to unfold, to reveal itself. If my connection between ancient Chinese philosophy and contemporary performance of medieval chant is less than convincing for you, nevertheless, I hope to show how the stylistic riches of the early sequence are revealed through the right action of the Schola's remarkable and highly original performances. Before I address the performances themselves, however, I would like to review briefly some of the basic background and stylistic features of the early sequence, as these have a bearing on performance practice.

Richard Crocker summed up the achievement of the early medieval sequence by noting that "from 850 to 1000 . . . the sequence represented one of the most important kinds of music produced in the West—important because of its intrinsic musical values as well as its historical significance for the development of style in general."[4] Sequences are a type of medieval chant, and as such represent a layer of monophonic music that came into being generations after the creation of the Gregorian Mass Propers. Sequences differ dramatically from these more ancient, Mediterranean chants, with the graceful, exquisite gestures of their antiphons, or the rhapsodically ornamental and effusive melismatic flights of their Graduals or Offertory verses. In stark contrast to these, sequences were Frankish creations, new and daring in the way syllabic text setting and a couplet structure, sometimes referred to as progressive parallelism, were used in conjunction with bold melodic style focused around the final or secondary tonal center that allowed melodies to span great distances, bringing melodic and textual material into a large-scale climax that was new to Western music and which had far-reaching implications.

Yet within these broad parameters there is great diversity, readily apparent with careful observation. As Crocker observed, "it must be stated that the items of this repertory are so marked by individual traits as to render many generalities invalid. This is perhaps the single most important conclusion to emerge from a consideration of the early sequence. . . . We need always to be reminded that throughout the Middle Ages individual composers labored and rejoiced to produce new works in new forms, or individual variations of old ones."[5] In other words, looking for "textbook" examples of early sequences is as elusive as looking for textbook fugues in the *Well-Tempered Clavier*. One

---

[1] Thomas Merton, *The Way of Chuang Tzu* (New York: New Directions, 1969), 110-11.

[2] *Medieval Sequences from Nonantola*, Schola Hungarica, dir. László Dobszay and Janka Szendrei (Quint CD, 903084, 1993).

[3] Parker J. Palmer, *The Active Life* (San Francisco: Harper, 1990), 55.

[4] *New Grove* (1980), s.v. "Sequence," by Richard Crocker.

[5] Richard Crocker, *The Early Medieval Sequence* (Berkeley: University of California Press, 1977), 370.

can observe clear principles, but the pieces are not the result of applying rigid formulas. When we realize this we can look deeper, honoring and delighting in the original details.

In selecting the program for the Schola Hungarica's recording of sequences, I focused on an Italian repertory because many Italian centers preserve microcosms of the entire spectrum of styles current in the genre around the year 1000. In a paper presented in 1990, I made a case in particular for the repertory from the northern Italian abbey of St. Silvester at Nonantola for a number of reasons.[6] These include: 1) the historical importance of the abbey; 2) the fine manuscripts copied there that preserve the repertory of sequences; 3) the make-up of the repertory itself; 4) the precise, diastematic musical notation with clefs, which in many cases offers the earliest readable versions of the East Frankish sequences; 5) the care with which music and text were notated; and 6) the level of Latinity displayed in the manuscripts. Furthermore, with its variety of styles the Nonantolan repertory gives rise to a wealth of possibilities of performance.

Performance Practice in the Early Medieval Sequence

Before addressing the Schola's live encounter with the Nonantolan sequences, brief mention is in order of some characteristics of the transmission of sequences that make the genre among the most problematic categories in all of chant with respect to performance practice. Little is known about the performance of sequences in the ninth and tenth centuries. Their preservation in the earliest East and West Frankish manuscripts in both syllabic and melismatic versions suggests a range of possibilities. Examples of this are well known to specialists, but for those who may be unfamiliar with the Western manuscript tradition, I include a few facsimiles that reveal the possibilities.

Sequence melodies are preserved in two versions: syllabically above the text and melismatically, either in the margins in East Frankish sources, or in separate sections of *sequentiaria* in West Frankish sources. Notker's sequence *Congaudent angelorum chori* is shown in figs. 2.1 and 2.2, from the East Frankish manuscripts Munich 14083 (a *cantatorium* from St. Emmeram, Regensburg, copied in the second half of the eleventh century) and Bamberg lit. 5 (a cantatorium from Reichenau copied in 1000-01). The melodies are represented by notation *in campo aperto* in the margins. The Bamberg manuscript also has neumes above each syllable. This type of syllabic notation is not as useful as the marginal versions because the overall shape of the melody cannot be adequately conveyed in non-diastematic notation in a syllabic style—we have basically a series of individual pitch-indicators (*virgae* and *puncta*), which does not give us a sense of the gestalt of the melodic phrase.[7]

The next facsimile (see fig. 2.3), an excerpt from the Easter sequence *Victimae paschali laudes* from the twelfth-century manuscript Einsiedeln 366, also uses both syllabic and melismatic settings, but now with the clear diastematic notation, including staff lines and clefs. Figure 2.4 is from the famous tenth-century source St. Gall 484, where just the melismatic forms of the sequence melodies, the *sequentiae*, are preserved along with their curious and often puzzling titles. Another puzzling aspect of this manuscript is that the melodies are read from the bottom of the page up. A convincing explanation for the reversing of the normal pattern has not yet been set forth. The fifth facsimile (fig. 2.5) juxtaposes a section of the *prosarium* and *sequentiarium* from the manuscript Paris, Bibliothèque Nationale, lat. 1121, where syllabic and melismatic versions of the melodies are preserved in different parts of the same manuscript. Since the West Frankish sources were diastematic from early on, and hence the syllabic settings readable, the melismatic versions presented as *sequentiae* were not necessary to communicate the melodic profile, as they were in the East Frankish sources.

---

[6] Brunner, "Nonantolan Sequences: Toward an Anthology of Recorded Sound," paper read at the fourth meeting of the International Musicological Society study group Cantus Planus, Pécs, Hungary, 4 September 1990. Since that time, I completed an edition of the entire repertory of sequences from Nonantola: *Early Medieval Chants from Nonantola, Part IV: Sequences*, in Recent Researches in the Music of the Middle Ages and Early Renaissance, vol. 33 (Madison: A-R Editions, 1999). The introduction to this volume (pp. xi-xxvi) contains a more extensive discussion of the Nonantolan repertory and its place in the history of the early medieval sequence.

[7] For a thorough discussion of the notation of sequences in East Frankish sources and the implications for performance, see Andreas Haug, *Gesungene und schriftlich dargestellte Sequenz: Beobachten zum Schiftbild der ältesten ostfränkishen Sequenzenhandschriften* (Neuhausen-Stuttgart: Hänssler-Verlag, 1987).

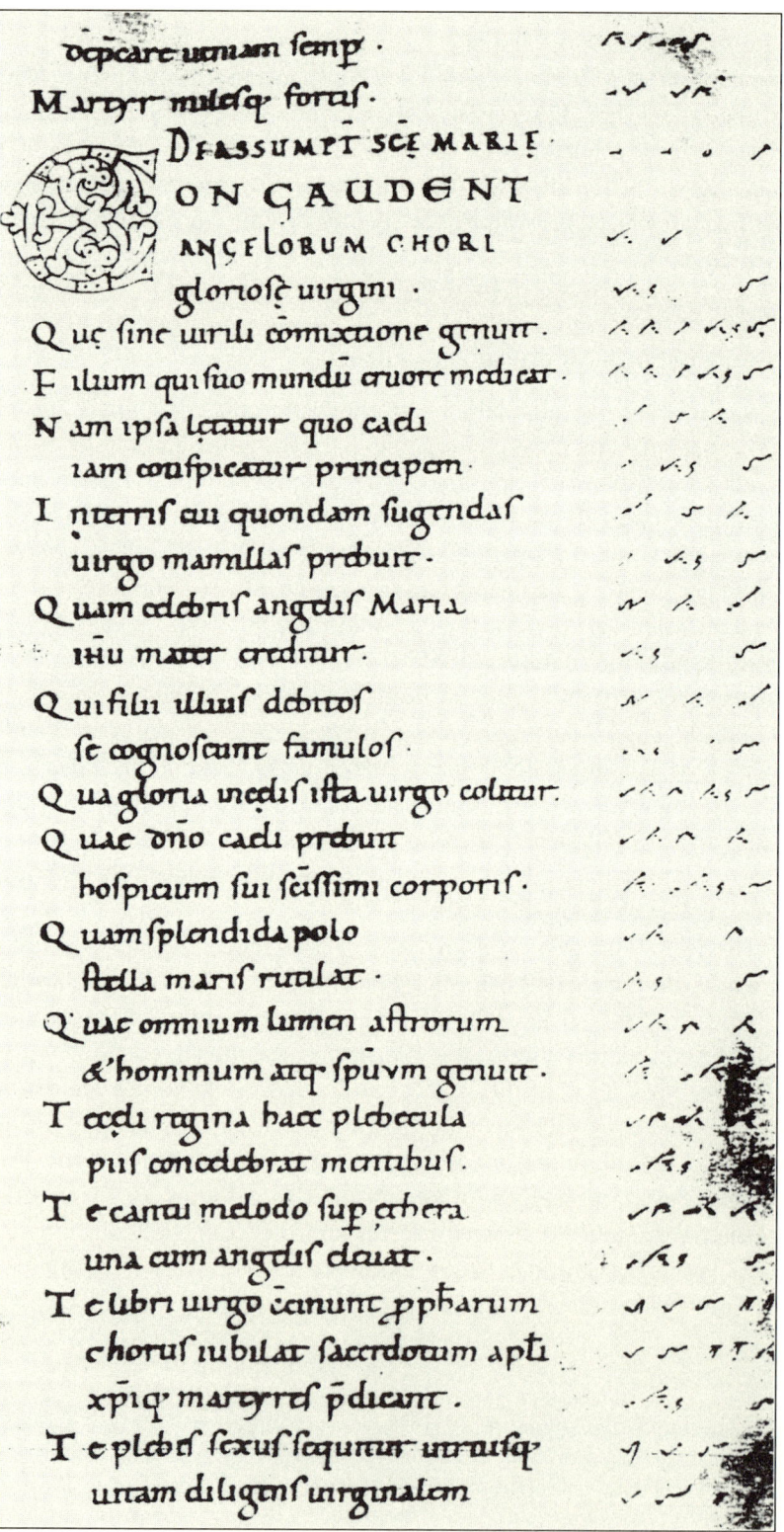

Fig. 2.1. *Congaudent angelorum chori*,
Munich, Bayerische Staatsbibliothek, Ms. Clm 14083, f. 23v.
Manuscript is from St. Emmeram in Regensburg

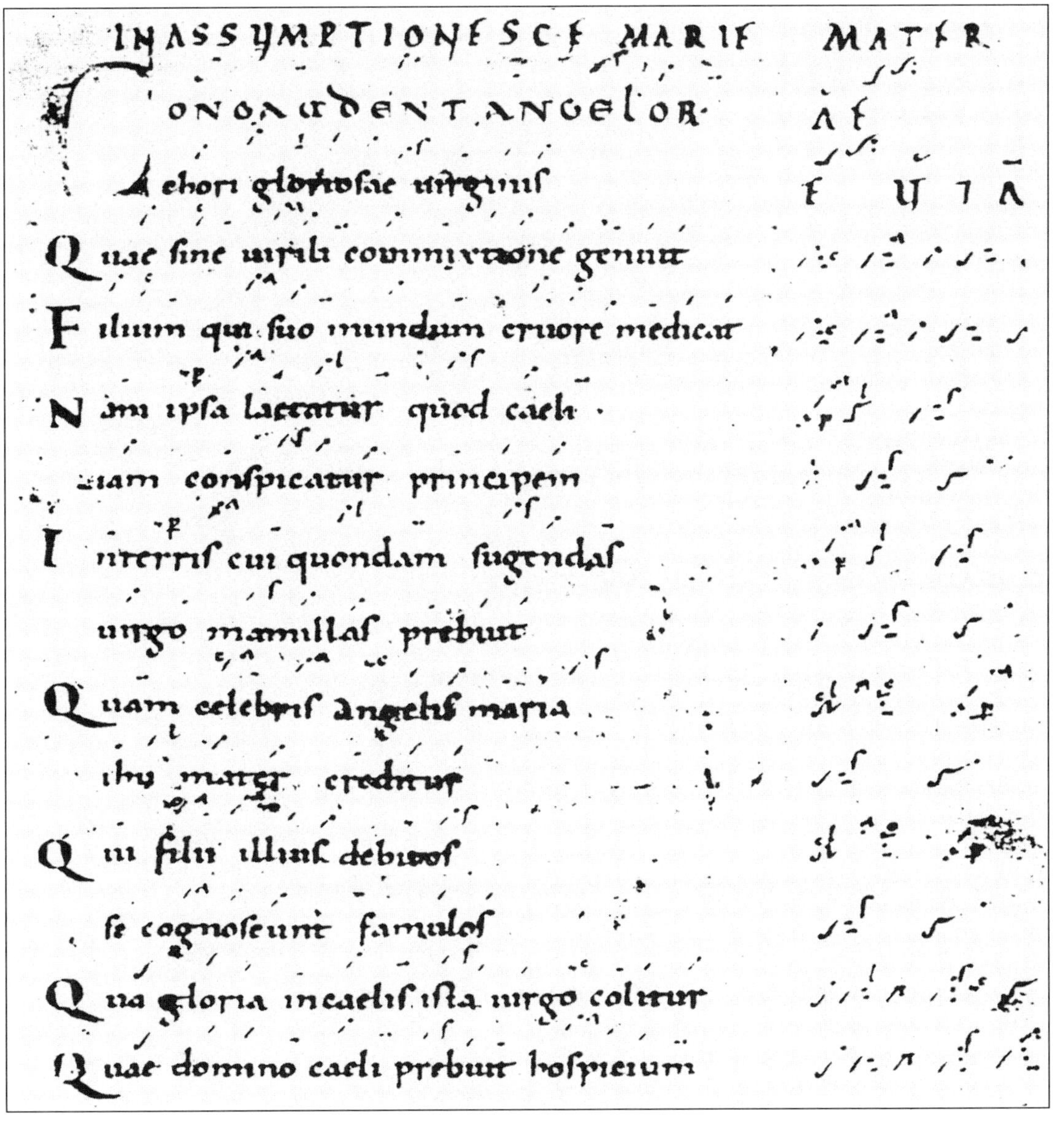

The Tao of Singing

IN ASSVMPTIONE SCE MARIE   MATER
Congaudent angelorum   AE
   chori gloriosae uirginis   E   VIA
Quae sine uirili commixtione genuit
Filium qui suo mundum cruore medicat
Nam ipsa laetatur quod caeli
   iam conspicatur principem
Interris cui quondam sugendas
   uirgo mamillas prebuit
Quam celebris angelis maria
   ihu mater creditur
Qui filii illius debitos
   se cognoscunt famulos
Qua gloria incaelis ista uirgo colitur
Quae domino caeli prebuit hospicium

Fig. 2.2. *Congaudent angelorum chori*,
Bamberg, Staatsbibliothek, Ms. lit. 5, f. 122

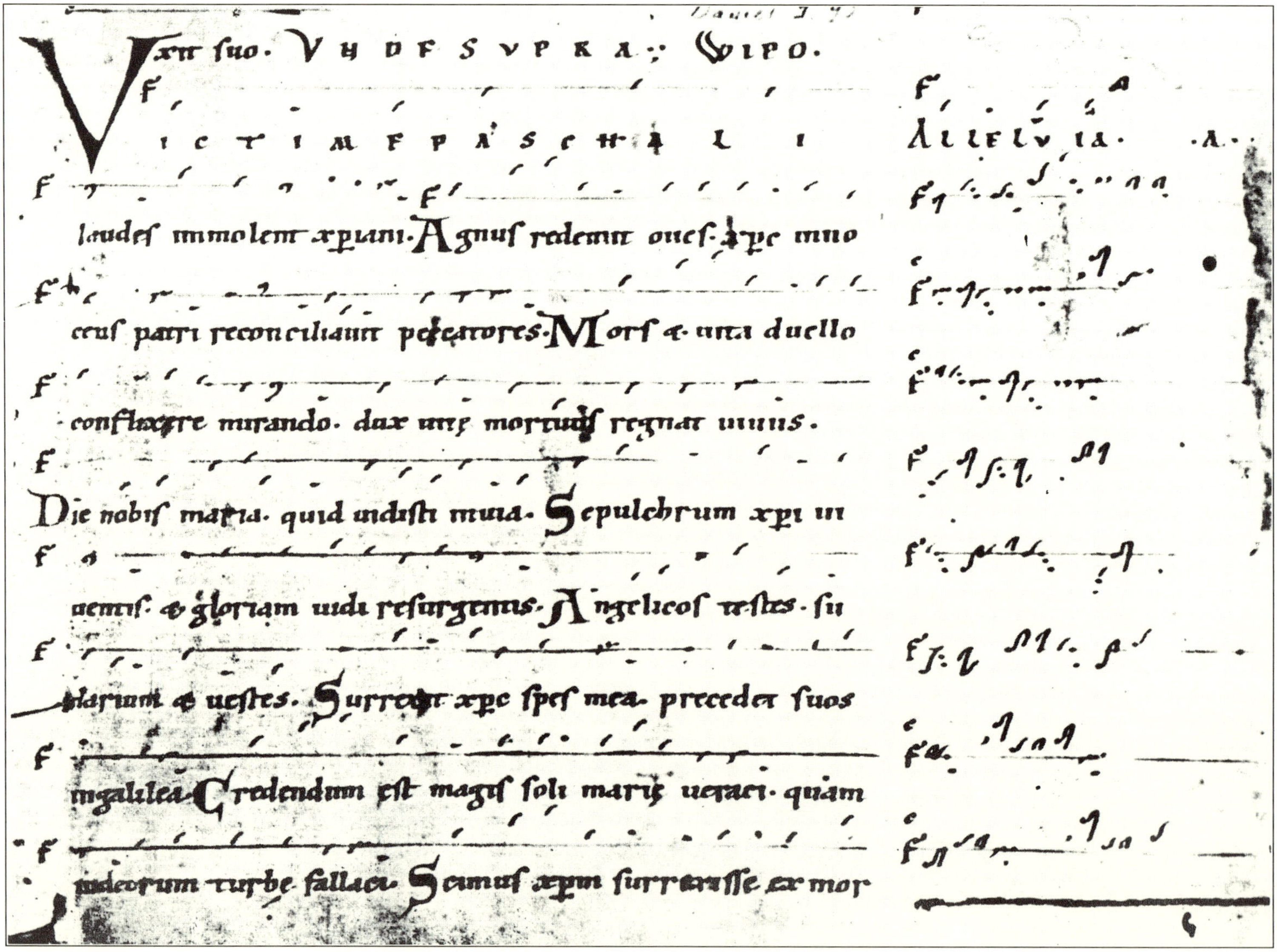

Fig. 2.3. *Victimae paschali laudes*, Einsiedeln, Stiftsbibliothek, Ms. 366, p. 17

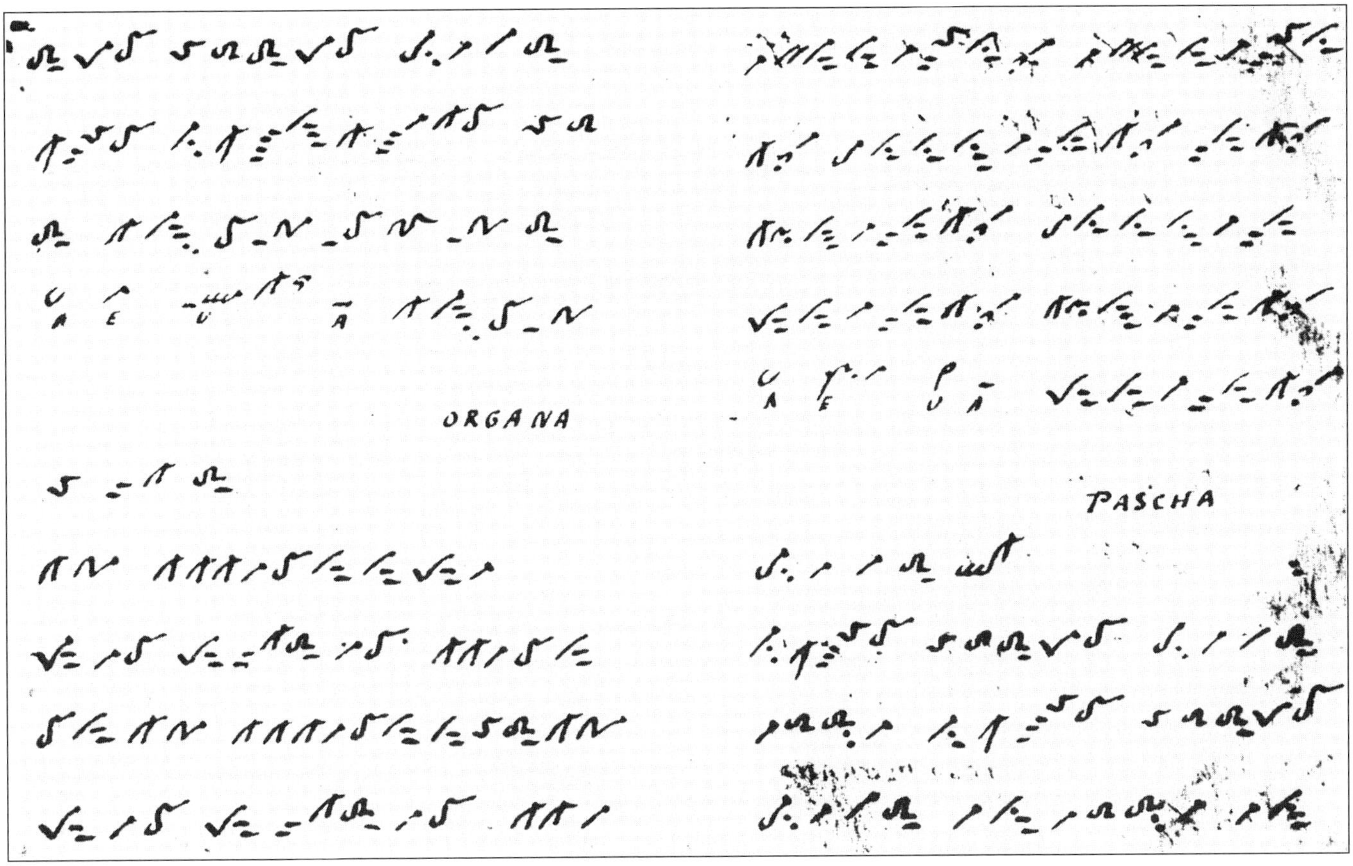

Fig. 2.4. *Sequentia* from St. Gall, Stiftsbibliothek, Ms. 484, pp. 274-75

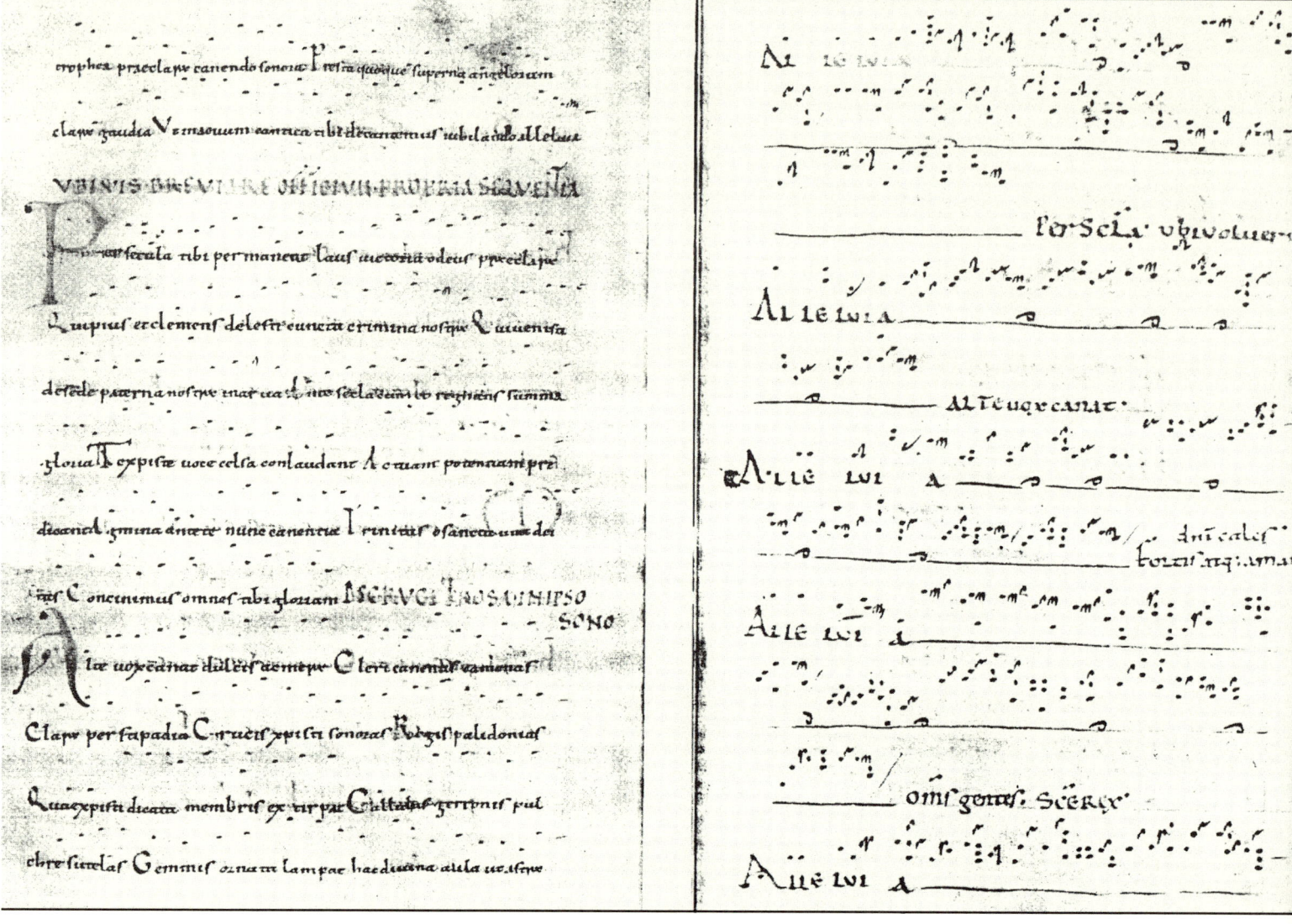

Fig. 2.5. Portion of the *Prosarium* and portion of the *Sequentiarium*,
Paris, Bibliothèque Nationale, Ms. lat. 1121, ff. 197v and 68r

The relationship of the syllabic and melismatic versions of the melodies in the written script has given rise to considerable speculation on performance. There are four general theories about how the melismatic versions were performed: 1) The melismatic versions were not performed at all, but rather simply provided a clearer idea of the melodic profile than the syllabic settings.[8] 2) The melismatic versions were performed after each verse as melismas on the syllable "a."[9] 3) The melismatic versions were performed simultaneously with the texted, syllabic setting.[10] And 4) the melismatic versions were performed on musical instruments.[11]

---

[8] Jacques Handschin, "Trope, Sequence, and Conductus," *New Oxford History of Music*, 2: *Early Medieval Music up to 1300*, ed. Anselm Hughes (Oxford: Oxford University Press, 1954), 158.

[9] Heinrich Husmann, "Sequenz und Prosa," *Annales musicologiques* 2 (1954): 61-91.

[10] Smits van Waesberghe, "Zur ursprünglichen Vortragsweise der Prosulen, Sequenzen und Organa," *Bericht über den siebenten Internationalen Musikwissenschaftlichen Kongress, Köln 1958* (Kassel: Bärenreiter, 1959), 251-54.

[11] Ewald Jammers, *Musik in Byzanz, im päpstlichen Rom und im Frankenreich* (Heidelberg: Carl Winter, 1962), 287-89; Andreas Holschneider, "Instrument Titles to the Sequentiae of the Winchester Tropers," in *Essays on Opera and English History in Honor of Jack Westrup*, ed. F. W. Sternfeld, et al. (Oxford: Blackwell, 1975), 8-18.

These theories are neither casual suggestions nor wild speculation. Rather, each has been set forth by an eminent medievalist who summons impressive evidence to support his hypothesis. If one includes considerations of soloistic or choral performance and the possibilities of alternating performance forces between halves of the couplet, these basic theories expand into well over a dozen possibilities of performance. Some of the theories seem less convincing when actually performed. An example would be the solution on the recording of the West Frankish sequence *Epiphaniam Domino* performed by the Accademia Monteverdiana, directed by Denis Stevens.[12] Stevens uses the second approach given above—that is, singing the melismatic versions after each syllabically sung verse. The phrases are doubled in length and the melodic phrases are heard four times in each couplet, rather than just twice. The melismatic versions also seem plodding in this performance and produce tedium, rather than the crisp momentum set up by text and music in the straight syllabic version.

It is also quite likely that performance differed from time to time and place to place. Indeed, in his study of the Winchester tropes, Alejandro Planchart cites examples of divergence in performance from one occasion to another even in the same church. As he appropriately puts it, sequences "seem to have remained in a no man's land between choral and soloistic performance."[13] In all of his work on the sequence, Crocker has written relatively little about performance questions, which is interesting since his scholarship is informed by his own considerable experience in singing and conducting chant. In his *New Grove* article "Sequence," however, he advocates playing it safe:

> Given the inconclusive nature of the evidence, and for other reasons as well, it seems advisable to consider the primary form of the work of art to be the singing of the melody with text, straight through, as found in the prosaria. This form, at least, gives a reliable base for stylistic judgments, which can then be modified to take into account other possible modes of performance.[14]

Schola Hungarica's Performances

The Schola Hungarica essentially decided *not* to sing the melodies straight through, to present "just the facts," but to shape their performance around the particular features of the Nonantolan sequences. Table 2.1 lists the sequences contained on the Schola Hungarica's recording, along with probable origins of the texts and the titles of the melodies. The table also displays in abbreviated form how the performance forces were used in each piece, as well as any unusual aspects to the performance. The fifteen sequences reveal fifteen different approaches to performance. These differences stem not from an attempt to produce variety for its own sake, or for commercial consideration, but rather arose out of the "live encounter" with each piece, allowing its hidden potential to be realized in creative ways that respect the notated source.

We can approach discussion of performance from three broad perspectives. First, it can be approached from the perspective of form and the division of performance forces, that is, how performance decisions highlight, emphasize, and articulate various aspects of the form. On the most superficial level, as is well known, early sequences are similar, exhibiting predominantly syllabic settings and couplet structure (i.e., *a bb cc dd . . . yy z*). Yet these characteristics reflect only general principles and provide at best only a crude container. Focus on such a level alone would make listening and further commentary unnecessary, something like passing over the first movement of a Mozart or Haydn sonata or string quartet by noting it is in the "standard sonata form." Obviously, as with later music, the tension and interaction between form and content, container and process, have been the focus of a great deal of creative energy and hence are an area of interest to us. Table 2.1, in the column on the far right, reveals how varied the use of performance forces is in rendering individual sequences in performance. Strong contrasts in groupings, as in *Ecce vicit* where the men (M) alternate with the whole ensemble (T = *tutti*), highlight the individual phrases and emphasize the couplet structure. *Summi triumphum* lies at the opposite end of the spectrum

---

[12] Cf. the recorded collection *The Worcester Fragments* (Nonesuch H-71308).

[13] Alejandro Planchart, *The Repertory of Tropes at Winchester*, vol. 1 (Princeton: Princeton University Press, 1977), 51.

[14] *New Grove* (1980), s.v. "Sequence," by Richard Crocker.

Table 2.1
Sequences from Nonantolan Repertory
Recorded by Schola Hungarica [Quint 903084]

Incipit	Text[a]	Melody Title	Performance forces/Notes[b]
1. Ecce vicit	WF	Concordia	M/T(M,W,C) [w/out All 1b]
2. Dic nobis	WF	Romana	W½/T(W)
3. Summi triumphum	EF/N	Captiva	M½/M½
4. Benedicta semper sancta	?	Benedicta sit	M/T(M,W)
5. Stans a longe	WF	Metensis minor	C dir.; M sing mel. simultaneously
6. Laeta mente	EF/N	Exsultate Deo	W dir. [w/out All 1b]
7. O quam mira	EF/N	Confitemini	C,W dir.
8. Haec sunt sacra	It	Eia turma	M solo/M solo
9. Sanctae crucis celebremus	It	"Sanctum diem"	M/W [w/out All 1b]; G finalis held throughout, alt.
10. Alme mundi rex	It	"Hodiernus sacratior"	M/T(M,W) [w/C 6, 8]
11. Pretiosa solemnitas	It	?	W dir [W,C on cadential echo, b]
12. Sancti merita benedicti	It	Occidentana	W/T(W,M) [final cadence = parallel organum]
13. Laurenti David magni	EF/N	Romana	W½/W½
14. Congaudent angelorum chori	EF/N	Mater	W solo/T(W) [5a,b alt.; 8b alt.]
15. Alma fulgens	It	—	M/T(M,W,C) [C only All 1b]

Texts: Italian [6]; Notker [5]; W. Frankish [3]; ? [1]

[a] Abbreviations of text origin as follows: EF = East Frankish; EF/N = Notker; WF = West Frankish; It = Italian.

[b] The following abbreviations are used: C = Children; M = Men; W = Women; T = Tutti; All 1b = Alleluia after first phrase of sequence; dir. = direct performance (i.e., without alternation); / = divides 1st and 2nd half of couplet [e.g., M/W, Men sing 1a, 2a, 3a, etc., Women sing 1b, 2b, 3b, etc.]; alt. = alternation; mel. = melismatic.

in that just the men, divided into two groups, sing. The effect is to conceal or downplay the melodic repetitions, giving more of a sense of continuous flow, musically and textually, from start to finish. As the table suggests, many possibilities are explored between these poles of maximum contrast and continuity.

Second, we could discuss performance from the perspective of the articulation of the lines and phrases themselves. Here we can examine two levels: that of the phrase and that of the motive (or smaller gestures, many of which are common figures—or "shared idioms," as Crocker calls them—that are found in many melodies in the early sequence). In rendering a phrase in performance the larger-scale units of text and melody are the foundation for making a host of subsidiary decisions. For example, tempo is not an independent problem for the Schola Hungarica, but rather a means, in service of bringing coherence to the overall phrase. Also, whether the lines will have internal articulation of subphrases or motives through caesuras or lengthened notes is a matter that can be decided in relation to the overall sense of the phrase. This will become clearer when we look at the specific examples below.

Third, we could discuss performance from the perspective of unusual or experimental approaches that reveal particular aspects of the pieces. I have mentioned a few of these already, but more details will be pointed out in the discussion of individual excerpts.

Let us begin by examining an excerpt from the Easter sequence *Ecce vicit*, which is given in fig. 2.6 and ex. 2.1.[15] The Schola's performance creates a high degree of contrast between phrases and what are clearly sets of motives within the phrases. Men alternate with the entire Schola (men, women, and children) in singing the two phrases of each couplet, making the progressive parallelism and overall form very clear. The motives within phrases are set off by slightly lengthening the final note, as indicated by the horizontal stroke above the notes. The emphasis on the motivic construction of the phrases tends to break up the sense of line, but creates a mosaic quality and reveals

---

[15] At the Cantus Planus meeting the examples presented here were played and discussed during the presentation. The written version will best be followed and understood in conjunction with the CD recording (see n. 2, above).

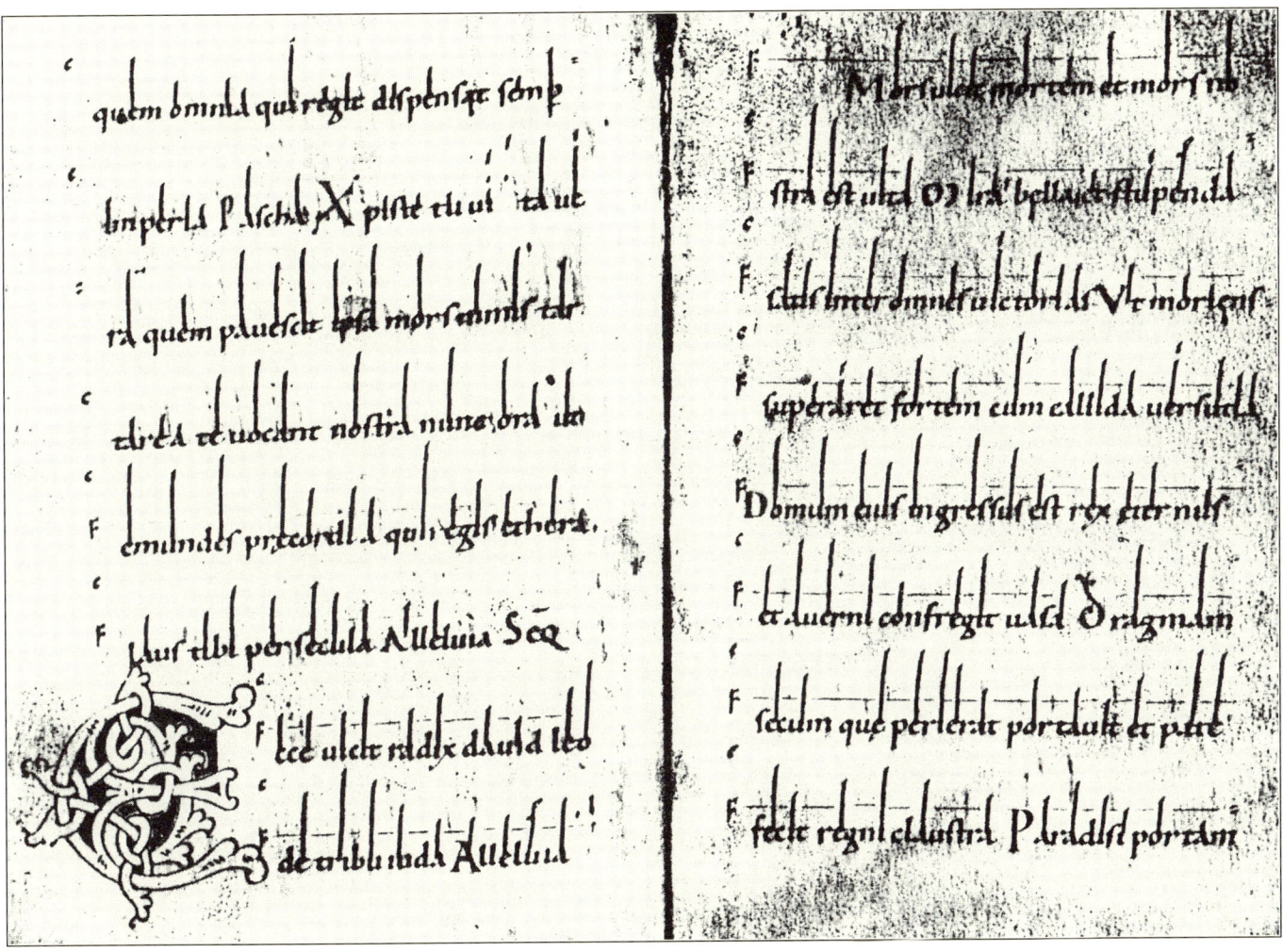

Fig. 2.6. *Ecce vicit*, Rome, Biblioteca Casanatense Ms. 1741, ff. 76v-77

how these units are combined to create longer phrases.[16] This musical articulation of the text seems to be primarily musically motivated, as it does not particularly reveal or highlight aspects of the text, but the musical effect is striking, offering us a clearer understanding of the building blocks of the melodies.

The Schola's performance of *Dic nobis* (see ex. 2.2) downplays the contrast between the two halves of each couplet by alternating half the women with the whole women's section. Furthermore, the motivic structure of the phrases is emphasized by singing phrases straight through on a single breath with a strong sense of directed motion.

The performance of the Ascension sequence *Summi triumphum* (see ex. 2.3) presents the opposite end of the spectrum from *Ecce vicit*. The men are divided into two equal groups that alternate in performing phrases of each couplet. They use a technique popular in some east European folk-song traditions of overlapping the end of a phrase and the beginning of the next, creating a seamless performance that has the quality of an exhilarating headlong rush from beginning to end.

The performances of the shorter sequences *Stans a longe* (see ex. 2.4) and *Laeta mente* (ex. 2.5) offer some unusual but convincing interpretations. For *Stans a longe* the Schola adopts Smits van Waesberghe's radical suggestion about performance of prosulas by having the men sing the melismatic versions of the melody simultaneously with the children, who sing words and music in direct performance throughout.[17] The recording shows that the results

---

[16] *Ecce vicit* is set to the melody "Concordia." For a detailed discussion of this melody, see Bruno Stäblein, "Die Sequenzmelodie 'Concordia' und ihr geschichtlicher Hintergrund," in *Festschrift Hans Engel zum siebzigsten Geburtstag*, ed. H. Heussner (Kassel: Bärenreiter, 1964), 364-92.

[17] See van Waesberghe, ibid.

Example 2.1. *Ecce vicit* (excerpt), Rome, Casanatense Ms. 1741, ff. 76v-77.

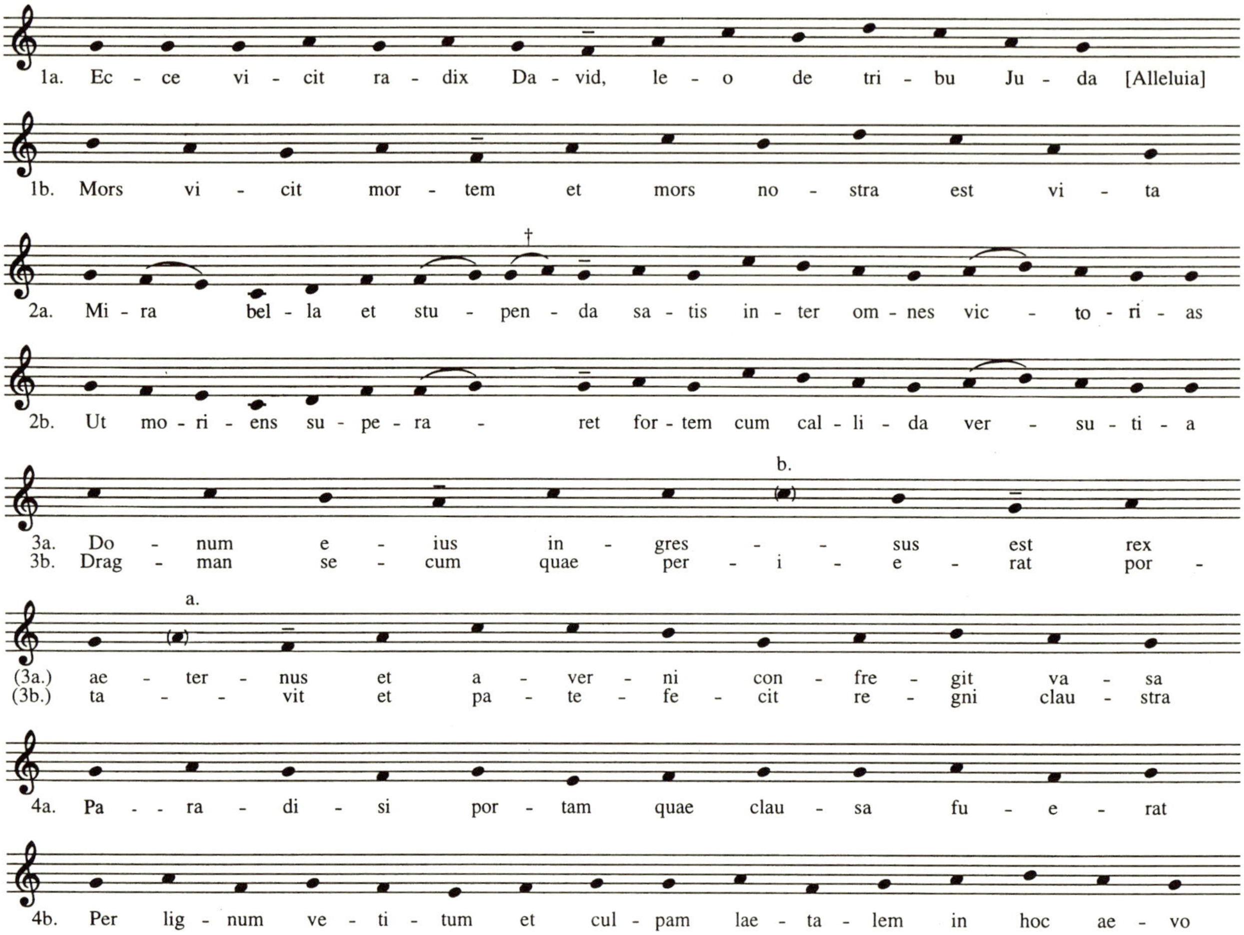

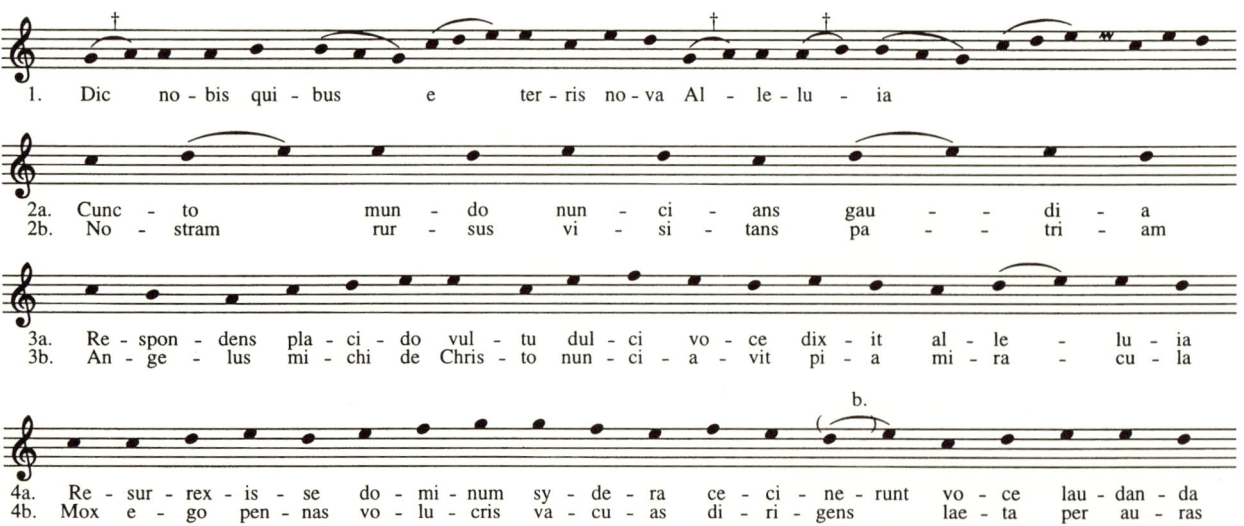

Example 2.2. *Dic nobis* (excerpt), Rome, Casanatense Ms. 1741, ff. 81v-82.

Example 2.3. *Summi triumphum* (excerpt), Rome, Casanatense Ms. 1741, ff. 90v-91.

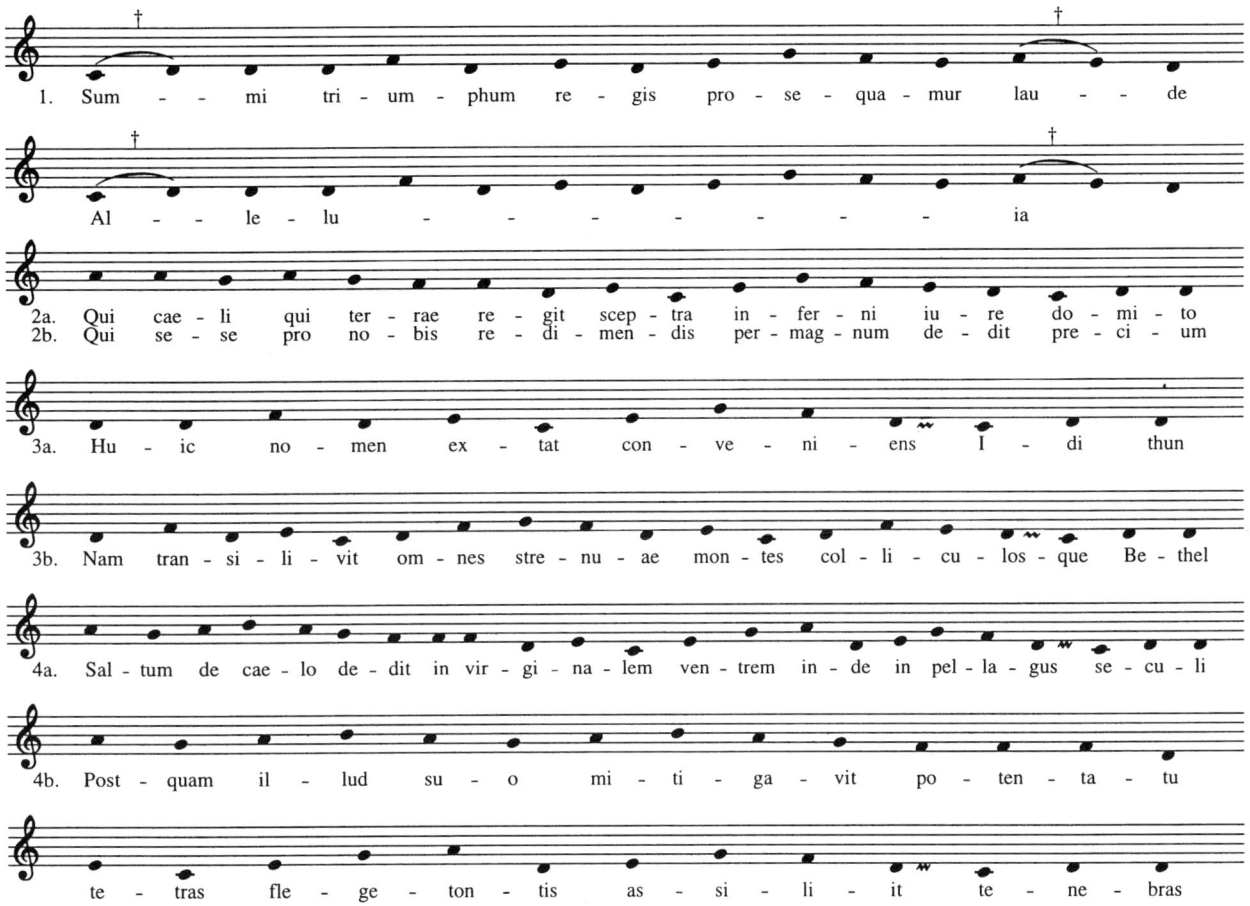

Example 2.4. *Stans a longe* (excerpt), Rome, Casanatense Ms. 1741, ff. 131-131v.

Example 2.5. *Laeta mente*, Rome, Casanatense Ms. 1741, ff. 131-132, with Alleluia *Exultate Deo*.

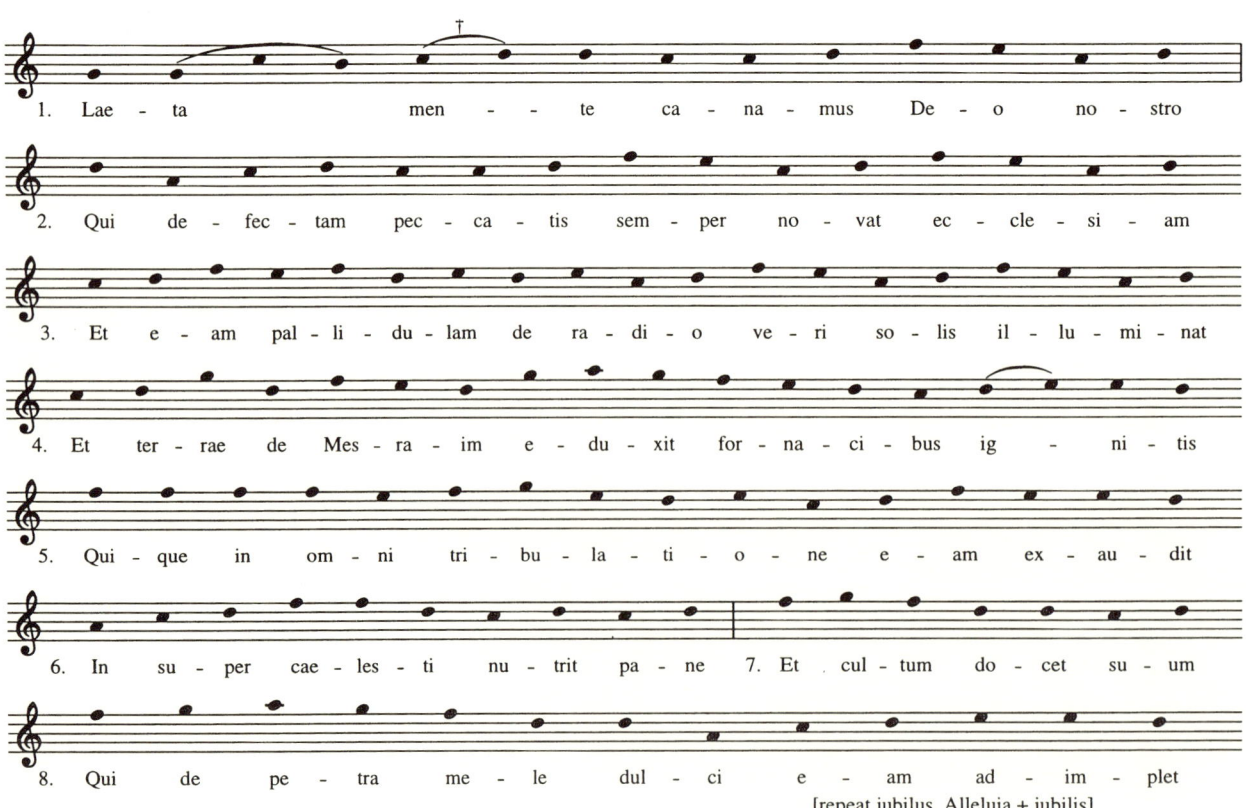

of such an interpretation can be aesthetically convincing. The men's voices add more depth and resonance to the overall sound, while the text remains clear and crisp in its articulation by the younger voices.

The Schola's interpretation of *Laete mente* (see ex. 2.5) is more radical and lacks, to my knowledge, any historical precedent. The sequence uses the same incipit as the Alleluia *Exultate Deo*, which precedes it. The sequence ends on the co-final, *d*, rather than the final, *g*. Since the jubilus of the Alleluia essentially moves from co-final to final, the Schola uses the jubilus at the end of the sequence to return to the final, and then repeats the Alleluia and jubilus. The effect is to frame the sequence with the Alleluia respond, as if the sequence were a second verse. This interpretation has some significant implications, implying that the sequence may have been a prosula on an original melisma or jubilus, and may have once been framed by the repetition of the Alleluia at the end. The Schola's interpretation, however, seems to be primarily motivated by aesthetic considerations, rather than historical hypothesis. The jubilus does bring a sense of closure in its gradual descent to the final, and the Alleluia respond creates a fine sense of balance. These observations, of course, represent my own, modern judgments, but the potential for such unusual interpretations is implicit in the written record, and their realization challenges us and offers us a richer understanding of the music itself.

The pieces of Italian origin often depart significantly from stylistic norms that characterize their northern counterparts. *Sanctae crucis celebremus* (see ex. 2.6) represents a very different style than most northern pieces. This relatively short piece for the feast of the Invention of the Holy Cross winds its way around its final *g*, which is the central focus of all the phrases. This focus on a single pitch is markedly different from the most popular northern melodies, which explore other points of reference, often moving to a climactic high point by the end of the piece. The gentle opening up of the strict syllabic style with periodic neumatic elaboration also tends to soften the highly directed motion of the northern pieces. The Schola's reading alternates between men's and women's voices, but each group sustains the *g*-final for the duration of the next phrase. This pedal serves as a central axis around which the melody is woven. Sustaining the final throughout emphasizes what a powerful organizing force the final serves in this particular piece.

Example 2.6. *Sanctae crucis celebremus* (excerpt), Rome, Casanatense Ms. 1741, ff. 85v-86.

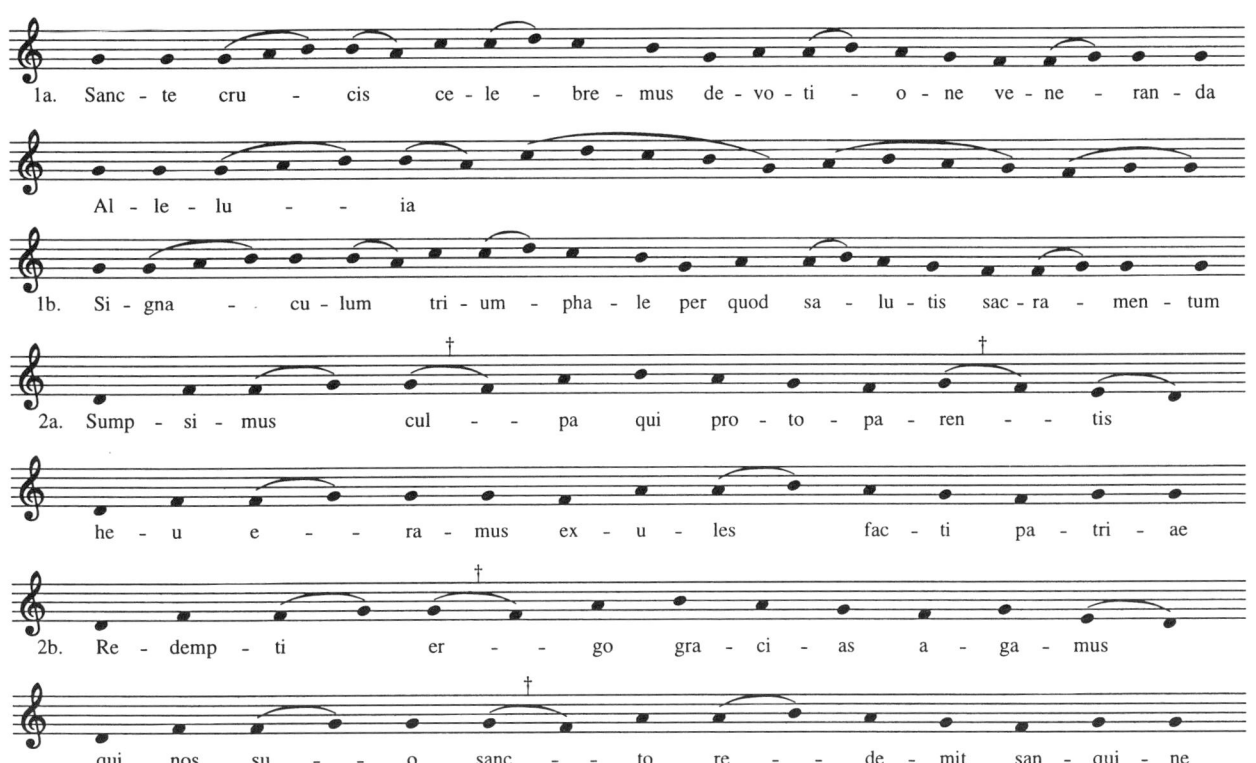

Other Italian sequences on the recording merit examination, as well, but in the interest of space I shall simply point these out. The melismatic elaborations in *Alma fulgens* open up the range of interpretation inherent in flourishes freed from constraints of text declamation. The structure of *Pretiosa solemnitas* invites an unusual echo effect at the end of the second half of each couplet, since these phrases are extended by the repetition of the final four notes. Listening to these pieces, as well as the rest not discussed here, results in a rich tour through the performance possibilities inherent in the genre.

It seems to me that the artistic success and magic of the Schola Hungarica's performances are due to several factors. At the foundation is a disciplined, intelligent musicality, born out of excellent music education and a relationship to music that is enviable. In addition, the Schola Hungarica has been singing together for twenty-five years under Dobszay's and Szendrei's direction, and, although the personnel has changed over time, there is a continuity and tradition that is very powerful.

Where is the equivalent of the "fasting," of what Khing, the woodcarver, went through to purify his heart and mind? I might suggest it is more than just the sacrifice of hard work in learning notes and working out interpretations. The fasting that informs the right action of these songs comes, in a sense, more from a different diet, that is, the discipline of the prolonged engagement in—the living encounter with—an authentic monophonic music tradition that was preserved into the twentieth century essentially out of the influence of the mainstream of European music. I am referring to the monumental ethnomusicological work of, among others, Zoltan Kodály and Béla Bartók in recording and preserving the folk traditions of central Europe. Dobszay, Szendrei, and many colleagues and students have been involved in the transcription and editing of this music for decades.

In a paper on chant performance given at several American universities in 1989, László Dobszay observed:

> To teach the limits and possibilities of the performance [of Gregorian chant] the best masters are other kinds of ancient monophonic cultures . . ., [including] the old folk music cultures, if they are akin to Plainchant in their tonal world, in the presence of the *parlando-rubato*, in the same connection between music and text or function. That means that folk music is not a direct model for chant performance but a fine musical background for the singer. When the leaders of the Schola Hungarica wanted to elaborate their performing style they were inspired by an intense folk music research done over many years, including the experience of transcribing thousands of pieces of folk music. But this activity did not give ideas directly; the classic forms, the impersonal style of performance in folk music let them learn a strict discipline and know the technical arsenal of a monophonic music culture, hardly attainable for a musician who has been trained exclusively in the eighteenth-nineteenth century European music.[18]

The Schola Hungarica's directors developed over time new strategies, instincts, a different consciousness about the possibilities of monophonic music beyond the often plodding, bland readings of many chant performances that have allowed chant to be easily assimilated into the "New Age" bins in record stores, so that the music can be used as soothing, ethereal wallpaper, mindless music to reduce stress, produce pleasant environments, and so forth, rather than spirited multifaceted musical expressions. As we all know, singing just the individual notes as written can produce lifeless and drab performances. We can hear a powerful demonstration of how far a performance can differ from the historical record in notation in Janka Szendrei's edition of the recordings of sixteenth and seventeenth century tunes in folk memory.[19] The folk performances are as different from the notated versions as a healthy living person is to a skeleton. But this kind of "resurrection" of old notated sources requires a "live encounter" with the material, and some type of disciplined, long-term engagement with a monophonic music tradition.

In the same paper, Dobszay made clear how the Schola Hungarica works out the delicate relationship between music and text, sound and sense:

---

[18] László Dobszay, "Chant Performance: Some Problems and Solutions," paper read at the University of Kentucky, and other universities, October 1989.

[19] Cassette recording *16th- and 17th-Century Tunes in the Folk Memory*, ed. Janka Szendrei (Budapest: MTA Zenetudományi Intézet, 1993).

> [The notation of] Gregorian music offers two sure points of departure. One is the grammar of the text. The articulation and caesuras of the text lead us to start from the whole musically as well: first to grasp the largest units, then the subordinate phrases, and finally consider the smallest details. The second factor is the row of the notes themselves, in the sense of how they correspond to the tonality or, perhaps better said, how they realize the tonality. Again, we must first see the larger units, to hear the main notes—the centers of these greater units—and also their interrelationships. Next we must determine the skeletal or structural notes that lead one through the unit. *I want to emphasize that these two things are essential to the clarity of a good performance.* Only after this level can we turn to the details. How does the piece prepare the arrival to the main notes? Which are the second-range main notes? How do we go over from one note to another? And finally: What is the role of a single note in the small details? A careful analysis shows that the function of the melodic and ornamental melismas are different and they can be distinguished in the living performance too.[20]

We can appreciate the fruits of such a method by listening to and looking at the individual pieces, phrase by phrase, as Dobszay and Szendrei did, to understand just how the Schola Hungarica reveals in the complete set of fifteen sequences the range of possible solutions to the resurrection of the music, and how convincing and fresh are the particular choices settled upon. Of course we cannot undertake such an exhaustive study within the limited space available here. But you can rightly see in this discussion my attempt to honor this remarkable group, to explore and share something of their "secret" and to express my gratitude, admiration, and respect to its directors.

To invoke the ancient Chinese practice of Taoism and its spiritual alchemy may seem off the mark, or even bizarre—but there is a serious intent behind the connection. "The Tao that can be told is not the eternal Tao," the ancient text of the *Tao Te Ching* reminds us.[21] So much of what we value about the experience of music or its historical record cannot be spoken nor discovered through analysis alone. "To understand," the Danish novelist Peter Høeg recently wrote," is an attempt to recapture something that has been lost."[22] We cannot recapture this experience through the ways we go about explaining music, with our elegant words, efficient tables and statistics, our clever symbols, particularly when we are considering the most obvious musical characteristics, those that lend themselves most easily to verbal or symbolic representation. Rhythmic subtleties, vocal color, ornamental grace, qualities of energy, tension and release, directed movement, the relationship between sound and silence, are more difficult to capture, yet these aspects are essential to a convincing and satisfying performance. Our words and conceptual understanding are most valuable, it seems to me, when they lead us back into participation, engagement—that is, to a "live encounter," which, when then named, leads us to the nameless and back again. It is the direct connection that involves both head and heart, mind and body.

It is obvious to me that one of the reasons for the great power of what the Schola Hungarica has accomplished is the relationship they cultivate between practice and theory, experience and concept, doing and non-doing (*wu wei*), where each informs the other, and the whole process deepens, has the power of the spirit of "live encounter." In this sense Dobszay and Szendrei are to my mind the equivalent of Taoist masters.

Working with the Schola Hungarica for ten days in the making of the sequence recording, I saw much more than a skillful musical ensemble. I witnessed a vital learning community. The education the children in the Schola Hungarica receive in the process of singing is far more than musical: it is social and moral education as well.[23] Current scholarship on community development has demonstrated how important this type of activity is for building healthy communities.[24] The type of community that making music on this level can build is something many in our high-tech world are groping for, yet often in the wrong places and in unskilled ways. In this world of distraction, we too easily forget the transformative power of music and its attentive making.

---

[20] Dobszay, ibid.

[21] *Tao Te Ching*, trans. Stephen Mitchell (New York: Harper & Row, 1988), 1.

[22] Peter Høeg, *Smilla's Sense of Snow*, trans. Tiina Nunnally (New York: Farrar, Straus, Giroux, 1993), 37.

[23] Dobszay, *After Kodály: Reflections on Music Education* (Kecskemet: Zoltan Kodály Pedagogical Institute of Music, 1992). See, for example, the first chapter, "Principles," 13-24, for a discussion of Kodály's thinking about the place of music in human development.

[24] See, for example, Robert D. Putnam, *Making Democracy Work: Civic Traditions in Modern Italy* (Princeton: Princeton University Press, 1993).

3

A Didactic Musical Treatise from the
Late Middle Ages:
Ebstorf, Klosterarchiv, Ms. V,3

Karl-Werner Gümpel

The Protestant convent of Ebstorf in Lower Saxony, Germany, possesses among its manuscript sources a Latin treatise which deserves special attention since it originated at a place dedicated to the monastic reform of the late Middle Ages. Ebstorf had become a priory of nuns under the rule of St. Benedict in the late twelfth century, following the departure of Premonstratensian monks who had formerly lived there.[1] As a Benedictine settlement the convent appears first in 1197, when the name of "Thydericus prepositus de Ebbikesdorp" is mentioned in the founding document of another convent located in Altdorf (Buxtehude). Ebstorf's monastic tradition came to an end during the Reformation. In 1565 its nuns accepted the Lutheran faith and established a Protestant place of religious life.

About one hundred years before this time, the convent was the place of a well-documented and thorough reform under the leadership of Ebstorf's prior, Mathias von dem Knesebeck (d. 1493) and several other reform-minded personalities.[2] It lasted from May 1469 through 1476. During this time of renewal significant influence was exerted on Ebstorf by the Benedictine monastery in Bursfeld (or Bursfelde), a leading reform center and head of the so-called Bursfeld Congregation. As can be gathered from a contemporary report, the singing of Gregorian chant received particular consideration among the things to be improved in Ebstorf. All initial reform efforts failed however because the nuns "did not yet properly know the regulations regarding the performance of chant,"[3] not to mention a general resistance concerning the introduction of the monastic liturgy. As a result, six sisters on each side of the choir were carefully familiarized with the art of proper singing and later given the task of instructing the other nuns. At the same time the use of the organ was reduced, if not forbidden, while new chant books[4] found their way into Mass and Liturgical Hours. In another part of the report one reads: "We changed the choral singing and melodies belonging to it."[5] This observation seems to indicate the use of melodies from the newly introduced chant books.

Chant practice and its reform represent an important aspect of fifteenth-century musical activities and writings on music. During the 1460s and 70s, Conradus de Zabernia visited numerous cathedrals, collegiate churches, and

---

[1] For a detailed history of Ebstorf see Klaus Jaitner, "Ebstorf," in *Die Frauenklöster in Niedersachsen, Schleswig-Holstein und Bremen*, Germania Benedictina, 11, ed. Ulrich Faust, O.S.B. (St. Ottilien: EOS, 1984), 165-92. A second study by Jaitner was published under the title "Das Benediktinerinnenkloster Ebstorf im Mittelalter (ca. 1165-1550)," in *Das Benediktinerinnenkloster Ebstorf im Mittelalter: Vorträge einer Tagung im Kloster Ebstorf vom 22. bis 24. Mai 1987*, Quellen und Untersuchungen zur Geschichte Niedersachsens im Mittelalter, 11, ed. Klaus Jaitner and Ingo Schwab (Hildesheim: Lax, 1988), 1-25.

[2] Valuable information about this part of Ebstorf's history is presented in Ulrich Faust's article "Monastisches Leben in den Lüneburger Klöstern," in *Das Benediktinerinnenkloster Ebstorf im Mittelalter*, 34-36.

[3] Report 1, from which this passage has been quoted, can be found in Conrad Borchling, "Litterarisches und geistiges Leben im Kloster Ebstorf am Ausgange des Mittelalters," *Zeitschrift des historischen Vereins für Niedersachsen* (1905), 388-96.

[4] It should be noted in this context that most of Ebstorf's library holdings were abandoned during the years of reform and replaced with new manuscripts and books.

[5] Borchling, "Litterarisches und geistiges Leben."

monasteries in southern Germany in order to improve the choral singing of chant.[6] His approach was very much practice-oriented and was undertaken with the help of a clavi-monochord, on which he demonstrated the elements of music theory and the art of properly singing Gregorian melodies.[7] As to the production of musical treatises within the monastic reform movement, the Benedictine abbey of Melk in Austria[8] stands out because of a considerable number of texts which were written with the purpose of educating its monks and assisting them in their daily performance of Gregorian chant. Interestingly enough, the Ebstorf treatise shows a remarkable closeness to practice-oriented writings of the fifteenth century, in particular those of Anonymous XI (CS III), Ladislaus de Zalka, Magister Szydlovita,[9] and several treatises from Melk. Its provenance, elementary text, format, and illustrations clearly indicate that it was created as a teaching device for the musical training of students and nuns in Ebstorf.

* * * * *

Ms. V,3 is a volume of 264 folios measuring 217 x 160 mm. According to the catalog by Renate Giermann and Helmar Härtel it dates from the last third of the fifteenth century and originated in Ebstorf.[10] The manuscript has five separate sections, with the musical treatise on ff. 199-203 as its fourth part. In the other sections, hymnological texts (among them commentaries in the Low German language), grammatical writings, and a Latin-German glossary (fragment) have been copied. The treatise on music theory is written in textura and bastarda style and its various exercises employ Gothic neumes. Ff. 200v and 201 display colored pen-and-ink drawings of the *Manus Guidonica* (see fig. 3.1) and tonal system (see fig. 3.2). These are complemented by illustrations which in part depict activities related to musical education at a Benedictine convent.[11] Apart from its tonal letters, the Guidonian hand is filled with explanatory texts in prose and verse form. Additional texts appear above and below it. In the drawing of the tonal system the hexachords are represented as seven towers surrounded by texts and illustrations, while the letters Γ through *ee* are found on the left margin in alternating blue and red color.

The present edition closely follows the spelling of the Ebstorf treatise. As the only exception from this procedure, the letters *u* and *v* were adapted to the classical orthography, and the use of initial capital and lowercase letters was standardized. All vocal exercises were transcribed into modern notation, with their four-line staffs and letter clefs remaining unchanged.[12]

---

[6] See Gümpel, *Die Musiktraktate Conrads von Zabern*, Akademie der Wissenschaften und der Literatur, 3 (Mainz: Abhandlungen der Geistes- und Sozialwissenschaftlichen Klasse, 1956), 154-57.

[7] A vivid account of Conradus' teaching methods was given around 1500 by Rutgerus Sycamber de Venray in his *Dialogus de musica*, ed. Fritz Soddemann, Beiträge zur Rheinischen Musikgeschichte, 14 (Köln: Arno Volk, 1963), 9-10, 38-39, 44-45, 49, and 57. Like Wolfgang Trefler (see Gümpel, 155-56), Rutgerus had been a student of the Magister.

[8] Besides Austrian monasteries, Melk's extensive reform activities, which began in 1423, included numerous Benedictine abbeys in Bavaria and Suevia. Repercussions of the movement are also found in Hungary and Switzerland. The musical aspect of the reform has been extensively studied by Joachim Angerer, O. Praem., especially in *Die liturgisch-musikalische Erneuerung der Melker Reform*, Österreichische Akademie der Wissenschaften (Vienna: Philosophisch-historische Klasse, 1974), Sitzungsbericht 287, no. 5, "Veröffentlichungen der Kommission für Musikforschung 15." For plainchant theory at Melk during the fifteenth century, see the following sources from the Stiftsbibliothek: Ms. 662 (f. 104v); Ms. 873 (pp. 199-215); Ms. 949 (ff. 2-34); Ms. 950 (ff. 127-83, 183-88v, 222v-29); Ms. 985 (ff. 143v-57v); Ms. 988 (ff. 340b-342b); Ms. 1094 (ff. 201v-16); Ms. 1099 (pp. 23-36 and 103-10); Ms. 1835 (pp. 25-27).

[9] Richard Joseph Wingell, "Anonymous XI (CS III): An Edition, Translation, and Commentary" (Ph.D. diss., University of Southern California, 1973); Waclaw Gieburowski, "Die 'Musica magistri Szydlovite': Ein polnischer Choraltraktat des XV. Jahrhunderts" (Ph.D. diss., University of Breslau; Posen: St. Albert-Druckerei, 1915); Dénes von Bartha, *Das Musiklehrbuch einer ungarischen Klosterschule in der Handschrift von Fürstprimas Szalkai (1490)*, Musicologia Hungarica, 1 (Budapest: Magyar Nemzeti Múzeum / Az Orsz. Széchényi Könyvtár Kiadása, 1934).

[10] Renate Giermann and Helmar Härtel, *Handschriften des Klosters Ebstorf*, Mittelalterliche Handschriften in Niedersachsen, 10 (Wiesbaden: Harrassowitz, 1994), 133-39.

[11] The drawings have been studied by Brigitte Uhde-Stahl, "Figürliche Buchmalereien in den spätmittelalterlichen Handschriften der Lüneburger Frauenklöster," *Niederdeutsche Beiträge zur Kunstgeschichte*, 17 (Munich: Deutscher Kunstverlag, 1978), 28a-29b (with a reproduction of f. 200v and 201) and 54a-b (note 22-26). See also Birgit Hahn-Woernle, *Kloster Ebstorf: Die Bauplastik* (Ebstorf, 1980), 28 and 29 (plate 6 = f. 201) and 37. Another description and reproduction of the illuminated pages was published in Cord Meckseper, ed., *Stadt im Wandel: Kunst und Kultur des Bürgertums in Norddeutschland, 1150-1650*, 1 (Stuttgart-Bad Cannstatt: Cantz, 1985), 486-87, no. 339. As Uhde-Stahl surmises, the drawings were made by a nun from Ebstorf familiar with music lessons (f. 200v) and local customs, during a study break (f. 201).

[12] The author of this article wishes to kindly thank Frau Irmgard von Funcke, Abbess of Ebstorf, for her permission to publish the musical treatise from Ms. Ebstorf V,3.

Edition

(f. 199)

1 [G]amma-ut, est linea? Est. Quot voces habet? Unam. Quam? Ut. Quando habet ut? Semper.

2 [A]-re, est spacium? Est. Quot voces habet? Unam. Quam? Re. Quando habet re? Semper.

3 [B]e-mi, est linea? Est. Quot voces habet? Unam. Quam? Mi. Quando habet mi? Semper.

4 [C]e-fa-ut, est spacium? Est. Quot vo[ces] habet? Duas. Quas? Fa et ut. Quando habet fa? In primo b♮-durali in ascendendo et descendendo. Quando habet ut? In primo naturali in ascendendo et descendendo.

5 [D]e-sol-re, est linea? Est. Quot vo[ces] habet? Duas. Quas? Sol et re. Quando habet sol? In pri[mo] b♮[-durali] in as[cendendo] et des[cendendo]. Quando habet re? In primo naturali in as[cendendo] et des[cendendo].

6 [E]-la-mi, est spacium? Est. Quot vo[ces] habet? Duas. Quas? La et mi. Quando habet la? In pri[mo] b♮[-durali] in as[cendendo] et des[cendendo]. Quando habet mi? In primo na[turali] in as[cendendo] et des[cendendo].

7 [F]-fa-ut, est linea? Est. Quot vo[ces] habet? Duas. Quas? Fa et ut. Quando habet fa? In primo naturali in as[cendendo] et des[cendendo]. Quando habet ut? In primo bi-molli in as[cendendo] et des[cendendo].

8 [G]e-sol-re-ut, est spacium? Est. Quot vo[ces] habet? Tres. Quas? Sol, re et ut. Quando habet sol? In primo naturali in as[cendendo] et des[cendendo]. Quando habet re? In primo bi-molli in as[cendendo] et des[cendendo]. Quando habet ut? In secundo b♮-durali in as[cendendo] et des[cendendo].

9 [a]-la-mi-re, est linea? Est. Quot vo[ces] habet? Tres. Quas? La, mi et re. Quando habet la? In primo naturali in as[cendendo] et des[cendendo]. Quando habet mi? In primo bi-moli in as[cendendo] et des[cendendo]. Quando habet re? In secundo b♮-durali in as[cendendo] et des[cendendo].

10 [b]e-fa-b-mi, est spacium? Est. Quot vo[ces] habet? Duas. Quas? Fa et mi. Quando habet fa? In primo bi-molli in as[cendendo] et des[cendendo]. Quando habet mi? In secundo b♮-durali in as[cendendo] et des[cendendo].

11 [c]e-sol-fa-ut, est linea? Est. Quot vo[ces] habet? Tres. Quas? Sol, fa et ut. Quando habet sol? In primo bi-molli in as[cendendo] et des[cendendo]. Quando habet fa? In secundo b♮-durali in as[cendendo] et des[cendendo]. Quando habet ut? In secundo naturali in as[cendendo] et des[cendendo].

12 [d]e-la-sol-re, est spacium? Est. Quot vo[ces] habet? Tres. Quas? La, sol et re. Quando habet la? In primo bi-molli in as[cendendo] et des[cendendo]. Quando habet sol? In secundo b♮-durali in as[cendendo] et des[cendendo]. Quando habet re? In secundo naturali in as[cendendo] et des[cendendo].

13 [e]-la-mi, est linea? Est. Quot vo[ces] habet? Duas. Quas? La et mi. Quando habet la? In secundo b♮-durali in as[cendendo] et des[cendendo]. Quando habet mi? In secundo naturali in as[cendendo] et des[cendendo].

14 [e]f-fa-ut, est spacium? Est. Quot vo[ces] habet? Duas. Quas? Fa et ut. Quando habet fa? In secundo naturali in as[cendendo] et des[cendendo]. Quando habet ut? In secundo bi-molli in as[cendendo] et des[cendendo].

15 [g]e-sol-re-ut, est linea? Est. Quot vo[ces] habet? Tres. Quas? Sol, re et ut. Quando habet sol? In secundo naturali in as[cendendo] et des[cendendo]. Quando habet re? In secundo bi-molli in as[cendendo] et des[cendendo]. Quando habet ut? In tercio b♮-durali in as[cendendo] et des[cendendo].

16 [a]a-la-mi-re, est spacium? Est. Quot vo[ces] habet? Tres. Quas? La, mi [...].

(f. 199v-200)

(f. 200v)

17 Musica est motus vocum proporcionabiliter, et sic arsi et thesi, id est elevacione et deposicione.

18 Et deswevit a multo tempore musica,

19 Quia torpor et invidia cuncta tulere studia.

20 Dira quidem pestis tulit omnia commoda terris.

21 Invidie telum perimat dilexio cecum.

NOTES FOR EDITION:

1-16 Quot] Quod *Ms.*

4 [C]e-fa-ut] [ ]cfaut *Ms.* | primo¹] prima *Ms.*

11 [c]e-sol-fa-ut] [ ]esoluaut *Ms.* | fa et ut] ua et ut *Ms.*

17 proporcionabiliter] proporcionbiliter *Ms.*

21 Invidie] Invidia *Ms.*

Guidonian Hand

Inscribed letters and texts
[Thumb (top to bottom)]:
    22 G in latino.
    23 Γ grecum, et est propositum a latinis propter congruum.
    24 A aliquibus antiphanis et cantibus descendendum.
    25 Gamma in greco, G in latino.

[Pointer]:
    e - f - g - C

[Middle finger]:
    d - dd - aa - D

[Ring finger]:
    c - cc - bb♮ - E

[Little finger]:
    b♮ - a - G - F

[Palm]:
    26 Nota: Quecumque clavis fuerit in linea, eius octava erit in spacio, et econtra. 27 Item primus cantus b♮-duralis incipit in linea, naturalis in spacio, bi-mollis in linea, et econtra, id est secundus cantus b♮-duralis in spacio, et sic de aliis.

[Wrist]:
    28 Claves octo graves, septem dicuntur acute.
    29 Quatuor excellunt, quas inchoat aa duplicatum.
    30 Cantus in manu sunt tres in genere et septem in specie.
    31 In c natura, f bi-mol, g[que] b♮-dura.
    32 In a natural, d bi-mol, eque b♮-dural.

[Below wrist]:
    33 Voces sunt sex:
    34 Ut, re, mi, fa, sol, la modulandi sint tibi signa.
    35 Ut queant laxis.
    36 Claves [secundum usum] sunt decem et novem in manu. 37 Sed secundum artem additur ee-la ad complendum tercium cantum b♮-duralem, et hoc extra manum.
    38 Clavium alie sunt unice et sunt quatuor. 39 Alie duplices et sunt decem, quarum due non sunt mutabiles.
40 Alie triplices et sunt sex.

    * *Illustration (left side): Seated Benedictine nun playing a portative organ with her right hand, from which flows music in Gothic neumes on a staff with letter clefs. Above are two billy goats under a tree with a bird's nest.*

    * *Illustration (right side): Seated Benedictine nun holding a music book on her lap with Gothic neumes and pointing at the first note of the recto page. A girl sitting in front of her uses a stylus to show the same note and identifies it with the words "prima in F." On top of this scene, which represents a music lesson at a Benedictine convent, is a stork's nest.*

(f. 201)
    41 Manus artificialis constat ex decem lineis et totidem spaciis, ut patet inspicienti.
    * *Illustration: Owl and monkey looking at a mirror.*

---

    31 natura] natural *Ms.*

A Didactic Musical Treatise from the Late Middle Ages

Fig. 3.1. Pen-and-ink drawing of the Manus Guidonica in
Ebstorf, Klosterarchiv, Ms. V,3, f. 200v.

Tonal System

ee							la
dd						la	sol
cc						sol	fa
bb♮						fa	mi
aa					la	mi	re
g					sol	re	ut
f					fa	ut	
e				la	mi		
d			la	sol	re		
c			sol	fa	ut[42]		
b♮			fa	mi			
a		la	mi	re			
G		sol	re	ut			
F		fa	ut				
E	la	mi					
D	sol	re					
C	fa	ut					
B	mi						
A	re						
Γ	ut						

[next to B-mi]:

43 Unica si fuerit, vox invariata manebit.

    * *Illustration: Two girls, guided by two seated Benedictine nuns, lead their rabbits on a rope among the trees of a* hortus conclusus. *Uhde-Stahl (p. 28) interprets this scene as a study break, during which teachers and students stroll in the convent garden.*

[next to E-la-mi]:

44 Si duplex detur, decet hanc ut bis varietur.

    * *Illustration: Two dogs chasing a rabbit.*

[next to G-sol-re-ut]:

45 Vox si sit terna, tunc fit mutacio sena.

    * *Illustration: Pair of dogs on a rope playing around a tree.*

[next to c-sol-fa-ut]:

46 Inspice et videbis que voces sub unaquaque continentur clavi et cuius et quoti cantus sit queque vox.

47 b♮-durum mi canit, b-molle fa dulce frequentat.

[next to g-sol-re-ut]:

48 Ubicumque ponitur ut, ibi incipitur aliquis cantuum. 49 Ubicumque la, ibi finitur.

    * *Illustration: Stag and hind playing among trees.*

[next to bb♯-fa-mi]:

50 In b-fa-♮-mi duas voces volo demi,

    * *Illustration: Ornament.*

51 Quas non mutabis, quia duplex tibi clavis.

    * *Illustration: Trees (next to E-la-mi) and flowers (C-sol-faut; a-la-mi-re; F-fa-ut). The first illustration of flowers carries at its bottom the words "vel auca."*

---

[42] c-sol-fa-ut] c sol so ut *Ms.*

[43] manebit] manenebit *Ms.*

[44] decet hanc] hanc decet *Ms.*

[46] unaquaque] unaqueque *Ms.*

[50] b-fa-♮-mi] b♮mi | duas] *suprascr.* fa *Ms.*

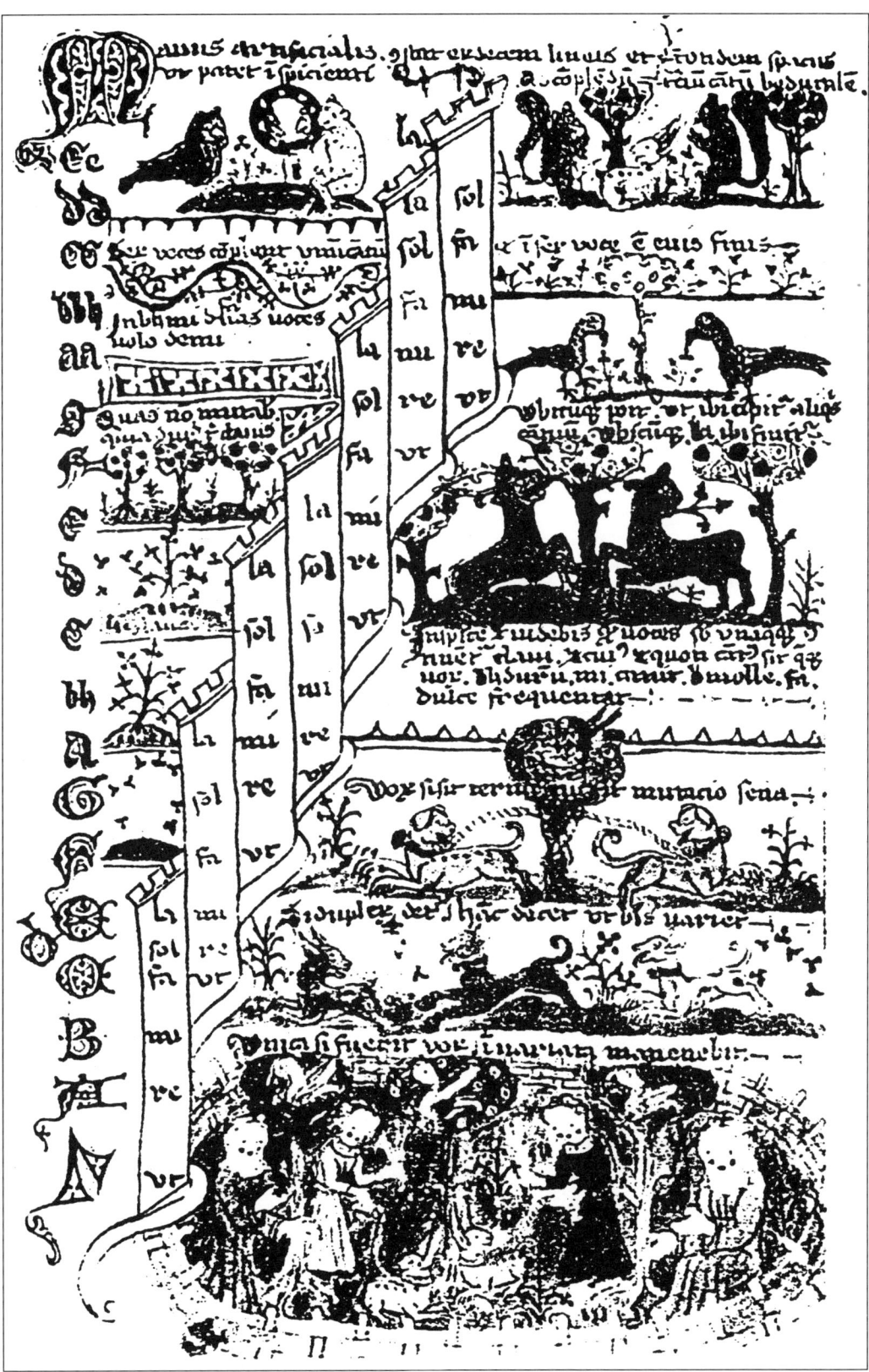

Fig. 3.2. Pen-and-ink drawing of the tonal system in
Ebstorf, Klosterarchiv, Ms. V,3, f. 201

[next to cc-sol-fa]:

52 Sex voces complent unum cantum et in sex[ta] voce est eius finis.
* *Illustration: Vines with grapes| Two birds facing one another.*

[next to ee-la]:

53 Ad complendum tercium cantum be-duralem.
* *Illustration: Rabbit between two feeding squirrels.*

---

52 eius] euis *Ms.*

Example 3.1. Ebstorf, Klosterarchiv, V,3, f. 201v, exercise.

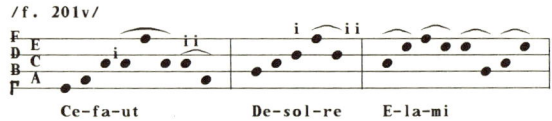

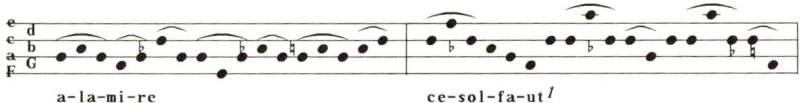

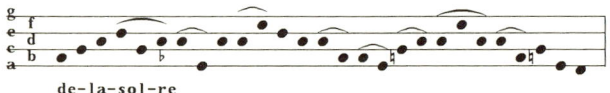

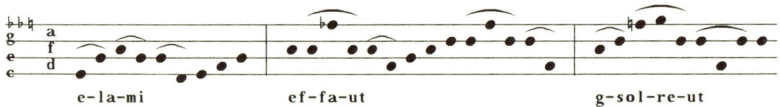

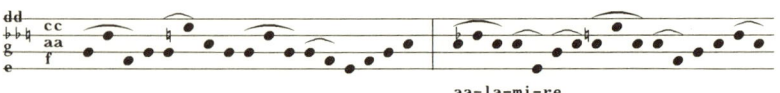

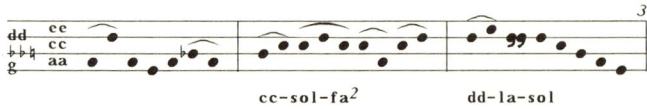

1 ce-sol-fa-ut] Ce sol ua ut *Ms.*

2 cc-sol-fa] CC sol ua *Ms.*

3 In addition to ex. 3.1, the manuscript contains on f. 201v a five-line staff with the following notation:

Both melodic formulae correspond with those in ex. 3.3b, where they are notated separately.

A Didactic Musical Treatise from the Late Middle Ages

Example 3.2. Ebstorf, Klosterarchiv, V,3, f. 202, exercise.

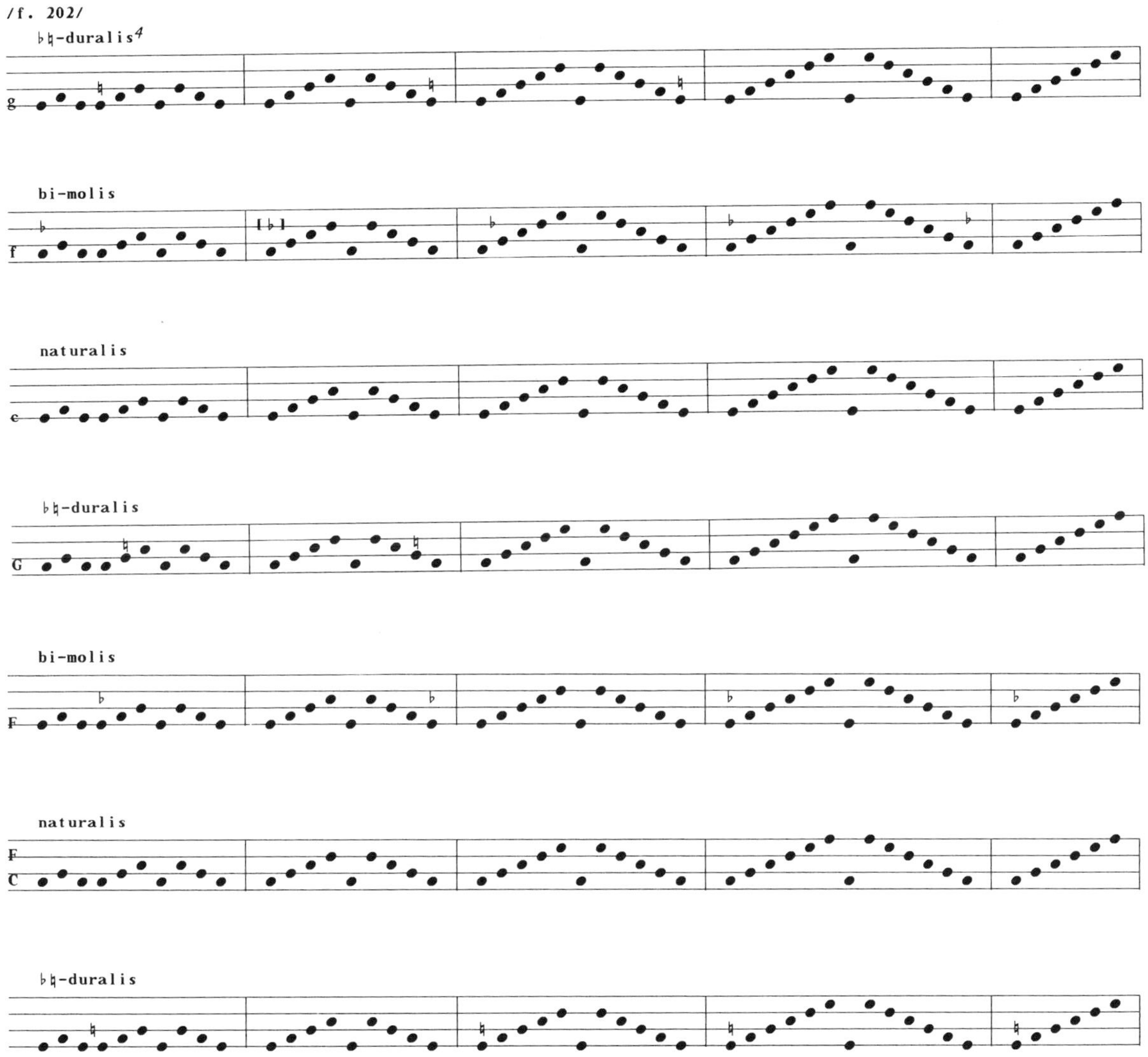

/f. 202/

♭♮-duralis[4]

bi-molis

naturalis

♭♮-duralis

bi-molis

naturalis

♭♮-duralis

---

[4] The names of the hexachordal species are placed in ex. 3.2 to the left of the individual staves and in ex. 3.3a alternately on the left and right margin.

Example 3.3a. Ebstorf, Klosterarchiv, V,3, ff. 202v-203, exercise.

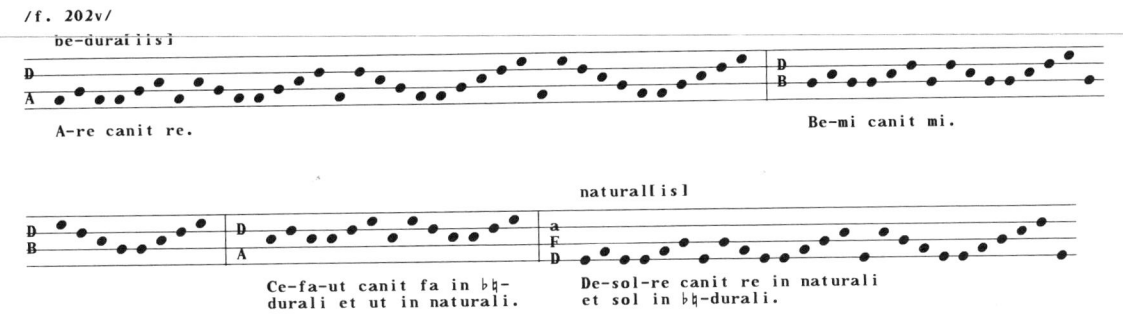

/f. 202v/

be-duralis

A-re canit re.

Be-mi canit mi.

natural[is]

Ce-fa-ut canit fa in ♭♮-durali et ut in naturali.

De-sol-re canit re in naturali et sol in ♭♮-durali.

Continued

Example 3.3a.—*Continued*

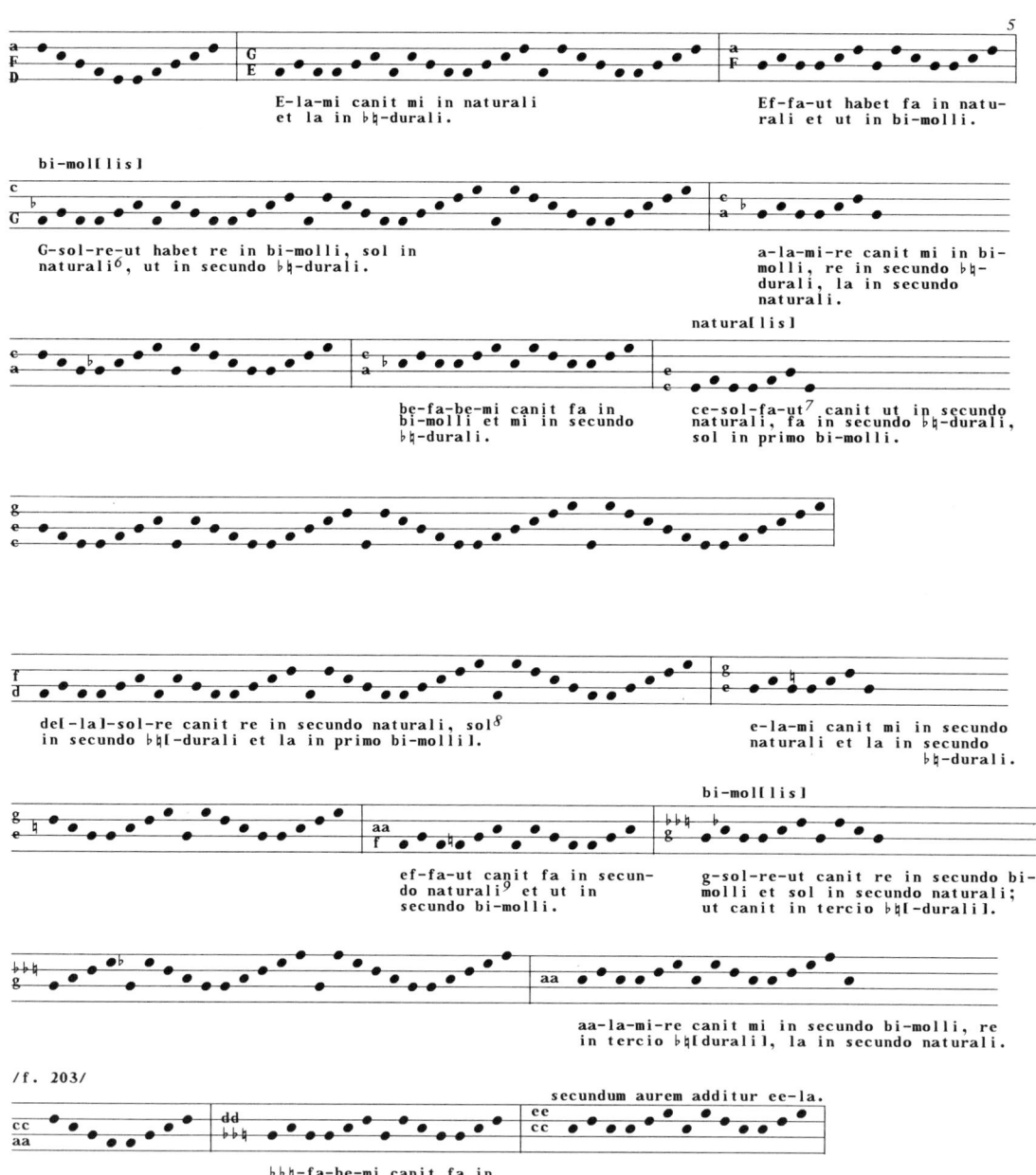

/f. 203/

---

[5] Note on right margin: . . . (?). Ms.

[6] naturali] b♯ durali Ms.

[7] ce-sol-fa-ut] csoluaut Ms.

[8] sol] et sol Ms.

[9] naturali] narali Ms.

[10] in secundo *stated twice:* Ms.

Example 3.3b. Ebstorf, Klosterarchiv, V,3, f. 203, exercise.

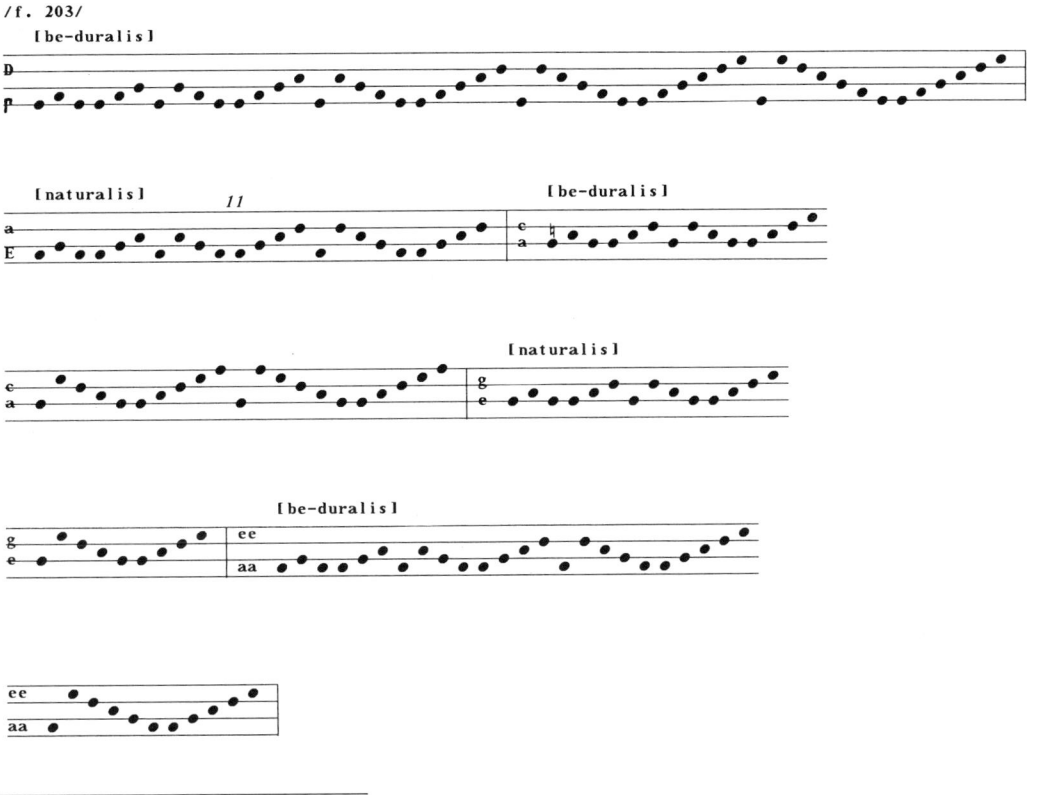

11 E *stated three times: Ms.*

Commentary

1-16: In this first part the anonymous author familiarizes his students with three basic elements of music theory: tonal letters and their location on the staff, solmization syllables (*voces*) and respective hexachords (*cantus*). The text is written in question-and-answer form and uses identical phrasing for each sentence.[13] At the same time its subject matter is only presented with an eye to performance practice. It is therefore necessary to consult other sources in order to provide a more complete interpretation and understanding of the text. One of the points in question pertains to notating the tonal letters on lines and spaces. Whereas the Ebstorf treatise simply states that Γ-*ut* "is" a line, *A-re* a space (and so on), Magister Szydlovita informs us "quod quelibet clavis [= littera] cum sua diccione in manu posita, tangens membrum impar, ponitur in linea, et quelibet tangens membrum par ponitur in spacio."[14] Besides formulating the principle underlying staff notation, Szydlovita and Ladislaus de Zalka offer several verses which explain the internal order of *linea* and *spatium*, among them these two: "Ex (De) facili cernes (cernas), que clavis linea sistit; / Linea sit prima clavis spaciumque secunda."[15] Unfortunately, the opening section

---

[13] The didactic method of question and answer was commonly used to educate young students in the elements of music. In his treatise of 1419 Johannes Floeß thus prefaces a dialogue on the *voces*, *claves*, and *mutationes* with the words "Pro iuvenum expertissima informatione." See Peter Cahn, "Eine Reichenauer Handschrift in Frankfurt am Main: Der Musiktraktat des Johannes Floeß (1419)," *Renaissance-Studien: Helmuth Osthoff zum 80. Geburtstag*, ed. Ludwig Finscher, 18 (9-27) (Tutzing: Hans Schneider, 1979).

[14] Gieburowski, 13, lines 8-10. See also Hugo Spechtshart von Reutlingen, *Flores musicae*, verses 52-53: "Impar iunctura sit quaevis linea dicta, | Vult numeroque pari spatium iunctura vocari"—ed. Gümpel, Akademie der Wissenschaften und der Literatur, 3 (Mainz: Abhandlungen der Geistes- und Sozialwissenschaftlichen Klasse, 1958), 105-06.

[15] Gieburowski, 13, lines 12-13; Bartha, 70, section 26.

of the Ebstorf treatise breaks off in *b-fa-n-mi*, which is followed by two empty pages. Although it is not known why our text was left incomplete, one can assume that ff. 199v and 200 were intended to contain further information on rudimentary matters.

17: Part 2 of the treatise begins with the definition of music as melodic motion (*motus vocum*). Its roots are found in Guido's *Micrologus*, cap. 16: "Musica motus est vocum," and "Igitur motus vocum . . . fit arsis et thesis, id est elevatio et depositio. . . ."[16] The reader will notice that the text version of the Ebstorf manuscript has been expanded by the adverb "proporcionabiliter" in order to identify the aspect of balanced progression (or "motio congrua") in Gregorian melodies. A definition with similar phrasing is included in the *Tractatus de musica*, cap. 1, of Hieronymus de Moravia: "Musica est motus vocum congrua proportione inter se consonantium."[17]

18-19: These two verses were taken from Guido's *Regulae rhythmicae*.[18] They dwell on the old topos of a world grown unaccustomed to music because envy and torpor took away all study. The Ebstorf treatise uses in both verses a text version hitherto unknown.

20-21: Guido Aretinus, *Micrologus*, verses 4 and 5 of the introductory acrostic hexameters (in reverse order).[19] Continuing the preceding topos, the text invokes the image of a ravaging pest (envy) which has robbed the land of all agreeable things, followed by the wish that love (of studying music) frustrate the spear of blind envy.

22-23, 25: Both notes are intended to distinguish the Greek letter *Γ* of the tonal system from its subsequent Latin letters. It is first mentioned in the Pseudo-Odonian *Dialogus* and *Musica*[20] from the early eleventh century and reflects the extension of the Systema teleion (*A-aa*) by one whole step at the lower end.

24: This statement relates to the limited use of *A-re* within the Gregorian chant repertory where it is found in melodies (in particular great responsories and antiphons) of the second mode. Incidentally, the Guidonian hand remains in Ms. Ebstorf without letter *B*, which was obviously forgotten.

26-27: See **31-32**.

28-29: Both verses signifying the traditional distinction between eight *littere graves*, seven *acute* and four *excellentes* are stated by Anonymous XI in his first treatise.[21]

30: For a more detailed discussion of this subject matter see Magister Szydlovita: "Notandum primo, quod tres sunt cantus in genere, scilicet durus sive asper, naturalis sive planus et mollis sive dulcis. . . . In specie autem cantus septem in numero, scilicet tres h durales, duo naturales et duo b molles."[22] The distinction between *cantus* (= hexachords) *in genere* and *cantus in specie* is also addressed by Ladislaus de Zalka.[23]

---

[16] Guido Aretinus, *Micrologus*, ed. Joseph Smits van Waesberghe, Corpus scriptorum de musica [hereafter CSM], 4 (American Institute of Musicology, 1955), 184 and 179-180, sentence 9.

[17] Hieronymus de Moravia, O.P., *Tractatus de musica*, ed. Simon M. Cserba, O.P., Freiburger Studien zur Musikwissenschaft, 2, no. 2 (Regensburg: Pustet, 1935), 7, lines 19-20.

[18] Guido Aretinus, *Regulae rhythmicae*, ed. Joseph Smits van Waesberghe, with Eduard Vetter, Divitiae musicae artis A.IV (1985), 116, verses 167-68.

[19] Guido, *Micrologus*, ed. Smits van Waesberghe, 80.

[20] Martin Gerbert, *Scriptores ecclesiastici de musica sacra potissimum* (St. Blasien: Typis San Blasianis, 1784), vol. 1, 253b-254a and 265b.

[21] Wingell, 9, sentence 55. In the second verse, Anonymous XI uses the form "excellent" instead of "excellunt," and "duplicata" instead of "duplicatum."

[22] Gieburowski, 16, lines 7-9, 25-26.

[23] "Cantus sunt tres in genere, scilicet cantus h duralis, naturalis et b mollis et sunt septem in specie" (Bartha, 70, section 27).

31-32: In these verses the three hexachordal species (*naturalis*, *molle*, and *durum*) are presented with regard to their beginning and ending tones.[24] The second hexameter is of special interest since only Anonymous XI can be identified as its source.[25] Verse 1, on the other hand, shows identical wording in Ladislaus de Zalka's treatise.[26] The subject of beginning and ending tones (as well as their position on the staff) is again addressed by Ladislaus de Zalka in the marginal notes on f. 37b: "Primus cantus b duralis incipit in G-ut in linea et finit in e-lami in spatio. Primus cantus naturalis incipit in c-faut in spatio et finit in a-lamire in linea. . . . Primus b mollis incipit in f-faut in linea et finit in d-lasolre in spatio. . . . Secundus b duralis incipit in g-solreut in spatio et finit in e-lami in linea . . .," etc.[27]

34: Cf. Magister Szydlovita[28] and the *Alius tractatulus metricus de musica* (1462) in Ms. Melk 950 (f. 223vb), where this verse appears. Next to it the reader is reminded of the Vespers hymn in honor of Saint John the Baptist, "Ut queant laxis resonare fibris," as the chant from which the six solmization syllables originated.

36-37: The subdivision of the *claves* "secundum usum" (*Γ-dd*) und "secundum artem" (*Γ-ee* extra manum) as a part of elementary theory is also presented by Magister Szydlovita[29] and Ladislaus de Zalka.[30] Both authors include the following verses in their texts: "Claves in numero reperimus decaque novem, / Ecce figura manus tenet has (ars) et quilibet usus."

38-40: As a means of preparing students for a more thorough knowledge of the tonal system, solmization and mutation, the *claves* are here identified according to their respective number of solmization syllables (*voces*). There are four letters with only one syllable (*Γ, A, B, ee*) called "claves unice"; ten letters carrying two syllables ("claves duplices" = *C-F, b♮, e-f,* and *bb♮-dd*, with *b♮* and *bb♮* excluded from mutation for being *non mutabiles*); and finally six letters with three syllables ("claves triplices" = *G-a, c-d,* and *g-aa*).[31] As to *claves/voces mutabiles* or *non mutabiles*, the same expression is used in the *Speculum musicae*, lib. VI, cap. 65, of Jacques de Liège:[32] ". . . quae voces invicem sunt mutabiles et quae non." See also Johannes Tinctoris, *Expositio manus*, cap. 7.[33]

41: The term "manus artificialis" can be related to the fact that the illustration on f. 201 reflects the tonal system *secundum artem*, i.e., including *ee* (see above, **36-37**).

43-45, 50-51: In its text on mutation the Ebstorf treatise limits itself to presenting five verses widely used in writings from the late Middle Ages. The first three verses determine the number of mutations with regard to the

---

[24] Verses about the same detail can also be found in the marginal notes to verse 96 of Hugo Spechtshart's *Flores musicae* (ed. Gümpel, 111): "Versus de ♮-durali: . . . Incipit in G primus, finem facit in e"; "De cantu naturali: . . . In c principiat, finem dat in a-la-mi-re:" "De cantu b-molli: F-fa-ut principiat primum, quoque terminat d-la."

[25] Wingell, 11, sentence 74: "in A naturalis, D b mollis, E que b duralis." See also Hugo Spechtshart's *Flores musicae*, verse 101, Marg. (ed. Gümpel, 112).

[26] Bartha, 69, section 25.

[27] Ibid., 76 sentence 50. See also Anonymous XI: ". . . ubi sit primum G in manu, ut hic gammaut, ibi incipitur primus cantus b duralis; et ubi secundum G, ibi incipitur secundus [*sic!*] cantus b duralis; eodem modo dicatur de C [*sic!*] et F. Item notandum quod cantus naturalis finitur in A et b mollis in D, et b duralis in E" (Wingell, 11, sentences 72-74).

[28] Gieburowski, 11, lines 18-19.

[29] ". . . claves in tota manu secundum usum sunt decem et novem, et hoc computando b fa, h mi pro una clave. . . . Sed loquendo secundum artem, tunc claves in numero sunt viginti, quia extra manum additur ela propter compleccionem et perfeccionem tercii cantus h duralis" (Gieburowski, 12, lines 50-52, and 13, lines 5-7).

[30] Bartha, 69-70, section 26.

[31] Cf. Magister Szydlovita, who in describing mutation makes the following statement: "Sciendum secundo, quod sex sunt dicciones in manu, habentes per tres voces et per sex mutaciones, octo autem per duas voces et eciam per duas mutaciones, ut patet practicanti. Et iterum quatuor sunt dicciones, habentes per unam vocem et per nullam mutacionem, scilicet Γ ut, A re, h mi et e la" (Gieburowski, 20, lines 11-16). The same subject matter is presented by Ladislaus de Zalka (Bartha, 71, section 31; 72, section 33).

[32] Jacobus Leodiensis, *Speculum musicae*, ed. Roger Bragard, CSM 3, no. 6 (1973), 179, sentence 1.

[33] Johannes Tinctoris, *Opera theoretica*, ed. Albert Seay, CSM 22, no. 1 (1975), 48, sentence 3.

individual syllables of a given *clavis*. If only one syllable is attached, no *varietas vocum* may take place, while *claves* with two and three syllables allow for four and six mutations, respectively. Both *b*♮ and *bb*♮ remain without hexachordal change because their syllables *fa* and *mi* entail two different pitches (verses 4-5). Among the sources reflecting this part of Ms. Ebstorf are Anonymous XI, Magister Szydlovita, Ladislaus de Zalka, and the Anonymous secundum Johannem Valendrinum.[34] See also Ms. Melk 950 (f. 223va), 873 (p. 204), and 1099 (p. 36, only verses 4-5).

47: See Ladislaus de Zalka, who includes this verse in his treatise.[35]

48: A similar text is stated by Ladislaus de Zalka: "Pro regula: ubicumque in manu ponitur ut, semper ibi incipitur aliquis cantus in specie, et ubi non ponitur ut, ibi nullus incipit cantus."[36]

Vocal exercises: The treatise is followed on ff. 201v-203 by various vocal exercises. These are designed to train and prepare students with regard to the practice of Gregorian chant.[37] Example 3.1 offers short melodic phrases for those *claves* of the tonal system on which mutation may take place (*C-a*; *c-aa*; *cc-dd*). Quite obviously students would sing the appropriate solmization syllables and mutate from one hexachord to another whenever required.[38] In order to clearly determine the scale degree of a given note, all lines and spaces of the seven staffs have been assigned letter clefs.

In ex. 3.2, singing and solmization within the individual hexachords (as represented on seven staffs) are implied. This exercise is based on a melodic pattern of ascending and descending scales as well as leaps, which gradually unfold the intervals and full range of each hexachord. The same pattern serves in ex. 3.3a to train students in recognizing how many solmization syllables belong to individual *claves* and in which of the seven hexachords these syllables are found. An explanatory text extends from *A-re* to *bb-fa*♮*-mi*, while the musical formula for *cc-sol-fa* is provided with a note describing its uppermost *clavis* (*ee*) as being added "secundum aurem." At the same time, marginal notes identify the hexachordal species on which the melodic formulas are based (*A-C* and *cc* = cantus duralis; *C-F* and *c-f* cantus naturalis; *G-b*♮ and *gg-bb*♮ = cantus mollis). Each formula starts on its *clavis* tone and extends from there to the upper end of the respective hexachord.

Example 3.3b may be considered a supplement. Besides the musical patterns on Γ, *E*, and *e*, it offers for the *claves a-la-mi-re* and *aa-la-mi-re* a melodic formula, which in contrast to ex. 3.3a is based on the (second and third) cantus duralis, thus requiring ♮*-mi* during solmization. It should also be noted that the scale degrees *E*, *e*, *a*, and *aa* function as ending and subsequently opening tones within the five formulas of this exercise: Γ*-E*, *E-a*, *a-e*, *e-aa*, and *aa-ee*. At the same time, *ee* is presented as an integral part of the tonal system.

---

[34] Wingell, 12, sentence 81; 13, sentence 84; 13, sentence 89; and 14, sentence 97; Gieburowski, 19, lines 34-20, line 27; Bartha, 71-72, sections 31-33; Fritz Feldmann, *Musik und Musikpflege im mittelalterlichen Schlesien*, Darstellungen und Quellen zur schlesischen Geschichte, 36 (Breslau: Trewendt & Granier, 1938), 171.

[35] Bartha, 69, section 25.

[36] Bartha, 70, section 27.

[37] For detailed observations on the important subject of vocal exercises in medieval treatises see Michel Huglo, "Exercitia vocum," in *Laborare fratres in unum: Festschrift László Dobszay zum 60. Geburtstag* (Hildesheim and Zurich: Weidmann, 1995), 117-23.

[38] The examples for *C-fa-ut* and *D-sol-re* contain numerals (*i* and *ii*) to indicate where a mutation takes place (*C-fa-ut*: *i* = fa→ut; *ii* = fa←ut; *D-sol-re*: *i* = sol→re; *ii* = sol←re). All other examples are without numerals.

4

Some Sixteenth-Century "Thematic" Madrigal Anthologies

James Haar

Printed anthologies of music are as old as printed part-music itself; Petrucci's publications of motets and of French and Italian-texted secular music were, with a single exception, all anthologies.[1] In this they resembled manuscript collections of the time, nearly always compilations of the work of several or a number of composers. Volumes of Masses devoted to a single composer were an important part of Petrucci's output, though even in this genre he also published anthologies.[2] In Italy secular music, the newly fashionable madrigal, was after 1530 to take the lead in prints devoted to single musicians, but never to replace anthologies altogether.[3] In France, on the other hand, the overwhelming preference of the royal music printer Pierre Attaingnant was for anthologies.[4]

Attaingnant, who for more than twenty years had a near-monopoly of music printing in France, was content to entitle his prints by the number of pieces they contained.[5] In Italy, where after 1510 the business of music printing was much more competitive, publishers began to designate series and even single volumes with distinctive names: *Corona, Fortuna, Serena, Fioretti, Croce* are early examples.[6] These were meant to be eye-catching, a form of advertising, rather than to refer to the contents of the books in any substantive way.[7] The process of attaching such qualifiers persisted, growing ever more elaborate as the century progressed, but the colorful words rarely meant anything more than title-page (= dust-jacket) advertising.

In his careful study of sixteenth-century madrigal anthologies, Franco Piperno gives attention to collections of every sort while at the same time singling out what he calls the "antologia a soggetto," which I shall term the thematic anthology.[8] (A list of these anthologies is provided in the appendix to this study.) The first thing to note

---

[1] The exception is *Musica de meser Bernardo pisano sopra le Canzone del petrarcha* of 1520.

[2] Examples are RISM 1505[1] (*Fragmenta missarum*) and 1509[1] (*Missarum diversorum authorum*). A particularly opulent Mass anthology of the period is RISM 1516[1], Antico's *Liber quindecim missarum.*

[3] The madrigals of Verdelot and Arcadelt were published in collections during the 1530s; some of these volumes contained madrigals by other composers as well.

[4] See Daniel Heartz, *Pierre Attaingnant, Royal Printer of Music* (Berkeley: University of California Press, 1969).

[5] See the index of titles in ibid., 381-90.

[6] See RISM 1514[1], 1519[1], 1519[4], [ca.1526][5], 1526[6], 1530[2].

[7] On this point see Franco Piperno, *Gli "Eccellentissimi musici della città di Bologna" con uno studio sull' antologia madrigalistica del Cinquecento* (Florence: Olschki, 1985), 4-5, in connection with volumes of madrigals advertised as the work of Verdelot, even when the bulk of the pieces were by "other excellent composers."

[8] Piperno, ch. 1, esp. 12-16. He deals with anthologies of all sorts, a far larger body of material than is my concern here. His "thematic" categories, both quite broad, are *ambiente* (place) and *argomento* (poetic theme, occasion). Marco Giuliani, ed., *I lieti amanti. Madrigali di venti musicisti ferraresi e non* (Florence: Olschki, 1990), 5-31, gives a less detailed survey of the anthology than Piperno's, but touching on some of the same volumes discussed here. I came upon Giuliani's book only after completing this study.

about this list is that it is limited to madrigals. Chansons, motets, and instrumental collections could also be and were prepared with a theme in mind, but it is the madrigal where the practice chiefly flourished.[9]

The volumes in this list must nearly all have been commissioned or at least assembled in the fairly certain knowledge that the support of a patron or group of patrons was forthcoming. Piperno's categories (see n. 8) are satisfactorily inclusive, but they do not emphasize the reasons behind the formation of these anthologies. Among these reasons are local or dynastic pride, flattery of important persons, and the desire to achieve success through novelty of poetic-musical conceit. These volumes, surely modeled on *cinquecento* poetic anthologies, contributed in an important way to the development of the music print as a book, to be read (sung) aloud or to be conned silently in order of content, a phenomenon that began to affect the nature of individual-composer prints by the late sixteenth century.[10] The rise and success of the madrigal comedy is not my subject here, but it is clearly related to the thematic anthology, as are staged musical performances, *intermedi*, and the early opera when they were given circulation in print.[11] Thematic anthologies must have been seen by printers as valuable in contributing to their own prestige, and they did not have to sell widely since they must have been subsidized wholly or in part by their patrons.

1. The clearest instances of patron-supported anthologies are volumes glorifying rulers. The first and one of the most celebrated of these is Antonio Gardano's publication of music performed at the wedding festivities for Cosimo I de' Medici and Eleanora of Toledo (RISM 1539^{25}; see appendix no. 1). Nine of the pieces in this volume are by Francesco Corteccia, *maestro* of the chapel at the Duomo and S. Giovanni in Florence; of these seven madrigals were reprinted by Gardano in 1547 in volumes devoted to Corteccia, here termed *maestro* of the ducal chapel (the introductory motet in the volume would subsequently appear in a 1564 motet collection).[12] Later anthologies include both music that was to be republished as well as madrigals already published, especially the work of well-known composers, though many pieces (and even some of the composers) are to be found only within their covers. There is no dedication in the 1539 print, but Gardano could hardly have had access to the music or been able to afford publishing it without subvention, and the Medici court (it is reasonable to assume) must have been the source for this support. Corteccia's 1547 madrigal volumes are dedicated by the composer to Cosimo; although the composer speaks of "paying his debt" to the duke, these volumes must also have been supported by Medici patronage.[13]

Gardano's volume contains, along with Corteccia's music and madrigals by other Florentines and by Costanzo Festa—notably absent are works by Arcadelt, the most prominent Florentine madrigalist of the 1530s[14]—a group of texts referring to Apollo and his *lira*; these were presumably sung as accompanied monodies. They were part of an elaborate *trionfo allegorico* praising the Medici and including references to Tuscan cities and rivers.[15] The *tavola* of Gardano's print tells us that its contents represent music for three separate occasions: Eleanora's entry into

---

[9] Some examples include *Le rossignol musical*, 1597^{10} (chanson); *Epithalamia in honorem... D. Nicolai Leopardi*, 1588^{21} (motet); *Pratum musicum*, 1584^{12} (instrumental music). In instrumental collections, fancy names are common but organized thematic content is rare.

[10] Madrigal volumes by Wert, Marenzio, Pallavicino, and Monteverdi are often wholly or in part "thematicized," with formal or informal cycles of stanzas from Tasso's *Gerusalemme liberata* and scenes from Guarini's *Pastor fido* accounting for much of their contents.

[11] See below and appendix nos. 30, 32 for anthologies with suggestions of dramatic representation.

[12] Mary S. Lewis, *Antonio Gardano, Venetian Music Printer, 1538-1569: A Descriptive Bibliography and Historical Study*, vol. 1, 1538-1549 (New York: Garland, 1988), nos. 105-06, pp. 566-71.

[13] See Mario Fabbri, "La vita e l'ignota opera-prima di Francesco Corteccia, musicista italiano del rinascimento (Firenze: 1502–Firenze 1571)," *Chigiana* 22 (1965), n.s. 2, 185-217, esp. 202-03. In his will Corteccia mentioned volumes of "libri stampati" of his compositions. He must have received these by contract with the publisher; whether he had to pay for them we do not know. For the dedications in his madrigal books, see Frank A. D'Accone, ed., *Music of the Florentine Renaissance*, 8: Corteccia, *Collected Works*, 1 (American Institute of Musicology, 1981). The Medici-Toledo arms are on the title pages of Corteccia's madrigal books.

[14] Arcadelt had probably settled in Rome by the time of the wedding. For speculation that he may have taken an anti-Medicean position after Duke Alessandro's murder in 1537, see Haar, "The Florentine Madrigal, 1540-1560," in *Music in Renaissance Cities and Courts: Studies in Honor of Lewis Lockwood*, ed. Jessie Ann Owens and Anthony M. Cummings (this publisher, 1997), 141-51.

[15] Henry W. Kaufmann, "Music for a Noble Florentine Wedding (1539)," in *Words and Music: The Scholar's View*, ed. Laurence Berman (Department of Music, Harvard University, 1972), 161-88, esp. 167-69.

Florence (on June 19); a wedding banquet, with the *trionfo* (on July 6); and a performance of Antonio Landi's comedy *Il commodo*, with musical intermedi (on July 9). All of this is described in detail in a letter of Pierfrancesco Giambullari, published, together with the play's text, in Florence shortly after Gardano's volume came out.[16]

For this anthology we thus have a full context including dates of first performance and a dramatic scheme. Not until the end of the century, when another Medici wedding (1589) was similarly recorded, is there another dynastic event so fully preserved. It is extraordinary to see Gardano's volume, the work of a struggling printer in the second year of his business (produced in the Venice that harbored Lorenzino de' Medici, the murderer of Cosimo's predecessor Duke Alessandro), and to think of it as paid for by the Medici themselves.[17] Cosimo I was intent from the beginning of his reign on creating and magnifying the reputation of the Medici *principato*. There being no established music printer in Florence, he turned to a young publisher in Venice, the city already recognized as the center of music printing in Italy (Lorenzino could be, and indeed was, taken care of later). This publication must have been a real triumph for Gardano, who after experiencing some setbacks in 1540 went on to become the best known music printer in Italy; thus the value of such an anthology to its publisher was established early.

The music for *intermedi* performed with a comedy given at the 1589 Medici wedding (1591[7]; appendix no. 5) has been widely discussed and needs no further comment here.[18] There were of course other occasions celebrated by the Medici court—weddings, births, deaths, festive entrées for visiting dignitaries—during the years between 1539 and 1589.[19] Of these only fragments of music in print and manuscript copies of single pieces survive.[20] Among the most elaborate of these festivities were the celebrations of Grand Duke Francesco I's two marriages, to Giovanna of Austria in 1565 and to Bianca Cappello in 1579; for both of these Alessandro Striggio supplied a good deal of the music.[21] Most of this is lost, but from the 1579 wedding, celebrated both in Florence and in Bianca Cappello's native Venice, a few pieces are extant; in addition there are two madrigal anthologies (1579[3], 1586[11]; appendix nos. 3-4) honoring the bride. It is not clear where and in what context their contents were performed, though the strongly Venetian list of composers suggests in Venice rather than in Florence.

Bianca Cappello, whose personal life made her by turns infamous and famous, was in Florence as early as 1563; she became the mistress of Francesco de' Medici and married him after the death of the Grand Duchess Giovanna in 1578. She was in a position of power before this. In 1574 Vincenzo Galilei dedicated his *Primo libro a 4 & 5* to her. Many of the texts set in this book may be by Francesco de' Medici himself.[22] Full descriptions of the 1579 wedding survive, but neither on this occasion nor that of his first marriage did Francesco have the music published (his brother

---

[16] The letter and the play appear in translation in Andrew C. Minor and Bonner Mitchell, eds., *A Renaissance Entertainment: Festivities for the Marriage of Cosimo I, Duke of Florence, in 1539* (Columbia: University of Missouri Press, 1968). Kaufmann's essay (see n. 15), though published later, was written before this volume appeared. Giambullari criticized the handling of the poetic texts in Gardano's print, which evidently came out shortly before his letter was published; see Kaufmann, 165n.

[17] On Gardano's early career, see Lewis, 17-34. For Lorenzino, see the references in Haar, "The Florentine Madrigal."

[18] See D. P. Walker, ed., *Les Fêtes du mariage de Ferdinand de Médicis et de Christine de Lorraine, Florence, 1589* (Paris: Editions du Centre National de la Recherche Scientifique, 1963).

[19] Federico Ghisi, *Feste musicali della Firenze Medicea (1480-1589)* (Florence: Vallecchi, 1939); Alois Nagler, *Theatre Festivals of the Medici, 1539-1637* (New Haven: Yale University Press, 1964).

[20] An example is the fragment of music by Alessandro Striggio surviving from a celebration of a Habsburg entry into Florence in 1569; see Ghisi, xxx-xxxiv; Haar, "Madrigals from three Generations: The Ms. Brussels, Bibl. du Conservatoire royal, 27.731," *Rivista italiana di musicologia* 10 (1975): 242-64, esp. 252-55.

[21] On music for the 1565 wedding, see Oscar G. Sonneck, "A Description of Alessandro Striggio and Francesco Corteccia's Intermedi 'Psyche and Amor,' 1565," *Musical Antiquary* 3 (1911): 40-53; Howard Mayer Brown, "Psyche's Lament: Some Music for the Medici Wedding in 1565," in *Words and Music*, 1-27. For the 1579 wedding, see Leo Schrade, "Les Fêtes du mariage de Francesco dei Medici et de Bianca Cappello," in *Les Fêtes de la renaissance*, vol. 1, ed. Jean Jacquot (Paris: Editions du Centre National de la Recherche Scientifique, 1956), 107-31.

[22] Schrade, 108-09. 1574 was the year of Cosimo I's death, following which praise of Bianca Cappello voiced openly presumably became acceptable. Marenzio's *Libro tertio a 6* (1585) is also dedicated to Bianca. Only a single partbook of Galilei's *Primo libro* of 1574 survives, but in his *Fronimo* (1584[15]) one piece from it may be found; see Howard Mayer Brown, *Instrumental Music Printed before 1600: A Bibliography* (Cambridge: Harvard University Press, 1965), 1584[5], and Schrade, 4 and fig. 3.

and successor Ferdinando did give a Venetian printer the music for the *intermedi* performed at his own wedding in 1589, which was fifty years after the wedding of his father Cosimo I). Several pieces from Massaino's *Trionfo di musica* (appendix no. 3) seem to come from the 1579 wedding celebration, and two others by Striggio were printed later.[23]

The *Corona di dodici sonetti* (1586[11]; appendix no. 4) must have been assembled some time before its printing; Marenzio's contribution to it was published in 1584.[24] In his dedicatory letter G. B. Zuccarini, the author of the twelve sonnets, writes that he had "woven a crown" of sonnets for Bianca Cappello at the time of her wedding, not being able to afford a more substantial gift, and that afterwards twelve of the century's best musicians, being "inamorati" with the verses because of their subject matter (praise of the Grand Duchess), overlooked the roughness of the verse and changed its "rude shingle" into a crown of the brightest stars, worthy to offer Bianca.[25] This letter, other-wise in the usual adulatory tone, is remarkable in placing the merits of the music above the merits of the poetry. One might credit Zuccarini with becoming self-worth,[26] but he did assemble a list of distinguished composers, including Marenzio, Monte, Palestrina, G. M. Nanino, Vecchi, and Porta, in addition to Venetians (among whom are the two Gabrielis). They must have been paid, or assured that they would share in the hoped-for gift from the Cappelli or from the Florentine court, in order to have become "inamorati" enough to set these texts. Zuccarini contributed poems to a number of anthologies over a twenty-five-year period; there must have been something in it for him as well.[27]

Florence, of course, was not the only court where elaborate festivities took place. Other Italian city-states, especially Mantua and Ferrara, were noted for them, as were royal courts outside Italy. One place where Italian influence was strong, and money freely if irregularly spent, was the Bavarian court at Munich. In the dedication of his fourth book of five-voice madrigals (1567) Orlando di Lasso, *maestro* of the chapel of the Bavarian duke Albrecht V, remarked that the muses were cultivated in far-off "Germania."[28] In the very next year Lasso and the muses were worked overtime at the elaborate entertainments accompanying the wedding of the ducal heir Wilhelm. A full description of this occasion, written by the Neapolitan singer-composer Massimo Troiano, was published in 1569.[29] This account mentions a good deal of the musical component of the various wedding banquets and entertainments, but does not include the music itself. In 1569 Troiano produced another publication, this one of music: *Musica de' virtuosi della florida capella dell' Illustr. et Ecc. S. Duca di Baviera* (1569[19]; appendix no. 2a).

In his dedicatory letter to Albrecht V, Troiano speaks of Lasso and other musicians in ducal service, and the volume is indeed made up entirely of music by singers and instrumentalists at the Munich court. The wedding music itself is not there; Troiano may have planned another publication that could have included some of it.[30] The anthology does have a plan of its own—it opens and closes with music of Lasso, and the texts set are presumably mostly, as

---

[23] See Ghisi, xxxvii-xl, and Schrade, 118, 122, 124.

[24] Marenzio's madrigal is in his *Libro quarto a 5*. Andrea Gabrieli, another contributor to 1586[11], died in 1586.

[25] For the dedicatory letter, see Gaetano Gaspari, *Catalogo della Biblioteca musicale G. B. Martini di Bologna* ([Bologna, 1890-1905]; facs., ed. Bologna: Forni, 1961), 3:28-29.

[26] In the view of Alfred Einstein, *The Italian Madrigal* (Princeton: Princeton University Press, 1949), 2:638, Zuccarini was "a miserable writer of occasional poems."

[27] His verses are to be found in 1567[13], 1568[16], 1592[11], and 1594[6]. He may have written the texts for Vecchi's *Canzonette libro terzo*; see Emil Vogel, *Bibliothek der gedruckten weltlichen Vocalmusik Italiens aus den Jahren 1500-1700* (1892), ed. Alfred Einstein (Hildesheim: Olms, 1962) [hereafter, Einstein-Vogel], 2:282.

[28] See Haar, "*Le Muse in Germania*: Lasso's Fourth Book of Madrigals," in *Orlandus Lassus and His Time,* ed. Ignace Bossuyt, Eugeen Schreurs, and Annelies Wouters (Peer: Alamire, 1995), 49-72.

[29] Troiano's *Discorsi . . . delle cose più notabili* of the 1568 wedding was published in Munich in that year. In 1569 an enlarged edition was printed in Venice under the title *Dialoghi di Massimo Troiano . . . nelle nozze dello Ill. & Ecc. Prencipe Guglielmo VI* [sic]. For a facsimile of this, see Horst Leuchtmann, ed., *Die Münchner Fürstenhochzeit von 1568. Massimo Troiano: Dialoge* (Munich: Katzbichler, 1980).

[30] 1569[15] is styled *Libro primo*; Troiano may have intended another volume to follow. But in 1570 he fled Bavaria, a fugitive from justice, and was never heard of or from again; see Leuchtmann, 428-32; cf. Leuchtmann, ed., *Musik der bayerischen Hofkapelle zur zeit Orlando di Lassos* (Wiesbaden: Breitkopf und Härtel, 1981), viii.

the title page says, *rime* of Antonio Minturno, a Neapolitan ecclesiastic, poet, and theorist with whom Troiano may have been acquainted.[31] Two texts are identified by author (Ariosto and Manrique). No mention of Minturno is made apart from the title page, but the longer poems (a double sestina and a single sestina, each with *commiato*, and each stanza set by a different composer) must be by Minturno, their setting commissioned by Troiano. None of the poetry makes reference to the recent ducal wedding. The oddest feature of this anthology is the final piece, a French chanson by Lasso.[32]

A *Secondo libro . . . de floridi virtuosi* (1575[11]; appendix no. 2b) was gathered by the Florentine lutenist-composer Cosimo Bottegari, in Bavarian ducal service at the time. Once again, all the composers were members of Albrecht V's musical establishment, but this time they appear to have contributed pieces they had ready; no unifying theme is apparent.[33]

2. The Munich anthologies belong to the category of dynastic celebration and at the same time to the next category to be considered, anthologies of madrigals by composers active in a single place. There are quite a few of these; the list given in the appendix, nos. 6-22, is surely not complete.[34] It is not surprising to find these, as sales and patronage in the vicinity must have been more or less guaranteed. Prominent among the patrons, poets, and on occasion the composers, represented in these anthologies are members of local academies.[35] Rome, Ferrara, and Mantua lead in the number of volumes in which the local provenance is explicitly named. There are many anthologies of predominantly Venetian cast; lack of specific identification may reflect Venetian pride and self-confidence.

Among the more interesting volumes celebrating local composers are those issued by the "musici di Roma" (appendix nos. 9, 13), the group that was to become the Accademia di Santa Cecilia.[36] Dedicated to Roman prelates, these anthologies are entirely the work of Roman composers, who by the time of the publication of *Le gioie* (1589[7]; appendix no. 13) were formally members of an academy whose *maestro* was Felice Anerio.[37] The Roman musicians were themselves dedicatees of a Mantuan anthology, *L'amorosa caccia* (1588[14]; appendix no. 12). The Accademia Filarmonica of Verona, recipient-dedicatee of numerous anthologies, itself prepared at least one, a manuscript collection of ca. 1580 honoring Laura Peverara.[38] The "Rinnovati" of Ferrara, not documented formally as an academy, was responsible for assembling the *Lauro secco* and *Lauro verde* volumes, also for Peverara (1582[5], 1583[10]; appendix nos. 24-25).[39] It is likely that many more "local" anthologies had some kind of backing by an academy.

---

[31] On Minturno, see Leuchtmann, *Musik der bayerischen Hofkapelle*, x; Bernard Weinberg, *A History of Literary Criticism in the Italian Renaissance* (Chicago: University of Chicago Press, 1961), 2:737-43, 755-59, 971-73. I have not been able to consult Minturno's *Rime et prose* (Venice: Rampazetto, 1559).

[32] The chanson is "Chanter je veux," a popular and often-printed piece. The "Catherine" referred to in its text is puzzling; the conjecture by Wolfgang Boetticher, *Orlando, di Lasso und seine Zeit, 1532-1594* (Kassel: Bärenreiter, 1958), 388, that the lady is Catherine de' Medici seems improbable.

[33] This volume contains the first printed music by Giovanni Gabrieli, who was in Munich for a time in the 1570s; see Leuchtmann, *Musik der bayerischen Hofkapelle*, xiii.

[34] See Piperno, 12-13.

[35] See the index in Einstein-Vogel, 2:544, for a list of dedications to academies. The dedicatory letter of Nasco's *Madrigali a 5* (1548) contains an early and full statement about the importance of academicians as patrons and critics of music; see Einstein-Vogel, 2:8.

[36] See Remo Giazotto, *Quattro secoli di storia dell'Accademia nazionale di Santa Cecilia* (Rome: Accademia di Santa Cecilia, 1970), 1, *parte prima*; Nino Pirrotta, "'Dolci Affetti': I musici di Roma e il madrigale," *Studi musicali* 14 (1985): 59-104.

[37] The academy was recognized in a papal bull of 1585; see Giazotto, 1:15.

[38] Anthony Newcomb, "The Three Anthologies for Laura Peverara, 1580-1583," *Rivista italiana di musicologia* 10 (1975): 329-45. Egon Kenton, "A Faded Laurel Wreath," in *Aspects of Medieval and Renaissance Music: A Birthday Offering to Gustave Reese*, ed. Jan LaRue (New York: Norton, 1966), 500-18, gives a description and an index of the contents of the manuscript (Verona, Accademia Filarmonica 220); there are twenty-two madrigals by eighteen composers.

[39] Ferrarese musicians, perhaps connected with the Rinnovati, are represented in *I lieti amanti* (1586[10]) and *La gloria musicale* (1592[14]), both dedicated to the Veronese academician Mario Bevilacqua. See Newcomb, 334-35. On *I lieti amanti*, see Giuliani, *I lieti amanti: Madrigali di venti musicisti ferraresi e non*.

3. A third category of anthology commemorates a single occasion or person, one other than a ruler or a dynastic event. The most popular and influential of all anthologies, *Trionfo di Dori* (1592[11]; appendix no. 27), may be put into this group, even if the occasion for its compilation is not entirely clear. *Trionfi di Dori* was reprinted six times up to 1628 in Venice and Antwerp; two German versions, one of them "spiritualized," appeared in the second decade of the seventeenth century, and a celebrated English anthology inspired by *Dori*, Thomas Morley's *Triumphes of Oriana*, was published in London in 1601.[40] The Italian *Dori* is dedicated by Angelo Gardano to Leonardo Sanudo (1544-1607), a Venetian patrician who is credited in the dedication with having commissioned both texts and music for the twenty-nine madrigals in the volume. The poems, their authors identified in the print, sketch a pastoral scenario in which nymphs, shepherds, and even Cupid join in honoring a lady (each poem ends with "Viva la bella Dori" (= Morley's "Long live fair Oriana"). Sanudo's wife is the presumed honoree. He had married Elisabetta Zustinian in 1577; even if, as it is stated in the dedication, it took some years ("industria di qualch'anno") to get the poetry collected and set, a volume of 1592 is a late wedding present. Still, the volume is in honor of a single person and perhaps at least the commemoration of a single occasion. The list of composers, including Palestrina, Marenzio, Monte, Vecchi, and Giovanni Gabrieli, is a distinguished one; it must have caused Sanudo a good deal of trouble and expense to obtain this poetry and music.[41]

The poetry is chiefly the work of local Venetian writers. Among them is G. B. Zuccarini, whom we have encountered as poet and compiler of the *Corona di dodici sonetti* (1586[11]; appendix no. 4), and whom we will meet again. He clearly belonged to a group, always numerous in Venice, of poets who wrote occasional verse on commission.[42] Their names turn up in these anthologies with some regularity, just as do certain composers below the top rank, men such as Lelio Bertani, Hippolito Baccusi, and Giovanni Cavaccio.

Leonardo Sanudo's name also appears with some frequency. He is the dedicatee of Croce's *Mascarate* of 1590, perhaps performed in his house.[43] In the *Madrigali pastorali . . . intitolati il Bon Bacio* (1594[6]; appendix no. 33), dedicated to Ottaviano Malipiero, Gardano's letter mentions that the latter had induced Sanudo to put the anthology together.[44] And the dedication of *I diporti della villa in ogni stagione* (1601[7]; appendix no. 35), dedicated to the collection's poet Francesco Bozza, states that Sanudo, "steadfast lover and supporter" of *virtuosi*, had taken the poetry and had it set to music.[45] It is clear that Sanudo was not merely a patron but an active force in the poetic-musical circles responsible for a number of these anthologies. One wonders how many others of his class were such active patrons. The effort for such a person was considerable. A theme was chosen; poets were contacted and advised about the form and content of their contributions, not just general adherence to the theme but use of details such as inclusion of certain words, use of a refrain or a chain-verse scheme (each poem beginning with the last line of its predecessor), etc. Then musicians had to be approached, not so easy if the list of composers was a peninsular or even international one. An editor could and doubtless did do much of the work, but the patron would have had to exercise a good deal of supervision—and of course to have paid the bills. Musical patronage, often considered less complex and less active than in the other arts, reached new levels in at least some of the anthologies here under consideration.

---

[40] See E. H. Powley, "Il Trionfo di Dori: A Critical Edition," 2 vols. (Ph.D. diss., Eastman School of Music, University of Rochester, 1975), 1:28-35. On the *Triumphes of Oriana*, see Joseph Kerman, "Morley and the Triumphs of Oriana," *Music & Letters* 34 (1953): 185-91. I would like to thank Professor Powley for his generosity in lending me microfilms of a number of the anthology prints here under discussion.

[41] Only Marenzio's madrigal had previously been published, in his *Quinto libro a 6* (1591), but Gardano in his dedicatory letter assures Sanudo that "è pero cosa sua, perchè da lei gli fu mandato le parole."

[42] Zuccarini seems to have been a friend of Orazio Vecchi; see above, n. 27. It is perhaps no coincidence that Vecchi set the third stanza, written by Zuccarini, of the canzone that opens the *Trionfo di Dori* or that this stanza follows one by Francesco Bozza, another poet frequently encountered in these anthologies (see below, n. 45).

[43] Croce, *Mascarate piacevoli et ridicolose per il carnevale.* In the dedication of this work the publisher Vincenti speaks to Sanudo of "queste Mascarate de quali con quanto sodisfatione siano stati piu volte rapresentate"; see Einstein-Vogel, 1:194.

[44] *Il bon bacio* (1594[6]), dedication: "havendo lei [Ottaviano Malipiero] fatto animo al Clariss. Sig. Lionardo Sanauto, di far ridur' à questo numero & a questo perfetione la sequente copia di Madrigali."

[45] *I diporti della villa* (1601[7]), dedication: "Havendomi ne' giorni passati il clarissimo Signor Lionardo Sanuto Gentil'huomo gratiossissimo, & perpetuo amatore & fautore de' virtuosi, fatto capitare in mano alcune Canzonette . . . & per opra d'esso Signore post' in Musica da diversi Autori eccellentissimi. . . ." Bozza, who wrote the whole of *I diporti*, contributed poems to *Trionfo di Dori* and *Il bon bacio* as well.

An important example of an anthology for a single occasion is *Corona della morte dell'illustre signore . . . Anibal Caro* (1568[16]; appendix no. 23). Its editor, Giulio Bonagiunta, brought out a number of volumes for the publisher Girolamo Scotto in the mid-1560s. The year before *Corona*, he edited Striggio's comic *Cicalamento delle donne al bucato*. Caro was a poet of some importance in the development of the madrigal; this volume may be regarded as fitting tribute.[46] Bonagiunta's dedicatory letter implies that he did all the work and that the dedicatee Giovanni Ferro was merely a friend ("quanto il Caro fosse caro a V. Sig.").[47] The poetry consists first of ten sonnets linked by last-line-first-line repetition; these are all presumably by G. B. Caro, nephew of Anibale.[48] After this come sonnets and *risposte* and a final dialogue, the latter along with one of the sonnets the work of our old friend G. B. Zuccarini.[49] Each sonnet is printed, inside a Valentine-like ornamental border, opposite its musical setting, a practice picked up in several later anthologies.[50] The composers are chiefly Venetians, but Palestrina, a remarkably frequent contributor to these anthologies, is also present.

Individual madrigals in praise of, say, a lady of beauty or a soldier of valor are not uncommon. A whole volume celebrating a single person (other than a ruler) is on the other hand rare.[51] An example is *Vittoria amorosa* (1596[11]; appendix no. 28). The pun in the title of this anthology is typical of its poetic texts, in which a lady named Vittoria repeatedly wins victory in amorous warfare. Who might this lady, not identified in the volume, be? The odd dedicatory letter, addressed to a Milanese nobleman, tells the dedicatee that the madrigals were intended for someone else, one whose name resounds everywhere in the volume.[52] Like many anthologies, this one probably took some time to assemble; it includes contributions by Palestrina (d. 1594) and Wert (d. 1595). The poems celebrate Vittoria's beauty but, more important, her unrivalled skills as a singer. One person leaps to mind as the most probable candidate: Vittoria Archilei, a singer of great fame throughout Italy, but especially in Florence and Rome, at this time.[53]

4. Some of the most famous sixteenth-century anthologies are volumes containing settings of a single text. *Sdegnosi ardori* (1585[17]; appendix no. 29) is a collection of thirty-one settings of Guarini's madrigal "Ardo sì ma non t'amo," along with several compositions on Tasso's *risposta* "Ardi e gela à tua voglia." This collection has been thoroughly studied by George Schuetze.[54] Here it might only be noted that the book, published by Adam Berg in

---

[46] On Caro, noted scholar, poet, and epistolary writer, see Claudio Mutini, in *Dizionario biografici degli italiani* (Rome: Istituto della Enciclopedia Italiana, 1960), 20:497-508.

[47] Ferro is the dedicatee of Alessandro Striggio's *Cicalamento delle donne al bucato* (1567), of Francesco Adriani's *Primo libro de madrigali a 6* (1568), and of Giovanni Ferretti's *Secondo libro delle canzoni alla napolitana a 5* (1569).

[48] Only the last of the first ten sonnets is attributed to G. B. Caro in the print, but Bonagiunta's dedication implies that he wrote all ten: "ho raccolto alquanti sonetti composti sopra la morte dell'eccellente Sig. Anibal Caro dal Sig. Giovan Battista suo amantissimo nipote."

[49] Others are by Cardinal Boba (set by Palestrina), Girolamo Fenaruolo, and Domenico Venier. On Boba see Lino Marini, "Marcantonio Bobba," *Dizionario biografico*, 10:807-13. For Fenaruolo and Venier, see Martha Feldman, *City Culture and the Madrigal at Venice* (Berkeley: University of California Press, 1995), ch. 4, "Ritual Language, New Music: Encounters in the Academy of Domenico Venier," pp. 83-119.

[50] The Ferrarese printer Vittorio Baldini used this format in *Il lauro secco* (1582[5]) and *Il lauro verde* (1583[10]).

[51] One possible instance of this category is a print I have not seen: 1586[7], *Armonia di scelti authori a 6 voci sopra altra perfettissima armonia di bellezza d'una gentil donna senese in ogni parte bella* (Venice: Scotto), a collection dedicated, without letter, to Giovanni Bardi. The collector-dedicator of this anthology may be Andrea Feliciani, at the time *maestro* at the Duomo in Siena and composer of the volume's second piece, which is also found in his *Primo libro a 6* of 1586. The first madrigal in the collection is Andrea Gabrieli's "Chiaro sol di virtute," clearly a dedicatory piece. It is also to be found in the *Concerti* of Andrea and Giovanni Gabrieli of 1587; for a modern edition see A. Tillman Merritt, ed., *Andrea Gabrieli: Complete Madrigals*, vols. 9-10, Recent Researches in the Music of the Renaissance, 49-50 (Madison: A-R Editions, 1983), p. 162.

[52] The dedication, to Count Teodoro Trivulci, is written by Geronimo Vaiano, who assures the Count that the anthology is not about a "soggetto vile" but a "Cavalier grande come V.S." The gender appears to refer to the *soggetto*, not to "Vittoria."

[53] On Vittoria Archilei, see Warren Kirkendale, *The Court Musicians in Florence during the Principate of the Medici* (Florence: Olschki, 1993), no. 52, pp. 262-76. Here is a sample text (set by Wert) from the collection: "Scherza nel canto a piace / Madonna hor pioggia hor scende hor con veloce / & hor con lento voce alletta e sface / Eccon le note care / Da belle labbra ond' ardo ogn' hor sì vago / ch'all udir ch'al mirar duo sensi appago / O dolce variare / Pago in due modi hor sono / Godon gl'occhi à Rubin' gl'orecchi al suono." Wert's madrigal is suitably virtuosic in character. For a modern edition of it, see Carol MacClintock, ed., *Giaches de Wert: Opera omnia* (American Institute of Musicology, 1961-77), 11:21.

[54] George C. Schuetze, ed., *Settings of "Ardo si" and Its Related Texts*, 2 vols., Recent Researches in the Music of the Renaissance, 78-81 (Madison: A-R Editions, 1990).

Munich, was prepared by one Italian and dedicated to another, at least one of them connected with the Bavarian court.[55] The ducal musicians contributed much of its context, with Lasso writing two settings and his sons Rudolf and Ferdinand each contributing one (their lone ventures in madrigal writing). This familial note echoes that of an earlier anthology of largely Roman content, *Il quarto libro delle Muse a 5* (1574[4]) in which a piece by Palestrina's son Ridolfo accompanies a group by his father.[56]

The other famous single-text anthology is *L'amorosa ero* (1588[17]; appendix no. 30). Dedicated by the musician Antonio Morsolino to the Brescian nobleman M.A. Martinengo, the volume contains eighteen settings, advertised as all in the same mode ("nel medesimo tuono"), of Martinengo's poem on Hero and Leander.[57] Martinengo, something of a musician, made a setting of his own text to lead off the volume. This piece is of interest in its demonstration that amateur composers were still, in the 1580s, writing in the manner of Arcadelt—a demonstration that a sort of madrigalian *stile antico* was being taught. The rest of the music is chiefly the work of north Italian composers, complemented by a Roman group including Marenzio and Nanino. Resemblances among the musical settings suggest that at least some of the composers saw each other's work as the compilation proceeded.[58] The print's title says that Ero is "rappresentata" by musicians. Under the dedicatory letter is a square frame inside which the poetic text is given, beneath the title "Madrigale. Soggetto dell'opera." As undramatic a volume of eighteen settings of a single text, all in the same mode, as this volume may be, the language suggests the *favola in musica*, which rose to popularity at the end of the sixteenth century.

5. An important if unavoidably eclectic category of anthology comprises pieces linked by similar subject matter or by the thematic conceit (appendix nos. 32-36). This group includes songs in dialect (1564[16]; appendix no. 31), settings of poems celebrating the seasons and the beauty of the villas of Frascati (1601[7], 1609[7]; appendix nos. 35-36), a sort of madrigal-cantata on a pastoral theme, *Florindo et Armilla* (1593[3]; appendix no. 32), and anthologies devoted to laughter and to a "good kiss" (*Le risa a vicenda*, 1598[8]; appendix no. 34), *Il bon bacio* (1594[6]; appendix no. 33). Each of these deserves comment, but there is not room for that here. A word might be said about *Florindo e Armilla*, of which only two partbooks survive; it contains (apart from three unrelated madrigals at the end) an eighteen-stanza *canzon pastorale* set by eighteen composers, with Monte and Lasso leading off. Its existence is further proof of the close connection of the polyphonic madrigal and the new monodic style in the realm of the pastoral.[59] *Il bon bacio* is of particular interest in that it is first of all a thematic poetic anthology; nearly every one of its texts (one of which, set to music by Vecchi, is by the composer himself) includes a phrase containing "bon bacio" or "baciollo."[60]

---

[55] The anthology's collector was Giulio Gigli da Imola, a musician in the service of the Duke of Bavaria. It is dedicated to Giovanni Battista Galanti. On Gigli (I have no information on Galanti), see Horst Leuchtmann, *Orlando di Lasso*, 2 vols. (Wiesbaden: Breitkopf und Härtel, 1976-77), 1:108, 155, 192, 200; 2:83, 105.

[56] See Einstein-Vogel, 2:684. Once again, the collection was of music not entirely new: Ridolfo Palestrina died in 1572; Animuccia, also a contributor, died in 1571. The three pieces by G. M. Nanino in this collection are among his earliest published works.

[57] See Harry B. Lincoln, ed., *The Madrigal Collection L'Amorosa Ero (Brescia, 1588)* (n.p.: State University of New York Press, 1968). Some pieces are in the first mode on D, others in that mode are transposed to G.

[58] Similarity in the openings and a few other details in many of the madrigals suggest that the setting the Brescian musician Lelio Bertani made—according to the dedication, at Martinengo's request before the other pieces were commissioned—was circulated, possibly together with the patron's own piece, to all the composers involved in the project.

[59] According to Piperno, 15, n. 31 the text of *Florindo e Armilla* is by G. B. Marino. He gives no authority for this, and it seems unlikely on chronological grounds. The text is actually the work of Maffei Venier; see James Chater, *Luca Marenzio and the Italian Madrigal, 1577-1593*, 2 vols. (Ann Arbor: UMI Research Press, 1981), 1:25.

[60] *Il bon bacio* is another anthology long in the making. It was published in 1594. Wert's contribution to it is in his *Libro decimo a 5* of 1591; of the other contributors, Lasso died in 1594, Striggio and Ingegneri in 1592. *Le risa a vicenda* is a Sicilian-Roman volume in which a short poem about the tears and laughter of love ("Son le risa a vicenda") and its *risposta* ("Non son rise a vicenda") appear in nine different settings, introduced and concluded by madrigals referring to the theme and alternating with freely chosen pieces; see Paolo Emilio Carapezza, ed., *Le risa a vicenda* (Florence: Olschki, 1993).

6. One anthology stands apart from all the others in that it seems to be the product of a collector's urge, a volume containing the musical "property" of a connoisseur who also owned paintings, antiquities, and a fine collection of Roman medals. This print, *La Eletta di tutta la musica intitolate Corona* (1569[20]; appendix no. 37), is noted for its inclusion of four madrigals from Willaert's *Musica nova* of 1559. The Venetian nobleman Antonio Zantani, the dedicatee of the *Corona* anthology, is the collector in question.[61] By the mid-1550s he had assembled, with the aid of one Zuan Iacomo da Zorzi (who wrote the dedication of the volume and may have printed it), a collection of madrigals, in the words of the dedication, "così stampate come non stampate." These pieces, which may have been performed at private gatherings of musicians sponsored by Zantani, were mostly drawn from printed sources, but among them were unpublished works by Donato and Perissone Cambio, members of Willaert's circle, as well as the four four-voice madrigals of *Musica nova*, not yet in print.[62]

Zorzi obtained a license and then a privilege to print the *Corona* in 1556-57; in March of 1557 the privilege was transferred to Zantani.[63] At the same time Prince Alfonso of Ferrara, heir to Duke Ercole II, was negotiating, through the Ferrarese composer Francesco Viola, with Antonio Gardano and with authorities in Venice, Rome, and Florence for privileges in expectation of publishing *Musica nova*. Alfonso had already purchased the music from its owner Polissena Pecorina, so that collection was now *his* property. Alfonso was furious to discover that he did not possess the only copy of the music, and set out to prevent Zantani from including the four-voice Willaert pieces in his *Corona*. The story (fully told by Martha Feldman and by Richard Agee and Jessie Ann Owens, who include all relevant surviving documents) ended with Zantani's reluctant agreement to put off publication of *Corona* for ten years. After some delays over the various privileges, Gardano published *Musica nova*, dedicated by Viola to Alfonso, in 1559.[64]

Printing of the *Corona* volume seems to have begun before 1559. There is some evidence to suggest the work was interrupted, and that if it was completed later some of the music near the end of the collection may have been a later addition.[65] Zantani, who in 1548 had published a book of medals with elaborately engraved illustrations,[66] was apparently a painter and engraver of at least amateur fame.[67] For the *Corona* print he designed "notes and staves of a new kind" ("il novo carraterre et righe per lui ritrovate").[68] The *Corona* volume is indeed unusual in appearance, with notes resembling the rounded forms of cursive handwritten notation and with continuous staves, unlike those of single-impression type; it looks (from a microfilm copy) like an early example of engraved music.[69]

---

[61] Feldman, 63-81. I am grateful to Professor Feldman for lending me a microfilm copy of the *Corona* print.

[62] On Zantani's patronage of Venetian musicians, see Feldman, 67-68, citing Orazio Toscanella's *I nomi antichi, et moderni delle provincie, regioni, città . . .* (Venice, 1567), a work dedicated to Zantani. The dedication is reproduced by Feldman (appendix E, pp. 433-34). In Zorzi's dedicatory letter to the *Corona* volume Zantani is styled "padre de musici, de i letterati, de gli scultori, de gli architetti, dei Pittori, Antiquarij."

[63] See Richard J. Agee and Jessie Ann Owens, "La stampa della *Musica nova* di Willaert," *Rivista italiana di musicologia* 24 (1989): 219-305, documents 4-10.

[64] See above, nn. 61 and 63.

[65] A letter (December 1558) from the Ferrarese ambassador in Venice to Ercole II in Ferrara informs that Zantani had printed "parte alcuna" of the music; see Agee and Owens, 272. It was certainly printed by 1567, according to Toscanella's *I nomi antichi* (see Feldman, 434). The pagination of the *Corona* volume begins with capital letters A through H; then, near the end of the first section, devoted to Willaert, and in the midst of the *Musica nova* pieces ending this section, there is a shift to numbered pages (in all four partbooks), possibly indicating a break in the printing process.

[66] *Le imagini con tutti I riversi trovati . . . libro primo* (Venice, 1548); see Feldman, 73-78. The engraver was Enea Vico, whose name appears on the title page. The book's colophon is identical with that of the 1569 *Corona*. Sartori, *Dizionario degli editori*, lists Zorzi (q.v.) as printer of the *Corona*; whether he helped print the *Imagini* as well would be hard to say.

[67] In Toscanella's words, Zantani "dipinge, ricama, & intaglia sopra ogni credenza bene"; see Feldman, 73, 434. Feldman's translation of "ricama" as "embroider" may be too literal: Toscanello probably meant something allied to *intarsia* or engraving.

[68] See Agee and Owens, " document 9, p. 248.

[69] Without examination of the print itself (the one surviving copy is in the Bayerische Staatsbibliothek in Munich), it is hard to be sure. The noteheads in *Corona* are similar to a type font developed by Robert Granjon in Lyons in the late 1550s; see *New Grove* (1980), s.v. "Robert Granjon," by Samuel Pogue. Aside from an early example of lute music, ca. 1535, the volumes produced by Simone Verovio in Rome in the 1580s and 1590s are usually said to represent the beginnings of musical engraving; see *New Grove* (1980), s.v. "Simone Verovio," by Thomas Bridges.

As for the book's contents, their hoped-for novelty consisted of the four Willaert madrigals from *Musica nova*, five pieces by Baldissera Donato, and three unpublished works by Perissone Cambio. By 1569 the Willaert pieces had of course been in print for ten years, and all of Donato's were included in his *Secondo libro a 4* of 1568; thus only the three madrigals of Perissone (out of four in the volume) were Zantani's "property" in the sense that they had not been published elsewhere.[70] For modern scholars there is a bonus in the eight pieces by Giovanni Contino and the single madrigal by Sperindio Bertoldo, probably first printed in volumes now lost.[71] The single madrigal by Berchem is known from earlier printed sources but is only here attributed to him.[72] It is odd to see included five pieces by Francesco Viola, editor of *Musica nova* and thus hardly a friend to Zantani. The volume begins with the work of Willaert and Donato, but the madrigal by the other Venetian, Perissone, comes near the end; it is hard to find logic in this order.

The printed sources from which Zorzi and/or Zantani drew materials for this anthology are well-known ones.[73] The sense in which Zantani could have regarded this music as "his" is not easy for us to grasp. But other people must have owned copies of engravings and medals in Zantani's possession; why should music have been regarded differently? By publishing the madrigals under his sponsorship and in a distinctive notational appearance, he asserted his ownership just as he had done with Roman medals. Printed music in this case becomes, more than in any of the other commissioned anthologies we have been dealing with, an *objet de vertu*, evidence of a nobleman's cultural distinction.

* * * * *

These anthologies are far from a unified group. Even the categories I have divided them into are somewhat arbitrary and contain considerable overlap. The music contained in them is not in any way different from the various stylistic types of the madrigal as a whole. Yet these books have a good deal to tell us about the madrigal as a social and cultural phenomenon. First of all, there is their emphasis on the poetic texts. Most of the thematic anthologies identify the poets, and in many of them the texts were commissioned or specially written for the particular musical settings and for the purpose at hand. These volumes are in fact poetic as well as musical anthologies, books to be read as well as for the purposes of singing from them. The composers were often local musicians, some known only from their presence in these volumes; these men were presumably glad to fulfill any commission coming their way. What is surprising is the range of composers involved, from the most obscure to the most famous, the latter sometimes far away from the source of the commission. There must have been a lot of correspondence involved, and composers must have received directions (about range/cleffing and mode, and in some cases they may have received copies of one or more musical settings already composed, ready for *imitatio* or its avoidance). They were certainly aware of being involved in a group project.

The greatest madrigalists of the later sixteenth century contributed to these volumes. Monte, Lasso, Palestrina, the Gabrielis, Marenzio, Wert, and many others of established reputations fulfilled these kinds of commissions often enough to make us think that these volumes were important to them. Monteverdi is nearly alone in his avoidance

---

[70] The entry for *Corona* in Einstein-Vogel, 2:414 (Vogel), 676-77 (Einstein) is, apart from its irritating alphabetic arrangement of composers, not accurate. "Se quel dolor che va inanzi" is not anonymous but the work of Donato (as Einstein knew; he cites the setting in *The Italian Madrigal*, 2:673). One piece, Donato's "Fuggi se sai fuggir," is omitted altogether.

[71] Bertoldo's *Primo libro a 5* (1561) is called, in its dedicatory letter, "questo 2do parto del mio piccolo ingegno," suggesting that a book *a 4* must have preceded it. Contino's *Primo libro a 5* (1560) has a dedication which states "havendo io gia dato in luce il mio primo Libro de madrigali a Quattro voci"; see Einstein-Vogel, 1:91, 179; Giuliani, *I lieti amanti*, 9 n. 11.

[72] In *Il primo libro . . . de diversi ecc. autori a misura di breve* (1542[17]) this piece, "Che giova saettar" (no. 25), is attributed to Hubert Naich; it is anonymous in reprints of the volume. Don Harrán thinks the *Corona* attribution to Berchem convincing on stylistic grounds; see Harrán, ed., *The Anthologies of Black-Note Madrigals* (American Institute of Musicology, 1978-81), lix, 95.

[73] Aside from the prints mentioned above, others include the *Primo libro a 4* of Rore (1550), of Viola (1550), of Nasco (1554), and the anthologies 1549[31] (*Il vero terzo libro . . . a note negre*) and 1554[28] (*Il quarto libro . . . a note bianche*). All of these were published in Venice and were doubtless purchased by Zantani.

of the thematic anthology.[74] The frequent presence of the apparently ever-obliging Monte is not surprising. More instructive is the participation of Lasso, known for his desire to control the publication of his music. The case of Palestrina is particularly interesting; the number of his madrigals published in anthologies of all kinds far exceeds those issued in volumes appearing under his name.[75] His music is found in many anthologies of a general character; of the thematic volumes under review here, he contributed to seven. Two were local projects in Rome (appendix nos. 9, 13) in which his participation might be expected. But the others (appendix nos. 4, 23, 27, 28, 32), chiefly Venetian in origin, show that Palestrina was widely valued as a madrigalist, and that, despite his declarations about avoidance of secular themes, he continued to take an active interest in the madrigal and was aware of stylistic and rhetorical trends in the genre.[76] Much remains to be learned from these anthologies. I hope this hurried survey will prompt their further study.

APPENDIX

Some anthologies with thematic content are listed here in chronological order according to categories discussed in the text of this article. Each anthology is listed by its RISM number— *Répertoire international des sources musicales: Recueils imprimés, XVIe-XVIIe siècles*, ed. François Lesure (Munich-Duisberg: Henle, 1960)—followed by its number (in parenthesis) in Einstein-Vogel. The contents are often given in Einstein-Vogel in alphabetical order of composers. Where there is a published listing in the original order it is referred to here.

A. Dynastic celebration

1. 1539^{25} (1539^1) Musiche fatte nelle nozze dello ill. Duca di Firenze il sig. Cosimo de Medici et della ill. Consorte sua mad. Leonora da Toledo. Venice: Antonio Gardane.
   No dedication.
   Contents: see Lewis, *Antonio Gardano*, 1, no. 14.
   Modern edition: Minor and Mitchell, eds., *A Renaissance Entertainment*.

2a. 1569^{14} (1569^1) Musica de' virtuosi della florida capella dell' ill. et ecc. S. Duca di Baviera a 5 voci con le rime del S. Antonio Minturno. Libro Primo. Venice: Girolamo Scotto.
   Dedication: Albrecht V, by Massimo Troiano.
   Contents: see modern edition.
   Modern edition: Leuchtmann, *Musik der bayerischen Hofkapelle*.

2b. 1575^{11} (1575^1) Il secondo libro de madrigali a 5 voci de floridi virtuosi del Ser. Duca di Baviera. Venice: L'herede di Girolamo Scotto.
   Dedication: Albrecht V, by Cosimo Bottegari.
   Contents: see modern edition.
   Modern edition: Leuchtmann, *Musik der bayerischen Hofkapelle*.

3. 1579^3 (1579^2) Trionfo di musica di diversi a 6 voci, libro primo. Venice: L'herede di Girolamo Scotto.
   Dedication: Granduchessa di Toscana, by Tiburtio Massaino.
   Contents: Einstein-Vogel 2:693-94.

---

[74] Monteverdi did contribute to one anthology, *Madrigali del Signor Cavaliero Anselmi* (1624^{11}); see Gary Tomlinson, *Monteverdi and the End of the Renaissance* (Berkeley: University of California Press, 1987), 197, 200, 204.

[75] See Piperno, 20, 22, 39-40.

[76] In the dedications of several of his sacred volumes, Palestrina lamented his youthful indiscretions in the realm of the secular madrigal; see F. X. Haberl et al., eds., *Pierluigi da Palestrina's Werke*, vol. 28 (Leipzig: Breitkopf und Härtel, 1862-1907), iii. Haberl assembled a "third book" out of a number of Palestrina madrigals found in collections; many more than these are extant.

4. 1586^{11} (1586^4)   Corona di dodici sonetti di Gio. Battista Zuccarini alla Gran Duchessa di Toscana . . . a 5 voci. Venice: Angelo Gardano.
Dedication: Donato Baglioni and Roberto Strozzi, by G. B. Zuccarini.
Contents: Einstein-Vogel 2:713-14.

5. 1591^7 (___)   Intermedi et concerti fatti per la Commedia rappresentata in Firenze nelle nozze del ser. Don Ferdinando Medici, e Mad. Christiana de Lorena, granduchi di Toscana. Venice: Giacomo Vincenti.
Dedication: Gran Duchessa Cristiana, by Cristofano Malvezzi, who mentions that Emilio de'Cavalieri, having been ordered "di far fedelmente stampare . . . le Musiche fatte per gli Intermedij della Commedia," gave the job of editing the music to him.
Contents: see modern edition.
Modern edition: see Walker, ed., *Les Fêtes du mariage*.

B. Collections defined by place

6. 1548^8 (1548^1)   Madrigali de la fama a 4 voci. Venice: Girolamo Scotto.
No dedication.
Contents (1548^7): Lewis, *Antonio Gardano*, 1, no. 126. Though nothing about it is said on the title page, this is a completely Ferrarese anthology, thus the earliest of those devoted to a single center. Gardano, who reprinted the collection (1548^7), identifies its three composers—Rore, Francesco Viola, Francesco Manara—on the title page and groups their work in that order. Lewis points out that "Fama" refers to a printer's device of Scotto, whose edition presumably preceded that of Gardano.

7. 1570^{15} (1570^3)   Il dolci frutti: Primo libro de vaghi et dilettevoli madrigali . . . a 5 voci. Venice: Girolamo Scotto.
Dedication: Gaspare Pignatta da Ravenna, by Cornelio Antonelli da Rimini [detto il Turturino].
Contents: Einstein-Vogel, 2:679. Though not specified as Venetian in content (and not restricted to Venetian composers) this collection deserves mention here because of its inclusion of an eleven-stanza canzone, "Questo si ch'è felice e lieto giorno," set by eleven composers, on a Venetian victory.

8. 1574^{5-6} (1574^{2-3})   Il primo [secondo] libro delle villanelle alla napolitana a 3 voci de diversi musici di Bari. Venice: li figli . . . di Antonio Gardano.
Dedication: Daniello Centurione, by Giovanni de Antiquis.
Contents: see modern edition.
Modern edition: Villanelle alla napolitana a 3 voci di musicisti baresi del secolo xvi (Rome: Istituto italiano per la storia della musica, 1941).

9. 1582^4 (1582^2)   Dolci affetti: Madrigali a 5 voci de div. ecc. musici di Roma. Venice: L'herede di Girolamo Scotto.
Dedication: Ottavio Bandini, by "L'Accademico anomato" [= G. M. Nanino?].
Contents: see modern edition.
Modern edition: Nino Pirrotta, ed., *I musici di Roma e il madrigale* (Rome: Accademia di Santa Cecilia, 1993).

10. ___ (1583^7)   Villotte mantovane a 4 voci. Venice: Angelo Gardano.
No dedication.
Contents: Einstein-Vogel, 2:703-04. Einstein's supposition (704) that the volume may be the work of Alessandro Striggio is unsupported; see *New Grove* (1980), s.v. "Striggio" by Iain Fenlon.

11. 1586^{10} (1586^6)   I lieti amanti. Primo libro de madrigali a 5 voci di div. ecc. musici. Venice: Giacomo Vincenti & Ricciardo Amadino.
Dedication: Mario Bevilacqua, by Hippolito Zanluca.
Contents: see modern edition.
Modern edition: Giuliani, ed., *I lieti amanti*. Ferrarese and "foreign" musicians alternate regularly in this volume.

12. 1588^{14} (1588^4)   L'amorosa caccia de div. ecc. musici mantovani nativi a 5 voci. Venice: Angelo Gardano.
    Dedication: "I signori musici di Roma," by Alfonso Preti, Gentil'huomo mantovano.
    Contents: Einstein-Vogel, 2:723-24. Preti's "La bella cacciatrice" sets the tone for the volume.

13. 1589^7 (1589^5)   Le gioie: Madrigali a 5 voci di div. ecc. musici della compagnia di Roma. Venice: Ricciardo Amadino.
    Dedication: Pietro Orsino, by Felice Anerio.
    Contents: see modern edition.
    Modern edition: Pirrotta, ed., *I musici di Roma* (*Le gioie* is edited by Giuliana Gialdroni).

14. 1589^{11} (1589^6)   Ghirlanda di fioretti musicali composta da div. ecc. musici a 3 voci. Rome: Simone Verovio.
    Dedication: Vincenzo Stella, by Verovio.
    Contents: Einstein-Vogel, 2:732.

15. 1590^{13} (1590^8)   Le gemme: Madrigali a 5 voci di div. ecc. musici della città di Bologna. Milan: Francesco & heredi di Simone Tini.
    Dedication: Monsig. Gio. Angelo Arcimboldi, by Francesco Lucini.
    Contents: Piperno, 54.

16. 1590^{15} (1590^5)   Novi frutti musicali. Madrigali a 5 voci di div. ecc. musici. Venice: Giacomo Vincenti.
    Dedication: Giovan Paolo Oliva, by Paolo Bellasio.
    Contents: Einstein-Vogel, 2:738-39. Another "crypto-Venetian" volume, this anthology contains a twelve-stanza canzone on a Venetian theme, "Ninfa che del superb' Adriatico." Bellasio contributed settings of the ninth and twelfth stanzas, and another madrigal; he may have been responsible for putting the volume together.

17. 1591^{12} (1591^{16})   Canzonette a 4 voci, composte da div. ecc. musici. Rome: [Simone Verovio].
    Dedication: Cardinal of Lorraine, by Verovio ["... queste canzonette Romane"].
    Contents: see modern edition.
    Modern edition: Alfred Wotquenne, ed., *Chansons italiennes de la fin du xvie siècle pour quatre voix mixtes* (Leipzig: Breitkopf & Härtel, n.d.).

18. 1591^{19} (1591^{15})   Giardino di musici ferraresi. Madrigali a 5 voci. Venice: Giacomo Vincenti.
    Dedication: Alfonso II, by Vincenti.
    Contents: Einstein-Vogel, 2:744.

19. 1591^{14-16} (1591^{17-19})   Canzonette per cantar et sonar di leuto a 3 voci [three books]. Venice: Giacomo Vincenti.
    No dedication.
    Contents: Einstein-Vogel, 2:744. In the edition of 1601^8 the books are said to be "de div. ecc. musici romani."

20. 1592^{14} (1592^5)   La gloria musicale di div. ecc. autori a 5 voci. Venice: Ricciardo Amadino.
    Dedication: Mario Bevilacqua, by Filippo Nicoletti.
    Contents: Einstein-Vogel, 2:751. This is a Ferrarese anthology, though not designated as such; see above, n. 39.

21. 1598^7 (1598^2)   Laudi d'amore. Madrigali a 5 voci da div. ecc. musici di Padova. Venice: Ricciardo Amadino.
    Dedication: Guglielmo Adorne Borusso, by Girolamo Boni.
    Contents: Einstein-Vogel, 2:766.

22. 1609^{16} (1609^1)   Teatro de madrigali a 5 voci de div. ecc. musici napolitani. Naples: G.R. Gargano & Lucretio Nucci.
    Dedication: Niccolo Ponzi, by Scipione Riccio.
    Contents: Einstein-Vogel, 2:799-800.

C. Anthologies for a single occasion or person

23. 1568[16] (1568[1])   Corona della morte dell' ill. sig. il Sig. Comendator Anibal Caro. Venice: Girolamo Scotto.
Dedication: Giovanni Ferro, by Giulio Bonagiunta.
Contents: Einstein-Vogel, 2:675.

24. 1582[5] (1582[1])   Il lauro secco. Primo libro di madrigali a 5 voci di div. autori. Ferrara: Vittorio Baldini.
Dedication: "A virtuosi lettori," by "I Rinovati." The letter mentions that the academicians' sincerity of intention obviates the necessity of "ammantarsi della protettione di alcun Principe, come ricerca il costume d'hoggi tanto pij." See Gaspari, 3:27.
Contents: Einstein-Vogel, 2:695.

25. 1583[10] (1583[3])   Il lauro verde: Madrigali a 6 voci di div. autori. Ferrara: Vittorio Baldini.
Dedication: no dedicatory letter; but Tasso's sonnet "Laura del vostro lauro in queste carte" is on the reverse of the title page. Like 1582[5], this volume is intended for Laura Peverara.
Contents: Einstein-Vogel, 2:701-02.

26. 1586[7] (1586[1])   Armonia di scelti autori a 6 voci sopra altra perfettissima armonia di bellezze d'una gentil donna senese in ogni parte bella. Venice: herede di Girolamo Scotto.
Dedication: no dedicatory letter, but title page says "Al' ill. sig. et mio patrone osservan. il S. Giovanni Bardi de Conti di Vernio." The dedicator may be Andrea Feliciani; see above, n. 51.
Contents: Einstein-Vogel, 2:712.

27. 1592[11] (1592[2])   Il trionfo di Dori descritto da diversi et posto in musica a 6 voci da altretanti autori. Venice: Angelo Gardano.
Dedication: Leonardo Sanudo, by Gardano.
Contents: see modern edition.
Modern edition: Powley, "Il Trionfo di Dori." Authors of the poetic texts are identified in the *tavola* and at the head of each piece.

28. 1596[11] (1596[5])   Vittoria amorosa de div. autori a 5 voci. Venice: Giacomo Vincenti.
Dedication: Count Teodoro Trivulci, by Geronimo Vaiano.
Contents: Einstein-Vogel, 2:760.

D. Anthologies on a single poetic text

29. 1585[17] (1585[5])   Sdegnosi ardori. Musica di div. autori sopra un istesso soggetto di parole a 5 voci, raccolti insieme da Giulio Gigli da Immola. Munich: Adam Berg.
Dedication: G. B. Galanti, by Giulio Gigli.
Contents: see modern edition.
Modern edition: Schuetze, *Ardo sì ma non t'amo*.

30. 1588[17] (1588[7])   L'amorosa Ero rappresentata de' piu celebri musici d'Italia con l'istesse parole & nel medesimo tuono. Brescia: Vincenzo Sabbio.
Dedication: Marc' Antonio Martinengo, by Antonio Morsolino.
Contents: see modern edition.
Modern edition: Lincoln, *The Madrigal Collection L'Amorosa Ero*.

E. Anthologies based on a poetic conceit

31. 1564[16] (1564[1])   Di Manoli Blessi [= Antonio Molino]: Il primo libro delle greghesche con la musicha disopra composta da diversi autori a 4, a 5, a 6, a 7, & a 8 voci. Venice: Antonio Gardano.
Dedication: Paulo Vergeli, Claudio da Currezo, Francesco Bunaldi, by Manoli Blessi.

Contents: see modern edition.
Modern edition: Siro Cisilino, ed., *Greghesche: Libro I, 1564* (Padua: Zanibon, 1974).

32. 1593³ (1593²)   Florindo et Armilla. Canzon pastorale ornata di musica da diversi de piu celebri compositori de tempi nostri & con altri madrigali novamente posta in luce a 5 voci. Venice: Ricciardo Amadino.
Dedication: Giulio Morosini (to whom "hà piacciuto di far ornare di Musica le presente Canzoni"), by Amadino.
Contents: Einstein-Vogel, 2:753. Here the alphabetic listing is misleading. The volume contains an eighteen-part canzone set, in order, by Monte, Lasso, Porta, Bell'haver, Ingegneri, dalla Casa, Mosto, Croce, Colombano, Nanino, Baccusi, Marenzio, Anerio, Merulo, Pallavicino, Spontone, Bertani and Stabile. Three madrigals, by Palestrina, Giovanelli, and Milleville, are added at the end.

33. 1594⁶ (1594⁴)   Madrigali pastorali descritti da diversi et posti in musica da altri tanti autori a 6 voci, intitolati il Bon Bacio. Venice: Angelo Gardano.
Dedication: Ottaviano Malipiero, by Gardano.
Contents: Einstein-Vogel, 2:774. All texts identified by author, in the *tavola* and with each piece.

34. 1598⁸ (1598¹)   Le risa a vicenda. Vaghi e dilettevoli madrigali a 5 voci posti in musica da div. autori. Raccolti ... di Gio. Pietro Flacconio siciliano di Milazzo. Venice: Giacomo Vincenti.
Dedication: Francesco Maria Cardinal dal Monte, by Flacconio (dated Rome, 20. viii. 1598).
Contents: see modern edition. A pair of related texts appears in nine settings alternating with free madrigals and with an introductory and a closing piece on the theme of love's pains and pleasures, forming a very symmetrical whole.
Modern edition: Paolo Emilio Carapezza, ed., *Le risa a vicenda*, Musiche Rinascimentali Siciliane, 12 (Florence: Olschki, 1993).

35. 1601⁷ (1601³)   I diporti della villa in ogni stagione. Spiegati in quattro canzoni dell' ill. S. Francesco Bozza Cavaliere et posti in musica da div. famosi autori a 5 voci. Venice: Angelo Gardano.
Dedication: Francesco Bozza, by Gardano.
Contents: see modern edition.
Modern edition: Siro Cisilino, ed., *I diporti della villa* (Milan: Carisch, 1961).

36. 1609¹⁷ (1609²)   Sonetti novi di Fabio Petrozzi romano sopra le ville di Frascati & altri posti in musica a 5 voci da div. ecc. musici. Rome: G. B. Robletti.
Dedication: Cardinal Arigone, by Petrozzi.
Contents: Einstein-Vogel, 2:800.

F. A collector's anthology

37. 1569²⁰ (1569³ᵃ)   La eletta di tutta la musica intitolata corona di diversi ... libro primo. [Venice: Zorzi].
Dedication: Antonio Zantani, by Zuan Jacomo di Zorzi.
Contents: Einstein-Vogel, 2:677 (but see above, n. 70).

5

An Organ Building Project of the Sixteenth Century: The Large Organ of St. Vitus Cathedral in Prague

Lilian P. Pruett

Archives and libraries in Prague and Vienna preserve records of what must be described as one of the most complicated—and ill-fated—organ construction projects in the history of music.[1] It began when Ferdinand I, then king of Bohemia and Hungary, made plans for the refurbishment of his residence and of the official rooms in Prague Castle. Among the innovations, he specified that a new large organ should be built for the cathedral church in the castle. Since the king was rarely in Prague, his son, Archduke Ferdinand II, governor of Bohemia, was delegated to serve as the local supervisor. Beginning in 1552, Ferdinand II sought to engage a well-known organ builder, Friedrich Pfanmüller (also Phanmüller, ca. 1490-1562) of Amberg, for the job. Correspondence of 7 July 1553 reveals that first contacts had been made in the summer of 1552, when Pfanmüller was building an organ in Eger. He had been asked to come to Prague, but as there had been no firm contract, he stopped in Pilsen to work on an organ there.[2] On 22 July 1553, the Bohemian Chamber informed the king that Pfanmüller had been ordered to appear in Prague by September 1, and asked for permission to complete negotiations with him.[3] King Ferdinand wrote to his son on 12 September 1553, indicating he had received the advice and opinions of his beloved chapelmaster, Petrus Maessenus, advising that Pfanmüller be summoned to Prague to work out the details, and, at the same time, sending a sample organ pipe according to which kind and measure the organ should be constructed.[4] Archduke Ferdinand responded October 4 that he had already negotiated the deal before receiving his father's letter of September 12. The agreement specified that Pfanmüller be provided with all the tin, lead, wire, iron, coal, and lights necessary for the making of the organ, and also wood for heating, and free housing for himself and his helpers. For his work he was to receive 600 taler, distributed over the more than two years that the work was likely to take. He was not to be responsible for the case for the organ, which would be built by a carpenter.[5]

The slight disconnection in these communications is indicative of the difficulties that accompanied this organ's birth. Seen in retrospect, the process was fraught with difficulties: failed communications, problems with personnel, including deaths, missed deadlines, lack of records, and expanding overruns of modern-day defense-budget proportions. The surviving records reveal a picture of personal involvement by ruling heads that is surprising in its intensity and detail, but show also that the most personal imperial involvement could not at times overcome the inertia of the multi-level bureaucracy of the Habsburg governmental institutions.

---

[1] Many of the documents have been gathered together in the *Jahrbuch der kunsthistorischen Sammlungen des a. h. Kaiserhauses*, published in Vienna late in the nineteenth century, specifically in vols. 5 (1887), 10 (1889), and 12 (1891); henceforth these will be referred to as *Jahrbuch*, vol. number, and document number. Others remain in the Statní Ústřední Archív, as well as in the Hradčanski Archív, both in Prague.

[2] *Jahrbuch* 10, no. 6149.

[3] Ibid.

[4] Ibid.

[5] Ibid., no. 6151.

The king approved the arrangement with Pfanmüller, but that did not translate into the work starting immediately. On 30 March 1554, the builder pleaded he was too ill and weak to travel to Prague, and requested he be permitted to finish a job he had started in Dachau.[6] On 30 October 1554, the Bohemian Chamber reported to the king that Pfanmüller has been ordered to stop all other work and come to Prague to begin construction of the great organ. Pfanmüller agreed to this, but, since there was an outbreak of the plague in Prague, and it would be more convenient to start work on the roof, pipes, chest, and keyboards in Amberg, he requested that materials be sent to him there.[7] And by the end of the month he received twelve hundredweight of tin.[8]

Five years later, on 24 November 1559, Pfanmüller wrote to (now emperor) Ferdinand I that Christmas 1559 will mark four years that he has been working on the organ. He reported that the requisite 3000 pipes as well as the keyboards had been completed, and that he could finish the remainder and install and tune the pipes in another six months, provided the case for the organ and the stonecutters' work (on the footing and the gallery) had been done. But, in another example of delayed action, court carpenter Hanns Sauerloch had earlier reported having had the model in hand since April, when he estimated to be able to have the case finished in nine months, but, lacking confirmation of the commission for the work, that he has not yet started.[9] Although the emperor tried to force an early completion date, he had to acquiesce to the proposals of carpenter and organ builder.[10] Interested in keeping the project on track, by 25 September 1559 he again inquired about the progress of the organ,[11] and on October 13 he wrote to his son in Prague, distressed that the carpenter has not yet done any work on the case, and the organ builder still had to construct the big pipes and complete considerable other work. He worried that the latter was an old, wornout man who might fall ill unexpectedly and even die before the elegant design can be completed, which, should it happen, could mean all the monies expended could come to naught and the construction be completely halted.[12]

One document is difficult to interpret. Dated 9 October 1559, it is a request from the organist at Prague Castle, Burian Waldeck, for a raise of one taler weekly so he can hire a "big" calcant, necessary for the "new large instrument," which is so large that he alone cannot handle it and place it in its "futteral." Was part of the new organ perhaps operative at that time?[13]

The emperor's concerns notwithstanding, there seems to have been no progress in the construction of the case. Hearing that Pfanmüller was inactive in Prague, waiting for the case to be completed, the mayor of Vienna petitioned the emperor on 4 January 1561 to allow the builder to come to Vienna at Easter-time to repair the two organs in St. Stephen's church, work that should not take longer than eight to ten weeks.[14] On January 16, Ferdinand I relayed the request to Ferdinand II.[15] The latter responded March 19 with concerns that Pfanmüller was too old and feeble to travel, but proposing to send the builder's son, organist in Eger and also a skilled builder. Ferdinand even suggested that Pfanmüller, Jr., could be retained to complete his father's job in the event of his death.[16] This seems not to have pleased, for on April 14 Ferdinand made another proposal: he will send both young Pfanmüller and Ciprian Waldeck,

---

[6] Ibid., no. 6153.

[7] Ibid., no. 6156.

[8] This was not the first shipment; 400 hundredweight of tin had already been relayed to him on 3 August 1553; see Hradčanski Archív, Antiquitates, carton 1, no. 134.

[9] *Jahrbuch* 5, no. 4289.

[10] Ibid, no. 4293, 19 January 1559.

[11] Ibid., no. 4303.

[12] Ibid., no. 6171.

[13] Hradčanski Archív, carton 2, no. 168: ". . . dieweil ich aber zum solchen Instrument ainen starcken Calcanten bedarff dann es ziemlich groß und schwer wird ainner es allain Inn das futteral nicht bringen kann, wie mir denn jetzendt dardurch ein großer Schaden wiederfaren und das silber darvon abgebrochen auch etlich Pfeiffen daraus genommen worden sein. . . ."

[14] Statní Ústřední Archív, fond. SM, signatura B, svazek 26/2, nos. 7-8.

[15] Ibid., nos. 5-6.

[16] *Jahrbuch* 12, no. 7966.

brother of the Prague organist Burian Waldeck, to Vienna to have their qualifications examined by experts, and the emperor may decide whom to engage for Prague. This, also, was not satisfactory, and ultimately Archduke Ferdinand had to give in, recommending that the elder and the younger Pfanmüller both go to Vienna, the elder instructing his son on what was to be done and returning in two to three weeks, the younger staying at least two months to complete the repairs.[17]

The documentary evidence is silent on whether the two builders went to Vienna. It is not likely, for by Whitsuntide, Pfanmüller's widow petitioned for a pension, and was granted 32 taler annually for four years, and a one-time payment of 50 Schock Meissenisch (13 July 1564).[18] She died as well before receiving the payment for the full four years. Her heirs, in requesting the residual amount, pointed out that father, mother, and two sons had spent their lives working on the organ.[19] And so the first decade, 1552-62, ended without completion of the instrument.

There is no further mention of young Pfanmüller as successor to his father on the project. Instead, Jonas Scherer, organ builder from Klosterneuburg, was dispatched to Prague (payment made 20 August 1562),[20] and Archduke Ferdinand's organ builder from Innsbruck, Georg (Jörg) Eberth,[21] was also engaged to build some pipes.[22] During the period 1563-65 most of the decoration, painting, and gilding of the organ-wings and case were completed, with much delay and great expense. Ferdinand II's own court painter, Francesco de Tertiis, was commissioned to furnish the paintings for the two wings, while the gilding provided a special challenge: for a long time, no suitably skilled painters could be found in Vienna or Prague, and an artisan was summoned from Milan. Before he could arrive, a craftsman from Prague, Hans Gerschnig, demonstrated his skills in gold-leafing, a process Archduke Ferdinand recommended as more radiant and longer-lasting than the usual gold paint, although admittedly more time-consuming and expensive. Once the Milanese artist, Domenico Pozzo, had arrived, he was retained to paint the walls and ceilings of the Landrechtsstube in the castle, work still seen there today.[23]

In the meantime, Jonas Scherer, proud of his reputation as an organ builder, rejected a collaboration with the younger Georg Eberth, who was then dismissed. The emperor's letter of 2 May 1563 reports that Scherer has been given permission to go on "Kur" for his ailing health, before he is to move to Prague.[24] By June 18, authorization is given for payments covering Scherer's move for himself, his wife, assistants, two wagons with eight horses, and their coachmen, as well as twenty-five gulden in travel money.[25] All the lumber and other materials he needed to construct the "positif" had already been ordered on March 26, and on July 20 the Bohemian Chamber authorized payment for three hundred prepared skins, which were to be used for the organ bellows.[26] Scherer also received the emperor's permission to call for the assistance of another builder, Joachim Rudner from Budweis, in order to speed up construction.[27]

What began so promisingly was to deteriorate in a short time. During this period the financial situation of the empire worsened as the Habsburgs' income was challenged by the increasing costs of establishing and maintaining lavish courts, while also providing for armies fighting the ever-threatening Turkish forces, as well as the Protestants.

---

[17] Ibid., no. 7967.

[18] Hradčanski Archív, carton 2, no. 189. A Schock is a weight measurement by which coins were dispensed.

[19] Statní Ústřední Archív, SM/B/26/2, no. 9.

[20] *Jahrbuch* 5, no. 4325.

[21] Builder of the oldest extant two-manual Renaissance organ still in close to authentic condition, located in the Court Church in Innsbruck. See Egon Krauss, *Die Ebert-Orgel in der Hofkirche zu Innsbruck (1558)* (Innsbruck: Edition Helbling, 1989).

[22] *Jahrbuch* 5, no. 4341, 10 April 1563.

[23] Among the documents pertinent to the decoration are *Jahrbuch* 5, nos. 4340-41, 4345-47, 4356-57, 4362, 4380; 10, no. 6204; 12, nos. 7987, 8000, 8011.

[24] *Jahrbuch* 5, no. 4345.

[25] Ibid., no. 4349.

[26] Ibid., no. 4341.

[27] *Jahrbuch* 10, no. 6205.

In 1561 Archduke Ferdinand had still been concerned about the hardships Pfanmüller encountered after the 600 taler for which he had contracted to build the organ in 1553 had been long spent, and felt the builder should be provided with an appropriate weekly disbursement for the upkeep of himself and his assistants.[28] But three years later Jonas Scherer's letter of 1 April 1564 reported to the emperor that he had been working all this time "on the mighty huge organ" without receiving payment for himself and his ten to eleven helpers, for whom he is obliged to provide wine and beer and four decent meals daily. Scherer accused the Bohemian Chamber of being deaf to his requests, noting he had been productive despite the difficult conditions and had completed the wind chest as well as many pipes and other work. He petitioned for the money to be provided in weekly payments of ten to eleven taler.[29]

Ferdinand I died 25 July 1564. There is no evidence he responded to Scherer's letter. However, the newly-elected emperor, Maximilian II, ordered on 23 September 1564 Ulrich Dubantzky, merchant in Prague, to provide 1,100 taler for the organ building at St. Vitus' church, and instructed the Bohemian Chamber to provide money, room, and board for Scherer and his helpers. Since Scherer was now ready to install and tune the organ, he was to have access to all the necessary workmen, locksmiths, and carpenters.[30] This was to no avail, for Scherer died 2 August 1565. Maximilian, attempting to trace the expenditures for the organ years later, was informed by "Baumeister" Bonifacius Wohlmut, the official responsible for overseeing all construction at the court, that Scherer had not received any payment whatsoever from his office.[31] Discontent with the services that Wohlmut had, or rather had not, provided, was considerable, and, a few years later, in early 1570, after investigations into his alleged incompetence and laziness, Maximilian ordered his dismissal.[32]

Meanwhile, Archduke Ferdinand and Maximilian were eager to have the organ construction project brought to completion. Ferdinand reported to his brother that he had hired the highly recommended Joachim Rudner from Budweis to carry on the work, after Rudner's examination by Ferdinand and Carl II of Styria, then on a visit to Prague, who had found him to be most qualified to finish the organ, which "has no equal anywhere in Christendom, and which is almost done." Rudner, familiar with the situation, was reluctant to take on the job without guarantees that the Bohemian Chamber would deal with him more responsibly than had been done with Scherer. He took the precaution of listing precisely what still needed to be done to the organ, and mentioned that he could not predict the time required for the work.

After twelve years of more or less continuous work, the list of items still to be completed seems unduly long: 1) the registers for the chest; 2) the pulls for the registers; 3) the installation of the complete works; 4) the pedalboard with the proper closures; 5) the installation of the "Rückpositif" and connecting it to the wind chest; 6) connecting the "Prustpositif" and its chest to the wind supply; 7) constructing the chest for the "großen Pusaun und auch die Pusaunen noch zumachen"; and finally, the construction of some four-hundred remaining pipes, as well as the alteration of many pipes already made.[33]

We do not know what assurances Rudner was given, but he, his sons, and his assistants worked diligently, including nights, as there was too much going on in the church during the daytime for him to do the tuning. On 20 November 1567—fifteen years after the planning had begun—he reported to Maximilian that the organ was finished, and requested payment of 2200 Rhenish gulden for his efforts. He also requested an annual pension (as had been given his predecessor, Friedrich Pfanmüller), in exchange for which he was to see to the upkeep of the instrument.[34]

In support of the demand for the large sum, Rudner provided an affidavit listing the items he had built. He opened with a statement that he had personally been informed by Jonas Scherer that emperor Ferdinand I had

---

[28] Ibid., no. 6181.

[29] Hradčanski Archív, carton 2, no. 183.

[30] Ibid., nos. 191 and 195, respectively.

[31] *Jahrbuch* 12, no. 8055, 6 February 1569. Scherer was more successful with Archduke Ferdinand, who authorized payment of 200 Schock Meissner groschen after Scherer threatened to leave—ibid., no. 7974, 5 August 1564.

[32] *Jahrbuch* 5, no. 4444, 15 April 1570. Nevertheless, he remained an active player in the story of the organ.

[33] Hradčanski Archív, carton 2, no. 214.

[34] *Jahrbuch* 12, no. 8009, and Hradčanski Archív, carton 2, no. 268, respectively.

promised him 3000 Schock and all expenses when he completed the great organ. He stressed that no other master but himself had the knowledge or skill to complete this work. Supporting his claim for the sum, as well as living expenses, he points out that in past work he has done for persons of noble or aristocratic birth, and for monasteries or other religious establishments he was never expected to spend any of his money for his own expenses. The itemization that follows exceeds the first estimate he made before he started working. He claims to have constructed 1) two chests for the pedal which house the great principal pipes and twenty registers for them; 2) a "positif" for the "Brustwerk," a new chest for it with three registers, along with connecting it to the wind supply of the great works and providing it with a register which can be opened or closed, if one finds it too heavy to play; 3) housings for the Posaunen for both manuals and pedals in which the pipes are standing, and also ten registers for them with rollers and connecting the whole construction into the Brustwerk; 4) a register to let the wind out of the bellows when they are not engaged; 5) built and erected the "Rückpositif." There had been one standing, but the chest was damaged, so he had to take it down, dismantle it, and ventilate it anew, then re-erect it. To this he made a new chest holding the trumpets and krumhorns to supplement the first, plus twelve registers and two hundred and thirty-one angled hooks to hang the entire "Rückpositif" together; 6) built a channel for the wind from the bellows through the works and the flooring, through the timber-work to the "Rückpositif," and made a register for the wind; 7) made the pedal to move and close off so it can be pulled to and fro, together with closures and three iron plates on which the pedal stands. He had to redo the pedal; Jonas had begun it, but had not gotten to the closures; 8) built the keyboards anew, having to strengthen them as the organworks demanded; 9) constructed anew the trumpets, great and small krummhorns and also three voices in the regal, which had been made, but as they did not agree nor fit with the others, had to be redone; 10) lastly, he installed the entire works, and tuned the pipes, having to work nights, because of all the singing during the day, for which effort he used up untold lights and endured freezing temperatures. The organ had been completed four days before Christmas.[35]

The Bohemian Chamber allowed him a payment of 100 taler, advising him to get the remainder directly from Maximilian during his next visit to Prague. Maximilian, in turn, approved the small payment, instructing Rudner to remain in Prague at imperial expense until he could get there, in case the builder should be needed for any adjustments or to correct any minor faults in the grand works.[36] Here began a tortuous trail of supplications, counter-supplications, explanations, and justifications, as one authority after another tried to make someone else responsible for the payment.

It was customary practice at the Habsburg court, when dealing with large, long-term, and costly projects, to have the completed work examined and evaluated by experts in the field, who considered its value and the labor spent on it, and arrived at a total monetary assessment. The Bohemian Chamber recommended this procedure for the organ. Joachim Rudner, however, objected strenuously, stating that his work could not be judged by anyone, for the simple reason that such an instrument had never been built before. He was angry that people who would not know one end from the other in most components of the organ should make the evaluation. He pointed out that others had worked on the organ without making the beginning, middle, and end meet, and he cites his ingenuity and labors in bringing the plan to reality. Should there be a master builder anywhere who had constructed such an organ, he would accept his judgment; but to let organists and others, who know nothing about the matters in question, make the evaluation was unthinkable. He also stated that to see all the intricacies, the instrument would have to be dismantled, and then there would be no guarantee that it would not suffer damage when put together again. He pleaded with the emperor to pay him what was his due, so he could return to his home in Budweis.[37]

Having arrived in Prague in the meantime, Maximilian issued the order to pay Joachim Rudner 2200 Rhenish gulden for the completion of the organ.[38] However, without a formal assessment and at a loss concerning the proper course of action, the Bohemian Chamber delayed payment and decided to assemble a commission consisting of the retired chief contracting officer, Bonifacius Wohlmut, the secretary of the contracting office, Michael Keck, as well

---

[35] Ibid., no. 8085, 20 May 1570.

[36] Ibid., no. 8029.

[37] Ibid., no. 8075, 7 March 1570, and no. 8074, before 13 February 1570.

[38] Hradčanski Archív, carton 3, no. 369.

as the chief craftsmen who had been involved in the building, among them master carpenters Hans Sauerloch and Hans Eissbauer, master locksmiths Georg Schmitthammer and Mathes Handschuh, and any other artisans who had worked on the instrument and who were knowledgeable in the crafts. They were to examine the instrument carefully, evaluate the builder's work and artistry, and provide an assessment, attesting it by their signatures and seals. That commission's written report provided no solution. In it the members explain that it is extremely difficult to fulfill their charges since all the previous master builders were dead; no inventories had been kept of materials delivered, used, and remaining at their deaths, or of how many helpers each one had used; there was no one among the present personnel who was knowledgeable about the art of organ building, and no one who had complete knowledge of the contributions of each worker; seeing many parts and not seeing others, they had no understanding of the nature and extent of the work involved, and so forth. In the end, the commission recommended that an equitable accommodation be made with Joachim Rudner, as it had already recommended once before.[39]

Meanwhile, trying to assure some source of steady income, Joachim Rudner's son, Albrecht, petitioned 14 April 1570 to be given a monthly stipend of 4 Rhenish gulden for maintaining the organ his father had built with such care, as well as 25 gulden annually for two years, so he could further learn the craft of organ building. (These were provisions that had been granted to Pfanmüller's son.) The petition was supported by Philippe de Monte, chapelmaster, and Wilhelm Formellis, court organist, curiously the only documented involvement of court musicians in the entire organ saga to date beyond the initial involvement of Petrus Maessenus in the specifications for the organ.[40] On 7 November 1570 the Bohemian Chamber again instructed the above-mentioned commission to inventory, assay, and assess the materials remaining after the completion of the organ construction. Not having been informed of the results, the Chamber renewed the instructions 22 January 1571, this time receiving the response that there was very little material of any value left, but that Master Joachim had offered to buy it all for 30 taler, along with the recommendation that the offer be accepted.[41]

In the summer of 1570, when the emperor's instructions to pay Rudner 2200 gulden were not carried out, Maximilian tried to gain some insight into the utterly confused record of expenditures, and he appears to have questioned the contracting secretary, Michael Keck. This becomes evident from a letter addressed to the emperor in which Keck seeks to distance, justify, and explain himself in such a way that he could not be held accountable. The letter is interesting in that it portrays the contractor's office as completely dysfunctional. Stating first that the organ project was not really his responsibility, he explains the lack of accounting procedures by the fact that he was so overworked that he had not the time to keep track of the monies taken in and spent:

> ... in the great rush to settle accounts with the craftsmen and workers, the draymen, and other persons, I shorted myself and forgot to make out receipts for many things, and, as easily happens when one has to deal with expenditures of money, neglected to do so to my detriment. Thus, when I would receive—usually on a Saturday—often 1000 Schock and more, then pay out the money on the following day or thereafter to hundreds of different persons, some of it would not be accounted for, as I can prove by several workmen who help me with the disbursements [who will corroborate this]. The time was not sufficient to make out proper receipts for all the monies paid out. . . .

In the letter, the accountant throws himself to the pity of the emperor, begging to be forgiven, and to have the debts struck. Concerning the problems with the organ he, rejects assuming the responsibility:

> As Your Majesty knows, Archduke Ferdinand had graciously ordered me, at the start of the sixty-first year, to take on the church, the great tower, and the organ here at the Prague Castle (which is not within my jurisdiction), which I have done for four years, and executed with much diligence and effort until the organ was finally finished and completed. And I have accounted regularly for all the

---

[39] *Jahrbuch* 12, no. 8094, after 14 October 1570.

[40] Hradčanski Archív, carton 3, no. 361, and *Jahrbuch* 12, no. 8079. Maximilian gave his approval on April 27.

[41] *Jahrbuch* 12, no. 8096.

> monies I received for that purpose, for which I have received a proper clearance. Now, for this labor, as Your Majesty will remember, I was to be given 25 gulden Bohemian, of which I have not received a penny to this day. But I leave it to Your Majesty to determine what you will graciously give for my proven fidelity, diligent efforts, and services. . . .

Keck concludes with a renewed plea for forgiveness and begs that his salary not be cut in half until the rest of the debt is paid, evidently a punishment the emperor threatened.[42] There is no record of Maximilian's response, but Michael Keck continued to function as contracting secretary for many years.

Rudner was not giving up quietly; he continued to write to the emperor and the Bohemian Chamber, reminding always of what he had been promised by Archduke Ferdinand (in the presence of the officials from the Chamber), listing what he received, and itemizing the expenses he had to absorb since being forced to remain in Prague after the organ's completion in 1567. The Chamber responded by asking for several more reports by different agencies as to the sums that had been paid out to the organ builder.[43]

Clearly wishing to put an end to the matter, Maximilian issued an order that Rudner be paid 1000 gulden. By 12 September 1571, Rudner again complained to the emperor that, although agreement was reached at 1000 florins, the Bohemian Chamber had not paid him the money in cash; deductions had been made at 30 Schock Meissnisch a year for housing, in violation of the emperor's directive that he remain in Prague at the emperor's expense (see document no. 8029), and in spite of the fact that Rudner had already paid 18 Schock annually for housing. He reiterated that he had been paying wages and daily upkeep for his four to five assistants, without whose help the organ could not have been completed, and that he had thus lost much money. In order to survive the three years in Prague thus far, he had to sell all his possessions in Budweis. Being an old man now, nearly blind, and in dire need, he requested a yearly pension for himself and, after his death, for his wife, who was an essential contributor to his labors. To speed up the official reviews of the request for the pension, Rudner begged the emperor to write a personal letter in his behalf. That letter was written 12 September 1571, but it was not presented to the Bohemian Chamber until 31 January 1572. The Chamber responded February 7 by asking its accountants to make another list of payments made to Rudner, then on 26 August 1572 wrote to the emperor asking for a decision on Rudner's pension! At this time, evidently tired of the entire problem, Maximilian ruled that Rudner's work had been fully paid, Rudner had received 1000 gulden "out of graciousness," and he turned down the request for the pension.[44]

Joachim Rudner is not heard from after this. The same cannot be said about the organ. In the following decade, Emperor Rudolf II ordered the organ repaired and renovated by Albrecht Rudner, the son of the maker who had applied (and been approved) to do maintenance work on the instrument in 1570. The contract spells out his responsibilities; he must 1) replace the present frames of the wings with new ones, remove and store the wing paintings so they will not be damaged, then rehang them in the new frames, decorate and paint the frames appropriately. He must make sure that the new wings cover the organ completely and tightly, so that no dust should enter, but they must be easily maneuverable, whether with ropes or wires, whatever is most workable. 2) The whole works shall be renovated and tuned. 3) The Principal, which had been damaged in the fire and had fallen out, shall be repaired, its missing parts replaced, and put in good working order. 4) He shall install a tremulant without adversely affecting the other vocal stops. 5) He is also to adjust two keyboards, the one at the great works not to have too deep a touch, the other at the Rückpositive to have a lighter touch. 6) He is to do whatever else is necessary and is determined by designated and knowledgeable organists, especially remove some non-functioning pipes and replace them. . . . For all this, he should receive 400 taler to be paid in installments: 100 taler at the start, 50 on the feast of St. Jacob, 50 on the feast of St. Michael, the remaining 200 after the completed work had been attested to by organists and masters. From this amount (400 taler), Albrecht Rudner is to pay all costs of locksmiths, carpenters, painters, laborers, and calcant (to help with the tuning), as he will need such persons.[45]

---

[42] Hradčanski Archív, carton 3, no. 386, 6 October 1570.

[43] *Jahrbuch* 12, nos. 8098-99.

[44] Ibid., no. 8120.

[45] Ibid., no. 8214, 17 April 1581.

The renovation took considerably longer than the elder Rudner's completion of the organ. Beginning in 1586 and extending to December 1590, an acrimonious dispute is documented between Albrecht Rudner and Carl Luython, organist, with the latter accusing the former of not only not having done the work for which he was contracted, but also of worsening the condition of the instrument through his ineptitude. As the documents reveal, the conflict was not limited to professional opinions but became intensely personal and even physical on some occasions. The emperor's musicians were deeply divided, as one organist undercut another before the Bohemian Chamber. The documentation is too lengthy to be quoted here, but some of the communications are reproduced in the *Jahrbuch* and in Albert Smijers's accounts of the imperial chapel in this period;[46] other notices are to be found in Prague archives.[47] Briefly, the dispute was as follows: Carl Luython reported (18 June 1586) that, after five years of renovations, the organ was worse than before, the keyboards less usable than at the start of the renovation, the wind supply poorer, the "tracturen" and "stöckh" completely unregulated, the action noisier than before, and the instrument tuned a half step higher than normal. Consulted about the situation, Paul von Winde, imperial organist, hedged in his response: he cannot judge the merits of the complaints since the renovation work was not yet finished (November 1586). On Easter 1587 Luython refused to play services on the instrument, claiming it was unplayable. But Achatzius Goltzig, the emperor's "pusauner und organist," informed the Chamber (27 April 1587) that he has played the organ and cannot see why Luython found it unplayable. It is at this point that chapelmaster Philippe de Monte entered the dispute for the second time, attesting that the organ is in bad condition: it is tuned too high, hence unusable with instruments and causes the singers to yell.[48] Albrecht Rudner had so ruined the instrument that Monte can think of no organmaster who would undertake to put it in good working order, further observing that Rudner was engaged to maintain the instrument regularly, but had allowed dust and dirt to almost destroy it.

The records remain silent about the further progress of this affair. It is a reasonable assumption that the organ was never put right, as the emperor, besieged by the mounting difficulties of his realm, withdrew more and more from daily transactions of the court. What had repeatedly been described as an "organ so grand as had never before been seen in Christendom,"[49] had taken fifteen years to complete, taken several human lives in the process of becoming, and swallowed up uncounted resources. The organ seems to have been allowed to fall into oblivion as far as the court records are concerned. In the succeeding decades—during the turmoil of the last years of Rudolph's reign, the transfer of the imperial court under Ferdinand II from Prague to Vienna in 1619, and the tribulations of the Thirty Years War—concerns about further repairs to an organ must have seemed insignificant and appear to have faded away. The instrument itself survived—in whatever condition—close to two hundred years, finally falling victim to an artillery attack on Prague on 3 June 1757 during the Seven Years War.[50]

---

[46] Ibid., nos. 8239-40, 8244, 8247-48, 8252-54, 8277; and Albert Smijers, "Die kaiserliche Hofkapelle von 1543-1619," 2. Teil, *Studien zur Musikwissenschaft* 7 (1920): 111-18.

[47] Statní Ústrední Archív, SM B 26/2, nos. 14-25.

[48] Michael Praetorius discusses the pitch distinction in use at the Prague cathedral—see *Syntagma musicum*, vol. 2: *De organographia* (1619), trans. Harold Blumenfeld (1962; reprint, New York: Da Capo, 1980), 15. The organ had been customarily tuned at chamber pitch, thus making possible cooperation with wind and string instruments. Raising it by a half step meant that instruments could not be used in church. Evidently Albrecht Rudner had assumed the organ had been at choral pitch, normally a whole tone lower than chamber pitch, and just raised it, clearly not having communicated with the local musicians.

[49] Rudolf Quoika, in *Die Musik in Geschichte und Gegenwart*, 10, col. 1163, describes it as the "Kaiserorgel," an instrument with four manuals and seventy-four speaking ranks. According to a citation in the same author's "Die Prager Kaiserorgel," *Kirchenmusikalisches Jahrbuch* 36 (1952): 35-46, the description is based on a surviving disposition in Dresdner Handschrift Orgeldispositionen, no. 60.

[50] Ibid., 43.

6

The Unknown Letters of Marco da Gagliano

EDMOND STRAINCHAMPS

In 1889 Emil Vogel's monograph on Marco da Gagliano appeared in *Vierteljahrsschrift für Musikwissenschaft*, which published it in two lengthy installments.¹ It was the first scholarly study of Gagliano, who "stood for more than thirty years at the very peak of musical life in Florence and surpassed all [his contemporaries] in artistic greatness," as Vogel characterized him,² and its value was much enhanced by an appendix of thirty-three pertinent documents. These formed for Vogel, and have for later scholars also, the bedrock for understanding Gagliano's life, his relationships with his contemporaries, and his personality. They have added valuably, as well, to our knowledge of the context for music in Florence in the last decades of the sixteenth century and the first half of the seventeenth.

Twenty-nine of the items in Vogel's appendix are letters that Gagliano sent to the court in Mantua, and they are extant now in the Archivio Gonzaga of the State Archive. Nearly all of them are addressed to Ferdinando Gonzaga,³ the second son of Duke Vincenzo and Eleanora de' Medici. They span the years from 1607 to 1623, a period during which Prince Ferdinando ended his student days to assume a cardinalate and, renouncing that, became the duke of Mantua in 1612 upon the death of his older brother.

It has been widely assumed since Vogel's day that his publication contained all of Gagliano's correspondence that has survived, but this is not the case. In fact, twenty-seven additional letters—nearly equaling the number in Vogel's appendix—can now be reported as having come down to us. Two of these are in Florence, written to a Florentine, and twenty-five are in the Archivio Gonzaga, addressed to Prince/Cardinal/Duke Ferdinando, either directly or by way of one of the court secretaries, or in the case of the last two, to his wife, Duchess Caterina de' Medici.

The twenty-nine letters that Vogel published are all contained in the *Autografi* of the Gonzaga archive, a rich subsection of files that was created by culling from the vast holdings those letters that were judged to be the most significant and organizing them by author. Within these Autograph files there are individual fascicles of letters (each chronologically ordered internally) from, for instance, Peter Paul Rubens, Ottavio Rinuccini, Claudio Monteverdi, Jacopo Peri, and Giulio Caccini, as well as from Marco da Gagliano (keeping to a single generation). The Autograph file with Gagliano's letters holds two more than Vogel published,⁴ so that, all told, there are thirty-one letters by

---

¹ Emil Vogel, "Marco da Gagliano: Zur Geschichte des Florentiner Musiklebens von 1570-1650," *Vierteljahrsschrift für Musikwissenschaft* 5 (1889): 396-442, 509-68.

² Ibid., 405.

³ Vogel, 550, asserted that the first five of the Gagliano letters he printed were intended for Prince Francesco and not for his younger brother, Prince Ferdinando. There is, however, no evidence of this; on the contrary, every indication is that all the letters were written to Ferdinando except for the last two, which were sent to Ferdinando's wife, Caterina de' Medici, duchess of Mantua. Nor did Vogel recognize the duchess as the addressee.

⁴ Vogel, 424, discloses the fact that the twenty-nine letters he published were sent to him by the Mantuan archivist, Stefano Davari. This may indicate that Vogel never searched the Archivio Gonzaga himself.

Gagliano in the *Autografi*. The twenty-three remaining letters in Mantua are spread through various files that make up the great bulk of the archive. These, arranged by provenance and date, contain letters of *diversi* (as opposed to the files with letters from princes, ambassadors, prelates, et al.).

The overall total of Gagliano's extant letters, then, is fifty-six,[5] which number breaks down as: twenty-nine published by Vogel (all from the Autograph series); twenty-five additional letters in the Archivio Gonzaga (two of these in the *Autografi*), and twenty-three spread through the rest of the archive; and two letters in Florence in the Biblioteca Medicea Laurenziana.

The Florentine letters are both from 1608, and both are addressed to the poet Michelangelo Buonarroti in Florence.[6] The more important of the two is dated March 8 and was sent from Mantua, where Gagliano spent the half year from late December 1607 to mid-June 1608. The letter makes known how some of Gagliano's musical responsibilities at home were taken care of during his prolonged absence. It reads in part:

> I did not wish to fail to give you an account of everything, and of how his most illustrious Signor Cardinal [Ferdinando Gonzaga] wrote to Signor Jacopo Peri, begging him to rehearse my music for one, two, and three voices for me. And I wrote to Signor Benci and likewise begged him to be so kind as to be present when the madrigals for eight voices are rehearsed, knowing that everything will go very well in this manner, as though I myself were present—and may your Lordship have no doubts about this. Meanwhile, I beg you to act so that they are rehearsed and to be present yourself, for I know how important your advice is.[7]

Michelangelo Buonarroti and Antonio Franceso Benci, of the three men Gagliano was depending upon (Jacopo Peri needs, of course, no identifying remark) were both noblemen and musical dilettantes active in Florentine cultural life. Benci was a colleague of Gagliano in the Accademia degli Elevati, for which he was *consolo* for a time; Buonarroti may also have been a member of the academy.[8] The music by Gagliano referred to in the letter is likely some of that used in the sumptuous wedding festivities for Crown Prince Cosimo de' Medici and Archduchess Maria Magdalena, which took place in October 1608. Gagliano's publications of 1615 and 1617 may contain the pieces he mentioned.

In turning to the large body of Gagliano letters that are in the Archivio di Stato in Mantua, it should first of all be observed that the most musically informative of them are those in the *Autografi* (a result of the selection of composers' letters that primarily deal with music). But the newly found letters—most of them not in the Autograph series—are also valuable. Not only do these provide new data of various sorts, adding to our understanding of musical life in Florence, Mantua, and Rome at that time, but they sharpen our reading of the letters already published by expanding upon information they contain, and they fill gaps in the continuity of the previously known letters so that the entire correspondence, old and new together, now seems a complete and unified whole.

The new letters also reveal in greater detail the complex and evolving relationship that existed between Gagliano and Ferdinando Gonzaga during more than fifteen years—that is, for most of the nobleman's adult life (he died in 1626 at the age of thirty-nine). Music was only one of Ferdinando's interests that Gagliano served. He also read and commented on Ferdinando's poetry—a passion that was equal to that Ferdinando had for music[9]—and aided him in his collecting of flowering plants and bulbs. In fact, it is from these letters of Gagliano that a fuller picture of Ferdinando's deep and abiding interest in gardening emerges.

---

[5] Appendix 1, below, lists all the known letters of Gagliano.

[6] The two letters are published in Maria Giovanna Masera, *Michelangelo Buonarroti il giovane* (Turin: Bona, 1941), 105f. They are also printed in appendix 2, below, along with all the other letters by Gagliano that Vogel did not publish.

[7] See appendix 2 in Letters from Florence at the date 8 March 1608 for the Italian text.

[8] Strainchamps, "New Light on the Accademia degli Elevati of Florence," *Musical Quarterly* 62 (1976): 510-12.

[9] An excellent and thorough analysis of Ferdinando Gonzaga's personality and activities is presented in Susan Parisi, "Ducal Patronage of Music in Mantua, 1587-1627: An Archival Study" (Ph.D. diss., University of Illinois, 1989), chapter 5, and her "*Licenze alla Mantovana*: Frescobaldi and the Recruitment of Musicians for Mantua, 1612-1615," in *Frescobaldi Studies*, ed. Alexander Silbiger (Durham: Duke University Press, 1987), 55-91.

The two probably first met in the Compagnia dell'Arcangelo Raffaello, the most important of the lay religious confraternities in Florence, which both were members of from early boyhood.[10] Gagliano, a rising star in the world of Florentine music, became Ferdinando's teacher in composition and was an important contact for him within the Florentine community of musicians—both professionals and dilettantes—and literati that Ferdinando enjoyed cultivating. And Ferdinando was often in the company of Florentines, both in Florence, where, as a prince and the grandnephew of the grand duke, he was welcome, and in Pisa, where he was a student at the university, and where the Medici court was accustomed to spend a part of each year.

Even when Prince Ferdinando was absent from Tuscany, his lessons with Gagliano continued. The letters, old and new alike, indicate that his compositional efforts in music, and also in poetry, were regularly sent to Florence to be corrected and improved by Gagliano.[11] Sometimes Gagliano would offer encouragement or support, as occurs in the new letter of 19 August 1608 (see fig. 6.1), in which he wrote, in part:

> I took great delight in hearing that your most illustrious Lordship is writing a *favola* adorned with many different affects, being assured that [these] will succeed excellently and will have a marvelous effect. I felt great distress at hearing that you have ripped up the *Adonis*, a work truly more worthy of living eternally than of being buried.
>
> I am awaiting the terzets, expecting to hear some fine invention, consistent with your usual [practice]. As to the sonnet that you sent me, it seems to me that I answered that it pleased me extremely.[12]

Gagliano often praised Ferdinando's work, both his poetry and his music, and in early 1608, when his *Dafne* was given its premiere in Mantua (very likely through the efforts of Ferdinando), Gagliano's approval of his pupil led him to include three arias by Ferdinando in the opera.[13] Gagliano also served Ferdinando by sending music of his own to him and by searching out music by other Florentines to be transmitted to Ferdinando. In June 1607, Gagliano was instrumental in founding the Accademia degli Elevati in Florence, for which Ferdinando was asked to serve as protector,[14] and, to judge from subsequent letters, Ferdinando's demands for music became even greater with his expectation that the academy's members, in addition to Gagliano, would now supply his seemingly insatiable desire for Florentine compositions. Gagliano's letter of 9 September 1608 gives an indication of how he was ever seeking new music for the cardinal—on this occasion, extra-Florentine music:

> I went to messer Paolo to have him give me the English book which was [however] taken away six months ago by the gentleman from England who was the owner of it. But I believe that some of it was copied by messer Vergilio, the companion of messer Paolo, who, being sick (and gravely so), it did not seem proper to me to ask for it. But I shall see that you are served as soon as possible.[15]

---

[10] Strainchamps, "Marco da Gagliano and the Compagnia dell' Arcangelo Raffaello in Florence: An Unknown Episode in the Composer's Life," in *Essays in Honor of Myron P. Gilmore* (Florence: La Nuova Italia, 1978), 473-87, explores the relationship of Gagliano and Prince Ferdinando in the sodality.

[11] Examples of this can be found in Vogel, ibid., in the letters of 15 and 29 July and 5 August 1608, to cite three instances.

[12] The full letter can be seen in transcription in appendix 2 at the date 19 August 1608. A photograph of the letter appears as fig. 6.1. I am grateful to the State Archive of Mantua, Archivio Gonzaga, and to Dottoressa Adele Bellù, the former director, for kind permission to publish the four plates included in this article.

[13] The arias, "Chi da' lacci d'Amor vive discolto," "Pur giacque estinto al fine," and "Un guardo, un guardo appena," which Gagliano stated in the *Dafne* preface had been composed by a principal accademician, were first ascribed to Cardinal Ferdinando Gonzaga by Vogel, 438. (Vogel, however, thought there were four arias rather than three, apparently from his misreading of Gagliano's remark about them.) Jacopo Peri, in a letter to Cardinal Ferdinando of 23 April 1608 (Mantua, Archivio di Stato, Archivio Gonzaga, *Autografi* 6), praised two of Ferdinando's *Dafne* arias himself and thanked the cardinal for having sent them to him. Peri's letter is printed in Angelo Solerti, *Gli albori del melodramma*, vol. 1 (Milan: Sandron, 1904), 88f.

[14] Ferdinando's role in the academy is detailed in Strainchamps, "Accademia degli Elevati," 507-35.

[15] The full Italian text for this letter is in appendix 2 at the date 9 September 1608.

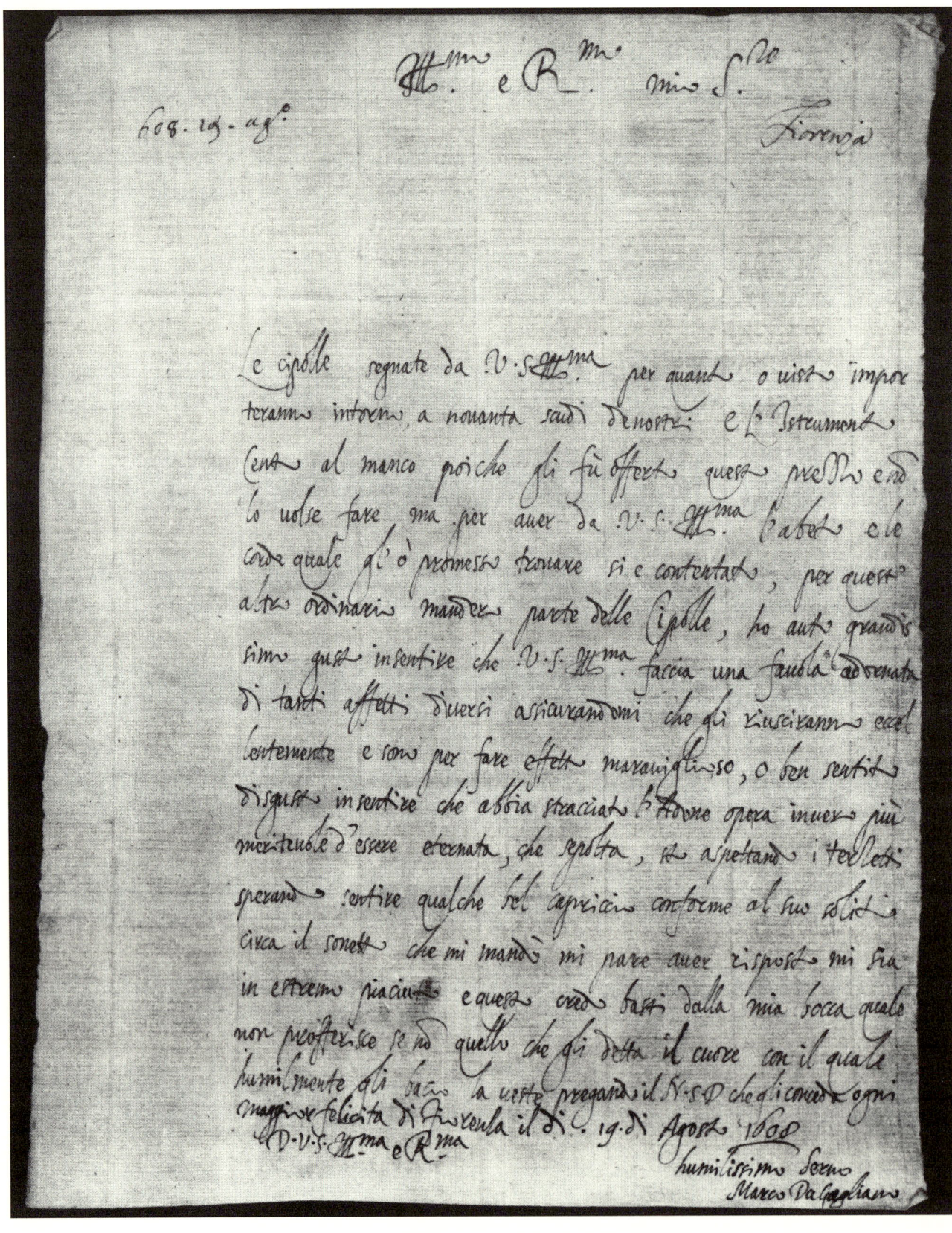

Fig. 6.1. Letter of Marco da Gagliano to Ferdinando Gonzaga, 19 August 1608
(Mantua, Archivio di Stato, Archivio Gonzaga, *busta* 1126)

The new letters also augment the evidence of Gagliano's frequent forwarding of his own music to Ferdinando. In letters of 16 September and 12 November 1608, it is clear that Gagliano was sending a selection of madrigals from his Fifth Book, along with portions of *La Dafne*. The latter, printed shortly after in Florence, but certainly underwritten by the Gonzagas, was undoubtedly especially valued by them, since it added in no small degree to Mantua's prestige as an important cultural and artistic center. They may have been particularly gratified that they, and not the Medici, had produced the first opera of the gifted young Florentine. And of course, the printed score, with its long preface written by Gagliano describing and praising *Dafne*'s performance there, would broadcast in Italy and beyond how liberal and progressive Mantua was in its patronage of music, even reaching, when necessary, beyond its own remarkable group of artists to import more from rival Florence.

On 9 November 1613 Gagliano wrote for the last time in the newly unearthed letters about sending music to Ferdinando (see fig. 6.2):

> I am sending to your most serene Highness a duo that I have composed in keeping with the memory that I retain of one that I heard sung by Signora Adriana [Basile] and her sister in the chamber of the most serene grand duke; [a duo] than which, truly, I have never heard anything more exquisite.[16]

Almost two years later, Gagliano published his *Musiche a una, dua e tre voci* (Venice, 1615; the dedication is dated October 15), which includes nine duets with continuo accompaniment. Perhaps the three-part setting of Pietro Bembo's sonnet "Cantai un tempo," with its combining of lyrical and coloratura vocal lines, is the very duet that Gagliano referred to in this letter.

Gagliano's helpfulness in satisfying Ferdinando's passion for music extended as well to his arranging for and overseeing the building of keyboard instruments for him in Florence. Gagliano's activity in this regard began soon after his return to Florence in June 1608 from his half-year sojourn in Mantua. In a number of letters that Vogel printed, this matter is taken up; in one of them, that of 17 June 1608, Gagliano described instruments proposed for the cardinal, instruments that Ferdinando did subsequently order built:[17]

> I went to see maestro Vincenzio, and I spoke to him about the upright instrument for your most illustrious Lordship ([he] will consider it a favor to serve you), and he said to me that a double instrument can be made that is strung [*accordato*] in front and in back, one [set of strings] separate from the other. And it seems to me that it would be well if one were to be tuned to the octave [of the other]. Upon it both can be played with only one keyboard, and if there should seem to be too much harmony, one of them at a time—whichever pleases most—could be played. And all can be done with the greatest ease, and if your Lordship is of my frame of mind, you will not deprive yourself of such a remarkable thing. Be advised that maestro Vincenzio is capable of making an instrument easily that can sound a concert of viols, imitated with naturalness, and one can play [on it] in all the ways that the viol itself does. But your most illustrious Lordship must send word to have the *fondi* made of pine, which I think will be [found] in Mantua, if not in Verona. The quality must be like the sample I am sending to you, and the length of the planks the same as [that of] the [enclosed] thread.[18]

Further communication on instrument building occurs in two of the new letters. Those of 19 August and 9 September 1608 make clear the effort Gagliano had had to make on Ferdinando's behalf to get Vincenzio to accept less money than he had believed he was due, and how Gagliano, who had been forced to importune the cardinal to have sent to the builder the pine planks and the strings needed, had finally had to take it upon himself to find these essentials so that the project might be completed. Some years later, Gagliano oversaw the building of additional

---

[16] The Italian text for the full letter is in appendix 2 at the date 9 November 1613. A photograph of the letter appears as fig. 6.2.

[17] This is known from Gagliano's letters of 1 and 8 July 1608. Transcriptions of them are published in Vogel, 552f.

[18] The Italian text for the portion of the letter quoted here is in Vogel, 552 (though Vogel mistakenly gave the date as two days earlier, 15 June 1608). Omissions of portions of the letters in Vogel's publication of them range from phrases to whole paragraphs; in the case of this letter, he left out the long opening paragraph.

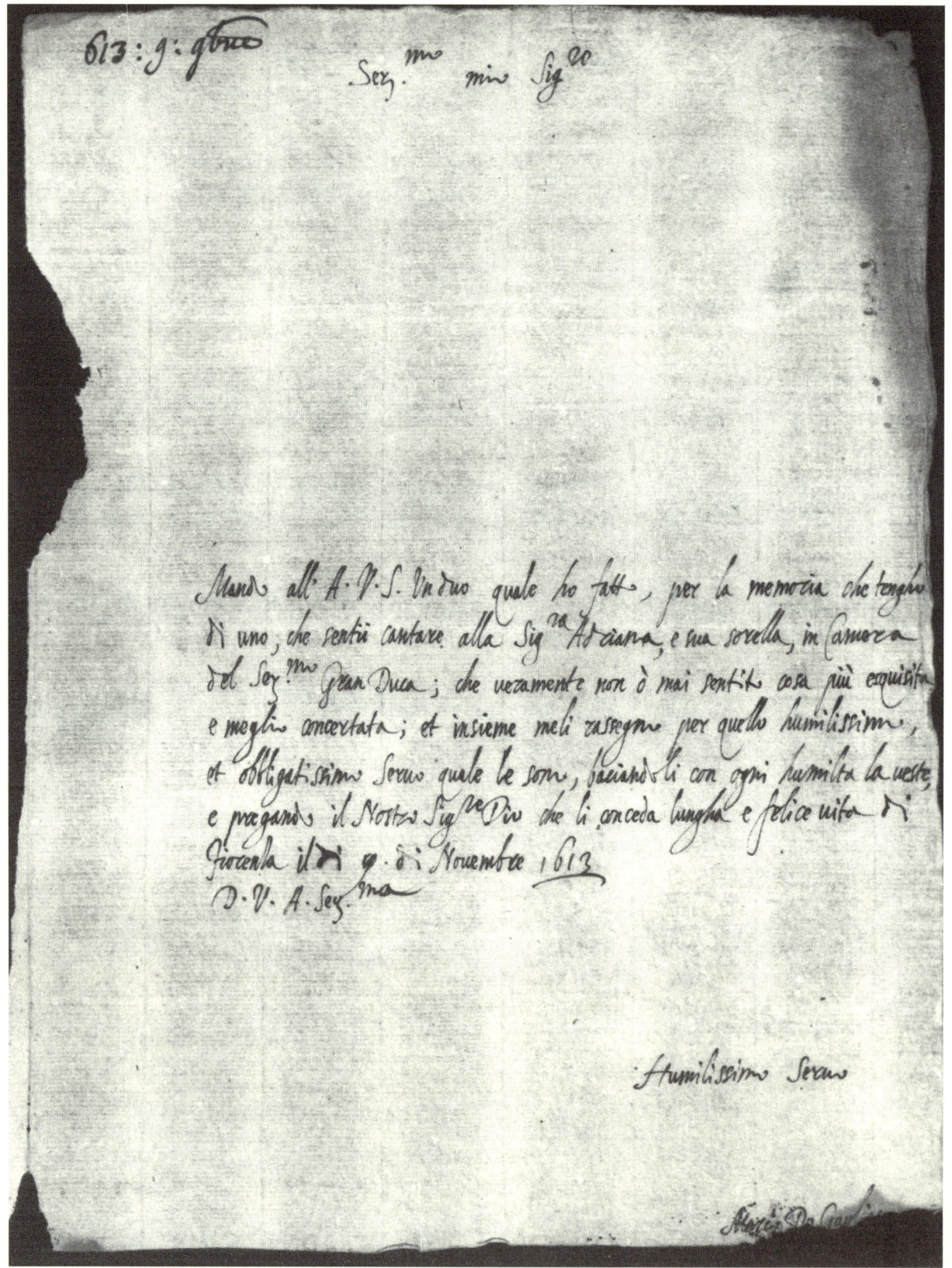

Fig. 6.2. Letter of Marco da Gagliano to Ferdinando Gonzaga, 9 November 1613 (Mantua, Archivio di Stato, Archivio Gonzaga, *busta* 1127)

instruments for the cardinal in Florence, though the letters in which this subject reappears are not among the new series, but are part of the Mantua *Autografi* file that Vogel investigated.

At the end of 1608 the series of letters—both old and new—is disrupted. After this year, during which for a time there was a letter every week, there was now none for nearly fifteen months. As letters in the old series indicate, the break was caused by the cardinal's fury over an advancement of Gagliano's career in Florence. In October of that year Luca Bati, *maestro di cappella* of both the Florentine cathedral, Santa Maria del Fiore, and the grand ducal court, died, and Gagliano, after hesitating for some weeks, asked for Bati's position. As he later said, he had been told that he was certainly favored over other candidates, but he wanted an indication from Ferdinando that he would approve and that he would recommend him for the post. What Gagliano was not told, but may have suspected, was that Ferdinando had intended Gagliano for his own service. The cardinal's plan, as later correspondence of Ottavio Rinuccini discloses, had been to appoint Gagliano as *maestro di cappella* for the chapel he would form at his new residence in Rome. Why he could not have done so in the fall of 1608, or did not tell Gagliano of his intention, is a mystery (though he probably awaited the endorsement and a stipend for this from his father, Duke Vincenzo).

Ferdinando's reaction to Gagliano's need for a decisive response was to make several ambiguous statements that Gagliano and others who saw them read as an encouragement for him to seek the Medici post. Ferdinando did finally address to the grand duke a recommendation along with a request that Gagliano be appointed. But when Gagliano was chosen, Ferdinando was enraged, believing that Gagliano was aware of his true desire, and that he had deliberately deceived and taken advantage of him. Gagliano, in fact, sounds honest and sincere when expressing his upset at having gone against Ferdinando's wishes, even though they had not been told to him. But the cardinal, unforgiving and probably unpersuaded, apparently broke all contact with Gagliano at that point[19]—at least for over a year.

Perhaps the relationship would have ended for good had Ferdinando not needed Gagliano's continued help in searching out and supervising the shipment to him of the flowering plants and bulbs that were best obtained in Florence and its environs. Overcoming his red-hot anger—or perhaps it had faded of its own accord[20]—at the *maestro di cappella* debacle, Ferdinando renewed contact with Gagliano. The first of Gagliano's letters to Ferdinando after the hiatus is dated 13 March 1609/10;[21] it is brief and refers to an order that Gagliano had received from Signor Don Rainero, acting for the cardinal. Soon, certainly at the prompting of Ferdinando, Gagliano once again corresponded with him not just about plants and bulbs, but about musical matters—singers, instruments, and new compositions in particular.

There is a tone of reserve in Gagliano's letters written after 1610, perhaps because he was wary of Ferdinando following the rupture that had occurred in 1608. From 1612 on, Gagliano increasingly wrote to court secretaries who conveyed Ferdinando's messages. This must have been primarily due, however, to the enormous changes that occurred in Ferdinando's life after his brother's sudden death, at age twenty-six, in December 1612. Soon Duke Ferdinando was faced with a war, with economic problems in the state, with a contesting of his succession to the dukedom, and with all sorts of other political complications. His distractions from all these troubles were still with music and poetry, but now, more than ever, with gardening. Botanical interests, especially the collecting of flowering bulbs and plants, became the new craze in Italy and elsewhere in the early seventeenth century. A number of aristocrats, as well as a few commoners, took up this new avocation—some, like Ferdinando, obsessively (though it was only in the Netherlands that an actual economic crash occurred, brought on by the overspeculation in bulbs).

The collecting of plants and bulbs had, indeed, always been apparently one of Ferdinando's pursuits, and Gagliano, who was apparently highly knowledgable in the matter, not only served Ferdinando as an agent, but advised and instructed him. From the first letters of 1607, gardening matters had been one of the chief subjects,

---

[19] My paper on this affair, "Marco da Gagliano in 1608: Choices, Decisions, and Consequences," delivered at the meeting of the American Musicological Society in Boston, 1998, and the Eighth Biennial Conference on Baroque Music at the University of Exeter, England, 1998, is forthcoming in the *Journal for Seventeenth-Century Music*.

[20] Perhaps the image should not be one of "fading," but of "reversing." Susan Parisi, "Music in Mantua," 282, with a careful reading of the extensive report of 1615 by the Venetian ambassador to Mantua, Giovanni da Mulla, suggests that Ferdinando was a manic-depressive.

[21] Until 1750, the new year began in Florence on March 25. Thus, the date of Gagliano's letter from Florence is 1609 in the Florentine style, but 1610 in modern style. Similar conversions of date are supplied throughout this article.

but at the beginning it was not so important as music. Later, as is evidenced by the new letters, plants and bulbs eclipsed music as the main topic of the correspondence. Of course, as duke, Ferdinando had at his disposal a large company of musicians in Mantua, a very different state of affairs from that of his days as a young cardinal with a small *cappella* and in need of help from Florence to realize his musical plans of creating the finest group of musicians ever known in Rome, as Aurelio Recordati, Mantuan ambassador in Rome, reported.[22]

Gagliano's letters on botanical matters from the new group range from the practical, in which he shows himself to be cautious and frugal in buying plants and bulbs for Ferdinando, to those that demonstrate his resourcefulness in looking out for special opportunities, to instructive, as is the case when he gives advice on planting and cultivation. His letter of 20 July 1618, addressed to Ferdinando's secretary, mixes some of these traits:

> I am sending through Francesco, doorkeeper of his most serene Highness, the bulbs and plants named on the enclosed list, in conformity with what was ordered of me in your last [letter]. And if it is not the number that his Highness wanted, it is because a part cannot be had, and as to another part, it is not time to send them, as it would be for rosebushes, fragrant asphodels and such. However, I shall not rest in seeking to complete said list. All were paid for in conformity with the prices that I sent, except for the rosy double anemones, which had been noted at 5 lire a plant and 6 lire were paid because most of them were rotted. And I think I did well [in the transaction]. The cost comes to 570 lire and 19 soldi. I have given Francesco 140 lire, for he told me he had an order for it from you, and 1 lira and 5 soldi for paper and string to pack them, so that everything comes to 712 lire and 4 soldi. I am left with 48 scudi and 1.16 lire on hand, which I shall keep to perform what shall be ordered of me and to pay the rest of what must be provided for. . . .[23]

Another letter, this one from about fourteen months later, dated 17 September 1619, demonstrates the kind of essential advice Gagliano gave to Ferdinando, while indicating his superior knowledge on gardening matters. Again written to a secretary, the letter reads in part:

> I arranged for the crocus bulbs, and they have already been sent in your direction. I was not able to fill the number of 100 bushels because in many places where they had been promised to me, they dig them up at the end of the month, so that, believing that it might be too late with respect to your country, I resolved not to wait any longer, and I have sent 80 bushels of them. If his Highness wants a greater number, they will be provided next year. Be advised that as soon as the rain has come, so that the earth is wet, have them planted. I am sending you instructions for how they are to be placed, cared for, and the fruit taken from them. . . .[24]

In an earlier letter, dated 16 April 1610, Gagliano, ever aware of values for Ferdinando, pointed out the better prices to be had in Florence and recommended a purchase. He continued by telling the cardinal of a rare opportunity, the chance to buy the noted collection of flowering plants belonging to Giulio Caccini. In Florence and abroad, Caccini had long been celebrated not only as a musician but as a gardener. (As early as 8 April 1589, the Ferrarese ambassador to Florence wrote to Duke Alfonso II, d'Este, exclaiming over Caccini's feat of making flowers bloom even out of season. He went on to suggest that Caccini should be hired as a musician and given responsibility for the ducal gardens as well.[25]) Gagliano's letter (see fig. 6.3) reads, in part:

> I am sending your most illustrious Lordship the enclosed notice of bulbs and plants with the prices, which seem to me very reasonable. And if you should decide that you want them, be assured that they will be in good condition. I have seen the list of prices that were set in Flanders last year, which are higher. Consequently, I believe it will be more advantageous to get them here, besides the certainty of their being authentic.

---

[22] Parisi, "Music in Mantua," 285.

[23] The Italian text for this letter is in appendix 2 at the date 20 July 1618.

[24] The Italian text for this letter is in appendix 2 at the date 17 September 1619.

[25] *New Grove*, s.v. "Caccini, Giulio," by H. Wiley Hitchcock.

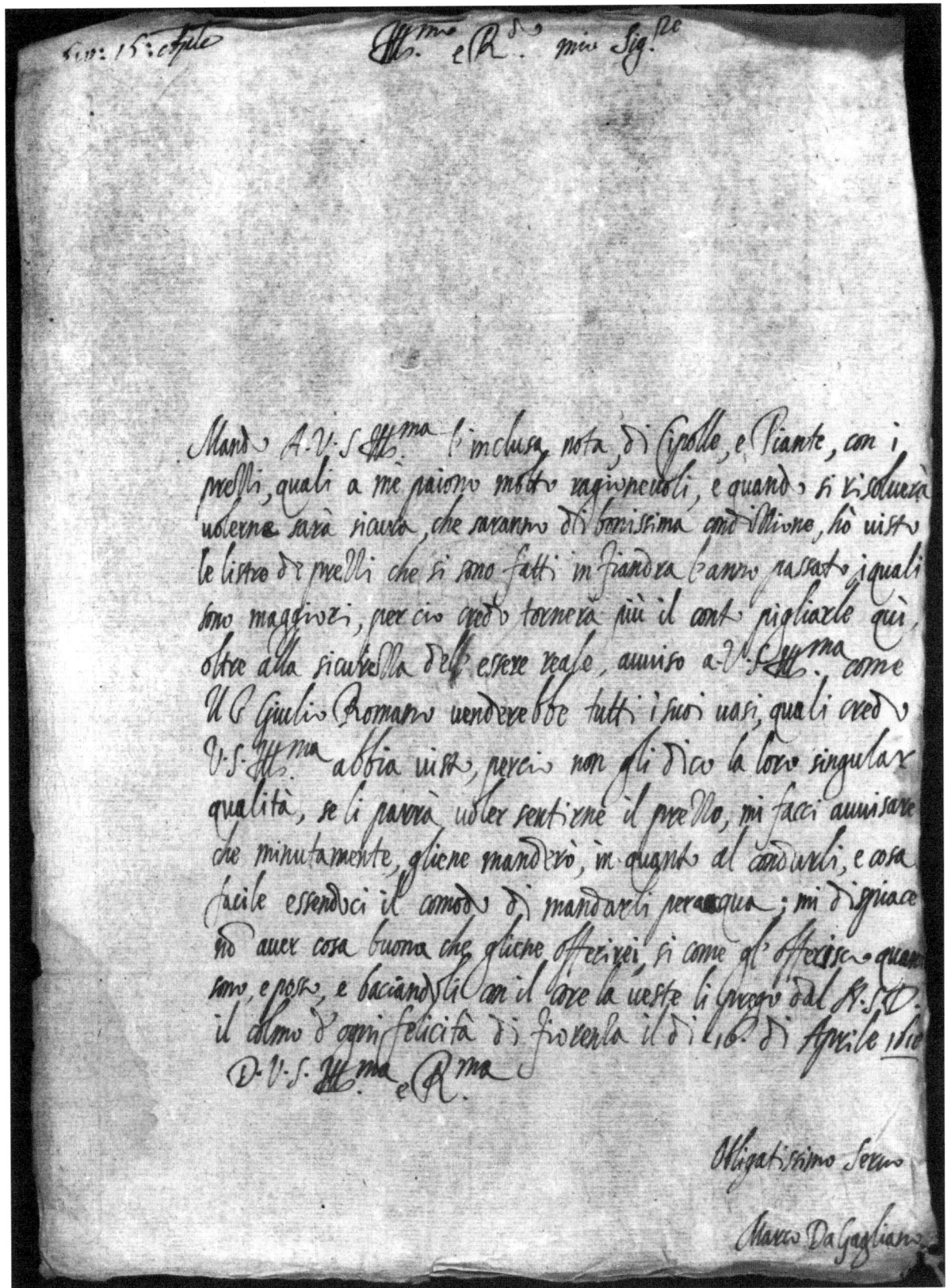

Fig. 6.3. Letter of Marco da Gagliano to Ferdinando Gonzaga, 16 April 1610
(Mantua, Archivio di Stato, Archivio Gonzaga, *busta* 1128)

> I advise your most illustrious Lordship that Signor Giulio Romano [Caccini] would sell all his vases, which I believe your most illustrious Lordship has seen; therefore, I will say nothing to you about their remarkable quality. If you think you want to hear about the price of them, let me know, and I will send them [*sic*] to you in detail. As to how to transport them, that is easy, since there is the convenience of sending them by water. . . .[26]

Gagliano, too, had a garden, and he sometimes sent small gifts of his own special bulbs to Mantua. There would have been little space for much gardening within the cloister of San Lorenzo, where Gagliano was a canon, and perhaps only slightly more, even if he restricted himself to jardinieres (as Caccini apparently had), at the house nearby on via dell'Amorino that he owned after 1610 with his brother, Giovanni Battista da Gagliano.[27] All the same, he seems to have cultivated rare specimens of which he was very proud.

In addition to the letters, there was probably a good deal of communication between Gagliano and Ferdinando Gonzaga that took place in person. As indicated above, Ferdinando in the early years was often in Florence and Pisa, and there was, in addition, the six-month period in 1608 when Gagliano was in Mantua, and probably much in contact with the cardinal. Even after 1608, though pre-occupied with increasing and varied responsibilities, Ferdinando visited Florence not infrequently, and he and Gagliano were likely to have been in touch with one another. Some of Ferdinando's stays in Florence would probably not have allowed informal talk, however, such as that on music and plants. Gagliano's letter of 15 January 1612/13 refers to one such visit; on this occasion, though, Gagliano could not even pay his respects to the duke:

> When your most serene Highness arrived in Florence, I came to [Palazzo] Pitti to kiss your gown and to dedicate myself to you as that most indebted and most humble servant, [for] I live as such for you. But since your Highness was very busy, and having seen the great number of gentlemen who were there to make reverence to you, I was not eager to do so, thinking I would have a good opportunity the following day, which did not come to pass, since your Highness was gone when I arrived at Pitti. . . .[28]

Several times during the fifteen years of the correspondence, Ferdinando invited Gagliano to visit Mantua and to take part in musical events there, but Gagliano never did go, except for his trip in the winter of 1608. On 19 June 1610, Gagliano declined an invitation because of the confinement of the grand duchess, which required him, as *maestro di cappella*, to be present to provide music in her private apartment in Pitti Palace or nearby.[29] And in the last of the new letters, Gagliano wrote about an aborted trip to Mantua, disappointing Ferdinando once more, though this time Gagliano had actually begun the voyage. The letter (see fig. 6.4), dated 4 January 1621/22, is here given in full:

> My Most Serene Lord:
>
> Sunday morning I set out from Florence in your direction with the two sopranos, as we had been ordered to do by your most serene Highness. And then Monday I had a letter through a man sent especially from their most serene Highnesses that told me that the nuptials for the empress were to be held so soon that there was no longer time to prepare the comedy. Therefore, their Highnesses ordered that I turn back, not wishing that I come in such awkward times and on such a dangerous trip in vain; upon which, I returned to Florence full of melancholy.

---

[26] The Italian text for this letter is in appendix 2 at the date 16 April 1610. A photograph of it appears as fig. 6.3.

[27] Mario Fabbri and Enzo Settesoldi, "Aggiunte e rettifiche alle biografie di Marco e Giovanni Battista da Gagliano: Il luogo e le date di nascita e di morte dei due fratelli musicisti," *Chigiana* 21 (1964): 141.

[28] The Italian text for this letter is in appendix 2 at the date 15 January 1612/13.

[29] See Angelo Solerti, *Musica, ballo e drammatica alla corte medicea dal 1600 al 1637* (Florence: Bemporad e Figlio, 1905), in which excerpts from Cesare Tinghi, the Medici court diarist, report such occasions for both the grand duke and duchess in Florence.

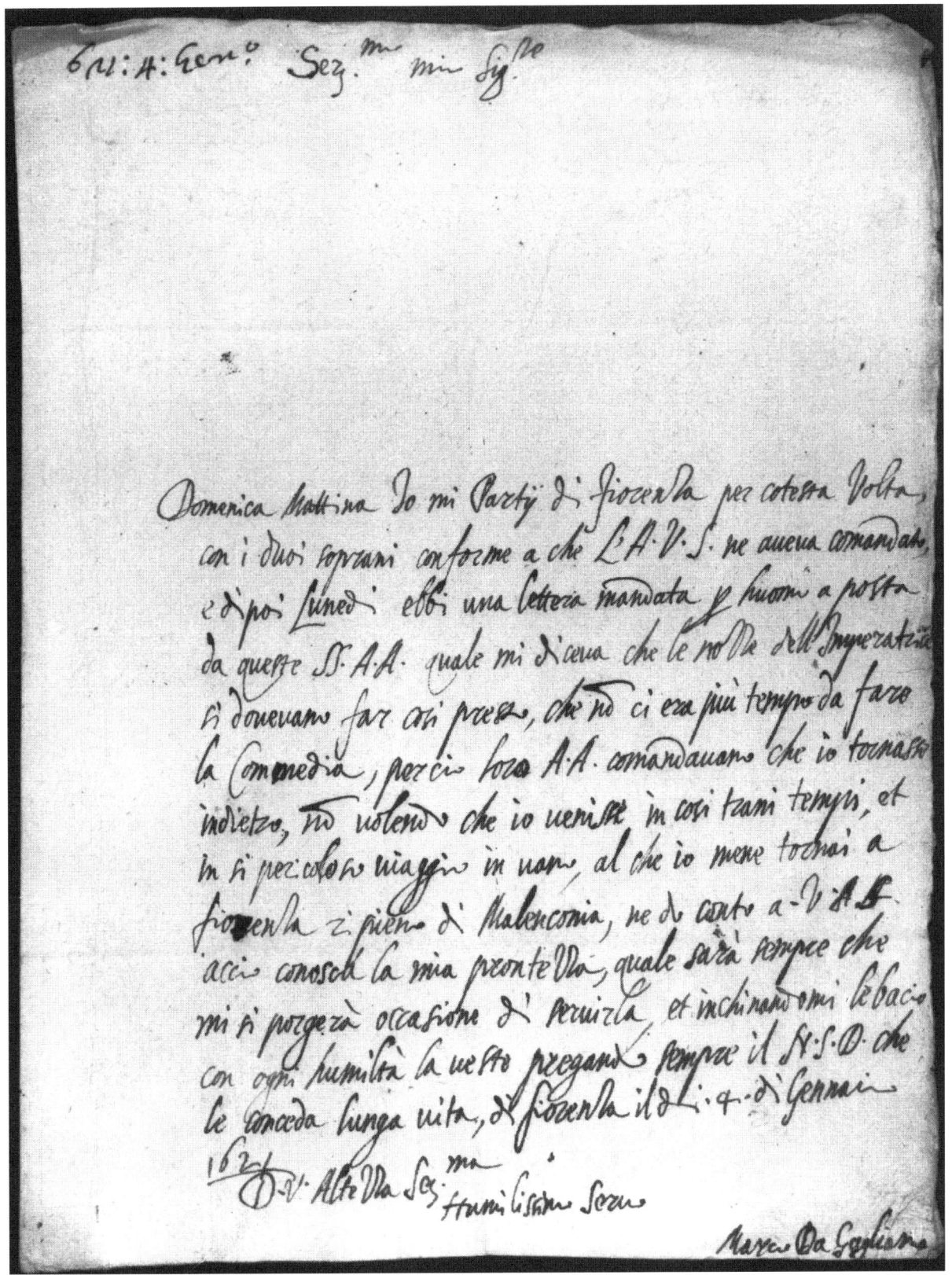

Fig. 6.4. Letter of Marco da Gagliano to Ferdinando Gonzaga, 4 January 1621/22
(Mantua, Archivio di Stato, Archivio Gonzaga, *busta* 1131)

> I give an account of this to your most serene Highness so that you may know of my readiness, which will always exist when the opportunity to serve you presents itself. And making a reverence to you, I kiss your gown with all humility, ever praying to our Lord God that He grant you long life.
> From Florence, the fourth day of January 1621 [1622]. From your most serene Highness's most humble servant,
>
> Marco da Gagliano[30]

The nuptials for the empress and the comedy Gagliano referred to in this letter were the marriage of Eleonora Gonzaga, Duke Ferdinando's sister, to Emperor Ferdinando II (which took place on January 6) and Gagliano's opera *Lo sposalizio di Medoro ed Angelica* (now lost), the performance of which was planned as one of two large theatrical entertainments to be presented during the wedding festival. The Medici called Gagliano back to Florence, as they explained to the Gonzaga, because they believed there would not be sufficient time to prepare the opera's performance before the newlyweds left Mantua, and they didn't want the composer's health put at risk in a pointless winter journey.[31] And with Gagliano not present in Mantua, the production of *Il Medoro* had to be cancelled,[32] no doubt causing embassassement to the Mantuans, and in particular to Duke Ferdinando.

The letter of 4 January 1622, the last of the new series, ends Gagliano's correspondence with Ferdinando, though not with the court. He wrote twice more to Mantua, to Ferdinando's wife, Caterina de' Medici, duchess of Mantua. These final letters, both from early 1623, were written to accompany the sending of the score of *Il Medoro*, whose libretto by Andrea Salvadori was printed with a dedication to Ferdinando Gonzaga early the next year.[33] That Gagliano now dealt with the duchess and that, to judge from the extant letters, there was no more communication with Ferdinando after 1622 (although the duke lived four more years) suggest that Ferdinando again broke off contact with Gagliano. When the lapse in their relations occurred in 1608, it was caused by Ferdinando's anger at Gagliano's advancement in Florence. It may be hypothesized that a rupture in 1622 was caused by another very angry response on the part of Ferdinando, this time to the cancelling of Gagliano's planned visit to Mantua by the Medici. In both cases, Ferdinando was thwarted by the Florentine nobility in realizing his plans, and in both Gagliano was blamed.

Finally, it may be observed that the newly found letters reported here, which amplify those long known through Vogel's publication and increase our knowledge of the context for music in several centers of the time, are perhaps most striking for what is learned in them about the relationship between Marco da Gagliano and Ferdinando Gonzaga. The peculiarities in the association of these two men produce questions for which no certain answers come easily to mind. And so it remains for another day to speculate on why Gagliano, though carrying such heavy responsibilities in Florence, would so readily accede to the excessive demands of Ferdinando Gonzaga, who had, after all, no authoritative role in his life. In the meantime, awaiting this investigation, it is gratifying to recognize how these new letters enhance our understanding of this endlessly fascinating period in the history of music in Florence.

---

[30] The Italian text for this letter is in appendix 2 at the date 4 January 1621/22. It also appears in Parisi, "Music in Mantua," 355. A photograph of it appears as fig. 6.4.

[31] See Parisi, "Music in Mantua," 316, 354f., for further on *Medoro* and the Gonzaga, and for the text of the Medici letter sent to the Gonzaga on recalling Gagliano.

[32] Vogel, "Marco da Gagliano," 520, states that the opera was performed in Mantua during Carnival 1622, but no evidence of this is known.

[33] Excerpts from the letters dated January 31 and February 7 are in Vogel, 564. Angelo Solerti, *Musica, ballo e drammatica*, 150, reviews the various ideas put forward in musicological literature on the possibility of *Il Medoro* having been published. See also *Il luogo teatrale a Firenze*, vol. 1 of *Spettacolo e musica nella Firenze Medicea: Documenti e restituzioni* (Milan: Electa, 1975), 148. In his thorough study of Florentine presses, Tim Carter, "Music-Printing in Late Sixteenth- and Early Seventeenth-Century Florence: Giorgio Marescotti, Cristofano Marescotti and Zanobi Pignoni," *Early Music History* 9 (1990), esp. 68-72, reports no evidence of a *Medoro* publication.

APPENDIX 1

This appendix contains a listing of all the letters of Marco da Gagliano now known, chronologically arranged within each of two groupings: Letters to Mantua, and Letters to Florence. The former, much the larger of the two, contains letters that are in the Archivio Gonzaga (A.G.) of the Mantua Archivio di Stato (ManAS). Archivio Gonzaga files that hold Gagliano letters are found in the section arranged by provenance and date or in the *Autografi*, a sub-section of files arranged by author. The two letters extant in Florence are in the Biblioteca Medicea Laurenziana (FlorBML), Buonarroti Collection. In the list, those letters published by Emil Vogel (ibid., 550-68) are so labeled, as are the two letters in Florence published by Maria Giovanna Masera (ibid.). Unpublished, previously unknown letters are labeled "new"; they are further distinguished by appearing in boldface type. "Vogel*" indicates the letter is incomplete in his publication of it.

Letters to Mantua

1.	23 July 1607	(ManAS, A.G. *Autografi* 6)	Vogel
2.	28 July 1607	(ManAS, A.G. *Autografi* 6)	Vogel
3.	20 August 1607	(ManAS, A.G. *Autografi* 6)	Vogel
4.	26 October 1607	(ManAS, A.G. *Autografi* 6)	Vogel
5.	3 December 1607	(ManAS, A.G. *Autografi* 6)	Vogel
6.	17 June 1608	(ManAS, A.G. *Autografi* 6)	Vogel*
7.	**24 June 1608**	**(ManAS, A.G. 1126)**	**new**
8.	1 July 1608	(ManAS, A.G. *Autografi* 6)	Vogel
9.	8 July 1608	(ManAS, A.G. *Autografi* 6)	Vogel*
10.	15 July 1608	(ManAS, A.G. *Autografi* 6)	Vogel*
11.	21 July 1608	(ManAS, A.G. *Autografi* 6)	Vogel
12.	29 July 1608	(ManAS, A.G. *Autografi* 6)	Vogel*
13.	5 August 1608	(ManAS, A.G. *Autofrafi* 6)	Vogel
14.	12 August 1608	(ManAS, A.G. *Autografi* 6)	Vogel*
15.	**19 August 1608**	**(ManAS, A.G. 1126)**	**new**
16.	**26 August 1608**	**(ManAS, A.G. 1126)**	**new**
17.	**2 September 1608**	**(ManAS, A.G. 1126)**	**new**
18.	**9 September 1608**	**(ManAS, A.G. 1126)**	**new**
19.	**16 September 1608**	**(ManAS, A.G. 1126)**	**new**
20.	30 September 1608	(ManAS, A.G. *Autografi* 6)	Vogel*
21.	21 October 1608	(ManAS, A.G. *Autografi* 6)	Vogel
22.	**4 November 1608**	**(ManAS, A.G. *Autografi* 6)**	**new**
23.	**12 November 1608**	**(ManAS, A.G. 1126)**	**new**
24.	**13 November 1608**	**(ManAS, A.G. 1126)**	**new**
25.	25 November 1608	(ManAS, A.G. *Autografi* 6)	Vogel
26.	16 December 1608	(ManAS, A.G. *Autografi* 6)	Vogel
27.	30 December 1608	(ManAS, A.G. *Autografi* 6)	Vogel
28.	30 December 1608	(ManAS, A.G. *Autografi* 6)	Vogel
29.	**13 March 1609/10**	**(ManAS, A.G. *Autografi* 6)**	**new**
30.	**16 April 1610**	**(ManAS, A.G. 1127)**	**new**
31.	19 June 1610	(ManAS, A.G. *Autografi* 6)	Vogel
32.	**23 October 1610**	**(ManAS, A.G. 1127)**	**new**
33.	18 August 1612	(ManAS, A.G. *Autografi* 6)	Vogel*
34.	1 September 1612	(ManAS, A.G. *Autografi* 6)	Vogel
35.	22 September 1612	(ManAS, A.G. *Autografi* 6)	Vogel
36.	6 October 1612	(ManAS, A.G. *Autografi* 6)	Vogel
37.	1 December 1612	(ManAS, A.G. *Autografi* 6)	Vogel
38.	**15 January 1612/13**	**(ManAS, A.G. 1128)**	**new**

39.	9 November 1613	(ManAS, A.G. 1128)	new
40.	23 June 1618	(ManAS, A.G. 1130)	new
41.	3 July 1618	(ManAS, A.G. 1130)	new
42.	20 July 1618	(ManAS, A.G. 1130)	new
43.	21 October 1618	(ManAS, A.G. *Autografi* 6)	Vogel
44.	29 October 1618	(ManAS, A.G. 1130)	new
45.	6 May 1619	(ManAS, A.G. 1130)	new
46.	27 May 1619	(ManAS, A.G. 1130)	new
47.	17 September 1619	(ManAS, A.G. 1130)	new
48.	8 October 1619	(ManAS, A.G. 1130)	new
49.	12 November 1619	(ManAS, A.G. *Autografi* 6)	Vogel
50.	21 May 1621	(ManAS, A.G. 1131)	new
51.	14 August 1621	(ManAS, A.G. 1131)	new
52.	4 January 1621/22	(ManAS, A.G. 1131)	new
53.	31 January 1622/23	(ManAS, A.G. *Autografi* 6)	Vogel*
54.	7 February 1622/23	(ManAS, A.G. *Autografi* 6)	Vogel*

Letters to Florence

1.	8 March 1608	(FlorBML Buonarroti 46)	Masera
2.	9 July 1608	(FlorBML Buonarroti 46)	Masera

APPENDIX 2

In this appendix appear the complete, original texts of the unknown letters of Marco da Gagliano. They are presented here in chronological order within each of the two categories of letters to Mantua and letters to Florence. The original spelling has been preserved, along with punctuation and, for the most part, capitalization. Abbreviations are often expanded, however, along with alterations in the formatting of the original letters for the sake of consistency. The locations of all the letters are indicated with designations explained in appendix 1, above. Most of the letters are from archival files that lack numbering for individual folios; but where folio numbers are available, they are given. A few of the letters are contained on more than a single sheet, though no indication of this has seemed necessary here.

Letters to Mantua

24 June 1608. (ManAS, A.G. 1126)

Illustrissimo e Reverendissimo mio Signore:

    Gli mando una listra di tutte le cipolle e piante che per ora si può avere, con i lor prezzi i quali a me sono ragionevoli. Starò aspettando che da Vostra Signoria Illma mi sia accennato quello deva fare et eseguirlo come conviene a servitore devotissimo et obligatissimo qual le son io. E facendoli humilmente con il core riverenza, gli prego dal nostro Signore Dio il colmo d'ogni felicità.

Di Fiorenza, il dì 24 di Giugno 1608
Di Vostra Signoria Illma e Rev.^{ma}

                                                          Humilissimo Servo
                                                          Marco da Gagliano

19 August 1608. (ManAS, A.G. 1126)

Ill.mo e Rev.mo mio Signore:

Le cipolle segnate da Vostra Signoria Ill.ma per quanto ò visto importeranno intorno a novanta scudi de' nostri, e l'istrumento cento al manco poiché gli fu offerto questo prezzo e non lo volse fare, ma per aver da Vostra Signoria Ill.ma l'abeto e le corde quale gl'ò promesso trovare, si è contentato. Per quest'altro ordinario manderò parte delle cipolle.

Ho auto grandissimo gusto in sentire che Vostra Signoria Ill.ma faccia una favola adornata di tanti affetti diversi, assicurandomi che gli riusciranno eccellentemente e sono per fare effetto maraviglioso. Ò ben sentito disgusto in sentire che abbia stracciato l'Adone, opera invero più meritevole d'essere eternata che sepolta.

Sto aspettando i terzetti, sperando sentire qualche bel capriccio conforme al suo solito. Circa il sonetto che mi mandò, mi pare aver risposto mi sia in estremo piaciuto, e questo credo basti dalla mia bocca, quale non profferisce se non quello che gli detta il cuore. Con il quale humilmente gli bacio la veste, pregando il nostro Signore Dio che gli conceda ogni maggior felicità.

Di Fiorenza, il dì 19 di Agosto 1608
Di Vostra Signoria Ill.ma e Rev.ma

                                                          Humilissimo Servo
                                                          Marco da Gagliano

26 August 1608. (ManAS, A.6. 1126)

Ill.mo e Rev.mo mio Signore:

La pollizza di cambio si avrà per quest'altro procaccio, conforme mi scrive il Signor Vergilio.

Mando a Vostra Signoria Ill.ma alcune cipolle, quale mi trovavo apresso. Se non sono conforme al suo desiderio, scusi la mia povertà. Ne ò fatto listra, acciò non fussino cavate. Troverrà quattro cipolle di diacinti tardivi odorati: so certo sono cosa rare, sì di colore come d'odore. Quest'altra settimana s'invierà la cassetta grande, dove saranno gran parte di quelle che Vostra Signoria Ill.ma compera, e già sono all'ordine, ma l'occasione del mandarla ben condizionata non ci è. Fra tanto me li ricordo humilissimo servitore e gli bacio con il core la veste. Dio gli conceda il colmo d'ogni felicità.

Di Fiorenza, il dì 26 di Agosto 1608
Di Vostra Signoria Ill.ma e Rev.ma

                                                          Humilissimo Servo
                                                        Marco da Gagliano

2 September 1608. (ManAS, A.G. 1126)

Ill.mo e Rev.mo Signor mio:

Domani consegnerò al condottiere la cassa delle cipolle, entrovi la listra di esse. Vostra Signoria Ill.ma le faccia riscontrare, ché per esser cosa singulare portono qualche risico, e avvertisca sieno quanto prima messe in terra giaché è il tempo. L'altre che mancano non si sono mandate per non essere ancora il tempo di cavarle se non con progiudicarli, ma quanto prima sarà possibile le manderò. Credo sarà servita bene, giaché sono tutte da fiore e bellissime.

Circa il servitore da me pro[po]stoli dal Rev.do Padre Civitella, avrà informazione de' suoi costumi, del tempo e della nascita. Lui si rimente [sic] nella voluntà di Vostra Signoria Ill.ma e la servirà in tutto quello che gli sarà comandato, se bene a me pare fussi buono per aiutante in camera, e credo ne avrebbe particular gusto. Pur tuttavia quando Vostra Signoria Ill.ma si risolva di servirsi della sua persona, lo potrà esp[e]rimentare. E per fine humilmente gli bacio la veste. Dio gli conceda ogni maggior felicità.

Di Fiorenza, il dì 2 di Settembre 1608
Di Vostra Signoria Ill.ma e Rev.ma

                                                          Humilissmo Servo
                                                        Marco da Gagliano

Giunchigli, cipolle	30
Pennachi persiani, cipolle	4
Iacinti orientali tardìi, cipolle	2

Gradiolo di Costantinopoli, cipolle	10
Iacinti orientali, cipolle	12
Bellundi, cipolle	2
Iride bulbosa di più colori, cipolle	12
Anemone rosso doppio, più piante	
Tazzette del fior piccolo, cipolle	4
Argemone del fior doppio, più piante	
Muschi greci, cipolle	2
Iacinti tardì odorati, cipolle	2
Tulipani di Costantinopoli, cipolle	6
Bottoni alessandrini, cipolle	3
Narcisi doppi, cipolle	12
Narcisi coronati, cipolle	12

9 September 1608. (ManAS, A.G. 1126)

Ill.mo e Rev.mo mio Signore:

Ho riceuto stamattina due lettere di Vostra Signoria Ill.ma, una con la polizza di cambio quale è stata accettata, e ò pensato dare ottanta scudi a conto di cipolle e piante, e gl'altri venti a maestro Vincenzio per l'istrumento.

Sono stato da messer Paolo per farmi dare il libro inghilese il quale fu portato via sono sei mesi da un gentiluomo d'Inghilterra, che ne era padrone, se bene credo ne fussi copiate alcune da messer Vergilio compagno di messer Paolo. Il quale essendo malato e grave, non mi è parso a proposito il domandargliene, ma vedrò quanto prima resti servita.

Sto aspettando le parole che mi dice voler mandare, non avendo altro desiderio che servirla. Con che humilmente li bacio la veste. Dio gli conceda ogni maggior felicità.

Di Fiorenza, il dì 9 di Settembre 1608
Di Vostra Signoria Ill.ma e Rev.ma

Humilissimo Servo
Marco da Gagliano

16 September 1608. (ManAS, A.G. 1126)

Ill.mo e Rev.mo mio Signore:

Credo che Vostra Signoria Ill.ma abbia riceuto la cassetta delle cipolle, giaché son passati dieci giorni che la consegnai al condottiere, quale è Antonio del Rosso. L'altre piante a lor tempo le manderò.

La Dafne è in sul finirsi, e per quest'altro ordinario gliene manderò. E per fine humilmente gli bacio la veste. Dio gli conceda il colmo d'ogni felicità.

Di Fiorenza, il dì 16 di Settembre 1608
Di Vostra Signoria Ill.ma e Rev.ma

Humilissimo Servo
Marco da Gagliano

4 November 1608. (ManAS, A.G. *Autografi* 6, f. 26)

Ill.mo e R.mo mio Sig.re:

Sono stato sempre talmente benificato e favorito da V. S. Ill.ma che con parole non posso esprimerli l'obbligho qual le devo, e ora maggiormente mi vien da lei porto favori, e tali, che sopravanzano di gran lunga il merito mio, e adempiano il mio desiderio, tal che sono restato confuso nel pigliar risoluzione di quello, che deva fare, e conosciendomi in atto a ciò mi son rimesso nel giudizio di alcuni gentiluomini da quali ne spero bonissimo consiglio. Assicuro V. S. Ill.ma che stimo tanto il servirla che se conosciessi nel appigliarmi qual mi fusse la servitù impedita non ci aurei auto pensamento alcuno quando fusse strata ancora migliore occasione, e con ogni umiltà rendendoli gratie infinite di tanti oblighi quali le devo gli bacio con il core la veste pregando il N. S. D. che gli conceda il colmo d'ogni felicità.

Di Fiorenza, il dì 4 di Novembre 1608
Di V. S. Ill.ma e R.ma

Humilissimo Servo
Marco da Gagliano

12 November 1608. (ManAS, A.G. 1126)

Ill.mo e Rev.mo mio Signore:

Ho consegnato alla condotta di Antonio del Rosso la cassetta entrovi le piante che erono rimaste, conforme alla listra, insieme con quattro elicrisi e uno euconio bianco doppio, aute dal Signor Cosimo Cini, quali manda a Vostra Signoria Ill.ma. Ò dato a Francesco una muta del mio quinto libro, conforme mi fu da lei comandato.

Circa il mio negozio, dal Signor Cosimo Gianfigliazzi li sarà detto tutto quello che è passato e che passa, potendo egli meglio a bocca raguagliare Vostra Signoria Ill.ma che io per lettera. Con ogni humiltà li bacio la veste, pregando il nostro Signore Dio che gli conceda il colmo d'ogni felicità.

Di Fiorenza, il dì 12 di Novembre 1608
Di Vostra Signoria Ill.ma e Rev.ma

Humilissimo Servo
Marco da Gagliano

13 November 1608. (ManAS, A.G. 1126)

Ill.mo e Rev.mo mio Signore:

Mando a Vostra Signoria Ill.ma la listra delle piante che sono nella cassetta inviatali; farà avvertire che la calta palustre sia coperta per cagione del freddo, quale è contrarissimo e non si conserverebbe. Con che humilmente li bacio la veste, pregando il nostro Signore Dio che gli conceda il colmo d'ogni felicità.

Di Fiorenza, il dì 13 di Novembre 1608
Di Vostra Signoria Ill.ma e Rev.ma

Humilissimo Servo
Marco da Gagliano

Listra delle piante che sono nella cassetta mandata sotto il dì 13 di Novembre 1608.

Piante 1 Calta palustre
      2 Leuconio giallo doppio
      2 Lecchinide silvestre doppie bianche
      6 Primavere doppie
      1 Primavera gialla accioche, doppia
      4 Asphedelo odorato giallo
      4 Primavere prolifere
      1 Peonia incarnata doppia

Dal Signor Cini
      4 Eliclisi
      1 Leuconio bianco doppio

13 March 1609/10. (ManAS, A.G. *Autografi* 6, f. 32)

Ill.mo e R.mo mio Signore:

Con l'occasione del mandare alcuni fogli a V. S. Ill.ma con ordine auto dal Signor Don Rainero, non ò volsuto tralasciare di ricordarmeli per quello obbligatissimo servo quale gli sono, e con humiltà farli reverenza, pregando il N. S. Dio che gli conceda il colmo d'ogni felicità.

Di Fiorenza, il dì 13 di Marzo 1609.
D. V. S. Ill.ma e R.ma

Humilissimo Servo
Marco da Gagliano

16 April 1610. (ManAS, A.G. 1127)

Ill.mo e Rev.mo Signore:

Mando a Vostra Signoria Ill.ma l'inclusa nota di cipolle e piante, con i prezzi, quali a me paiono molto ragionevoli, e quando si risolverà volerne sarà sicura che saranno di bonissima condizzione. Ho visto le listre de' prezzi che si sono fatti in Fiandra l'anno passato, i quali sono maggiori, perciò credo tornerà più il conto pigliarle qui, oltre alla sicurezza dell'essere reale.

Avviso a Vostra Signoria Ill.ma come il Signor Giulio Romano venderebbe tutti i suoi vasi, quali credo Vostra Signoria Ill.ma abbia visto, perciò non gli dico la loro singular qualità. Se li parrà voler sentirne il prezzo, mi facci avvisare, che minutamente gliene manderò. In quanto al condurli, è cosa facile essendoci il comodo di mandarli per acqua. Mi displace non aver cosa buona che gliene offerirei, sì come gli offerisco quanto sono e posso. E baciandoli con il core la veste, li prego dal nostro Signore Dio il colmo d'ogni felicità.

Di Fiorenza, il dì 16 di Aprile 1610
Di Vostra Signoria Ill.ma e Rev.ma

Obligatissimo Servo
Marco da Gagliano

23 October 1610. (ManAS, A.G. 1127)

Ill.mo e Rev.mo mio Signore:

Non mando a Vostra Signoria Ill.ma le cipolle che desiderava, perché la persona dalla quale dovevo averle mi à mostrato che tutte ànno messo, e che quando cavasse il numero notato da Vostra Signoria Ill.ma, guasterebbe il giardino, cosa che dice non poterlo fare per rispetto del suo padrone. Talché non ò possuto con maniera alcuna indurlo a farmi il piacere, se bene dice che quando abbino fatto il fiore potrà Vostra Signoria Ill.ma restar servita di quel numero che li piacerà. Et invero che quando le avessi date, sono sicuro che per quest'anno la maggior parte avrebbono disperso il fiore, per rispetto dell'essere tanto inanzi, talché Vostra Signoria Ill.ma non avrebbe cavato gusto alcuno. Non ò volsuto tentare altra strada per averle, perché non m'assicuro del non essere ingannato; oltre che tutte sono nel medesimo grado.

La polizza di cambio se da Vostra Signoria Ill.ma non mi sarà ordinato altro, la rimanderò indietro. E con ogni humiltà li fo riverenza, rassegnandomi per quello obbligatissimo e devotissimo servitore qual le sono, pregando il nostro Signore Dio che li conceda il colmo d'ogni bene.

Di Fiorenza, il dì 23 di Ottobre 1610
Di Vostra Signoria Ill.ma e Rev.ma

Humilissimo Servo
Marco da Gagliano

15 January 1612/13. (ManAS, A.G. 1128)

Serenissimo mio Signore:

Quando Vostra Altezza Ser.ma arrivò in Fiorenza, io venni a Pitti per baciarli la veste e rassegnarmele per quello oblighatissimo e humilissimo servo quale le vivo. Ma per essere l'Altezza Vostra molto occupata e per aver visto il gran numero di gentiluomini che erano quivi per farli reverenza, non ardii ciò fare, pensando di aver comodo il seg[u]ente giorno, il che non fu giaché Vostra Altezza era partita quando arrivai a Pitti. Hora avendo in me tanta allegrezza di ogni sua esaltazione, non mi sono potuto contenere di non manifestargliene con queste quattro righe e pigliare ardire di infastidirla, restando con pregare di contìnovo il nostro Signore Dio ne' miei sacrifizzi che lunghamente la conservi e li conceda quello che desidera. Con che gli bacio con il core la veste.

Di Fiorenza, il dì 15 di Gennaio 1612 [1613]
Di Vostra Altezza Ser.^{ma}

Obligatissimo Servo
Marco da Gagliano

9 November 1613. (ManAS, A.G. 1128)

Serenissimo mio Signore:

Mando all'Altezza Vostra Ser.^{ma} un duo quale ho fatto, per la memoria che tengo di uno che sentìi cantare alla Signora Adriana e sua sorella in camera del Ser.^{mo} Gran Duca, che veramente non ò mai sentito cosa più esquisita e meglio concertata. Et insieme me li rassegno per quello humilissimo et obbligatissimo servo quale le sono, baciandoli con ogni humiltà la veste e pregando il nostro Signore Dio che li conceda lunga e felice vita.

Di Fiorenza, il dì 9 di Novembre 1613
Di Vostra Altezza Ser.^{ma}

Humilissimo Servo
Marco da Gagliano

23 June 1618. (ManAS, A.G. 1130)

Molto Illustre Signor mio Osservandissimo:

Dalla sua intendo il desiderio di Sua Altezza circa le cipolle da fiori, e perché resti servita ho digià cominciato a farne listra. Ma perché non sono per ancora cavate tutte di sotto terra, perciò non ho possuto per questo ordinario inviarla, ma credo che non passerà quest'altro che la manderò. Fra tanto prego Vostra Signoria Molto Illustre a favorirmi di ricordarmi a cotesta Ser.^{ma} Altezza per quello humilissimo e obligatissimo servo qual le sono, e a lei bacio la mano offerendomi prontissimo a ogni suo comando, con pregare Dio per ogni sua felicità.

Di Fiorenza, il dì 23 di Giugno 1618
Di Vostra Signoria Molto Ill.^{re}

Affezionatissimo Servitore
Marco da Gagliano

3 July 1618. (ManAS, A.G.1130)

Molto Illustre Signor mio Osservandissimo:

Gli mando le tre incluse listre di fiori, quali si potranno avere, con i loro prezzi. Ho fatto mettere in dua la quantità che ne possono dare, nell'altra non si è notato perché non sono per ancora cavate tutte di sotto terra, e si trova che molte ne sono infradiciate. Vostra Signoria potrà presentarle a Sua Altezza, et io starò aspettando mi sia comandato quello che devo fare. La prego a proccurare la resoluzione quanto prima, perché così vengo pregato da' venditori, avendo altre occasioni di smaltirle, e mi favorisca di rappresentare a Sua Altezza Ser.^{ma} come le vivo humilissimo et obligatissimo servo. Et a lei bacio la mano, offerendomi sempre pronto per servirla, con che le prego da Dio ogni bene.

Di Fiorenza, il dì 3 di Luglio 1618
Di Vostra Signoria Molto Ill.^{re}

Obligatissimo Servo
Marco da Gagliano

20 July 1618. (ManAS, A.G. 1130)

Molto Illustre Signor mio Osservandissimo:

Mando per Francesco, portiere di cotesta Altezza Ser.^ma, le nominate cipolle e piante nella inclusa listra conforme a che mi fu ordinato per l'ultima sua. E se non sono il numero che desiderava Sua Altezza, procede che parte non si possono avere, e l'altre non è il tempo di mandarle, come sarebbe rosai, asfedele odorata e simile, se bene non resterò di cercare di complire detta listra. Si sono pagate tutte conforme a' prezzi che mandai, accettuato l'anemone incarnatino doppio, quale si era notato lire 5 la pianta e si è pagato lire 6 perché è la maggior parte infradiciato e mi pare averne auto piacere. Il costo importa lire cinquecento settanta soldi 19. Ho dato a Francesco lire centoquaranta ché mi à detto averne ordine da lei e lira una soldi 5 in carta e spago per rinvoltarle, talché tutto importa lire settecentododici soldi 4. Mi rimane in mano scudi quarantotto lire 1.16, quali terrò per eseguire quello mi sarà ordinato e per pagarne il restante che si deve provvedere. Mando a Vostra Signoria una scatoletta di cipolle del mio giardinetto: gli piacerà accettarle, et insieme favorirmi di qualche comandamento, offerendomi prontissimo sempre per servirla, pregandola a farmi grazia di ricordarmi a cotesta Ser.^ma Altezza per quello humilissimo et obligatissimo servo qual le vivo. E gli bacio la mano, pregando il nostro Signore Dio che li conceda il colmo d'ogni bene.

Di Firenze, il dì 20 di Luglio 1618
Di Vostra Signoria Molto Illustre

Obl.^mo Servo
Marco da Gagliano

29 October 1618. (ManAS, A.G. 1130)

Molto Illustre Signor mio:

Ho consegnato alla condotta per cotesta volta le cipolle e piante notate nell'inclusa listra, quali sono in dua cassette e saranno condotte in Mantova da' Giroldi di Bologna. Gli piacerà farsele consegnare e accusarle a Sua Altezza, dicendoli che non si è potuto adempire l'intero numero rispetto alla perdita grande che si fece ancora qua l'invernata passata. Nella cassetta dove sono le cipolle vi è un rinvolto per il Signor Conte Anibale Chieppio, sopra il quale vi è scritto il nome, ed è il maggiore di tutti. Mi farà grazia pigliarlo e fargliene consegnare. Et io ricordandomeli servitore, gli bacio la mano, pregando sempre il nostro Signore Dio che li conceda il colmo d'ogni bene.

Di Fiorenza, il dì 29 di Ottobre 1618
Di Vostra Signoria Molto Illustre

Obligatissimo Servo
Marco da Gagliano

Anemone ortensie, tenui folio, coccineo colore, intus capitulo nigro, circa quod aliquantum albicante folia simplex n.° 50
Asphodelus odore perfusus, flore luteo n.° 30
Rannunculus silvestris, pleno flore purpurescente n.° 30
Rosa belgica duplex pulcherrima n.° 2
Rosa semper florens, duplici flore carneo n.° 4
Rosa duplex carnea rubris, virgulis aspersa n.° 2
Rosa lutea duplex pulcherrima n.° 3

Hiacinti fogliati n.° 3
Hiacinti primaticci del Nerli n.° 50
Muschi greci n.° 18
Hemorocalli di più fiori overo ricci della Signora n.° 7

6 May 1619. (ManAS, A.G. 1130)

Molto Illustre Signor mio:

Sento dalla sua il desiderio di Sua Altezza circa le cipolle da zafferano, e perché sono informato che sia di meglio qualità quello che fa nello stato di Siena, perciò ho fatto diligenza in quella parte acciò possa Sua Altezza sapere la quantità che se ne potrà avere et il prezzo. E per andarne meglio giustificato, ò fatto ancora diligenze in altri luoghi dello stato dove se ne faccia quantità, talché quanto prima sarà avvisata di quello si potrà fare. Fra tanto non passa il tempo, perché non si mette sotto terra le cipolle prima che a Settembre; intenderò ancora come si custodischino e che sorte di terreno sia approposito, e di tutto ne sarà informata. Fra tanto mi favorisca di baciar la veste in mio nome a Sua Altezza e ricordarmele humilissimo servitore. Et io a lei offerendomi prontissimo in servirla, gli bacio la mano, con pregare il nostro Signore Dio per ogni sua maggior grandezza.

Di Fiorenza, il dì 6 di Maggio 1619
Di Vostra Signoria Molto Ill.re

Affezionatissimo Servitore
Marco da Gagliano

27 May 1619. (ManAS, A.G. 1130)

Molto Illustre Signor mio:

Per quanto ho potuto intendere fino a qui circa le cipolle da zafferano, se ne potrà avere quella quantità che vorrà Sua Altezza, et il prezzo sarà circa dua lire lo staio. È ben vero che intendo voglino il terreno magro, talché non so come possino far frutto in coteste parti. Il tutto dico per avviso, aspettando quanto prima ordine di quello deva fare, sendo adesso il tempo di tramutarle. Con che offerendomi prontissimo in servirla, gli bacio la mano pregando il nostro Signore Dio per ogni suo bene.

Di Fiorenza, il dì 27 di Maggio 1619
Di Vostra Signoria Molto Ill.re

Obligatissimo per Servirla
Marco da Gagliano

17 September 1619. (ManAS, A.G. 1130)

Molto Illustre Signor mio:

Feci la provvisione delle cipolle da zafferano e già sono inviate per cotesta volta. Non ò possuto adempire il numero di cento staia perché in molti luoghi dove mi erono state promesse le cavano alla fine del mese, talché credendo non fusse troppo tardi rispetto al paese, mi sono risoluto non aspettar più e ne ò mandate ottanta staia. Se Sua Altezza ne vorrà maggior numero si provederanno quest'altro anno. Avverta che subito che è venuto la pioggia in modo che sia spento il terreno, si faccino seminare. Gli mando l'istruzione come si accomodino, si custodicano e se ne cavi il frutto. Ancora gli mando nota della spesa, con il saldo di quello spesi l'anno passato e che mi era rimasto in mano. Mi farà grazia darne conto a Sua Altezza et insieme in mio nome baciarle la veste con ricordarmi humilissimo et obligatissimo servo. E a lei offerendomi prontissimo a' suoi comandi, gli bacio la mano pregando Dio che gli conceda il colmo d'ogni bene.

Di Fiorenza, il dì 17 di Settembre 1619
Di Vostra Signoria Molto Ill.re

Obligatissimo Servo
Marco da Gagliano

Scudi 150 furno quelli che io hebbi l'anno passato per polizza di cambio da' Signori Capponi	sc. 150
Per il presente anno lire ottantadua dal clarissimo Signor Vincenzio Giugno	sc. 11.5
In tutto	sc. 161.5

Le prime cipolle che si mandorno l'anno passato costorno lire cinquecentosettantotto e soldi nove	sc. 82.4.9
Scudi venti hebbe Francesco portiere detto lo Spagnuolo	sc. 20—
Le seconde cipolle e piante che si mandorno importorno lire centoventisei	sc. 18—
Per dua cassette e porto e gabella di una cassa venuta di Pisa lire dieci soldi undici denari otto	sc. 1.3.11.8
Il presente anno per n.° 80 staia di cipolle da zafferano lire centoottantadua	sc. 26
Per le casse e ammagliatura di dette cipolle lire novantacinque	sc. 13.4
In tutto	sc. 161.5.0.8

8 October 1619. (ManAS, A.G. 1130)

Molto Illustre Signor mio:

Ho inteso per due sue la ricevuta delle cipolle e la diligenza fatta con Sua Altezza della spesa sì delle presenti come delle mandate l'anno passato, del che gliene rendo grazie, offerendomi sempre pronto a' suoi comandi. Con che baciandoli la mano le prego da Dio il colmo d'ogni bene.

Di Fiorenza, il dì 8 d'Ottobre 1619
Di Vostra Signoria Molto Ill.re

Obligatissimo Servo
Marco da Gagliano

21 May 1621. (ManAS, A.G. 1131)

Serenissimo mio Signore:

Non mi si può rappresentare maggior favore e grazia che l'aver occasione di servire l'Altezza Vostra Ser.ma in essequizzione di quanto comanda. Vedrò quanto prima quello si potrà avere e ne manderò nota con i prezzi. Sento con molto gusto i fiori che di nuovo à l'Altezza Vostra Ser.ma e credo che qua non ci sieno, del che ne voglio far diligenza e restarne informato. Rendo infinite grazie a l'Altezza Vostra Ser.ma di tanto favore, me li ricordo humilissimo et obligatissimo servo, et inchinandomi con ogni humiltà le bacio con il core la veste, pregando Dio che li conceda lunga e felice vita.

Di Fiorenza, il dì 21 di Maggio 1621
Di Vostra Altezza Ser.ma

Humilissimo Servo
Marco da Gagliano

14 August 1621. (ManAS, A.G. 1131)

Serenissimo mio Signore:

Mando a Vostra Altezza Ser.ma una listra di quelle cippolle che qua si possono avere, con i prezzi conforme che in essa è notato. So che saranno sicure e buone, perciò starò aspettando mi sia comandato quello deva fare. E ricordandomeli per humilissimo et obligatissimo servo, con ogni maggior reverenza me li inchino e li bacio la veste, pregando sempre il nostro Signore Dio che li conceda lunga vita.

Di Fiorenza, il dì 14 di Agosto 1621
Di Vostra Altezza Ser.ma

Humilissimo et Oblig.mo Servo
Marco da Gagliano

4 January 1621/22. (ManAS, A.G. 1131)

Serenissimo mio Signore:

Domenica mattina io mi partii di Fiorenza per cotesta volta con i duoi soprani conforme a che l'Altezza Vostra Ser.ma ne aveva comandato, e dipoi lunedì ebbi una lettera mandata per huomo a posta da queste Ser.me Altezze quale mi diceva che le nozze dell'Imperatrice si dovevano far così presto che non ci era più tempo da fare la commedia, perciò loro Altezze comandavano che io tornasse indietro, non volendo che io venisse in così [s]trani tempi et in sì pericoloso viaggio invano. Al che io me ne tornai a Fiorenza ripieno di malenconìa. Ne do conto a Vostra Altezza Ser.ma acciò conosca la mia prontezza, quale sarà sempre che mi si porgerà occasione di servirla. Et inchinandomi le bacio con ogni humiltà la veste pregando sempre il nostro Signore Dio che le conceda lunga vita.

Di Fiorenza, il dì 4 di Gennaio 1621
Di Vostra Altezza Ser.ma

Humilissimo Servo
Marco da Gagliano

Letters to Florence

8 March 1608. (Florence, Medicea Laurenziana, Buonarroti 46, c.686)

Molto Illustre Signor mio:

    Già credevo essere in Fiorenza dove avrei potuto servire i miei patroni conforme all'obligho mio, ma poi che queste Altezze si sono compiaciute ch'io le serva in queste nozze e non è valsuto addurre scusa nessuna, non ò volsuto mancare di darli conto del tutto e come l'Ill.mo S.r Cardinale à scritto al S.r Iacopo Peri con pregarlo che voglia per me esercitare le mie musiche per una voce, per due e per tre. Et io ò scritto al S.r Benci e similmente pregato a favorirmi di trovarsi presente quando si prova i madrigali a otto, sapendo che il tutto in questa forma passerà benissimo come s'io fussi presente, e di ciò V. S. non dubiti. Fra tanto la prego a operare che sieno esercitate e trovarsi presente, che so quanto importi il suo consiglio. E per fine me li offero prontissimo in servirla e li bacio la mano. Dio nostro Signore gli conceda ogni bene.

Di Mantova, il dì 8 di Marzo 1608
D.V. S. Molto Ill.e

                                                Aff.mo per Servirla
                                                Marco da Gagliano

9 July 1608. (Florence, Medicea Laurenziana, Buonarroti 46, c.687)

Molto Ill.e S.r mio:

    Per non essere il S.r Bozzaghi in Firenze, bisogna indugiare a provare il coro a un altro giorno. Gliene avviso acciò non pigli disagio, e me li ricordo servitore.

Di Scuola, il dì 9 di luglio 1608
D.V. S. Molto Ill.e

                                                Aff.mo Servitore
                                              Marco da Gagliano

7

The "Staging" of Genres Other Than Opera in Baroque Italy

CAROLYN GIANTURCO

Previous research has indicated that in Baroque Italy there were not only sacred oratorios but also sacred and moral operas; and there were sacred and moral cantatas as well.[1] Although an opera, oratorio, and cantata might have been concerned with the same subject, what identifies the genre is not its subject matter but its treatment of the subject: oratorios and operas are dramas—the former in two parts and the latter in three acts—but cantatas are not; they are descriptive accounts, sometimes in dialogue form, in either one or two parts. It is here proposed to continue the investigation of genre but from yet another point of view, that of "staging." One often reads accounts of cantatas (also called serenatas)[2] which mention a theater, a stage, stage setting, and so forth; descriptions of oratorios presented on a stage are also to be found. We need to know exactly what "staging" meant in each case during the seventeenth century and the first half of the eighteenth in Italy, and we need to be aware of what this could indicate as to the genre of a work.

* * * * *

As a general introduction to the subject (but with no intention of becoming macabre), I want to begin with a description of the non-musical arrangements for the funeral of Eleonora Boncompagni Borghese held at the Church of Santa Lucia dei Ginnasi in Rome on 16 September 1695. There were candelabras holding 240 candles arranged quite splendidly about a catafalque. As her husband informs us:

> The church was sumptuously decorated in mourning with drapings in gold and silver and with the coat of arms of Her Excellency the Princess, and with paintings, well-done, depicting death in diverse attitudes. In the center of the church was the catafalque made of three levels: the first two were covered in black cloth with white silk veiling on each of its corners. On each of the four sides of the first level [of the catafalque] was the coat of arms of the defunct princess, held by two [allegorical] figures; on the sides of the second level, that is those facing the entrance to the church and main altar, there were two paintings with portraits of the Princess, and on the other sides were two other paintings with inscriptions. The third level [of the catafalque] was covered with gold brocade bordered with velvet embroidered with gold, and on it was a large cushion on which rested a golden crown.[3]

---

[1] See my essays "Opera sacra e opera morale: due *altri* tipi di dramma musicale," in *Il melodramma italiana in Italia e Germania nell'età barocca*, ed. Alberto Colzani, Norbert Dubowy, Andrea Luppi, and Maurizio Padoan (Como: A.M.I.S., 1995), 170-77, and "*Cantate spirituali e morali*, with a Description of the Papal Sacred Cantata Tradition for Christmas 1676-1740," *Music & Letters* 73 (1992): 1-31.

[2] For examples of works from the seventeenth century where there is interchangeable labeling of cantatas/serenatas, see the section devoted to "Secular Cantatas with Instrumental Accompaniment," in Gianturco and Eleanor McCrickard, *Alessandro Stradella (1639-1682): A Thematic Catalogue of His Compositions* (Stuyvesant, N.Y.: Pendragon Press, 1991), 67-105.

[3] "Essendo la chiesa suntuosamente apparata di litto con tocche di oro, et argento, armi di detta Ecc.ma S.ra Principessa, e figure di morte ben dipinte, che facevano attioni diverse. In mezzo poi detta chiesa vi era il catafalco composto di tre ordini, li due primi erano coperti

Figures 7.1 and 7.2 show two other catafalques, both from Naples: the structure in fig. 7.1 (with its many burning candles) was designed for Signor Don Antonio Miraballo in 1695, and that in fig. 7.2 (showing part of the Church of San Lorenzo) was made in 1746 for Philip V of Spain.

Sometimes an architect was called upon not just to "dress up" an occasion, but to improve the look of a place. In 1697, when Pope Innocent XII visited Prince Pamphilj in Nettuno in the countryside not far from Rome, it was decided that the simple buildings adjacent to the palace marred the grandeur of the Pamphilj country residence, and should be hidden. After the Pope passed through a triumphal arch, constructed temporarily for the occasion, and whose devices alluded to his good works, he proceeded to the Pamphilj palace. There, lighted by torches from behind, a huge painted screen covered the facades of the several buildings making them seem to be constructed of marble of various colors, with columns of lapislazuli, and statues towering above.[4] Naturally all of this decorative material would have been thrown away once it had served its purpose; but throwing away fruits of hard labor was never a problem in Italy in this period.

Perhaps the most evident proof of the ephemeral nature of such structures is to be gotten from those which were made to be burned. Figures 7.3 and 7.4 show two structures. The apparatus (as it was then called) in fig. 7.3 was designed to be placed in Piazza di Casandrino in Naples to celebrate the pregnancy of the Austrian Empress Elizabeth, wife of Phillip IV, in 1723;[5] and the one in fig. 7.4 was made for the coronation of Charles as King of Sicily in 1736 and erected in the square before the Royal Palace in Palermo.[6] In such cases, an elaborate structure such as these, made of wood, was illuminated by all sorts of fireworks (as is charmingly depicted in fig. 7.4), a spectacle which would culminate in the flaming consumption of the structure itself—to the delight of the viewers.[7]

As art historian Germain Bazin has written, "Theatre was one of the essential features of the life of the [Baroque] period; it was certainly the most characteristic art form of the time. . . . [Moreover], the theatre had a considerable influence on the formal language of the other arts." The function of Baroque art was "to astonish, excite, enchant, transport."[8] While there are hundreds of accounts of sacred and secular non-operatic music being presented simply, it is no surprise to find other accounts which reveal that some musical works were performed in settings created with the same desire "to astonish, excite, enchant, transport"—which is so apparent, for example, in funeral catafalques, in false building facades, and in structures built to be illuminated and then destroyed with fireworks—and we now look at some such musical works.

On the evenings of 23-24 August 1705 Alessandro Scarlatti's oratorio *Il regno di Maria Assunta in cielo* was given not indoors, but in the courtyard of the Ottoboni palace so that as many of the nobility as possible could attend. A contemporary account informs us that Cardinal Pietro Ottoboni had instructed his engineer to transform the courtyard

---

di panno nero scorniciati per tutte le cantonate di velo bianco di seta. A tutto le quattro facciate del primo ordine vi era una grand'arme della S.ra principessa defonta sostenuta da due figure che facevano diversi significati; nella facciata poi del secondo ordine, cioè nelle due che riguardavano una la porta della chiesa, l'altre l'altar maggiore vi erano due quadri simili con l'inscrittione. Il terzo ordine era coperto con una coltre grande di broccato d'oro con le fascie attorno di velluto con recamo d'oro, e sopra detta coltre vi era un gran cuscino sopra il quale vi era una corona dorata." In *Diario del Sig. Principe Don Giovanni Battista Borghese del Primo Novembre 1693 alli 4. dicembre 1701*, cited in Fabrizio Della Seta, "I Borghesi (1691-1731): La musica di una generazione," *Note d'Archivio* 1 (1983): 159.

[4] "La sera si vidde illuminato con torce un arco trionfale eretto da quel pubblico con molte imprese, e motti allusivi all'opere eroiche di S. Beatitudine. Nella piazza avanti il palazzo di detto S.r Principe era eretto in tela dipinta un teatro che fingeva più portici, i quali si univano col suddetto palazzo, e ciò per ricuoprire la deformità e rustichezza di molte casette, che sono intorno alla medesima piazza. Erano le tele trasparenti, a segno che la sera accesasi di dietro una quantità grandissima di lumi, compariva agl'occhi un teatro assai vago, parendo di un marmo di varii colori, e le colonne di lapis lazoli, con statue di sopra che davano finimento all'opera." In *Viaggio da Roma a Nettuno della S.ta di N.S. papa Innoc.o XII Dom.ca XXI aprile 1676 dedicato all'Ill.mo et Ecc.mo Sig.re il Sig.r Principe Borghese*, cited in ibid., 161.

[5] *Veduta della Machina di Foco artificiale fatta erigere nella Piazza di Casandrina per lo Giorno di S. Carlo Dal marchese Sig. D. Francesco Maria Salerni Degnissimo Commissario di Campagna per la Faustissima Nuova della Gravidanza dell'Augustissima Imperatrice D. G. nel 1723* (Biblioteca Nazionale, Rome).

[6] Pietro La Placa, *La Reggia in trionfo per l'acclamazione, e coronazione della Sacra Real Maestà di Carlo Infante di Spagna, Re di Sicilia, Napoli, e Gerusalemme* (Palermo, 1736), "Machina de fuochi artificiali" (between pp. 156 and 167). The structure, which represented the Temple of Ephesus, appeared to be made of various kinds of marble, decorated with precious stones (see the description on pp. 156-57).

[7] *Enciclopedia dello spettacolo* (Rome: Le Maschere, 1954-66), s.v. "Pirotecnica" by Elena Povoleda.

[8] Germain Bazin, *The Baroque Principles, Styles, Modes, Themes* (London: Thames and Hudson, 1968), 46 and 49 respectively.

into a "theater." (It is important to remember that in the Renaissance and Baroque "theater" was the term assigned to a place of celebration—a room, a salon, a hall, a courtyard, whatever.[9]) The engineer, therefore, had a temporary stage built on one side of the courtyard. It had balustrades, staircases, large twisted columns, and painted scenes representing the virtues; in the center, at an opening in the front balustrade, was a platform for the four singers. The one-hundred some instrumentalists were arranged on a staircase. The audience sat in open carriages that had been transported to the courtyard before the event and lined up one next to the other.[10]

For Handel's oratorio *La Resurrezione* presented at the Ruspoli palace in Rome on Easter Sunday, 8 April 1708, a proscenium-framed and curtained stage was constructed and elaborately ornamented in a large salon of the palace.[11] The stage had semicircular elevations for the orchestra with a special platform for the concertino. The backdrop of the stage was a large painting within which could be seen "the resurrection of our Lord with a 'glory' of babes and cherubim, and the angel sitting on the tomb announcing the aforementioned resurrection to Saint Mary Magdalene and Mary Cleopha, with Saint John the Evangelist beside a mountain, and the fall of the demons into the abyss."[12] Above the proscenium and extending across the full width of the hall was a large representation of an ornate frontispiece bearing the title of the oratorio. Elaborate and colorful drapery hung from the walls of the stage, and the entire hall was lavishly decorated and illuminated.

During Lent in 1646 the archconfraternity of Santa Maria dell'Orazione e Morte in Rome organized a series of didactic, but yet pleasurable, evenings.[13] The church was draped in black, and the tribune or raised dais of the high altar served as a stage. Here flats, extending from the tribune to the vault of the church, depicted clouds and angels. For every Monday of the month a different "mystery" was chosen, and this was explained in a sermon and rendered in a sacred cantata. Each "mystery" was illustrated in a two-dimensional scene arranged on the stage. These scenes, as well as the clouds and angels, were illuminated by torches placed behind them. According to a contemporary report, the settings for the sermons and sacred cantatas were the following: first Monday, March 5: "Jesus praying in the garden with the apostles"; second Monday, March 12: "Jesus at the column being whipped by two scoundrels who are in the act of beating him"; third Monday, March 19: "*Ecce homo*, when they show Him [Christ] to the people

---

[9] *Enciclopedia dello spettacolo*, s.v. "Teatro, II. Età moderno," by Elena Povoledo.

[10] The following are the relevant passages in the long account (Rome, Biblioteca Apostolica Vaticana [hereafter, Rvat], Urb. lat. 1406, ff. 1-4v): "Oratorio esposto al publico e fatto rappresentare nel cortile della Cancelleria con sontuoso apparato intitolato il Regno di Maria Assunto [*sic*] in Cielo dall'Em.mo Card. Pietro Ottobono dal medesimo dato in luce il quale fu cantato la sera delli 23 e 24 agosto 1705 . . . chiamato il S.r Cavaliere Giovan Francesco Pellegrini . . . ingegnere celebre, e rappresentatoli che voleva esponere questo oratorio al publico, volendo che nel giro di poche hore formasse il teatro per ivi rappresentarlo in forma che vi potessero stare molto ben commodi più di 100 professori de' più celebri di Roma, cioè d'arco come di trombe et altro e musici che doveano cantarlo . . . nella facciata del cortile fatt'erigere un gran palco la grandezza del quale prendeva da una parte e l'altra con un risalto in fuori per più commodo de' musici; serviva di base a detto palco un gran piedestallo dipinto di pietra . . . sopra del detto palco vi erano in forma triangolare rialzato sette commodi gradini, dove stavano a sonare i professori, ambe due de' quali havevano il lor leggio . . . le facciate di detti scalini erano tutti dipinti in fiori. . . . Sopra de' piedestalli, quattro figure . . . che andavano scherzando con alcuni leoni, e queste rappresentavano diverse virtù, nell'apertura delle dette balaustrate vi era situata una gran tavola sostenuta parimente da diverse figure, nella qual tavola cantavano li 4 musici. . . . Da i lati delle scale si fingeva per ogni parte un gran colonnato, a due per 2, le quali erano ritorte, adornate con quantità di vasi di fiori . . . in lontananza diversi arazzi finti . . . et infine di essi palazzi, e fontane era [*sic*] in bellissima positura eretti sopra del palco in quattro gran gradini, quattro gran vasi finti d'albastro . . . e torcie gramischiate per render luminoso detto palco. . . . Nel gran tela che posava la facciata dell'archi vi era dipinto in una cartella le seguenti lettere: Il Regno di Maria Assunta in Cielo. . . . Venivano apparati i ricchi tappeti sino quasi all'estremità del tetto ove poscia in mezzo fu posto in tela trasparente il ritratto della Beata Vergine Assunto in Cielo. . . . Furono presi i posti delle carrozze scoperte, dal giorno avanti lasciate nel cortile senza cavalli, e strette in forma che ciascheduna toccava l'altra . . . con infinità di popolo. . . ."

[11] Information on the oratorio is to be found in Ursula Kirkendale, "The Ruspoli Documents on Handel," *Journal of the American Musicological Society* 20 (1967): 222-73, in particular 231-39 and the related documents, especially nn. 11, 12, 16-19 on pp. 256-64.

[12] "la resuretione dell'Sig.re con gloria di putti, e cherubini, e l'angelo à sedere sul sepolcro, che anuncia la resuretione sud.ta alle S. Maria Madalena, e M: Cleofe, con S. giovanni Evangelista in Contorno dell' Monte, e la Caduta delli demonij nell'abbisso." Given in Kirdendale, 161, document 17, bills from the painter Michelangelo Cerruti.

[13] The following information is from the Archivio dell'Arciconfraternita, Libro della Banca dal 1627 al 1668, p. 129, as reported by Augusto Bevignani, *L'Arciconfraternita di S. Maria dell'Orazione e Morte in Roma e le sue rappresentazioni sacre* (Rome: R. Società Romana di Storia Patria, 1910), document 9, pp. 133-34. Howard E. Smither, *A History of the Oratorio*, 1: *The Oratorio in the Baroque Era* (Chapel Hill: University of North Carolina Press, 1977), 165, calls these works simply "dialogues."

crowned with thorns, [positioned] above behind a railing, and within was seen a room decorated with taffetta with many people . . . and in the middle of the scene there was a 'glory' of angels with the Sacred Host"; fourth Monday, March 26: "Jesus crucified between two thieves on Mount Calvary."[14]

Metastasio's sacred Christmas cantata, set to music by Giovanni Battista Costanzi in 1727 for the members of Rome's Arcadia, was another work commissioned by Cardinal Ottoboni. It was performed in the indoor theater of his palace which had been designed by Juvarra. As may be seen in fig. 7.5,[15] the stage set is mainly a series of twisted columns arranged to give the illusion of depth; three singers are seated in the center of the stage, flanked by about thirty-six instrumentalists; twenty more instrumentalists are in the orchestra pit.

* * * * *

Before turning to secular works, cantatas and serenatas, the "staging" of the oratorios and sacred cantatas mentioned thus far should be evaluated. First of all, a distinction must be made between works performed in what is essentially and solely an attractive setting—whether this was in a permanent or temporary theater or on a permanent or temporary stage—and works which relied for their execution and essence on visual simulation which the trappings of a proper theater provided. By "trappings" is intended scenery relevant to the environment of the particular work, therefore implying several scene sets which changed in order to suit the course of a plot, and costumes which clothed characters according to their respective roles in the drama. Moreover, one expects that such characters continually entered and exited from these stage sets, again in order to enact an ongoing and ever-changing story.

None of the examples offered here—and they are representative of Baroque oratorios and sacred cantatas in general—is a theatrical piece in the usual understanding of the term. It is true that they were performed on a stage, but in single-scene settings. The decorative settings did not attempt to recreate a particular story-connected environment; the performers were not in costume, as far as one can tell; they certainly did not frequently enter and exit the set. Each oratorio and sacred cantata could have been performed off-stage and in a completely undecorated setting and still have achieved the fullness of its literary-musical genre.

* * * * *

As far as secular cantatas and serenatas are concerned, their settings were equally varied. Of course, the importance of the occasion determined the splendor of the apparatus. Sometimes only the general setting was special, as when on 26 July 1681 the Spanish ambassador in Rome had the entire facade of his palace illuminated with burning torches to celebrate the birthday of the Queen Mother of Spain, but did not request the addition of other decorations to accommodate the performance of the celebratory serenata.[16]

A more particular setting is documented for the festivities offered by the Spanish ambassador to Rome beginning on 30 April 1701 to celebrate the name day and birthday of Philip V. Now, we are told, "a stage such as is in a theater" was erected in Piazza di Spagna to hold the singers and instrumentalists while they performed a cantata.[17] A Frenchman described the scene in the following manner:

---

[14] "Giesù orante nell'orto con gli Apostoli," "Giesù alla colonna fragellato da dui manigoldi che stavano in atto di dare," "*Ecce homo* quando lo mostrano al popolo coronato di spine sopra una ringhiera, che dentro appariva una stanza apparata di tafetani con molte fighure . . . et in mezzo alle tavole vi era una gloria d'angioli con il santissimo," "Giesù crucifisso in fra dui ladroni sul monte Calvario."

[15] The engraving is in the libretto *Componimento sacro per la festività del SS. Natale in occasione della solita annua adunanza de' signori Accademici Arcadi nel Palazzo della Cancelleria Apostolica* (Rome, 1727), between pp. 6 and 7 (Rvat Stamp. Barberini J.J.J.IX.30, int. 22). Smither, 269, considers the work an oratorio, even though confirmation is to be found in the libretto (p. 6) that the *componimento* is a "cantata."

[16] "Il S. Ambasc. Cattolico per il giorno natalizio della Reg. madre di Spagn.a sabato sera fece illuminare tutta la facciata del Palazzo del Re con torce accese a fare nella Piazza di essa una serenata in musica ed sinfonie." Munich, Bayerische Staatsbibliothek, Cod. ital. 193, Avvisi di Roma, f. 158r, dated 2 August 1681, given in Thomas Edward Griffin, "The Late Baroque Serenata in Rome and Naples: A Documentary Study with Emphasis on Alessandro Scarlatti" (Ph.D. diss., University of California, Los Angeles, 1983), 75.

[17] "Fu cominciata Sabbato sera l'allegrezza in Piazza di Spagna, con una cantata di numerosi Musici, e suoni de migliori della Città, per i quali era fatto un palco a modo di Teatro con vaghissime pitture, e notti, ornato di moltitudine di Doppieri, che con lumi accesi facevano una sontuosa comparsa." Macerta, Biblioteca Comunale Mozzi-Borghetti, Avvisi, III (1700-35), given in Griffin, 328.

The figure of the King on horseback, surrounded by trophies, was centered on a pedestal above the roof [of the stage]; several figures representing his virtues extended around the roof. Some chandeliers bearing three hundred torches which illuminated this spectacle were placed between two [of the Virtues] and in several other positions. The labors of Hercules were painted in gilt bas-relief on the facades of the two pedestals at the two sides of the amphitheater—upon which this monarch's arms were raised—and on the facade of the roof. Behind this structure there was the illusion of a forest, which produced a fine effect.[18]

Aquatic settings were also popular. For example, on 8 August 1695, a serenata was performed to honor the Viceroy Duke d'Osseda during his summer stay in Messina, Sicily. To hold the musicians, a platform—or stage—simulating a wooded hill was constructed on the edge of the sea coast. The character Venus, on a silvery seashell, began to sing as she was being transported to the platform by sea monsters. The viceroy and his wife listened to the music from a ship anchored nearby; other guests were also in boats.[19]

On Sunday, 1 September 1720, the Viceroy of Naples, Wolfgang-Annibale von Schrattenbach, arranged a party in the great hall of the royal palace. Figure 7.6 is a print of the occasion.[20] As a contemporary tells us, the evening included a "serenata in praise of the Most August Ruler [Empress Elisabetta] entitled *Scherno festivo tra le ninfe di Partenope*, performed in a beautiful theatre, which represented a lush wood with a view in the distance of the sea." The print confirms the wood and sea setting. The account continues that the serenata (which we know was composed by Domenico Sarro) "was sung by the best male and female virtuosos with 140 instruments."[21] One can see the five singers seated on stage, two on the left and three on the right, apparently waiting their turn to sing. But even counting the heads of instrumentalists placed in unlikely positions for accompanying the serenata—that is, not only at the base of the stage but arranged on both sides of the stage and on top of the central arch—the count comes nowhere near 140 instruments. Be that as it may, the rest of the print shows some guests sitting in front of the stage and others being served at table. (The account also notes the viceroy's generosity in the variety of the refreshment; see fig. 7.6.) The following Wednesday, September 4, Metastasio's first important work for music was heard. It had been set by Porpora, and one of his young students, the castrato Farinelli, made his debut in it. The entertainment was offered by Prince Caracciolo. A contemporary accounts informs us that "In his lodge he [Prince Caracciolo] had a luxuriant garden made, in the midst of which, in a beautiful theatre, he had performed by six voices a serenata entitled *Angelica e Medoro*...." The rest of the evening offered a ball, gambling, and "a noble supper," and ended at daybreak.[22]

---

[18] "Au milieu et dessus de l'attique, sur un grand pied d'estail, étoit la figure du Roy à cheval, environnée de trophées; plusieurs figures, représentantes ses virtues, régnoient sur le tour de l'attique. Des candélabres étoient posséz entre deux et en plusieurs autres endroitz, qui portoyent trois cens flambeaux qui éclairoient ce spectacle. Dans les faces des pieds d'estaux, qui étoyent aux deux extrémités de l'Amphitéâtre, sur lesquels étoyent élevées les armes de ce Monarque et, sur la face de l'attique, les Travaux d'Hercule y étoyent peints en bas-reliefs, rehaussez d'or. Derrière cet édifice, on avoit feint un bois, qui faisoit un fonds ltès avantageux pour l'effet." Given in Anatole de Montaiglon, *Correspondance des Directeurs de l'Académie de France à Rome*, vol. 3 (Paris: Charavay Frères, 1889), 76, no. 1089, letter of Houasse to Mansart dated Rome, 3 May 1701, given and translated in Griffin, 329-30.

[19] Enrico Mauceri, *Messina nel Settecento* (Napoli: Remo Sandron, 1924; reprint, Messina: Libreria Bonanzinga, 1918), 21-22, citing from a manuscript by Giuseppe Cumueo in the Museo Nazionale of Messina (no further source information given).

[20] *Adornamento della Sala, detta de' Vici Re e del Teatro in essa, fatto reparare per il giorno Natalizio di Sua M.^{ta} Ces. e Cat.ca d'Elisabetta Imperatrice Regnante dall'Em. sig. Cardinal di Schrattembach.*[sic] *Vice Re, Luogot. e Capitan Generale in questo Regno di Napoli, a 28 Agosto del 1720.*

[21] "... col medesimo Sig. Vice-Re goderono nella gran Sala di Palazzo la detta Serenata in lode dell'Augustissima Regnanta [*sic*] intitolata *Scherno festivo tra le Ninfe di Partenope*, rappresentata in un bel Teatro; che figurava un delizioso Bosco con veduta di lontananza di Mare, cantata dalli primi, e prime Virtuose con 140. istromenti, tutta quella gran Sala rappresentava un chiaro giorno per il riflesso de' gran lumi, che ripercuotevano in quella gran quantità di Specchi, e pendevano dalla diversità de' nobili lampadari di cristalli; La nobiltà tutta si trattenne per quella notte a godere quel nobil festino, & a spassarsi ne' giuocchi, essendo in detta Sala, e negl'altri appartamenti accomodati di diversità di Tavolini, e qui l'Eminenza Sua non tralasciando di praticare la sua solita grandezza interpellamente fece godere con diversità di rinfreschi, e dolci gl'atti della generosità." *Diario ordinario* (Rome: Chracas, 1720), n. 492, dated Naples, 3 September 1720.

[22] "... nella sua loggia [Principe Caracciolo] fece erigere un delizioso Giardino, in mezzo del quale in un bel Teatro fece recitare a 6. Voci una Serenata intitolata *Angelica, e Medoro* dedicata al Sig. Principe di Zinzendorff: cio terminata tutte le Dame, e Cavalieri entrarono nell'appartamento di detto Sig. Principe, che vedevasi tutto ben ornato di ricche suppellettili, e vaghezza di lumi, & ivi si trattennero ne' guoochi de' tavolini, &

An interesting example of distinctions between opera and serenata in this period is offered by the celebrations in honor of the birth of Prince Phillip, King Charles's first son and heir to the throne, clearly an important event. The celebrations began on 4 November 1748 and ended on November 19.[23] On the second evening Hasse's opera *Siroe*, to Metastasio's libretto, was presented at the Teatro San Carlo; it was not repeated. On the third evening, November 6, Giuseppe de Majo's serenata *Il sogno d'Olimpia*, to a text by Calzabigi, was performed in the palace theater (see fig. 7.7). It was repeated on the 9th, the 12th and the 15th of the month, however in the Teatro San Carlo (shown in fig. 7.8). The fifth and last performance was held on November 16, now back in the palace. Obviously two different stage sets had to be made for the serenata, as one can see. The engravings show, however, that both sets depicted a garden with trees, a fountain, and a temple, and the singers were richly dressed (as the printed account of the festivities noted) in high fashion. Certainly the serenata was the main event of the festivities, not the opera. In fact, while two engravings of the serenata were inserted in the printed description of the festivities (which included as many as six balls, as well as gambling, and fireworks), not a single print of the opera was included.

* * * * *

All of these examples show that cantatas/serenatas, like the so-called "staged" oratorios and sacred cantatas, were presented in single-scene settings. As was noted for the sacred works, the setting of a cantata or serenata may have been elaborate, but it did not attempt to recreate the environment of the text of the musical composition. Singers were beautifully garbed, but not in conformity with their roles.[24]

* * * * *

Theater treatises—from Angelo Ingegneri's of 1598 to Pier Jacopo Martello's of 1715, to Antonio Planelli's of 1772[25]—stress the necessity of "pretending" in order to simulate nature convincingly and thereby move the spectator. Scenery, costumes, gestures: all was to be in conformity with the work's environment and with its various roles. This was considered essential, however, only for works conceived as dramas, either with or without music, and only for works written expressly for presentation in the theater. No treatise on theater mentions either oratorios or cantatas, because these are not theatrical genres. In treatises on Italian literature—including those by Salvadori, Crescimbeni, Quadrio, and Muratori[26]—oratorios and cantatas are discussed separately from opera: oratorios are said to be dramas, and are said to be sung but not portrayed; cantatas are never called dramas and are said simply to have been "done" (*fatte*), some with great magnificence.

---

intanto a tutti si davano ogni sorte di rinfreschi, dolci e frutti aggiacciati, che in diverse foggie, anco al naturale si vedevano espresse. Di là poi si passa alla Sala del ballo, dal quale dopo le 9. ore italiane [ore 3-4] al num. di 40. tra Cavalieri, e Dame si presentarono ad un nobil Cena, che terminò nel far giorno." Ibid., n. 495, dated Naples, 10 September 1720.

[23] *Narrazione delle solenne reali Feste fatte celebrare in Napoli da Sua Maestà il Re delle Due Sicilie Carlo Infante di Spagna duca di Parma, Piacenze, &c. &c. per la nascita del suo primogenito Filippo Real Principe delle Due Sicilie* (Napoli: [Palazzo Reale], 1749) is the source of the following information as well as the illustrations. A list of events is presented on p. 4 of the *Narrazione*, and their description occupies the following pages.

[24] It is opportune here to repeat what Ursula Kirkendale, 235, n. 44, asserted in 1967: "We now know that not a single oratorio in Italy before 1750 was acted." To that statement one could substitute "staged" for the last word and retain the same meaning. The affirmation should also be applied to cantatas/serenatas, whether sacred or secular.

[25] Angelo Ingegneri, *Della poesia rappresentativa & del modo di rappresentare le favole sceniche* (Ferrara: Vittorio Baldini, 1598; facsimile, Bologna: A.M.I.S., 1971); Pier Jacopo Martello [Martelli], *Della tragedia antica e moderna* [1714/R1715], in *Saggi critici e satirici*, ed. A. S. Noce (Bari: Laterza, 1963), in *Scrittori d'Italia*, vol. 205, pp. 283-84; English translation by Piero Weiss, "Pier Jacopo Martello on Opera [1715]: An Annotated Translation," *Musical Quarterly* 66 (1980), 378-403. Antonio Planelli, *Dell'opera in musica* (Naples: Donato Campo, 1772), critical edition by Francesco Degrada (Fiesole, Florence: Discanto Edizioni, 1981).

[26] Giuseppe Gaetano Salvadori, *Poetica toscana all'uso* (Naples: Gramignani, 1691); Giovanni Mario Crescimbeni, *L'istoria della volgar poesia*, 3rd ed., 6 vols. (Venice: Lorenzo Basegio, 1730-31); Francesco Saverio Quadrio, *Della storia e della ragione d'ogni poesia*, 5 vols. (Bologna and Milan: F. Pissari and F. Agnelli respectively, 1739-52); Ludovico Antonio Muratori, *Della perfetta poesia italiana*, 2 vols. (Modena: Bartolomeo Soliani, 1706).

Therefore, what can the fact that a musical composition was performed on a stage tell us about its genre? In itself, nothing. Only study of several factors will reveal whether the stage as such—with all that that implies—was a necessary ingredient in presenting the work or whether it was simply an accidental characteristic of the particular performance in question.

*   *   *   *   *

Yet another example will serve to highlight the question and the problems it poses. As a test case, it might initially be found puzzling. In 1668 Leopold de' Medici was made cardinal, and in the spring he went to Rome to be installed in his honored position by the pope. Among the many invitations he received while there, was one from Princess Olimpia Pamphilj to spend May 16 at her villa, called Belvedere, in the country town of Frascati.[27] He and the other guests enjoyed the spectacular gardens of the villa and were served a marvelous meal. They were then invited to the "Apollo" salon for a musical entertainment. At one end of the highly decorated room (fig. 7.9) was a fountain representing Mount Parnassus with Apollo and the Muses, each with a musical instrument in hand. A delightful feature of the wooden sculpture was that it was mobile: when the fountain was activated, each figure moved as though playing its instrument; in fact actual music was heard as the water ran. (The kneeling figure of a gentleman with a ball in the foreground of the engraving shows that the air pressure issuing from an escape valve was strong enough to have supported the ball of copper.)

The musical entertainment itself opened with Circe coming to visit the tomb of her son, Telegono (Telegonus), the founder of the ancient city of Tusculum, the site of Frascati. A bright light surprises and disturbs her and she calls on Algido, after whom the river in Frascati is named, to explain it. He tells her it is due to the presence of a Medici. After Circe has an "echo" conversation with Zeffiro (Zephyrus), God of the Wind, he also appears. Zeffiro then specifically names Leopold, saying that no praises are sufficient for him. In his own account of the festivity, Leopold noted that a piece of scenery representing woods was added to both sides of the Mount Parnassus fountain, and it was from behind this setting that the three characters emerged one by one as the work proceeded. The score of the piece, entitled *La Circe*, by Alessandro Stradella, contains only the music and text.[28] Instead, on the autograph manuscript of the text by Giovan Filippo Apolloni[29] there are several important indications. For example, from it one learns that Circe was dressed as a queen, complete with crown, scepter, and a rich cape. (It would make sense that the other two characters were also dressed appropriately, even though this is not stated.) The manuscript also suggests that Zeffiro should seem to be flying when he comes out from behind the fountain. After the three characters quickly agree that Leopold must be honored with gifts, Algido decides to transform the waters of Tusculum into crystal. The directions state that at that point a beautifully dressed page should hand Leopold a crystal vase. Zeffiro chooses to offer Leopold flowers, and the directions indicate that a little winged zephyr should give him beautiful silk flowers; finally, as Circe's gift, a shade from Elysium is to present Leopold with perfume. During the closing ensemble, the three are to offer Leopold other gifts, which we know from his own account were fans and gloves in a beautiful box. At the end of their trio, the directions stipulate that the fountain with its music was to be activated and the characters were to retreat behind it.

At this point one needs to ask: what is the genre of this secular musical entertainment? A cantata, of course. It is certainly not a drama; it is simply a series of laudatory comments in honor of Leopold de' Medici put into a mythological context. What about the staging? As usual, the stage set is a single one—the Mount Parnassus fountain with a painted flat added on both sides. Although wonderfully decorative, the apparatus is not particularly relevant to the environment

---

[27] There are several sources for the day's events: Leopold's letter to his brother, Granduke of Tuscany, dated 19 May 1668 (Florence, Archivio di Stato, Mediceo del Principato, 5508); Marquis Francesco Riccardi's letter to the Granduke written the same day (ibid., 3939); an *avviso* bearing the same date (Rvat, Barb. lat. 6369); another *avviso*, this one cited by Alessandro Ademollo, *I teatri di Roma nel secolo decimosettimo* (Rome: L. Pasqualucci, 1888; reprint with new pagination, Rome: A. Borzi, 1969), 101.

[28] Modena, Biblioteca Estense, Mus. F. 1151.

[29] Rvat, Chigi L.VI.193, ff. 4 -10v.

suggested by the text. What of the staggered entrances of the characters and their costumes? These were delightful contrivances, more than was apparently customary, but they are not sufficient in themselves to turn the work into a musical drama, that is, into an opera. What of the gifts and the extras—the page, little zephyr, and shade—who presented the gifts to Leopold? Since Circe, Algido, and Zeffiro do not address the extras or Leopold directly, his actually being given the gifts is outside the work itself: once again, it was a charming but extraneous touch.

* * * * *

What the directions for *La Circe* and the descriptions of other so-called "staged" oratorios and cantatas tell us, however, is that a musical score may not reveal the whole story, and that many non-operatic works could have been performed in quite elaborate settings. At the same time, we must not be tricked into believing that when words such as "stage" or "theater" are associated with a musical composition that these necessarily imply the work was a drama, or that it received a complete theatrical peformance.

The "Staging" of Genres Other Than Opera in Baroque Italy

Fig. 7.1. Catafalque for the funeral of Sig. Don Antonio Miraballo, Naples, 1695 (Biblioteca Nazionale, Rome)

Fig. 7.2. Catafalque for the funeral of Philip V of Spain, Naples, 1746 (Biblioteca Nazionale, Rome)

Fig. 7.3. Fireworks structure for the pregnancy of Empress Elizabeth of Austria. Naples, 1723 (Biblioteca Nazionale, Rome)

Fig. 7.4. Fireworks structure for the coronation of King Charles of Sicily, Palermo, 1736 (Biblioteca Nazionale, Rome)

Fig. 7.5. Stage set for Metastasio's *Componimento sacro per la festività dell SS. Natale* set to music by Giovanni Battista Costanzi, Palazzo Ottoboni, Rome, 1727 (Biblioteca Vaticana, Rome)

Fig. 7.6. Stage set for *Scherno festivo tra le ninfe di Partenope*, set to music by Domenico Sarro, Palazzo Reale, Naples, 1720 (Biblioteca Nazionale, Rome)

The "Staging" of Genres Other Than Opera in Baroque Italy

Fig. 7.7. Stage set for Ranieri de' Calzabigi's *Il sogno d'Olimpia*, set to music by Giuseppe de Majo, Palazzo Reale, Naples, 1748 (Biblioteca Vaticana, Rome)

Fig. 7.8. Stage set for Ranieri de' Calzabigi's *Il sogno d'Olimpia*, set to music by Giuseppe de Majo, Teatro San Carlo, Naples, 1748 (Biblioteca Vaticana, Rome)

Fig. 7.9. Stanza d'Apollo, Villa Aldobrandini, Frascati (Rome) site of Giovan Filippo Apolloni's *La Circe*, set to music by Alessandro Stradella in 1668 (Biblioteca Vaticana, Rome)

8

Oil and Opera Don't Mix:
The Biography of S. Aponal, a Seventeenth-Century Venetian Opera Theater

JONATHAN E. GLIXON AND BETH L. GLIXON

It is not entirely unreasonable to think of buildings, like people, as having lives that can be chronicled in a biography.[1] Like people, buildings are born, develop and mature with time, are involved in relationships with others (in this case, inhabitants, guests, and neighbors, both human and architectural), grow old, decay, and die. In the case of prominent buildings, as with prominent people, these life stories can often be extensively documented. We can look back not only to their births, but often to their conceptions, and even, in some cases, to when they first became a gleam in the eyes of their patrons or creators. Scholars can trace buildings' lives in detail, documenting each event, each changing relationship, each moment of growth or decay, up until their sometimes catastrophic deaths. More modest structures, like less prominent individuals, have biographies that are considerably more obscure. Their births are often undocumented, their life stories, though sometimes eventful, are rife with gaps, and their deaths are frequently slow and shrouded in mystery.

The opera theaters of Venice provide examples of both extremes. The noblest of them all, and the last to be built, La Fenice, is, not surprisingly, the best documented.[2] We can trace its long history in considerable detail, from the formation in 1790 of the company that built it and the plans of the architect hired for the job, to the illustrious composers and performers that have graced its stage for nearly two centuries. Most dramatically, and tragically, we can learn of the several disastrous fires that consumed La Fenice, including that of January 1996. Fortunately, after each one of those untimely deaths, the theater, true to its name, has risen again from the ashes.

The humbler, middle-class Teatro Sant'Apollinare, better known by its nickname in Venetian dialect as Sant'Aponal, had a very different kind of life.[3] Its birth, as might be expected, is obscure. The earliest known document to make reference to it dates from 1635.[4] Although described there as "the place where they performed comedy" (*il*

The research for this article was facilitated by grants from the Gladys Krieble Delmas Foundation, the National Endowment for the Humanities, and the University of Kentucky.

[1] The idea of writing a biography of a non-human entity is, of course, not a new one. Biographies of cities are quite frequent. Most notable are several by Christopher Hibbert: *Rome: The Biography of a City* (Harmondsworth: Penguin, 1987), *Venice: The Biography of a City* (New York: Norton, 1989), and *Florence: The Biography of a City* (New York: Norton, 1993). See also Anthony Read and David Fisher, *Berlin Rising: Biography of a City* (New York: Norton, 1994).

[2] See Franco Mancini, Maria Teresa Muraro, and Elena Povoledo, *I teatri di Venezia e il suo territorio, Imprese private e teatri sociali*, I teatri del Veneto, vol. 1, no. 2 (Venice: Corbo e Fiore, 1996), 185-297.

[3] For previous histories of the theater, see Nicola Mangini, *I teatri di Venezia* (Milan: Mursia, 1974), 67-69, and Franco Mancini, Maria Teresa Muraro, and Elena Povoledo, *I teatri di Venezia. Teatri effimeri e nobili imprenditori*, I teatri del Veneto, vol. 1, no. 1 (Venice: Corbo e Fiore, 1995), 362-78.

[4] Archivio di Stato di Venezia (henceforth ASV), Archivio notarile, Atti Agostino Cavertino, busta (henceforth b.) 2863, f. 132, 17 September 1635.

luoco ove si recitava la Comedia), the first use of S. Aponal as a theater may not have occurred much before that date, since it is not mentioned in Gerolamo Priuli's listing of theaters presenting comedies in the first part of the century.[5] The property, located in the Corte de Ca' Petrian (sometimes also known as the Corte del Botter) off the Grand Canal on the side opposite San Marco just south of the Rialto Bridge, apparently had belonged to the stonemasons' guild[6] and then became the property of the Belaviti family, forming part of the dowry of Lucieta Belaviti.[7] In a decision of the Giudici del Proprio (one of Venice's financial courts) after Lucieta's death, the property passed to her children Zuanne, Anzola, and Anneta Panizzi. Most likely, at this point, it was structured as a warehouse, with two rooms on the ground floor, and above, with a separate entrance, another room several stories in height but apparently unencumbered by permanent floors or other structures.[8]

The two floors of the building had somewhat different, although crucially intertwined stories. In 1622, perhaps in settlement of a debt or fine, the Officio del Sopragastaldo (a magistracy that executed certain court orders) sold a two-thirds interest in the ground floor warehouses to the oil merchant Santo Grigis (or perhaps another member of his family), who three years later purchased the remaining third directly from Anzola Panizzi.[9] Santo, and then his son Bortolo, and his descendants retained control of both warehouses for more than four decades, using them for storage of barrels of oil.

The upper room of the property apparently remained in the family of its earlier owners, in the person of the merchant Pietro Ceroni, Anzola Panizzi's husband, perhaps in trust for her children. At some point, probably between 1626 and 1635, this upper room had been altered for use as a theater for the production of comedies. When in 1635 Pietro Ceroni rented the room to Bortolo Grigis, who already owned the lower floor, for a period of eight years at a rent of fifty ducats per year, he obligated himself to "wall up those doors, windows, and openings that had been made in that place for the purpose of [presenting] comedies."[10] The wood that had been used for the theater's internal structures, some of which was still attached to the walls, would become the property of Grigis, who perhaps was hoping to expand his business.

While Grigis, as mentioned above, maintained possession of the ground-floor warehouses for several decades, a situation that would have serious consequences for the theater, the taller upper-floor room took on a life of its own, probably after the expiration of Grigis's eight-year rental agreement in 1643. It seems likely, based on information in a later document, that this upper room was next rented to one Francesco del Mesa, a Jewish merchant who used the space to store his goods, paying an annual rent of between thirty and forty ducats.[11] After the death of Pietro Ceroni, the building, along with other properties, passed, shared evenly, one half to Ceroni's sons Francesco, a lawyer, and Giovanni Battista and the other to their cousin, Zanetta Diamante.[12]

Teatro Sant'Aponal can truly be said to have come of age in 1650, when Francesco Ceroni and Zanetta Diamante rented it for three years (with an option for another three) to the young author Giovanni Faustini, who sought a

---

[5] Priuli's diary is dated 1607, but according to Mangini, 34, the description of the theaters of S. Cassiano, S. Moisè, and S. Luca dates from 1626, when Priuli made additions to his diary.

[6] ASV, Dieci savi sopra le decime in Rialto, b. 387, no. 690. In the absence of more precise documentation, the story of the early years of this property has been inferred primarily from two later documents that discuss, sometimes ambiguously, previous episodes: ASV, Archvio notarile, Atti Giulio Pincio, b. 1175, f. 19, 18 August 1666 (a declaration from Bortolo Grigis to Francesco Ceroni concerning a legal action by Zanetta Diamante), and Dieci savi sopra le decime in Rialto, b. 387, no. 690 (Francesco Ceroni's property tax declaration). For more on the latter, see below, pp. 139-40.

[7] ASV, Archivio notarile, Atti Giulio Pincio, b. 1175, f. 19, 18 August 1666.

[8] There were also one or more small storerooms under the stairway that led to the upper floor; see ibid., ASV, Dieci savi sopra le decime in Rialto, b. 387, no. 690.

[9] ASV, Archivio notarile, Atti Pietro Bracchi, b. 906, f. 537v, and Atti Giulio Pincio, b. 1175, f. 19, 18 August 1666.

[10] ASV, Archivio notarile, Atti Agostino Cavertino, b. 2863, f. 132, 17 September 1635.

[11] ASV, Dieci savi sopra le decime in Rialto, b. 387, no. 690.

[12] Pietro Ceroni had died by 17 June 1641; see ASV, Archivio notarile, Atti Alessandro Basso, b. 996, f. 85. Diamante's name has been cited erroneously in much of the literature as "Zanetta Piamonte."

venue to produce his body of libretti.[13] In order to assess the significance of Faustini's involvement with S. Aponal, it is helpful to look at his career in the years preceding 1650. Faustini had begun his association with the composer Francesco Cavalli at the Teatro S. Cassiano in 1642; at that time Cavalli himself led a company at the theater. In 1644 Cavalli turned over the operation to a group of noblemen, but he and Faustini remained active there.[14] While other composers such as Francesco Manelli, Benedetto Ferrari, Francesco Sacrati, and Claudio Monteverdi had helped to establish the musical side of the Venetian operatic machine, it was Cavalli who would achieve the most durable presence as a composer for the Venetian stage, and it was the ongoing partnership of Cavalli and Giovanni Faustini that created a standard pattern for the Venetian opera plot.[15]

The Venetian theaters were closed for the 1645-46 and 1646-47 carnival seasons because of the war of Crete.[16] By the time they reopened for the 1647-48 season, Giovanni Faustini had decided to immerse himself in the business of opera. Whereas previously he had been a librettist, perhaps with some financial interest in production, he was now the impresario, in control of his own theater, S. Moisè. This theater (which would later feature premieres of Rossini's operas) was one of Venice's oldest. During the mid-*seicento*, it vacillated between productions of commedia dell'arte and opera. On 26 September 1647 Giovanni Faustini signed a three-year contract with the owner, Almorò Zane, to mount operas there.[17] Faustini's first production was his opus 6, *L'Ersilla*, with music, according to the chronicler of Venetian opera, the cleric and librettist Cristoforo Ivanovich, by "diversi," perhaps including Cavalli. For the second year, 1649, the venerable team of Faustini and Cavalli was reunited for *L'Euripo*.

In October of 1649, while involved in preparations for his third season at S. Moisè, in which he planned to present two operas, *Oristeo* and *Rosinda*, Faustini learned that Almorò Zane wished instead to present comedies. Although he had already hired, and in one case begun to pay, singers, Faustini terminated his contract with Zane, temporarily ending his career as an impresario. Within seven months, however, Faustini had found a new venue for his operatic talents: the Teatro S. Aponal.

Faustini's rental of S. Aponal may have been facilitated by some typically Venetian personal and business relationships. Ceroni and Marco Faustini, Giovanni's brother, would probably have known each other, as both were lawyers. Zanetta Diamante, the other owner of the S. Aponal property, knew Elena Bottoni, the Faustinis' first cousin, and her husband Alvise.[18] On 4 May 1650 Francesco Ceroni authorized Diamante to conduct business regarding S. Aponal, and on May 19 she rented the theater to Giovanni Faustini.[19]

The Teatro S. Aponal held one distinct advantage: its rent, sixty ducats a year, was quite small, substantially lower than that of the other theaters in Venice. The debts Faustini had incurred earlier—he mentioned them in the foreword to *Oristeo* and *Rosinda*—and had hoped to recoup with performances of those works at S. Moisè, might well have prevented him from aspiring to a more prestigious theater. The grand SS. Giovanni e Paolo rented for 1200 ducats, or so it had, apparently, several years earlier. Even the theaters devoted to spoken comedy rented for

---

[13] The years from 1650 through 1657 were examined by Jane Glover in her dissertation "The Teatro Sant'Apollinare and the Development of Seventeenth-century Venetian Opera" (D.Phil. diss., Oxford University, 1975). Glover's research was largely based on the librettos and extant scores of the operas performed at S. Aponal, as well as the documents in ASV, Scuola Grande di San Marco (henceforth SGSM), bb. 188 and 194. New information concerning the theater during those years was introduced in Beth L. Glixon and Jonathan E. Glixon, "Marco Faustini and Venetian Opera Production in the 1650s," *Journal of Musicology* 10 (1992): 48-73. Further new documentary material will appear in Glixon and Glixon, *Marco Faustini and Venetian Opera Production in Mid-Seventeenth-Century Venice* (forthcoming).

[14] On Cavalli and his company at S. Cassiano, see Giovanni Morelli and Thomas Walker, "Tre controversie intorno al San Cassiano," in *Venezia e il melodrama nel seicento*, ed. Maria Teresa Muraro (Florence: Olschki, 1976), 97-120.

[15] See Ellen Rosand, *Opera in Seventeenth-Century Venice: The Creation of a Genre* (Berkeley: University of California Press, 1991), especially 169-75.

[16] Lorenzo Bianconi and Thomas Walker, "Dalla *Finta pazza* alla *Veremonda*: Storie di Febiarmonici," *Rivista italiana di musicologia* 10 (1975): 416-17; Rosand, 108.

[17] ASV, Archivio notariale, Atti Taddeo Federici, b. 6075, f. 41, 5 October 1649.

[18] For documents connecting Diamante and the Bottoni family, see ASV, SGSM, b. 195, no. 30, and b. 188, letter of Diamante to Bottoni, 2 June 1653 (to be found in the "Bottoni" papers, rather than those pertaining to Faustini and the theater). Elena Bottoni's mother, Daria Vecellio Ugoni, was the sister of the Faustinis' mother, Isabetta Vecellio Faustini; see Glixon and Glixon, *Marco Faustini and Venetian Opera*.

[19] For Ceroni's authorization to Diamante, see ASV, Archivio notarile, Atti Taddeo Federici, b. 6053, f. 64v, 4 May 1650; for Diamante's rental to Faustini, ASV, SGSM, b. 194, ff. 179-83 (copy of the notarial act of Alberto Mastaleo).

considerably more; a payment of at least 600 ducats was customary.[20] S. Aponal's sixty ducats is, then, shockingly low by comparison, although perhaps commensurate with its condition and size, as Faustini complains in his dedication, stating that it was not really an improvement over S. Moisè, already described as too small:

> It is true that the theater built by me is not dissimilar to the one [S. Moisè] where *Ersilla* and *Euripo* appeared, and there these twins [*Oristeo* and *Rosinda*] should have been seen.[21]

The low rent probably also reflected the current state of the upstairs room at S. Aponal; it had not been used as a theater for many years, and perhaps had never possessed the boxes typical of an opera theater. Potential impresarios rented, in essence, a floor, a ceiling, and four walls, inside which they would have had to construct from scratch, at considerable expense, everything from the boxes with the stairs and corridors needed for access to them, to the stage and spaces above and below required for the production.

In addition, the building itself was in poor condition, and Ceroni and Diamante agreed to make the repairs. The contract stated:

> It is declared also that the said lessors are obligated to secure the floor of the said place, which trembles, fix the roof, reinforce the windows, which are not secure, repair the stairway, and take care of other things that are necessary and required in that place. It is not intended that the present rental shall begin, nor shall Signor Faustini be compelled to pay the aforesaid rent, if first the above lessors have not performed the said repairs, and in particular the repair of the aforesaid floor, notwithstanding that it is written above that the rental should begin this coming June 21. It is declared that the aforesaid repairs shall be done with the money from the first payment of the rent in the present rental.[22]

Faustini later agreed to contribute part of the funds necessary to repair the building.[23]

Giovanni Faustini's plans for the theater were doubly ambitious. He planned to mount two productions per year, a goal he met with *Oristeo* and *Rosinda* the first year and with *Calisto* and *Eritrea* the second; no other theaters at this time produced more than one opera per season. Faustini's other coup was the securing of the experienced Francesco Cavalli as the composer for his theater. During the 1651 and 1652 seasons the other theaters—SS. Giovanni e Paolo, SS. Apostoli, and S. Cassiano—offered the works of other, more junior composers: Francesco Lucio, Antonio Cesti, and Gasparo Sartorio. Although the extent of Faustini's financial backing is not entirely clear, he did receive some assistance from two noblemen, Alvise Duodo and Marc'Antonio Correr. Faustini paid homage to them as the dedicatees of *Oristeo* and *Calisto* (*Eritrea*, which premiered after Giovanni Faustini's death, also was dedicated to one of the noblemen).

During his second year at S. Aponal, Giovanni Faustini, perhaps at the instigation of his older brother Marco, capitalized on the idea of an expanded season. While the season typically started with the beginning of Carnival, which that year commenced December 26, *Calisto* opened on November 28, nearly a month earlier. Preparations for the show began inauspiciously, however, as the lead contralto Bonifacio Ceretti became ill and died twenty-five days later, on December 5.[24] Two weeks following, on December 19, Giovanni Faustini himself died after several

---

[20] A document of 1644 mentions the rent of a theater owned by Giovanni Grimani (i.e., the Teatro SS. Giovanni e Paolo) as 1200 ducats (ASV, Archivio notarile, Atti Taddeo Federici, b. 6047, f. 327, 14 December 1644). The small Teatro S. Moisè rented for 900 ducats in 1642 (ASV, Archivio notarile, Atti Paolo Moretti, b. 8504, f. 11, 7 April 1642), but for only 600 ducats ten years later (ASV, Archivio notarile, Atti Francesco Simbeni, b. 12042, f. 111, 13 May 1652).

[21] "E vero, che non dissimile dall'Orchestra sudetta, nella quale comparsero Ersilla, et Euripo, e dove di poi dovevano farsi vedere questi gemelli, è il Palco da me eretto. . . ." Giovanni Faustini, *Oristeo* (Venice: Pinelli, 1651), 3-4.

[22] "Dichiarando ancora che detti signori locatori siino obligati ad'assicurare il suolo di detto loco, che trema, acconciarli il colmo, stropar i balconi, che non vi sono sicuri, accomodar la scala, et altre cose bisognose e necessarie in detto luoco. Non intendosi per principiata la presente affittatione, ne meno esso Signor Faustini astretto all'esborso dell'affitto antedetto se prima non sarà stato dalli sopradetti signori locatori affettuato li concieri sudetti et in particolar il conciero del suolo predetto, nonostante, che di sopra si è detto che la presente affittatione debba principiar li 21 [22] giugno prossimo venturo. Dichiarando, che li concieri sudetti debbino esser fatti delli danari della prima ratta dell'affitti della presente affittatione." ASV, SGSM, b. 194, f. 180.

[23] ASV, SGSM, b. 194, ff. 181v-182, 20 September 1650.

[24] ASV, Provveditori alla Sanità, Necrologio, b. 877, 5 December 1651.

days of illness, at the age of thirty-six.²⁵ *Calisto* had not been drawing large crowds. Not even Faustini's death sparked new interest, however, and the opera closed on December 31, after eleven performances. The second opera, *Eritrea*, opened on January 17, with mention in the libretto of the deaths of Ceretti and Faustini.²⁶ *Eritrea* fared well, with 3423 tickets sold at twenty-three performances. (Ironically, *Eritrea* is largely unknown today, while *Calisto* has been performed successfully in a number of venues on both sides of the Atlantic.)

Giovanni Faustini's rental contract bore the customary phrase "for himself, his heirs and successors" (*per se, heredi, et successori suoi*), so that Marco, his only surviving relative, inherited his brother's interest in the theater, both literally and figuratively. At first, however, he must have decided not to pursue the enterprise in the absence of Giovanni: notarial documents show that Marco sublet the theater, as of 30 October 1652,²⁷ to Bortolo Castoreo (who had earlier been an impresario at S. Cassiano²⁸), Annibale Basso, and Paulo Morando.²⁹

The appearance of a new company at S. Aponal represented a change in outlook, stature, and, most importantly, the prestige of its creative artists. In the place of the leading librettist in Venice, the subrenters included a one-time librettist (Bortolo Castoreo was the author of *Armidoro*, performed at S. Cassiano in 1650-51³⁰), and two artisans, an embroiderer (Basso) and a woodturner with experience in costuming (Morando). Although Castoreo had been one of the renters at S. Cassiano when Cavalli's *Giasone* was produced, the composer chose not to mount his new works there, preferring the more established Teatro SS. Giovanni e Paolo. Francesco Lucio was available for the first year (with *Pericle effeminato*, his third opera [1652-53])³¹; the next season saw the operatic debut of Pietro Andrea Ziani, with *La guerriera spartana* (1653-54).³² The librettist for these two works was Giacomo Castoreo, the brother of Bortolo.³³

It appears that the new company used the theater to present plays as well as opera. According to information in Leone Allacci's *Drammaturgia*, Pietro Urbano's *Astrilla* and Giacomo Castoreo's *Eurimene* were performed there.³⁴ The Teatro S. Aponal, then, served as a creative outlet for the Castoreo brothers, much as it had for Giovanni Faustini.³⁵

---

²⁵ Ibid., 19 December 1651. According to the parish death records, Giovanni Faustini died at the age of thirty-six; this age agrees with the record of his birth written by his father. Angelo Faustini specifies the date as 19 May 1615 (ASV, SGSM, b. 117), as do the baptismal records of the parish of San Geminiano (Archivio Storico del Patriarcato di Venezia, Parrocchia di San Geminiano, Battesimi 1563-1674, f. 170). Marco Faustini, on the other hand, apparently to enhance his brother's status as a prodigy, seems to have promulgated Giovanni's age at the time of his death as thirty-two (the age that appears on his tombstone in the church of S. Vidal in Venice, as well as in some of the forewords to the librettos).

²⁶ On the death of Giovanni Faustini: "While a feigned death of Eritrea will sweetly please Your Illustrious Lordship's ear, the unfortunately real one of Signor Giovanni Faustini will sorrowfully move your spirit" ("Mentre una finta morte d'Eritrea lusingherà a V.S. Illustriss. dolcemente l'orecchio, la pur troppo ver del Sig. Giovanni Faustini le commoverà dolorosamente l'anima"). Several sentences later: "[Eritrea] has also lost the companionship of the virtuoso Bonifacio, whose steps halted at the beginning of the path of life" ("Ha pur anco smarrita in dietro la compagnia del virtuoso Bonifatio, che nel principio del camino fermò col passo la vita"). Giovanni Faustini, *L'Eritrea* (Venice: Giuliani, 1652), 5.

²⁷ ASV, Archivio notarile, Atti Camillo Pincio, b. 10983, f. 365. Faustini, in a document dated 26 February 1653, refers to an agreement of 30 October 1652.

²⁸ See Morelli and Walker, 114-17.

²⁹ Morando's connections with theatrical activity in Venice can be traced back as far as 1640, when he was guarantor for the rental of the benches (*scagni*) at the Teatro Novissimo (ASV, Archivio notarile, Atti Andrea Calzavara, b. 3055, f. 49, 10 March 1642).

³⁰ Castoreo's libretto may have been set by Gasparo Sartorio; see *The New Grove Dictionary of Music and Musicians* (1980), s.v. "Sartorio, Gasparo," by Edward H. Tarr.

³¹ Lucio's first two operas were *L'Orontea* (1649) and *Gli amori d'Alessandro Magno e di Rossane* (1651).

³² Documents concerning the production of this year list only Castoreo and Basso as the "interessati"; see ASV, Archivio notarile, Atti Camillo Lion, b. 8019, f. 136v, 14 February 1654.

³³ Although no documentation found thus far specifically states that the two were brothers, they both were the sons of Giovanni Antonio Castoreo.

³⁴ Leone Allacci, *Drammaturgia di Lione Allacci accresciuta e continuata fino all'anno 1755* (Venice: Giambattista Pasquali, 1755), cols. 124, 317. *Astrilla* and *Eurimene* both bear a publication date of 1652. A copy of *Astrilla* at the University of California, Los Angeles (published by Nicolini), lists S. Apollinare as the location of the performance; see Irene Alm, *Catalog of Venetian Librettos at the University of California, Los Angeles* (Berkeley: University of California Press, 1993), 52. We have no evidence as to when *Astrilla* was performed; Castoreo's *Eurimene*, with its dedication date of 17 January 1652 (1653 modern style), would have been mounted simultaneously with *Pericle effeminato* if it was indeed performed at S. Aponal.

³⁵ Castoreo continued to publish plays with intermedi designed for music after his association with S. Aponal. *Il prencipe corsaro* (1658) and *Il pazzo politico* (1659) specify a performance at the Teatro "Saloni."

Although not involved in the productions, Marco Faustini carefully monitored the activities at S. Aponal. He apparently still controlled the boxes and the income derived from their rental, and would, therefore, have had a clear interest in seeing that the productions went on as planned.[36] Faustini complained to Morando, Basso, and Castoreo on 24 November 1652 of insufficient progress towards the production of an opera for that season.[37] The second year, the company faced problems when the prima donna, Anna Felicita Chiusi, fell ill, disrupting the performances.[38] By the following spring, Faustini had decided to involve himself once again in opera production; the extant evidence of his plans for the 1654-55 season begins on 1 May 1654.[39]

Marco Faustini's return to the Teatro Aponal as its impresario was accompanied by several changes. He brought with him a new investor in the theatrical company, one Bortolo Pasinetto. Pasinetto supplied 70% of the operating capital for the 1654-55 season; indeed, it is likely that Pasinetto's participation made the return possible. Pasinetto, a *cartoler* (maker and seller of playing cards), as was his father before him, was a young man, aged twenty-four at the time of his first involvement with Faustini. Moreover, he was a lover of music, or at least a lover of musical instruments. At the time of his death in 1667 he left a spinet, a harpsichord, a viol, and fourteen different plucked instruments.[40] It should be noted that Alvise Duodo and Marc'Antonio Correr still maintained connections with the company, but they did not serve as primary investors.

Faustini and Pasinetto chose, as had the interim impresarios, to produce only one opera per year rather than the two that Giovanni Faustini had initiated. Giovanni had been an assiduous writer of librettos, and had left a number unfinished at his death. Not surprisingly, Marco Faustini chose to produce one of his brother's works for the new season.[41] The original intention of the company must have been to once again present an opera by Francesco Cavalli. Indeed, Alvise Duodo had been negotiating a contract with the composer during the summer of 1654. Cavalli, however, was displeased with the details of the arrangements, and ultimately the negotiations must have broken down entirely.[42] Faustini fell back on Pietro Andrea Ziani, who had composed the opera for the previous year at S. Aponal, and it was he who set Giovanni Faustini's *Eupatra* for the 1654-55 season.

It is difficult from our vantage point to assess the reasons behind the success or failure of a seventeenth-century opera, especially when, as in this instance, a score is lacking. Ticket sales, however, attest to the popularity of *Eupatra*. Thirty performances were given, with 4232 tickets sold, and only four performances had fewer than ninety in attendance (the highest figure for attendance for any of the years for which records are extant is 338, on the first night of *Eupatra*). The popularity may in part have been due to the participation of Anna Renzi, the most celebrated operatic diva during the previous decade in Venice, who had become famous in Giulio Strozzi's and Francesco Sacrati's *La finta pazza* (1640-41).[43]

---

[36] The contract between Faustini and the new company has not turned up; on the box rentals for those years (1652-53, 1653-54), see below.

[37] ASV, Archivio notarile, Atti Camillo Pincio, b. 10983, f. 361.

[38] On this incident, see Beth L. Glixon, "Private Lives of Public Women: Prima donnas in Mid-Seventeenth-Century Venice," *Music & Letters* 76 (1995): 509-31, especially 520-21.

[39] Documentary materials concerning the production at S. Aponal for the 1654-55 season appear in the "account book" (ASV, SGSM, b. 113) and the receipt book (ASV, SGSM, b. 118); see Glixon and Glixon, "Marco Faustini," 62-66.

[40] Pasinetto committed suicide in March of 1667 by jumping out of a window. One of the apprentices in the Pasinettos' shop was Antonio Albinoni, who eventually inherited the business. Albinoni was the father of the composer Tomaso, born in 1671. On the business connections between the Pasinettos and Albinonis, see Gastone Vio, "Per una migliore conoscenza di Tomaso Albinoni: documenti d'archivio," *Recercare* 1 (1988): 111-22, in particular 112-14.

[41] Throughout his remaining years as an impresario, Marco Faustini maintained a commitment to bring his brother's unperformed works to the stage. Marco stated this goal explicitly during his recruiting for the 1666-67 season at SS. Giovanni e Paolo; see Rosand, 193-94.

[42] Cavalli's displeasure was voiced in a letter of 23 July 1654 (ASV, SGSM, b. 188, f. 14); see Glover, *Cavalli* (New York: St. Martin's Press, 1978), 22, and Glixon and Glixon, "Marco Faustini," 62-64.

[43] On Renzi, see Claudio Sartori, "La prima diva della lirica italiana: Anna Renzi," *Nuova rivista musicale italiana* 2 (1968): 430-52, and Rosand, 228-30; see also Glixon, "Private Lives of Public Women," 512-19.

Renzi did not appear in the next year's production, but the new work, *Erismena*, a collaboration between Cavalli and Aurelio Aureli, received thirty-two performances, with a total of 5418 tickets sold. Cavalli had not returned to S. Aponal in his previous capacity as "house composer," for *Erismena* competed against another of his works, *Xerse*, performed at the Grimani theater (SS. Giovanni e Paolo), and Cavalli did not himself conduct the opera. His participation at S. Aponal had contributed to a successful season, however, and that year the company must have earned a profit, although the surviving figures are not entirely conclusive.[44] The composer of the next year's offering (1656-57) was once again Pietro Andrea Ziani, this time with a libretto by Aurelio Aureli, *Le fortune di Rodope e Damira*. Anna Renzi also appeared again at S. Aponal, in a role that allowed her to perform one of her famous portrayals of madness. *Le fortune di Rodope e Damira* was probably the last true opera to grace the stage of S. Aponal.

In previous writings about the theater, Lorenzo Bianconi, Jane Glover, Ellen Rosand, and Thomas Walker have stressed the "middle class" heritage of the Teatro S. Aponal, and have interpreted the involvement of Duodo and Correr as lending a more aristocratic aura (such as was present at other theaters) to the enterprise. Surviving documents, however, show that the audience comprised both classes. Faustini's record keeping has provided us with box assignments for four years: 1652-53 through 1655-56—that is, two years under the aegis of Morando, Basso, and Castoreo, and two under Faustini himself.[45] S. Aponal had three levels, or orders, with sixteen boxes each. In general, the first two orders of boxes were rented by the same sort of aristocrats as at the more prestigious theaters. The list of renters at S. Aponal included, besides ordinary Venetian patricians, several of the highest rank, including a number of the Procuratori di San Marco (one of the most distinguished of all government positions). In addition, some boxes in the first order were occupied by such eminent foreigners as the dukes of Brunswick and Parma, and the Papal Nuncio. For the 1653 season, Giovanni Antonio Curti, a businessman with connections to Faustini, was one of several non-noblemen in the second order; Faustini himself was the only person below the level of patrician to have a box in the first order. The first order also had a box reserved "per le donne"—that is, for some of the better class of courtesans, a practice that may have been traditional in Venetian opera houses.

In Faustini's accounting of the boxes, the top order is mostly blank, so that those particular boxes would have been rented out each night on demand. For 1655, Curti appears as one of the few annual renters in this top row, along with Nicolò Personè (who was Pietro Andrea Ziani's brother-in-law and a cloth merchant with ties to the opera business) and three other non-nobles; only in 1656 were they joined by two noblemen. It may not have been unusual for businessmen to rent boxes in the top order in Venetian theaters. In another list of box-holders in the Faustini papers, quite possibly from SS. Giovanni e Paolo, the top order included Giovanni Maria Savioni, a close associate of Ziani; Girolamo Squadron, the brother of a Venetian doctor; Aureli (the librettist); and "Franceschi" (probably the agent of the Grimani family, Gabriel Angelo Franceschi), as well as a number of noblemen, including two Procuratori.[46]

Our attention has thus far been focused on the creative aspects and results of opera production. Teatro S. Aponal, however, like much other property in Venice, served its owners as collateral, or income that could be put to other uses. Many Venetians acquired debts of various kinds, and came up with a variety of means of satisfying them. Zanetta Diamante appears to have led a rather uneventful fiscal existence. Francesco Ceroni, on the other hand, owed money to the nobleman Sebastian Mocenigo at least as far back as May 1642. Four years later, on 18 August 1646, the figure owed to Mocenigo was just over 352 ducats.[47] In 1651 Ceroni began to have his portion of the rental fees of the theater directed towards the repayment of that debt. Through a series of court actions, Marco Faustini was eventually ordered in 1653 to pay the rent to the noblemen Ottavian Bon and Francesco Grimani, to whom Mocenigo owed money.[48] While legal proceedings unfolded over the years, on 25 October 1655 Zanetta

---

[44] For a list of expenditures and income for *Calisto*, *Eritrea*, *Eupatra*, and *Erismena*, see Glixon and Glixon, "Marco Faustini," 63. The figures for *Erismena* probably represent only a portion of the expenses.

[45] ASV, SGSM, b. 194, ff. 92ff.

[46] Ibid., f. 18.

[47] Ibid., f. 192. For the evidence of the Ceronis' debts to Sebastiano Mocenigo, see ASV, Archivio notarile, Atti Francesco Beazian, b. 655, f. 353v, 17 May 1642; also see Glover, "The Teatro Sant'Apollinare," 330-32.

[48] ASV, SGSM, b. 194, f. 210, 26 August 1653.

Diamante renewed the rental of her half of the theater to Marco Faustini. She also authorized him to act on her behalf in disagreements over property with Ceroni.⁴⁹ Relations between Ceroni and Faustini must have worsened over the next few months. On 4 May 1656, just two months after the success of *Erismena*, Ceroni wanted Faustini out of the theater, and ordered him to pay 500 ducats in rent if he wished to stay. Ceroni's motivations are not entirely clear from the surviving documentation. Perhaps he now judged the rent of sixty ducats too small for a moderately successful theater. Difficulties between the two lawyers continued, and on 16 March 1657 Faustini agreed to give Ceroni back his portion of the theater.⁵⁰ Less than two months later, on May 5, Faustini rented another, larger theater, Teatro S. Cassiano, the oldest opera house in Venice.⁵¹

Faustini may have turned over "Ceroni's portion" of the theater, but he continued to rent the other half from Diamante (that agreement would be in force until 1662). Because Faustini's partners Correr, Duodo, and Polifilo Zancarli sought assurance that the smaller theater would not compete with S. Cassiano, in their agreement of incorporation they specified that S. Aponal, while in Faustini's possession, could not "perform operas for profit that could jeopardize the Teatro S. Cassiano, and in particular, that they should never compete with that theater."⁵² It was in Faustini's interest to find another use for the theater, and his solution was quick at hand. On 20 June 1657 he sublet the theater for a period of one year to the "Signori Accademici Imperturbabili."⁵³

The Imperturbabili have been known by virtue of their publication of two libretti, *Tolomeo* (1658) and *La pazzia in trono* (1660?). They differed from more prominent Venetian academies such as the Incogniti, whose members included some of the most prestigious writers of the time (such as Giovanni Francesco Loredano, the founder of the Incogniti, Giovanni Francesco Busenello, Pietro Michiel, and Giulio Strozzi, to name just a few), and whose publications were numerous and impressive.⁵⁴ The Imperturbabili, rather, have been nearly invisible. Until the recent discovery of the Faustini papers relating to this academy, none of the members' names were known. The signatures on Faustini's rental contract include Lauro Tamburin, Michel dall'Acqua, Giacomo di Franceschi, Giacomo Rizzardi, Jacomo Renier, and Emanuel Calafato. None of these men is known to have been prominent in Venetian business or government, or in arts and letters.⁵⁵

In the foreword to *Tolomeo*, the Imperturbabili state their mission: "to pass, in honest and virtuous recreation, the most dangerous days of the year"⁵⁶ (i.e., carnival), and they refer to *Tolomeo* as the second of their offerings. The notarial archives of Venice reveal that the academy had indeed been active a year earlier, mounting a production at a theater somewhere near the "Misericordia" (the Scuola and Abbazia della Misericordia lie in the outer region of Cannaregio, not far from the church of Madonna dell'Orto).⁵⁷ The academicians found a more central location in the Teatro S. Aponal, and one that by now had acquired the reputation of presenting respectable entertainment for carnival. Faustini took advantage of the situation: he charged the academicians twice the fee that he and his brother

---

⁴⁹ Ibid., f. 168.

⁵⁰ Ibid., f. 169.

⁵¹ Ibid., ff. 69, 71.

⁵² ". . . dovendo esso Signor Faustini, mentre haverà la patronia del Theatro di Sant Apponale, non permetter, che in esso siano recitate opere in musica con pagamento, dalle quali potesse pregiudicarsi al Theatro di San Cassano, et in particolare, che mai s'incontrino con San Cassano, et questo patto espresso, et particolare"—ibid., f. 24v. On the company at S. Cassiano, see Lorenzo Bianconi and Thomas Walker, "Production, Consumption and Political Function of Seventeenth-Century Opera," *Early Music History* 4 (1984): 211-99, especially 221-27.

⁵³ The rental agreement (ASV, SGSM, b. 113), first cited in Glixon and Glixon, "Marco Faustini," is reproduced in Mancini, Muraro, and Povoledo, I Teatri di Venezia. Teatri effimeri 372.

⁵⁴ The Incogniti have been discussed in many recent publications. For an overview, see Rosand, 37-40. For the Incogniti, and their view on women, see Wendy Beth Heller, "Chastity, Heroism, and Allure: Women in the Opera of Seventeenth-Century Venice" (Ph.D. diss., Brandeis University, 1995), especially ch. 2; for a somewhat less adulatory view of the group and its members, see also Bernard Aikema, *Pietro della Vecchia and the Heritage of the Renaissance in Venice* (Florence: Istituto Universitario Olandese di Storia dell'Arte, 1990), chs. 4 and 5.

⁵⁵ Jacomo Renier may have been the son of the painter, Nicolò Renier. A Giacomo Renier, son of Nicolò, helped to appraise some paintings in 1657; see ASV, Archivio notarile, Atti Angelo Maria Piccini, b. 11060, f. 211, 7 July 1657.

⁵⁶ ". . . di passare in honesta, e virtuosa recreatione i giorni più perigliosi dell'anno. . . ." *Il Tolomeo* (Venice: Valvasense, 1658), 5.

⁵⁷ ASV, Archivio notarile, Atti Camillo Lion, b. 8021, f. 39v, 15 May 1657.

had paid, 120 ducats. The contract specified that they could not charge admission to their performances ("far recitar a pagamento"); moreover, they could not "compete" on any nights that opera would be performed at S. Cassiano, a condition with-out which "Faustini would not have realized the present rental."[58] Faustini devised a plan by which he would notify the academicians the evening in advance of a "dead" night at S. Cassiano, thus giving them time to distribute tickets.

If Giovanni Faustini and his successors found the Teatro S. Aponal to be small and humble, the academicians proudly displayed the name of their new home on the title page of their libretto. *Tolomeo* comprises a prologue and three acts, in the manner of an opera (Giacomo Castoreo, in his plays for S. Aponal and other theaters, often resorted to the more "classical" five acts). The libretto specifies that Pier Simon Agostini—then about twenty-three years old—composed music for the prologue and ballets, as well as some canzonette, his earliest datable pieces.[59]

Unable to charge admission for their offering, the Academici apparently ran short of money. This lack of income affected not Ceroni and Diamante, but Marco Faustini. The Imperturbabili failed to turn back their keys to the theater after their year's rental; eventually Faustini had the locks on the theater changed, and he threatened to dismantle the boxes and the stage. The Imperturbabili were intent on keeping the theater, however. On 11 January 1659, well into the traditional carnival season, Emanuel Calafati agreed to turn over to Faustini the interest from some of his investments in order to cover the previous debts, and on January 26[60] Faustini rented the theater to Calafati (not to the acadamicians en masse) through the period of Lent.[61] In extending the rental agreement for another season, Faustini relaxed his previous prohibitions: he granted the academy the right to present entertainment on the same nights as the Teatro S. Cassiano two times during the last week of carnival. Had he not done so, S. Aponal would have remained dark for much of February, for the show at S. Cassiano ran for seventeen consecutive nights, from February 8 through February 24 (carnival ended that year on February 25).[62] The Faustini/Calafati rental contract was drawn up just one day after Cavalli's *Antioco* had commenced performances at the Teatro S. Cassiano. The Imperturbabili evidently presented *La pazzia in trono*, an "opera di stile recitativo" by Domenico Gisberti, although the much later publication of the work—in the author's *Talia* of 1675—gives 1660 as the year of the performance.[63]

The dangers of operating a theater on the second floor of a building became evident at the end of the season. The weight of the boxes and their occupants split three beams in the oil warehouse below, costing its owner, Bortolo Grigis, more than 100 lire to repair,[64] a sum he undoubtedly billed to Ceroni and Diamante (although the cost might, in the end, have been passed on to Faustini or the Imperturbabili). This incident was the first sign of what would become a serious conflict between the building's two functions, the theater and the oil warehouses.

La pazzia in trono represents our last link to the activities of the Imperturbabili, and it seems that S. Aponal lay fallow after the departure of the academy, while Faustini continued to pay thirty ducats per year to Zanetta Diamante. According to the 1661 property tax declaration of Francesco Ceroni,[65] S. Aponal apparently remained empty in what turned out to be the final year of Faustini's rental. This document states that although Faustini was still the leaseholder, the theater was not rented out. Ceroni declared no income from the property, with no operas currently in performance:

---

[58] "Che quelle sere, che si reciterà l'opera a San Casano non si possa recitar a Sant'Apponale per non incontrarsi, et questo per patto spetiale, senza il quale detto Signor Faustini non sarebbe venuto alla presente locatione"—in ASV, SGSM, b. 113.

[59] On Agostini, see *The New Grove Dictionary of Opera* (1992), s.v. "Agostini, Pier Simone," by Harris S. Saunders.

[60] This contract renewal is partially transcribed in Mancini, Muraro, and Povoledo, *I Teatri di Venezia. Teatri effimeri*, 372. We have interpreted the date of the renewal as *more veneto* (i.e., January 1659), while Mancini, Muraro, and Povoledo place it in the previous year.

[61] A copy of the notarial document drawn up by Ascanio Scarella (11 January 1658 [m.v.]) can be found in ASV, SGSM, b. 117, *mazzo* A.

[62] The performance dates for Cavalli's *Antioco* at S. Cassiano are taken from Faustini's account book, found in ASV, SGSM, b. 194; see Bianconi and Walker, 223-24.

[63] Domenico Gisberti, *Talia* (Monaco: Jecklino, 1675). In 1660 Gisberti went on to form an academy of his own, the Angustiati, on the island of Murano; see Venice, Biblioteca Nazionale Marciana, Ms. cl. x, 121 (7197), "Costituzioni delle Accademie degli Angustiati . . .," 1660.

[64] ASV, Monastero di SS. Giovanni e Paolo, b. XXV, loose sheet dated 12 March 1659.

[65] ASV, Dieci savi sopra le decime in Rialto, b. 387, no. 690.

> Item, in the same district, in Corte de Ca' Petriani, a large warehouse, which previously belonged to the stonemasons' guild, in which were produced comedies; when there were boxes, they performed operas, and a rent of sixty ducats a year was paid, that is, for my half, thirty ducats. But now it is unrented, and it is not known when it will be rented, according to the notice made by the Excellent Marco Faustini, leaseholder. In earlier times, when it was used to hold merchandise, it was rented for thirty to forty ducats a year to the Jew Franco del Mesa, which would be, for my half, twenty ducats.[66]

It seems that, in his earlier attempt to gain a greater income, Ceroni had ended up the loser. Faustini continued to pay Diamante rent for her half of the theater per his agreement of 1655, while Ceroni, apparently, would only receive rent if a new sublet agreement were negotiated with a third party, or if Faustini decided to resume his own operatic activities there. Although Faustini's agreement with Diamante, giving him rights to half the theater, was still in force, it seems probable that Ceroni would have been able to prevent any use of the theater unless paid his half of the original rent. In the case of the Imperturbabili, it is likely that Faustini had agreed privately with Ceroni to resume payments (since the contract with the Accademia makes no mention of rental payments to anyone but Faustini).

The tax declaration also provides some more information about the state of the lower-level warehouse:

> Item, under the said property [the theater] there are two oil warehouses, subject to the same conditions of inheritance, which are possessed by the heirs of the late Santo Grigio, son of the late Vido; at present I am suing to recover them, and when that occurs, I will give further notice.[67]

Ceroni apparently believed that one or both of the two sales involving the warehouses (by the Officio del Sopragastaldo in 1622 or by his mother in 1625) were invalid. Zanetta Diamante reached the same conclusion in 1666, and she managed, at least in the initial stages, to void the sales.[68] The *catastico*, or property census, compiled at the same time as Ceroni's tax declaration, offers similar information about the theater ("at present to be rented, and it used to be rented . . . for sixty ducats"), although it makes no mention of the warehouses below in connection with Ceroni and Diamante's property.[69] Instead, they are listed along with other properties in the parish rented by Bortolo Grigis, confirming Ceroni's statement in his tax declaration:

> The said [Grigis] possesses as his own property two other warehouses in the aforementioned Corte de Ca' Pitrian, combined into one, and these he keeps for his own use.[70]

The relative stability, at least in terms of function, that had persisted throughout the twelve years of control by the Faustini family came to an end in early 1662, after Marco Faustini made his last payment to Diamante on March 7.[71] At Christmas time of that year the theater was rented, perhaps for the carnival season or only for a period of a few days, to a company headed by Iseppo Bellato, in order to run a dance hall and a food stand, with its own kitchen ("farsi ballo e furatola con cusina").[72] This new venture immediately faced a serious challenge. Bortolo Grigis, apparently

---

[66] "Item in detta contrà in Corte de Ca Petriani un magazeno grande fu della Scola di Piera nel quale si faceva Comedie, e quando vi erano i palchi si recitava opere [e] si escavano ducati sessanta all'anno, cioè per mia mettà D.30. Ma hora essendo inaffitato, non si sa quando s'affiterà, stante il cognito fatto dall'Eccellente Domino Marco Faustini condutore. Nelli tempi antecedenti da metter mercantie si è affitato D.30 et son D.40 all'anno a Franco del Mesa ebreo, si che se così fosse sarebbe per mia mettà D20"—in ASV, Dieci savi sopra le decime in Rialto, b. 387, no. 690.

[67] "Item sotto detto loco vi sono due magazeni da oglio soggetti allo stesso fidei commisso, quali sono possessi dalli heredi del quondam Santo Grigio quondam Vido, per quali presentemente son in litte la recupera d'essi, che quando seguirsi si darà notta più nonc"—ibid.

[68] ASV, Archivio notarile, Atti Giulio Pincio, b. 1175, f. 19, 18 August 1666.

[69] ". . . al presente d'affittar, e si soleva affittar . . . ducati sessanta"—in ASV, Dieci savi sopra le decime in Rialto, b. 423, f. 239v, no. 160. Also listed (at no. 159) is a small storeroom under the stairs of the theater, which yielded an annual rent of three ducats.

[70] ASV, Dieci savi sopra le decime in Rialto, b. 423, f.234, no. 63: "Il detto possiede di sua ragione due altri magazeni nella sodetta corte da Ca Pitriani, riddotti in uno, e quelli tiene per suo uso."

[71] ASV, SGSM, b. 118, f. 61, 7 March 1662.

[72] ASV, Monastero di SS. Giovanni e Paolo, b. XXV.

still in possession of the oil warehouses, had evidently used one of them as part of the dowry of his niece Isabetta. Though Isabetta came from a family of oil merchants, her new husband was someone quite different. Francesco Corner was a member of one of the most distinguished of Venice's patrician families, and the son of the powerful Giovanni Battista Corner, Procuratore di San Marco. Whatever the reasons for this unusual match (money was most likely involved, as the Grigis family, though of the merchant class, was quite rich), the arrival on the scene of a powerful nobleman caused drastic changes in the life of the theater. Corner quickly recognized the danger presented to his wife's property by the presence of a kitchen on the floor above. Citing a recent fire in adjacent houses the preceding October, he appealed, through his influential father, to the Capi of the Council of Ten, the government body charged, among other things, with public safety, who immediately ordered that Bellato and his companions vacate the premises. The "place above the oil warehouse" (*loco . . . sopra il magazen da oglio*) was then rented to the cooper who lived in the courtyard, presumably to serve as a warehouse, and probably at the low rent suitable for such a humble function.

Despite its small size and poor condition, the possibility of renting an opera theater for not much more than a tenth of the going rate continued to attract potential impresarios to S. Aponal. In mid-July of 1665, a year in which three other opera houses already had seasons planned (and a fourth would get underway soon), Ceroni and Diamante signed a three-year rental contract, designating the building this time as "the place where they do comedy, that is the theater" [*il luoco della comedia sive teatro*] with Don Sebastian Enno and one Camillo Nebbia, at the usual rate of sixty ducats per year.[73] Enno, a canon at the Cathedral of San Pietro di Castello, had considerable experience with singers and opera. He was an active singing teacher, and had himself performed at least once on the Venetian stage, in Francesco Lucio's and Giacinto Andrea Cicognini's *Gl'amori di Alessandro magno, e di Rossane*, at Teatro SS. Apostoli in 1650-51.[74] Since S. Aponal had not been used for opera for several years, the renters were required, as had been Giovanni Faustini, to build *palchi* from scratch, and permission to do so was included in the contract. Ceroni and Diamante apparently had hopes that the theater would continue to present operas even after the three years of the rental, as they agreed to reimburse Enno and Nebbia for the value of the *palchi*, as determined by an outside evaluator, at the termination of the contract. In addition to the annual rent, the owners were to receive, as was standard practice, a box (with its locks and keys) free of charge.

On August 23 Enno and Nebbia reached a formal agreement between themselves regarding the income and expenditures of the theater, a necessity given that they had both begun to expend funds to prepare the season.[75] They agreed that out of the combined income from the rental of the boxes, the food concession, and the sale of librettos, they should first be reimbursed for any expenses either had made, records of which they were each obligated to keep. Any income in excess of these expenditures would be divided between them equally. They also agreed that at the end of the three years of the rental of S. Aponal, the scenery and other apparatus would be appraised and again divided equally. They clearly hoped that the profits would be abundant.

Unfortunately for them, obstacles had already been thrown in their path. Nearly two weeks before their agreement, August 11, Francesco Corner, who had successfully stopped Iseppo Bellato from operating a dance hall in S. Aponal three years earlier, again complained to the Capi of the Council of Ten.[76] Once more he cited the danger of fire, which, he said, had already occurred at two theaters, S. Cassiano and S. Luca, and which would be exceptionally dangerous in the area of Teatro S. Aponal.[77] The theater would be a threat not only to the oil in his warehouse, but

---

[73] Two of the theaters, SS. Giovanni e Paolo and S. Luca, were continuing in operation from previous years. Plans for the season at the Teatro S. Moisè, which had not mounted opera since 1654, had commenced by 30 June; see ASV, Archivio notarile, Atti Giovanni Grandis, b. 6762, f. 12. For Enno and Nebbia, see ASV, Archivio notarile, Atti Camillo Testagrossa, b. 12671, f. 83 [145], 23 July 1665. Teatro S. Cassiano, which had not presented opera since Faustini's departure in 1660, would begin by early October; see ASV, Archivio notarile, Atti Francesco Simbeni, b.12055, f. 208v, 5 October 1665.

[74] On problems with this production, see Beth Glixon, "Music for the Gods?: A Dispute Concerning F. Lucio's *Gl'Amori di Alessandro Magno, e di Rossane* (1651)," *Early Music* 36 (1998): 445-54.

[75] ASV, Archivio notarile, Atti Cristoforo Brombilla, b. 1165, f. 98, 23 August 1665.

[76] ASV, Monastero di SS. Giovanni e Paolo, b. XXV.

[77] The Teatro S. Cassiano had burned down in 1629, and S. Luca in 1652; see Mangini, 36, 51.

to the entire district—one, Corner affirmed, "of narrow streets, rotten buildings, and near a bakery, that is to say, ready to burn, because of the canes and wood found there." He asked that construction of the theater (that is, conversion of the warehouse) be prohibited.

Unidentified persons, perhaps Enno and Nebbia themselves, testified against the prohibition, citing the funds they (referred to as "a company of virtuosi") had already expended and the potential financial benefits (after first overstating the rent they paid, at eighty instead of sixty ducats):

> They have, to this point, spent a great deal in wood and hardware, and it would be a shame to dismantle what they had already done. To repay this, they are content to use what they will gain from the boxes, which are fifty-seven in number, and, rented at twenty ducats each, would yield in total rents about 1200 ducats.[78] From this sum, first of all the rent [of the theater] would be subtracted, and then the other expenses, in wood, hardware, canvas, scene painter, costumes, and other things to be employed to stage the opera, about 600 ducats in all. The remainder (always referring to the income from the boxes) shall be the profit, not only this year, but also in future years, which will be rather considerable, since it will no longer be the case that so many expenses are necessary.[79]

It should be noted that several of the most significant expenditures of an operatic season are not mentioned here: the composer, the singers, and the nightly expenditures for musicians, dancers, extras, and stagehands. Also not mentioned is income from the sale of tickets (*bollettini*). Presumably, Enno and Nebbia hoped that ticket receipts would cover all those musical costs, though the experiences of other impresarios, such as Marco Faustini, should have demonstrated that this was not necessarily a realistic projection.[80]

A later section of the testimony reveals that the impresarios had reached a compromise with Bortolo Grigis, still the owner of the other oil warehouse, in which he would, for the Carnival season, reduce the amount of oil stored there, in exchange for an unspecified payment, one the impresarios were willing to make even though it would have substantially lessened their profits:

> One portion [of the profits] should be for the carpenter, who will thus be satisfied, for labor, wood, hardware, nightly assistance every evening there is a performance, and also to provide a night watchman; another portion would be for the investors [Enno and Nebbia], and the other two would be for the Most Excellent Signor Bortolo Grigis, until the entire agreed upon sum shall be paid. After the period [of the opera season] shall be finished, he shall continue as before without any contradiction, but during those two months of the year keeping as little oil as possible in the warehouse underneath [the theater].[81]

We can only imagine the discussions that might have occurred between Grigis and his niece's husband, who apparently held completely opposite opinions on the relationship between the theater and their oil warehouses. The testimony concludes with information on the opera they planned to perform:

---

[78] Enno and Nebbia apparently planned to increase the number of boxes, from the forty-eight that had been in the theater during the Faustini years, to fifty-seven. Although the boxes would undoubtedly have been smaller, the projected annual rent, twenty ducats each, was unchanged.

[79] "Questi sino hora hanno fatto moltissime spese in legnami et feramenti che sarebbe peccato il disfare quanto da loro fu operato. Per questo si contentano che quello si caverà delli palchi, che sono numero 57, ch'affitandoli a ducati 20 l'uno renderano di affito ducati mille et doi cento in circa. Che primieramente il affito sudetto sii levi et poi tutte le spese che saranno fatte, si di legnami, feramenti, telle, pitore, habbiti, et altre che andassero per meter in cena l'opera, che potrebbe importar in circa ducati seicento. Il resto sarà il guadagno [inserted: "intendendo sempre delli palchi"] si di questo anno, come anco delli anni venturi, qual sarebbe di non poca consideratione mentre non si haverebbe di far più tante spese"—in ASV, Monastero di SS. Giovanni e Paolo, b. XXV.

[80] Even if they were unaware of the specific circumstances of the finances of earlier impresarios, it must have been common knowledge that opera production was a risky business.

[81] "Una parte fusse del marangone, così contentandosi lui per le sue fatture, legname, ordegni, assistenza di assistere ogni sera si recitarà, con farli anco la custodia la notte [inserted: "una altra parte alli interesatti"], le altre tre [changed to "doi"] parte sarebbero del Clarissimo Signor Bortolo Grigis sino al'intiero pagamento di quello si resterà d'accordo. Che fornito il suo tempo debbi lasciar seguitar senza contraditione tenendo in quelli doi mesi del anno meno oglio sii possibile nel magazeno di sotto"—in ASV, Monastero di SS. Giovanni e Paolo, b. XXV.

> The opera that they will present will be Rosane, a work of Cicognini, made most noble, and with all the songs changed.[82]

This "Rosane" was to be a new setting of Cicognini's *Gli amori di Alessandro magno, e di Rossane*, the opera that Enno had had a part in years earlier.

It seems, however, that none of the arguments of the impresarios was successful—not their noting the potential of lost income, not their willingness to compromise with the owner of one of the oil warehouses, not even their mentioning the artistic merits of the proposed opera—and the Capi of the Council of Ten acceded to Corner's request.[83]

Following the failed attempt to revive S. Aponal as an opera theater in 1665, the building began its inevitable, if slow, decline. In 1669, the theater (or at least Ceroni's half) was rented to Angelo Monelli at a rate of forty ducats a year.[84] At some point after that, Ceroni again rented his half of the theater (no mention is made of Diamante) to the Frenchman Monsù Battista for thirty-six ducats a year, eighteen of which in 1673 he assigned to the notary Vincenzo Vincenti in repayment of a debt.[85] The contracts for these two rentals have not turned up, nor have any other indications regarding Monelli's or Battista's plans for the space. However, given that the property in these documents is referred to, respectively, as "il luogo della comedia" and as the "Teatro a S. Aponal," and that the rent is at the higher level normally charged when the building was used as a theater (in contrast to the thirty or forty ducats for both halves when rented as a warehouse), one is tempted to think that it might have continued to serve as a theater of some kind. In any event, Monsù Battista's rental agreement must have been near its end at this point, or was of brief duration, as only three years later, in March 1679, Ceroni and Diamante, once again cooperating, agreed to rent the building, this time to Zuanne Facino, for the small annual sum of twenty-two ducats, "because of the long time, of many years, that it has been empty without being rented to anybody."[86] Facino's contract, again with no purpose indicated, was to last until 1686. It was to be Ceroni's obligation to fix the roof, but the new tenant was obligated to repair the floor and some of the windows, all of which was necessary for the building, now referred to as "the theater, that is, large warehouse" (*il Teatro, sive magazen grande*) to function properly for its intended purpose. This evidence supports the statement of Ivanovich, who, in his chronicle of Venetian theaters in 1681, referred to S. Aponal as "locked up, with little hope of reopening."[87] Also in the 1670s, Ceroni apparently managed to reacquire one of the warehouses, which had been out of his family's control for fifty years, although it is uncertain whether this came about as a long awaited result of his earlier legal actions against Bortolo Grigis or more simply through a direct purchase. In 1677 he rented it for five years (a contract that was renewed through at least 1686) to Zuanne Girardi, a sausage-maker whose shop was also in Corte de Ca' Petrian.[88]

---

[82] "L'opera che si reciterà che sarà la prima sarà la Rosane, opera del Cichognini fatta ancora ch'è nobilissima, et gli sono mutatte tutte le cansoni"—ibid.

[83] We have not yet located a governmental decree banning the operation of the theater, but it is clear the performances never took place. Because Enno had already begun to recruit singers, and since he could not offer them the promised payment, he needed to find other work for them. The heightened competition in that season provided him with an outlet: he approached Marco Faustini, now at the Teatro SS. Giovanni e Paolo, and arranged a contract for two singers, Catterina Masi and Saretta Sabbatini (ASV, SGSM b. 188, f. 64). Enno and Nebbia, however, did not abandon plans for their own production: the following year they rented the Teatro S. Moisè, and presented the opera they had hoped to offer at S. Aponal, although not without considerable difficulty and controversy. Irene Alm introduced new documentary evidence for that production in "A Singer Goes to Court: Virginia Camuffi and the Disaster of *Alessandro amante* (1667)," paper presented at the meeting of the American Musicological Society, Baltimore, November 1996.

[84] Nine months' rent = 92, or thirty ducats, was collected in payment of a debt to Grigis in February 1670—in ASV, Archivio notarile, Atti Pietro Bracchi, b. 907, f. 374.

[85] ASV, Archivio notarile, Atti Francesco Simbeni, b. 12063, f. 331, 13 October 1673. "Monsù" is the usual Italian colloquial form of the French "monsieur."

[86] ASV, Archivio notarile, Atti Iseppo Bellan, b. 1342, 24 March 1679.

[87] ". . . ora è serrato con poca speranza di riaprirsi." Ivanovich, *Minerva al tavolino*, 400, as cited in Mancini, Muraro, and Povoledo, *I Teatri di Venezi. Teatri effimeri*, 378.

[88] ASV, Archivio notarile, Atti Giovanni Antonio Generini, b. 6799, f. 441, 21 October 1677 and ibid., Atti Raffaele Todeschini, b. 12769, f. 134, 4 July 1682. The documentary situation surrounding these properties is complicated by the presence in Corte de Ca' Petrian of other warehouses, unconnected with the theater, owned by either Ceroni or Girardi, and, in one case, rented by Girardi from Ceroni.

The plans of the owners to resurrect the theater one last time in 1696 were cut short before they bore fruit, once again on account of oil. By this date, the oil warehouses (or at least one of them) had become a "doganetta publica" (apparently a small clearinghouse for oil), and its directors, fearful, as had been their predecessors, of fire, appealed successfully to the Council of Ten to ban the proposed theatrical performances.[89] By 1713 the doganetta, owned now by one Giovanni Terzi, was vacant, although it had usually rented for fifty ducats annually, a large figure that—especially in light of the fact that neither the theater nor any other warehouse appears in the listings of properties in Corte de Ca' Petrian at this date—might imply that the entire building was now included.[90] Another possibility is raised by the appearance of only one property in the Corte associated with the name Ceroni: a house rented by Ceroni's sons Giovanni Pietro and Giacomo to a certain Piero Dazii for the familiar sum of sixty ducats—perhaps the theater was now a house.[91] In the tax census for 1740 not only are the theater and warehouses gone, but so also is the large house previously owned by Ceroni's heirs. In its place were several smaller houses owned by the Tassis family, who possessed a number of properties in the Corte.[92] This corresponds with the statement of Carlo Bonlini, who wrote in 1730 that the area of the theater had become small dwellings, owned by the Tassis family.[93] As had been the case for most of its life, the death of the Teatro Sant'Aponal was a modest event—there was no spectacular fire or sudden collapse, just a gradual decline and a final reabsorption into the Venetian fabric out of which it had emerged a century earlier.

---

[89] ASV, Compilazione leggi, b. 138, f. 148 (26 September 1696), as cited in Mangini, 69. The document does not make specific reference to the owners of the theater.

[90] ASV, Dieci savi sopra le decime in Rialto, b. 430, S. Aponal no. 31: "Doanetta d'oglio, hora non affittata, di raggione del Signor Domino Zuanne Terzi, e si affitta————D.50:—."

[91] Ibid., no. 39. This volume also contains one other remnant of the earlier episodes of the story, one property in the nearby Campo dei Meloni owned by the heirs of "Nobil Donna Elisabetta Grigis Corner," the oil merchant's niece who became a noblewoman.

[92] ASV, Dieci savi sopra le decime in Rialto, b. 437, S. Aponal.

[93] Mancini, Muraro, and Povoledo, *I Teatri di Venezia. Imprese private*, 364. In his *Le glorie della poesia e della musica* (Venice, [1730]), Carlo Bonlini wrote that the area of the theater had become small dwellings, owned by the Tassis family; see pp. 23-24.

9

The Influence of Architect and Playwright Sir John Vanbrugh and His Musical Taste on the London Stage, 1696-1711

CAROLINE S. FRUCHTMAN

John Vanbrugh (1663-1726) exerted a significant influence on the changing tastes of London theatergoers during the first decade of the eighteenth century. Most famous for his great houses of Blenheim, Castle Howard, and the Queen's Theatre in the Haymarket, Vanbrugh also wrote nine plays, the ninth completed after his death by Colley Cibber. All were published. Only two of his comedies produced during his lifetime are entirely original, the rest are adaptation-translations of existing dramas. For the dozen years following the run of his first play, he was, to quote Arthur Huseboe, "an indispensible part of the London stage," serving in a variety of capacities, as author of plays, theatre architect, manager of a theatre company, and opera impresario.[1]

Vanbrugh's reputation as a Restoration playwright rests most securely on his two original plays: *The Relapse* (1696), written and staged as a sequel to Cibber's *Love's Last Shift* (1696), and *The Provok'd Wife* (1697). These successful comedies augured a promising career as a dramatist for the recently released prisoner from France, who had been held for a time in the Bastille. Indeed, during the short interval 1696-1705, when all his plays but the last were on London stages, Vanbrugh was considered, with Etherege, Wycherley, Congreve, and Farquhar, as one of the most skilled writers of the comedy of manners then in vogue.[2] At the same time, Vanbrugh, who was a friend or acquaintance of some of the most powerful and wealthy figures in the government, held posts and sinecures that prepared him to choose architecture as a profession and to abandon his work as a playwright.[3] Three years after the production of his first play, *The Relapse*, Vanbrugh was appointed architect to Charles Howard, the third Earl of Carlisle, and in 1702 he was appointed Comptroller of His Majesty's Works.

Almost as a sideline to Vanbrugh's multifarious career, and pursued while Comptroller to His Majesty's Works, and at the height of his popularity as a dramatist, was his role in bringing Italian-style opera to London audiences. In the context of Vanbrugh's other career activities, this rather minor pursuit has seized the attention of scholars in the present century, especially theater historians who have questioned Vanbrugh's judgment as theater manager and promoter of Italianate opera sung throughout—efforts they claim hastened the demise of the English style of dramatic opera.[4] There is yet another aspect of Vanbrugh's extraordinary career that reflects transition in the theater, and that is his gradual relinquishing of songs and dances within the acts of the plays he created—it is almost as if there is a calculated decrease in music present in the succession of stage pieces. This observation, though of less importance

---

[1] *Sir John Vanbrugh* (Boston: G. K. Hall, 1976), 28, 116-32, passim.

[2] Gerald M. Berkowitz, *Sir John Vanbrugh and the End of Restoration Comedy* (Amsterdam: Rodopi, 1981), i.

[3] After his return to England from imprisonment in France, Vanbrugh joined the Kit-Cat Club, "... among whose aristocratic members he was to find his most enthusiastic patrons for the building projects which he would undertake beginning in 1699." See Frank McCormick, *Sir John Vanbrugh: The Playwright as Architect* (University Park: Pennsylvania State University Press, 1991), 17.

[4] Robert D. Hume, "The Sponsorship of Opera in London, 1704-1720," *Modern Philology* 85, no. 4 (1988): 420-32, voices the most ardent and persuasive criticism of Vanbrugh's judgment in the period he was the manager of the Queen's Theatre, 1705-08.

to architecture historians, adds one more piece of evidence supporting Vanbrugh as a key figure who stimulated, and also reflected, a fluctuating fashion in the performance arts in London at the turn-of-the-eighteenth-century.

* * * * *

There is documentation for examining Vanbrugh's multiple careers, from the time he was a prisoner in France accused of espionage in 1689-93, to his service in the military, his careers as playwright, Comptroller of His Majesty's [Public] Works, Clarenceux herald in the College of Arms, architect for the building or remodeling of more than a dozen great houses, and architect and manager of the Queen's Theatre in the Haymarket. The records include the following categories: 1) more than 250 surviving letters—invaluable for their detailed information on building projects, references to governmental affairs, prominent individuals, the antagonism between Vanbrugh and the Duchess of Marlborough concerning aesthetic and fiscal issues during the building of Blenheim Castle, and Vanbrugh's close friendship with the Earl of Carlisle over the twenty years of the construction of Castle Howard;[5] 2) theater documents preserved by Sir Thomas Coke, Vice-Chamberlain and primary overseer of theatrical matters (1706-27) during the tenure of Lord Chamberlain Henry Grey, Earl of Kent;[6] 3) the views of contemporaries concerning Vanbrugh as a playwright and as an architect;[7] 4) seventeenth- and eighteenth-century commentaries on music in London theaters (stage plays, English dramatic operas, Italianate operas).[8]

The present study takes a look at John Vanbrugh's evolving careers in the light of how his career choices came to affect theater music in London in one of the most turbulent times in the history of English drama. To aid in reining in the "mettlesome horses"[9] of Vanbrugh's careers, the appendix gives a chronology of important events in his life, focusing on the years when he was most identified with London theaters, 1696-1711.[10] Included in the listing are titles of works and details concerning productions—some with no connection to Vanbrugh—to illustrate the variety of musical offerings in the theaters of Drury Lane/Dorset Garden, Lincoln's Inn Fields (1695-1705), and Vanbrugh's

---

[5] See *The Complete Works of Sir John Vanbrugh* (Bloomsbury: Nonesuch Press, 1928), vol. 4: *The* [234 numbered] *Letters*, ed. Geoffrey Webb; Arthur R. Huseboe, "Additions to Vanbrugh's Correspondence," *Philological Quarterly* 53 (1974): 135-40; Albert Rosenberg, "New Light on Vanbrugh [eight letters]," *Philological Quarterly* 45 (1966): 606-13.

[6] The documents are available in a modern edition; see Judith Milhous and Robert D. Hume, eds., *Vice Chamberlain Coke's Theatrical Papers 1706-1715, Edited from the Manuscripts in the Harvard Theatre Collection and Elsewhere* (Carbondale: Southern Illinois University Press, 1982), 1-122; also see Milhous, "New Light on Vanbrugh's Haymarket Theatre Project," *Theatre Survey* 17 (November, 1976): 143-61.

[7] For some contemporary views, see Arthur S. Huseboe, "Pope's Critical Views of the London Stage," *Restoration and Eighteenth-Century Theatre Research* 3 (May 1964): 25-37; Colley Cibber, *An Apology for the Life of Colley Cibber*, ed. B. R. S. Fone (Ann Arbor: UMI Press, 1968); McCormick, *Sir John Vanbrugh*; Kerry Downes, *Sir John Vanbrugh: A Biography* (New York: St. Martin's Press, 1987); Laurence Whistler, *Sir John Vanbrugh, Architect and Dramatist* (New York: Macmillan, 1939); *The Complete Works of Sir John Vanbrugh*, vols. 1-3, ed. Bonomy Dobree; Graham F. Barlow, "Vanbrugh's Queen's Theatre in the Haymarket, 1703-1709," *Early Music* 17 (November 1989): 515-21.

[8] Excerpts from some of the commentaries are published in the following studies: Curtis Price, *Music in the Restoration Theatre* (Ann Arbor: UMI Research Press, 1979), ch. 5, which concerns the infiltration of Italian opera and imbroglios of theatrical companies that plagued London stages during the first decade of the eighteenth century; Roger Fiske, *English Theatre Music in the Eighteenth Century* (London: Oxford University Press, 1986), chs. 1 and 2; Lowell Lindgren, "*Camilla* and *The Beggar's Opera*," *Philological Quarterly* 59 (1980): 45-61; Philip Olleson, "Vanbrugh and Opera at the Queen's Theatre, Haymarket," *Theatre Notebook* 26 (spring 1972): 94-101.

[9] Madeleine Bingham, *Masks and Facades* (London: George Allen & Unwin, 1974), 142.

[10] The order of the chronological events is indebted to Geoffrey Beard, *The Works of John Vanbrugh, Illustrated by Anthony Kersting* (New York: Universe Books, 1986), 70-73. The only plays listed in the chronology are by Vanbrugh except for the play by Cibber that inspired Vanbrugh's first theater production. Most of my additions to the information in Beard's chronology concern operatic productions at London theaters. Titles, names of librettists, translators, arrangers, composers, and dates of English dramatic operas and of Italian operas performed during this period were culled from the following: D. F. Cook, "Françoise Marguerite de l'Epine: The Italian Lady?" *Theatre Notebook* 35 (1981): 58-69 and 104-13; Fiske, *English Theatre Music*, chs. 1 and 2; Todd S. Gilman, "Augustan Criticism and Changing Conceptions of English Opera," *Theatre Survey* 36, no. 2 (November 1995): 1-35; Hume, "The Sponsorship"; Lindgren, "*Camilla* and *The Beggar's Opera*"; *The London Stage 1600-1800: A Calendar of Plays*, ed. William Van Lennep, Emmett L. Avery, Arthur H. Scouten, G. Winchester Stone Jr., and C.B. Hogan (Carbondale: Southern Illinois University Press, 1960-68), vol. 1: *1660-1700*, and vol. 2: *1700-1729*; Richard Luckett, "Exotic but Rational Entertainments: The English Dramatic Operas," in *English Drama: Forms and Development*, ed. Marie Axton and Raymond Williams (London: Cambridge University Press, 1977), 123-41; Milhous and Hume, *Vice Chamberlain Coke's Theatrical Papers*; Donald Mullin, "The Queen's Theatre, Haymarket: Vanbrugh's Opera House," *Theatre Survey* 6 (November 1967): 84-105; Olleson, "Vanbrugh and Opera"; Price, *Music in the Restoration Theatre*.

Queen's Theatre during the period. In order of importance in Vanbrugh's life, undoubtedly his profession as an architect comes first. The next in importance to posterity is his career writing stage plays, then the influences he exerted as comptroller of works and member of the Greenwich Hospital board, and, lastly, the most controversial, the decisions he made as theater manager and impresario.

The first evidence of Vanbrugh's interest in architecture is in a letter he wrote 25 December 1699 to Charles Montague, fourth Earl (later Duke) of Manchester:

> I have been this Summer at my Ld Carlisle's, and Seen most of the great houses in the North, as Ld Nottings [Daniel Finch, 1647-1730, 2nd Earl of Nottingham and Secretary of State]; Duke of Leeds [Thomas Osborne, 1631-1712, 1st Duke of Leeds and father of Peregrine Osborne, who was Vice-Chamberlain 1694-1706 and briefly Vanbrugh's partner at the Queen's Theatre]; Chattesworth [William Cavendish, 1640-1707, 1st Duke of Devonshire] &c. I stay'd at Chattesworth four or five days. . . . I shew'd him all my Ld Carlisle's designs. . . . He absolutely approved the whole design. . . .[11]

Lord Manchester (1656-1722) was ambassador to Venice (1697), to Paris (1699), and again to Venice (July 1707-October 1708). It was during this second stay in Venice that he attended a performance of Handel's opera *Agrippina* and invited the young composer to visit the English court.[12] About the same time he employed Vanbrugh to rebuild Kimbolton Castle. There was another Charles Montague (1661-1715), Earl of Halifax, who was Chancellor of the Exchequer and ambassador to the Elector's court in Hanover, First Lord of the Treasury; he was also a friend of Vanbrugh. The man for whom Vanbrugh had drawn the designs referred to in the letter to Manchester was Charles Howard (1669-1738), third Earl of Carlisle and Lord Treasurer. He had engaged William Talman (architect for Chatsworth) to build a great house on the site of one burned down at the family estate near York. They were unable to agree on financial terms, and Carlisle replaced Talman with Vanbrugh, who at that time had not designed any buildings. That Carlisle, in planning a grandiose castle, would place his trust in an untried builder is an early indication of Vanbrugh's ability to inspire confidence.

Vanbrugh's stature as successful playwright (with three plays) and member (with Carlisle) of the Kit-Cat club gave him an entrée to potential patrons that more experienced builders lacked. He also benefited from an association with Nicholas Hawksmoor (1661-1736), an experienced architect who was a protegé and assistant to Sir Christopher Wren. The preparatory elevations for Castle Howard are in Hawksmoor's hand. We know that in 1700 Vanbrugh indicated to Carlisle that Hawksmoor ". . . [is] a man of experience in dealing with builders and craftsmen. . . ."[13] Concurrently with beginning construction of Castle Howard (1701), Vanbrugh staged his fifth play, an adaptation of Fletcher's *The Pilgrim* (1700). He also started to build for himself in Whitehall what Swift dubbed "Goose Pie House" (1696).[14] In the following year he produced his sixth play (an adaptation), *The False Friend*. He was also appointed Comptroller of His Majesty's Works, and it is known that he discussed with Kit-Cat members a plan to build a theater in the Haymarket (see chronology), a project that would take another three years to complete. That same year (1705) Vanbrugh was appointed architect for Blenheim Palace.

In January 1705, Queen Anne granted John Churchill the estate of the Royal Manor of Woodstock, famous in English history for its occupancy by Fair Rosamond, the mistress of Henry II, in the twelfth century. On June 9 Lord

---

[11] Webb, *Letters*, 4-5. In the same letter is also mention of opera: "Liveridge [Leveridge, singer and composer] is in Ireland, he owes so much money he dare not come over, so for want of him we han't had one Opera play'd this Winter; tho' [Daniel] Purcell has set one New One [? John Oldmixon's *The Grove, or, Love's Paradice*, DL, 1700] and Fingar another [? *The Rival Queens, or the Death of Alexander the Great*, DL, 1701, dramatic opera with music by Daniel Purcell and Godfrey Finger].

[12] H. C. Robbins Landon, *Handel and His World* (London: Weidenfeld & Nicolson, 1984), 54-55.

[13] Until about the mid-eighteenth century the architecture profession in the modern sense did not exist; on this point, see John Summerson, *Georgian London*, 3rd ed. (Cambridge: MIT Press, 1978), 70, cited in McCormick, *Sir John Vanbrugh*, 150, n. 42. Hawksmoor is given credit as co-architect with Vanbrugh of Castle Howard, Blenheim Castle, and Easton Neston; see Kerry Downes, *Hawksmoor* (New York & Washington: Praeger, 1969), 9-47, passim. Speculation about stylistic influences on Vanbrugh's architecture has ranged from Palladian (Downes, Beard, Whistler, Summerson), to medieval "bastion"; to French, especially the Chateau at Vincennes where Vanbrugh was incarcerated briefly before he was sent to the Bastille (McCormick, Summerson).

[14] Jonathan Swift, "Van's House/Built from the Ruins of Whitehall that was Burnt" (1703), quoted in Whistler, 304-07.

Treasurer Godolphin (whose son had married John Churchill's daughter) "at the request and desire of the said Duke of Marlborough," signed a warrant appointing John Vanbrugh surveyor of all the works and buildings which the duke had "resolv'd to erect" at Woodstock, the gift from a grateful nation for Marlborough's victory at the decisive battle of Blenheim.[15] Vanbrugh's conception of his assignment is expressed in his letter of 30 September 1710 to Lord Poulett, a later Lord Treasurer:

> . . . I found it the Opinion of all people & of all partys I convers'd with, that altho the Building was to be calculat'd for, and Adapted to, a private Habitation, Yet it ought at ye same time, to be consider'd as both a Royall and a National Monument . . . that it might have ye. Qualitys proper to such a Monument, Vizt. Beauty Magnificence, and Duration. . . .[16]

Throughout the eleven years Vanbrugh worked at Blenheim, the Duchess of Marlborough, Sarah Churchill, was a vociferous critic of the designs, procedures, and especially the exorbitant costs of the work. Reaching the limit of his patience, unable to secure proper and timely wages for the workmen, and with little prospect of collecting his own fees, Vanbrugh resigned from the project. Blenheim Palace was later completed by Hawksmoor between 1722 and 1725. The Duchess was the only client with whom Vanbrugh fell out of favor. All his other building projects ran on concurrently with his other enterprises, and his relations with other patrons remained amicable.[17] John Summerson refers to Blenheim:

> At Blenheim the English Baroque culminates. Vanbrugh was to build, or remodel, some seven or eight more great houses, and one or two . . . are perhaps even more surprisingly original. But Blenheim is inexhaustible and represents the whole varied mind of its creator—and of Hawksmoor his collaborator. . . . Blenheim is both a palace and a castle. The massive pavilions with their arched attics give that impression . . . [and] Vanbrugh had a feeling . . . for the qualities of the medieval fortress. When he remodelled Kimbolton Castle for Lord Manchester and Lumley for Lord Scarborough he enjoyed the experience of merging his own weighty classic with the massiveness of a Gothic fortress, and he liked to pretend [his own house at Greenwich] was a Bastille.[18]

Several deductions may be made concerning Vanbrugh's position in London during these crucial years. First, he was under obligation to several patrons and potential supporters for commissions to build houses and for his sinecure in His Majesty's Works. There were forty-eight members of the elite Kit-Cat Club, a society of men who by and large favored the Whig party and were against any meddling by royals or the papacy in British affairs.[19] Most of their portraits, painted by Sir Godfrey Kneller, are now in the National Gallery in London. Along with Vanbrugh's portrait are those of several landowners who commissioned him to build or remodel their great houses: the Duke of Marlborough (Blenheim), the third Earl of Carlisle (Castle Howard), the Earl of Halifax (Kimbolton), the Earl of Clare, later Duke of Newcastle (Claremont), and the Earl of Scarborough (Lumley Castle). In addition to these friends and patrons, Vanbrugh also had some contact with the Lords Chamberlain (appointees of the crown to operate the royal household), whose duties included supervising London's theaters. The actual day-to-day dealing with theater matters was the responsibility of the Vice-Chamberlain. From 1704 to 1710 Henry Grey, Earl of Kent, was Lord Chamberlain; his vice-chamberlains were Peregrine Bertie (1694-1706), third Earl of Lindsey (later second Duke of Leeds), long-time friend and distant cousin to Vanbrugh, and Thomas Coke (1706-27).[20] Vanbrugh's obligations to, and association with, these influential individuals in the private sector and government were most demanding precisely at a time when he was staging his own plays and supervising the construction of Castle Howard.

---

[15] Beard, 38.

[16] Webb, 45.

[17] A lengthy account of Vanbrugh's involvement with Blenheim Palace, and the travails he endured with the Duchess of Marlborough, is in Bingham, 162-318, passim.

[18] John Summerson, *Architecture in Britain, 1530 to 1830*, 4th rev. ed. (Harmondsworth: Penguin Books, 1963), 166-67.

[19] Bingham, 88-99.

[20] Milhous and Hume, xxiv-xxix.

A second aspect of Vanbrugh's propulsion into a position of influence was his awareness of innovations in the theater. It was a time when Italian opera began to compete seriously with English dramatic opera ("semi-opera") in London. The most enthusiastic supporters of Italian opera in England were mainly from the wealthier classes and the nobility, along with theatergoers who were familiar with opera on the continent. These were the patrons of Vanbrugh and of his fellow Kit-Catters, William Congreve, Charles Addison, and Richard Steele. Vanbrugh's personal preference for Italian opera is difficult to document before he planned his theater, but he was privy to the artistic tastes of his supporters. By proposing the need for a new theater he could satisfy his own desire to build and also provide a venue that would appeal to devotees of Italian opera. London, unlike other European capitals, never had an opera house. English dramatic operas, from their early appearances in the 1670s, were performed under the auspices of the patent theater companies.

The earliest reference to a new London theater is in a letter Vanbrugh wrote to Jacob Tonson (another Kit-Cat member) on 13 July 1703: "I have drawn a design for the whole disposition of the [theater's] inside, very different from any Other House in being. . . ."[21] Dorset Garden Theatre (designed by Wren, 1671) had always been the most suitable venue for mounting large productions, but was then in need of remodeling. Vanbrugh and William Congreve had reason to believe that the time was ripe for London to have a house large enough to mount elaborate stage productions and that would be suitable for Italian vocal performances.[22] They went ahead with plans to build the first new theater in London since the construction of Sir Thomas Wren's Theatre Royal (in Drury Lane) in 1674. In the article describing his reconstruction based on Vanbrugh's original designs for the playhouse, Graham Barlow has written a brief summary of how the new theater came to be:

> The theatre was built to house the company currently under the direction of Thomas Betterton performing at . . . Lincoln's Inn Fields. They had occupied this theatre since 1695 when they seceded from the United Company which operated from both the Theatre Royal in Drury Lane and the Duke's Theatre, Dorset Garden [the last two under one management]. . . . Vanbrugh raised the capital by prevailing upon 29 wealthy aristocrats and fellow members of the Whig Kit-Cat Club to covenant 100 guineas each towards the project.[23]

The theater project was controversial from the beginning on several fronts. For one, Christopher Rich, manager of the theaters in Drury Lane and Dorset Garden, recognized the potential competition and produced Clayton's *Arsinoe, Queen of Cyprus*, an Italianate opera that Vanbrugh's company had scheduled for the opening of the new theater. Also significant, Vanbrugh, Betterton, and Congreve had difficulty raising the number of subscriptions to make the enterprise financially viable. Further, the building was not completed by the date anticipated. And, most damaging, the new playhouse had considerable deficiencies in its design. Many years after the completion of the theater (fall 1705), and after its remodeling (1708-09), Colly Cibber wrote his often-quoted remarks on the theater's acoustics:

> . . . at the first opening it, the flat ceiling, that is now [after alteration] over the orchestra, was then a semi-oval arch that sprung fifteen feet higher from above the cornice: the ceiling over the pit, too, was still more raised, being one level line from the highest back part of the upper gallery to the front of the stage. . . . The tone of a trumpet, or the swell of an eunuch's holding note, 'tis true, might be sweetened by it; but the articulate sounds of a speaking voice were drowned by the hollow reverberations of one word upon another.[24]

---

[21] Webb, 9. The most thorough study of the theater's architectural design is Barlow, "Vanbrugh's Queen's Theatre in the Haymarket." The following are indispensible sources for anyone attempting to sort out the causes and effects of the intrigues and bitter competition in playhouse management: Milhous, "New Light on Vanbrugh's Haymarket"; Hume, "The Sponsorship"; Milhous and Hume, *Vice-Chamberlain Coke's Papers*; and Price, *Music in the Restoration Theatre*.

[22] London already had "operatic spectaculars," such as *The Tempest, The Prophetess*, and Henry Purcell's semi-operas that were performed at Dorset Garden. Most of these shows seem to have succeeded in covering even their extravagant expenses; see Hume, 421.

[23] Barlow, 516.

[24] Cibber, *An Apology*, quoted in Mullin, 87-88.

Graham Barlow has suggested that Vanbrugh intentionally designed a multi-purpose theater that would accommodate stage plays, and would have the capacity (ca. 900 seats) and the grandeur for producing operatic spectacles:

> The structure that emerges [from Barlow's calculations] reflects the extent to which Vanbrugh was influenced by classical and Palladian theatre architecture. . . . This is particularly demonstrated in Vanbrugh's method of relating both parts of the house—stage and auditorium—to create an aesthetically satisfying, unified architectural structure that would in its own terms echo the harmony of the music to be performed within its walls. . . .[25]

The first performance in the new Queen's Theatre, *Gli Amori d'Ergasto* on 9 April 1705 (see the chronology), was not a success, in part because the theater was not finished. But there were other reasons: the all-sung opera was performed in Italian by imported Italian singers, and the work itself, and the cast's performance, were received "indifferently by the gentry."[26]

The year 1705 appears to have been a critical juncture both in the annals of opera in England and in the biography of Vanbrugh. As mentioned above, Christopher Rich had preempted Vanbrugh's plan to mount the first all-sung opera, and in January had produced *Arsinoe*, set to music by Clayton and sung by English singers in English. By April at the unfinished Queen's Theatre, Vanbrugh, Congreve, and Owen Swiney managed to put on only five performances of the inaugural *Gli Amori d'Ergasto*. Over the next several months Vanbrugh attempted unsuccessfully to persuade Christopher Rich and the vice-chamberlain to agree to merge the Drury Lane and Queen's theater companies. Meanwhile on June 18 the foundation-stone for Blenheim was laid at Woodstock. In the same month, the Vanbrugh company of Betterton and actors moved back to Lincoln's Inn Fields Theatre to work until the Queen's Theatre was ready for occupancy. William Congreve withdrew from the management partnership with Vanbrugh in December, having lost more money in the project than he could sustain.[27]

As the prolonged theater crisis neared its culmination, the rival playhouse managers (Rich at DL/DG and Vanbrugh-Swiney at QT) attempted to predict which type of stage fare would be most popular with the majority of the limited number of theatergoers: plays with incidental music (overtures and music between acts, and often also songs and dance music within acts), English dramatic operas (incorporating scenes of dialogue and scenes of all-sung entertainments), or all-sung Italianate spectacles in Italian or in translation, these apparently more favored by wealthy subscribers. As Robert Hume has pointed out, financial security of the two patent theaters was not to be solved by creating one theater exclusively for operas:

> We can only wonder what demon of perversity had seized Vanbrugh that he should imagine a separate opera company to be financially viable. . . . Opera had never been performed night after night . . . [and] in divorcing music from theatre Vanbrugh was separating his company from the entire repertory of semi-opera [dramatic opera], which obviously could not be performed without actors [implying that opera singers were incapable of taking speaking roles].[28]

For the 1705-06 season the playhouses continued to compete, both staging musical productions and straight plays. In the following season Vice-Chamberlain Coke issued the decree permitting DL/DG to produce plays and operas and limiting the Queen's Theatre to plays with *no* music. During the summer of 1706 Vanbrugh spent a month in Hanover. As Clarenceux King of Arms, he and Lord Halifax, ambassador to the court of Hanover, were appointed by Queen Anne to invest then Prince Elector (afterwards George II) with the Order of the Garter. In August 1706 Vanbrugh turned over the management of his playhouse to Owen Swiney, though he continued to seek either a union of both theaters or a monopoly in the staging of opera for the Queen's Theatre. The division along genre lines between the two theaters prevailed until 31 December 1707, when Lord Chamberlain Kent ordered:

---

[25] Barlow, 516.

[26] John Downes, *Roscius Anglicanus (1708)*, ed. Montague Summers (New York & London: Benjamin Blom, 1929; reprint, 1968), 48.

[27] Milhous and Hume, xx.

[28] Hume, 422.

> That all Operas and other Musicall presentments be perform'd for the future only at her Majesty's Theatre in the Hay Market . . . and I do hereby strictly charge and forbid . . . from and after the 10th day of January next [1708] to represent any Comedys Tragedys or other Entertainments of ye Stage that are not set to Musick. . . .[29]

Now that his theater in the Haymarket was given the monopoly for opera, Vanbrugh repurchased his interest from Swiney (January 1708) and resumed negotiations with Italian soloists under contract, including the celebrated castrato Valentino Urbani. On February 24 he wrote to Lord Manchester, ambassador in Venice:

> I'll . . . Acqaint y^r Ldship, that at last I got the Duke of Marlbor: to put an end to the Playhouse Factions, by engaging the queen to exert her Authority, by means of which, the Actors are all put under the Patent at Coventgarden House [Theatre Royal at Drury Lane], And the Operas are Establish'd at the Haymarket. . . . This Settlement pleases so well, that people are now eager to See Operas carry'd to a greater perfection, And in order to it the Towne crys out for a Man and Woman of the First Rate to be got against Next Winter from Italy. But at the Same time they declare for the future against Subscriptions, and have not come into any this Winter . . . [also] to Acquaint you, that if Nicolini and Santini will come Over (my Ld Hallifax telling me this morning y^r L^{dsh} very much desired they shou'd) I'll venture as far as A Thousand Pounds between 'em . . . if you please to give your Self the trouble of making the Agreement.[30]

Ever optimistic, Vanbrugh confided in the same letter that, because they had not raised sufficient subscriptions to support opera expenses, he had appealed to Marlborough to request financial help from the Queen. He had reason to think there would be a positive response from the Lord Treasurer, but a royal subsidy was not forthcoming. However, Lord Manchester did respond to Vanbrugh's request to engage singers from Italy: Niccolino Grimaldi, a male soprano, arrived in England in the fall of 1708 as part of Lord Manchester's entourage returning from Italy.[31] "Nicolini" enjoyed popular acclaim, notably in *Rinaldo*, Handel's first opera performed in England in 1711.[32] From January through May Vanbrugh resumed his managerial duties, and the Queen's Theatre staged three major operatic productions (see chronology). He was unable to prevent further financial losses, and in May 1708 he once again leased his opera house to Swiney.[33]

London now had an opera house designed, and briefly managed, by England's greatest Baroque architect, and it was not effective for spoken drama or English dramatic opera with dialogue, though in size it was as large as any Italian theater of the time, and its acoustic "responsive to trained Italian voices."[34] In 1709, the unique theater in the Haymarket was altered to correct its imperfections: the width of the interior was lessened by the addition of boxes on each side and the very high ceiling was lowered to remedy the complaint of excessive reverberation, though its physical beauty was compromised. Managers of the Queen's Theatre continued to incur financial liabilities for the remainder of its existence. One of the better known examples of its insolvency occurred in the period 1720-28, when it served as the venue for some of Handel's best operas—productions sponsored by the Royal Academy of Music. Ironically, the end of Vanbrugh's opera house came when a disgruntled Italian singer set it ablaze in 1789.[35]

Vanbrugh's efforts to save the new playhouse from financial disaster had included the staging of his *The Confederacy* (30 October 1705) as the featured play for the first full season after the company moved back into the recently completed Queen's Theatre. Interspersed with operatic productions of the 1705-06 season were his *The Mistake* (December 1705) and a revival, in January 1706, of *The Provok'd Wife* (May 1697). All three plays helped the playhouse to survive for

---

[29] Ibid., 49.
[30] Webb, 16-17; see also Milhous and Hume, 83-84, for "Vanbrugh's Proposal for Subsidy by the Queen," 21 February 1708.
[31] Olleson, 100.
[32] Webb, 257.
[33] Milhous and Hume, 106.
[34] Luckett, 139.
[35] Mullin, 104; Barlow, 520.

that first season, but could not avert the Queen's Theatre from its mounting financial difficulties.[36] *The Mistake* was the eighth and last of the full-length plays Vanbrugh wrote or adapted, except for the uncompleted *Journey to London*, finished by Cibber and successfully staged in 1728 as *The Provok'd Husband*. It is likely his activities in the world of theater as a builder and impresario helped bring to a halt his playwriting. During the last three years of his theater career (1705-08) he was also supervising the construction of Castle Howard in Yorkshire and Blenheim Palace at Woodstock near Oxford, agreeing to design and supervise alterations to Audley End in Essex, and to rebuild Kimbolton in Cambridgeshire.[37] The physical exertion and distances involved in traveling between locations left little time for writing and staging plays.

* * * * *

Sir John Vanbrugh's first play, *The Relapse, or, Virtue by Danger: Being the Sequel of The Fool in Fashion*, was representative of the successful comedies staged in London theaters at the end of the Restoration. It opened at the Drury Lane Theatre 2 November 1696 with a generally young cast comfortable with a less traditional mode of acting, one more realistic and suitable to Vanbrugh's often breezy text.[38] Eight money-making productions (except, perhaps, the first run of his *The Country House*) in nine years assured his reputation as a playwright. As someone whose plays came after Wycherley's comedies of manners and before Richard Steele's full-blown sentimental comedies, Vanbrugh is understandably labeled as a transitional figure. But he was not unassertive, or, as Gerald Berkowitz has put it, "not a passively transitional figure, but an active instigator and shaper of . . . changes [in dramatic style]. Both Vanbrugh and Farquhar, without sacrificing comedy or lapsing into sentimental moralizing, give serious consideration to moral and psychological problems. . . . It would be an overstatement to assert that he caused the transition, but it is important to see that he helped to shape it, and indeed, to make it possible."[39] Vanbrugh denied the sentimentality of Cibber's *The Fool in Fashion* where the virtuous heroine converts her dissolute husband by "appealing to his feelings and reducing him to tears." In Vanbrugh's *The Relapse*, the sequel to Cibber's play, the husband returns to his libertine ways and "the world, stripped of sentimental gloss, is shown in its true colors. . . ."[40] His third produced play, *The Provok'd Wife*, probably written while Vanbrugh was in prison, is another example that reveals his interest in social and ethical issues of the day, particularly as these affected the aristocracy whose social morals and predicaments he was familiar with through his patrons. The play deals with two main social problems: a younger brother's difficult circumstances due to the law of primogeniture, and marital incompatibility.[41]

In addition to reflecting social problems of contemporary society, Vanbrugh's plays also reflect the playhouse audience's changing musical tastes. From the beginning of the Restoration period, the spoken play contained, in addition to incidental music played before the first act and between successive acts, dances and songs within the acts performed by professional singers (playing small roles) and often by the dramatic actors themselves. A theater that put on plays in London was expected to be "as much a concert hall as it was . . . for the presentation of spoken drama," for, in the words of Curtis Price, "the audience expected the music to be . . . ever-changing as the plays in which it appeared."[42] In some plays the playwright might include stage directions that merely indicated, "A Song" or "Musick Without," and the actors or stage managers made the appropriate musical selections. When a song poem was written in the play by its author, it was more likely to be given a musical setting by a composer accustomed to working in the theater, for example, John Eccles, Henry Purcell, Daniel Purcell, Godfrey Finger, or others writing for

---

[36] Huseboe, 56.

[37] Beard, 84-134, passim.

[38] The cast included Colley Cibber, the author and one of the actors in *The Fool in Fashion*, with actresses Kent, Rogers, Cross, Powell, and actors Powell, Bullock, Mills, and veterans Doggett and Jo Haines. See *The Relapse*, ed. Curt A. Zimansky (Lincoln: University of Nebraska Press, 1970), xiv.

[39] Berkowitz, ii-23, passim.

[40] *Twelve Famous Plays of the Restoration and the Eighteenth Century*, with an introduction by Cecil A. Moore (New York: Modern Library, 1933), xvi-xvii.

[41] Paul Mueschke and Jeannette Fleisher, "A Re-evaluation of Vanbrugh," *Publications of the Modern Language Association of America* 49 (1934): 848-89, quoted in Berkowitz, 126, n. 6.

[42] Price, 94-112, passim.

the theater. By the end of the century (around 1700), there was growing interest in Italian instrumental music played at public concerts, in venues such as the York Building. Concomitantly with the advent of public concerts and declining enthusiasm for plays overloaded with music, there was increasing audience interest in dramatic operas and, as we have seen, in Italian all-sung operatic productions. Playwrights were less obligated to include directions for songs and instrumental music in their plays. Traditional masques declined in importance, and masque-like entertainments survived as autonomous pieces performed at act finales, as entr'actes, and as afterpieces.[43]

When we examine directions for music in Vanbrugh's plays, we find this trend substantiated. *The Relapse* (DL, 1696) has one specified song (act 4, scene 2): "I smile at Love and all its arts," a poem of two twelve-line stanzas. In act 5, scene 5, three and one half pages before the last line of the play comes the stage direction "They sit and the masque begins." The text of the masque is a "Dialogue Between Cupid and Hymen." It consists of eight stanzas of varying length, two specified for chorus.[44] From the beginning of the Restoration, masque scenes had been incorporated nearly as often in comedies as in tragedies. In the list of forty-four published tragedies and comedies with masques from the period 1663 to 1703 that Curtis Price has compiled, more than a third were performed in the seven-year period 1695-1703 of his survey.[45] The insertion of a masque or an entertainment, antick dance, entry—that is, a loosely-defined musical episode not germane to the dramatic action—in comedies was somewhat more frequent just at the time Vanbrugh began his career in the theater. His second play, *Aesop* (1697), act 1 calls for one dance, a Troop of Musicians, and a Dialogue Song, all in the final act. His third published play—the first he wrote—*The Provok'd Wife* (1697), has stage directions for five songs: one each in acts 1, 3, 5, and two in act 2. Vanbrugh's poems for the five songs are representative of sometimes pastoral, sometimes bawdy, sometimes lightly veiled satiric songs of the time. In act 3, scene 2 of *The Provok'd Wife*, Vanbrugh casually introduces the lyrics into the conversation: "What a pother of late/Have they kept in the state." Sitting at a table, drinking, are Lord Rake, Sir John Brute, and Colonel Billy. Lord Rake (sings):

> What a pother of late/Have they kept in the state/
> About setting our consciences free!
> A bottle has more/Dispensation in store,/
> Than the king and the state can decree.
>
> When my head's full of wine,/I o'erflow with design,/
> And know no penal laws that can curb me.
> Whate'er I devise/Seems good in my eyes,/
> And religion ne'er dares to disturb me.
>
> No saucy remorse/intrudes in my course/
> Nor impertinent notions of evil;
> So there's claret in store,/in peace I've my whore,/
> And in peace I jog on to the devil.[46]

If indeed Vanbrugh wrote this play while in prison, he must have added "What a Pother" later for the play's performance and publication. The political references reflect contemporary events and his own recent experiences as a sympathizer with supporters of William III. The text of Vanbrugh's fourth play, *The Country House* (1698), an adaptation, has no stage directions for music. His fifth, *The Pilgrim* (1700), is a revision of Fletcher's *The Pilgrim* (1621), and was intended for a benefit performance for John Dryden, who died several days after the production's first night. Dryden had added

---

[43] Ibid.

[44] Unless otherwise stated, references to Vanbrugh's texts are from *The Complete Works of Sir John Vanbrugh*, ed. Bonomy Dobree, 3 vols. (Bloomsbury: Nonesuch Press, 1928).

[45] Price, 28-34 and 256.

[46] *The Provok'd Wife*, act 3, scene 2. The Toleration Act of 1689 and the Quaker Act of 1696 granted dissenters "liberty of conscience." "Dispensation" refers to the power of the king to suspend the law in an individual case; it was invoked by James II to confer military offices on Catholics. The reference to "penal laws that can curb me" does not seem to reflect the actual situation in England where the laws were rarely enforced against Catholics, though in Ireland, beginning in 1695, the laws were enforced with severity; see the editorial notes in *The Provok'd Wife*, ed. James L. Smith (London & Tonbridge: New Mermaids, 1974), 54.

the prologue, epilogue, and *Secular Masque*, the last set to music by Daniel Purcell.[47] Apparently Vanbrugh had nothing to do with specifying music. His sixth, seventh, and eighth plays—all adaptations—have neither stage directions for music nor poems for songs. *The False Friend* (1701) was produced at the Drury Lane Theatre, where resources were available for music performance. *The Confederacy* (1705) and *The Mistake* (1705), as noted earlier, were produced at his house, the Queen's Theatre, where there were actors who sang.[48] Whatever his specific reasons for eliminating directions for instrumental music and song poems from the text, Vanbrugh's last three plays reflect the general tendency of dramatists at this time to remove from their plays songs and dances of no organic importance. Masques as afterpieces continued to appear throughout the first quarter of the century, most often as anonymous entertainments.[49]

Vanbrugh's plays also entertained later London audiences. During the Garrick years (1747-76) there were 134 performances of *The Provok'd Wife*, and in the nineteenth century there were at least forty-three performances of *The Confederacy*.[50] In the twentieth century, in London alone, *Wife* has had at least seven different revivals by professional companies and six revivals by amateur troupes.[51] In London in 1963 *The Relapse, or, Virtue in Danger* was adapted as a musical, *Virtue in Danger*.[52]

* * * * *

Playhouse management in early eighteenth-century London, convoluted as the system might appear to us to have been, set the course for opera in England for the next centuries. In the early years no one was more involved than Vanbrugh in his brief struggle to win from the Lord Chamberlain a decision favorable to his theater and his clients. A short while later, during the so-called "golden years of Italian opera in eighteenth-century England," management was in even greater distress. The Royal Academy of Music, subsidized by George II, with a roster of the best singers anywhere (Senesino, Cuzzoni, Faustina), and the world-famous composer George Frideric Handel at the helm, was forced to dissolve (1734) in favor of the Opera of the Nobility. The Handel-John Rich company moved from the King's Theatre—that is, from Vanbrugh's house in the Haymarket—to the Covent Garden Theatre, which had been built in 1732. Replacing them at the Vanbrugh Theatre was the Opera of the Nobility, which lasted three years before collapsing in 1737.[53] More than two centuries later, opera's financial instability continues today in London with the renowned, but debt-ridden, Covent Garden Opera House. John Vanbrugh, in realizing his desire to build a theater suitable for Italianate opera, could never have anticipated the consequences of that ambition.

The two great houses, Castle Howard and Blenheim Palace, which Vanbrugh began to build while still intimately involved with theatrical enterprises, are today occupied by descendants of their builders.[54] They are acknowledged the best work of the architect and of the short-lived Romantic-Baroque style he and Hawksmoor created. Had John Vanbrugh not chosen to become an architect, and instead remained closely identified with the theater as playwright and/or impresario, his contributions would still be considerable. In the context of his entire oeuvre, Vanbrugh's ten years in the world of drama and music are all the more remarkable: he demonstrated perseverance in a sphere of conflicting personalities, and, along with others, was a force in initiating changes in the artistic tastes of London theatergoers.

---

[47] In the publication of 1700 a "Dialogue Song" is printed after the play. This song was probably sung in act 3 or in the Madhouse Scene in act 4. There is also a ceremonial scene requiring music at the end of the finale, but this is not a part of the masque; see *Works*, 2:143-45.

[48] In *Works*, 3: 282, Dobree notes that songs and dances were *added* in revivals of *The Mistake*. In *Journey to London* (1728), Cibber's posthumous revision of *The Provok'd Husband*, a Masquerade opens act 1, and Henry Carey wrote words and music for two songs in act 4, scene 1, and act 5, scene 5; see *Works*, 3: 239, 266.

[49] Price, 40, has observed that "a few playwrights realized [ca. 1700 and later] that if most of the music sprinkled throughout the acts . . . were concentrated at the end of the final scene, then the drama would be left intact and practically unaffected by the music and dance."

[50] McCormick, 162, nn. 4-5.

[51] The years of the professional revivals are 1919, 1936, 1950, 1953, 1963, and two in 1973; see Vanbrugh, *The Provok'd Wife*, ed. Smith, xxvi-xxvii.

[52] The titles of some of the songs for the musical are "Fortune, thou art a bitch," "Stand back, Old Sodom," and "I shall have to cuckold someone"; see Vanbrugh, *The Relapse*, ed. Zimansky, xxiii.

[53] Daniel Nalback, "Opera Management in Eighteenth-Century London," *Theatre Research* 13, no. 1 (1973): 75-91.

[54] Castle Howard served as the setting for Masterpiece Theatre's television production of *Brideshead Revisited*.

APPENDIX

Chronology

1664 — 24 January JV born in parish of St. Nicholas Acons, London, to Giles van Brugg, merchant from Haarlem and Elizabeth, youngest daughter of Sir Dudley Carleton, Imber Court, Surrey. **1667**—family moved to Chester. **1681**—JV worked for his cousin, William Matthews, a wine merchant. January **1686**—JV commissioned as captain in Earl of Huntingdon's Foot Regiment; resigned during summer. Summer **1687**—JV a Bailiff in retinue of James Bertie, Earl of Abingdon, High Steward of Oxford (cousin to JV).

1688 — February JV removed as Bailiff by order of King James II. Late summer [or early 1689] arrested in France for talking about William of Orange; imprisoned at Calais, then Vincennes (**1691**) and finally in the Bastille (**1692**). April **1693**—JV released from prison; returned to England. May (**1693**)—JV became **Auditor**, Southern Division, Duchy of Lancaster (relinquished post in 1702).

1695 — United (theatre) Co. dissolved; Patent Co. remained with Rich at Drury Lane/Dorset Gardens. Betterton and rebel actors received license to play at Lincoln's Inn Fields. JV commissioned **Captain** of Marines (regiment disbanded in 1698). DG/DL (Rich) produced dramatic opera *The Indian Queen* (Dryden-H. Purcell).

1696 — DG/DL (Rich) produced dramatic opera *Bonduca* (Powell-H. Purcell). DL (Skipworth) produced Colley Cibber's play *Love's Last Shift; or, The Fool in Fashion*; was successful. November, JV staged his first play ***The Relapse, or Virtue in Danger*** (DL), sequel to Cibber's *Love's Last Shift*, very successful. December, JV staged his second play *Aesop*, 1 (DL).

1697 — March, JV produced *Aesop*, Part 2 (DL). April, JV staged ***The Provok'd Wife*** (LIF) (work probably begun while in Bastille); was very successful. DG/DL (Rich) produced dramatic opera *Cinthia & Endimion* (Durfey-D. Purcell et al.); was successful.

1698 — January, JV produced ***The Country House*** (DL), his translation and adaptation of Dancourt's *La Maison de Campagne*, not successful until 1703. March, Jeremy Collier published criticisms of JV's dramatic works in his *Short View of the Immorality and Profaneness of the English Stage*. June, JV published ***A Short Vindication of the Provok'd Wife and The Relapse from Immorality and Profaneness***. LIF (Betterton) produced dramatic opera *Rinaldo and Armida* (Dennis-Eccles), was unsuccessful.

1699 — JV supplanted William Talman as **architect** to 3rd Earl of Carlisle, prepared plans for Castle Howard. JV travelled during the summer to see "most of the great houses in the North" (Webb, *Letters*, 4). DL (Rich) produced dramatic opera *The Island Princess* (Fletcher/Motteux-J. Clarke et al.); was successful.

1700 — April, JV staged his version of Fletcher's ***The Pilgrim*** with Dryden's *Secular Masque* (DL); was successful. JV began to build '**Goose Pie House**' in Whitehall for himself (from rubbage left from fire of 1698 that destroyed Whitehall Palace).

1701 — Spring, work began for 3rd Earl of Carlisle at **Castle Howard**. DL/DG (Rich) produced dramatic opera *The Virgin Prophetess* (Settle-Finger); was successful.

1702 — February, JV produced ***The False Friend*** (DL), adaptation in English of Lesage's translation (*Le Traitre Puni*) of Zorilla's *La Traicion busca el Castigo*; was successful. March, JV became captain in Huntingdon's regiment. June, appointed **Comptroller**, successor to Talman, of His Majesty's Works.

1703 — With William Congreve and Thomas Betterton (at LIF), JV planned to build a new theatre in **Haymarket**. June, JV appointed **Carlisle Herald** by Earl of Carlisle. August, JV appointed to Board of Directors of Greenwich Hospital.

1704 — March, JV appointed **Clarenceux Herald** in the College of Arms. April 18, foundation stone of **Haymarket Opera House** laid by Lady Sunderland, daughter of John Churchill, first Duke of Marlborough. December, JV and Duke of Marlborough chose site for house at Woodstock; Nicholas Hawksmoor began to plan its appearance and layout.

1705	January 18, Queen Anne granted Duke of Marlborough estate of Royal Manor of Woodstock, eventual **Blenheim Palace**. January, DL mounted *first* Italianate (all-sung) opera, *Arsinoe, Queen of Cyprus*, pasticcio of Stanzani's verses translated by Motteux, set to music by Clayton, scenic design by Thornhill; English singers at DL included Hughes, Mrs. Cross, Leveridge, Mrs. Tofts; work was very successful. April, model of **Blenheim** sent to Kensington for Queen Anne's approval. Spring, Betterton & LIF actors moved into **Queen's Theatre**, unfinished 'Opera House' at Haymarket. April 9, **QT** (Vanbrugh & Congreve) produced Italianate (all sung) pastoral *Gli Amori d'Ergasto* (text, anon.—music, Greber), imported Italian singers; was unsuccessful. Summer, JV proposed union of **QT** & DG-DL theatres but rebuffed. Late summer, Congreve withdrew from management of **QT**. 18 June, foundation stone of **Blenheim Palace** laid. JV appointed its surveyor.
(1705)	29 June, **QT** closed for four months. Betterton & Co. moved back to LIF until completion of QT. October, JV produced ***The Confederacy*** (**QT**), his translation and adaptation of Dancourt's *Les Bourgeoises a la mode*; was successful. 27 December, JV produced ***The Mistake*** (**QT**), his translation and adaptation of Moliere's *Le Depit amoureux*; was successful.
Season 1705-06	**QT** staged English dramatic operas: February 1706, *The British Enchanters* (Granville—Eccles); was successful; March 1706, *Wonders in the Sun* (Durfey—Draghi/Eccles); was unsuccessful; Italianate all-sung in English pasticcio *The Temple of Love* (text?/trans. Motteux—Saggione); was unsuccessful.
1706	Summer, Lord Chamberlain decreed for 1706-07 season DL permitted to mount plays and operas; **QT** only plays (no opera, masque or entr'acte). Summer, JV as **Clarenceux Herald** and Charles Montague (later Earl of Halifax) took insignia of Order of the Garter to court of Hanover to invest Prince Elector (later King George II). Summer, **Castle Howard** main block well advanced, east wing near completion. August, JV turned over management of **QT** to Swiney, but still sought union of both theaters or opera monopoly for **QT**.
Season 1706-07	DL (Rich) 30 March 1706 produced Italianate all-sung in English *Camilla* (Stampiglio/trans. Motteux—G. Bononcini/Haym); was very successful. December 1706, first appearance in London of castrato "Valentini" (who sang in Italian, Mrs. Tofts in English) in *Camilla*. April 1707, pasticcio *Thomyris* (Motteux—Italian airs collected by Heidigger, recit. by Pepush); was successful. March 1707, Italianate *Rosamond* in English (J. Addison-T. Clayton); was unsuccessful; dramatic operas, all revivals: *Island Princess, Bonduca, King Arthur, Tempest, Indian Queen, Timon of Athens, Macbeth*, all successful. **QT** (JV/Swiney) not allowed to stage any musical productions.
1707	**Blenheim Bridge** under construction. East wing of house to cornice level. December 31, Lord Chamberlain (Earl of Kent) concerned by competition between two companies (and probably pressured by JV) issued decree: after 10 January 1708 DL (under Rich) given exclusive rights to plays, **QT** given exclusive rights to operas thus becoming *London's first Opera House*.
1708	January, JV repurchased Swiney's interest in **QT**; musical directors Haym and Heidegger produced Italianate opera *Love's Triumph* (Ottoboni/Motteux—Gasparini et al.), sung in English except for Valentini; January, revival of *Thomyris*; February, revival of *Camilla*. Finances precarious, May 10, JV again leased **QT** to Swiney. May 11, JV's letter to Earl of Manchester, ". . . have parted with my whole concern to Mr. Swiney . . ." (Webb, *Letters*, p. 20). JV built screen and two-flight staircase at **Audley End**, Essex. JV involved in rebuilding **Kimbolton** for Charles Montague, Earl of Manchester.
Season 1708-09	**QT** (Swiney) sold subscriptions for two new operas with recently arrived castrato Nicolini: December 1708, bi-lingual performance *Pyrrhus & Demetrius* (A. Morselli, trans. Swiney—songs by A. Scarlatti and N. Haym); was successful. March 1709, bi-lingual performance *Clotilda* (*La forza della Virtu*, trans. anon.—songs by Italian composers); was unsuccessful.
1709	June, Lord Chamberlain (Earl of Kent) removed Rich as manager of DL; no activity at DL for six months; **QT** under Swiney and joint managers (Wilks, Doggett, Cibber) permitted to stage operas *and* produce plays. June, JV quarrelled with Duchess of Marlborough over repairs at Woodstock to the **Old Manor House** (JV wished to preserve 'Rosamund's Bower,' she wanted it demolished). The main block at **Blenheim** almost ready for its roof. Summer, **QT** (Wilks, Dogget, Cibber, and Swiney) remodeled to remedy acoustics detrimental to speaking voice. November, JV built house for himself, **Chargate**, near Esher, Surrey. December, DL reopened under managers William Collier and Aaron Hill; DL permitted to stage plays and produce musical entertainments *but not* operas, **QT** (Swiney, Wilks, Doggett, Cibber) to continue to stage operas *and* plays.

1710	January, **QT** Italianate opera *Almahide* (text? arr. Heidegger—Bononcini) sung in Italian with vocal intermezzi sung in English between acts; was successful. March, **QT**'s *L'Idaspe Fidele* (text?—F. Mancini), sung entirely in Italian, successful. October, Duchess of Marlborough (temporarily) stopped all work at **Blenheim**. November 6, Lord Chamberlain (Kent) transferred Swiney and *all* actors back to DL; **QT** once again an *opera house*, now managed by Collier and Hill. December, treasury allocated 7,000 pounds to complete work on **Blenheim**; work resumed on the decoration of Hall and Saloon.
1711	January, **QT** staged pasticcio *Etearco* (text?—Bononcini). February 24, **QT** staged *first* opera by Handel in England: Italian style, all sung *Rinaldo* (English scenario by Hill trans. to Italian by Rossi).
1712	Queen Anne stopped all Treasury money for building at **Blenheim**. Duke and Duchess of Marlborough left for the Continent. JV began work for Eduard Southwell (Secretary of State for Ireland) on **King's Weston**, Glouchestshire. Carlisle moved into Castle Howard.
1713	JV dismissed as **Comptroller** of Her Majesty's Works, his patent revoked for writing a letter to the Mayor of Woodstock, ". . . in which I say the Duke of Marlborough has been bitterly and barbarously persecuted" (Webb, *Letters*, p. 55).
1714	JV altered London house for Duke of Newcastle. August, George I acceded to throne; Marlboroughs returned from abroad. December 19, JV **knighted** by king.
1715	JV reappointed **Comptroller** of His Majesty's Works and (June) appointed **Surveyer** of Gardens and Waterworks belonging to Royal Palaces. May, JV began work on interiors of **Hampton Court** for George, Prince of Wales, completed 1718. JV appointed **Garter King of Arms** (in 1717, position reverted to John Anstis). May, JV began alterations at **Chargate** that he had sold to the Earl of Clare (Duke of Newcastle who renamed it **Claremont**). JV altered **Walpole House**, Chelsea for Sir Robert Walpole.
1716	JV appointed **Surveyor** at Greenwich Hospital. April, work resumed at **Blenheim**. May, Duke of Marlborough had a stroke; JV now dealt with Duchess. June, Marlboroughs in residence, east wing of **Blenheim**. JV acquired land at Greenwich. November, JV severed all connection with **Blenheim**.
1718	February, date of design for forecourt of **King's Weston**. JV built four **houses** for himself and his brothers at **Greenwich**. JV started building at **Eastbury Park** for George Bubb Dodington (Baron Melcome). August, JV paid his first visit to **Seaton Delaval** in Northumbria, owned by Admiral George Delaval.
1719	January, JV, aged 54, married at York to Henrietta Maria (1693-1776) daughter of Colonel James Yarburgh of Heslington Hall, York. Daughter born to them but died soon after. JV proposed alterations to **Nottingham Castle** (Webb, *Letters*, pp. 107-11) and completed a 'New Room' at **Claremont**, both for Duke of Newcastle.
1720	Son Charles born to JV and his wife; he died 1745. Office courts at **Eastbury** completed.
1721	August, JV inspected work in progress at **Seaton Delaval**, and visited **Lumley Castle** (owned by Richard Lumley, Earl of Scarbrough) to "form a General Design for the whole" (Webb, *Letters*, p. 138). November, JV prepared response to Chancery suit brought by the Duke of Marlborough "against everybody concern'd in the Building at Blenheim" (Webb, *Letters*, p. 140).
1722	January, son John was born to JV and his wife (he died in infancy 1723). June 16, Duke of Marlborough died at Windsor Lodge, aged 73 years. **1722-25**—Hawksmoor completed work at **Blenheim**.
1723	Duchess of Marlborough had outworks at **Blenheim** finished. JV supervised alterations to **Prince's Rooms** at Hampton Court. August, JV called on 2nd Duke of Ancaster at **Grimsthorpe** to "discuss the General Design I made for his Father last Winter" (Webb, *Letters*, p. 151).
1724	February, work proceeded on the outworks at **Castle Howard**, and on **Eastbury**, according to JV's second design.

1725   February, JV's design for the Four Winds Temple at **Castle Howard** approved by Earl of Carlisle. July-August, JV undertook six-week tour with his wife and Earl of Carlisle and daughters. They visited Woodstock, but by instruction of Duchess of Marlborough, Vanbrughs were not allowed "to see either House, Gardens, or even to enter the Park" at **Blenheim** (Webb, *Letters*, p. 167). September, JV received 1700 pounds in fees due for his work at **Blenheim**; still owed 300 pounds (Webb, *Letters*, p. 169).

1726   March 26, JV died at his house in **Whitehall** after short illness, was buried in family vault at St. Stephen Walbrook. Hawksmoor continued work at **Castle Howard** (completed Temple, 1731), began erection of Mausoleum; completed after Hawksmoor's death (1736) by Daniel Garrett, 1737-42.

1727   C. Cibber produced *The Provok'd Husband* (1728) incorporating JV's unfinished ***A Journey to London*** (also known as *The Provok'd Husband*); was successful. *The Beggar's Opera* (ballad opera), book by John Gay, music 17th- and 18th-century ballads selected and arr. by Pepusch, very successful.

10

The Correspondence of the Impresario Luca Casimiro degli Albizzi: An Index

WILLIAM C. HOLMES

My offering to Robert Weaver, who, together with his wife Norma, has contributed so much to our knowledge of Florentine opera in the seventeenth, eighteenth, and nineteenth centuries, is in a format with which both of the Weavers are quite familiar: an extensive index of a large number of documents relevant to Florentine theater in the first half of the eighteenth century. The index, containing as it does many references to the production of Florentine opera and to the musicians who performed in the city, is meant to serve as a complement to the Weavers' pioneering work in the field and, I hope, as a further stimulus to research in Florence.[1]

    The documents indexed here are but a small part of the archive of the historic Florentine family of the Albizzi, which contains papers and documents covering a period of over half a millenium, from 1181 to 1786, the year of the death of Lorenzo Casimiro degli Albizzi, last of his line. The Albizzi holdings eventually reached another historic Florentine family, the Guicciardini, through a series of marriages and inheritances which saw the legacy of Lorenzo Casimiro's sister, Caterina degli Albizzi, who married Lorenzo Pucci in 1730, pass to her sister-in-law Elisabetta Pucci. Elisabetta had married into the Guicciardini family, and after the death of her brother Lorenzo the precious holdings were transferred to the Guicciardini, with whom they have remained over the centuries. Presently, the Albizzi documents and papers are housed in the Palazzo Guicciardini on the Via Guicciardini in Florence. In recent years the archive, which can be visited by appointment once permission has been obtained, has been systematically reordered, and various categories pertaining to the Albizzi's personal fortune, the day-to-day running of their houses and estates, their role in Florentine politics, economics, and society are readily available to the interested scholar. More recently, documents concerned with musical matters have been cataloged and put into order by the eminent Florentine archivist Gino Corti, who kindly called my attention to their existence.

    The present index deals with the outgoing and incoming correspondence of Marchese Luca Casimiro degli Albizzi (1664-1745), whose role as impresario of the Teatro la Pergola in Florence formed the basis of my book *Opera Observed*.[2] The Teatro la Pergola, along with the Teatro del Cocomero, was one of the most important public opera houses in Florence. Eventually, the Pergola became the city's prime venue for opera seria, whereas the Cocomero produced comic opera as well. The Pergola was owned and administered by the members of Accademia degli Immobili, a society of noblemen whose support and subscriptions, along with subventions from the ruling Medici family, helped keep the theater going.[3] By virtue of his birth—Albizzi was the scion of an ancient and distinguished Florentine family—and

---

    [1] In my work I have relied especially on the Weavers' *A Chronology of Music in the Florentine Theater, 1590-1750: Operas, Prologues, Finales, Intermezzos and Plays with Incidental Music*, Detroit Studies in Music Bibliography, 38 (this publisher, 1978).

    [2] *Opera Observed: Views of a Florentine Impresario in the Early Eighteenth Century* (Chicago: University of Chicago Press, 1993). In a review in *Cambridge Opera Journal* 7, no. 2 (July 1985): 176, Ellen Harris lamented the fact that there was no complete listing of all of the Albizzi documents pertaining to music. The present contribution, I hope, will at least partially remedy that lack.

    [3] Though it is no longer responsible for running the theater, the Accademia degli Immobili is still extant and its archive is kept in its quarters within the theater. The standard work on the Immobili and their theater is Ugo Morini, *La R. Accademia degli Immobili ed il suo Teatro "La Pergola," 1649-1925* (Pisa: F. Simoncini, 1926).

his connections, Luca Casimiro was a logical choice as impresario. His musical education and his experience with opera had begun at an early age. As a child he was welcomed at the grand-ducal residence, where he became a close friend of the grand prince Ferdinando (1663-1713). Ferdinando, the most musical of the later Medici, was passionately devoted to opera. While still a young man, he instituted a series of operatic productions at his private theater in the magnificent Medici villa at Pratolino. From 1679 to 1710, one opera was produced there every year, including new works by Giovanni Legrenzi, G. M. Pagliardi, and Alessandro Scarlatti, among others.[4] Both Luca Casimiro and his father, Marchese Luca degli Albizzi (1638-1708), advised Ferdinando on business and musical matters dealing with some of those operatic productions and were in correspondence with singers, composers and librettists on the prince's behalf. With such a background and experience, it seems only natural that Luca Casimiro, long a very active member of the Accademia degli Immobili, should eventually be chosen by his peers to act as impresario of their theater.

For a good many years before Albizzi's tenure as impresario, the Teatro la Pergola had had a checkered history. Indeed, aside from annual productions between 1657, the year of the Pergola's opening, and 1661, the theater remained closed for much of the second half of the seventeenth century and the first decade of the eighteenth. It was not to reopen officially until June of 1718, after which it became, as mentioned, the principal place for the performance of opera seria in Florence. Albizzi had been a member of the Accademia degli Immobili since the 1680s; he held important posts within the academy, and was among those members who raised money in order to refurbish the Pergola before its much anticipated reopening. From 1718 onwards, he exerted great influence on the artistic policies of the theater, as attested by records in the archive of the Accademia degli Immobili. In 1724 he was appointed impresario to the first of his many three-year terms. It was a role that he clearly relished and fulfilled with gusto for a number of years, relinquishing it only when the burden of advancing years, the death of grand duke Gian Gastone de' Medici in 1737, and the arrival of the new Austrian grand dukes forced him reluctantly to step aside. When he retired in 1738 he was seventy-four years old.

Albizzi's correspondence, especially that from the period of his official connection with the Teatro la Pergola, is a goldmine of information about how an opera house, one that was both an academic and a public theater, operated in the first half of the eighteenth century. There are contracts with workmen engaged to make changes or additions to the theater itself; there are negotiations about salary and terms of employment with singers, composers, and set designers; instructions to music copyists and librettists and suggestions to composers; there are bits and pieces of professional gossip gleaned from the letters of other impresarios, and there are even law suits, or threats of them. It is not difficult for a reader leafing through the many pages of correspondence to form an accurate picture of the behind-the-scenes functioning of a major opera theater over an extended period of time. Some, but by no means a great portion, of these letters furnished the background for my published account of various moments in Luca Casimiro's career as an impresario at the Teatro la Pergola. Understandably, there are many, many other unpublished letters containing a wealth of information regarding singers, dancers, librettos, the operatic situation in other cities—witness one London correspondent writing Luca Casimiro of Handel's imminent operatic failure in 1734 and another from St. Petersburg speaking of the rage for Italian singers there in 1735—which will continue to furnish scholars with important and very useful information. It is precisely for this reason—as an aid to future research—that the present index has been compiled.

The outgoing correspondence is found in three letter-books, catalogued as A.769, A.770, and A.771. These contain letters from ca. 1680 until 1745, the year of Albizzi's death. The largest volume of correspondence occurs, with a few notable gaps, between 1725 and 1738—that is, during the years of his incumbency as impresario. There are fewer letters after this date, during the years when Albizzi acted principally as an agent for a number of singers. Much of the incoming correspondence is perhaps lost, as can be seen from the smaller number of extant letters from roughly the same period. This incoming correspondence is collected alphabetically by the senders' name in various folders numbered from A.718-A.799 (excluding, of course, the above mentioned A.769, A.770, and A.771) and from A.801-A.808, A.810, A.812, A.814-A.818, A.820-A.821, and A.823-A.825.

---

[4] For a general account of the princely operatic venture, with particular reference to Scarlatti's role in it, see Mario Fabbri, *Alessandro Scarlatti e il Principe Ferdinando de' Medici* (Florence: Olschki, 1961); see also Weaver and Weaver, 31-41. An eminently readable account of Ferdinando's life is in Harold Acton's *The Last Medici*, rev. ed. (London: Methuen, 1958).

I should note that for reasons of space I have limited the present index only to the outgoing and incoming correspondence of Luca Casimiro from the period after 1700. Documents from the last three decades of the seventeenth century, many of which were written by his father, Luca degli Albizzi, or received by him have been excluded. Some idea of the content and style of these latter, however—those dealing with operatic patronage by grand prince Ferdinando at his theater in Pratolino between 1679 and 1686—appear in *Opera Observed*.[5] I should note further that the contents of all the outgoing correspondence has been fully indexed, while the incoming correspondence lists only the names of the senders and the dates and place of origin of their letters. Some of the letters indexed here have already appeared in print, either in whole or in part. These are marked in the appropriate places with an asterisk followed by a page reference in parentheses to either *Opera Observed*, siglum OO, or to Gino Corti's article "Il teatro la Pergola," siglum RIM.[6] Finally, I should also point out that consecutive dating is not always consistent with the order of folio numbers in a given volume.

Index of the Albizzi correspondence

Outgoing letters

Entries for outgoing letters appear in the following order: name of the addressee in italics, place, date (by year, day and month), volume number, and folio number. Names, in roman type, and places and works of musical interest receive separate entries with reference to the letters in which they appear. An asterisk before an entry indicates that the letter has been published, in whole or in part, in either RIM or OO. References to these latter appear within parentheses immediately after the entry in question. In Albizzi's time the Florentine new year still began on March 25, the feast of the Assumption. In my listings all dates have been changed to conform to modern usage.

Acciaioli, Angelo (Napoli). 1736/22/5, A.770, 610v; 1736/7/8, A.770, 643v; 1736/14/8, A.770, 648v; 1736/4/9, A.770, 657; 1736/18/9, A.770, 666; 1736/25/9, A.770, 668v; 1736/1/10, A.770, 671; 1736/8/10, A.770, 673; 1736/15/10, A.770, 675; 1736/22/10, A.770, 679v; 1736/29/10, A.770, 682; 1737/8/1, A.771, 31v; 1737/15/1, A.771, 34; 1737/22/1, A.771, 36v; 1737/5/2, A.771, 42; 1737/12/2, A.771, 45; 1737/19/2, A.771, 48; 1737/12/3, A.771, 54v; 1737/14/5, A.771, 70; 1738/26/8, A.771, 199; 1738/9/9, A.771, 201; 1738/16/9, A.771, 204; 1738/6/10, A.771, 205v; 1738/27/10, A.771, 212; 1738/25/11, A.771, 218; 1738/9/12, A.771, 222; 1738/22/12, A.771, 225; 1738/30/12, A.771, 226v; 1739/13/1, A.771, 229v; 1739/27/1, A.771, 233; 1739/20/4, A.771, 240v; 1739/29/4, A.771, 242; 1739/2/6, A.771, 245v; 1739/9/6, A.771, 247v; 1739/16/6, A.771, 252; 1739/23/6, A.771, 255; *1739/7/7, A.771, 268 (OO, 140); *1739/12/10, A.771, 305 (OO, 142); 1741/20/3, A.771, 417v.

Addato, Domenico di, detto Minelli. *See* Vivaldi, 1739/14/10; 1739/28/10.

Agliata, Tommaso (Pisa). 1735/7/6, A.770, 472v; 1735/14/6, A.770, 444; 1736/30/6, A.770, 630v; 1736/24/7, A.770, 639; 1739/9/6, A.771, 248v; 1739/16/6, A.771, 251v; 1739/27/6, A.771, 262v; 1739/11/7, A.771, 271; 1739/14/7, A.771, 273v; 1739/8/9, A.771, 295v.

Alamanni, Vincenzo, marchese (Firenze). 1733/20/5, A.770, 253v.

Albinoni, Tomaso (Venezia). 1734/6/3, A.770, 324v; *see also* Visconti, 1734/21/9.

Aldegati, Carlo (Mantova). 1733/14/4, A.770, 235.

---

[5] Appendix 2, 168-71.

[6] "Il teatro la Pergola di Firenze a la stagione d'opera per il carnevale, 1726-1727: Lettere di Luca Casimiro degli Albizzi a Vivaldi, Porpora ed altri," *Rivista italiana di musicologia* 15 (1980): 182-88.

Aldrovandi, Filippo, conte (Bologna). 1735/9/7, A.770, 487v; 1735/26/7, A.770, 495v; 1735/30/7, A.770, 497v; 1735/2/8, A.770, 501; 1735/6/8, A.770, 502v; 1735/9/8, A.770, 506v; 1735/13/8, A.770, 508; 1735/16/8, A.770, 511; 1735/20/8, A.770, 511v; 1735/23/8, A.770, 514; 1737/14/12, A.771, 129v; 1737/21/12, A.771, 131v.

Alessandri, Margherita. *See* Nozzoli, S. T., 1740/5/4.

Ambrogi, Averardo (Firenze). 1735/20/10, A.770, 531v.

Amorevoli, Angelo. *See* Acciaioli, 1738/6/10; Antinori, 1733/7/11; Baratti, P., 1739/1/8; Gualandi, 1737/1/6; Tesi, 1740/5/10.

Anderlini, Pietro. *See* Prini, 1733/28/4; Saladino del Borgo, 1733/2/5; 1733/9/5; 1733/19/5; 1733/26/5; Schianteschi, 1732/28/6.

Angioletta. *See* Vivaldi, 1735/20/8; 1736/5/5; 1736/12/5; 1736/19/5.

Annibali, Domenico. *See* Lucchesini, 1739/11/8; Nozzoli, F. M., 1732/22/7; Porpora, 1733/19/9.

Antinori, Luigi (Bologna). 1725/10/3, A.769, 182v; (Venezia) 1733/12/9, A.770, 288; 1733/24/10, A.770 297v; *1733/31/10, A.770, 298 (OO, 58); 1733/7/11, A.770, 300; 1733/14/11, A.770, 301; 1733/2/11, A.770, 301v; *see also* Cottini, 1733/9/10; 1733/16/10; 1733/24/10; 1733/30/10; 1734/6/3.

Appianino (Appiani). *See* Della Rovere, 1735/2/8; 1735/9/8; Donatelli, 1735/3/5; 1735/7/5; 1737/8/6; Lucchesini, 1739/9/6; 1739/23/6; 1739/4/8; 1739/11/8; Niccolini, G. L., 1739/4/8; Niccolini, M., 1735/14/6; Salviati, A. M., 1735/7/6; Vivaldi, 1736/23/3.

Aquilanti, Francesco (Venezia). 1732/4/4, A.770, 104v; 1732/18/4, A.770, 106v; 1732/7/6, A.770, 124; 1734/9/1, A.770, 310; 1734/23/1, A.770, 313v; 1734/6/2, A.770, 316v; 1734/20/2, A.770, 320v; 1734/6/3, A.770, 324; 1734/13/3, A.770, 325v; 1734/20/3, A.770, 327v; 1734/26/3, A.770, 329v; 1734/2/4, A.770, 335v; 1734/9/4/, A.770, 337v; 1734/16/4, A.770, 341; 1734/23/4, A.770, 432v; 1734/7/5, A.770, 346v; 1734/29/5, A.770, 350v; 1734/26/6, A.770, 366; 1734/10/7, A.770, 373v; *see also* Broschi, 1731/23/1; 1731/6/2; Brunoro, 1739/7/2; Corsini, 1736/28/2; 1736/6/3; 1736/13/3; 1736/20/3; Cottini, 1734/19/6; 1734/10/7; Donatelli, 1734/23/4; Grimaldi, 1731/27/1; Pinacci, 1731/26/3; Pompeati, 1737/12/2.

Arrigoni, Carlo (Londra). 1733/25/4, A.770, 239v; 1733/19/6, A.770, 263; 1733/15/8, A.770, 282; 1734/28/1, A.770, 422v; 1735/24/2, A.770, 443v; (Lione) 1736/7/8, A.770, 644; (Vienna) *1737/23/11, A.771, 121v (OO, 154); *see also* Acciaioli, 1737/22/1; Dreyer, 1735/15/1; 1735/26/2; 1735/17/3.

Aureli, Maria Caterina. *See* Uttini, 1734/7/5.

Babbi, Gregorio. *See* Della Rovere, 1737/27/8; Prini, 1736/21/2; Saladino del Borgo, 1734/2/3; Valletta, 1731/6/2; 1731/13/2; 1731/24/2; 1731/3/3.

Bagnano, Francesco Antonio da (Modena). 1738/22/7, A.771, 187v.

Bagnolesi, Anna. *See* Agliata, 1736/30/6; Baratti, P., 1739/13/6; Broschi, 1731/23/1; Donatelli, 1737/25/5; Grimaldi,1731/27/1; Martelli, 1732/15/7; Pinacci, 1731/26/3; Pucci, 1732/6/9; Ridolfi, 1732/16/8; Roperini, 1732/1/11; Zambeccari, 1739/16/6.

Banchieri, Antonio, monsignor governatore (Roma). *1726/21/5, A.769, 268 (OO, 125).

Baratti, Pietro (Modena). 1733/10/11, A.770, 300v; 1734/12/4, A.770, 338v; 1734/11/5, A.770, 348; 1734/27/9, A.770, 494v; 1734/9/10, A.770, 406v; 1735/2/4, A.770, 451v; 1735/16/4, A.770, 459; 1735/30/4, A.770, 465v; 1735/7/5,

A.770, 468v; 1735/4/6, A.770, 471; 1735/11/6, A.770, 474; 1735/18/6, A.770, 478v; 1735/28/6, A.770, 481v; *1735/ 4/7, A.770, 485v; 1735/30/7, A.770, 498; 1735/6/8, A.770, 504; 1735/13/8, A.770, 508; 1735/17/9, A.770, 522v; 1735/23/9, A.770, 523v; 1735/20/10, A.770, 532v; 1735/19/11, A.770, 542; (Bologna) 1737/4/5, A.771, 67v; 1738/ 31/5, A.771, 175v; 1738/21/6, A.771, 181; 1738/28/6, A.771, 182; 1738/4/7, A.771, 183v; 1738/12/7, A.771, 185; 1738/19/7, A.771, 186; 1738/26/7; 1738/23/8, A.771, 197v; 1738/31/10, A.771, 213; (Milano) 1738/ 25/11, A.771, 218; 1738/9/12, A.771, 222v; 1738/16/12, A.771, 224; 1738/30/12, A.771, 226v; 1739/13/1, A.771, 230; 1739/27/1, A.771, 232v; 1739/20/4, A.771, 240v; (Bologna) 1739/13/6, A.771, 249; 1739/20/6, A.771, 254; 1739/23/6, A.771, 259; 1739/27/6, A.771, 261v; 1739/11/7, A.771, 271; 1739/18/7, A.771, 274v; 1739/25/7, A.771, 278; 1739/1/8, A.771, 280v; 1740/28/5, A.771, 338; *see also* Acciaioli, 1738/16/9; 1738/6/10; Corsini, 1739/27/5; Grisi,1735/20/10; Niccolini, 1734/22/6; Nozzoli, F. M., 1738/6/10; Saladino del Borgo, Giovanni, 1733/20/6; 1733/27/6; 1734/2/3; Vivaldi, 1735/20/8.

Baratti (Baratta), Teresa (Bologna). 1739/17/4, A.771, 240; 1739/2/5, A.771, 243; *see also* Acciaioli, 1738/16/9; 1738/ 6/10; 1738/27/10; 1738/25/11; 1738/22/12; 1738/30/12; 1739/13/1; 1739/27/1; 1739/20/4; 1739/29/4; 1739/2/6; 1739/9/6; 1739/16/6; 1739/23/6; Baratti, P., 1735/4/6; 1735/11/6; 1735/18/6; 1735/30/7; 1735/23/9; 1735/20/10; 1738/26/7; 1738/23/8; 1738/31/10; 1739/27/1; 1739/17/4; 1739/13/6; 1739/23/6; 1739/27/6; 1739/25/7; 1739/1/8; Corsini, 1738/27/5; Lucchesini, 1740/17/5; Orlandini, 1736/23/6; Saladino del Borgo, 1734/18/9; 1734/21/9; 1734/ 27/9; 1734/9/10; Vivaldi, 1735/30/7; 1735/20/8.

Barbara. *See* Nozzoli, F. M., 1733/28/7; Orlandini,1734/16/10; Saladino del Borgo, 1734/16/10.

Barberina. *See* Nozzoli, F. M., 1733/28/7; Vivaldi, 1734/9/10.

Barbieri, Antonio (Venezia). 1734/20/3, A.770, 328; 1734/23/4, A.770, 342; 1734/15/5, A.770, 333; 1734/7/5, A.770, 347v; 1734/29/5, A.770, 352; *1734/12/6, A.770, 356v (OO, 198, n. 38); 1734/26/6, A.770, 366v; 1734/10/7, A.770, 373v; 1734/24/7, A.770, 382v; 1734/7/8, A.770, 386v; 1734/16/10, A.770, 409; 1734/27/11, A.770, 419v; *see also* Baratti, P., 1734/12/4; Cottini, 1734/2/4; 1734/15/5; Orlandini, 1733/28/7.

Barbieri, Lucia Bassi. *See* Barbieri, 1734/23/4; 1734/7/5; 1734/29/5; 1734/16/10; Cottini, 1734/15/5; Orlandini, 1734/ 12/10.

Barbieri, Santi. *See* Corsini, B., 1738/27/5.

Barbuzzietta (Barbuzetti). *See* Cottini, 1736/13/4; Della Rovere, 1737/17/9; Vivaldi, 1735/30/7; 1735/7/10; 1735/28/10; 1736/3/3; 1736/17/3; 1736/23/3; 1736/15/9; 1737/1/6.

Barlocci, Francesca (Checca). *See* Corsini, B., 1738/27/5; Prini, 1737/21/5; 1737/28/5; 1737/4/6; 1737/8/6; 1737/15/6.

Baroni. *See* Saladino del Borgo, 1733/25/7.

Barsotti. *See* Valletta, 1731/27/2; 1731/3/3.

Bartolommei, Ferdinando, marchese (Vienna). 1737/25/5, A.771, 73v; *1737/14/12, A.771, 127 (OO, 159); *1737/28/12, A.771, 132v (OO, 157); *1738/4/1, A.771, 135 (OO, 160); 1738/11/1, A.771, 136; *1738/1/2, A.771, 139v (OO, 161); 1738/8/2; 1738/22/2, A.771, 146; 1738/7/3, A.771, 151; 1738/5/4, A.771, 156v; 1738/12/4, A.771, 159v; 1738/3/5, A.771, 165v; 1738/14/6, A.771, 178; 1738/19/7, A.771, 187.

Bartolommei, Giovanni, marchese (Villa San Marco). 1731/22/12, A.770, 90v.

Bassi, Caterina (Bologna). 1736/17/7, A.770, 636v; *see also* Grimani, 1737/11/2; Orlandini, 1736/9/6.

La Beccaretta. *See* Fachinelli, Lucia.

Befeli, Francesca. *See* Albinoni, 1734/6/3.

Belisani Buini, Cecilia. *See* Martelli, D., 1732/15/7.

Bentivoglio, Guido, marchese (Genova). 1738/11/1, A.771, 137v.

Berenstadt, Gaetano (Firenze). 1733/10/11, A.770, 301; *see also* Aldegati, 1733/14/4.

Bernacchi (Barnacchi, Barnacco), Antonio. *See* Donatelli, 1737/29/6; 1737/6/7; 1737/7/12; 1737/17/12; Lucchesini, 1739/11/8; Mari, 1737/1/7; Pinacci, 1731/16/4; Saladino del Borgo, 1734/13/3; Visconti, 1735/20/10.

Bernardi, Francesco detto Senesino (Siena), 1737/14/12, A.771, 129; *1739/7/6, A.771, 248 (OO, 133); *1739/16/6, A.771, 250 (OO, 134); 1739/21/6 (=copy of a letter to be sent by him), A.771, 255v; 1739/23/6, A.771, 257v; (Pisa) *1739/25/6, A.771, 260 (OO, 137); (Siena) 1739/30/6, A.771, 264; *1739/7/7, A.771, 267 (OO, 139); *1739/11/7, A.771, 268 (OO, 140); 1739/14/7, A.771, 272v; 1739/19/7, A.771, 274; 1739/21/7, A.771, 276; 1739/25/7, A.771, 277; *1739/28/7, A.771, 279 (OO, 141); 1739/4/8, A.771, 283; 1739/11/8, A.771, 286v; 1739/15/8, A.771, 287v; 1739/22/8, A.771, 290; 1739/29/8, A.771, 291v; 1739/1/9, A.771, 292v; 1739/5/9, A.771, 294; 1739/8/9, A.771, 295; (Napoli) 1739/15/12, A.771, 314v; (Siena) 1740/21/3, A.771, 323; 1740/25/3, A.771, 323v; 1740/29/3, A.771, 324; 1740/5/4, A.771, 326v; *see also* Acciaioli, 1739/23/6; 1739/7/7; 1739/12/10; Baratti, P., 1739/18/7; 1739/25/7; 1739/1/8; Bernardi, 1739/21/6; 1739/25/6; Della Rovere, 1736/22/2; Donatelli, 1737/25/5; 1737/13/12; Lucchesini, G., 1739/9/6; 1739/16/6; 1739/23/6; 1739/30/6; 1739/14/7; 1739/28/7; 1739/4/8; 1740/22/2; 1740/29/2; 1740/13/3; 1740/28/3; Migliorucci, 1726/29/3; Mijone, 1737/11/6; Prini, 1741/29/8; Pucci, 1733/31/7.

Beroardi, Filippo (Venezia), 1720/17/8, A.768, 1101; 1720/31/8, A.768, 1103; 1720/9/11, A.768, 1120.

Bertolli. *See* Orlandini, 1733/28/7.

Bettina. *See* Saroni, Elisabetta.

Bibiena. *See* Ridolfi, 1732/2/8.

Bisagi, Natalizia. *See* Agliata, 1735/7/6; 1735/14/16; Corsini, 1738/27/5; Della Rovere, 1737/6/8; 1737/27/8; 1737/3/9; 1737/10/9; 1737/17/9; Donatelli, 1735/7/6 (called Polverini); 1735/11/6; Grimani, 1736/25/2; Mochi, 1736/21/2; 1736/21/7; 1736/28/7; Nozzoli, S. T., 1735/19/4; 1736/21/7; 1736/28/7; 1741/29/8; 1741/5/9; 1741/9/9; Orlandini, 1736/16/6; 1736/26/6; Prini, 1741/29/8; 1741/5/9; 1741/16/9; Vivaldi, 1735/30/7.

Boni, Giacomo Antonio (Genova). 1739/16/6, A.771, 253; 1739/23/6, A.771, 259v.

Bonifazzi, Domenico. *See* Donatelli, 1737/29/6.

Bordoni, Faustina. *See* Broschi, 1731/23/1; 1731/6/2; Della Rovere, 1733/21/4; Donatelli, 1733/25/4; Grimaldi, 1731/27/1; Lucchesini, 1740/17/5; Migliorucci, 1726/7/12; Nozzoli, F. M., 1726/5/3; Schianteschi, 1724/7/10.

Borghesi, Alessandro (Firenze). 1739/9/10, A.771, 303v; *see also* Grimani, 1739/19/7; 1739/1/8; 1739/15/8; 1739/5/9; 1739/12/9; 1739/2/10; 1739/9/10.

Borghesi, Gabriello Antonio (Bologna). 1736/26/6, A.770, 628v; 1737/10/8, A.771, 102; *see also* Cottini, 1736/16/6.

Brantani, Maria. *See* Nozzoli, F. M., 1740/2/8.

Bresciani, Donato. *See* Lucchesini, 1739/14/7.

Brivio. *See* Donatelli, 1735/7/5.

Broschi, Carlo (Farinelli)(Torino). 1731/23/1, A.770, 28v; 1731/6/2, A.770, 30v; *see also* Della Rovere, 1736/22/2; Donatelli, 1734/29/5; 1737/25/5; Grimaldi, 1731/27/1; Lucchesini, 1739/30/6; Nicolini, 1737/23/3; 1737/22/4; Pinacci, 1731/16/4; Saladino del Borgo,1734/13/3; 1734/20/3; Schianteschi, 1726/13/7; Tanara, 1726/13/7.

Brunoro, Giuseppe (Venezia). 1739/7/2, A.771, 235v.

Buini, Rosalba (La Buina). *See* Donatelli, 1737/7/12; 1737/13/12; Orlandini, 1734/12/10; 1734/16/10.

Caffarello (Caffariello). *See* Majorano, Gaetano.

Campioni, Antonio (Milano). 1735/30/7, A.770, 497; (Venezia) 1736/21/4, A.770, 599v; 1736/5/5, A.770, 604; 1736/25/8, A.770, 651v; 1736/8/9, A.770, 659; *see also* Colucci, F., 1736/18/8; Corsini, B., 1735/27/12; Gasparini, 1736/8/9; Vivaldi, 1736/3/3; 1736/17/3; 1736/23/3; 1736/6/4; 1736/1/9; 1736/8/9; 1736/15/9.

Cangiano. *See* Schianteschi, 1739/11/8.

Canini, Settimio. *See* Coppoli, 1737/10/8; Corsini, 1738/27/5; Grimani, 1736/25/2; 1736/10/3; 1736/23/3; Mochi, 1736/21/2; Niccolini, 1739/18/8; 1739/25/8; 1739/1/9; Orlandini, 1736/19/6; Prini, 1736/21/2; Vivaldi, 1735/7/10; 1735/19/10; 1735/28/10; 1735/12/11; 1736/30/6.

Caraffa, Lelio. *See* Baratti, P., 1734/12/4; Corsini, B., 1735/8/11.

Carasale (Carassale), Angelo. *See* Acciaioli, 1738/9/9; 1739/13/1; 1739/27/1; 1739/20/4; 1739/29/4; 1739/2/6; 1739/9/6; 173916/6; 1739/23/6; 1739/7/7; Baratti, P., 1739/13/1; 1739/20/4; 1739/13/6; 1739/20/6; 1739/23/6; 1739/11/7; Baratti, T., 1739/17/4; 1739/2/5; Bernardi, 1739/16/6; 1739/23/6; 1739/25/6; 1739/30/6; 1739/7/7; 1739/11/7; 1739/19/7; 1739/25/7; 1740/25/3; Lucchesini, 1740/28/3; Nozzoli, F. M., 1726/19/3; 1740/2/8; 1740/23/8; 1740/13/9.

Carestini, Giovanni (Napoli). 1732/8/7; (Venezia) 1732/30/8; 1732/6/9, A.770, 159v; 1732/20/9, A.770, 166v; (Piacenza) 1732/27/9, A.770, 170v; 1732/9/10, A.770, 175; *see also* Castore, 1732/27/9; 1732/17/10; Corsini, B., 1739/15/9; Della Rovere, 1736/22/2; Donatelli, 1734/29/5; 1737/25/5; 1737/8/6; 1737/15/6; Grisi, 1732/8/7; 1732/22/7; 1732/9/8; Lucchesini, 1739/30/6; 1740/5/7; Martelli, D., 1732/15/7; Nicolini, 1737/23/3; 1737/22/4; Nozzoli, F. M., 1732/22/7; Pinacci, 1731/26/3; 1731/16/4; 1731/8/5; Pucci, 1733/31/7; Ridolfi, 1732/16/8; Roperini, 1732/1/11; Schianteschi, 1726/13/7; Tanara, 1726/13/7; Tesi, 1740/5/10.

Carlotti, Alessandro, marchese (Verona). 1739/8/8, A.771, 284v.

Castore, Antonio Castor (Perugia). 1732/27/9, A.770, 170; 1732/17/10, A.770, 176.

Castris, Francesco de (Roma). 1720/10/12, A.768, 1130; 1720/25/12, A.768, 1134; 1721/8/1, A.768, 1136; 1721/14/1, A.768, 1139; 1721/21/1, A.768, 1141.

Caterina. *See* Ristorini, 1736/18/2.

Catani, Andrea. *See* Barrati, P., 1739/25/7; 1739/1/8; Colucci, O., 1737/4/5.

Cavana, Giuseppe. *See* Marchesini, 1726/16/6; 1726/22/6.

Cermenati, Antonia (La Napoletana) (Roma). 1731/27/2; *see also* Valletta, 1731/6/2; 1731/27/2; Zambeccari, 1739/16/6.

Chaumont, Giovanni. *See* Vivaldi, 1735/23/9.

Checco lucchese. *See* Aquilanti, 1734/9/1; 1734/16/4; Corsini, B., 1736/17/1; 1736/24/1; Grimani, 1735/30/7; Vivaldi, 1734/9/10.

Chiara (Chiaretta). *See* Aquilanti, 1734/9/1; Colucci, O., 1736/15/9; Corsini, B., 1735/27/12; 1736/17/1; Grimaldi, 1731/27/1; Saladino del Borgo, 1734/20/3.

Chiavistelli. *See* Corsini, B., 1735/27/12; 1736/28/2; 1736/6/3.

Colucci, Filippo (Venezia). 1736/18/8, A.770, 649; 1736/1/9, A.770, 656; 1736/8/9, A.770, 658; *see also* Vivaldi, 1736/15/9.

Colucci, Orsola (Venezia). 1736/15/9, A.770, 664; 1737/23/3, A.771, 58; (Verona) 1737/8/4, A.771, 63; 1737/4/5, A.771, 66v; 1737/25/5, A.771, 74; 1737/8/6, A.771, 81v; (Venezia) 1737/29/6, A.771, 90; 1737/13/7, A.771, 94r; 1737/27/7, A.771, 98; 1737/3/8, A.771, 100; *1737/10/8, A.771, 102 (OO, 152); 1737/17/8, A.771, 103v; (Milano) 1740/19/4, A.771, 330v; *see also* Acciaioli 1737/22/1; Campioni, 1736/21/4; 1736/5/5; Colucci, F., 1736/18/8; 1736/8/9; Cottini, 1740/9/4; Della Rovere, 1737/6/8; Gasparini, 1736/8/9; Grimani, 1736/23/3; 1736/13/4; 1736/5/10; 1737/11/2; Mijone, 1737/30/7; 1737/6/8; Saroni, 1737/5/2; Vivaldi, 1735/7/10; 1735/28/10; 1736/3/3; 1736/17/3; 1736/23/3; 1736/28/3; 1736/6/4; 1736/21/4; 1736/5/5; 1736/12/5; 1736/1/9; 1736/15/9; 1737/4/5; 1737/1/6; 1737/19/3; 1737/22/4.

Coluzzi, Orsola. *See* Colucci, Orsola.

Compstoff, Ermanno. *See* Aquilanti, 1734/6/2; Lucchesini, 1739/28/7; 1740/22/2; 1741/24/1; 1741/31/1; Schianteschi, 1739/11/8; 1739/15/8; 1739/25/8; 1739/1/9; Spada, 1743/13/7.

Conti, Gioacchino (Giziello). *See* Della Rovere, 1736/22/2; Mochi, 1736/10/3.

Coppoli, Ranieri, marchese (Bologna). 1737/10/8, A.771, 101.

Corsini, Bartolomeo, principe (Roma). 1731/11/12, A.770, 89; (Parma) 1733/1/9, A.770, 284v; (Napoli) *1735/8/11, A.770, 536v (OO, 94); *1735/27/12, A.770, 552v (OO, 42); (Roma) 1736/17/1, A.770, 558v; 1736/24/1, A.770, 560v; 1736/31/1, A.770, 562v; 1736/7/2, A.770, 565; 1736/21/2, A.770, 571; 1736/28/2, A.770, 574; 1736/6/3, A.770, 577; 1736/13/3, A.770, 580; 1736/20/3, A.770, 584; 1736/9/4, A.770, 595; (Napoli) 1736/22/5, A.770, 611; 1736/10/7, A.770, 634; *1736/17/7, A.770, 636 (OO, 96); 1736/31/7, A.770, 641v; 1736/21/8, A.770, 650v; (Palermo) *1738/26/4, A.771, 163v (OO, 100); *1738/27/5, A.771, 174 (OO, 100); *1738/21/6, A.771, 181v (OO, 101); 1739/15/9, A.771, 296v; 1741/22/8, A.771, 455v; 1744/18/2, A.771, 611; *see also* Acciaioli, 1736/22/5; 1736/4/9.

Corsini, Maria Vittoria Altoviti, principessa (Roma). 1736/11/9, A.770, 661v; *1736/18/9, A.770, 666v (OO, 44).

Costa, Antonia (Bologna). 1735/23/4, A.770, 462v; *see also* Baratti, P., 1735/30/4; Donatelli, 1735/20/4; 1735/30/4; 1735/7/5; 1735/7/6; 1735/11/6; Mochi, 1736/21/7; Nozzoli, S. T., 1735/19/4; 1736/21/7; 1736/28/7; Orlandini, 1736/23/6.

Cottini, Giovanni Domenico (Venezia). 1725/15/9, A.769, 206v; 1725/28/9, A.769, 208; 1726/1/6, A.769, 273; 1726/8/6, A.769, 275; 1726/16/6, A.769, 276v; 1726/22/6, A.769, 277; 1726/29/6, A.769, 280; 1728/24/4, A.769, 391v; 1732/5/1, A.770, 93; 1732/22/1, A.770, 94v; 1733/1/8, A.770, 279; 1733/12/9, A.770, 280; *1733/26/9, A.770, 294 (OO, 68); 1733/9/10, A.770, 296; 1733/16/10, A.770, 297; 1733/24/10, A.770, 298; 1733/30/10, A.770, 298v; 1733/7/11, A.770, 299v; *1734/6/3, A.770, 324v (OO, 68); 1734/2/4, A.770, 335; 1734/15/5, A.770, 332v; 1734/19/6, A.770, 362; 1734/10/7, A.770, 374; 1734/24/7, A.770, 382; 1734/7/8, A.770, 386v; 1734/21/8, A.770, 394; 1734/6/11, A.770, 414; 1734/27/11, A.770, 420; 1735/26/2, A.770, 444v; 1735/23/4, A.770, 462; 1735/7/5, A.770, 469; 1735/14/10, A.770, 528v; 1735/12/11, A.770, 539v; 1736/17/3, A.770, 583; 1736/28/3, A.770, 590; 1736/6/4, A.770, 592; 1736/13/4, A.770, 596v; 1736/21/4, A.770, 600; 1736/16/6, A.770, 623; 1737/7/12, A.771, 124; 1740/9/4, A.771, 328v; *see also* Donatelli, 1737/7/12.

Craon, Principe di (Firenze). 1737/14/12, A.771, 128; *see also* Bartolommei, 1737/14/12; 1737/17/12; 1738/4/1; 1738/1/2; 1738/22/2; 1738/12/4; 1738/3/5; Cottini, 1737/7/12; Tomii, P., 1737/7/12; Zambeccari, 1737/17/12.

Croci, Rosa (Bologna). 1724/11/7, A.769, 136; 1731/13/2, A.770, 32; 1731/24/2, A.770, 34v; 1731/3/3, A.770, 37; *see also* Donatelli, 1737/17/12; Valletta, 1731/13/2; 1731/24/2; 1731/27/2; 1731/3/3.

Cuzzoni Sandoni, Francesca (Bologna). 1737/11/5, A.771, 68v; 1737/18/5, A.771, 70; 1737/25/5, A.771, 75v; 1737/7/12, A.771, 125; *see also* Della Rovere, 1733/21/4; Donatelli, 1733/25/4; 1734/29/5; 1737/13/12; 1737/17/12; Lucchesini, 1740/17/5; Mari, 1737/1/7; Migliorucci, 1726/7/12; Nozzoli, S. T., 1740/27/8; Pinacci, 1731/26/3; 1731/16/4; 1731/8/5; Sandoni, P., 1731/27/4.

dancers. *See* Aquilanti, 1732/7/6; 1734/23/1; 1734/6/2; 1734/26/6; Corsini, B., 1736/17/1; 1736/31/1; 1736/7/2; Cottini, 1733/26/9; Pieri, 1734/27/11; Sabioni, 1735/11/6; Vivaldi, 1734/18/9; 1734/6/11; 1734/27/11; 1735/6/8.

Davia, Filippo (Lucca). 1733/19/9, A.770, 290; 1733/23/9, A.770, 293v.

Della Ciaia, Annibale (Venezia). 1728/31/7, A.769, 407v; 1729/10/12, A.769, 465v; 1735/12/11, A.770, 538v; 1735/26/11, A.770, 543v.

Della Rovere, Francesco (Genova). 1732/3/6, A.770, 123v; 1732/17/6, A.770, 128; 1732/29/7, A.770, 142v; 1732/5/8, A.770, 145v; 1732/12/8, A.770, 148; 1732/2/9, A.770, 158; 1732/9/9, A.770, 161; 1732/16/9, A.770, 165v; 1732/30/9, A.770, 172; 1733/1/4, A.770, 229; 1733/14/4, A.770, 235v; 1733/21/4, A.770, 238v; 1733/28/4, A.770, 244; 1735/26/7, A.770, 496v; 1735/2/8, A.770, 502; 1735/9/8, A.770, 505; 1736/22/2, A.770, 571v; 1737/12/3, A.771, 54v; 1737/6/8, A.771, 101; 1737/27/8, A.771, 108v; 1737/3/9, A.771, 110v; 1737/10/9, A.771, 112; 1737/17/9, A.771, 113; 1738/18/3, A.771, 153v; 1738/22/4, A.771; 1738/6/5, A.771, 168; 1739/2/6, A.771, 246; 1739/9/6, A.771, 247v; 1741/1/8, A.771, 449v; 1741/22/8, A.771, 456; 1742/3/7, A.771, 514.

Della Taia, Giulio (Siena). *1735/9/7, A.770, 486 (OO, 90); 1735/12/7, A.770, 488; 1735/2/8, A.770, 502.

Del Rosso, Cristofano (Pisa). 1737/22/6, A.771, 87v; 1739/20/6, A.771, 253v; 1739/14/7, A.771, 273v.

Denzi, signora (Venezia). 1733/27/6, A.770, 266; *see also* Saladino del Borgo, 1733/20/6; 1733/27/6.

Dolci, Paolo. *See* Mijone, 1737/27/8.

Dolfino, Vettor (Venezia). 1731/12/5, A.770, 46v; 1731/23/6, A.770, 51.

Donatelli, Rocco Agostino (Bologna). 1731/3/3, A.770, 36v; 1733/25/4, A.770, 241v; 1733/16/5, A.770, 250v; 1733/30/6, A.770, 260v; 1734/20/3, A.770, 328v; 1734/2/4, A.770, 335; 1734/9/4, A.770, 337v; 1734/16/4, A.770, 340v; 1734/23/4, A.770, 341v; 1734/1/5, A.770, 346; 1734/7/5, A.770, 347; 1734/22/5, A.770, 343; 1734/29/5, A.770, 351v; 1734/20/11, A.770, 417v; 1735/20/4, A.770, 463; 1735/30/4, A.770, 464v; 1735/3/5, A.770, 467; 1735/7/5, A.770, 468v; 1735/7/6, A.770, 473; 1735/11/6, A.770, 473v; 1735/25/6, A.770, 481; 1735/1/7, A.770, 483v; 1736/11/8, A.770, 646v; 1737/11/5, A.771, 69; 1737/18/5, A.771, 72; 1737/25/5, A.771, 73v; 1737/1/6, A.771, 78; 1737/8/6, A.771, 81; 1737/15/6, A.771, 85v; 1737/22/6, A.771, 88; 1737/29/6, A.771, 89v; 1737/6/7, A.771, 91v; 1737/7/12, A.771, 124; 1737/13/12, A.771, 125v; 1737/17/12, A.771, 130v; 1739/13/6, A.771, 249; *see also* Fontana, Agostino, 1734/5/6.

Dreyer (Dreier), Giovanni (Venezia). 1735/15/1, A.770, 431v; 1735/29/1, A.770, 436; 1735/26/2, A.770, 444v; (Pietroburgo) 1735/17/3, A.770, 449v; 1735/1/7, A.770, 484v; (Berlino) 1736/14/2, A.770, 567; *see also* Donatelli, 1734/20/11; Orlandini, 1736/9/6.

Durazzo, Giovanni Stefano (Genova). 1724/19/9, A.769, 155; 1724/5/12, A.769, 170; 1724/13/12, A.769, 170v; 1725/2/1, A.769, 173v.

Eberhard, Giustina. *See* Porpora, 1726/20/7.

Elmi, Agata (Agatina). *See* Acciaioli, 1739/20/4; 1739/29/4; Baratti, P., 1738/25/11; 1739/20/4; 1739/13/6; 1739/20/6; 1739/11/7; 1739/18/7; 1739/1/8; Baratti, T., 1739/17/4; Uttini, 1734/7/5.

Evans, Carlo (Pisa). 1732/16/9, A.770, 165v.

Fabbri, Anibale Pio (Il Ballino) (Napoli). 1724/23/5, A.769, 127; 1726/30/11, A.769, 314v; 1739/23/6, A.771, 259v; *see also* Baratti, P., 1735/30/4; Boni, 1739/16/6; 1739/23/6; Costa, 1735/23/4; Della Rovere, 1737/12/3; Donatelli, 1735/20/4; 1737/15/6; 1737/29/6; Grimani, 1736/10/3; 1736/21/4; Porpora, 1726/20/7; Vivaldi, 1735/19/11.

Fabri, Anibal Pio. *See* Fabbri, Anibale.

Facchinelli, Lucia (La Beccaretta). *See* Acciaioli, 1738/25/11; 1738/9/12; 1738/30/12; 1739/20/4; 1739/23/6; Baratti, P., 1739/20/6; 1739/1/8; Baratti, T., 1739/17/4; Bernardi, 1739/23/6; 1739/28/7; 1739/25/8; 1739/29/8; Dreyer, 1735/29/1; Grimani, 1732/6/12; Lucchesini, 1740/17/5; Nozzoli, F. M., 1732/25/11.

Fachner, Giovan Francesco. *See* Grimani, 1735/27/8.

Faini. *See* Della Rovere, 1732/30/9; 1733/1/4; 1733/21/4; 1733/28/4; Evans, 1732/16/9.

Faini, Anna Maria. *See* Corsini, 1738/26/4; 1738/27/5.

Faliconti, Giuseppe Polverini (Roma). 1740/11/7, A.771, 348; 1740/19/7, A.771, 351; 1740/26/7, A.771, 354; 1740/2/8, A.771, 356; 1740/9/8, A.771, 359v; 1740/16/8, A.771, 363v.

Farinelli. *See* Broschi, Carlo.

Faus, Menichina. *See* Orlandini, 1736/9/6.

Ferrari, Caterina. *See* Ristorini, 1736/25/2.

Ferrari, Giacomina. *See* Orlandini, 1736/16/6; 1736/19/6; 1736/26/6.

Ferretti, Ottaviano (Ancona). 1734/21/4, A.770, 341.

Fieschi, Urbano (Milano). 1721/21/1, A.768, 1141; 1721/4/2, A.768, 1144.

Finazzi, Filippo (Bologna). 1736/12/6, A.770, 621v; 1736/1/9, A.770, 656v; *1736/3/11, A.770, 683 (OO, 45); *see also* Marini, 1736/9/6; 1736/11/8; Orlandini, 1736/9/6; Visconti, 1735/20/10.

Fini, Michele. *See* Grimani, 1733/9/5.

Fontana, Agostino (Bologna). 1734/5/6, A.770, 354; 1734/27/11, A.770, 419v; *see also* Donatelli, 1734/20/3; 1734/2/4; 1734/9/4; 1734/16/4; 1734/23/4; 1734/1/5; 1734/7/5; 1734/29/5; 1735/7/5; Orlandini, 1733/21/7; 1734/12/10; Pinacci, 1731/16/4; Saladino del Borgo, 1734/20/3; 1734/21/8, A.770, 394v; Salviati, 1735/7/6.

Fontana, Antonio (Roma). 1724/6/6, A.769, 130v; 1724/11/7, A.769, 137; 1724/20/7, A.769, 132v; 1724/27/7, A.769, 133; 1725/21/8, A.769, 197; 1725/28/8, A.769, 200v; 1725/4/9, A.769, 202; 1725/11/9, A.769, 203v; 1725/13/9, A.769, 205; 1725/18/9, A.769, 207v; 1726/12/3, A.769, 246; 1727/25/11, A.769, 368v; 1727/6/12, A.769, 370v; *1734/21/8, A.770, 394v (OO, 69); *1734/27/11, A.770, 419v (OO, 70).

Forano, Principe di (Roma). 1736/10/7, A.770, 633v.

Forcellini, Diacinta (Bologna). 1736/14/7, A.770, 634v; 1736/20/11, A.771, 16; *see also* Montemar, 1736/17/11; 1736/20/11; Orlandini, 1736/9/6; 1736/19/6; 1736/26/6; 1736/6/7; 1736/14/7; Prini, 1736/10/11; 1736/17/11; 1736/20/11; Turcotti, 1736/26/6.

Forsanino. *See* Della Rovere, 1732/29/7.

Fortini, Lorenza (Genova). 1740/30/4, A.771, 333v; (Lucca) 1741/21/1, A.771, 402v; 1741/28/1, A.771, 405; 1741/21/2, A.771, 412v; *see also* Lucchesini, 1741/17/1; 1741/21/2; 1741/7/3; 1741/20/3; Paghetti, 1737/17/8; 1737/24/8.

Frescobaldi, Francesco (Firenze). 1738/29/9, A.771, 205.

Frizzi, Maria Maddalena. *See* Orlandini, 1736/9/6; Vivaldi, 1735/30/7; 1735/20/8.

Fumagalli, Caterina. *See* Lucchesini, 1740/17/5.

Fusano. *See* Aquilanti, 1734/9/1; Bagnano, 1738/22/7; Lucchesini, 1739/23/6.

Gaggiotti, Pellegrino. *See* Corsini, 1738/27/5; Della Rovere, 1733/1/4; 1733/14/4; 1733/21/4; 1733/28/4.

Galletta La. *See* Aquilanti, 1734/9/1; 1734/9/4.

Galletti, Domenico Giuseppe. *See* Della Rovere, 1732/30/9.

Gallo, Giustina (Venezia). 1736/6/4, A.770, 592; *see also* Agliata, 1736/24/7; Cottini, 1736/17/3; 1736/28/3; 1736/6/4; 1736/13/4; 1736/21/4.

Gasparini, Matteo (Parma). 1736/8/9, A.770, 658v; *see also* Colucci, F., 1736/8/9; Vivaldi, 1736/8/9.

Georgi, Filippo. *See* Saladino del Borgo, 1734/2/3.

Gerardini, Maria Maddalena (La Sellarina). *See* Grimani, 1739/1/8; Mochi, 1736/3/3; Ristorini, 1736/25/2; Vivaldi, 1736/3/3.

Giacomazzi. *See* Vivaldi, 1735/20/8.

Giacomelli. *See* Baratti, P., 1735/4/7; Lucini, 1735/4/7.

Giacomina, Napoletana. *See* Saladino del Borgo, 1734/18/9.

Giardini (Del Delfino), Rosa. *See* Orlandini, 1736/9/6; 1736/16/6; 1736/19/6; 1736/26/6; 1736/30/6; Vivaldi, 1736/17/3; 1736/23/6; 1736/30/6.

Gieri. *See* Saladino del Borgo, 1734/21/9.

Giovannino. *See* Vivaldi, 1735/28/10.

Giraud, Annina. *See* Cottini, 1735/14/10; 1735/12/11; Finazzi, 1736/12/6; Grimani, 1736/10/3; Ridolfi, 1732/2/8; Vivaldi, 1735/16/4; 1735/30/4; 1735/4/6; 1735/18/6; 1735/1/7; 1735/9/7; 1735/28/10; 1735/12/11; 1735/19/11; 1736/3/2; 1736/28/3; 1736/6/4; 1736/13/4; 1736/21/4.

Giuliano. *See* Della Rovere, Francesco, 1733/28/4.

Gizzi, Domenico (Roma). 1726/22/3, A.769, 247.

Grandi, Cesare (Pisa). 1737/18/4, A.771, 65; *see also* Pasquetti, 1744/15/2.

Grassi, P. M. de, marchese (Bologna). 1724/17/6, A.769, 132v.

Grimaldi, Niccola (Venezia). 1731/27/1, A.770, 29v; *see also* Broschi, 1731/23/1; 1731/6/2.

Grimani, Michele (Venezia). 1726/5/10, A.769, 306; 1732/6/12, A.770, 195v; 1733/9/5, A.770, 249v; 1735/30/7, A.770, 497v; 1735/13/8, A.770, 509; 1735/20/8, A.770, 512; 1735/27/8, A.770, 514; 1735/10/9, A.770, 521; 1736/25/2, A.770, 573v; 1736/10/3, A.770, 579; 1736/23/3, A.770, 586; 1736/6/4, A.770, 593v; 1736/13/4, A.770, 597v; 1736/21/4, A.770, 600v; 1736/1/9, A.770, 655; 1736/15/9, A.770, 662; 1736/5/10, A.770, 672v; 1737/11/2, A.771, 47; 1739/19/7, A.771, 274v; 1739/1/8, A.771, 280; 1739/15/8, A.771, 287v; 1739/5/9, A.771, 194v; 1739/12/9, A.771, 296v; 1739/2/10, A.771, 301v; 1739/9/10, A.771, 303; 1741/18/3, A.771, 417; *see also* Borghesi, A., 1739/9/10; Colucci, O., 1737/3/8; Della Rovere, 1737/3/9; Lucchesini, 1739/21/7; 1739/11/8; 1739/1/9; Vivaldi, 1736/17/3; 1736/5/10.

Grisi, Francesco (Brescia). 1732/8/7, A.770, 132v; (Mantova) 1732/22/7, A.770, 141; 1732/26/7, A.770, 142v; (Brescia) 1732/9/8, A.770, 145v; 1732/16/8, A.770, 150; 1733/18/4, A.770, 236; 1733/16/5, A.770, 252; 1733/23/5, A.770, 254v; 1733/20/6, A.770, 263v; 1733/25/7, A.770, 274; 1733/1/8, A.770, 279; 1735/16/7, A.770, 490; 1735/20/10, A.770, 532; 1737/22/1, A.771, 37; 1737/29/1, A.771, 39; *see also* Cottini, 1735/12/11; Martelli, 1732/15/7; Mochi, 1736/21/2; 1736/3/3; Orlandini, 1733/28/7; Prini, 1736/21/2; Saladino del Borgo, 1733/20/6; 1733/25/7; Vivaldi, 1735/13/8.

Groppo, Antonio. *See* Cottini, 1732/5/1; 1732/22/1.

Gualandi, Margherita (La Campioli) (Venezia). 1724/10/6, A.769, 131; 1726/19/3, A.769, 251v; 1726/29/6, A.769, 280v; 1726/20/7, A.769, 287; 1737/18/5, A.771, 72; 1737/1/6, A.771, 71v; 1737/15/6, A.771, 85; *see also* Durazzo, 1725/2/1; Nozzoli, F. M., 1726/5/3; 1726/12/3; 1726/19/3; 1726/15/4; Pieri, B., 1737/1/6.

Guetta, Giovanna (Firenze). 1733/19/9, A.770, 291; *see also* Niccolini, 1734/26/1; Pola, 1733/19/9; Saladino del Borgo, 1734/2/3.

Gugliantini, Pietro. *See* Lucchesini, 1739/14/7.

Guiducci, Niccolò (Firenze). 1733/3/8, A.770, 279v.

Handel, [George Frederick]. *See* Pucci, 1734/11/5.

[Hasse, Adolfo], Il Sassone. *See* Aquilanti, 1732/18/4; Imer, G., 1736/24/11; Nozzoli, S. T., 1736/17/11; 1736/24/1.

Iaco, Filippo (Roma). 1741/20/3, A.771, 417v.

Imer, Giuseppe (Venezia). 1736/24/11, A.771, 17.

Imer, Marianna and Teresa. *See* Grisi, 1737/22/1; 1737/29/1.

Lacchetti, Gaetano. *See* Lucchesini, 1739/11/8.

Lafond. *See* Schianteschi, 1736/22/9.

Landuzzi, Anna Maria. *See* Donatelli, 1739/13/6; Nozzoli, S. T., 1739/13/6; Valletta, 1731/13/2; 1731/24/2; 1731/27/2; 1731/3/3.

Lanzetti, Lucia (La Grechetta) (Piacenza). 1726/16/3, A.769, 249v; (Ferrara) 1726/12/4, A.769, 256v; (Modena) 1726/11/5, A.769, 263v; (Bologna) *1726/5/10, A.769, 305 (RIM, 187); *see also* Porpora, 1726/20/7.

Lapi, Neri de (Lungone). 1733/6/6, A.770, 259; 1733/20/6, A.770, 264; 1733/1/8, A.770, 279v.

Laurenzani (Lorenzani), Maria Anna. *See* Guetta, 1733/19/9; Nozzoli, F. M., 1726/5/3.

Lebecche. *See* Venturini, 1744/14/3.

Leo, Leonardo. *See* Acciaioli, 1736/18/9; 1736/25/9; 1736/1/10; 1736/8/10; 1736/22/10; 1737/8/1; 1737/15/1; Corsini, M. V., 1736/18/9; Niccolini, 1734/22/6; Orlandini, 1736/8/10; 1736/21/10.

LoFredi. *See* Saladino del Borgo, 1734/27/9.

Lolli, Dorotea. *See* Orlandini, 1736/9/6; 1736/16/6; 1736/19/6; Uttini, 1734/7/5.

Longini, Lucrezia. *See* Martelli, 1732/8/7; Saladino del Borgo, 1733/20/6.

Lorenzani. *See* Laurenzani, Maria Anna.

Lorenzoni, Signor. *See* Cottini, 1733/30/10; Della Rovere, 1737/6/8.

Lottini, Antonio. *See* Della Rovere, 1733/1/4.

Lucchesina, La. *See* Acciaioli, 1737/22/1; 1737/5/2.

Lucchesini, Girolamo, marchese (Modena). 1734/12/4, A.770, 340; 1736/6/3, A.770, 576v; 1737/15/1, A.771, 34; (Reggio) 1739/9/6, A.771, 248; 1739/16/6, A.771, 252; 1739/23/6, A.771, 256; 1739/30/6, A.771, 263; 1739/7/7, A.771, 269; 1739/14/7, A.771, 272; 1739/21/7, A.771, 276; 1739/28/7, A.771, 278v; 1739/4/8, A.771, 282v; 1739/11/8, A.771, 285; 1739/15/8, A.771, 288; 1739/25/8, A.771, 291; 1739/1/9, A.771, 293v; 1739/8/9, A.771, 295v; 1739/15/12, A.771, 314; *1740/22/2, A.771, 319v (OO, 148); *1740/29/2, A.771, 320 (OO, 148); 1740/14/3, A.771, 321; 1740/28/3, A.771, 323v; *1740/17/5, A.771, 336 (OO, 103); 1740/7/6, A.771, 339v; 1740/21/6, A.771, 342; 1740/5/7, A.771, 346; 1740/1/11, A.771, 387; 1741/17/1, A.771, 402; 1741/24/1, A.771, 403; 1741/31/1, A.771, 405v; 1741/21/2, A.771, 412v; 1741/7/3, A.771, 416v; 1741/20/3, A.771, 417v; 1741/13/6, A.771, 430v; *see also* Bernardi, 1739/7/7; 1739/14/7; 1740/21/3; 1740/25/3; 1740/29/3; Fortini, 1741/21/1; 1741/28/1; 1741/21/2; Rangoni, 1739/22/9; Tesi, 1740/5/10.

Lucini, Giulio Antonio (Milano). 1735/4/7, A.770, 485; 1735/23/8, A.770, 514.

Maffei, Scipione. *See* Vivaldi, 1731/13/11.

Majorano, Gaetano (Caffarello). *See* Donatelli, 1737/25/5; Nozzoli, F. M., 1736/7/2.

Mancinelli, Costanza (Recanati). 1732/2/8, A.770, 144; *see also* Carestini, 1732/6/9; Niccolini, 1732/9/8; 1732/26/8; 1732/2/9; 1732/6/9; 1732/23/9; 1732/25/10; 1732/28/10; Porro, 1732/13/10.

Mancini, Giovanni Battista (Lucca). 1733/19/9, A.770, 290v; 1733/23/9, A.770, 293v; *see also* Davia, 1733/19/9; 1733/23/9.

Mancini, Rosa (Padova). 1737/22/6, A.771, 88v; *see also* Corsini, 1738/27/5; Donatelli, 1737/25/5; Nozzoli, F. M., 1736/6/3; Rangoni, 1732/15/7; Ridolfi, 1732/16/8; Tesi, 1737/25/5; Vivaldi, 1731/6/11.

Manzuoli, Giovanni. *See* Della Rovere, 1735/26/7; 1735/2/8; 1735/9/8; Nozzoli, S. T., 1735/26/7; 1735/2/8.

Marcello, Aurelia. *See* Vico, 1726/20/7.

Marchesini, Santa (Bologna). 1726/20/4, A.769, 258; 1726/16/6, A.769, 276v; 1726/22/6, A.769, 278v; 1726/6/7, A.769, 282v.

Marchi, Damiano, dottore (Cascina). 1735/1/1, A.770, 427; *see also* Corsini, 1736/21/8; Orlandini, 1736/8/10.

Mari, Giovanni Battista de, marchese (Torino). 1735/2/8, A.770, 500; 1735/16/8, A.770, 511; 1736/20/3, A.770, 583v; 1737/18/6, A.771, 86v; 1737/1/7, A.771, 91; 1737/6/8, A.771, 100v.

Marini, Maria Anna (Bologna).   1736/9/6, A.770, 621; 1736/11/8, A.770, 647v; *1736/3/11, A.770, 683v (OO, 45); *see also* Della Rovere, 1739/2/6; 1739/9/6; Nozzoli, S. T., 1739/13/6; Orlandini, 1736/9/6.

Martelli, Domenico, abbate (Roma).   1732/8/7, A.770, 133; 1732/15/7, A.770, 136; 1732/22/7, A.770, 138v; 1733/28/7, A.770, 275v; 1734/19/4, A.770, 341; 1734/27/4, A.770, 344v; 1734/3/5, A.770, 345.

Mazzanti, Rosaura (Venezia).   1726/5/10, A.769, 305v.

Merighi, Antonia (Bologna).   1733/5/9, A.770, 285; *see also* Donatelli, 1733/16/5; Grimani, 1732/6/12; Nozzoli, F. M., 1733/28/7; 1740/23/8; 1740/30/8; Orlandini, 1733/28/7; 1733/1/8; Visconti,1735/20/10; Vivaldi, 1735/19/11.

La Maestina.   *See* Tomii, Antonia.

Metastasio, Pietro.   *See* Barbieri, A., 1734/12/6; Bartolommei, 1737/25/5; Cermenati, 1731/27/2; Corsini, 1736/21/8; Niccolini, 1734/15/6; Nozzoli, S. T., 1740/17/9; 1740/8/11; Valletta, 1731/24/2.

Migliorucci, Pier Giuseppe (Londra).   1726/29/3, A.769, 253v; *1726/7/12, A.769, 315v (RIM, 188).

Mijone, Signor (Torino).   1735/2/8, A.770, 500; 1735/16/8, A.770, 510v; 1735/20/9, A.770, 523; 1737/12/3, A.771, 54; 1737/11/6, A.771, 83v; 1737/11/7, A.771, 90v; 1737/30/7, A.771, 99; 1737/6/8, A.771, 100v; 1737/27/8, A.771, 108; *see also* Ambrogi, 1735/20/10; Collucci, O., 1737/3/8; 1737/10/8; Corsini, 1735/27/12; 1736/21/2; 1736/28/2; Cottini, 1736/28/3; 1736/6/4; Grimani, 1735/10/9; 1736/5/10; Mari, 1735/2/8; 1735/16/8; 1736/29/3; Pompeati 1737/12/2; Schianteschi, 1736/22/9; Vivaldi, 1736/17/3; 1736/5/10.

Minelli.   *See* Addato, Domenico di.

Minelli, Giovanni Battista.   *See* Della Rovere, 1733/28/4; Donatelli, 1735/25/6; Durazzo, 1725/2/1; Pinacci, 1731/16/4.

Minucci (Roma).   1736/7/8, A.770, 644.

Mochi, Raffaello (Livorno).   1736/21/2, A.770, 570v; 1736/3/3, A.770, 575v; 1736/10/3, A.770, 579; 1736/21/7, A.770, 638; 1736/28/7, A.770, 640v; *see also* Nozzoli, S. T., 1741/29/8.

Molarini, Maria Maddalena (Bologna).   1733/22/9, A.770, 292; 1733/10/11, A.770, 300v; 1733/10/11, A.770, 301; 1733/21/11, A.770, 302; *see also* Guetta, 1733/19/9; Niccolini, 1734/26/1; 1734/9/3; 1734/16/3; Nozzoli, F. M., 1733/28/7.

Molinari, Carlo Francesco (Venezia).   1720/3/8, A.768, 1093; 1720/31/8, A.768, 1103; 1720/14/9, A.768, 1108; 1720/21/9, A.768, 1111; 1720/7/12, A.768, 1128; 1720/14/12, A.768, 1131; 1721/18/1, A.768, 1140; 1721/1/2, A.768, 1144.

Montemar, duca di (Pisa).   1736/17/11, A.771, 11v; 1736/20/11, A.771, 16.

Monticelli, Angelo Maria (Milano).   1736/24/3, A.770, 587; *see also* Baratta, P., 1734/12/4; 1734/11/5; Nozzoli, F. M., 1736/7/2; Valletta, 1731/13/2; Visconti, 1735/22/11; 1736/24/3; 1736/8/5; 1736/15/5.

Moretti.   *See* Pieri, B., 1737/1/6.

Moro, Anna.   *See* Grimani, 1736/1/9; 1736/15/9; 1736/5/10; Vivaldi, 1736/5/10.

Moro, Elisabetta.   *See* Grimani, 1737/11/2.

La Naveresi.   *See* Nozzoli, F. M., 1740/23/8.

Negri, Maria Caterina.   *See* Sacchetti, 1739/25/7; 1739/4/8.

Nenci, Domenico (San Miniato). *1738/4/1, A.771, 136 (OO, 160).

Nesti, Giovanni Battista. *See* Scaramuccia.

Niccolini, Giovan Luca, monsignore (Roma). 1732/22/7, A.770, 140; 1732/9/8, A.770, 146v; 1732/19/8, A.770, 151v; 1732/26/8, A.770, 154v; 1732/2/9, A.770, 157; 1732/6/9, A.770, 160; 1732/23/9, A.770, 168; 1732/23/9, A.770, 169; 1732/25/10, A.770, 179; 1732/28/10, A.770, 180v; 1732/29/11, A.770, 191; 1732/2/12, A.770, 194; *1733/22/11, A.770, 306v (OO, 61); 1733/15/12, A.770, 306v; *1734/26/1, A.770, 315 (OO, 62); *1734/2/2, A.770, 315v (OO, 64); 1734/9/3, A.770, 325; 1734/16/3, A.770, 326v; 1734/15/6, A.770, 358; 1734/22/6, A.770, 363; 1735/7/6, A.770, 473v; 1735/14/6, A.770, 476v; 1735/21/6, A.770, 479v; 1735/28/6, A.770, 481v; 1735/4/7, A.770, 485v; 1735/12/7, A.770, 490; 1739/4/8, A.771, 283; 1739/18/8, A.771, 289; 1739/25/8, A.771, 290v; 1739/1/9, A.771, 293; *see also* Martelli, 1732/15/7.

Nicolini, Mariano (Roma). 1735/14/6, A.770, 475v; 1735/21/6, A.770, 479; *1735/28/6, A.770, 482 (OO, 37); (Brescia) 1737/23/3, A.771, 57v; 1737/22/4, A.771, 65v; 1737/14/5, A.771, 69v; *1737/4/6, A.771, 79v (OO, 152); *see also* Acciaioli, 1737/12/3; 1737/14/5; Baratta, P., 1738/25/11; Della Rovere, 1737/12/3; Niccolini, G. L., 1735/7/6; 1735/14/6; 1735/21/6; 1735/28/6; 1735/4/7; 1735/12/7; Salviati, Anton Maria, 1735/7/6.

Novello, Felice (Bologna). 1736/24/7, A.770, 639v; 1736/31/7, A.770, 642; 1736/11/8, A.770, 647v; *see also* Donatelli, 1736/11/8.

Nozzoli, Filippo Maria (Napoli). 1724/11/7, A.769, 136; 1724/25/7, A.769, 139v; 1724/8/8, A.769, 142; 1724/22/8, A.769, 145v; *1726/5/3, A.769, 244 (OO, 108); 1726/12/3, A.769, 246v; 1726/19/3, A.769, 250v; *1726/8/4, A.769, 257 (OO, 108); *1726/15/4, A.769, 257 (OO, 109); 1726/21/5, A.769, 268v; 1726/8/6, A.769, 275; 1727/2/7, A.769, 282; 1727/25/11, A.769, 368; 1732/22/7, A.770, 140v; 1732/25/11, A.770, 190v; 1733/28/7, A.770, 276; 1733/11/8, A.770, 280v; 1734/25/5, A.770, 349; 1736/6/3, A.770, 576v; 1736/7/2, A.770, 564v; 1736/9/4, A.770, 594v; 1738/6/10, A.771, 206; 1740/2/8, A.771, 357; 1740/23/8, A.771, 368; 1740/30/8, A.771, 372v; 1740/13/9, A.771, 376.

Nozzoli, Sebastiano Tommaso (Livorno). 1726/11/5, A.769, 264v; 1728/7/8, A.769, 409; 1728/11/9, A.769, 415; 1735/19/4, A.770, 459r-v; 1735/26/7, A.770, 496; 1735/2/8, A.770, 501v; 1736/28/1, A.770, 561; 1736/21/7, A.770, 638v; 1736/28/7, A.770, 641v; 1736/17/11, A.771, 13; 1736/24/11, A.771, 18; 1739/13/6, A.771, 249; 1740/5/5, A.771, 326; 1740/9/8, A.771, 361; 1740/13/8, A.771, 363; 1740/16/8, A.771, 364; 1740/20/8, A.771, 365; 1740/23/8, A.771, 369v; 1740/27/8, A.771, 371; 1740/30/8, A.771, 372v; 1740/6/9, A.771, 374; 1740/10/9, A.771, 375; 1740/13/9, A.771, 376v; 1740/17/9, A.771, 377v; 1740/8/11, A.771, 388v; 1740/29/11, A.771, 394v; 1741/29/8, A.771, 458; 1741/5/9, A.771, 460; 1741/9/9, A.771, 460v; 1741/13/10, A.771, 467; 1741/17/10, A.771, 468; 1741/18/10, A.771, 468v; 1741/21/10, A.771, 468v; 1741/24/10, A.771, 469v; 1741/28/10, A.771, 470v; 1741/31/10, A.771, 472.

Obizzi, Ferdinando, marchese (Padova). 1740/7/5, A.771, 334v; 1740/28/5, A.771, 337v.

operas:

    Achille in Sciro. *See* Bernardi, 1739/21/6; 1739/23/6; Lucchesini, 1739/4/8; 1740/14/3; Nozzoli, S. T., 1740/20/8; 1740/23/8.

    Adriano in Siria. *See* Antinori, 1733/7/11; 1733/14/11; Cottini, 1733/26/9; 1733/9/10; 1733/30/10; 1733/7/11; Molinari, 1733/10/11; Sabatini, 1739/16/10.

    Alessandro nell'Indie. *See* Corsini, 1736/10/7.

    Alessandro severo. *See* Carestini, 1732/27/9; 1732/9/10.

    Amor costante. *See* Corsini, 1736/10/7.

    Anibale. *See* Pinacci, 1731/16/4.

Antigone. See Venturini, 1724/2/9.

L'Arianna. See Cottini, 1728/24/4.

Arianna e Teseo. See Frescobaldi, 1738/29/9.

Arminio. See Carestini, 1732/20/9.

Arsace (=Amore e maestà). See Corsini, 1736/10/7; Donatelli, 1731/3/3; Frescobaldi, 1738/29/9; Orlandini, 1731/17/2; Valletta, 1731/13/2; 1731/15/2; 1731/24/2.

Artaserse. See Spada, 1743/29/6.

Astianatte. See Fontana, Antonio, 1724/6/6; 1724/11/7; 1724/20/7; 1724/27/7.

Bajazette. See Vivaldi, 1734/9/10.

Il bottegaio gentiluomo. See Durazzo, 1724/19/9.

Camilla. See Lucchesini, 1740/22/2.

Cesare in Egitto. See Baratti, P., 1735/4/7; 1735/6/8; Lucini, 1735/4/7; 1735/23/8; Porro, 1735/9/8; 1735/23/8; 1735/13/9; 1735/27/12; Vivaldi, 1735/17/9; 1735/23/9.

Il Cid, (Il gran Cidde). See Acciaioli, 1736/18/9; 1736/25/9; 1736/1/10; 1736/8/10; Carestini, 1732/9/10; Corsini, M., 1736/18/9; Finazzi, 1736/1/9; Marini, 1736/11/8; Minucci, 1736/7/8; Niccolini, 1734/22/6; Nozzoli, S. T., 1740/9/8; 1740/13/8; 1740/20/8; 1740/23/8; 1740/30/8; 1740/6/9; 1740/10/9; 1740/13/9; 1740/17/9; Orlandini,1736/8/10.

La Clemenza di Tito. See Cottini, 1735/26/2.

Cleopatra regina d'Egitto vinta da Augusto. See Grimani, 1739/19/7; 1739/1/8; 1739/2/10.

Demetrio. See Aquilanti, 1732/4/4; Carestini, 1732/30/8; 1732/6/9; 1732/20/9; Nozzoli, S. T., 1741/13/10; 1741/17/10; 1741/21/10; 1741/24/10; 1741/28/10; 1741/31/10.

Il Demofoonte. See Lucchesini, 1740/22/2; 1740/5/7; Niccolini, 1733/22/1; Nozzoli, S. T., 1740/16/8; 1741/17/10; 1741/21/10.

Didone. See Fontana, Antonio, 1724/11/7; 1725/21/8; 1725/28/8; Nozzoli, F. M., 1724/11/7; 1724/25/7; 1724/8/8; 1724/22/8; Prini, 1737/5/1; 1737/12/1.

Dionisio longino. See Bentivoglio, 1738/11/1.

Ezio. See Barbieri, 1734/12/6; 1734/26/6; 1734/10/7; 1734/24/7; 1734/7/8; Carestini, 1732/20/9; 1732/27/9; Cottini, 1734/10/7; 1734/24/7; 1734/7/8; 1734/21/8; Fontana, Agostino, 1734/21/8; Niccolini, 1734/15/6; 1734/22/6; Sabatini, 1739/16/10; Uttini,1734/21/8; Visconti, 1734/24/8; 1734/2/11.

Faramondo. See Orlandini, 1721/9/8.

Farnace. See Fabbri, 1739/23/6; Fontana, Antonio, 1725/21/8; 1725/28/8; 1725/4/9; 1725/11/9; 1725/13/9; 1725/18/9; 1726/12/3; Lucchesini, 1741/21/2; Niccolini, 1732/29/11; Nozzoli, S. T., 1728/11/9; Orlandini, 1732/5/11; Roperini, 1732/1/11; Schianteschi, 1733/24/1; Spada, 1743/29/6; Valletta, 1731/17/2; Vivaldi, 1736/6/4; 1736/21/4.

La forza del sangue. See Cottini, 1725/15/9.

Gianguirre. See Carestini, 1732/30/8; 1732/20/9.

Ginevra. See Baratti, P., 1735/4/7; 1735/30/7; Orlandini, 1721/13/9; 1721/20/9; 1721/27/9; Vivaldi, 1735/18/6; 1735/6/8; 1735/17/9; 1735/23/9; 1735/7/10; 1735/12/11; 1735/19/11; 1736/28/2.

Il Giocatore. See Lapi, 1733/6/6; 1733/1/8.

L'inganno e disinganno. See Spada, 1732/10/5.

Ipermestra. See Cottini, 1726/1/6; 1726/16/6; Grimani, 1726/5/10.

L'innocenza difesa. See Castris, 1720/10/12.

Lucio Papiro. See Venturini,1724/5/8; 1724/19/8; 1724/2/9.

Merope. See Vivaldi, 1735/23/7.

Nerone. See Mazzanti, 1726/5/10.

Nino. See Niccolini, G. L., 1733/22/11; 1733/15/12.

Olimpiade. See Bartolommei, 1738/1/2; Nozzoli, S. T., 1740/8/11.

Ormisda. See Donatelli, 1737/17/12; Spada, 1743/29/6.

La Pellegrina. See Lapi, 1733/20/6.

Rodelinda, regina de'Longobardi. See Corsini, 1736/10/7; 1736/31/7; 1736/21/8; Donatelli, 1736/11/8; Marini, 1736/11/8; Novello, 1736/24/7; 1736/31/7; 1736/11/8; Orlandini, 1736/8/10.

Semiramide. See Niccolini, 1734/26/1; Nozzoli, S. T., 1740/17/9; Vivaldi, 1731/6/11.

Siroe. See Cermenati, 1731/27/2; Croci, 1731/3/3; Orlandini, 1731/17/2; 1731/24/2; 1731/3/3; Valletta, 1731/15/2; 1731/24/2; 1731/27/2; 1731/3/3.

Telemaco. See Fontana, Antonio, 1725/11/9; 1725/18/9.

Temistocle. See Bartolommei, F., 1737/25/5; Nozzoli, S. T., 1740/6/9; 1740/10/9; 1740/13/9; Spada, 1743/29/6.

Teseo. See Cottini, 1728/24/4.

Tito Manlio. See Barbieri, 1734/7/8; 1734/16/10; Orlandini, 1734/12/10; Visconti, 1734/21/9; 1734/28/9.

Tradimento traditore di se stesso. See Carestini, 1732/30/8; 1732/9/10; Della Rovere, 1732/29/7; 1732/5/8; Orlandini, 1721/9/8.

La verità nell'inganno. See Cottini, 1725/15/9; Fontana, Antonio, 1725/4/9.

Vincislao. See Saladino del Borgo, 1734/9/3.

Orlandini, Giuseppe (Bologna). 1721/8/7, A.768, 1168; 1721/19/7, A.768, 1170; 1721/19/7, A.769, 3; 1721/26/7, A.769, 4; 1721/29/7, A.769, 5; 1721/2/8, A.769, 6; 1721/5/8, A.769, 6v; 1721/9/8, A.769, 8; 1721/16/8, 9v; 1721/18/8, A.769, 10; 1721/6/9, A.769, 15; 1721/9/9, A.769, 16; 1721/13/9, A.769, 18; 1721/20/9, A.769, 19; 1721/27/9, A.769, 20v; 1721/13/10, A.769, 21; 1722/14/3, A.769, 32v; 1722/21/3, A.769, 33; 1724/10/6, A.769, 132; 1731/17/2, A.770, 33v; 1731/20/2, A.770, 34; 1731/24/2, A.770, 35; 1731/3/3, A.770, 36v; 1731/9/3, A.770, 37v; 1732/5/11, A.770, 182; (Pistoia) 1733/21/7, A.770, 272v; 1733/28/7, A.770, 277; 1733/1/8, A.770, 278; 1734/12/10, A.770, 406v; 1734/16/10, A.770, 408v; (Bologna) 1736/19/5, A.770, 608v; 1736/9/6, A.770, 619; 1736/16/6, A.770, 623v; 1736/19/6, A.770, 625; 1736/23/6, A.770, 627; 1736/26/6, A.770, 628; 1736/30/6, A.770, 629v; 1736/6/7, A.770, 631v; 1736/10/7, A.770, 633v; 1736/14/7, A.770, 634v; *1736/8/10, A.770, 673 (OO, 45); 1736/21/10, A.770, 679; *see also* Acciaioli, 1736/8/10; 1737/22/1; 1737/19/2; Baratti, P., 1735/23/9; 1739/1/8; Carestini, 1732/6/9; 1732/20/9; Castore, 1732/17/10; Corsini, B., 1731/11/12; Donatelli, 1734/2/4; 1734/9/4; 1734/1/5; 1736/11/8; 1737/7/12; 1737/13/12; Fontana, Agostino, 1734/27/11; Martelli, 1732/15/7; Niccolini, 1733/22/11; 1734/2/2; Novello, 1736/11/8; Nozzoli, F. M., 1727/25/11; Saladino del Borgo, 1734/2/3; 1734/9/3; 1734/13/3; Turcotti, 1736/26/6; Valletta, 1731/15/2; 1731/24/2; 1731/27/2; 1731/3/3; Vinci, 1727/25/11; Visconti, 1734/24/8; 1734/28/9; 1734/2/11; 1735/20/10; Vivaldi, 1735/7/10.

Pacini, Andrea *(Il Lucchesino)* (Lucca). 1725/15/9, A.769, 205v; *see also* Fontana, Antonio, 1726/12/3.

Paghetti, Giovanni Battista (Bologna). 1735/23/7, A.770, 494; 1735/30/7, A.770, 499; 1735/13/8, A.770, 508; 1735/16/8, A.770, 510; 1737/10/8, A.771, 102v; 1737/17/8, A.771, 104; 1737/24/8, A.771, 107.

Pagnini, Francesco Massimiliano (Reggio). 1726/21/5, A.769, 269; 1726/28/5, A.769, 271; *see also* Fortini, 1740/30/4.

Panacci, Antonio Bastiano (Siena). 1732/9/9, A.770, 161v.

Pandolfini, Palmieri. *See* Pinacci, 1726/11/5.

Parmigiana, La. *See* Vivaldi, 1734/13/11.

Pasquetti, Alessandro (Livorno). 1744/15/2, A.771, 611.

Pasi. *See* Orlandini, 1736/30/6.

Pelli (Peli), Francesco (Modena). 1731/16/4, A.770, 40v; 1739/22/9, A.771, 299v.

Pellizzari, Antonio. *See* Lanzetti, 1726/16/3; Nozzoli, F. M., 1726/19/3.

Pepoli Bentivoglio, Maria Anna, marchesa (Ferrara). 1735/16/7, A.770, 491.

Perez, David. *See* Corsini, B., 1738/21/6; 1739/15/9.

Pertici. *See* Bagnano, 1738/2/27; Baratti, P., 1738/12/7; 1739/19/7; Corsini, B., 1738/26/4; 1738/27/5; Della Rovere, 1732/30/9; Evans, 1732/16/9.

Petrillo (Pietrillo). *See* Grimani, 1735/13/8; Lucchesini, 1739/23/6; 1739/30/6; 1739/7/7; 1739/14/7; 1739/21/7; 1739/4/8; 1739/15/8; 1739/15/12; Vivaldi, 1734/23/10.

Peruzzi, Anna Maria (La Perrucchiera) (Genova). 1736/31/1, A.770, 562; (Bologna) 1736/19/2, A.770, 569v; *see also* Baratti, P., 1739/25/7; Boni, 1739/23/6; Dreyer, 1735/29/1; Fabbri, 1739/23/6; Lucchesini, 1740/17/5.

Pieri, Antonio (Venezia). 1742/23/9, A.771, 530v.

Pieri, Bartolomeo (Venezia). 1734/27/11, A.770, 420; 1737/1/6, A.771, 77.

Pieri, Maria Maddalena. *See* Acciaioli, 1738/26/8; 1738/9/9; 1738/16/9; 1739/23/6; Aldrovandi, 1735/9/7; Aquilanti, 1732/18/4; Barbieri, 1734/20/3; Bernardi, 1739/16/6; Broschi, 1731/23/1; 1731/6/2; Cermenati, 1731/27/2; Corsini, 1736/17/7; 1738/27/5; Cottini, 1734/6/11; 1734/27/11; Croci, 1731/13/2; 1731/3/3; Della Rovere, 1733/14/4; 1733/21/4; 1733/28/4; Donatelli, 1733/25/4; 1735/25/6; Dreyer, 1735/17/3; 1735/1/7; Durazzo, 1724/5/12; Fontana, Antonio, 1727/25/11; Grimaldi, 1731/27/1; Grimani, 1732/6/12; 1739/15/8; Gualandi, 1726/19/3; 1737/18/5; Lucchesini, G., 1736/6/3; 1739/9/6; 1741/24/1; 1741/31/1; 1741/21/2; Mari, 1736/20/3; Marini, 1736/9/6; Niccolini, 1734/16/3; Nozzoli, F. M., 1733/28/7; 1733/11/8; 1734/25/5; Nozzoli, S. T., 1728/11/9; Orlandini, 1736/19/5; Pieri, A., 1742/23/9; Pinacci, 1726/21/5; 1726/28/5; 1731/26/3; 1731/16/4; 1731/8/5; Rangoni, 1732/15/7; 1739/22/9; Ridolfi, 1732/16/8; Sabatini, 1739/16/10; Salviati, M., 1733/22/9; Sandoni, 1731/27/4; Stampa, 1735/13/12; Valletta, 1731/13/2; Vinci, 1727/25/11; Visconti, 1736/24/3; Vivaldi, 1731/6/11; 1734/4/9; 1734/24/9; 1734/16/10; 1734/6/11; 1735/18/6; 1735/30/7; 1735/20/8; 1736/6/4; 1736/13/4; 1736/2/6; 1736/30/6.

Pieri, Teresa. *See* Bernardi, 1739/16/6; Fontana, Antonio, 1727/25/11; Grisi, 1733/25/7.

Pietrino. *See* Vivaldi, 1734/24/9; 1734/9/10; 1734/13/11.

Pinacci, Giovanni Battista (Modena). 1726/11/5, A.769, 260v; (Reggio) 1726/14/5, A.769, 265; 1726/21/5, A.769, 269; 1726/28/5, A.769, 270v; (Roma) 1731/26/3, A.770, 39v; 1731/16/4, A.770, 41; 1731/8/5, A.770, 44; *see also*

Agliata, 1736/30/6; 1736/24/7; Banchieri, 1726/21/5; Baratti, P., 1739/13/6; Broschi, 1731/6/2; Del Rosso, 1737/22/6; Della Rovere, 1732/9/9; Gualandi, 1737/1/6; Martelli, 1732/15/7; Porro, 1735/29/11; 1735/27/12; Pucci, 1732/6/9; Ridolfi, 1732/16/8; Roperini, 1732/1/11; Salviati, A., 1732/12/8.

Pola, Camillo bali, fra (Venezia). 1733/12/9, A.770, 289; 1733/19/9, A.770, 291; 1737/22/6, A.771, 87v; 1737/6/7, A.771, 92v; 1738/11/1, A.771, 137v.

Polverini. *See* Bisagi, Natalizia.

Pompeati, Angelo (Venezia). 1736/5/10, A.770, 671v; 1737/12/2, A.771, 46v; *see also* Colucci, F., 1736/18/8; 1736/8/9; Colucci, O., 1737/8/4; 1737/4/5; 1737/25/5; 1740/19/4; Vivaldi, 1736/8/9; 1737/4/5; 1737/19/3.

Porpora, Nicola (Venezia). *1726/20/7, A.769, 287v (RIM, 186); *1726/17/8, A.769, 293v (RIM, 186); 1733/5/9, A.770, 285v; 1733/19/9, A.770, 290v; *see also* Acciaioli, 1737/19/2; Barbieri, 1734/10/7; Della Ciaia, 1728/31/7; Gualandi, 1726/20/7; Nozzoli, F. M., 1727/25/11; Vinci, 1727/25/11.

Porro, Pompeo, conte, abbate don. (Livorno). 1732/13/10, A.770, 176; (Milano) 1735/9/8, A.770, 504v; 1735/23/8, A.770, 513; 1735/30/8, A.770, 516; 1735/6/9, A.770, 519; 1735/13/9, A.770, 521v; 1735/17/10, A.770, 530; 1735/29/11, A.770, 543v; 1735/27/12, A.770, 553; 1744/24/3, A.771, 619.

Porta, Giovanni. *See* Acciaioli, 1737/19/2; Vinci, 1727/25/11.

Posterla, Costanza. *See* Valletta, 1731/3/3.

Postini. *See* Donatelli, 1734/23/4.

Prasca, Giacomo Maria, abbate (Genova). 1712/3/1, A.768, 544; 1712/3/8, A.768, 547; 1713/7/2, A.768, 687; 1713/11/4, A.768, 700; 1713/9/5, A.768, 708; 1713/11/7, A.768, 714; 1713/18/7, A.768, 715; 1713/24/10, A.768, 728; 1713/5/12, A.768, 728; 1714/1/1, A.768, 742; 1714/17/4, A.768, 757.

Preati, Giulia (Bologna). 1737/25/6, A.771, 89; *1737/27/7, A.771, 98 (OO, 153); *see also* Turcotti, 1737/10/8.

Predieri, Luca Antonio. *See* Broschi, 1731/6/2.

Prini, Pier Gaetano (Pisa). 1733/28/4, A.770, 242; 1736/21/2, A.770, 570; 1736/10/11, A.771, 7; 1736/17/11, A.771, 12; 1736/20/11, A.771, 15; 1737/5/1, A.771, 31; 1737/12/1, A.771, 33; 1737/21/5, A.771, 73; 1737/25/5, A.771, 75; 1737/28/5, A.771, 76; 1737/4/6, A.771, 79; 1737/8/6, A.771, 82; 1737/15/6, A.771, 85v; 1737/22/6, A.771, 88v; 1741/29/8, A.771, 457v; 1741/5/9, A.771, 455v; 1741/16/9, A.771, 463; *see also* Del Rosso, 1737/22/6.

Pucci, Vincenzo (Londra). 1732/6/9, A.770, 160; 1733/31/7, A.770, 277v; 1734/11/5, A.770, 331v.

Puttanino. *See* Lucchesini, 1739/7/7; Vivaldi, 1737/1/6.

Radif. *See* Baratti, P., 1733/10/11; Prini, 1737/5/1; 1737/12/1; Valletta, 1731/27/2.

Raffaelli, Antonio. *See* Lucchesini, 1740/17/5.

Rambaldi, Rambaldo, conte (Verona). 1739/29/8, A.771, 292.

Rangoni, Lodovico, marchese (Modena). 1732/15/7, A.770, 137; 1736/5/10, A.770, 671; 1739/22/9, A.771, 299.

Raperino. *See* Della Rovere, 1735/26/7; 1735/2/8.

Redi, maestro. *See* Della Rovere, 1741/22/8.

Regale, Signora. *See* Paghetti, 1737/10/8; Vivaldi, 1737/9/11.

Reginelli. *See* Turcotti, 1735/18/1.

Richecourt, Conte di. *See* Bartolommei, F., 1738/11/1; 1738/1/2; 1738/22/2; Bernardi, 1739/25/6; 1739/30/6; Lucchesini, 1739/23/6.

Ridolfi, Giuseppe (Bologna). *1732/2/8, A.770, 144 (OO, 80); 1732/16/8, A.770, 150v.

Righini. *See* Ridolfi, 1732/2/8; Saladino del Borgo, 1733/26/5; Schianteschi, 1732/28/6; 1732/12/7; 1732/19/7; 1732/26/7; 1732/2/8; 1732/9/8; 1732/16/8; 1732/23/8; 1732/30/8; 1732/6/9; 1732/13/9; 1732/3/10; 1732/10/10; 1732/8/11; 1732/15/11; 1732/6/12; 1732/27/12; 1733/24/1; 1733/31/1; 1733/7/2; 1733/28/2; 1733/7/3.

Ristorini, Antonio (Parma). 1724/6/5, A.769, 126; 1724/23/5, A.769, 127v; 1724/27/5, A.769, 128; (Bologna) 1736/18/2, A.770, 569v; 1736/25/2, A.770, 572; *see also* Orlandini, 1736/9/6.

Roperini, Cristofano (Piacenza). 1732/1/11, A.770, 181.

Rosana. *See* Colucci, O., 1736/15/9; Sabioni, 1735/30/4; Saroni, 1737/5/2; Vivaldi, 1739/14/11.

Rosina. *See* Saladino del Borgo, 1734/18/9.

Rospigliosi, Clemente (Pistoia). 1735/20/10, A.770, 531.

Rospigliosi, Lorenzo Felice (Pistoia). 1732/11/11, A.770, 183.

Rossermini, Ranieri (Pisa). 1735/19/10, A.770, 530v; 1735/31/10, A.770, 534v; *see also* Agliata, 1736/24/7.

Rossi, Alessandra, de'. *See* Saladino del Borgo, 1734/18/9; 1734/21/9; Tesi, 1737/25/5.

Rossi, Giuseppe. *See* Agliata, 1739/9/6; 1739/16/6; 1739/11/7; 1739/14/7; Prini, 1737/4/6; 1737/8/6; 1737/15/6; 1737/22/6.

Rubini Monteviali, Angelica. *See* Agliata, 1739/8/9.

Sabatini, Paolo (Modena). 1739/16/10, A.771, 306v.

Sabioni (Sabbioni), Francesco (Venezia). 1735/30/4, A.770, 467; 1735/11/6, A.770, 475; 1735/18/6, A.770, 478; *see also* Corsini, 1735/27/12; 1736/17/1; 1736/21/2; 1736/28/2; 1736/6/3; 1736/20/3; Grimani, 1735/30/7; 1736/5/10; Pompeati, 1737/12/2; Saroni, 1737/5/2.

Sacchetti Caprara, Maria Verginia, contessa (Bologna). 1739/25/7, A.771, 278; 1739/4/8, A.771, 283v.

Saladino del Borgo, Giovanni (Pisa). 1733/2/5, A.770, 245v; 1733/9/5, A.770, 249; 1733/19/5, A.770, 252v; 1733/26/5, A.770, 255v; 1733/13/6, A.770, 260; 1733/20/6, A.770, 264v; 1733/27/6, A.770, 266v; 1733/21/7, A.770, 272; 1733/25/7, A.770, 274v; 1733/1/8, A.770, 279v; 1734/2/3, A.770, 323; 1734/9/3/, A.770, 325; 1734/13/3, A.770, 325; 1734/20/3, A.770, 329; 1734/18/9, A.770, 400; 1734/21/9, A.770, 402; 1734/27/9, A.770, 403v; 1734/9/10, A.770, 405v; 1734/16/10, A.770, 409v.

Salè, Madama. *See* Baratti, P., 1737/4/5; Lucchesini, 1741/17/1.

Salimbeni, Felice. *See* Donatelli, 1737/11/5; 1737/18/5; 1737/25/5; 1737/1/6; 1737/8/6; 1737/15/6; 1737/22/6; Mari, 1737/18/6; Porpora, 1733/5/9; 1733/19/9.

Salvai, Maria Maddalena (Bologna). 1737/13/12, A.771, 126v; *see also* Aldrovandi, 1737/14/12; 1737/21/12; Donatelli, 1737/13/12; 1737/17/12; Nozzoli, F. M., 1726/8/4; 1726/15/4; Zambeccari, 1737/17/12; 1737/24/12.

Salvatici, Michel. *See* Marchesini, 1726/22/6.

Salvi. *See* Corsini, 1736/31/7; Vivaldi, 1735/18/6.

Salviati, Alamanno, cardinale (Roma). 1732/12/8, A.770, 148.

Salviati, Anton Maria, duca (Roma). 1720/18/12, A.768, 1132; 1735/7/6, A.770, 473; 1741/22/8, A.771, 455v.

Salviati, marchese (Reggio). 1733/22/9, A.770, 293.

Sammartini, Eleonora (La Polacca). *See* Saladino del Borgo, 1733/20/6; 1733/25/7; Venturini, 1733/25/7; Visconti, 1734/1/6.

Sandoni, Pier Giuseppe (Bologna). 1731/27/4, A.770, 42.

Sangiorgio. *See* Grimani, 1735/13/8; Lucchesini, 1741/17/1; Mijone, 1737/30/7; Vivaldi, 1736/23/3; 1736/22/9.

Sani, Prudenza. *See* Corsini, 1738/27/5; Della Rovere, 1742/3/7; Grimani, 1737/11/2; Lucchesini, 1739/4/8; Nozzoli, F. M., 1736/6/3; Nozzoli, S. T., 1740/20/8; 1740/23/8; 1740/27/8; 1740/6/9.

Santini. *See* Cottini, 1733/1/8; Saladino del Borgo, 1733/1/8.

Saroni, Lisabetta (Elisabetta, Bettina) (Napoli). 1736/22/5, A.770, 610; 1737/5/2, A.771, 42; 1737/31/3, A.771, 60v; *see also* Acciaioli, 1736/22/5; 1736/18/9; 1737/8/1; 1737/5/2; 1737/19/2; Ambrogi, 1735/20/10; Aquilanti, 1734/9/4; Campioni, 1735/30/7; 1736/21/4; Colucci, O., 1736/15/9; 1737/8/6; Corsini, 1735/27/12; 1736/24/1; 1736/21/2; 1736/28/2; 1736/6/3; 1736/13/3; 1736/20/3; 1736/9/4; 1736/22/5; Gallo, 1736/6/4; Grimani, 1735/30/7; 1735/13/8; 1735/20/8; 1735/27/8; Mari, 1735/2/8; Mijone, 1735/2/8; 1735/16/8; 1735/20/9; Sabioni, 1735/30/4; Vivaldi, 1735/7/10; 1736/17/3; 1736/21/4.

Sarro, Domenico. *See* Acciaioli, 1736/7/8; 1736/4/9; 1736/18/9; 1736/8/10; 1737/15/1; 1737/19/2; Corsini, 1736/21/8.

Sauter, Francesco. *See* Lucchesini, 1739/7/7; Venturini, 1744/14/3; Vivaldi, 1736/23/3.

Scalzi, Carlo. *See* Della Rovere, 1737/6/8; Donatelli, 1737/29/6; Mari, 1737/18/6; 1737/1/7; 1737/6/8; Nozzoli, F. M., 1726/5/3; 1726/19/3; Pinacci, 1731/16/4; 1731/8/5; Pucci, 1733/31/7; 1734/11/5.

Scaramuccia (Giovanni Battista Nesti). *See* Carlotti, 1739/8/8; Colucci, O., 1737/4/5; Corsini, 1736/24/1; Della Rovere, 1737/6/8; 1737/17/9; Faliconti, 1740/11/7; 1740/19/7; 1740/26/7; 1740/2/8; 1740/9/8; 1740/16/8; Iaco, 1741/20/3; Rambaldi, 1739/29/8; Vivaldi, 1734/24/9; 1734/9/10; 1734/23/10; 1734/20/11; 1736/8/9; 1737/19/3; 1739/16/10.

Scarlatti. *See* Fontana, Antonio, 1725/11/9.

Scarlatti, Domenico. *See* Lucchesini, 1740/7/6.

Schianteschi, Domenico, conte (Parma). 1711/27/6, A.768, 474; 1711/22/8, A.768, 488; 1724/7/10, A.769, 158v; 1726/13/7, A.769, 284; *1728/12/6, A.769, 400v (OO, 90); 1732/28/6, A.770, 130; 1732/12/7, A.770, 134v; *1732/19/7, A.770, 136 (OO, 79); 1732/26/7, A.770, 141v; 1732/2/8, A.770, 144v; 1732/9/8, A.770, 146; *1732/16/8, A.770, 149 (OO, 81); *1732/23/8, A.770, 152v (OO, 80); *1732/30/8, A.770, 156 (OO, 78); 1732/6/9, A.770, 158v; 1732/13/9, A.770, 163v; 1732/3/10, A.770, 173v; 1732/10/10, A.770, 174v; 1732/8/11, A.770, 182v; 1732/15/11, A.770, 183; *1732/6/12, A.770, 194v (OO, 83); *1732/27/12, A.770, 201 (OO, 83); *1733/24/1, A.770, 219v (OO, 84); 1733/31/1, A.770, 214v; 1733/7/2, A.770, 216v; 1733/28/2, A.770, 222; *1733/7/3, A.770, 225 (OO, 85); (Modena)

1736/22/9, A.770, 667; 1737/25/6, A.771, 89; 1739/4/8, A.771, 282; 1739/11/8, A.771, 285v; 1739/15/8, A.771, 288; 1739/25/8, A.771, 291; 1739/1/9, A.771, 293v.

scores. *See* Della Rovere, 1732/12/8.

Senesino. *See* Bernardi, Francesco.

Serenissima Dorotea [Farnese]. *See* Schianteschi, 1732/6/9.

Signorini, Raffaello (Venezia). *1726/5/10, A.769, 305 (RIM, 187); *see also* Pinacci, 1726/11/5; 1726/21/5; 1726/28/5; Porpora, 1726/20/7.

Silvani, Francesco. *See* Nozzoli, S. T., 1740/17/9.

singers. *See* (in Russia) Arrigoni, 1735/24/2; Della Rovere, 1732/2/9; (in Russia) Dreyer, 1735/15/1; 1735/29/1; 1735/26/2; Grisi, 1732/15/8; Martelli, 1734/19/4; Rossermini, 1735/19/10; Vivaldi, 1734/18/9; 1735/6/8.

Spada, Paolo, marchese (Spoleto). 1732/10/5, A.770, 111v; 1743/22/6, A.771, 575; 1743/29/6, A.771, 576v; 1743/13/7, A.771, 578.

Stabili, Barberina (Barbera). *See* Porpora, 1726/20/7; Saladino del Borgo, 1733/21/7; 1733/25/7; 1734/18/9; 1734/21/9; 1734/27/9.

Stagi. *See* Vivaldi, 1735/19/11.

Stampa, monsignor (Roma). 1735/13/12, A.770, 547v.

Stampiglia, Luigi Maria. *See* Grimani, 1739/2/10.

Strada, Anna Maria. *See* Nozzoli, S. T., 1740/27/8; Pucci, 1734/11/5.

Suarez, Maria Anna Valvasoni, contessa (Firenze). *1737/17/9, A.771, 112v (OO, 153); *see also* Vivaldi, 1734/24/9.

Tanara, Giovanni Niccolò, marchese (Bologna). 1726/13/7, A.769, 284v; 1739/3/7, A.771, 264v.

Tanfani. *See* Visconti, 1734/27/4.

Taus, Domenica. *See* Coppoli, 1737/10/8.

Tearelli, Gerolama (Pisa). 1738/22/4, A.771, 162v; 1739/3/5, A.771, 166; *see also* Della Rovere, 1738/6/5; Porro, 1744/24/3.

Teatro
    Cocomero (Firenze). *See* Vivaldi, 1736/14/1; 1736/21/1; 1736/28/1; 1736/11/2; 1736/3/3.

    de' Fiorentini (Napoli). *See* Acciaioli, 1736/8/10.

    San Bartolomeo (Napoli). *See* Acciaioli, 1736/8/10; Paghetti, 1737/10/8.

    Alibert (Roma). *See* Niccolini, 1739/18/8; 1739/25/8.

    Argentina (Roma). *See* Faliconti, 1740/11/7; Paghetti, 1737/10/8.

    Capranica (Roma). *See* Banchieri, 1726/21/5; Fontana, Antonio, 1725/11/9; Marini, 1736/11/8; Niccolini, 1733/15/12.

    Grimani (Venezia). *See* Brunoro 1739/7/2.

    San Cassiano (Casciano) (Venezia). *See* Vivaldi, 1736/5/10; 1737/19/3.

San Giovanni Grisostomo (Venezia). *See* Cottini, 1735/26/2; Della Ciaia, 1729/10/12; Della Rovere, 1737/3/9; Grimani, 1736/23/3; Nozzoli, F. M., 1726/12/3; Venturini, 1744/14/3; Vivaldi, 1736/17/3.

San Moisè (Venezia). *See* Cottini, 1726/16/6; 1726/22/6; 1726/29/6.

San Samuele (Venezia). *See* Grimani, 1733/9/5; 1736/10/3; Tesi, 1726/8/6; Vivaldi, 1734/24/9.

Sant'Angelo (Venezia). *See* Vivaldi, 1739/14/11; 1739/28/11.

Tedeschi, Giovanni. *See* Niccolini, 1735/14/6; Obizzi, 1740/7/5; 1740/28/5; Zuccherini, 1740/21/5.

Tempesti. *See* Saladino del Borgo, 1733/25/7.

Tempi, Benedetto (Venezia). 1726/1/6, A.769, 272v.

Tesi Tramontini, Vittoria (Roma). 1726/7/5, A.769, 260; 1726/8/6, A.769, 274; 1726/29/6, A.769, 280; (Pisa) 1737/25/5, A.771, 74v; (Madrid) 1740/10/1, A.771, 319; 1740/5/10, A.771, 381; *see also* Acciaioli, 1738/26/8; 1738/9/9; 1738/16/9; 1739/23/6; Baratti, P., 1740/28/5; Bernardi, 1739/7/6; 1739/16/6; 1739/21/6; 1739/29/8; 1740/5/4; Corsini, 1736/17/7; Cottini, 1734/19/6; Donatelli, 1734/2/4; Grimani, 1739/12/9; Lanzetti, 1726/5/10; Lucchesini, 1739/9/6; 1739/16/6; 1739/23/6; 1739/28/7; 1739/4/8; 1739/11/8; 1739/25/8; 1739/1/9; 1739/15/12; 1740/14/3; 1740/28/3; 1740/7/6; 1740/21/6; 1740/5/7; 1740/1/11; Nicolini, 1737/14/15; Nozzoli, F. M., 1726/15/4; 1726/21/5; 1726/8/6; Nozzoli, S. T., 1726/11/5; Saladino del Borgo, 1734/2/3; 1734/9/3; 1734/13/3; 1734/20/3; Vivaldi, 1735/28/10.

Tessarini, Carlo. *See* Ferretti, 1734/21/4.

Testagrossa. *See* Colucci, O., 1737/4/5; 1737/25/5; Della Rovere, 1732/29/7; Grimani, 1735/13/8; 1735/20/8; 1735/27/8; 1735/10/9; Lucchesini, 1739/23/6; Vivaldi, 1736/22/9; 1737/22/4; 1737/4/5.

Tomii, Antonia Negri (La Maestina). *See* Aldrovandi, 1737/21/12; Aquilanti, 1732/18/4; Donatelli, 1737/7/12; 1737/13/12; 1737/17/12; Pola, 1737/22/6; Zambeccari, 1737/24/12.

Tomii, Pellegrino (Lucca). 1733/5/9, A.770, 285; (Venezia) 1737/7/12, A.771, 125; *see also* Aldrovandi, 1737/21/12; Cottini, 1737/7/12; Donatelli, 1737/7/12; 1737/13/12; Pola, 1737/22/6; 1737/6/7; 1738/11/1.

Tordoni. *See* Pepoli, Bentivoglio, 1735/16/7.

Torrigiani, Rafaello. *See* Aquilanti, 1734/13/3.

Tozzi, Maria Antonina (Parma). 1724/6/6, A.769, 130v.

Trapano. *See* Grimani, 1736/6/4.

Turcotti Checchini, Maria Giustina (Napoli). 1734/16/3, A.770, 326; 1734/5/4, A.770, 335v; 1734/7/12, A.770, 422v; 1735/4/1, A.770, 428; 1735/18/1, A.770, 428; 1736/26/6, A.770, 629; (Bologna) 1737/27/7, A.771, 98v; 1737/10/8, A.771, 101v; *see also* Acciaioli, 1739/23/6; Baratti, P., 1739/20/6; Bernardi, 1739/23/6; Borghesi, G., 1737/10/8; Dreyer, 1735/15/1; 1735/29/1; Lucchesini, 1740/17/5; Orlandini, 1736/9/6; Preati, 1737/25/6; Saladino del Borgo, 1733/20/6.

Ungherelli, Rosa. *See* Durazzo, 1724/5/12.

Uttini, Elisabetta (Bologna). 1734/12/4, A.770, 339; 1734/23/4, A.770, 342v; 1734/7/5, A.770, 347; 1734/15/5, A.770, 332v; 1734/25/5, A.770, 350; 1734/21/8, A.770, 394; (Perugia) 1734/16/10, A.770, 409; *1734/4/12, A.770, 421v (OO, 70); *see also* Costa, 1735/23/4; Nozzoli, S. T., 1735/19/4; Orlandini, 1733/28/7; Tanara, 1726/13/7; Valletta, 1731/27/2.

Valenti, Giuseppe (Padova). 1737/15/6, A.771, 85.

Valletta, Gaetano (Livorno). 1731/6/2, A.770, 31; 1731/13/2, A.770, 31v; 1731/15/2, A.770, 33; 1731/24/2, A.770, 34; (Pisa) 1731/27/2, A.770, 35v; 1731/3/3, A.770, 37; (Lisbona) 1743/26/3, A.771, 557v; *see also* Aldovrandi, 1735/9/7; 1735/26/7; 1735/30/7; 1735/2/8; 1735/6/8; 1735/9/8; 1735/13/8; 1735/16/8; 1735/20/8; Cermenati, 1731/27/2; Dolfino, 1731/12/5; 1731/23/6; Donatelli, 1734/20/11; Paghetti, 1735/23/7; 1735/30/7; 1735/13/8; 1735/16/8; 1737/10/8; Pelli, 1731/16/4; Porro, 1732/13/10; 1735/9/8; 1735/30/8; 1735/6/9; Vivaldi, 1735/19/11.

Vanneschi, Francesco Abbate. *See* Broschi, 1731/6/2; Pinacci, 1731/26/3; 1731/16/4; 1731/8/5.

Venturini, Francesco Maria (Venezia). 1724/5/8, A.769, 141v; 1724/19/8, A.769, 145; 1724/2/9, A.769, 149r-v; 1724/9/9, A.769, 150v; 1724/15/9, A.769, 152; 1733/25/7, A.770, 274; 1733/12/9, A.770, 288v; *1733/2/10, A.770, 295 (OO, 57); 1733/16/10, A.770, 297; 1744/14/3, A.771, 617; *see also* Cottini, 1733/9/10; 1733/16/10; Saladino del Borgo, 1733/25/7.

Vico, Diana (Parma). 1726/20/7, A.769, 285v; 1726/6/8, A.769, 290v; 1726/10/8, A.769, 293v; *see also* Porpora, 1726/2/7.

Vinci, Leonardo (Napoli). 1727/25/11, A.769, 368; *see also* Acciaioli, 1737/19/2; Fontana, Antonio, 1727/25/11; 1727/6/12; Nozzoli, F. M., 1727/25/11.

Visconti, Caterina (Milano). 1734/27/4, A.770, 345v; 1734/11/5, A.770, 348; (Genova/Milano), 1734/1/6, A.770, 352v; (Milano) 1734/9/6, A.770, 356; 1734/29/6, A.770, 368; 1734/24/8, A.770, 395; *1734/7/9, A.770, 398 (OO, 69); 1734/21/9, A.770, 402; 1734/28/9, A.770, 404; 1734/26/10, A.770, 411; 1734/2/11, A.770, 413; (Napoli) 1735/2/10, A.770, 525; 1735/20/10, A.770, 531v; 1735/31/10, A.770, 535; 1735/8/11, A.770, 537v; 1735/22/11, A.770, 542; (Milano) 1736/24/3, A.770, 587v; 1736/8/5, A.770, 605v; 1736/15/5, A.770, 607v; 1736/22/5, A.770, 610v; (Torino) 1737/19/3, A.771, 56; *see also* Baratti, P., 1739/13/1; Grimani, 1739/15/8; Lucchesini, G., 1739/9/6; 1739/23/6; 1739/30/6; 1739/4/8; 1740/29/2; 1740/14/3; 1740/28/3; 1740/17/5; 1740/7/6; Monticelli, 1736/24/3.

Vivaldi, Antonio (Venezia). *1726/6/7, A.769, 283 (RIM, 185); *1726/20/7, A.769, 287 (RIM, 185); *1726/17/8, A.769, 294v (RIM, 186); *1726/31/8, A.769, 297v (RIM, 187); *1727/28/3, A.769, 342 (RIM, 188); (Verona) 1731/6/11, A.770, 80v; (Mantova) 1731/13/11, A.770, 82v; (Venezia) 1733/26/9, A.770, 293v; 1734/13/2, A.770, 318; 1734/4/9, A.770, 397v; 1734/18/9, A.770, 400v; 1734/24/9, A.770, 403; 1734/9/10, A.770, 405; 1734/16/10, A.770, 407v; 1734/23/10, A.770, 410v; 1734/6/11, A.770, 413v; 1734/13/11, A.770, 416; 1734/20/11, A.770, 416; 1734/27/11, A.770, 420v; *1735/16/4, A.770, 457v (OO, 38); *1735/30/4, A.770, 465 (OO, 39); *1735/4/6, A.770, 471 (OO, 40); *1735/18/6 (OO, 40); *1735/1/7, A.770, 484 (OO, 41); 1735/9/7, A.770, 486v; 1735/16/7, A.770, 490v; 1735/23/7, A.770, 493v; 1735/30/7, A.770, 499; 1735/6/8, A.770, 503; 1735/13/8, A.770, 507; 1735/20/8, A.770, 511; *1735/17/9, A.770, 521v (OO, 41); *1735/23/9, A.770, 524 (OO, 42); 1735/7/10, A.770, 526; 1735/19/10, A.770, 530v; 1735/28/10, A.770, 533v; 1735/5/11, A.770, 535v; *1735/12/11, A.770, 539 (OO, 42); *1735/19/11, A.770, 541v (OO, 43); 1735/26/11, A.770, 543; 1735/10/12, A.770, 545; 1736/14/1, A.770, 557; 1736/21/1, A.770, 569; 1736/28/1, A.770, 651v; 1736/3/2, A.770, 563v; 1736/11/2, A.770, 565v; 1736/28/2, A.770, 572v; 1736/3/3, A.770, 575; 1736/17/3, A.770, 581; 1736/23/3, A.770, 584v; 1736/28/3, A.770, 589v; 1736/6/4, A.770, 592v; 1736/13/4, A.770, 596; 1736/21/4, A.770, 600v; 1736/5/5, A.770, 604; 1736/12/5, A.770, 606v; 1736/19/5, A.770, 609v; 1736/2/6, A.770, 614v; 1736/9/6, A.770, 623; 1736/23/6, A.770, 626v; 1736/30/6, A.770, 630v; 1736/6/7, A.770, 631v; 1736/1/9, A.770, 655v; 1736/8/9, A.770, 659; 1736/15/9, A.770, 663; 1736/22/9, A.770, 667v; 1736/5/10, A.770, 671; (Venezia) 1736/1/11, A.771, 3v; 1736/10/11, A.771, 7v; 1736/17/11, A.771, 14; 1737/26/1, A.771, 38; 1737/19/3, A.771, 59v; (Mantova) 1737/22/4, A.771, 65v; (Venezia) 1737/4/5, A.771, 67; 1737/1/6, A.771, 78r; 1737/9/11, A.771, 118v; 1737/16/11, A.771, 120r; 1739/14/11, A.771, 310; 1739/16/11, A.771, 306v; 1739/28/11, A.771, 312; *see also* Baratti, P., 1735/4/7; 1735/20/10; Campioni, 1736/21/4; 1736/8/9; Colucci, F., 1736/18/8; 1736/8/9; Cottini, 1734/27/11; 1735/23/4; 1735/12/11; 1736/21/4; Della Ciaia, 1735/12/11; 1735/26/11; Grimani, 1736/10/3; 1736/23/3; Grisi, 1735/20/10; Lucchesini, 1737/15/1; Nozzoli, F. M., 1727/25/11; Nozzoli, S. T., 1728/7/8; Orlandini, 1736/8/10; Pieri, B., 1734/27/11; Pompeati, A., 1736/5/10; Rangoni, T., 1736/5/10; Vinci, 1727/25/11.

Zambeccari, Paolo (Bologna). 1737/17/12, A.771, 130; 1737/24/12, A.771, 132; 1739/16/6, A.771, 252v.

Zanardi, Livia. *See* Tanara, 1739/3/7.

Zingoni. *See* Nozzoli, F. M., 1736/9/4.

Zuccherini, Tommaso (Pisa). 1740/21/5, A.771, 337v.

Incoming letters

Entries for incoming letters are arranged differently from those for outgoing letters. Since incoming letters are grouped into packets alphabetically according to the last name of the sender and placed within these in chronological order, I have thought it best to present the information accordingly, by name, volume number and date.

Acciaioli, Ottaviano. A.772: (Roma) *1726/2/3 (OO, 120); *1726/27/4 (OO, 122); 1726/15/5; 1726/18/5.

Agliata, Tommaso. A.772: (Pisa) 1733/31/8.

Albizzi, Giovan Luca degli. A.740: (Firenze) 1720/13/4.

Albizzi, Lucantonio degli, cavaliere. A.745: (Bologna) 1733/6/6; (Parma) 1733/7/7; A.741: (Napoli) 1736/1/5; 1736/8/5; 1736/15/5; 1736/22/5; 1736/29/5; 1736/10/7; 1736/17/7; 1736/24/7; 1736/31/7; 1736/7/8; 1736/16/10; *1739/1/4 (OO, 132).

Banchieri, Antonio, governatore. A.757: (Roma) *1726/1/6 (OO, 127).

Bartolommei, Ferdinando, marchese. A.764: (Vienna) 1721/15/2; 1721/22/3; 1724/19/2; 1725/6/1; 1725/17/3; 1725/1/9; 1725/6/10; 1725/10/11; 1725/17/11; 1726/5/1; 1726/19/1; 1726/9/3; 1726/18/5; 1726/31/8; 1726/21/9; 1726/26/10; 1727/8/3; 1727/30/8; 1727/29/11; 1728/3/1; 1728/2/8; 1728/30/8; 1728/6/9; (Graz) 1728/27/9; 1728/11/10; (Vienna) 1728/6/11; 1728/25/12; 1729/15/1; 1729/22/1; 1729/5/2; 1729/19/2; 1729/26/2; 1729/20/8; 1729/24/9; 1729/24/12; 1730/21/1; 1730/28/1; 1730/11/2; 1730/18/2; 1730/20/5; 1730/9/12; 1731/17/1; 1731/27/2; 1731/15/12; 1732/5/1; 1732/19/1; 1732/2/2; 1732/9/2; 1732/22/2; 1732/8/3; 1732/15/3; 1732/29/3; 1732/5/4; 1732/12/4; 1732/3/5; 1732/10/5; 1732/17/5; 1732/7/6; 1732/14/6; 1732/3/9; 1733/21/11; 1734/2/1; 1734/9/5; 1734/31/12; 1735/5/3; 1736/15/4; 1736/12/11; 1738/22/3; 1738/19/4; 1738/10/5; 1738/5/7.

Bernardi, Francesco detto Senesino. A.771: (Napoli) *1739/21/5 (OO, 136); A.776: (Napoli) *1740/26/1 (OO, 146); (Roma) 1740/19/3.

Capponi, Cappone. A.781: (Modena) 1711/29/5.

Corsini, Bartolomeo, principe. A.785: (Roma) 1732/10/2; 1732/24/3; (Parma) 1733/6/11; (Napoli) 1734/6/7; *1734/19/10 (OO, 93); *1735/27/9 (OO, n. 8, 208); *1735/22/10 (OO, 93); 1735/21/11; 1735/13/12; 1736/3/1; 1736/7/1; 1736/21/1; 1736/4/2; 1736/18/2; 1736/25/2; (Roma) 1736/3/3; 1736/17/3; 1736/32/3; 1736/7/4; (Napoli) 1736/15/5; 1736/26/6; *1736/24/7 (OO, 96); 1736/21/8; *1736/4/9 (OO, n. 23, 210); *1736/25/9 (OO, 97); *1736/30/10 (OO, 97); 1736/25/12; 1737/15/1; 1737/29/1; (Palermo) 1737/31/3; *1738/31/1 (OO, 99, 157); *1738/30/5 (OO, 101); *1738/27/6 (OO, 101); *1739/14/8 (OO, 145); 1739/9/10; 1739/6/11; *1739/20/11 (OO, 145).

Corsini, Maria Vittoria Altoviti, principessa. A.785: (Roma) 1736/15/9.

Ferrari, Girolamo, detto Silvio. A.791: (Livorno) 1712/2/9.

Fontana, Antonio, cavaliere. A.792: (Roma) 1722/13/9; 1722/19/9; 1722/3/10; 1722/17/10; 1726/2/3; 1726/23/3; 1726/30/3; 1726/13/4; *1726/21/5 (OO, 125).

Fontana, Domenico. A.792: (Roma) *1726/2/3 (OO, 119); *1726/13/4 (OO, 122).

Frosini, Tommaso, conte. A.792: (Dusseldorf) 1702/21/1.

Giudice, Niccolò del, cardinale. A.744: (Roma) 1735/9/7.

Grimani, Michele. A.795: (Venezia) 1730/1/5; 1736/2/2; 1736/3/3; 1736/17/3; 1736/29/9; 1736/13/10; 1738/22/3; 1739/26/9.

Gualandi, Margherita (La Campioli). A.796: (Venezia) 1726/31/8.

Laderchi, Pietro. A.797: (Faenza) 1728/7/1.

Lalli, Domenico. A.797: (Venezia) 1729/19/11.

Lucchesini, Girolamo, marchese. A.798: (Modena) 1725/29/6; 1727/25/7; 1727/1/8; 1729/5/2; 1733/16/1; 1733/23/1; (Reggio) *1739/10/6 (OO, 135); 1739/19/6; 1739/26/6; 1739/3/7; 1740/8/1; 1740/10/1; 1740/15/1; *1740/5/2 (OO, 147); *1740/4/3 (OO, 148); *1740/11/3 (OO, 149); 1740/18/3; 1740/9/9.

Maccarani, Paolo Maria. A.799: (Roma) *1726/27/3 (OO, 121); 1726/20/4; *1726/1/5 (OO, 123).

Maggio, Melchior, monsignore. A.799: (Roma) 1722/26/12.

Mari, Giovanni Battista de, marchese. A.788: (Torino) 1737/16/1; 1737/25/6.

Migliorucci, Pier Giuseppe. A.802: (Londra) 1725/19/3; 1726/29/4; 1726/10/6; 1726/29/7; 1726/1/11; 1727/7/2.

Monteleone, Marchese di. A.803: (Venezia) 1728/5/6; 1730/7/3.

Niccolini, Giovan Luca, monsignore. A.804: (Roma) 1725/20/1; 1727/13/12; 1731/3/3; 1731/10/3; 1733/10/1; 1733/10/1; 1734/6/2; 1739/3/1.

Nozzoli, Filippo Maria. A.805: (Napoli) 1717/5/12; *1726/26/2 (OO, 106); *1726/12/3 (OO, 107); *1726/12/4 (OO, 109); 1726/22/3; 1726/29/3; 1726/5/4; 1726/12/4; 1726/19/4; 1726/26/4; *1726/1/5 (OO, 110); *1726/14/5 (OO, 111); *1726/28/5 (OO, 112); 1734/20/7; 1734/17/8; 1734/2/11; 1735/2/8; 1736/20/8; 1736/16/10; 1737/8/1; 1738/19/8; 1740/20/9; 1740/15/11.

Nozzoli, Sebastiano Tommaso. A.805: (Livorno) 1726/10/4; 1726/19/6; 1734/2/6; 1735/31/1; 1737/6/2; 1737/4/3; 1740/12/2; 1740/23/9; 1740/14/11; 1740/2/12.

Olivieri, Fabio, cardinale. A.734: (Roma) 1730/18/11; 1730/9/12; 1731/3/3; 1731/8/3; 1732/1/3; 1732/22/3; 1732/14/6; 1732/26/7; 1733/31/7; 1734/20/2; 1734/17/7; 1735/21/1.

Orlandini, Giuseppe. A.806: (Bologna) 1721/27/5; 1721/30/5; 1721/7/6; 1721/14/6; 1721/17/6; 1721/28/6; 1721/1/7; 1721/4/7; 1721/8/7; 1721/15/7; 1721/19/1; 1721/22/7; 1721/25/7; 1721/29/7; 1721/5/8; 1721/18/8; 1721/19/8; 1721/25/8; 1721/26/8; 1721/29/8; 1721/2/9; 1721/9/9; 1721/13/9; 1721/16/9; 1721/23/9; 1721/27/9; 1721/14/10; 1721/18/10.

Orsini, Filippo, duca. A.806: (Solofra) 1726/1/6, includes an undated note from Albizzi, an unsigned note dated 17/5/26 and an undated note from Carlo Scalzi; 1726/30/7; (Napoli) 1731/21/9; 1732/8/1.

Pandolfini, Palmiro. A.808: (Firenze) 1721/19/6.

Pinacci, Giovan Battista. A.810: (Reggio) *1726/4/5 (OO, 123); *1726/11/5 (OO, 124); *1726/24/5 (OO, 126); (Roma) 1731/5/5; 1731/12/5; 1731/27/5; 1731/8/6.

Pola, Camillo balì, fra. A.811: (Venezia) 1729/22/1; 1729/5/2; 1729/19/2; 1729/5/3; 1729/23/4; 1739/19/12.

Pucci, Vincenzo. A.812: (Londra) 1728/7/6; 1729/7/3; 1731/11/1; 1731/12/3; 1731/29/11; 1733/23/3; 1733/25/5; 1733/19/7; 1734/6/9; 1734/27/9; 1734/27/9; 1734/22/11; 1735/16/4; 1735/18/7; 1735/5/10; 1735/6/11; 1736/23/1; 1736/2/4; 1736/20/8; 1736/1/10; 1737/1/7; 1738/17/3; 1738/1/5.

Riccardi, Bernardino. A.814: (Arezzo) 1736/17/12.

Righini, Pietro. A.763: (Parma) *1733/13/1 (OO, 84).

Romoli, Giuseppe Maria. A.815: (Firenze) 1727/5/10.

Salomoni, Giovan Battista. A.816: (Napoli) 1700/26/6; 1700/17/7; 1700/28/9; 1701/20/12; 1702/31/1; 1702/14/2; 1702/13/6; 1702/4/7; 1702/18/7; 1702/15/8; 1702/21/11; 1702/19/12; 1703/2/1; 1703/16/1; 1704/4/3.

Saroni, Elisabetta. A.817: (Napoli) 1736/12/5.

Salviati, Alamanno, monsignore, [later] cardinale. A.818: (Firenze) 1702/14/9; (Urbino) 1725/16/9; (Pesaro) *1725/7/10 (OO, 106); *1726/19/3 (OO, 34); 1726/13/12; (Urbino) 1726/30/6; (Roma) 1729/21/12; 1730/11/1; 1730/28/1; 1731/17/3; 1731/31/3; 1731/16/6; 1731/8/12; 1732/12/1; 1732/26/1; 1732/9/2; 1732/23/2; 1732/17/5; 1732/24/5; 1732/7/6; 1732/14/6; 1732/12/7; 1732/19/7; 1732/16/8; 1732/20/9; 1732/27/9; 1732/8/11; 1732/15/11; 1732/22/11; 1733/3/1; 1733/17/1; 1733/7/2; 1733/14/2.

Salviati, Anton Maria, duca. A.818: (Roma) 1735/25/6.

Schianteschi, Domenico, conte. A.763: (Parma) 1732/8/8; 1732/22/8; 1732/29/8; 1732/5/9; 1732/12/9; 1732/19/9; 1732/3/10; 1732/24/10; 1732/31/10; 1732/7/11; 1732/21/22; 1732/28/11; 1732/12/12; 1732/26/12; 1733/2/1; 1733/9/1; 1733/16/1; 1733/30/1; 1733/6/2; 1733/20/2.

Stampa, Gaetano, monsignore. A.765: (Venezia) 1722/3/1; 1722/17/1; 1722/31/1; 1723/30/1; 1723/26/6; 1723/6/11; 1723/4/12; 1724/15/1; 1725/3/2; 1725/7/7; 1725/18/8; 1725/10/11; 1725/24/11; 1725/8/12; 1725/22/12; 1726/12/1; 1726/14/9; 1727/15/11; 1727/29/11; 1729/5/3; 1729/19/3; 1729/17/12; 1730/11/2; 1730/25/2; 1730/13/5; 1730/27/5; 1730/25/11; 1731/24/11; 1731/15/12; 1732/12/1; 1732/2/2; 1732/15/3; 1733/5/1; 1733/2/2; 1733/16/3; 1734/23/1; 1734/30/1; 1734/6/2; 1734/20/3; 1734/12/6; 1734/7/8; 1734/6/11; (Roma) 1737/26/1; 1737/2/2; 1737/9/2; 1738/22/2.

Stoppani, Giovan Francesco, monsignore. A.820: (Venezia) 1739/28/11; 1740/2/1; 1740/27/2.

Strozzi, Francesco, marchese. A.820: (Mantova) 1732/3/7.

Tanara, Giovan Niccolò, marchese. A.821: (Bologna) 1709/21/5; 1709/4/6; 1716/9/6; 1718/9/8; 1718/16/8; 1718/23/8; 1725/30/1; 1728/9/1; 1728/16/1.

Tornaquinci, Giovanni Antonio, abbate. A.823: (Firenze) 1731/29/12; 1732/7/12; 1734/28/8; 1738/19/2.

Tornaquinci, Mario, generale. A.823: (Livorno) 1712/1/8; 1712/8/8; 1712/16/11; 1712/18/11; 1713/31/5.

Tron, Francesco. A.823: (Venezia) 1711/7/5; 1711/6/6.

Venturini, Francesco Maria. A.824: (Venezia) 1722/26/9, includes a letter from marchese Lancillotti from the same day.

Wolkra, Cristoforo, conte. A.825: (Vienna) 1710/1/2; 1710/8/3; 1710/5/4.

11

Johann Mattheson:
The Enlightenment, *L'Éclaircissement*, or *Die Aufklärung*

ERNEST HARRISS II

When dealing with Johann Mattheson's influence upon intellectual developments in the eighteenth century, one encounters a complex of philosophical problems of major dimensions. The two most common interpretations of Mattheson's philosophical perspective are fundamentally different. The more venerable scholarly tradition holds that Mattheson was a rationalist, heavily oriented toward French neoclassical ideals. Much of the literature in the twentieth century on Mattheson accepts this interpretation as valid. On the other hand, there are several studies which conclude that Mattheson was a pragmatist, enlightened in the method of the English empiricists. The advocates of this perspective have established a countercurrent to the rationalistic interpretation that has gained supporters during the last several decades. Though the conflict has emerged in the literature of this century, its roots are to be found in the eighteenth century. An additional aesthetic variable that must be taken into account is the Arcadian classicism that gained such an influential following in the field of music from the 1720s. The impact of the views of Pietro Metastasio in shaping this musical aesthetic, and the accompanying changes in style that occurred, cannot be ignored.

Since the ideas of Johann Christoph Gottsched are sometimes said to have relevance to discussions of Mattheson's views, it is important to remember from the outset that the German *Aufklärung* was little more than an imitation of ideas and ways of thinking that had first come to light during the period of the British Enlightenment and of the French *Éclaircissement*. The *Aufklärung* did not contain much of substance that could be called new. Voltaire's *Candide* is but one example of how *Aufklärung* thinking was held up to ridicule by the more sophisticated intellectuals of the day. Besides, Gottsched's well-know antipathy toward opera places him outside the mainstream of scholars writing about music. If for no other reason, this is true because opera was the most popular and influential genre of the day, generally attracting the best performers and composers. Further, changes in style and in aesthetic usually first occurred in one or another of the operatic genres.

Another and more serious confounding factor is that the dominant aesthetic of the decades under consideration is poorly understood. The Arcadian classical movement helped shape the most classical directions of the century from the 1720s. The pendulum moved away from the most extreme manifestations of the classical aesthetic and related musical styles by the 1740s. But it was only in the 1790s that this move toward the romantic and away from the classical became decisive. This pattern of development is not well-articulated, in part because much of the music in which these changes occur is not well known. This adds yet another layer of confusion to any effort to understand aesthetic changes during that time and their musical consequences.

The generous support of the Alexander von Humboldt Stiftung in Bonn is gratefully acknowledged. An earlier version of this study was presented as "Johann Mattheson's Influence on the Next Generation of Scholars," during "Sektion IV: Matthesons Einfluss auf die Musiktheorie und -praxis des 18. Jahrhunderts" of the Internationales Johann Mattheson-Symposium, Herzog August Bibliothek, Wolfenbüttel, 28 September 1981. The author notes with deep appreciation his special debt to his mentor Robert Lamar Weaver, whose guidance first led him to explore the striking ideas found in Mattheson's writings.

While Mattheson's ideas were influential (and while extensive evidence of his influence could be provided), it is much more important that a basis for understanding the philosophical confusions surrounding his views be identified in Mattheson's interaction with scholars. The source of these confusions appears to reside in the way in which eighteenth-century and modern writers utilized Mattheson's ideas, not in the ideas themselves. Though a great admirer of Mattheson, when Lorenz Christoph Mizler borrowed or commented upon Mattheson's ideas, this process was influenced by his own personal rationalist perspective.[1] When Quantz discussed the affections, he insinuated a distinctively different bias into his explanations.[2] The philosophical climates of Leipzig and Berlin caused the writers there to reinterpret Mattheson's views to bring them into conformity with their own thinking. Then, when conceptual models for studying the eighteenth century were developed in the early part of the twentieth century, Arnold Schering, Hermann Kretzschmar, and especially Hugo Goldschmidt traced the *Éclaircissement* or even the *Aufklärung* roots of a rationalistic aesthetic to Mattheson.[3] But what they really described was a Mattheson as interpreted by the eighteenth-century rationalists. For example, Goldschmidt states:

> Das Hauptwerk: "Der vollkommene Kapellmeister" . . . fasst alles das Angeführte zusammen, unterstreicht aber die rationalistische Neigung des Verfassers energischer. Der französische Einfluss ist auch äusserlich bemerkbar.[4]

Then, after a short discussion of Mattheson's attitude toward instrumental music, he continues:

> Aber diese in sich berechtigte Musik konnte der französische Rationalismus nicht anerkennen, und ihm unterwirft sich Mattheson. . . . Viel entschiedener tritt die Irrlehre hervor, die Musik könne deutlich und untrüglich Affekte schildern in der vokalen und instrumentalen Musik durch die engere Anlehnung an die Natur. Es schwebt ihm hier bereits vor, was er und nach ihm wieder Marpurg—in törichter Übertreibung—zur These erhob: die Gleichstellung mit der Poesie, durch Vermittlung von musikalischen Ideen von bestimmten musikalischen Wendungen Vorstellungen zu erwecken, wie sie sich in der Poesie an das Wort anschliessen.[5]

Goldschmidt thus projects Marpurg's philosophical perspective backward to Mattheson. As neoclassical ideals were gaining ground in 1915, when Goldschmidt's book was published, and since he was particularly vehement in his opposition to those ideals, he condemned the "rationalist" Mattheson without restraint.

But we must consider Mattheson's own intellectual environment and his own writings if we are to understand his point of view. In his fine biography of Mattheson, Beekman Cannon was quite right to focus our attention upon Hamburg and its British traditions.[6] Consistent with Cannon's emphasis, Gloria Flaherty has demonstrated that Hamburg was an important center for English pragmatism in Germany in the eighteenth century, and that Mattheson was a principal personality in establishing that intellectual orientation. She also traced a practical and empirical

---

[1] *The New Grove Dictionary of Music and Musicians* (1980) (hereafter, *New Grove*), s.v. "Mizler von Karlof, Lorenz Christoph," by George J. Buelow.

[2] Rudolf Schäfke, "Quantz als Ästhetiker," *Archiv für Musikwissenschaft* 4 (1924): 213-42, provides a listing of Quantz's illustrations relating to the affections. As an example of how far such ideas were taken, Schäfke selected Marpurg's very long discussion of recitatives and their affections. He states (p. 241), "Der grösste Teil der Definitionen ist Überhaupt unbrauchbar." In discussing the sources for Quantz's ideas, he notes "Von seinen ästhetischen Darlegungen liebe sich *a priori*... eine Abhängigkeit von J. Mattheson annehmen. Die Spuren seiner Schriften, besonders des 'Volkommenen Kapellmeisters' (1739), finden sich in der gesamten kritischen Literatur der Zeit, so auch bei Quantz" (ibid.).

[3] Arnold Schering, "Die Musikästhetik der deutschen Aufklärung," *Zeitschrift der internationalen Musikgesellschaft* 8 (1907): 263-71, 316-22; Hermann Kretzschmar, "Allgemeines und Besonderes zur Affektenlehre I," *Jahrbuch der Musikbibliothek Peters für 1911* 18 (1912): 63-77, and "Allgemeines und Besonderes zur Affektenlehre II," *Jahrbuch der Musikbibliothek Peter für 1912* 19 (1913): 65-78; and Hugo Goldschmidt, *Die Musikästhetik des 18. Jahrhunderts und ihre Beziehungen zu seinem Kunstschaffen* (Zurich and Leipzig: Rascher & Co., 1915), 58-68.

[4] Goldschmidt, *Musikästhetik*, 63.

[5] Ibid., 64.

[6] *Johann Mattheson: Spectator in Music* (New Haven: Yale University Press, 1947), 1-17.

attitude through his works.⁷ In a dissertation that appeared in the same year as Flaherty's book, Bellamy Hamilton Hosler also found the literature of the twentieth century to be filled with such philosophical distortions as those being considered in this essay. She reviewed eighteenth-century sources thoroughly and came to the same view of Mattheson's philosophy as Flaherty.⁸ Werner Braun did also, in his incisive analysis of Mattheson's philosophical perspective, stating:

> Mattheson mochte in seinen Kompositionen wohl unbewusst funktional empfunden haben. Er hütete sich aber, dieser Funktionalität eine zu grosse Rolle in seinem Bewusstsein einnehmen zu lassen, aus Furcht "metaphysisch" zu werden. Mattheson blieb als Theoretiker immer zugleich Empiriker und Praktiker. Wenn Mattheson Regeln gibt, dann sind das immer mehr allgemeine Richtlinien und Hilfsmittel.⁹

Thus, when Mattheson's working environment and his treatises are considered, he is seen to have been intuitive, practical, and empirical in approach. Once one understands his point of view, it is relatively easy to identify the numerous perversions of Mattheson's position found in the literature of this century. An illustration will serve to make the implications of this clearer.

One of the most important music scholars to have been directly associated with Mattheson was Johann Adolph Scheibe. Imanuel Willheim's dissertation on Scheibe provides us with a thoughtful study of Scheibe's literary endeavors.¹⁰ Willheim delineates Scheibe's basic philosophical position quite clearly, but also permits us to witness how distortions of Mattheson's views have affected modern scholarship. According to Willheim, Scheibe began as a rationalist, directly under the influence of Gottsched in Leipzig, but evolved into a spokesman for the new spirit which was then emerging.¹¹ This new attitude was intuitive and pragmatic. In his thinking, such English approaches more and more came to replace French neoclassical approaches. Scheibe is thus depicted as having moved away from a musical rationalism, a rationalism which Willheim, following Goldschmidt's lead, asserts is embodied in the writings of Johann Mattheson.¹²

Willheim thus continues the tradition in the earlier twentieth century of considering Mattheson to have been a rationalist; but, at the same time, he provides readers who consider Mattheson to have been a pragmatist with numerous illustrations of ways in which Scheibe can be seen to have followed very closely in Mattheson's footsteps. When considered from this point of view, Willheim's dissertation shows Scheibe to have been unswervingly loyal to the ideals which Mattheson espoused and to have been their primary spokesman for the next generation.¹³

Willheim's assumption that Mattheson was a rationalist results in numerous anomalies in his dissertation. He points out, for example, that Scheibe recognized Mattheson's intuitive approach, that Mattheson and Scheibe were allies in their anti-rationalistic attacks on Mizler, and that Mattheson even used a part of his *Der vollkommene Capellmeister* to object to some of Scheibe's ideas that Mattheson found overly rationalistic. Nevertheless, Willheim holds firmly to the notion that Mattheson was a rationalist. This causes Willheim to miss opportunities for realizing the full potential of the data with which he was working.¹⁴

There is one especially interesting example of this oversight. Willheim considers Scheibe's manuscript treatise *Compendium musices* rather carefully, noting that it may have been written in Leipzig in the years immediately before Scheibe moved to Hamburg, but that the copy which is at Yale University bears a date of 1736, the year Scheibe moved

---

⁷ *Opera in the Development of German Critical Thought* (Princeton: Princeton University Press, 1978), 37-92.

⁸ "Changing Aesthetic Views of Instrumental Music in Eighteenth-Century Germany" (Ph.D. diss., University of Wisconsin, 1978), 138-70.

⁹ "Johann Mattheson und die Aufklärung" (Ph.D. diss., Martin-Luther-Universität zu Halle-Wittenberg, 1952), 115-17.

¹⁰ "Johann Adolphe Scheibe: German Musical Thought in Transition" (Ph.D. diss., University of Illinois, 1963).

¹¹ Ibid., 24; *New Grove*, s.v. "Gottsched, Johann Christoph," by Buelow.

¹² Willheim, 95-96.

¹³ Ibid., 4, 14-17, 24, 33-34, 70-72, 95-96, 135-37, 203-05, 260-61.

¹⁴ Ibid., 70-72, 135-37, 95-96.

to Hamburg. Willheim reasons that if 1736 is the correct date, then the treatise must have been written in Hamburg. Further, he notes that the treatise is filled with non-German words, a feature not found in Scheibe's published writings.[15] Gottsched's advocacy of a purer German is usually clearly manifest in Scheibe's literary style.[16] In his description of this treatise, Willheim notes that the third part deals with melody and that Scheibe considered melody to be the heart of musical composition. As he evaluates its contents, he finds the manuscript to contain an early formulation of Scheibe's principal ideas, concepts which would have been contrary to Mattheson's presumed "rationalism."[17]

Closer examination of the treatise reveals a number of interesting points. First, the use of non-German words there is very similar stylistically to the way in which Mattheson employed non-German expressions in his early writings.[18] Though Mizler was in Leipzig during the years before Scheibe moved to Hamburg and had manifested an intense admiration for Mattheson's ideas, it is highly unlikely that Scheibe would have employed this literary style in the Leipzig of Gottsched. After all, as George Buelow has pointed out, "Gottsched's goal was to reform the German language," and Scheibe was "Gottsched's pupil and the musician most profoundly influenced by him."[19]

Second, the ideas about melody articulated in the manuscript are very similar to those published by Mattheson, with Scheibe's praise, in 1737 and again in 1739.[20] Mattheson's theory of melody, given here in a very concise form, is in an advanced state of refinement. Scheibe must have been exposed to these ideas first-hand in Hamburg. Other concepts in Scheibe's treatise are similar in tone and content to Mattheson's views.[21] It is therefore reasonable to assume, on the basis of literary style and content, that this treatise represents Scheibe's very successful synthesis of the striking ideas he encountered during his first few months in Hamburg. This would also explain the early date of 1736 on the copy found at Yale.[22] If Willheim had not considered Mattheson to have been a rationalist, such an interpretation would very likely have also occurred to him.

There is another dimension to the period 1736-39, during which Scheibe was in Hamburg, important to our present understanding of Mattheson.[23] Goldschmidt was of course quite correct when he pointed out that *Der vollkommene Capellmeister* of 1739 exhibits elements of rationalism found in Mattheson's earlier works.[24] Willheim again assists us in coming to understand why these rationalistic ideas are present so much more profusely. In a comparison of passages in Scheibe's *Der criticus Musicus* with similar passages in *Der vollkommene Capellmeister*, Willheim discovered that Mattheson, in his discussion of the affections as they relate to various musical styles, was responding directly to what Scheibe had written on the subject. Mattheson was in fact ridiculing Scheibe's classification of the passions, offering an alternative, and warning against borrowing ironclad rules from orators and applying them to music.[25] Hence the very sections of *Der vollkommene Capellmeister* that led writers such as Goldschmidt to call Mattheson a rationalist resulted, at least in part, directly from Mattheson's response to, refinement of, and cautioning against the rationalistic ideals

---

[15] Ibid., 33-34.

[16] *New Grove*, s.v. "Gottsched," by Buelow; and Willheim, 34.

[17] Willheim, 33-34. The centrality of melody to musical expression is Mattheson's fundamental theoretical assumption; see part two of *Der vollkommene Capellmeister*.

[18] Compare Mattheson, *Das neu-eröffnete Orchestre*, 1713. Indeed, the contents of the *Compendium* also parallel the contents of the *Orchestre* to a significant degree.

[19] *New Grove*, s.v. "Mizler" and "Gottsched," by Buelow.

[20] The key words Mattheson uses, "deutlich," "fliessend," and "leicht" appear, and the same types of structural concerns are also explored in some depth in the Scheibe treatise.

[21] While Scheibe explicitly acknowledges his debt to Mattheson's earlier published works in several places, the treatise is filled with ideas apparently borrowed from Mattheson, which Scheibe did not explicitly credit to him.

[22] This copy was made by Christoph Graupner; see Peter Benary, *Die deutsche Kompositionslehre des 18. Jahrhunderts*, Jenaer Beiträge zur Musikforschung, ed. Heinrich Besseler, 3 (Leipzig: Breitkopf und Härtel, 1960), 55. Scheibe's *Compendium musices* is printed as an appendix of this book.

[23] Willheim, 35-44.

[24] Goldschmidt, 63-65.

[25] Willheim, 34-35; see also Benary, 55-60, especially p. 58, providing another illustration of Scheibe's awareness of some of Mattheson's more advanced thinking, which tends to lend further support to the possibility that the treatise was in fact written in 1736 in Hamburg.

which Scheibe had brought from Leipzig. But Willheim, consistently holding the position that Mattheson was himself a rationalist and that he had in fact developed a formal *Affektenlehre*, nevertheless maintains that the basic difference between Scheibe and Mattheson was that the former moved away from the precepts of the *Affektenlehre* by not employing Mattheson's model for the various affections.[26] We now know that this view simply does not stand up under analysis.

Buelow has convincingly demonstrated that Mattheson did not develop a formal *Affektenlehre*, all modern scholarship to the contrary notwithstanding.[27] I have added the corollary that Mattheson, as a pragmatist and empiricist, simply would not have had any interest in developing such an abstract, intellectual conceptualization of the affections.[28] If one understands that Mattheson was reacting to the rationalistic views of Gottsched, as these had been imported into Hamburg by Scheibe, then the relationship between Mattheson and Scheibe becomes much clearer. In these years Scheibe indeed came to be an important spokesman for the intuitive, pragmatic, Hamburg tradition—i.e., Mattheson's tradition.

Mizler was another music scholar who admired Mattheson tremendously, but one who remained loyal to Gottsched's rationalistic principles. He was in fact the first important German writer on music of the eighteenth century who was a thorough-going rationalist. In the 1730s Mizler had a very positive attitude about Mattheson, dedicating his 1734 dissertation to Mattheson and beginning a series of lectures on Mattheson's *Das neu-eröffnete Orchestre* at the University of Leipzig in 1737.[29] He considered Mattheson to have been the most important contemporary writer on music. The fundamental philosophical difference that was to divide them did not become a problem until the interaction between Mattheson and Scheibe brought the conflict into the open.

The full force of this dispute became manifest with the publication of *Der vollkommene Capellmeister*. Mattheson devoted a large part of the twenty-three page foreword of this book to an attack upon Mizler's fundamental views. His perspective is especially clear when he is discussing the role of "musical mathematics."[30]

> Die Natur bringt den Klang, und alle seine, auch die grössesten Theils noch unbekannte Verhältnisse hervor. Das ist eine unstreitige Wahrheit. Der Mathematicus hat sich von ie her viele Mühe gegeben, diesen Klang und dessen Verhältnisse in Ordnung und Rechnung zu bringen, welches aber bis data noch gar nicht völlig geschehen ist, auch vermutlich in dieser Welt nimmer geschehen wird, weil es mit den Klängen ins Unendliche fortgehet. Der Musicus hergegen beurteilet und verbessert diese Magelhaffte, und gewisser Massen ohne Wirth gemachte Rechnung, und weiss sich so wohl damit zu behelffen, dass er seine Klänge zu einer wunderbaren Wirkung bringet. Wo steckt nun das *Principium*, der Ursprung, das Fundament und der Grundsatz aller Musik?[31]

Scheibe penned a poem praising Mattheson, which appears at the end of the foreword.[32] Here he extols Mattheson's intuitive approach.[33] Mizler, for his part, printed long excerpts from *Der volkommene Capellmeister*, but felt that

---

[26] Willheim, 95-96. Scheibe obtained his formal instruction in rationalism in Leipzig from Gottsched. Buelow notes (*New Grove*, s.v. "Gottsched"): "In the *Critische Dichtkunst* (1730), by rules of reason and by example, Gottsched formulated a scientific, classical method of creation for all the poetic arts. The baroque rationalism of imitating emotional states, the affections, received considerable emphasis as a goal of these arts. Rhetorical doctrine was the mechanism by which the goal was to be reached, and the centrality of the rules of rhetoric to Gottsched's reforms was in one sense the final outcome of more than a century of reawakened interest in rhetoric by German Baroque writers on music as well as the literary arts."

[27] "Johann Mattheson and the Invention of the 'Affektenlehre'," paper presented at the 19th annual meeting of the South-Central Chapter of the American Musicological Society, Louisville, Kentucky, April 1981.

[28] Harriss, "The Music of Johann Mattheson and the *Affektenlehre*," paper presented at the same meeting.

[29] *New Grove*, s.v. "Mizler," by Buelow. In lecturing on Mattheson's book, "He [Mizler] was the first to lecture on music at a German university for 150 years."

[30] His strong feelings are expressed emphatically in the section "Von der musikalischen Mathematik," on pp. 16-22 of this foreword.

[31] Ibid., 19.

[32] Ibid., 30-31.

[33] *Vorrede*, 16-22, and 31-32; Willheim, 70-72; and Franz Wöhlke, "Lorenz Christoph Mizler: Ein Beiträge zur musikalischen Gelehrtengeschichte des 18. Jahrhunderts" (Ph.D. diss., Friedrich-Wilhelms-Universität zu Berlin, 1940), 91-94.

it did not measure up to the intellectual ideals he cherished.[34] Scheibe contributed an anonymous letter, printed in Mattheson's *Ehrenpforte* of 1740, countering with an attack on Mizler.[35] In 1744, and again in 1754, Mattheson continued that philosophical attack on Mizler.[36]

While Mizler had complained of Mattheson's failure to conform to rationalistic guidelines in *Der volkommene Capellmeister*,[37] he apparently came to realize that the gulf between himself and Mattheson was based upon fundamental differences of perspective and was thus not subject to any significant degree of amelioration when dealing with specific issues. But whatever his motivation, Mizler chose not to take up the pen against Mattheson again, even in the face of the repeated assaults which were directed toward him by Mattheson.[38] Yet the rationalistic tradition in German music scholarship Mizler established was to have considerable influence in the following decades.

After Frederick the Great became king in 1740, Berlin gained greater importance as a musical center, even rivaling the established brilliance of the Dresden Hofkapelle.[39] With the French philosophical perspective of Frederick's court, and with the precedent found in Mizler's work, it is not surprising to find that the treatises and books that emerged from Berlin during the next decades had a strong rationalistic bias. One of the most fascinating questions one encounters in trying to assess Mattheson's impact upon other musicians in the eighteenth century relates to how his ideas were interpreted by the musicians and scholars associated directly or indirectly with Frederick's court. This concern gains considerable significance from the fact that sometimes more attention seems to have been paid to the books that emanated from the court than to the music. One simple example that might be mentioned is that many musicologists specializing in the music of the eighteenth century have studied Quantz's *Versuch*, but it is doubtful that even a majority have heard or carefully studied an opera by Capellmeister Karl Heinrich Graun.[40]

Mattheson's writings were certainly well known and read in Berlin. In addition, he dedicated a book defending opera to the king.[41] This book appeared in 1749, at the very moment when Frederick's musicians began publishing their own treatises.[42] It is possible that the king, having established the finest musical establishment in northern Germany, and having witnessed the broad impact that Mattheson's books were having, expressed a desire to have his best musicians display their erudition in a manner which would preserve forever the glory of his musical undertakings. One quiet word to Quantz during a royal flute lesson would certainly have been sufficient to start the process moving forward. Whatever the catalyst was, it is apparent that a great deal of interest in precisely such activities was in evidence during the 1750s. The king must have supported this, otherwise it would not have been permitted to continue, much less to prosper.

Though their personal relationship was pointedly ignored by one author,[43] Mattheson's interaction with Christoph Nichelmann provides us with a good illustration of the way in which Mattheson's ideas were transmitted directly to the

---

[34] *New Grove*, s.v. "Mizler," by Buelow. Mizler's *Musikalische Bibliothek* devotes considerable attention to Gottsched and Mattheson, including over 200 pages to the *Vollkommene Capellmeister*. As Buelow has observed, "while often genuinely impressed by Mattheson's ideas, Mizler criticized him for failing to create a systematic ordering of musical materials and a methodical presentation of the basic principles of part-writing."

[35] Wöhlke, 93.

[36] Johann Mattheson [Aristoxenus, der jüngere], *Die neueste Untersuchung der Singspiele* (1744), and *Matthesonii Plus Ultra* (1754).

[37] *New Grove*, s.v. "Mizler," by Buelow; and Wöhlke, 87, who notes that Mizler's "naturwissenschaftliche Betrachtungsweise zog ihm die Feindschaft Matthesons zu."

[38] Wöhlke, 94.

[39] Ortrun Landmann, "The Dresden Hofkapelle during the lifetime of Johann Sebastian Bach," *Early Music* 17 (1989): 17-30. Landmann's documentation shows that during the eighteenth century, in a comparison with the important musical centers of London, Mannheim, Leipzig, and Esterházá, the Dresden Hofkapelle had the largest forces for the longest period of time.

[40] "It [*Versuch*] is an invaluable work . . . worth far more than Quantz's compositions. It was enthusiastically received even in its own time, and can truly be said to be a product, in every sense of the word, of Frederick's patronage"; see Ernest Eugene Helm, *Music at the Court of Frederick the Great* (Norman: University of Oklahoma Press, 1960), 166-67.

[41] *Matthesons Mithridat wider den Gift einer welschen Satyre, genannt, La Musica*, 1749.

[42] The treatises by Quantz, C. P. E. Bach, Nichelmann, and Agricola appeared in the 1750s.

[43] Karl G. Fellerer, "Zur Melodielehre im 18. Jahrhundert," *Studia musicologica* 3 (1962): 109-15.

court of Frederick the Great and modified there. Nichelmann did not simply rehash Mattheson's theories in his *Die Melodie nach ihrem Wesen sowohl als nach ihren Eigenschaften* of 1755. As Werner Braun put it, "Sicher ist Nichelmanns Melodie-Traktat . . . durch Mattheson inspiriert worden, wenn auch jener zu anderen Ergebnissen gelangte."[44] Yet his impetus to write this treatise clearly came from Mattheson. Nichelmann had lived in Hamburg in 1733-39, during the formative years between the ages of sixteen and twenty-two, and had studied with Mattheson.[45] This is the very period in which Mattheson was bringing his own innovative theories on melody to their definitive form. Between 1736 and 1739 Scheibe had also been in Hamburg and had manifest an intense interest in Mattheson's theories on melody. While Nichelmann had worked, between the ages of thirteen and sixteen, under J. S. Bach's direction in Leipzig[46] (during a time when both Scheibe and Mizler were there), the ideas of Mattheson are the decisive influence on this treatise.

Further, in his *Der vollkommene Capellmeister* Mattheson specifically advocates the types of treatises that were written by C. P. E. Bach, Quantz, and Agricola.[47] Precedents for Bach's *Versuch* can certainly be found in Mattheson's *Kleine General-Bass-Schule* and in his *Grosse General-Baß-Schule*, as well as in works by other authors.[48] Quantz's *Versuch*, while reflecting the more rationalistic climate of Berlin, generally follows the wide-ranging format found in *Der vollkommene Capellmeister*. Evidence of Mattheson's influence is found throughout the *Versuch*.[49] Johann Friedrich Agricola patterned many of his observations on Mattheson's ideas in his transformation of Pier Francesco Tosi's little book into a major treatise. The scientific tone which his discussion of the vocal apparatus characterizes in his *Anleitung zur Singkunst* has led to the conclusion that he was a forerunner of modern voice science.[50] Kurt Wichmann, in comparing Tosi's original with Agricola's greatly-expanded verson, put it this way: "Trotz der Anlehnung an das Tosische, den Ideen der Renaissance verhaftete Gedankengut ist bei Agricola deutlich der Geist der Aufklärung zu spüren."[51] In this way French neoclassical values prevalent in Berlin are repeatedly insinuated into concepts adapted from Mattheson's writings.

In the final analysis, Willheim was correct in his description of the philosophical evolution in the arts during the eighteenth century.[52] The fundamental direction was toward the practical, intuitive approaches of the English empiricists and away from French neoclassicism. One reason that this tendency is poorly understood by music scholars is that there is an often unspoken assumption that the classical period was an outcome of a swing toward classical values some time between 1750 and 1780. However, these final decades were actually less classical and more romantic in their aesthetic than the decades between 1720 and 1750 had been.[53] Aesthetically and philosophically the bases for these changes in Germany are found in Hamburg, and specifically, in Mattheson's treatises.[54] Rationalism based on French ideas was already under heavy attack when Frederick ascended to the throne.[55] Though because

---

[44] Braun, 129.

[45] *New Grove*, s.v. "Nichelmann, Christoph," by Douglas A. Lee.

[46] Ibid.; Willhelm, 35-44; and *New Grove*, s.v. "Mizler," by Buelow.

[47] Braun, 469.

[48] William J. Mitchell provides a listing of precedents; see Carl Philipp Emanuel Bach, *Essay on the True Art of Playing Keyboard Instruments*, trans. and ed. Mitchell (New York: Norton, 1949), 11.

[49] Schäfke, 214 and 234-35. As Edward Reilly has aptly observed, in Quantz's *Versuch*, "all phases of performance, from phrasing, ornamentation and dynamics to the seating of the orchestra, are discussed. Quantz had models for certain portions of his work, but no similarly comprehensive manual had been attempted before." If one considers a Capellmeister to be a performer, then *Der volkommene Capellmeister* provides just such a precedent. Its tremendous influence on Quantz, as Schäfke has noted, would in fact make it the likely model.

[50] Harriss, "Agricola as an Early Voice Scientist," paper presented at the annual meeting of the Southern Chapter of the American Musicological Society, Lafayette, Louisiana, March 1978.

[51] Pier Francesco Tosi, *Anleitung zur Singkunst*, trans. Johann Friedrich Agricola, ed. Kurt Wichmann (Leipzig: VEB Deutscher Verlag für Musik, 1966), 12.

[52] Willheim, 4-17.

[53] See Harriss, "Johann Adolf Hasse and the *Sturm und Drang* in Vienna," *Hasse-Studien* 3 (1996): 24-53.

[54] Though the author makes several fundamental errors, on this point see Benary, 81-87; also see Flaherty, 81-92, and Hosler, 138-70.

[55] Gottsched's ideals were under attack in the 1730s and 40s. Lessing was effectively questioning rationalistic assumptions during the 1750s and later; see Flaherty, 102-16 and 201-32. On Frederick, see Gerhard Ritter, *Frederick the Great: A Historical Profile*, trans. Peter Paret

of the power of the king the neoclassical rationalist perspective enjoyed one final moment of glory, the movement was essentially moribund before the Seven Years War.[56] In the field of music scholarship the attack was led by Mattheson and Scheibe. The Arcadian classicism that helped shape the new musical style of the 1720s, the style that the king liked most of all, was also beginning a slow and long retreat from its more extreme manifestations.

In summary, though Mattheson's ideas received a considerable amount of attention from contemporary scholars, his philosophical concepts were also so altered in the process that today he might not recognize his own words. When one considers that the climate for musical scholarship changed during the course of the eighteenth century, as has been suggested in this essay, it becomes less surprising that scholars earlier in the present century were led to develop such highly formalistic theories as the *Affektenlehre*, the *Rhetoriklehre*, and the *Figurenlehre*, as if these theories had something to do with musical composition and performance.[57] It is also easier to understand why the earlier scholars who developed such intellectual models for the study of ideas in the eighteenth century searched for a basis for their conceptual points of view in the treatises of Mattheson.[58] If one accepts that Mattheson's approach was basically empirical, pragmatic, and intuitive, then it becomes apparent that these earlier twentieth-century scholars, in choosing Mattheson as the formulator of rationalistic theories, certainly selected an inappropriate person. Once the fundamental philosophical problem I have outlined has been satisfactorily resolved, we will have a better basis for understanding the life of Mattheson and the intellectual crosscurrents of his time.

(Berkeley: University of California Press, 1970). As Ritter (p. 51) states, "The philosophy of his [Frederick's] age was the doctrine of rationalism and of determined secularism. The more deeply he penetrated this body of thought, the more strongly he came to accept the belief that lay behind every aspect of the Enlightenment."

[56] The war (1756-63) brought an abrupt end to the most successful period of Frederick's patronage; on music in this period, see Helm, 126-39.

[57] See Harriss, "Johann Mattheson and the *Affekten-*, *Figuren-*, and *Rhetoriklehren*," paper presented at the Thirteenth Congress of the International Musicological Society, Strasbourg, 3 September 1982.

[58] Schering, "Musikästhetik"; Kretzschmar, "Affektenlehre"; and Goldschmidt, *Musikästhetik*.

12

Mozart's Milanese Theatrical Works

Kathleen Kuzmick Hansell

Before the age of twenty-five, when he was preparing for the premiere of *Idomeneo* at Munich in 1781, Mozart's only real experiences as a composer for the professional theater had occurred nearly a decade earlier in Italy. For Milan's Regio Ducal Teatro between 1770 and 1772 he provided two *opere serie*, *Mitridate, re di Ponto* and *Lucio Silla*, and a *festa teatrale*, *Ascanio in Alba*. Their composition and performance gave him first-hand knowledge of what all but the French then considered the most important domain for any young composer to conquer, namely Italian opera.

Naturally, Leopold Mozart was only too aware of this necessity, especially in view of the few and disappointing opportunities heretofore. Wolfgang's dramatic compositions up to the time of *Lucio Silla*, both sacred and secular, are listed in table 12.1, which includes pertinent details regarding the genre, librettist, dates of composition, and first performance. The first two works, his contribution to the school oratorio *Die Schuldigkeit des ersten Gebots* and the brief Latin intermedium *Apollo und Hyacinth*, both of 1767, were written for student amateurs; the intermedium was performed just once, and Mozart's portion of the oratorio on only two occasions.[1] Leopold of course had far different expectations for the third work, a full-length *dramma giocoso* composed with a professional cast in mind. However, the intended performance in Vienna of *La finta semplice* never materialized—this despite Wolfgang's keenness to please his singers by writing and rewriting according to their desires, and despite all his father's attempts to sway the intractable impresario of the Burg- and Kärntnertor theaters, which included a petition to the Emperor himself.[2] *La finta semplice* was finally produced, as the table indicates, a year later, not in a Viennese theater by well-known Italian stars of the opera buffa, but in Salzburg at the Archbishop's palace by local singers. Meanwhile, Wolfgang set to music the very brief arias and three ensemble pieces that make up the one-act singspiel *Bastien und Bastienne*. Neither the circumstances regarding the commission for this work nor its production have ever been satisfactorily explained, although after Mozart's death Constanze asserted that it had been given a private performance in 1768 in the garden of the Viennese "magnetist" Franz Mesmer.[3] In fact, the first documented production occurred only in 1890 in Berlin![4] Even from this brief survey we can understand what prompted Leopold Mozart finally to take the bull by the horns, so to speak, and set off with Wolfgang for Italy at the end of 1769.

---

[1] On the performances of both works see Alfred Orel's introduction to the critical edition of *Apollo und Hyacinth* in *Neue Ausgabe sämtlicher Werke* (Kassel: Bärenreiter), series 2, Werkgruppe 5, vol. 1 (1959), viii-x, xv-xviii.

[2] Leopold's petition, describing Wolfgang's travails, is given in English translation in Otto Erich Deutsch, *Mozart: A Documentary Biography* (Stanford: Stanford University Press, 1965), 80-83.

[3] This assertion, given in the early biography of Mozart (1828) by Constanze's second husband, Georg Nikolaus Nissen, was later rejected by Alfred Orel, "Die Legende um Mozarts *Bastien und Bastienne*," *Schweizerische Musikzeitung* 91, no. 4 (1951), as a mere legend; yet recent articles, such as Julian Rushton's entry on the work in the *New Grove Dictionary of Opera* (1992), 1:147, state it as a simple fact.

[4] See Deutsch, 159.

Table 12.1
Mozart's Early Dramatic Works

Köchel No.	Title	Genre	Librettist	Composed	First Performance
35	Die Schuldigkeit des ersten Gebots, Part 1	Oratorio (3 parts: 2 = J. M. Haydn; 3 = A. C. Adlgasser	I. A. von Weiser	Salzburg, early 1767	Salzburg, University, 12 March 1767
38	Apollo und Hyacinth	Latin intermedium (3 acts = Prologue + 2 Chori)	R. Widl	Salzburg, spring 1767	Salzburg, University, 13 May 1767
51/46a	La finta semplice	Dramma giocoso (3 acts)	M. Coltellini after Goldoni	Vienna, mid-1768	Salzburg, Palace of Archbishop, 1 May 1768
50/46b	Bastien und Bastienne	Singspiel (1 act)	F. W. Weiskern & J. A. Schachtner after Rousseau and Marie Favart	?Vienna, summer 1768	?Vienna, House of F. A. Mesmer, September-October 1768
87/74a	Mitridate, re di Ponto	Dramma per musica (3 acts)	V. A. Cigna-Santi, after Parini and Racine	Bologna & Milan, autumn 1770	Milan, Regio Ducal Teatro, 26 December 1770
118/74c	La Betulia liberata	Oratorio (2 acts)	P. Metastasio	Italy & Salzburg, spring 1771	for Padua; probably no performance
126	Il sogno di Scipione	Serenata (1 act)	P. Metastasio	Salzburg, ?April-August 1771	?possibly Salzburg, Palace of Archbishop, May 1772
111	Ascanio in Alba	Festa teatrale (2 parts)	G. Parini	Milan, August-September 1771	Milan, Regio Ducal Teatro, 17 October 1771
135	Lucio Silla	Dramma per musica (3 acts)	G. De Gamerra	Salzburg & Milan, autumn 1772	Milan, Regio Ducal Teatro, 26 December 1772

Before turning to the three Milanese commissions, let us review briefly the situation with regard to Mozart's other pre-1780 dramatic works. The table names two works written, apparently, between his first and second Italian journeys, neither of which can be unequivocally proven to have been performed during his lifetime. In a letter of 14 March 1771 from Vicenza, Leopold wrote to his wife about Wolfgang's most recent accomplishments and then added: "He also took on a job, however, since he must compose an oratorio for Padua, and he can do it at an opportune time."[5] And by July, from Salzburg, he noted that the composition to a text by Metastasio, *La Betulia liberata*, was well underway and would soon be sent to Padua to be copied and readied for performance.[6] Unfortunately, these plans seemingly came to nothing. Thirteen years later Wolfgang thought of taking up the work again and asked his sister in a letter of 21 July 1784 to have Leopold dig it out:

> If he [Papa] could also send me the old oratorio *Betulia liberata*, I would be very grateful. I must write this oratorio for the society I named above. Perhaps I could even reuse some pieces from it here and there.[7]

---

[5] *Mozart: Briefe und Aufzeichnungen*, ed. Wilhelm A. Bauer and Otto Erich Deutsch, 7 vols. (Kassel: Bärenreiter, 1962-75), 1:425: "Er bekamm aber auch eine Arbeit, indem er ein Oratorium nach Padua Componieren muss, und solches nach gelegenheit machen kann."

[6] Letter from Leopold Mozart to Count Gian Luca Pallavicini in Bologna of 19 July 1771; ibid., 1:428.

[7] Ibid., 3:319: "... wenn er [Papa] mir auch das alte Oratorium schicken könnte, wäre es mir recht lieb.—ich muss dieses oratorium für den hiesige Societät schreiben—vielleicht könnte ich doch Ja und da etwas davon Stückweise brauchen."

But once again there is no evidence either of any further revisions or performance by the Viennese Tonkünstler-Societät. A similar fate met Mozart's setting of another Metastasian text, the one-act serenata *Il sogno di Scipione*. According to Joseph Horst Lederer, editor of the critical edition, *Il sogno di Scipione* was most likely completed before the second journey to Italy— that is, before the beginning of September 1771. If intended for the old Archbishop of Salzburg, Schrattenbach, and the fiftieth anniversary of his priesthood in January 1772, his death a month earlier and the accession of the parsimonious Colloredo seem to have killed any hopes for a performance as well.[8]

And after *Lucio Silla*? For Munich Mozart wrote the three-act comic opera *La finta giardiniera*, which had its première on 13 January 1775. But the cast, according to Leopold Mozart, was incompetent, and it was further reduced by illness, so that it gave only two other performances, these incomplete.[9] Five years later the work had more success in German translation as a singspiel (that is, with spoken dialogue) under the title *Die verstellte Gärtnerin*. But in its original form it was not successfully produced until modern times. Also in 1775, for the visit of Archduke Maximilian Franz to Salzburg on April 23, Mozart set to music a revised and abbreviated version of Metastasio's serenata *Il re pastore*, cut down to two acts. Its single performance, about which there is little information, was entrusted (except for the title role) to local singers, and the work saw no revivals during Mozart's lifetime.[10] Finally, about two additional works there is even less reliable information. Beginning in 1773, and continuing apparently until 1779, Mozart provided various pieces used as incidental music for Tobias P. Gebler's play *Thamos, König in Ägypten*. The play (originally staged in 1773 in Bratislava) was revived in Vienna in April 1774 with two choruses by Mozart. Later productions by a visiting troupe in Salzburg probably occasioned Mozart's remaining contributions, but documentation regarding their performance is lacking.[11] In any case, the play soon fell out of the repertory, and with it any further dissemination of Mozart's music. Before *Idomeneo* there survive fragments of just one other dramatic composition, the unfinished two-act singspiel *Zaide* (*Das Serail*), composed the year before, in 1779. Portions of *Zaide* may have been used for a production then in Salzburg, but Mozart's later proposals to stage it in Munich in 1780, and Vienna in 1781, were never carried through.[12] A *duo-drama*, *Semiramis*, mentioned in reports of 1778, remains an unknown quantity: the music has never surfaced.

By comparison with these disheartening histories of performances—inadequate, partial or totally lacking—and with them the serious want of professional stimulus, the experiences at the Regio Ducal Teatro of Milan must be counted invaluable. They were of primary importance in Mozart's formation as a dramatist, for all that they were not followed up by any further commissions or employment. To understand better his obligations and how he met them, it is vital to know in a general way how works for Italian theaters were commissioned, prepared, and heard, as well as the particular circumstances at Milan.

By the 1770s only the major theaters of Italy regularly staged *opera seria*: it was a very expensive undertaking![13] The main season at Carnival, beginning the day after Christmas and lasting until the beginning of Lent, thus varied in length from year to year. According to when Easter fell, Carnival occupied anywhere from a minimum of seven weeks, in the shortest seasons, to a maximum of eleven. Most theaters staging heroic operas put on two, or at most

---

[8] *Neue Ausgabe sämtlicher Werke*, series 2, Werkgruppe 5, vol. 6 (1977), vii-viii. There is some indication that a performance may have been given for the installation of the new archbishop, possibly in May 1772; see Deutsch, 141-42.

[9] See Leopold's letters to his wife from Munich of 21 January and early February 1775 in *Mozart: Briefe und Aufzeichnungen*, 1:519-20.

[10] See the introduction by Pierluigi Petrobelli and Wolfgang Rehm to the critical edition of *Il re pastore* in *Neue Ausgabe sämtlicher Werke*, series 2, Werkgruppe 5, vol. 9 (1985), ix, xii-xiii.

[11] See Deutsch, 145.

[12] See Leopold's letter of 11 December 1780 and Wolfgang's of 18 January and 18 April 1781, in *Mozart: Briefe und Aufzeichnungen*, 3:53, 90, 107.

[13] In addition to Milan's Regio Ducal Teatro, these included just seven other theaters considered to be of the first rank, all staging opera seria during carnival season: the Regio of Turin, the San Benedetto of Venice, the Accademia Filarmonica of Verona, the Pergola of Florence, the Ducale of Modena, the Argentina of Rome, and the San Carlo of Naples. Second-tier houses putting on heroic operas either favored the annual spring and summer fair seasons, as did the Teatro Pubblico of Lucca and the Nuovo of Padua, or were more irregular in their presentations, as was true of the Teatro Comunale of Bologna, the S. Agostino of Genoa, and the Teatro delle Dame of Rome. The Teatro Pubblico of Reggio Emilia, which had numbered among the top-ranking theaters in the 1750s and early 60s, ceased putting on opera seria for over a decade from 1765.

three, works per season. Almost all were newly composed for the occasion. Until the 1820s and later no theaters in Italy followed the repertory system in which there were several different operas on the bill playing in alternation, with successful earlier productions being brought back from year to year.[14] Thus, in Mozart's time, a single opera played evening after evening, every day but Friday (a penitential day). In the case of the first opera of the season, the length of the run was determined by its relative success, while the end of Carnival time signaled the close of the second (or last).[15] Hence, theater managements usually scheduled what was expected to be the better-received work as the second opera, and they also designated a larger part of the budget for its production.[16] In the eighteenth century, once a heroic opera finished its run it was never taken up again at the same theater, and only very rarely would it ever be staged at another house.

The explanation for this practice lies not only in the idea that audiences expected completely new works. It also has to do with the fact that a particular musical setting was designed for the needs of a specific theater and specific performing forces. True, all productions of *opera seria* during the period shared certain characteristics in common. Among these were the size and composition of the typical cast.

There were usually six solo singers, occasionally seven, in a clear hierarchy. At the top were the *prima donna*, always a soprano, and *primo uomo*, a castrato singer who was most often a soprano as well, but sometimes a mezzo or, less often, a contralto. The salaries these two received were far above what the management paid out for any other aspect of the production. By the 1770s the *primo uomo* no longer had the status he had enjoyed earlier. The same may be said of the third principal singer, the *tenore*, who played the role of the father, ruler, or tyrant. At mid-century the most famous tenors had commanded fees nearly equivalent to those of the principal couple. But by the time Mozart came to Italy their fees had dropped by over fifty percent.[17] The other members of the cast included the *secondo uomo*, quite often a young castrato singer with a high voice, though sometimes this part was played by a female soprano, and the *secondo donna*, usually also a soprano. At the bottom level was the so-called *ultima parte*, a male singer who might be either a soprano or alto castrato or a tenor. If there were a seventh soloist it was normally a *terzo uomo*, that is, yet another castrato. Thus all the voices, male and female, were high; even contraltos were in a distinct minority. There were no baritones or basses in Italian heroic opera until around the turn of the century.

The hierarchical status of the singers was clearly a determining factor in the construction of heroic opera librettos and their subsequent musical settings. In fact, not infrequently the make-up of the cast was established before even the composers received their contracts and always long before the librettos were considered.[18] The same singers appeared in all the works staged at one theater in a particular season. Thus, the assurance of their participation was a top priority, since, more than any other factor, it was a stellar cast that would best guarantee the impresario's investment. The librettists, whether contributing entirely new texts or, as often the case, revising

---

[14] These conclusions are based on a review of schedules for all the major Italian theaters as available in published chronologies of individual houses and in the yearly editions of the series *Indice de' spettacoli teatrali*, which is now available complete in a reprint edition as *Un almanacco drammatico: L'indice de' teatrali spettacoli, 1764-1823*, ed. Roberto Verti, 2 vols. (Pesaro: Fondazione Rossini, 1996).

[15] In most of Italy this occurred on Shrove Tuesday (*martedì grasso*), but in Milan, which observed the Ambrosian rite, Carnival concluded on *sabato grasso*, allowing three more opera performances (Wednesday, Thursday, and Saturday). Leopold Mozart remarked with some humor on the custom in his letter of 27 February 1770; see *Mozart: Briefe und Aufzeichnungen*, 1:316-17.

[16] In Milan the impresario expected to take in 40% of the season's revenue from the first opera and the remainder during the run of the second. See my "Opera and Ballet at the Regio Ducal Teatro of Milan, 1771-1776: A Musical and Social History" (Ph.D. diss., University of California, Berkeley, 1979), 189, n. 7. A similar situation can be seen to prevail at other theaters whose accounts are readily available, such as those of Turin's Regio, as reported in Marie-Thérèse Bouquet, *Il teatro di corte dalle origini al 1788* (Turin: Cassa di Risparmio, 1976), vol. 1 of *Storia del Regio Teatro di Torino*.

[17] For comparisons and changes in singers' salaries in Milan and Turin between the 1750s and 70s, see Hansell, 217-21, and the tables on pp. 655-56. During this period seasonal fees for the *prime donne* and *primi uomini* reversed their relative positions, increasing for the women from an average of 6,000 to 8,500 lire and decreasing for the castrati from 8,200 to 6,200 lire; the tenors fared even worse, with their salaries diminishing from 2,500 to 1,800 lire.

[18] Surviving contracts and other documentary evidence reveal that agreements with principal singers were generally settled one year or two years in advance of the engagement, while those with composers could (as in the case of Mozart's for *Ascanio in Alba*) be issued a half-year or less before the scheduled premiere (the contract for *Ascanio* arrived in Salzburg in early April 1771 for a work to open on October 16).

favorite older ones, considered not only the general requirements for granting the various roles their allotted share of the drama: we know from contemporary documents that at least for the principal figures librettists clearly envisioned the performers who would create them.[19] Composers worked even more specifically for and around the interpreters. But, as in all other aspects of the *dramma per musica*, the vocal characterizations too followed certain traditions distinguishing the singers' rank, which we shall examine in detail presently.

Numerous other conditions common to the presentation of operas in *settecento* Italy influenced their general formal characteristics. An obvious one was the expected duration of the performance. A typical evening at the theater began at 5:30 or 6:00 and ended between 11 p.m. and midnight. Until late in the century most operas were in three acts, the first two lasting normally about one to one and one-quarter hours each, while the third act became progressively shorter. During the intervals between acts, until far into the nineteenth century, elaborate pantomime ballets were staged. By the time of Mozart's sojourns, as his father also mentions in a letter from Milan, the danced works following the first and second acts of the opera commonly lasted 45 minutes to one hour.[20] After the opera's last act, north Italian theaters also mounted shorter ballets which sometimes were connected thematically with the vocal work.[21] But it should be emphasized that the entr'acte ballets were normally completely independent of the operas with which they were staged, both in plot and music. The ballet music was not the responsibility of the opera composer but provided by other musicians. The operas themselves almost never had any dances, and this remained the general rule in Italy until about the time of Verdi's *Aida*.[22]

By modern standards, not only the overall length but the pacing of the theatrical presentations was *very* leisurely—intentionally so! The staged spectacles formed only part of the theater's *raison d'être*, and perhaps nowhere was this truer than in Milan. During the theater season the opera house was the principal center for social gatherings for all who could afford to attend. In many cities the boxes were rented by the season, and their patrons used them on nearly a nightly basis. At Milan, however, the boxes of all but the uppermost tier were not rented but owned outright by the city's prominent families, who paid a large annual fee for the privilege. Tickets were sold only for the fifth tier of boxes and for keys to seats in the parterre (then the least sought-after in the house).[23] The theater in question, it should be stressed, was not La Scala, as has all too often been stated, but its predecessor which occupied one wing of the Ducal Palace, just off the Piazza Duomo. Called therefore the Regio Ducal Teatro, it had been built in 1717 and continued in regular operation until destroyed by fire in February 1776.

Whether theater boxes were rented or in private possession is of less importance than the fact that the spectators filling them remained essentially the same throughout the entire season. The operas and ballets on stage formed a pleasant accompaniment to the many other diversions offered. At Milan, as in some other cities, these diversions included gambling and lotteries, which indeed were the impresario's major source of income. Refreshments and, in the boxes, even full dinners were served during performances. Friends visited each other, chatted, played cards or chess— all activities reported in the journals of foreigners visiting Italy at Carnival time. All these factors, taken together with the *en suite* method of opera production, had significant consequences for the structure of the staged works.

---

[19] A noted example is Metastasio's letter of 17 February 1772 to Anna de Amicis, prima donna in his and Hasse's *Il Ruggiero*, and the following year in Mozart's *Lucio Silla*: "From the first moment that I imagined and selected the subject of *Ruggiero* I thought that among the dramatic heroines known to me there was no one as absolutely suitable as Signora De Amicis to represent the part of Bradamante with fire, with boldness, with frankness, and with the expression necessary for such a character." *Tutte le opere di Pietro Metastasio*, ed. Bruno Brunelli, 5 vols. (Milan: Mondadori, 1952-54), 5:140.

[20] On 29 December 1770, following the premiere of Wolfgang's *Mitridate*, Leopold noted that "the opera with the 3 ballets lasts 6 good hours; but now they want to shorten the ballets because they last 2 good hours." *Mozart: Briefe und Aufzeichnungen*, 1:411.

[21] The two theaters where this custom prevailed most regularly and endured longest were those of Milan and Turin. During the 1770s the Teatro San Carlo of Naples occasionally staged three ballets as well, particularly with heroic operas whose first performances were given on the name-day of Saint Charles, November 4. Data regarding ballets at San Carlo, however, are still incomplete in all secondary sources on the theater, even the most recent such as *La cronologia, 1737-1987*, ed. Carlo Marinelli Roscioni, vol. 2 of *Il Teatro di San Carlo* (Naples: Guida, 1987).

[22] On the continuing relationship between Italian opera and ballet, see my chapter "Il ballo teatrale e l'opera italiana," in vol. 5 of *Storia dell'opera italiana* (Turin: EDT, 1988), 177-306; an English edition (Chicago: University of Chicago Press) is forthcoming.

[23] See the section "The Theater and Its Patrons" in my "Opera and Ballet," 158-82.

In the first place, the opera itself had to last long enough to provide a satisfying evening's entertainment, which meant at least three to three and one-half hours. Secondly, it should be put together in such a way as to allow comprehension and provide enjoyment without the necessity of uninterrupted attention. Important in this respect was the persistence of the "system" so much criticized by advocates of operatic reform but obviously preferred by the Italian public, namely the development of the plot chiefly in *recitativo semplice* in alternation with lyrical texts (mainly for arias), reflecting or commenting upon the action.[24] Thirdly, the aria settings were not only to vary in tone from one to the next but, since they were sung night after night to essentially the same audience, also allow room for the singers' elaborations. "A fine singer," commented one Milanese observer, "brings something new to his aria every evening."[25] That until late in the eighteenth century Italian heroic operas had very few ensemble numbers— usually one duet and perhaps a trio or quartet—and often no pieces for chorus may well be because these were much less susceptible to varied executions. Recitative accompanied by the orchestra was for special effects only and limited to a few highly dramatic scenes and usually to the principal singers. In general, elaborate orchestrations, if viewed as distracting too much attention from the vocal soloists, met only incomprehension.

With these general observations in mind, let us now turn to the three works Mozart wrote for the Milanese. The first point to note is that they represent two distinct genres. *Mitridate* and *Lucio Silla* are *opere serie*, commissioned in the usual way and performed during regular Carnival seasons. *Ascanio in Alba*, by contrast, is a *festa teatrale*, an occasional work written to enhance the celebrations accompanying the wedding of Archduke Ferdinand, the third surviving son of Empress Maria Teresa and new governor of Milan, with the princess Maria Beatrice d'Este in October 1771. As such, *Ascanio in Alba* differed in numerous respects from the seasonal operas right from the moment of drawing up the contracts. Let us begin therefore by examining the way in which the youthful Mozart received the commissions for these three works.

In March of 1770 the fourteen-year old composer had been in Milan with his father for some two months. It was the initial stage of their first Italian journey, but already crowned with success. They met important singers and composers and became acquainted with influential patrons, the most important of whom was the plenipotentiary minister of Milan, Count Karl Joseph von Firmian. Wolfgang gave several well-received concerts of his own works. After the last of them, at Firmian's residence on the 12th, Leopold wrote to his wife:

> . . . between this evening and tomorrow morning yet another thing will be agreed upon. That is, they want Wolfgang to write the first opera for the coming Christmas season. . . . If only the contract can be drawn up, then the libretto will be sent to us.[26]

Then on the 24th, from Bologna: "The *scrittura*, or written contract, is already drawn up and [copies] exchanged between us."[27] Wolfgang himself explained a month later, after a sojourn in Florence where he became reacquainted with the renowned castrato Manzuoli, that he had swayed opinion in his favor and earned Firmian's protection by proving his ability as a composer of Italian vocal music:

> Manzuoli is under contract with the Milanese to sing in my opera. In Florence he therefore sang four or five arias for me, including some of my own—those which I had had to compose in Milan

---

[24] Since the usage "secco" recitative is primarily a nineteenth-century derogatory term, eighteenth-century parlance is preferred here. I therefore adopt the eighteenth-century English equivalent, simple recitative.

[25] "Un bravo cantante ogni sera porta qualche novità nella sua aria"; letter of Pietro Verri of 19 August 1778, commenting on the effect of the inaugural opera at La Scala. *Carteggio di Pietro e di Alessandro Verri dal 1766 al 1797*, ed. Emanuele Greppi, Alessandro Giulini et al., 12 vols. (Milan, 1923-42), 10:54-55.

[26] ". . . zwischen heute abends und dem morgigen Tage wird auch noch eine andere Sache ausgemacht. Man will nämlich dass der Wolfg: die erste opera kommende Weinachten schreiben soll. . . . Wollte nun aber die Scrittura gemacht werden, so wird uns das Buch [libretto] geschickt. . . ." Letter of 13 March 1770 in *Mozart: Briefe und Aufzeichnungen*, 1:320.

[27] Ibid., 1:325: "Die Scrittura, oder der schriftliche Contract ist schon gemacht, und gegen einander ausgewechselt."

because they had not heard any theatrical things of mine, in order to see that I was capable of writing an opera. . . . As yet the libretto is not known. I've recommended one by Metastasio.[28]

The last remark was certainly ingenuous on Wolfgang's part. Rarely was a composer of that era in the position to determine the choice of libretto, and especially not one of his inexperience.

For *Mitridate*, as for the usual Carnival operas, since the theater impresario would have to bear any losses incurred it was he who made the decisions about the production, subject to government approval. The only irregular aspect here was Firmian's apparent intervention on Mozart's behalf. Otherwise normal procedures were followed, as in the terms of Wolfgang's contract, reported by his father on March 24:

> The recitatives must be sent to Milan in October, and on November 1 we must be in Milan so that Wolfgang can write the arias. The *prima* and *seconda donna* are Signora Gabrielli and her sister. The tenor is Signor Ettore. . . . The *primo uomo* and the others have not yet been decided.[29]

Wolfgang thus had his contract nine months before the intended premiere, a typical arrangement especially for a first Carnival opera. Naturally, a fledgling composer would scarcely have been entrusted with the season's more prestigious closing work. Regarding the cast, Leopold's uncertainties may simply reflect a lack of access to the proper channels of information. Normally the principal singers were engaged at least a year in advance of the performance in order to guarantee high quality in this all-important aspect of the season. As table 12.2 listing Mozart's Milanese casts illustrates, Leopold was mistaken in almost every case concerning *Mitridate*. Even so, all the main performers with whom Wolfgang would collaborate at Milan were, with a single exception (the tenor for *Lucio Silla*), among the best of the day.

Table 12.2
Mozart's Milanese Casts

Part	*Mitridate*	*Ascanio in Alba*	*Lucio Silla*
Iª Donna	Antonia Bernasconi (soprano)	Antonia Maria Girelli-Aguilar (soprano)	Anna de Amicis-Buonsolazzi (soprano)
Iº Uomo	Pietro Benedetti detto Sartorino (soprano)	Giovanni Manzuoli (mezzo-soprano)	Venanzio Rauzzini (soprano)
Iº Tenore	Guglielmo d'Ettore	Giuseppe Tibaldi	Bassano Morgnoni
2º Uomo	Giuseppe Cicognani (contralto)	Adamo Solzi (soprano)	Felicità Suardi (soprano)
2º Donna	Anna Francesca Varese (soprano)	Geltrude Falchini (soprano)	Daniela Mienci (soprano)
3º Uomo	Pietro Muschietti (soprano)		
Ultima parte	Gaspare Bassano (tenor)		Giuseppe Onofrio (tenor)

---

[28] Letter of 21 April 1770; ibid., 1:339: "Manzuoli steht im Contract mit den Mailändern, bey meiner Oper zu singen. Der hat mir auch deßwegen in Florenz vier oder fünf Arien gesungen, auch von mir einige, welche ich in Mailand componieren habe müssen, weil man gar nichts von theatral. Sachen von mir gehört hatte, um daraus zu sehen, daß ich fähig bin, eine Oper zu schreiben. . . . Man weiß auch noch nicht das Buch. Eins von Metastasio habe ich . . . recommandirt."

[29] Ibid., 1:325: "die Recitativ müßen im october nach Mayland geschickt werden, und den 1 Novemb: müßen wir in Mayland seyn, daß der Wolfg: die Arien schreibt. die prima und 2ᵈᵃ Donna sind die La Sgra. Gabrielli und ihre schwester. der Tenor ist il Sgr: Ettore. . . . der primo huomo und die übrigen sind noch nicht bestimmt."

The terms of the contract stipulating the order and dates for the delivery of the score were like those regularly accorded with all composers of the regular seasonal operas. The *scrittura* for *Lucio Silla* had the same obligations for the same dates two years later. The difference then was that for his second Milanese opera Wolfgang already had the contract in his pocket in March 1771, not nine but twenty-one full months ahead of time, indicating that confidence in his abilities had greatly increased. In both cases, as was the normal and very practical procedure, he was to deliver all the recitatives (meaning those accompanied by basso continuo) first. Since composition of the simple recitatives was generally less dependent on the individual performers, they could be turned over beforehand to the copyists for preparation of the necessary scores and vocal parts. Thus, both composer and copyists would be free later for the more demanding labor of finishing the arias and ensembles. Both the autograph scores and working copies of Mozart and his contemporaries in Italy give clear evidence that composers generally wrote out their operas in just this order—that is, they did not follow the sequence of the libretto. With the arias and ensemble pieces this was even more so.

And yet, we must be careful not to draw hasty conclusions regarding the actual planning and composition of an opera, as opposed to its final elaboration and scoring. Even a prodigy like Mozart planned his works well in advance, although he did not always commit every thought to paper. His letters confirm as much, as do the surviving sketches, which in the case of *Mitridate* exist in quite a large number. Although that is not true for *Lucio Silla*, the autograph score itself gives evidence of considerable reworking; Mozart had to revise the endings of over half the recitatives because he was forced to change the tonalities he had originally planned for the following arias in order to suit the singers. Figure 12.1, from the autograph of act 2 of *Lucio Silla* (preserved at Crakow, Biblioteka Jagiellonska), illustrates one of these instances, the last measures of Giunia's accompanied recitative preceding her aria "Ah se il crudel periglio" (no. 11). In B♭ major in the definitive version, the aria was originally planned in C, as the revisions of these cadential measures clearly indicate.

Fig. 12.1. From the autograph score of Mozart's *Lucio Silla* (Crakow, Biblioteka Jagiellonska), act 2, f. 43v. Mozart revised the concluding measures of Giunia's accompanied recitative to accommodate a change of key in the following aria (no. 11).

Even where the autographs show no changes, copies of the score made before the premiere sometimes reveal earlier versions of passages. Another passage from *Lucio Silla*—a portion of the simple recitative immediately preceding the previous example—shows in fig. 12.2a the original version of measures 62-67 as they appear in the score copy probably prepared for rehearsals and performance (preserved at the Bibliothèque Nationale in Paris), and then in fig. 12.2b the definitive version in the autograph. The revised version more effectively uses the diminished chord, beginning in measure 64 on the word "tiranno" and continuing the harmony until the G-minor resolution.

Fig. 12.2a. From a copy of the score of *Lucio Silla* (Paris, Bibliothèque Nationale), act 2, f. 47r. The copyist prepared the simple recitatives ahead of time, and these measures (62-67) are in Mozart's original version

Fig. 12.2b. From the autograph score of *Lucio Silla*, act 2, f. 41v. In the definitive version of the same measures Mozart altered both the harmonic scheme and the melodic line

On the other hand, copyists' scores, particularly those used during performances or those made for presentation to important patrons, may also contain additions or alterations in the hand of the composer—or in Mozart's case in the hand of his father as well—not found in the autograph, but representing later thoughts or notational refinements. Figure 12.3 shows a case in point: a page from a copy of *Lucio Silla* that the Mozarts probably commissioned toward the end of the opera's initial production for presentation to the Grand Duke of Tuscany (preserved at Turin, Accademia

Fig. 12.3. From a copy of the score of *Lucio Silla* (Turin, Accademia Filarmonica), act 3. A page from Cecilio's aria "Pupille amate" (no. 21) with dynamic indications added by Mozart

Filarmonica). Taken from Cecilio's act-three aria "Pupille amate," it is one of many pages in this copy on which Mozart himself carefully entered dynamic indications after the copyist had completed his work. None of those shown here appears in the autograph score, but the additions were the result of Mozart's work with the performing forces in the theater. Similar circumstances are also represented in the surviving copies of *Mitridate* and *Ascanio in Alba*.

The contract for *Ascanio in Alba* reached Mozart very shortly after that for *Lucio Silla*, in March 1771, just seven months before the performance. The notion of putting on a *festa teatrale*, in addition to the heroic opera by Johann Adolf Hasse already planned by Empress Maria Teresa for the imperial wedding seems to have originated in Milan rather than in Vienna. The sobriety of *Il Ruggiero*, the last Hasse-Metastasio collaboration, would be counterbalanced by a purely decorative lighter spectacle. The librettist of the *festa teatrale*, the well-known poet Giuseppe Parini, was already in the regular employ of Milan's theater. The cast, with the exception of the semi-retired castrato Manzuoli, in Metastasio's words "formerly the idol of Vienna,"[30] was chosen in Milan.[31] Mozart's appointment too was promoted by the Milanese, apparently favorably impressed by *Mitridate* the year before. Importantly, however, the entire expense for the production was to be covered by the imperial treasury and not by the local theater management.[32]

Rather than six or seven solo roles, *Ascanio in Alba* has only five, each of which was an allegorical representation of one of the primary personages associated with the wedding. Thus Ascanio symbolized the bridegroom, Archduke Ferdinand; Silvia his spouse, Maria Beatrice d'Este; and Venus the Empress Mother, while Aceste represented the Duke of Modena, governor of Milan and the bride's father, and Fauno Count Firmian. The interpreters, we note, were

---

[30] Letter of 13 October 1760; *Tutte le opere di Pietro Metastasio*, 4:167.

[31] On the process of selecting the cast, as revealed in archival documents in Milan and Vienna, see my "Opera and Ballet," 29-35.

[32] The economics of preparing and staging both works are discussed in ibid., 18-25.

singers normally employed for the *opera seria*. Thus their solo arias had vocal requirements similar to those of heroic opera. But in other respects the *festa teatrale* shows important structural characteristics clearly distinctive of this genre. Instead of three acts, it is in two parts of approximately equal length, connected by a ballet that is an integral part of the work. The plot, a pastoral scene, was just a thin disguise for presenting a series of picturesque effects.

Comparing the three diagrams showing the so-called *liason des scènes* of the works under discussion (see tables 12.3, 12.4, and 12.5),[33] one immediately notes another salient feature of *Ascanio in Alba* that is totally absent in *Mitridate* and present to a much more limited degree in *Lucio Silla*. The *festa teatrale* is replete with choral movements: seven different ones, some repeated several times, and a good number danced as well as sung. The arias, by contrast, are rather short in comparison with those usual in the *opera seria*, and especially in Mozart's *opere serie*. In *Ascanio in Alba* the kaleidoscopic effect of alternating solo and choral movements is enhanced musically by Mozart's varied orchestrations, and visually not only by the dancers but by stage machines and other scenic illusions long since discarded in heroic opera. For the moment let us defer discussion of the orchestrations, since this factor may profitably be taken up in comparing the music of the three works.

The diagrams also reveal another peculiarity of the *festa teatrale*. In an eighteenth-century *opera seria*, after singing an aria or participating in a solo ensemble, the principal singers always left the stage. Indeed, a major task of the librettist was to construct the scenes and the links (*liaisons*) between them so as to permit these exits in the most logical manner possible. The only exception to what was truly a rule of practice was the short *aria cavata* or *cavatina* of just one verse. This was used to introduce a character, and otherwise was reserved for particular effects in the popular *ombra* scenes. Now, in *Ascanio in Alba* we observe that very often even the principal singers remain on stage after their solo numbers. What is more, they may even do so in complete silence, not participating at all in the ensuing recitative (as indicated in table 12.2 with parentheses).

By comparison, the *liason des scènes* in *Mitridate* and *Lucio Silla* are managed following the usual custom of exit arias. The diagrams show in a clear way how the construction of scenes within each stage setting is highly regular in *Mitridate*, whereas the libretto of *Lucio Silla* has a more disparate construction, and not only in this respect. In *Mitridate* the overall proportions between acts is a normal one, if somewhat old-fashioned in the length of the third act. But in *Lucio Silla* act 2 is far longer than act 1, and it was even more so in the printed libretto, which has another aria for Silla that Mozart omitted. It is not surprising, therefore, that when the same libretto was used later in other settings (by Anfossi, J. C. Bach, and Mortellari) the second act was always cut down. Naturally, these various structural factors are attributable to the librettists and not the composers.

Mozart's *Mitridate* was based on a libretto written three years earlier by the Turinese poet Vittorio Amadeo Cigna-Santi. In its first setting, by Quirino Gasparini, the maestro di cappella of the cathedral of Turin, it had been performed in 1767 at Turin's Teatro Regio. For Milan Cigna-Santi's libretto was partially altered, perhaps by Parini. Following Metastasian models, it was a competent piece of work but in no way out of the ordinary. That the author of *Lucio Silla*, Giovanni De Gamerra, had very different aesthetic ideals is already evident in his libretto for Mozart, which was among his first.[34] De Gamerra is known to students of Italian literature as the author of some of the earliest Italian *drammi lagrimosi*, following French models (*pièces larmoyantes*). His poetry showed certain pre-Romantic inclinations, especially a preoccupation with death and the lugubrious. Concerning the musical theater, De Gamerra espoused ideas more in tune with those of the Viennese "reform" poets and French opera. He advocated a return in Italy to the use of spectacle in the form of choruses, integrated ballets and stage effects:

> Operas can no longer be called shows, because as they are despoiled of stage machines, ballets, and choruses, they have nothing by way of embellishment save harmonious orchestral numbers and voices supported by instruments.... Aerial entrances, flying chariots, scene transformations, and

---

[33] The indications of scenes in the diagrams (in arabic numerals) follow those of the librettos, as does my usage of the term here. In Italian opera through the latter part of the nineteenth century, the end of one scene and beginning of the next denoted the entrance or exit of a character and had nothing to do with a change of setting (called *mutazione di scena*).

[34] Among the most recent studies of De Gamerra, with many biographical details, is Rosy Candiani's chapter "Giovanni de Gamerra e il libretto di *Lucio Silla*" in her *Libretti e librettisti italiani per Mozart* (Rome: Archivio Guido Izzi, 1994), 13-45.

Table 12.3
Liaison des scènes in Mozart's *Mitridate*

MITRIDATE
Liaison des scènes

I,1		AS	SI			AR>	
I,2		**AS**	SI				
I,3			**SI**°				
---	---	---	---	---	---	---	---
I,4		AS		FA			
I,5		AS	SI	FA			
I,6		AS	SI	FA		**AR**	
I,7		**AS**	SI	FA			
I,8			SI	FA			
I,9				**FA**			MA>
			Marcia				
I,10				<u>MI</u>	IS	AR	
I,11		SI>		MI	FA>	**IS**	AR
I,12				MI		AR>	
I,13				**MI**°			
===
II,1					FA	IS	
II,2				MI		IS>	
II,3		AS		MI			
II,4		AS	SI	**MI**			
II,5		AS	SI				
II,6		AS	SI			AR>	
II,7		AS	**SI**°				
II,8		**AS**°					
---	---	---	---	---	---	---	---
II,9				MI	IS	AR	
II,10			SI	MI	FA	IS	AR
II,11			SI	MI	FA	IS	AR	MA>
II,12			SI	MI	FA	**IS**	AR
II,13			SI	MI	**FA**		AR>
II,14		AS	SI	**MI**			
II,15		**AS**°	**SI**°				
===
III,1		AS		MI		IS	
III,2		AS		MI			
III,3		AS		**MI**		AR>	
III,4		<u>AS</u>°					
III,5		AS>	SI				
III,6			SI				
---	---	---	---	---	---	---	---
III,7					FA		
III,8					FA		**MA**
III,9					**FA**°		
---	---	---	---	---	---	---	---
III,10			SI	MI		AR	
III,11		AS	SI	MI		AR	
III,12		**AS**	**SI**	**MI**>	**FA**	**IS**	**AR**

ABBREVIATIONS
AS = Aspasia (Prima donna)   IS = Ismene (Seconda donna)   **bold** = aria or ensemble
SI = Sifare (Primo uomo)   AR = Arbate (Terzo uomo)   ° = accompanied recitative
MI = Mitridate (Primo tenore) MA = Marzio (Ultima parte)   = = (aria) cavata
FA = Farnace (Secondo uomo)   \> = exit without aria
                                                               --- = change of setting

Table 12.4
Liaison des scènes in Mozart's *Ascanio in Alba*

			ASCANIO IN ALBA *Liaison des scènes*			
I,1	Coro: **SATB**					
			AS			VE
	Coro: **SATB/R**		AS			**VE**
I,2			**AS***			
I,3	Coro: **TB**					
	Coro: **TB/R**		AS	FA		
			AS	**FA**		
			AS	FA		
I,4	Coro: **SSATB**					
	Coro: **TB/R**	(SI)	[AS]	AC	[FA]	
	Coro: **TB/R**	(SI)		AC		
		(SI)		**AC**		
		SI		AC		
		SI		AC		
	Coro: **TB/R**	(SI)		AC		
I,5			AS			VE
	Coro: **SATB/R**		AS			VE

Ballo

- -

II,1	Coro: **SS**	**SI**				
II,2		SI*	AS*			
II,3		SI	AS	FA		
II,4		SI	**AS**			
		SI*				
	Coro: **SSA**	(SI)	AS			
II,5			**AS**			
II,6	Coro: **TB/R**	(SI)	(AS)	(AC)	(FA)	
		(SI)		AC		
	Coro: **SATB**	SI		AC		
	Coro: **SATB**	SI	AS	(AC)		
	Coro: **SATB/R**	(SI)	(AS)	AC		
		SI	AS	AC		VE
		SI	AS	AC		VE
	Coro: **SATB**	SI	AS	(AC)		VE

===

ABBREVIATIONS

SI = Silvia (Prima donna)
AS = Ascanio (Primo uomo)
AC = Aceste (Tenore)
FA = Fauno (Secondo uomo)
VE = Venere (Seconda donna)
S = sopranos
A = altos
T = tenors
B = basses

bold = aria or ensemble
* = accompanied recitative
═══ = cavatina
R = ripresa
_ _ _ = change of setting

Table 12.5
Liaison des scènes in Mozart's *Lucio Silla*

LUCIO SILLA
Liaison des scènes

Scene	Coro	GI	CC	SI	CN	CL	AU
I,1			CC		**CN**		
I,2			**CC***				
I,3				SI		**CL**	AU
I,4				SI			AU>
I,5		**GI**		SI			
I,6				**SI***			

[Instrumental Transition]

- - -

Scene	Coro	GI	CC	SI	CN	CL	AU
I,7			**CC***				
I,8	Coro: **SATB**	**GI**					
		GI					
I,9		**GI***	**CC***				

═══

Scene	Coro	GI	CC	SI	CN	CL	AU
II,1				SI			AU
II,2				SI>		CL>	
II,3			**CC***		CN		
II,4					CN	<u>CL</u>	
II,5		**GI***			CN		
II,6					**CN***		

- - -

Scene	Coro	GI	CC	SI	CN	CL	AU
II,7				SI			AU>
II,8		**GI**		SI			
II,9		**GI**	**CC***				
II,10		**GI**				CL	
II,11		**GI***					

- - -

Scene	Coro	GI	CC	SI	CN	CL	AU
II,12	Coro: **SATB**	**GI**		SI			AU
II,13		**GI**	CC	SI			AU
II,14		**GI**	**CC**	SI	CN>		AU>

═══

Scene	Coro	GI	CC	SI	CN	CL	AU
III,1			CC		CN	<u>CL</u>	
III,2			CC		**CN**		
III,3		GI	CC				
III,4		GI	CC				AU>
III,5		**GI***					

- - -

Scene	Coro	GI	CC	SI	CN	CL	AU
III,6				SI	CN	CL	
III,7		GI		SI	CN	CL	
III,8	Coro: **SATB**	**GI**	**CC**	**SI**	**CN**	**CL**	**AU**

═══

ABBREVIATIONS

- GI = Giunia (Prima donna)
- CC = Cecilio (Primo uomo)
- SI = Lucio Silla (Primo tenore)
- CN = Lucio Cinna (Secondo uomo)
- CL = Celia (Seconda donna)
- AU = Aufidio (Ultima parte = tenore)
- S = sopranos
- A = altros
- T = tenors
- B = basses

- **bold** = aria or ensemble
- * = accompanied recitative
- <u>=</u> = (aria) cavata
- \> = exit without aria
- - - - = change of setting

other things of this type are unsuited to spoken tragedy, but not to opera, because the nature of the *dramma* [*per musica*] is to maintain our minds, our eyes, and our ears in an equal state of enchantment.[35]

In his librettos he tried to get away from certain formal aspects of the Metastasian dramas. Clearly, Mozart was taken by some of the effects De Gamerra sought in his *Lucio Silla*, and they account for some of the most compelling moments in his score. The most obvious and the most forward-looking section is the great scene complex at the end of act 1, which even in schematic form (table 12.5) is set apart graphically from the rest.

The same diagram of *Lucio Silla* also indicates the unusually high number of orchestrally accompanied recitatives in Mozart's setting. In fact, the young composer showed himself to be surprisingly confident in constructing the *recitativi obbligati*, whereas those with continuo accompaniment often betray his inexperience. The lengthy simple recitatives in *Lucio Silla* lack the long-range tonal organization that gives those of the era's most distinguished composers such as Paisiello their direction and sense of inevitability.[36] In the accompanied recitatives of *Lucio Silla*, on the other hand, the problems associated with the freer style of the *semplici* were mitigated through the use of orchestral passages well defined in terms of thematic content and regular harmonic and rhythm patterns.

All three of Mozart's stage works for Milan underscore the cast hierarchy established in the librettos through musical means, both traditional and more innovative. One of the most obvious is to have the recitatives of the principal characters accompanied by the orchestra. In *Lucio Silla* Mozart uses this device far more than any other composer performed at Milan in the 1770s, indeed, more than perhaps any Italian of the time but Jommelli. We should recall that Wolfgang met Jommelli several times and heard two performances of his *Armida abbandonata* at Naples in 1771. While the young Mozart may have been impressed, the San Carlo audiences clearly were not. Jommelli's opera was almost a complete failure. I believe that in Mozart's case, too, an explanation for the lack of further commissions for Milan or any other Italian city has partly to do with his transgressing acceptable limits, as then understood, in his last Milanese opera. Neither *Mitridate* nor, of course, *Ascanio in Alba* had had similar consequences.

Mozart's arias set apart the characters to whom they are assigned through well-established conventions concerning tempo, meter, and tonality. Thus, only the principal roles have arias in slow tempos, in the *alla breve* meter and in minor keys or keys with many accidentals. But beyond these traditional means Mozart also uses formal schemes and orchestration to underline still further the characters' hierarchical position as well as certain traits associated with the dramatic action. For example, the more adventurous through-composed arias are reserved chiefly for the most important figure, namely the *prima donna*. Sonata-like formal designs belong to the principal roles, while the lengthy more old-fashioned full or slightly shortened da capo arias go most often to the subordinates.

A special scene, not peculiar just to Mozart's two *opere serie* but by then a regular feature of many *drammi per musica*, was reserved for the *prima donna* in the third act. This was the *ombra* scene, so called because the leading lady imagines or fears the shade or *ombra* of her beloved. It began and usually ended with orchestrally accompanied recitative and included at least one cavatina. The text, filled with more or less explicit allusions to death and the macabre, called forth innovative orchestrations, wailing oboes and flutes, pizzicato and muted strings, divided violas, and so forth. In *Lucio Silla* Mozart capitalized on the lugubrious tone of De Gamerra's libretto and the superb orchestra at his disposal for striking effects of this type, not only in the tomb scene of act 1, but particularly in Giunia's act 3 *ombra* scene, "Sposo, mia vita"/"Fra i pensieri più funesti di morte" (no. 22).

At the Regio Ducal Teatro Mozart found one of the largest and best orchestras in Italy. In a letter of 15 December 1770 Leopold described its constitution, which is included in table 12.6, comparing Italian opera orchestras from 1737 to 1845. A characteristic, common in Italy but apparently not found elsewhere, is the disposition of the lower

---

[35] "I drammi più chiamar non si possono spettacoli, da che spogliati delle macchine, dei balli, e dei cori non hanno per abbellimento, se non che i concerti armoniosi, e le voci sostenute dagl'istrumenti.... I voli, i carri volanti, le trasformazioni, e cose simili disconvengono alla tragedia, ma non all'opera, poiché la proprietà del dramma [per musica] si è di tener gli spiriti, gli occhi, e le orecchie in un eguale incanto." From De Gamerra's "Osservazioni sull'opera in musica," published at the end of his libretto *L'Armida* (Milan, 4 April 1771), 46-47; a copy is preserved at the Library of Congress, Washington, D.C.

[36] I discuss at length and compare the tonal organization of simple recitatives by Mozart, Paisiello, and Guglielmi in my "Opera and Ballet," 411-27.

Table 12.6
Disposition of Opera Orchestras at Turin, Milan, Rome, and Naples, 1737–1845

Parts	Naples 1737	Turin 1742	Milan 1747	Turin 1755	Rome 1758	Milan 1770	Turin 1771	Naples* 1771	Turin 1773	Milan 1778	Naples 1780	Turin 1780	Turin‡ 1790	Turin 1790	Naples 1796	Milan 1814	Naples 1818	Turin 1821	Turin 1845
Violini	24	17	22	21	14	28	27	36	28	30	32	26	36	23	25	25	24	21	21
Viole	6	4	6	5	4	6	4	?	5	8	4	4	6	6	4	6	6	4	4
Violoncelli	3	2	2	2	2	2	2	2	2		3	3	2	5	2	4	6	4	4
Contrabassi	3	2	5	2	4	6	6	5			5	6	2	7	6	8	7	6	6
Bassi (di ripieno)	—	5	—	6	—	—	2	—	8	13	—	—	9	—	—	—	—	—	—
Cembali	2	2	2	2	2	2	2	2	2	2	2	2	2	2	2	1	?	1	—
Flauti	—	—	—	—	—	2	—		—	2	—	—	—	—	—	2	2	2	3
Oboi	2	3	2	3	2	2	4		4	4	4	4	4	5	2	2	2	2	2
Clarinetti	—	—	—	—	—	—	—		2	2	2	2	2	2	2	2	2	2	2
Fagotti	3	2	2	2	—	2	2		4	2	2	3	3	3	4	2	2	2	2
Corni da caccia	—	2	—	—	4	4	4		4	4	—	4	4	4	4	4	4	4	4
Trombe (da caccia)	—	—	5	4	—	2	2		2	4	4	2	2	2	—	2	2	2	2
Tromboni	—	—	—	—	—	—	—		—	—	—	1	1	—	—	1	3	2	3
Timpani	—	[1]	1	[1]	—	[1]	1		1	1	1	1	1	1	[1]	1	1	1	1
Others	—	—	—	—	—	—	—		—	—	—	—	—	—	—	—	—	—	—
TOTAL	45	40	47	48	32	57	56	?	62	72	59	57	73	60	52	60	61?	56	57

* Based on Burney's report from Naples, which is incomplete.

† Based on the letter of Pietro Verri describing the inauguration of La Scala, when an unusually large orchestra was used. He lumps together all the lower strings as "Bassi."

‡ Based on the table given in Francesco Galeazzi's *Elementi teorico-practici di musica* (1797) showing the disposition of the orchestra pit of the Teatro Regio. The numbers were inflated by Galeazzi, as archival documents for the Turin carnival of 1789/90 (represented in the following column) show.

Fig. 12.4. A detail from the painting by Pietro Domenico Olivero of a performance at Turin's Teatro Regio in 1740, showing the principal cello and double bass players flanking the first harpsichord, reading from the score on the keyboard rack. The first bassoon and some of the "bassi di ripieno" are to their right

strings. For generations these included but two cellos against five or six instruments called either "bassi" or "contrabassi." The two cellos together with two large double basses accompanied all the recitatives, their players flanking the two harpsichordists and reading from the full score on the keyboard rack rather than from separate parts, a practice illustrated in fig. 12.4 (a detail from the well-known painting by Pietro Domenico Olivero showing a performance at Turin's Teatro Regio in 1740). The other string basses, which played during the overture and in all the solo and ensemble pieces, were of varying sizes, and certainly not all were what we would today term double basses. The bass line was further reinforced by two bassoons, which doubled the string parts whenever other winds were playing (as in the illustration), even though not notated in the scores. Similarly, two oboes frequently doubled the violins *ad libitum* and, as Leopold noted, the flutes always played along with the oboes when they had no separate parts.[37]

---

[37] "2 Flautotraversi, welche, wo keine flauti dabey sind, allzeit mit 4 Hautb: mit spielen." *Mozart: Briefe und Aufzeichnungen*, 1:408.

More than those of any of his Italian contemporaries, Mozart's scores for Milan consistently contain fuller and more continually varied orchestrations. Of course, the traditional ensemble of two oboes, two horns, and strings, as well as purely string accompaniments, are found too. But in many numbers, and particularly the arias for the principal singers, he employs different combinations of woodwinds, for instance giving the bassoons important independent parts. He much favored full brass choirs, and thus numerous pieces call for four horns or two horns and two trumpets—upon occasion there are altogether six brasses. But Mozart also treated the strings with care, frequently writing in four real parts, a practice which was still uncommon among most Italian composers. Divided violas appear as well with some regularity. A truly unusual ensemble is the one accompanying the shepherd's chorus in *Ascanio in Alba*: two flutes, two oboes, two bassoons, divided cellos and bass—no violins or violas. One of Ascanio's arias specifies two *serpenti* (or *serpentini*), the Milanese dialect term for English horns.[38] If not unknown to Gluck, for instance, these instruments were certainly a rarity south of the Alps.

Mozart's theatrical works for Milan, written when he was between the ages of fourteen and seventeen, veritably exploded with what was then called "music"—as opposed to simple recitative—and this was nowhere more true than in *Lucio Silla*. In addition to all the aspects already mentioned there was the simple fact of the proportions of its musical numbers. In this opera Mozart's arias are at least 50 percent longer than those of any comparable work of the time. In some cases the first section alone, in full sonata form, is the dimension of an entire aria by another of his colleagues.[39] Add this circumstance to the comparatively plentiful accompanied recitatives, the three substantial choral movements, and the orchestrations elaborate by standards of the time and place, and one can begin to understand why Mozart did not ever again have a chance to repeat the experience.

In 1771, the young Archduke Ferdinand had wished to take Wolfgang into his service in Milan, but his mother the Empress successfully discouraged the suggestion. Two years later, at the time of *Lucio Silla*, Leopold tried various stratagems to secure a post for his son in Florence at the court of another Austrian archduke, Leopold, but to no avail. The Mozarts left Italy for good in March of 1773. For the remainder of his life Wolfgang dreamed and schemed to write Italian opera, if not opera for Italy. But Italy was a very long time in repaying this loyalty. Not until our own century have his works gradually been fully accepted there. And the last of all to gain a firm place in Italian repertories have been just Mozart's Italian operas.

---

[38] See Luigi Ferdinando Tagliavini's introduction to the critical edition of *Ascanio in Alba* in *Neue Ausgabe sämtlicher Werke*, series 2, Werkgruppe 5, vol. 5 (1956), xiii.

[39] For more detail on the lengths and internal characteristics of arias from operas performed at Milan in the 1770s, see my "Opera and Ballet," 448-500.

13

Violence, Pathos, and Comedy in Salieri's *La finta scema*

JOHN A. RICE

September 1775 was not an auspicious time to present a new opera buffa in Vienna. Impresarios had run the two court theaters, the Burgtheater and the Kärntnertortheater, since 1766; but now Emperor Joseph II, eager to manage the Burgtheater himself, looked for an excuse to invalidate the contract by which the last of the impresarios was operating. "La troupe de l'opera buffa est détestable," he wrote to his brother Pietro Leopoldo on 20 August 1775.[1] On the same day he issued an ultimatum to Count Johann Keglevich, the impresario, threatening to take over the theaters if he did not "immediately make arrangements to put the opera buffa, the ballets, and also the German troupe on a more advantageous footing."[2]

Three weeks later, on September 9, Antonio Salieri, Keglevich's resident music-director since 1774, presented *La finta scema* in the Burgtheater. From box-office receipts that survive among Keglevich's papers in the Hungarian National Archive in Budapest (see fig. 13.1), we know that the premiere was followed by a ballet vaguely entitled "Divertimenti campestri." Salieri wrote his opera for the company that Joseph had dismissed as "détestable"; the emperor was not alone in his dissatisfaction with Keglevich's singers. Prince Johann Khevenhüller, who attended the troupe's debut at the beginning of the theatrical year 1775, had praise for only one newcomer:

> This evening one of the new opere buffe, *La frascatana*, was finally performed. Several new singers appeared: Caterina Consiglio, known as La Ciecatella [the little blind girl] because she squints very noticeably; Signor Marchetti, one of the best buffi I have ever heard; Signora Anna Paganelli Bernucci and Signora Anna Santori [Marianna Santoro], both of whom look better than they sing, and Signor Novi Seni [probably Giovanni Battista Seni], a weak tenor. The music by Signor Giovanni Paisiello, a Neapolitan, was nevertheless applauded with uncommon enthusiasm.[3]

Only one of these singers, the comic bass Baldassare Marchetti, had enjoyed a substantial career in Italy before coming to Vienna, singing important buffo roles in northern Italy since the 1760s. In 1774 alone he created roles in three operas that went on to win applause all over Europe for several years: Anfossi's *La finta giardiniera* (Rome, Carnival 1774), Paisiello's *La frascatana* (Venice, fall 1774), and Anfossi's *Il geloso in cimento* (also Venice, fall 1774). In Vienna he sang in all these operas, which dominated the repertory during 1775. His career culminated in a long engagement in St. Petersburg (1779-85), where he created the role of Basilio in Paisiello's *Il barbiere di Siviglia* (1782).

---

[1] Vienna, Haus-, Hof- und Staatsarchiv, Sammelbände, Karton 7.

[2] Quoted in Franz Hadamowsky, *Die Josefinische Theaterreform und das Spieljahr 1776/77 des Burgtheaters* (Vienna: Verband der Wissenschaftlichen Gesellschaften Österreichs, 1978), 3; English translation in John A. Rice, *Antonio Salieri and Viennese Opera* (Chicago: University of Chicago Press, 1998), 240.

[3] Johann Joseph Khevenhüller, *Aus der Zeit Maria Theresias: Tagebuch des Fürsten Johann Josef Khevenhüller-Metsch, Kaiserlichen Oberhofmeisters, 1742-1776* (Vienna: Holzhausen, 1907-72), 8:75 (29 April 1775).

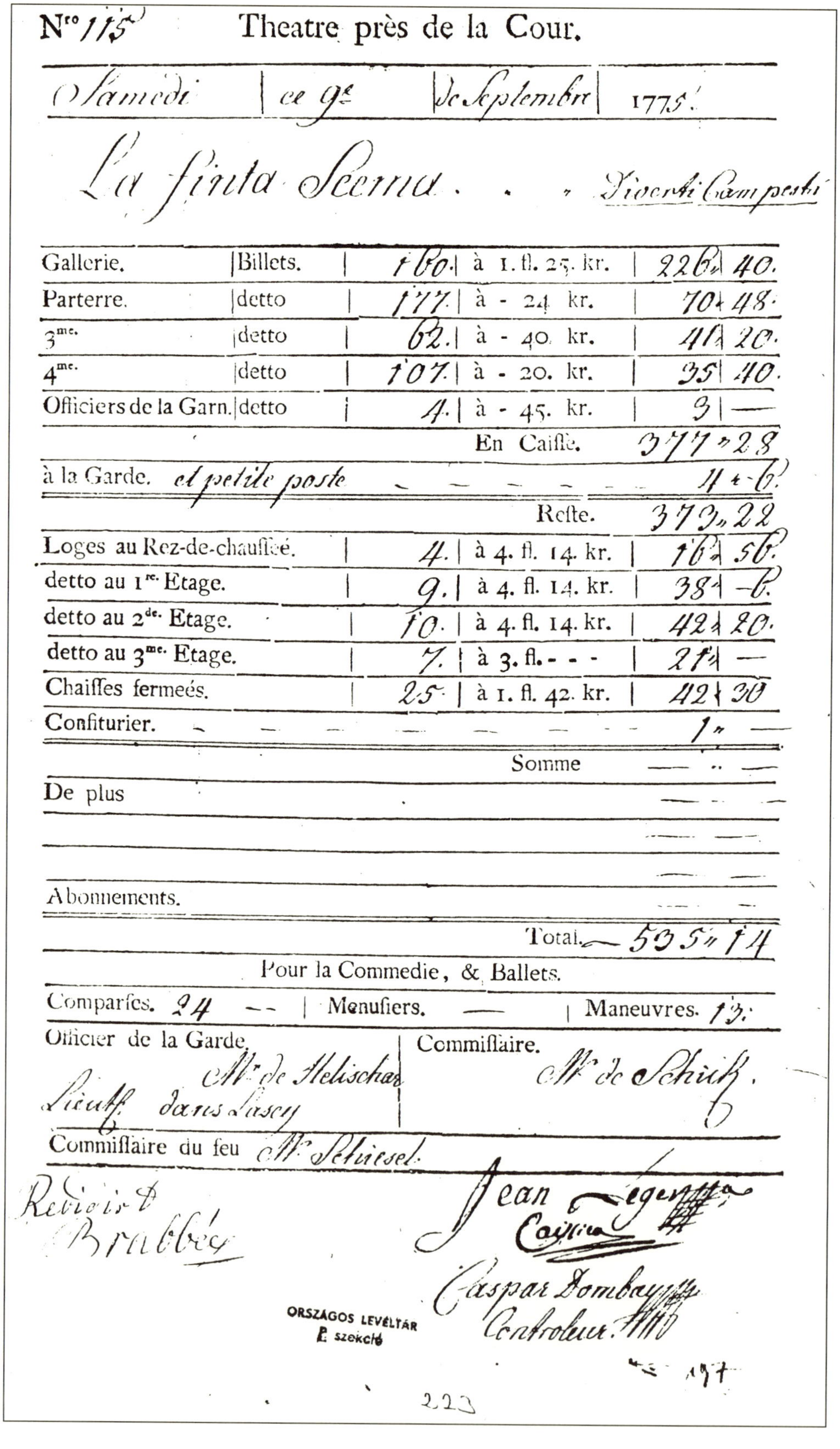

N^ro 115 Theatre près de la Cour.

Samedi	ce 9e	de Septembre	1775.

La finta Scema . . . Diverti Campestri

Gallerie.	Billets.	160.	à 1. fl. 25. kr.	226	40.
Parterre.	detto	177.	à - 24 kr.	70	48.
3me.	detto	62.	à - 40. kr.	41	20.
4me.	detto	107.	à - 20. kr.	35	40.
Officiers de la Garn.	detto	4.	à - 45. kr.	3	—
			En Caisse.	377	28
à la Garde. et petite poste				4	6
			Reste.	373	22
Loges au Rez-de-chaussée.		4.	à 4. fl. 14. kr.	16	56
detto au 1re Etage.		9.	à 4. fl. 14. kr.	38	6
detto au 2de Etage.		10.	à 4. fl. 14. kr.	42	20.
detto au 3me Etage.		7.	à 3. fl. - - -	21	—
Chaisses fermeés.		25.	à 1. fl. 42. kr.	42	30
Confiturier.				1	—
			Somme	—	—
De plus					
Abonnements.					
			Total	535	14

Pour la Commedie, & Ballets.

Comparses. 24 — | Menusiers. — | Maneuvres. 13.

Officier de la Garde Mr. de Helischar Lieutt. dans Lascy | Commissaire. Mr. de Schick.

Commissaire du feu Mr. Schiesel.

Receu Brabbée

Jean Legenti Caissier

Caspar Dombay Controleur.

ORSZÁGOS LEVÉLTÁR

E szekció

197

223

Fig. 13.1. Box office receipts for the premiere of Salieri's *La finta scema*. Budapest, Magyar Országos Levéltár (Hungarian National Archive), Keglevich Cs., V/18, f. 197

Paisiello's music and Marchetti's portrayal of Fabrizio in *La frascatana* made that opera a success in Vienna despite the mediocrity of the rest of the cast, but Salieri's *La finta scema*, performed four months later by a very similar cast, was not so fortunate. Keglevich had engaged a new theatrical poet at the beginning of 1775. Giovanni De Gamerra, like his predecessors Marco Coltellini and Giovanni Boccherini, had little experience with comic opera when he began to work in the court theaters. But that did not keep him from collaborating with Salieri, who throughout his career rarely let a librettist's lack of experience disqualify him as a potential collaborator.

De Gamerra, fond of theatrical polemics and eager to earn a name for himself as an operatic reformer in the manner of Calzabigi, prefaced several of his librettos with statements of artistic principle that reveal extraordinary verbosity and, at the same time, real flair for theatrical innovation. These two sides of his artistic personality are also evident in the librettos themselves. In the preface to *La finta scema* (reproduced in full as appendix 1) he sought to disarm potential critics by admitting the weaknesses of his first Viennese libretto, which he described as

> no less defective than the other *Buffe Rapsodie* that flood the theaters of Europe, dishonoring the stages, disgusting the senses, degrading the authors, and trampling both truth and nature.

At the same time he set himself up as a reformer of comic opera, promising

> to present to the public at another time a dramatic genre that is more rational, more interesting, and more useful; in which the situations and the naturalistic depiction of customs and of eccentric characters must enliven the action, without which there can be no interest, no life.
>
> The author does not intend as his only goal that thoughtless laughter that signifies only the wild fancy of a soul thrust outside the limits of reason, and after which the human heart is no less empty than before; rather he will seek to arouse that delightful interest, that fine, delicate, and yet penetrating smile that is born of the language of nature, and that is worth much more than the immoderate laughter that does not speak to the soul and that, being a product of ignorance, ought to be left to today's comic productions. If mixed sensations are the sweetest, the new genre that the author proposes should be one of the most delightful to those who love and cultivate the fine arts, who enjoy real beauty, and who pronounce their own judgments on the basis of solid principles, strength of conviction, and good sense.

Although De Gamerra did not claim *La finta scema* as an example of his projected reform, and the title refers openly to Goldoni's *La finta semplice*, this work departs significantly from Goldonian norms. It presents an unusually large cast, requiring ten singers. (Goldoni's operas rarely have more than seven.) Contrary to Goldoni's normal practice, De Gamerra inserted in his libretto many detailed instructions for singers' gestures and movements, either recording his activities as stage director or claiming for himself decisions that the Venetian librettist might have left to singers.

In his spoken dramas De Gamerra helped introduce the *comédie larmoyante*, the sentimental or pathetic comedy, to Italy. In *La finta scema* he experimented with the idea of opera buffa as *comédie larmoyante*. He was not alone. Several of the most successful operas of the mid-1770s followed Goldoni's *La buona figliuola* in placing their virtuous heroine in a situation in which the audience is asked to pity her, but they intensified her plight, making it much more dangerous and lugubrious than anything experienced by Cecchina. In Paisiello's *La frascatana* Violante is locked in a tower; and in Anfossi's *La vera costanza* (Rome, 1776) the mentally unstable Errico, who has secretly married Rosina, actually instructs another character to murder her. De Gamerra contributed to the increasing level of violence and pathos in opera buffa. In *La finta scema* he emphasized the danger of the situation in which the heroine finds herself almost to the point of tragedy, even bringing her close to being killed by another character.

Don Pisone, a country gentleman (bass, the role created by Baldassare Marchetti[4]), wants to marry the beautiful young Rosina (high soprano, Caterina Consiglio). She loves Ernesto (tenor, Luigi Righetti), one of Pisone's employees, and Ernesto loves her. To defend herself against Pisone's advances Rosina, like the Rosina in *La finta semplice*, pretends to be a simpleton. Pisone at first seems to be a straightforward *parte buffa*. Near the beginning of the opera he

---

[4] The original cast of *La finta scema* is listed in a copy of the score in Vienna, Österreichische Nationalbibliothek, Mus. Hs. 17842.

sings a big comic aria, "Questa gamba è all'Ercolina," in which he boasts of his strength and pleasing appearance. Writing for a comic bass Salieri—as his contemporaries in Vienna and Italy did so often—combined duple meter and a disjunct, march-like melody. Like countless comic arias for bass in D major, this one begins with a tune that exploits the octave between *D* and *d´*. The melody cleverly incorporates a bit of recitative, the effect of which is enhanced by the suddenly compressed declamation of text from the normal rate of two measures per line to one measure per line (ex. 13.1).

Example 13.1. Salieri, *La finta scema*, act 1, "Questa gamba è all'Ercolina," meas. 2-10. Source: Vienna, Österreichische Nationalbibliothek, Mus. Hs. 16608.

This leg is like that of Hercules, these shoulders are those of Atlas, this is a giant's body.... Pay attention to me, don't look that way.... This is a giant's body.

The autograph score of *La finta scema* is one of several in which Salieri, probably late in life, commented on each of the opera's numbers. His annotations (transcribed in appendix 2) tell us something of Pisone and the singer who created this role:

> The aria "Questa gamba è all'Ercolina" seems to me well made; the actor, of truly gigantic size, acted very well; but his naturally hoarse voice took away much of its musical effect, and it remained cold.

The aria's phrase "Questo corpo è da gigante" suggests (in light of Salieri's comment) that De Gamerra wrote the text with Marchetti in mind.

Marchese Argante (bass, Gabriele Messieri), an impoverished nobleman, arrives at Pisone's castle with his son Tiburzio (tenor, Giovanni Battista Seni) and his daughter Vanesia (high soprano, Caterina Cavalieri). Argante, another *parte buffa*, loves food; he introduces himself in an aria, "Quando ascolto il dolce moto," in which he describes the activities of a cook. Catalogue arias of the kind so brilliantly exemplified by Mozart's "Madamina, il catalogo è questo" are common in Goldonian opera buffa,[5] but De Gamerra took this type of aria in a new direction by bringing it into the kitchen.

The aria begins with an orchestral imitation of a noisy rotisserie. Salieri has the first violins repeat the pitch *f´*, tremolo, for seventeen measures, "sempre mezzo forte." In his autograph score he wrote: "The first violins must play this entire tremolo *in applicatura* [by which he may have meant "deliberately," or "firmly," or "with rhythmic precision"], making sure to produce a rough sound."[6] Salieri's setting of De Gamerra's culinary catalogue is comically

---

[5] On catalogue arias, see Daniela Goldin, *La vera fenice: librettisti e libretti tra Sette e Ottocento* (Turin: Einaudi, 1985), 23-25, 149-63; Stefan Kunze, "Elementi veneziani nella librettistica di Lorenzo da Ponte," in Maria Teresa Muraro, ed., *Venezia e il melodramma nel Settecento*, 2 vols. (Florence: Olschki, 1978-81), II, 279-92 (286-87); and John Platoff, "Catalogue Arias and the 'Catalogue Aria'," in Stanley Sadie, ed., *Wolfgang Amadeus Mozart: Essays on His Life and Music* (Oxford: Oxford University Press, 1996), 296-311.

[6] "Il primi violini devono suonare tutto questo tremolo in applicatura, procurando di cavarne una voce cruda"; quoted in Vittorio Della Croce and Francesco Blanchetti, *Il caso Salieri* (Turin: Eda, 1994), where it is suggested that the term "in applicatura" may have something to do with the German musical term *applikatur* ("fingering").

repetitious. But the aria is most drole when Argante's mouth begins to water. After a long series of two-measure phrases a sudden extension of phrase-length to three measures (beginning "Ah . . .") conveys Argante's ecstasy; descending scales befittingly depict the working of his salivary glands. In the following phrase Salieri's alternation between B♭ and B♮ and his repetition of C up and down an octave suggest something of the sensual pleasure with which Argante savors food, even in his imagination (ex. 13.2).

Example 13.2. Salieri, *La finta scema*, act 1, "Quando ascolto il dolce moto," meas. 25-49.

Now he pounds the porkchops, now he cleans the chickens, now he minces the herbs, now he quickly grates the cheese; now he slices the salami, now the bread, now he tastes, now he salts, now he touches . . . Ah, my mouth is beginning to water! What an agreeable spectacle!

Later in the opera Argante states his philosophy of life in "Gran teatro è questo mondo," an operatic version of "All the world's a stage." Argante takes food seriously, but the rest of life is a theatrical spectacle that he observes from afar and finds amusing; he describes this spectacle in a long catalogue of people and their activities. At the end of the aria-text De Gamerra wrote "Parte sempre mangiando" (exit eating). Argante's children did not inherit their father's Epicurean emotional detachment. Vanesia expresses sadness that she will be unable to find a husband because of her father's poverty; Tiburzio, meanwhile, is attracted to Rosina. In a duet, brother and sister tease each other about their amorous interests.

A strange new character appears, accompanied, according to the libretto, by the sound of "una nonagenaria caratteristica sinfonia" (an instrumental piece characteristic of or depicting a ninety-year-old). Salieri responded to De Gamerra's instructions with a march in D minor whose long descending sequence, with imitation between treble and bass, he intended to sound old-fashioned (ex. 13.3). Donna Ortensia (created by the distinguished comic bass Andrea Morigi) is the wife of Colonello Tremò, who is believed to have died in battle.

Ortensia used to be an operatic soprano until an illness changed her voice to that of a bass. But she can still sing some soprano and tenor as well as bass, as she demonstrates in a long comic scene, "Questa è un'aria d'Egiziello,"

Example 13.3. Salieri, *La finta scema*, act 1, "nonagenaria caratteristica sinfonia" accompanying Ortensia's entrance, meas. 1-16.

that incorporates parodies of opera seria arias for soprano, tenor, and bass, and compares her singing favorably with that of two famous seria singers, the male soprano Gioacchino Conti (known as Egiziello) and the tenor Anton Raaff. Part of the comedy of this scene comes from the actions of the other characters on stage, whose exits De Gamerra carefully timed:

> Questa è un'aria d'Egiziello;
> Il motivo è nuovo e bello,
> Par che fatta sia per me.
>   Cara, deh prendi in pace
>   L'estremo addio funesto,
>   L'ultimo pegno è questo
>   Del mio costante amor.
> Voi gli acuti ben sentite;
> Che ne dite? Così è.
> M'ascoltate. Oh che stupore!
> Ecco un'aria da tenore,
> Che assai ben mi s'adattò.
>   Pensa che sol per poco
>   Ritengo all'ire il freno,
>   Perché mi parla in seno
>   Un resto di pietà.

        Ah no che Raf nemmeno
           Si ben non cantò.
           Eccovi un'aria in basso;
           Ho l'organo un pò lasso
           Ma pur mi sforzerò.
                  (*Argante guarda l'orologio, e parte.*)
           Nel regno oscuro e muto
                  (*Appena Argante è partito fa lo stesso anche Don isone.*)
           Dell'implacabil Pluto
           Ombra dolente e pallida,
           Discendo ad ulular.
    Signori ditemi . . .
           Come? Scapparono?
           Qui mi lasciarono?
           Che se ne vadano,
           Non monto in collera,
           Il mio gran merito
           Non soffre ingiuria,
           Tutto lo lodano,
           Tutti l'ammirano,
           Sol quello stolide
           Testaccie d'asini
           Mi fanno ridere
           In verità.
           Ah ah ah ah (*Parte.*)

(This is an aria of Egiziello; the theme is new and beautiful: it sounds as if it had been written for me. "My dear, accept in peace my last mournful farewell; this is the last token of my faithful love." Listen to the high notes carefully. What do you say? Yes indeed. What amazement! And here is an aria for tenor that was well suited to my voice. "Consider that I can restrain my anger for only a short time, because a trace of pity speaks to me in my heart." No, not even Raaff sang so well. And here is an aria for bass. My voice is a little tired, but I will force myself to continue. (*Argante looks at his watch and leaves.*) "In the dark and silent (*As soon as Argante leaves Don Pisone does the same.*) reign of implacable Pluto, I descend, a weeping pale ghost, to weep." Tell me, gentleman . . . What? Have they escaped? Have they left me here? Let them go; I will not give way to anger. My great talent will not allow itself to be insulted. Everyone praises me, everyone admires me. Only those fools, those asses' heads, make me laugh. Ha, ha, ha, ha.)

From his use of falsetto in several operas (starting with *L'amore innocente* of 1770) we know that Salieri was fond of this comic technique, one that Haydn also exploited often, but that Mozart, in contrast, consistently avoided.[7] From the quotation and parody of Metastasio's arias in *La secchia rapita* (1772) we know that Salieri, despite his warm relations with the *poeta cesareo*, liked to make fun of Metastasian opera. Ortensia's *scena* requires both falsetto and parody, although the aria texts quoted are apparently not by Metastasio. The singer for whom De Gamerra and Salieri wrote this scene, the bass Morigi, could sing falsetto effectively, to judge from annotations by Salieri:

> The accompanied recitative "Questa è un'aria di Egiziello" and the aria for soprano "Cara deh prendi in pace," later in the tenor range and then in the bass, is *buffissima*; it makes a great effect when the singer has the ability to sing in all three registers, but the ability is not common.

Ortensia's imitation of Egiziello is suitably lyrical, beginning with a *messa di voce* of two measures. Salieri emphasized the comedy of Morigi's falsetto by having him dive to the bottom of his bass register at the word "l'estremo" (ex. 13.4).

---

[7] I am grateful to Caryl Clark (conversation in Vienna, 1994) for telling me of Haydn's fondness for falsetto in comic arias.

Example 13.4. Salieri, *La finta scema*, act 1, "Questa è un'aria d'Egiziello," meas. 5-14.

Thus he makes fun of the a-b-b´ melodic form from which eighteenth-century composers (including Salieri himself) derived so many noble, heroic, and pathetic melodies.[8]

In his aria for bass (ex. 13.5) Salieri parodied the ghost aria, a type of aria common in mid-eighteenth-century opera seria in which a character—usually a woman—imagines the ghost of lover or spouse, and expresses her grief and horror in music that frequently makes use of long notes and wide leaps in the melodic line.[9] Salieri, who had made fun of ghost-aria conventions in his first opera buffa, *Le donne letterate* of 1770, does so again here by having Donna Ortensia sing in her lowest register on the repeated "ululur" (wail).

Act 1, during which Argante frequently expresses his desire to eat, culminates in a finale that begins, luckily for Argante, with a banquet. Several of the finales in Salieri's earlier operas (for example, those in part 2 of *L'amore innocente* and act 1 of *La locandiera* of 1773) end with celebratory vaudevilles, ensembles in which each character sings a short solo before the rest of the cast answers with a refrain. The first finale of *La finta scema* makes dramatic use of the vaudeville convention by shifting the vaudeville forward, leading audiences to think that the finale is a very short one, and interrupting the vaudeville "Viva il bel tempo" with an entirely new plot development. As the characters express the pleasure and satisfaction the banquet has given them, suddenly the castle comes under attack. Confusion replaces celebration. De Gamerra supplied a description of the chaotic action that follows ("Rosina and D. Ortensia faint in convulsions. Vanesia and three servants help Rosina; Nanetta and three other servants help D. Ortensia . . ."), together with a description of the music and the sound effects that accompany it: "a very loud orchestral passage combined with gunshots, explosions and cries."

Near the beginning of act 2 we find what Salieri, in his annotations, called an "arietta francese," a song in French with which De Gamerra and his collaborator maintained the Goldonian (and also specifically Viennese) tradition of French songs within Italian comic operas. Marianna Santoro, who created the pants-role of Giannino, one of the Colonel's children, could pronounce French "marvelously," according to Salieri; it was not by accident that De Gamerra and Salieri assigned to her "En enfant timide."

Act 1, except for the finale's violent conclusion, is almost entirely comic; act 2, on the other hand, has several surprisingly serious scenes. Pisone sentences Rosina to prison. Believing that her beloved Ernesto is dead, she grieves in "Questo fioco urlo dolente," in which she imagines that she hears the cries of her dead lover (ex. 13.6). Unlike the parody of a ghost aria within Ortensia's comic scena in act 1, this is a real ghost aria. De Gamerra and Salieri clearly had no parodistic intent in composing "Questo fioco," which belongs, according to the composer, "in the tragic style." Rosina's words remind one of those that De Gamerra gave Giunia in her ghost scene in *Lucio Silla*. An orchestra that includes muted horns accompanies Rosina's plaintive, noble melody. Her mounting distress is

---

[8] The predominance of a-b-b´ melodies in opera seria of the third quarter of the eighteenth century is documented in Eric Weimer, *Opera Seria and the Evolution of Classical Style, 1755-1772* (Ann Arbor: UMI Research Press, 1984); see especially pp. 18-20.

[9] On ghost arias see Kathleen Hansell, "Opera and Ballet at the Regio Ducal Teatro of Milan, 1771-1776: A Musical and Social History" (Ph.D. diss., University of California, Berkeley, 1980), 289-303.

Example 13.5. Salieri, *La finta scema*, Questa è un'aria d'Egiziello," meas. 97-120.

Example 13.6. Salieri, *La finta scema*, act 2, "Questo fioco urlo dolente," meas. 14-31.

This faint, mournful wailing that comes to me fom far away is the voice of my beloved, who, trembling and covered in blood, speaks to me in a lifeless voice: "My love . . . farewell . . . I die . . . my love . . . I die for you."

signalled by the gradual breaking up of melodic units: from two measures ("Questo fioco urlo dolente") to one measure ("è la voce") to fragments of measures ("Cara. . . addio . . ."). When Rosina quotes the voice of her dead beloved, the sudden shift from major to minor is chilling.

De Gamerra and Salieri may have been inspired to insert such a scene into a comic opera by a similarly pathetic scene in Paisiello's *La frascatana*. Paisiello's heroine Violante was created in Venice and later sung in Vienna by the same Caterina Consiglio who created the title role in *La finta scema*. Violante, imprisoned in a tower, thinks she is seeing ghosts, and expresses her fear in an aria, "Dove son? Che cosa è questa," that resembles in both words and musical style the ghost arias in some contemporary serious operas.[10]

Pisone sings an aria of indecision—a kind of aria, very common in Goldoni's operas, in which a character, usually male, is faced with a dilemma, and often imagines that he hears voices giving him contradictory advice. Normally such arias are comic, but Pisone's indecision in "Entro all'asta in mano" (I enter with sword in hand) is about whether or not to kill Rosina. Pisone evolves before our eyes from a conventional *buffo caricato* to a real villain, something of a rarity in eighteenth-century opera buffa.

The finale of act 2 takes place inside a "dreadful underground prison." The spectacle of a sentimental heroine alone in a "gothic" setting near the end of act 2 was a common feature of comic operas during the 1770s. *La frascatana*, *La vera costanza*, and *La finta giardiniera* (in settings by Anfossi and Mozart) all offer good examples.[11] But a prison scene was unusual enough in Vienna in 1775 that an elaborate new piece of scenery had to be constructed. The scene painter and architect Alessio Cantini was paid fifty gulden, in addition to his regular salary, "for building a prison for the opera of *La finta scema*."[12] By choosing a prison for his "gothic" setting De Gamerra anticipated the many scenes in late eighteenth- and early nineteenth-century operas that take place in dark prisons or in underground chambers.[13]

Salieri took advantage of the dark associations of the key of E♭ (associations that he had already exploited in the first finale of *Il barone di Rocca Antica* of 1772, where the words "Ohimé che tetro orrore! che fiero oscurità!" are accompanied by a sudden modulation to E♭) in choosing it for the finale of act 2. Beginning with a pathetic monologue for the imprisoned Rosina, this long, complex finale reaches its dramatic climax as Pisone, enraged by Rosina's refusal to marry him, and about to stab her, is prevented from doing so by the Colonel's timely arrival. Salieri's early biographer Ignaz von Mosel found this finale particularly fine, perhaps because of its adumbration of the French rescue operas he knew and loved.[14]

In his preface to the libretto De Gamerra praised not only the composer but the singers who had been so harshly criticized by Khevenhüller and Joseph II:

> The author, however, considers himself fortunate to find himself at the side of a skillful and adventurous composer and a select company of experienced actors who, encouraged by their own merit, do not flinch before the painful difficulties that face them on a new, untrodden path.

In spite of De Gamerra's tactful praise, Salieri (in his annotations to the autograph score) blamed several of his principal singers for the opera's less than enthusiastic reception:

> From the duet "Fra il timore e la speranza" [near the beginning of act 2] through almost all the rest of this act, the naturally hoarse voices of the prima donna, the primo amante, and Don Pisone

---

[10] Ibid., 490-91.

[11] Mary Hunter, "Landscapes, Gardens, and Gothic Settings in the *Opere Buffe* of Mozart and His Italian Contemporaries," *Current Musicology* 51 (1993): 94-104. Anfossi's *La finta giardiniera*, like Paisiello's *La frascatana*, was performed very frequently in the Viennese court theaters during the months before *La finta scema* came to the stage.

[12] "Il Sgr. Leger pagherà al Sgr. Cantini cinquanta fiorini convenuti con esso per la fattura d'una prigione nell'opera della *finta scema*. Vienna 30. 7bre 1775. [signed:] Gontier direttore [signed below:] Alessio Cantini Pitore ed architetto teatrale 9 9bre 1775." Budapest, Magyar Országos Levéltár (Hungarian National Archive), Keglevich Cs., V/15, no. 27.

[13] Della Croce and Blanchetti, 437.

[14] Ignaz von Mosel, *Ueber das Leben und die Werke des Anton Salieri* (Vienna: Wallishausser, 1827), 50.

caused the opera to lose most of its musical effect because, being in an almost tragic style here and there, it requires clear, strong voices. The duet therefore remained cold.

Salieri had mixed feelings about Consiglio's performance of her most important aria, "Questo fioco," which he remembered as having been "well acted, but the singer's naturally indistinct voice always resulted in its losing half its effect." And he summed up the reception of the opera as follows:

> From everything that I have said of this opera, one might believe that in spite of some of the voices of the troupe, the opera nevertheless met with great success. Perhaps it would have been so; but the hoarse, indistinct voices were precisely those of the three leading roles; so I have to say that this music was esteemed more than it was applauded.

Salieri and De Gamerra should have shared some of the blame for the "moderate applause" that, according to Prince Khevenhüller, Viennese audiences bestowed on *La finta scema*.[15] The librettist and composer, in composing an opera with ten singing roles, unwisely stretched the resources of a troupe that under the best of circumstances was weak.

One might have thought the threats of Joseph II, in his letter of 20 August 1775, would encourage the impresario Keglevich to abandon Salieri's opera in favor of a new production that promised greater success. But Keglevich may well have concluded there was little he could do, in the short term, to stave off the emperor's plan to bring the Burgtheater under his personal control. With little confidence that his tenure would last beyond the end of the theatrical year 1775 (that is, the end of Carnival 1776), and with a large part of his income guaranteed by subscriptions, Keglevich preferred to let a marginally successful production run its course rather than pay the large expenses—for scenery, costumes, music-copying, and so forth—necessary to replace it with a new work. He let Salieri's opera remain in the repertory for the rest of the theatrical year, presenting it fourteen times in all. Salieri's opera was never revived, in Vienna or elsewhere. De Gamerra's libretto, retitled *Il castellano deluso*, was reset to music by Giacomo Rust (Parma, 1781), but that opera was performed no more widely than Salieri's.

Joseph II made good on his threat. During the winter of 1775-76 he ousted Keglevich and made the Burgtheater, which he renamed the Nationaltheater, home to a troupe of German actors employed by the court. Until 1778 an independent opera buffa troupe under Salieri's musical direction continued to perform Italian comic operas in the Kärntnertortheater and (when Joseph's German troupe was idle) in the Nationaltheater. But this troupe presented very few operas; Salieri contributed not a single comic opera to its repertory. It was not until 1784, a year after Joseph II founded an opera buffa troupe and made the Nationaltheater its home, that Salieri's career as a composer of Viennese opera buffa resumed.

---

[15] Khevenhüller, vol. 8, p. 98.

APPENDIX 1

Giovanni De Gamerra's preface to the libretto of *La finta scema*. Source: Vienna: Kurzböck, [1775]; transcribed in Edward Swenson, "Antonio Salieri: A Documentary Biography" (Ph.D. diss., Cornell University, 1974), 60-61.

 Tutto il pregio delle nostre Opere Buffe, generalmente parlando, consiste nella sola Musica. Il Poeta, che dovrebbe avere il diritto alla preminenza degli elogj, è per lo meno ignorato. Il rispettoso Autore, che per la prima volta affrontar deve il sensato giudizio del Pubblico Viennese, comprende pur troppo di dover incontrare nel suo presente giocoso Dramma la stessa sorte. Ma chi è sensibile agli stimoli dell'onore, e della lode, deve sull' ali del genio aprirsi una nova strada a traverso la folla dei Copisti, e fra le tenebre dell'ignoranza. Impresa veramente lodevole quando ella ha per meta l'ingrandimento, ed i progressi dell'Arte. Ma un tal progetto esser non può felicemente ultimato, se i Maestri, e gli Attori non concorrono a sostenerlo; i primi coll'oltrepassare i limiti, fra i quali gli ha circostritti il costume, l'infingardaggine; i secondi col rinunziare al dispotismo, ai pregiudizi, e all'indecenze.

 Si chiama per altro ben fortunato l'Autore ritrovandosi al fianco un virtuoso intraprendente Maestro, ed una scelta unione di sperimentati Attori, i quali animati dal proprio merito non si sbigottiscono all'incontro dell penose difficoltà, che si presentano nell'avanzarsi su d'un novo non calcato sentiero. Egli adunque promette al Publico di produrre in altro tempo un genere Drammatico più ragionato, più interessante, e più utile, ove le situazioni, e la natural pittura dei costumi, e dei caratteri stravaganti animar dovranno l'azione, senza di cui non v'è nè interesse, nè vita. L'Autore non si prefiggerà per unico fine l'eccitamento di quell'inconsiderato riso, che denota la stravaganza dell'anima spinta fuori dei limiti della ragione, e dopo di cui il core umano non resta men vuoto di prima; ma cercherà di destare quel delizioso interesse, e quel sorriso fino, delicato, e penetrante, che nasce dal linguaggio della Natura, e che ben vale assai più dei smoderati risi, che non parlano all'anima, e che appartenendo all'ignoranza lasciar si devono all'odierne Buffe Rappresentazioni. Se le sensazioni miste sono le più dolci, il novo genere, che l'Autor si propone esser deve de' più dilettevoli, e il più applaudito da una Nazione, che ama, e formenta le belle Arti, che gusta il vero bello, e che pronunzia i proprj giudizj con fondamento, solidità, e raziocinio. Ma non essendo questi un luogo adattato per diffondersi in una più lunga analisi, stima adunque a proposito l'umile Autore d'implorare dai degnissimi Viennesi un grazioso compatimento per la presente sua produzione sinceramente dichiarandosi di riconoscerla nulla meno difettosa delle altre Buffe Rapsodie, che inondano i Teatri d'Europa, avviliscono le Scene, disgustano i Sensati, degradano gli Autori, e calpestano la verità, e la Natura. Lusingasi però, che gl'Intelligenti non v'incontraranno nè duplicatà di scene, nè caratteri falsi, non conservati, e fuori del verosimile teatrale, il quale però richiede sempre un certo grado di giudiziosa economica esagerazione, onde la favola produca l'effetto della verità, ed il ridicolo sia più colorito, e piccante, nè vi si leggeranno degl'intrighi osceni, o dei motti indecenti, contentandosi piuttosto l'Autore di non sentirsi applaudire, che acquistare a un si vil prezzo le acclamazioni, e le lodi.

De Gamerra
Poeta de' Cesari Teatri

APPENDIX 2

Salieri's annotations to the autograph score of *La finta scema*. Source: Vienna, Österreichische Nationalbibliothek, Mus. Hs. 16608, as transcribed in Rudolph Angermüller, *Antonio Salieri: Sein Leben und seine weltlichen Werke unter besonderer Berücksichtigung seiner "grossen" Opern*, vol. 3 (Munich: Katzbichler, 1972), 7-10.

Il mio parere anche sopra la musica di questa mia opera.

La Sinfonia, puo passar come un'annuzio di nozze, di Ballo ecc. del che si parla nell'opera.

L'Introduzione—*Presto affrettiamoci*—spiega diverse cose, primo il carattere delle tre persone, che cantano la stessa Introduzione e qualque altro carattere, e il motivo che li muove di casa loro. Questo pezzo è sufficientemente allegro, ma un poco lungo; cagione forse le parole.

L'Aria—*Quando ascolto il dolce moto*—ha un'accompagnamento in principio [*sic*] molto espressivo alle parole, il restante è strepitoso come deve essere, e il tutto fa buon'effetto.

Il duetto—*Ecco il gentil sposino*—cantato da due personaggi subalterni, puo non esser cattivo, se è ben recitato.

La Cavatina—*Ah ah ah ah, il sorcio è il tropola*—è giudiziosamente composta, presta molto all'attrice, e fa rider con piacer il pubblico.

L'Aria—*Questa gamba è all'ercolina*—mi sembra ben fatta; l'attore, di figura veramente gigantesca, l'ha recitava molto bene, ma la voce di natura rauca, toglieva molto all'effetto musicale, e restava fredda.

L'Aria—*Vuoi qu'io mi fidi* aria amorosa; recitata con grazia e foco, puol esser buona.

Il Duettino—*Voi siete gentilissimo*—di stile antico, è giudiziosamente fatto, perché cantato da una vecchia Donna con affettazione, e con affettazione da un cavaliere corrisposta. questo picciolo pezzo fu sempre applaudito.

L'Aria—*Dritto dritto colla testa*—è tutta d'azione, e da questa dipende l'effetto.

Il Rec.^{vo} istromentato—*Giacché il Fato inumano*—col Duetto che segue—*So che fedel mi sei*—formano una scenetta seria accademica, quantunque si recitò, la più giovinetta delle due ragazze, che l'[h]anno cantata e recitata, non aven che dodici anni: cantò e recitò egualmente all'altra a maraviglia, e la scenetta piacque moltissimo.

Il Rec: strom.^{to}—*Questa è un aria d'Egiziello*—e l'aria in Soprano—*Cara deh prendi in pace*—è poi in Tenore e poi in Basso, è buffissima; fa molto effetto quando il Cantante ha il dono di queste tre chiavi, ma il dono non è comune.

Il finale—*Fra le tazze e fra i bicchieri*—comincia e seguita molto tempo con allegria. Vi so in quà e in là dei tratti d'accompagnamento istrumentale che fanno buonissimo effetto. La fine puol piacere o dispiacere second che viene recitata dalle due Donne svenute; i gridi fuori d'armonia ponno offender l'orecchio del pubblico, e render freddo la fine dell'atto primo, e farebbe torno forse all'atto 2.do, e tanto più l'atto 2.do, dopo le prime scene amorose, passa quasi allo stile tragico, come si vedrà.

Il mio parere sopra la musica di questo secondo e terzo atto.

Il pezzo a quattro che comincia l'atto—*Ogni strepito è svanito*—è allegro, armonioso, e fa buon'effetto dopo lo strepito della chiusa dell'atto I.^{mo}.

L'Arietta—*Se lo dovessi prendere*—è una cosetta semplice e proporzionata al carattere che la canta, ch'è una giovinetta.

L'Arietta francese—*En enfant timide*—quantunque del colore in certa maniera dell'antecedente, pure si stacca da quella di molto, e ciò per la diversità della lingua, e perché ancor questa giovinetta pronunciava il francese a maraviglia.

Dal Duetto che dice—*Fra il timore e la speranza*—per quasi tutto il restante di quest'atto, la voce rauca per natura della prima Donna del primo amante e di Don Pisone hanno fatto perder molto dell'effetto della musica, che essendo in quà e in là d'un genere quasi tragico abbisogna di voci chiari e forti. Il Duetto dunque è restato freddo.

Il Quintetto—*Se a questo segno o barbaro*—faceva per l'armonia sufficiente effetto, ma senza la sortita dal personaggio che dice: *Alto là, perché gridata*, personaggio d'una voce veramente militare come era il suo carattere, finiva fredamente anche questo pezzo, che fu però sempre applaudito mediante questo bel vocione.

L'Aria—*Quasi fossa debil zucca*—si sostenne con effetto perché cantata e recitata dallo stesso vocione che ha sostenuto il pezzo antecedente.

Il Rec.^{t} stromentato—*Come, che dite*—e l'aria—*Questo fioco urlo dolente*—appartiene allo stile tragico; mi lusingo sia ben composta: fu benissimo recitata, ma la voce velata per natura della Cantante, ne fece sempre perder la metà dell'effetto.

L'Aria—*Entro coll'Asta in mano*—faceva rider quando il personaggio piangeva. La cosa era in regola, e lo è, ma quando poi viene l'energico dell pezzo, la voce velata anche di questo personaggio come dissi altrove, faceva piuttosto languire che rinforzar l'effetto, come dovrebbe esser sempre in ogni pezzo di musica di questo genere.

L'Aria—*L'adorata mia speranza*—è cantata da un giovine con molta espressione e con una voce angelica, quantunque di personaggio subalterno, era molto applaudita. Per parte della composizione, non è piuttosto buona.

L'Aria—*Gran Teatro è questo mondo*—Quantunque cantata da una voce molto di gola, faceva musicalmente effetto; anzi il cattivo di quella voce in una figura per arte [illegible] molto panciuta, e pesante, era molto a proposito, e aumentava l'affetto del tutto.

L'Aria—*A trucidar quel barbaro*—è troppo forte per una giovinetta, e parte subalterna, ma era bene eseguita, e piaceva.

L'Aria—*Sogno . . . vaneggio*—fu cantata parimente da una voce poco grata, ma il Cantante ci metteva un foco di verità, che interessava il pubblico.

Alla fine del libro per il Finale e l'atto 3.^{zo}.

Il Finale dell'atto 2.do—*Infelice ove m'aggire*—era detto dal Pubblico: Il superbo Finalone—mi lusingo che questa lode non sia tutta mal fondata. L'orchestra ha degli accompagnamenti di buonissimo effetto. Il soggetto istesso del Poema ha in quà e in là delle cose interessanti, e che furono con intelligenza recitate. Il motivo a Rondo della chiusa, l'ha fatto terminar sempre con grandissimo applauso.

Atto terzo.

L'Aria—*Se spiegar potessi appieno*—è piuttosto seria, ma senza disconvenire al personaggio di condizione, che la canta. Fu anche eseguita a maraviglia da una bellissima voce, e piacque moltissimo.

L'Aria—*Ecco al suon degli stromenti*—piacque parimente, e parimenti perché cantata da una voce angelica. Queste due arie mi sembrano anche ben composte in musica.

Il Duetto—*Sposo diletta e fida*—malgrado che cantato da due voci, come dissi sopra, velate, rauche, non faceva cattivo effetto. Quello che segue appartiene al finaletto, che non è gran cosa.

Da tutto ciò che ho detto di questa mia opera, si potrebbe creder che malgrado alcune voci velate della compagnia, l'opera nulladimeno abbia avuto grand'incontro. Forse questo sarebbe stato: ma le voci rauche, velate, erano appunto dei tre primi personaggi: dunque devo dire che questa musica fu più stimata che applaudita.

14

Alfieri and the Revitalization of Opera Seria

Marita Petzoldt McClymonds

Profound changes in opera seria took place during the 1780s and 90s. Arcadian neoclassical dramaturgy with its succession of recitatives and arias gave way to through-composed scene complexes freely moving among textural options combining recitative, solo, ensemble, and chorus. As cavatinas not requiring exits became more prevalent and acceptable, these were included in such complexes ultimately stretching over several scenes and often encompassing entire stage settings. Librettists no longer confined themselves to classical or mythological subject matter but ventured into early modern history and even more recent history if the location was far enough removed from European politics and culture—like Mexico (*Motezuma*), Peru (*La vergine del sole*), or the South Seas *Capitano Cook*. Along with the general loosening of Arcadian restraints came the departures from the precepts governing good taste and verisimilitude, which had fostered the revision of tragic plots to come out happily and the avoidance of staged deaths.

The opera libretto cannot be considered an innovative genre. Its neoclassical Arcadian form was the product of the Arcadian literary movement originating in Rome in the 1690s, which had taken its inspiration from the seventeenth-century French classical theater of Racine and Corneille. The greatest early Arcadian librettist, Apostolo Zeno, differs little in style and rational from the great Italian playwright of the same period, Scipione Maffei. Their individual renderings of the Greek historical tale of Queen Merope, for example, dramatize quite different plots, yet they have much in common. Both have seven characters. Besides the four central characters, Maffei added a male and a female confidant for the widowed queen, Merope, and a male confidant for the usurper, Polifonte. In spite of all of the characters, Maffei maintains a single plot and draws out the point of mother-son recognition until well into the fifth act. The play suffers from the neoclassical use of a narrator to describe how the rightful son and heir rises up in the midst of the wedding preparations and kills the tyrant. Zeno's plot is more complex. In addition to the three main characters, there are four others: a love interest for the son, an ambassador, a city official, and a henchman for Polifonte. Zeno avoided the anticlimatic narrative at the end by having the son Epitide confront Polifonte, who is led off stage to be executed. The main plot of all of the Merope dramas hangs on the recognition of the long-lost son in time to stay his execution as his own murderer, so that he may avenge the deaths of his father and brothers by killing the usurper. The secondary plot in Maffei and Alfieri's dramas is to avoid Merope's enforced marriage to Polifonte. In Zeno, it is to counter Polifonte's efforts to frame Merope for the murder of her family. Both Maffei and Zeno used devices that Alfieri, writing seventy years later, dismissed as cheap means—such as the telltale ring and belt that the young stranger wears, which Merope recognizes as her own farewell gifts to her son. Alfieri would also have deplored all of the extraneous characters and the contrived complications.[1]

The French playwright Voltaire followed with his own version, *Mérope,* in 1734. The cast consists of the four principal characters, plus one confidant each for Mérope and Polyphonte. The plot is similar to Maffei's, but Voltaire's tyrant is hardly suited for the term, he has become so gentile. In courting the grieving queen, he even proposes to

---

[1] Vittorio Alfieri, "Invenzione," Alfieri, *Le tragedie*, ed. Pietro Cazzani (Milan: Mondadori, 1966), 1070-76.

become a father to her lost son, when and if he returns. Like Maffei, Voltaire was restrained by neoclassical conventions from staging the death of Polyphonte at the hands of the rightful heir, and the deed is narrated as it occurs offstage. Voltaire continually railed against the conventions governing verisimilitude. "Why," he queried in his *Discours sur la tragédie*, "are heroes and heroines on the French stage only permitted to kill themselves but no one else? Is the stage less bloody for the death of Atalide, who stabs himself for his love, than it would be for the death of Caesar?" He goes on to argue that exceptions should be made to the rules that forbid bloodying the stage, if masterfully handled and not excessive.[2] Italians and French alike looked northward to the uninhibited bloody plays of Shakespeare and his successors with a mixture of envy and disapproval.

The seemingly sudden change in attitude towards staged death and tragic endings in the 1780s begs for an explanation. Already in 1757, Diderot challenged the musical theater to imitate the "gut cry of nature — in all its nuances—violent and inarticulate."[3] The availability of Shakespeare's plays through Ducis's translations into French began with *Hamlet* in 1769. At the Bologna meeting of the International Musicological Society in 1987, I pointed out precedents in the operas of the librettist Verazi and laid a direct pathway from the bloody ballets of Noverre in Stuttgart, through similar collaborations by Angiolini and Gluck in Vienna, to their successful introduction into Italian opera houses in the late 1770s and early 80s.[4] The publication of the first two volumes of Alfieri's tragedies in 1783 appears to have been the final event leading to the shocking staged matricide in Prati's opera *La vendetta di Nino* performed in Florence in 1786. But Alfieri's thinking sparked changes not only in approaches to death and tragedy but also in the selection of more modern subject matter, in literary style, and in formal constructions.

Alfieri took issue with the idea that Maffei's *Merope* was an "almost perfect" play. He thought it should be simpler, warmer, and more pressing. In general he considered the diction of modern authors lacking in tragic vigor—too languid, and their verse too melodious, in sum, faded and castrated.[5] His own version of *Merope* was conceived as a challenge to the venerated position of the earlier play.[6] In a letter to Calzabigi, author of Gluck's "reform" operas, Alfieri outlined his goals—a play in five acts on a single subject, having the drama expressed by the principals without aid of confidants or spectators, as rapidly as the passion would allow, as simply as possible, as gloomy and ferocious as nature can be, and as passionate as his inner feelings.[7] His plays normally have only four characters. With rare exceptions, there are no peripheral incidents or spurious mechanisms and props such as ghosts, lightning, and thunder, eavesdropping on confidential conversations, useless killing, nonverisimilar recognitions, secret notes, locks of hair, and similar devices he called *mezzucci* or cheap means.[8] He believed that great heroes do not confide their thoughts to underlings and was a firm advocate of the soliloque.[9] He maintained that the dynamics of the action should be supplied by some simple and natural means suggested by the situation itself. The subject of the drama should never be introduced by a character created merely for that purpose, and that in the final act narrative should never substitute for what could be seen on the stage without offending common decency and verisimilitude. If a narrative could not be avoided it should be delivered by a main character and not by a messenger.[10] In his letters to both Calzabigi and

---

[2] François Marie Arouet de Voltaire, "Discours sur la Tragedie a Mylord Bolingbroke," *Brutus, Tragédie: Représentée, pour la première fois, le 11 Décembre 1730*, pp. 306-07; Voltaire, *Dissertations sur le théâtre* (Heidelberg: Karl Winter Universitätesverlag, 1949), 28.

[3] Denis Diderot, *Entretiens sur "Le fils naturel,"* 1757, extract in *Écrits sur la musique*, ed. Béatrice Durand-Sendrail (Paris: Éditions Jean-Claude Lattès, 1987), 126-27.

[4] McClymonds, "'La morte di Semiramide ossia La vendetta di Nino' and the Restoration of Death and Tragedy to the Italian Operatic Stage in the 1780s and 90s," *Atti del XIV Congresso della Società Internazionale di Musicologia, 27 agosto - 1 settembre 1987*, vol. 3 (Turin: EDT, 1990), 285-92.

[5] Alfieri, "Risposta dell'autore," response of 6 September 1783 to a letter from Raniero de' Calzabigi on his first four tragedies, *Le tragedie*, ed. Cazzani, 978-79.

[6] Franci Betti, *Vittorio Alfieri* (Boston: Twayne, 1984), 62.

[7] Alfieri, "Risposta dell'autore," 964.

[8] Alfieri, "Invenzione," *Le tragedie*, 1074.

[9] Alfieri, "Sceneggiatura," *Le tragedie*, 1080-83.

[10] Alfieri, "Invenzione," *Le tragedie*, 1074-75.

Cesarotti, he characterizes his stylistic goals as brevity, simplicity, dignity, and energy, though he admits to being somewhat obscure and stylistically harsh at times. The over-abundance of prepositions and monosyllables, he countered, was deliberately calculated to avoid the singsong trivialities that were emasculating Italian poetry of the time.[11] He supported enthusiastically the neoclassical belief that drama should both instruct and delight.

Though Alfieri's work had a profound influence on what happened to opera seria later in the decade, few of his plays were actually adapted for the musical theater in the eighteenth century. Opera by its very nature made some of Alfieri's goals almost impossible to achieve. Most plays required a great deal of modification for the musical theater. Plays had five acts rather than opera's three. They were performed in intimate, often private venues and did not involve elaborate stage settings. Most plays take place in a single location, while opera librettos normally had at least two settings per act, some in private and some in public locations. Opera librettos had to provide opportunities for arias, ensembles, and, late in the century, even for finales. Alfieri's plays presented even further problems because of his insistence on maintaining a single plot free of dependence on secondary characters as confidants and uncluttered with the subsidiary incidents they generated. His plays often have very few characters, and the action is private, familial, and introspective. *Virginia* was better suited for the musical theater than most because it has a cast of six characters (the same as an opera normally had), and it is more publicly oriented and action filled. The first of three "tragedies of liberty," it followed Alfieri's treatise *On Tyranny*, and came out of his studies of Machiavelli and Plutarch in 1777.[12] He thought there could not be a more grandiose, terrifying, and pitiful case.[13] He found within the event passions real, natural, and terrible. Nothing need be borrowed from religion, government, imagination, or destiny. Franco Betti points out that what is new about this tragedy is Alfieri's insistent, open attacks on exaltedness and nobility of rank, its corruption standing, in strong contrast to the virtue and spiritual nobility of the plebeians who finally rise to reclaim their liberty, an example that Alfieri hoped one day the Italian people would follow. The play was received enthusiastically at the time, and has since been considered one of his best.[14]

Virginia was surely known to *cognoscenti* before its publication in Alfieri's first volume of plays in 1783. Ranieri de' Calzabigi wrote a detailed and highly favorable commentary on the entire volume in August of the publication year.[15] Two years later (1785), the first of several operatic versions was produced in Florence on an anonymous libretto with music by Angelo Tarchi, followed by a second production a year later in Livorno, Calzabigi's home town. That Florence was first to produce an opera on an Alfieri play was undoubtedly due to the patronage of Archduke Leopold, ruler of Tuscany. This Habsburg prince was a youth in Vienna when Calzabigi, Gluck, and Angiolini were producing their radical masterpieces. Under his patronage, the Florentine theater led the way in freeing opera from the contrived happy endings and the crippling ban on staged death in an audacious, positive reaction to Alfieri's precepts. Already in 1783, the tragic triple suicides in *Piramo e Tisbe* were allowed to proceed without the fortuitous intervention that normally led to a happy ending. The year after *Virginia* was produced saw the staged matricide of Semiramide in *La vendetta di Nino*—a landmark in operatic history.

Virginia, the play, and the operas it spawned share a basic plot: Virginia, daughter of Lucio Virginio, betrothed to Icilio, has caught the eye of the Decemviro Appio Claudio. When she rejects his advances he initiates a plot with a henchman, who claims that Virginia was born to one of his slaves and therefore not Virginio's true daughter. In the forum, Appio, acting as judge, finds in favor of his henchman and against Virginio, who kills her rather than allow her to become the property of another.

In Alfieri's play, Virginia, her mother Numatoria, and her betrothed Icilio have been forced to deal with Appio's unwelcome advances and his associate Marco's claims, while Lucio Virginio is away with the Roman army. Icilio has already begun to gather citizens to their side when Virginio returns. At first Virginio counsels a peaceful route, but

---

[11] Betti, 13-16; Alfieri, "Risposta dell'autore," 976-77.

[12] Betti, 38-39.

[13] Alfieri, "Parere dell'Autore," on *Virginia: Le tragedie*, 1023.

[14] Betti, 40-42.

[15] Ranieri de' Calzabigi, "Lettera al signor conte Vittorio Alfieri sulle quattro sue prime tragedie," *Scriti teatrali e letterari*, ed. Anna Laura Bellina, vol. 1 (Roma: Salerno Editrice, 1994), 185-232.

his meeting with Appio makes it clear that Icilio is in mortal danger. Upon arriving in the forum for the hearing, Virginio learns that Icilio was attacked as a traitor to Rome, and after a valiant defense killed himself. Virginio denounces Appio and is arrested. Appio finds in favor of Marco. In a last embrace, Virginio stabs and kills Virginia. The people of Rome advance on Appio calling for his death, he is overwhelmed, his scepter falls. There is fighting and tumult.

To a degree, Tarchi's plot backs away from Alfieri's challenge. Icilio is still alive at the end of the opera, and Virginia's father kills her offstage, returning with a bloody dagger to report what he has done. He and Icilio exit threatening revenge, but the tyrant is still alive and unpunished when the opera closes. An anonymous critic addressing a similar situation at the end of Abate Pierantonio Meneghelli's play *Bianca de' Rossi* of the late 1780s considered it a fatal flaw: "The audience . . . wants and ought to want a penalty enacted before its eyes, he declared."[16]

Formally, acts 1 and 2 of Tarchi's opera begin and end in private or at least less public locations most in or near Appio's palace—the location also of act 3. The central scene is in the Roman Forum, site of Alfieri's entire play. The end of act 2 takes place in a gloomy underground place—evidence of Romantic stirrings, also to be found especially in Alfieri's Greek tragedies and anticipated even earlier in Coltellini and Traetta's dark opera *Antigona* for St. Petersburg in 1772.

In Tarchi's opera, Appio's henchman Publio has already taken Virginia into custody at the beginning of the opera. Her family encounters her on the streets and in the forum in chains and accompanied by lictors. Virginio shows his fidelity to Appio by ordering Virginia to comply with the Decemviri's orders and seeking Appio's advice in countering Marco's claims. Appio makes his wrong-headed decision awarding Virginia to Publio already in the middle of act 2, but the energy generated is expended through arias in which Icilio vents his despair and Virginio his anger. The remainder of act 2 is a typical operatic diversion designed to afford the prima donna a dramatic obbligato monologue and a rousing ensemble closing. Tullia, angered at Appio's infidelity, arranges a subterranean meeting between Icilio and Virginia. They miss each other, but Appio overhears Virginia believing she is speaking to Icilio and resolves to punish them both. Icilio and Virginio enter. Appio issues his threats and leaves them to express their reactions in a trio. Act 3 takes place entirely in Virginia's rooms. Virginio asks for a moment alone with Virginia. He returns with his bloody dagger just as Icilio comes rushing onto the scene. Thus the deed is done not only offstage but in private. There are no angry citizens to call for the death of the tyrant and only a threat of future revenge. The tragic ending in which the heroine dies and the villain goes free represents a flagrant departure from Arcadian precepts, while still observing some of its niceties. Virginia dies offstage in accordance with classical tradition, and the audience as well as the reigning patron are spared the treasonous spectacle of a figure of authority being overwhelmed by a mob seeking justice.

Tarchi's opera has another extraneous distraction in Appio's intended, Tullia, the seconda donna. In Alfieri's play the seconda donna is Virginia's mother, who has an active parental role. In Tarchi's opera there is no subsidiary plot for the seconda donna, and her role seems little more than residual. She mainly provides a lead into an aria—either her own or someone else's—sometimes as an ineffectual prick to Appio's conscience, and other times as a confidant. And, of course, she sets up the equally extraneous secret meeting initiating the final scene in act 2.

Most theaters did not yet have the stomach for either the violence or the tragedy being introduced to the public in Florence. The Roman version of Tarchi's libretto set by Albertini for production the next year, 1786, is much more moderate in its portrayal of Appio, and therefore closer to the typical Arcadian libretto in spirit. Alfieri's tyrant shows no qualms of conscience whatsoever, whereas Tarchi's tyrant expresses displeasure at having to resort to force when he would have preferred to win Virginia through courtship and is still hoping to persuade her at the beginning of act 2. In Albertini's opera Appio assumes the gentile characteristics of the Arcadian tyrant who will repent later on. In new scenes in acts 1 and 2 he feels sorry for Virginio, and admits to himself that he is doing the wrong thing, though he cannot control his desire for Virginia. He loses his patience at the end of act 2 when Virginia and Icilio try to escape, and expresses his anger in a trio, which becomes a quartet when Virginio arrives. Consistent with the conciliatory tone of the opera, Virginio remains persistently loyal to Appio, becoming angry only when Appio decides against him

---

[16] "Notizie storico-critiche sopra Bianca de'Rossi," in Pierantonio Meneghelli, *Bianca de'Rossi Tragedia*, Il teatro moderno applaudito, no. 22, pt. 1 (Venice, 1798), 73.

in the Forum. Act 3 is entirely new—resulting in a typical Arcadian happy ending. In the first scene Virginio has given Virginia a dagger with which to commit suicide. As she raises the dagger, Icilio arrives with the news that the people are against Appio's decree and are calling for her in the Forum. Staged battles and fights had become operatic fare by this time, and at the beginning of the final scene a battle is taking place between the citizens and the guards. Appio and Publio are overpowered. Their lives are spared, and everyone celebrates the restoration of liberty.

By 1794, when Pepoli's *Virginia* was written for La Fenice in Venice and set by Felice Alessandri, opera seria had been completely transformed. Choruses had become important dramatic entities, the number of arias had been greatly reduced and replaced with both active and static ensembles of all sizes, as well as arias with chorus and or soloists acting as *pertichini*. The traditionally stark contrast between recitative and aria was becoming increasingly blurred as instrumental obbligato accompanied more and more of the recitative and even invaded the set pieces. Staged deaths and tragic endings were no longer novelties.

Two aspects of Pepoli's opera exemplify how Alfieri was affecting opera formally and stylistically by the early 1790s. Formally, Calzabigi especially admired the tableau construction characteristic of Alfieri's acts.[17] In his *Virginia*, for example, all but the last act begins and ends with the same personnel, disturbed by the arrival and business of others, and left to reflect at the end of the action. For example, in act 1 Virginia's family plan a wedding. Marco enters with his claims. The family reflects on what this means. Once the exit aria convention began to give way, librettists were able to construct large integrated sections centered on a single action unbroken by exit numbers, even though some of the characters enter or leave. In Pepoli's opera these often occupy an entire stage setting. They normally contain at least one musical number, though they may not necessarily end with one. The practice of inserting comments or dramatic business between an exit number and a set change had become an important dramatic option. On the other hand, the extraordinary number of stage settings this technique generated in Pepoli's opera (six in act one, five in act two) seems undesirably disruptive. Stylistically, Pepoli's diction, like that of his contemporaries, has a vigorous, short-breathed, declamatory style. Gone for the most part are the long speeches and mellifluous verses so greatly admired during much of the eighteenth century and so harshly criticized by Alfieri.

Pepoli himself had strong opinions regarding opera subject matter and construction, which he enunciated in prefaces to several of his librettos. It is, therefore, hardly surprising that he treads his own course in his rendering of Virginia's story, notwithstanding clear borrowings from both Alfieri's play and Tarchi's opera. The opera opens in a public place for a ceremonial *Introduzione* with chorus. Otherwise, Pepoli follows established practice in having central public scenes—the Forum in act 1 and the Temple of Vesta in act 2—surrounded by more private locations. Like Alfieri's play, the last act takes place in public. Pepoli keeps Alfieri's name for Appio's henchman Marco. Virginia acquires a confidant, Camilla, who often lends a solo voice to the chorus of women. Numitorio, a maternal uncle, functions as a masculine substitute for Alfieri's Numitoria, Virginia's mother. The secondary characters generate no extraneous subsidiary scenes, and the plot can even be said to have no subsidiary incidents. Pepoli's Virginio is no longer conciliatory here. By this time liberty has become Europe's cause as well as Alfieri's, and the Italian people will soon have an opportunity to translate Alfieri's lessons into action. Act 2 is occupied with appeals to the people for support, Virginio's appeals to Appio, and Virginia's imprisonment. The closing quartet takes place in her prison. Like Alfieri, Pepoli saves the confrontation in the forum until the last act. When Appio finds in favor of Marco, Virginio keeps his promise to Virginia and kills her. In an action ensemble the Romans descend upon Appio, and Icilio kills him. This immediate retribution against an unspeakable tyrant would have pleased Meneghelli's critic and the spectators he represented. His death is even more explicit than it was in Alfieri's play, where it is assumed but hidden by the crowd. Clearly, opera seria had proven fertile ground for Alfieri's challenging precepts, whose key elements had played a vital role in the revitalization process that was transforming opera seria during the 1780s and 90s.

---

[17] Calzabigi, "Lettera al . . . Alfieri," 203-12.

15

Le finte pazzie of Ferdinando Rutini: A Rediscovered Florentine Opera Buffa of the Late Eighteenth Century

SUSAN PARISI

The ascendancy, in the late eighteenth century, of theatrical professionals whose interests lay in promoting their own works, to positions of influence in the musical life of Florence has been documented by Robert Lamar Weaver and Norma Wright Weaver.[1] These were the composers who also played the cembalo in the theater orchestras (and were therefore the directors of the orchestras), musicians in the orchestras, and the impresarios who favored them. The Tuscan repertory they promoted, unprecedented in its success in the local theaters—works by Luigi Barbieri, Vincenzio Bianciardi, Francesco Clerici, the young Luigi Cherubini, Alessandro Felici, Francesco Giuliani, Bernardo Mengozzi, Giuseppe Moneta, Michele Neri-Bondi, Ferdinando Rutini, and Antonio Riccomini—has in the last few years come under bibliographic control, thanks in large part to the catalogues of Weaver and Weaver, and Marcello De Angelis, and to the historical survey in the former.[2] There is need now for the composers and their operas and ballets to be studied more closely.[3] The present essay initiates an effort in that direction through focus on Ferdinando

---

I should like to thank the President's Research Initiative Program, University of Louisville for the Program's support of this research; Richard Griscom, former head of the Dwight D. Anderson Music Library, University of Louisville, for kind permission to reproduce folios from the score; and Dottore Mario Armellini of the Biblioteca Civico Museo Bibliografico Musicale, Bologna, for helping me to obtain the libretto. An earlier version of the essay was read at the annual meeting of the Italian Musicological Society, Florence, Italy, October 1995.

[1] Robert Lamar Weaver and Norma Wright Weaver, *A Chronology of Music in the Florentine Theater 1751-1800: Operas, Prologue, Farces, Intermezzos, Concerts, and Plays with Incidental Music*, Detroit Studies in Music Bibliography, 70 (this publisher, 1993; hereafter, Weaver and Weaver, *Chronology*, 35-91), in particular see table 3, "Performances of Works by Tuscan Composers," 83-87. The patronage of Grand Dukes Pietro Leopoldo (ruled 1765-90) and Ferdinando (ruled 1791-99, 1814-24), particularly the theatrical policies of the former, and the attitudes of the academicians who owned the theaters and hired the impresarios to run them, of course conspicuously influenced Florentine operatic music. The authors give a detailed analysis of this patronage.

[2] Complete titles of the operas, names of participants, location of extant scores and librettos, and references to operas in the local press are in Weaver and Weaver, *Chronology*, and Marcello De Angelis, *Melodramma, spettacolo, e musica nella Firenze dei Lorena*, vol. 2 (Florence: Giunta Regionale Toscana, 1991). Transcriptions of documents pertaining to regulation of the theaters are in the former. Other relevant studies include De Angelis, *Le Felicita in Etruria* (Florence: Ponte alle Grazie, 1990); John Rice, "Grand Duke Pietro Leopoldo as Patron of Florentine Music, 1765-1790," paper read at Patrons, Politics, and Art in Italy, 1738-1859: Conference for the Inauguration of the Ricasoli Collection, University of Louisville, March 14-18, 1989; Rice, "Emperor and Impresario: Leopoldo II and the Transformation of Viennese Musical Theater, 1790-1792" (Ph.D. diss., University of California, Berkeley, 1987); Marita Petzoldt McClymonds, "Mozart's 'La clemenza di Tito' and Opera Seria in Florence as a Reflection of Leopold II's Musical Taste," *Mozart-Jahrbuch* 1984/85 (Kassel: Bärenreiter, 1986), 61-70; Carlo Mangio, "Attività teatrale nella Toscana democratizzata (1799)," *Ricerche storiche* 17 (1987): 317-37; Aubrey S. Garlington, "Opera in Florence under French Domination: Social and Cultural Considerations," in *Opera & libretto*, vol. 1 (Florence: Olschki, 1990), 77-100; and biographical articles on Cherubini, Bartolomeo and Alessandro Felici, and Giovanni Marco and Ferdinando Rutini written by Mario Fabbri, "La giovanezza di Luigi Cherubini nella vita musicale fiorentina del sup tempo," *Luigi Cherubini nel II centenario della nascita*, ed. Adelmo Damerini, Historiae musicae cultores, 19 (Florence, 1962), 1-46; "Il terzo maestro di Luigi Cherubini: Alessandro Felici," *Musiche italiane rare e vive da Giovanni Gabrieli a Giuseppe Verdi*, Chigiana 19 (1962): 183-94; "Incontro con Ferdinando Rutini il dimenticato figlio musicista del primo maestro di Mozart," *Le celebrazioni del 1963 e alcune nuove indagini sulla musica italiana del XVIII e XIX secolo*, Chigiana 20 (1963): 195-205.

[3] The extant repertory is relatively small. Of approximately one hundred operas by Tuscan composers performed in Florence between 1781 and the end of 1800 only twenty operas are known to exist. Fifteen are comic operas. For the complete titles of these works, by

Rutini, the most prolific composer of this flourishing school. It undertakes an updated review of Rutini's career and an examination of his intermezzo *Le finte pazzie o sia la pupilla bizzarra* (1794), in light of new documentation and the discovery of the score.

Ferdinando Rutini (1763-1827) composed forty-four comic operas, almost all of them between 1786 and 1799, the years he was employed in Florence. He was the son of Giovanni Marco Rutini, himself a composer of nineteen operas, and of keyboard sonatas and oratorios, who in the 1760s and 1770s was one of the principal musicians residing in Florence.[4] Although the younger Rutini was not to become as prolific a composer of keyboard music as his father, his earliest dated works are for "cembalo pianoforte": two sets of sonatas, a capriccio, and a trio for cembalo and strings. The first set of *Tre sonate*, issued by the Florentine printer Pagani, appeared in 1784; an announcement in the *Gazzetta toscana* described it as Ferdinando's "first work."[5]

Ferdinando Rutini's career in the theater began two years later as a cembalo player in the orchestra of the Teatro in via S. Maria. His operatic composition came to public notice in the same year when a trio composed by him was inserted in a production of Cimarosa's *L'italiana in Londra*, organized by the Marchesa Ginevra Bartolommei, who sang one of the roles.[6] By 1789 Rutini was cembalist at both the S. Maria and the Intrepidi theaters. The first full-length operas he composed premiered in the same year: an intermezzo at the Cocomero Theater in Florence and a *dramma giocoso* at the Valle Theater in Rome. In the following decade he completed thirty-six works in the genres of intermezzo, farce, and *dramma giocoso*; all but seven opened in Florence. At the height of his popularity in the mid 1790s six new operas by Rutini premiered in a single year. He continued to perform as cembalist, moving in 1795 to the Cocomero Theater, where he remained through 1798.[7]

His activities were not limited to opera. During the Lenten season, when all the theaters except the Pergola were closed, the Armonici, a concert society, sponsored two or three concerts at the Porta Rossa Theater. From notices in the *Gazzetta toscana*, *L'Osservatrice fiorentina*, and *Gazzetta universale* we know that among works heard in these concerts were Rutini overtures and operatic scenes.[8] In *Nuova teoria di musica* (1812), Carlo Gervasoni mentions

---

Neri-Bondi, Moneta, and Rutini, see the following entries in Weaver and Weaver, *Chronology*: 1783[6], 1784[30], 1785[4], 1785[22], 1789[13], 1790[3], 1791[6], 1791[7], 1791[10], 1791[30], 1794[18], 1794[28], 1795[31], 1796[4], 1797[6]. The operas of Anfossi, Cimarosa, Gazzaniga, Guglielmi, Paisiello, Portogallo, Spontini, and Zingarelli, as well as operas by Mayr and Paer, were of course staged in Florence, and were popular with audiences, but Italian operas by composers active outside Italy rarely were performed. As Weaver and Weaver point out, one opera by Mozart was produced during the entirety of Grand Duke Pietro Leopoldo's reign (*Figaro* in 1788), and no other would be heard until 1817 (*Don Giovanni*); no operas by Haydn, and only two by Salieri, and three by Martin y Soler were performed during the reign of Grand Duke Ferdinando III. On the staging of *Die Zauberflöte* in 1818, see De Angelis, "The Magical Moment in Mozart's *Zauberflöte*, and a Note on the Production of the Opera at the Teatro di S. Maria in Florence in 1818," this volume.

[4] The total number of operas Ferdinando Rutini composed was not as large as the number by some composers of his and the previous generation, whose operas played in Italy in the 1790s: Anfossi, about 76 operas; Cimarosa, 65 operas; Gazzaniga, about 50 operas; Guglielmi, 91 operas; Paër, 55 operas; Paisiello, about 80 operas; Sarti, about 70 operas. See Elvidio Surian, "The Opera Composer," in *Opera Production and Its Resources*, ed. Lorenzo Bianconi and Giorgio Pestelli, *The History of Italian Opera*, vol. 4 (Turin, 1987; rev. ed., trans. Lydia G. Cochrane, Chicago: University of Chicago Press, 1998), 322. On Giovanni Marco Rutini, see Giorgio Pestelli, "Mozart e Rutini," *Analecta musicologica*, 18 (1978): 290; Weaver and Weaver, *Chronology*, 50-51; and *The New Grove Dictionary of Music and Musicians* [hereafter, *New Grove*] (1980), s.v. "Rutini, Giovanni Marco," by Giorgio Pestelli. The date of Ferdinando Rutini's birth is not certain. He was probably born during one of his father's temporary engagements outside Florence, and is probably the son whose birth the father announced in a letter of 3 December 1763 to Padre Martini: see *The New Grove Dictionary of Opera* (1992) [hereafter, *New Grove Opera*], s.v. "Rutini, Ferdinando," by Robert Lamar Weaver, and Fabbri, "Incontro con Ferdinando Rutini," 197, 200.

[5] "Il Giovane Sig. Ferdinando Rutini ha date alle stampe tre Sonate da Cembalo, sua prima opera, che, a giudizio degl' Intendenti, sono di un gusto delicato e brillante." *Gazzetta toscana*, 1784, p. 196, as quoted in Fabbri, "Incontro con Ferdinando Rutini," 203-04.

[6] The performance took place at the Teatro de' Tintori and was reported in the *Gazzetta toscana* and the *Gazzetta universale*; excerpts are in Weaver and Weaver, *Chronology*, 549.

[7] A full list of all of Rutini's compositions, including the operas, is in Susan Parisi, "Rutini, Ferdinando," *New Grove Dictionary*, 7th ed. (London: Macmillan, forthcoming). On Rutini's various theater appointments, see table 4 in Weaver and Weaver, *Chronology*, 93-96.

[8] According to the *Gazzetta toscana* (1793): 30, Rutini overtures were heard on the concerts of February 17 and March 5, and a Rutini concerto for cembalo on the concert of March 25. The following year Rutini directed the Armonici's first concert on March 9 and a *scena ed aria* from one of his operas was heard on the second concert on April 5—*Gazzetta toscana* (1794): 41, 57; *Gazzetta universale* (1794): 167, 232; excerpts in Weaver and Weaver, *Chronology*, 683-84, 700, 702. The membership of the Armonici comprised ten noblemen and forty citizens; see ibid., 74.

that Rutini composed a cantata for a wedding in Florence in 1789 and sang the principal part. A notice of 1796 in the *Gazzetta toscana* advertises the publication of his recently completed concerto for pianoforte and orchestra (another work apparently lost),[9] and another, of 1798, the opening of his music school. Nothing is known about the school, though an advertisement for the opening of Neri-Bondi's Fiesole School of Music in 1796 tells us that its curriculum included dancing and fencing, and that Domencio Somigli, then the leading Florentine librettist of comic operas, who collaborated with Rutini in several operas, was to give impromptu improvisations Sunday evenings between seven and ten o'clock.[10] At least one other non-operatic composition by Rutini dates from this period: *Voglio vergine pietoso: Canzoncina in cuore di Maria Sanctissima* for tenor and basso continuo of 1797.[11]

Less well-documented are Rutini's movements at the time of the French occupations of Florence, which lasted for three months in 1799, and then essentially from 1800 to 1814. The main Tuscan composers—Rutini, Neri-Bondi, Moneta, Riccomini, and Giuliani—all ceased composing for the theater. Rutini's comic operas continued to be staged, though by 1801 production had decreased to one new opera a year, staged at the Cocomero during carnival. No new opera by him was performed in 1805; the following year one of his earliest operas was repeated.[12] Apparently by 1804 Rutini had left Florence to assume the post of *maestro di cappella* in Ancona; his move to a church position in a less prestigious musical center has not been explained. The *Tre ore di agonia di N. S. Gesu Cristo* in the Ancona Library,[13] and the recently identified motets "Domine Deus," "Qui sedes ad dexteram," and "Quoniam tu solas" for solo voices and instruments, indicate some attention to church music. The motets are found in two manuscripts acquired by the University of Louisville in 1997, and probably date from the period when Rutini was working in central Italy, ca. 1800-04 to 1827. The decorated title page of one manuscript, with a lithographed pre-printed border depicting Orpheus and Eurydice (the same border appears on the other manuscript) is given as fig. 15.1.[14] Between 1812 and

---

[9] "Avvisi," *Gazzetta toscana* 13 (1796): 52: "E stato pubblicato da Giovacchino Pagani un bellissimo Concerto per cimbalo Piano forte combinato in maniera da potersi eseguire comodamente ancora sull'Arpa, questa è una nuova produzione del rinomato Sig. Maestro Ferdinando Rutini, nella quale vi si trova novità, buon gusto, e spirito. A norma del Manifesto si rilascia ai Sigg. Associati per il tenue prezzo di Paoli sei con tutte le parti cavate, e ai non Associati Paoli otto."

[10] "Avvisi," *Gazzetta toscana* 36 (1798): "Il nostro Sig. Maestro Rutini a norma del già pubblicato manifesto aprirà la sua Scuola di Musica posta in Via Nuova da S. Remigi al Num. 23 la mattina di Lunedi 10 corrente. Tendono le sue premure ad essere utile ai suoi amabili Concittadini, perciò implora incoraggiamento, e protezione." On Neri-Bondi's school, see *Gazzetta toscana* 7 (1796): 27-28: ". . . e ogni Domenica mattina dalle ore dieci a mezzogiorno Accademia di Scherma; oltre le sudd[ette] vi sara ancora Accademia d'Improvviso, a cui presiederà il Sig[nor] Domenico Somigli, ogni Domenico sera dalle ore 7 alle 10, e mezzo. Tali Accademie hanno avuto principio sino dalla sera del dì 11 stante cominciando dalla Musica; e saranno proseguito in tutto l'Anno fuori che nei Mesi di Giugno Luglio e Agosto. Gl'Istitutori si lusingano di essere favoriti da un numero di Dilettanti ed Apprendisti sufficiente a conservare un tale stabilmento. Per fissare l'onorario mensuale tanto per intervenire alle Lezioni che all'Accademie è incaricato il Sig[nor] Maestro Michele Neri Bondi reperibile alla predetta Scuola, e alla Copisteria di Musica dirimpetto a Badia." For Somigli, see *New Grove Opera*, s.v. "Somigli, Domencio," by Robert Lamar Weaver.

[11] The *Canzoncina In cuore di Maria Sanctissima* is located in the Dubrovnik Samostan Mala Braca, Glazbeni Arhiv Ms. 45/1262. An undated organ polacca is in the Biblioteca Casantense in Rome, Ms. Mus. 5902. Other undated instrumental works by Rutini are mentioned below.

[12] The opera was *La pianella perduta*, staged at the Cocomero. It was probably a version of the opera performed in Parma in 1790, and the same opera later performed in Milan in 1820. On changes opera theaters experienced between 1800 and 1814 when France governed Tuscany, see Garlington, 77-100; also see Weaver and Weaver, *Chronology*, 97-99. For discussion of the social and political ramifications, see *La Toscana nell'età rivoluzionaria e Napoleonica*, ed. Ivan Tognarini (Naples: Edizioni Scientifiche Italiane, 1985), and Eric Cochrane, *Florence in the Forgotten Centuries, 1527-1800* (Chicago: University of Chicago Press, 1973), 501-04.

[13] The manuscript, Ancona, Biblioteca Comunale, Ms. Mus. 83, apparently bearing a date of 1820, is incomplete: only the violoncello and basso parts are extant.

[14] The entry in the sale catalog lists the composer as "Rubini fiorentino" and the date as ca. 1800. However, the musician is clearly Rutini. Robert Weaver was the first to make the identification. The complete titles of the manuscripts are *Duetto "Gratias agimus tibi" del Sig.re M'ro Francesco Zannetti/Terzetto "Domine Deus" Del Sig.re M'ro Ferdinando Rutini/Quartetto "O salutaris Hostia" Del Sig.re M'ro Giuseppe Weigl /Con accompagno di Cembalo, o Piano-Forte* and *Versetti N.o 4. a Voce Sola di Soprano/Con accompagno di Piano-Forte, e Flauto obbligato/Due del M'ro Sig.re Giuseppe Rossi di Assisi, e/Due del M'ro Sig.re Ferdinando Rutini Fiorentino. In Roma. Presso Giovanni Jubilli Professore della Basilica Vaticana. Negoziante di musica antica e moderna.* "Domine Deus" is scored for two sopranos, alto, and pianoforte; "Qui sedes ad dexteram Patris" for soprano, flute, pianoforte; "Quoniam tu solus" for soprano, flute, pianoforte. The manuscripts are bound in quarter-calf with modern marbled boards. Both manuscripts also contain Anglican chants, copied later by a different hand. The chants in the first volume bear ascriptions to Philip Hayes, Crotch, Boyce, Alcock, and Beckwith. In the second volume there are five chants, one ascribed to Chard, another to Norris, to

Fig. 15.1. Title page (with lithographed pre-printed border) of manuscript containing *Domine Deus* by Rutini (Dwight D. Anderson Music Library, University of Louisville)

1816 Rutini held the post of *maestro di cappella* in Macerata. Two of his undated instrumental works were at one time owned by the Countess Girolama Campagnoni Marefoschi of Macerata, and have also recently come to light.[15]

In 1816 and 1817 Rutini took up composition for the stage once more, but apparently without real success. He produced three operas in Rome, two for the Apollo Theater and one for the Argentina, the latter especially criticized, even by the librettist, Jacopo Ferretti. His whereabouts in the next three years have not been documented, though eighteen years later Ferretti reminisced that Rutini became a *maestro di cappella* in Orvieto sometime after

---

the Earl of Mornington, one labeled "Lichfield Cathedral," and one without attribution. John Alcock was organist and vicar choral at Lichfield Cathedral. On the basis of the latter, the entry in the 1997 sale catalog indicates an owner of the manuscript may have lived close to Lichfield.

[15] The works are *Pianoforte Concerto Per Chitarra Francese e Pianforte Del Sig.re Ferdinando Rutini Per divertimento della Nobil'Doncella Signora Girolama Contessa Compagnoni Marefoschi* (copy in the Biblioteca Casantense, Rome, Ms. Mus. 6079; second copy in the Dubrovik Samostan Mala Braca, Ms. 45/1261), and *Violino Sonata per Cembalo e Violino Del Maestro Rutini* (cembalo part missing; also formerly owned by the [Contessa Girolama] Compagnoni Marefoschi of Macerata, and now in the private collection of Giancarlo Rostirolla in Rome, Ms. Mus. 1035). The opening incipits of the two works (I have not seen the compositions) are identical.

1817.[16] Nevertheless, a performance of his earlier farce, *La pianella perduta* took place at the Teatro Re in Milan in May 1820.[17] He was *maestro di cappella* in Aquapendente (a town very near Orvieto) from 1820 to 1825, and he then assumed the same position in Terracina until his death in 1827.[18]

The Extant Rutini Operas

Until a few years ago only the scores of four of Rutini's operas were thought to have survived. In the last five years the scores of two additional operas have surfaced: *Le finte pazzie o sia La pupilla bizzarra* (The feigned insane, or the high-spirited ward), an intermezzo of 1794 acquired by the University of Louisville,[19] and *La dama giardiniera* (The lady gardener) of 1791, to a libretto by Domenico Somigli adapted from a French farce, whose score is in the Parma Conservatory Library. Undoubtedly this is the same work whose libretto the Weavers and De Angelis, unaware of the survival of the score, list as *La baronessa giardiniera*.[20] The earliest of the other four surviving operas is *I tre desideri o sia il taglialegna* (The three wishes, or the woodcutter) of 1794, an intermezzo by Somigli adapted from a French play. The libretto gives the opera's opening as "carnival 1795."[21] The other three are *Il finto medico per amore*

---

[16] The operas at the Apollo were *La donna soldato*, to a libretto by Caterino Mazzolà, which opened 26 December 1816, and *Pulcinella* to a libretto by Jacopo Ferretti, performed during carnival 1817; and at the Teatro Argentina, *La Polissena*, which premiered 11 February 1817 and was replaced after one (according to the *Il corriere delle dame*) or two (according to the *Gazzetta musicale di Lipsia*) performances. In his diary, Prince Agostino Chigi described the opera as "molto cattiva."; excerpts are in Mario Rinaldi, *Due secoli di musica al Teatro Argentina* (Florence: Olschki, 1978), 532, 534-35. In *Alcune pagine della mia vita*, which he read to members of the Tiberina Academy in 1835, Jacopo Ferretti wrote: "In quell' anno medesimo [1817] scrissi una *Polissena* pel teatro de Argentina. La regalai per elemosina ad un maestro di cappella che s'ebbe 40 scudi per porla in musica. Il pubblico, conscio della mercede, si contentò di ridere modestamente in tutto il tempo che durò il canto, ma rispettò quello sventurato contrappuntista le cui melodiche ispirazioni partivano da una moglie digiuna e da cinque figli vestiti alla *sans culotte* che seco dormivano sulla paglia in una soffitta sopra assi di legno non mattonati. Regalai a quello stesso infelice una farsa pel teatro di Apollo di cui era impresario il comico Benferreri, celebre nei fasti degl' imbrogli teatrali. L'intitolai 'Pulcinella impresario' e ne scrissi la parte del protagonista in napolitano. La cantò il Tavassi, rinomato buffo bisceglese de teatro di San Carlino. Il maestro in undici rate ebbe in tutto dal Benferreri dieci scudi. Eva sapiente di contrappunto; le cantilene, però, le frasi, gli accompagnamenti risalivano a mode dotissime ma tarlate dal tempo. Anche per lui si verificò il post nubila Phoebus, perché gli morirono tre figli e passò maestro di cappella in Orvieto. Era il modello dell' onestà. Ricordomi di aver pianto a grosse lacrime quando dopo essermi arrampicato per lunga scala di legno, mi sentii serrare il core trovando sul mattino quel disgraziato ravvolto nella buona memoria di un tabarro che scriveva a lume di veramente fioca e povera lucerna su d'una sfracassata spinetta che vantava meno corde di una ghitarra, e ne toccava leggerissimamente i vedovi tasti per non destare la sua sconsolata Niobe e il quintetto elegiaco dei suoi Ugolini in erba. Aveva vegliata l'intera notte non bevendo che un gran fiasco d'acqua . . . simbolo forse d'altra vicina sventura, e consumando due once di stranutiglia. Dopo quello spettacolo che non lasciai di particolarizzare agli amici, s'avesse scritto un duetto a cinque parti reali e avesse cominciato un pezzo dalle cadenze avrei sempre giurato ch'era un miracolo. Fame! Cenci! Moglie digiuna! Cinque figli per copia conforme . . . Scrivete se vi da' l'animo la Cenerentola!" Quoted in Francesco Paolo Russo, ed., "Jacopo Ferretti, 'Alcune pagine della mia vita, Delle ricende della poesia melodrammatica in Roma, memoria seconda'," *Recercare* 8 (1996), 189.

[17] The performance, on 2 May 1820 at the Teatro Re, is listed in Franz Steiger, *Opernlexikon*, 2, no. 3: *Komponisten, N-Z* (Tutzing: Schneider, 1978), 966.

[18] Fabbri, "Incontro con Ferdinando Rutini," 201. It had not been established whether before his employment in Terracina, Rutini was active in both Orvieto and Aquapendente, or Ferretti (see n. 16) was mistaken.

[19] The title page on the score is *Le Finte Pazzie o Sia La Pupilla bizzarra Del Sig[no]re Rutini Rappresentata in Firenze nel R[eal]e Teatro di via d[e]l Cocomero Nel l'Autunno 1794*. The complete title as it appears in the libretto (in Bologna, Biblioteca Civico Museo Bibliografico Musicale, 32 pp.) is: *LE FINTE PAZZIE O SIA LA PUPILLA BIZZARRA. INTERMEZZO IN DUE ATTI Da Rappresentarsi nel Regio Teatro di via del Cocomero nell'Autunno dell'Anno 1794. SOTTO LA PROTEZIONE DELL'A. R. IL SERENISSIMO FERDINANDO III Principe Reale d'Ungheria e di Boemia Arciduca d'Austria Gran-Duca di Toscana. FIRENZE MDCCXCIV. Nella Stamperia di Ant. Gius. Pagani, e Comp. Con Approvazione.* On the history of the score, see below.

[20] The title page of the score is *La Dama Giardiniera 1791 Rutini farsetta in 1 atto alla francese poesia Sig[no]re Dom[eni]co Somigli fiorentino. La Dama Giardiniera. Farsetta in un Atto Alla Francese. Musica del Sig[or]re M[aest]ro Ferdinando Rutini, Eseguita in Firenze nel Regio Teatro degli Arrischiati, Posto sulla Piazza Vecchia Di S[an]ta Maria Novella L'anno 1791.* Based on notices in the *Gazzetta toscana*, *L'Osservatrice fiorentina*, and (for a later performance) *Indice de' spettacoli teatrali*, Weaver and Weaver identify Somigli as the librettist. Excerpts from the local press are in *Chronology*, 637, 662.

[21] The work is designated an intermezzo on the title page of the score, but is called a farce on the title page of the libretto. The title page of the score reads: *I tre desiderij o sia il taglia legna. Intermezzo d'un sol atto. Musica di Ferd[inand]o Rutini. Rappresentato per la prima volta in Firenze nel teatro posto in Borgo Ognisanti la sera di 26 Xbre 1794*. The libretto (1 act, 19 pp.) gives the librettist as "Domenico Somigli fra gl'Arcadi Lisindo Teresiano": *I Tre desideri o sia il Taglialegna. Farsa nuova di un atto in prosa, e in musica alla francese da rappresentarsi in Firenze nel Teatro di*

(The feigned doctor of love), an intermezzo by Somigli of 1796;[22] *Lo sposo per oracolo* (The bridegroom by decree), a farce of 1796;[23] and *La principessa pescatrice* (The princess fisherwoman), an intermezzo that probably dates from 1797, though the score is undated. This last, with chorus, is probably the work referred to as *La pescatrice fortunata* in the *Indice de' spettacoli teatrali*, which calls it a *dramma giocoso* and mentions the "musica nuova con cori."[24]

Each of the six opera scores survives in a single full-score manuscript copy. Figure 15.2, the title page of the *Le finte pazzie* score, shows the hand of the principal scribe, as yet unidentified. The scores tend not to be paginated: in some instances there are insertions of a few alternative scenes, and in other instances there are character and dialogue

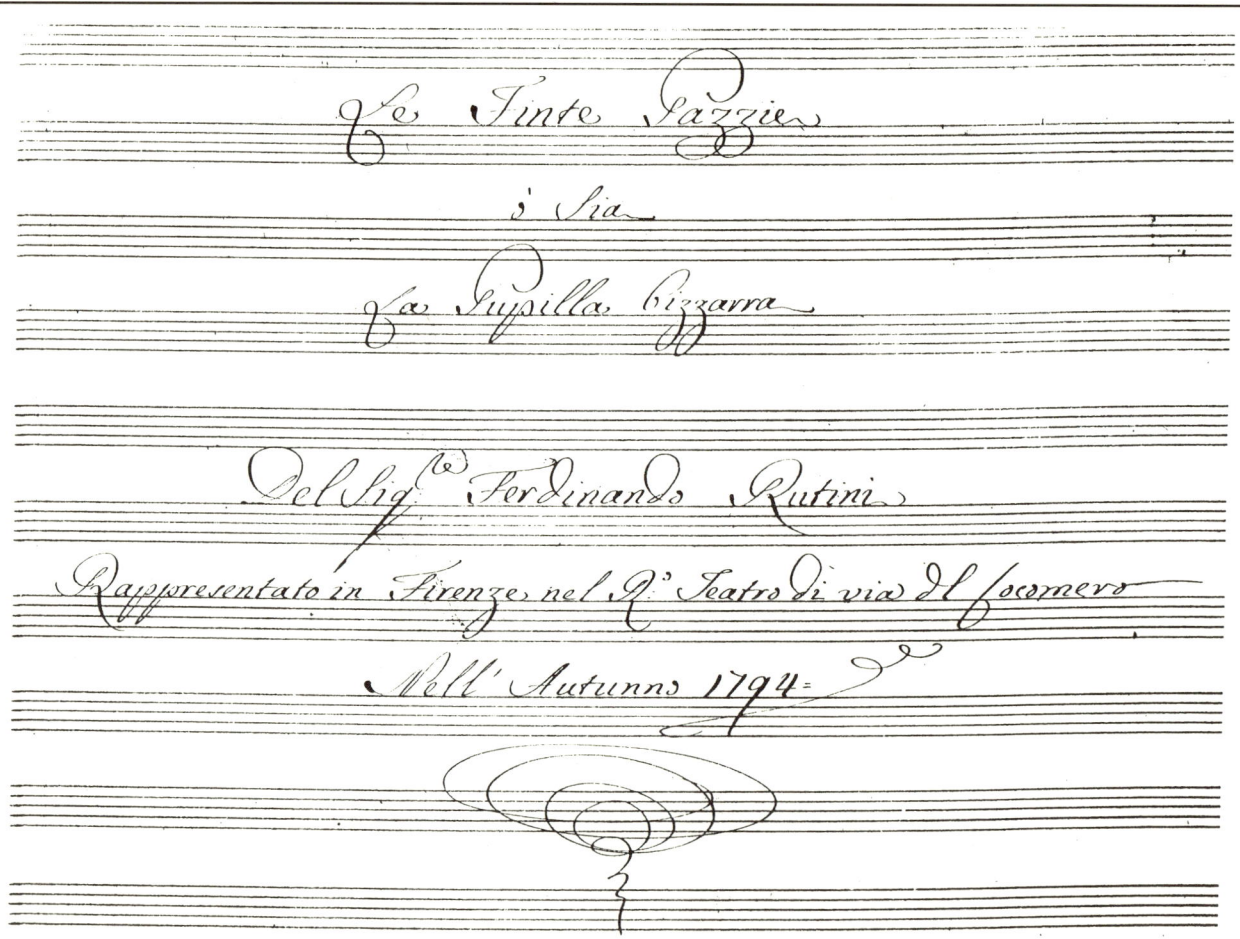

Fig. 15.2. Title page of manuscript score of Rutini's *Le finte pazzie*
(Dwight D. Anderson Music Library, University of Louisville)

Borgo Ognissanti il carnevale del 1795. Firenze, Stamperia gia Albizziniana, MDCCXCIV. The libretto is in the Biblioteca Nazionale Centrale, Rome; a manuscript copy is in the music section of the Bibliothèque Nationale, Paris. This second exemplar gives an added cover page titled "Il Taglialegni [*sic*] a Farsa in Prosa e in Musica del Rinnomato Maes[tr]o Rutini" and the added notation" = G.B," evidently a mistaken attribution to Giovanni Marco Rutini. Weaver and Weaver, *Chronology*, 712-13, suggest that the opera is a translation of Jean-François Guichard's *Le Bûcheron ou les trois souhaits*.

[22] The title page on the score is *Carnevale 1796 nell Regio Teatro della Piazza Vecchia Di S. Maria Novella Intermezzo a 6 voci Il Finto Medico per Amore Del Sig*[no]*r Ferdinando Rutini*. Weaver and Weaver, *Chronology*, 731, give the premiere as 27 December 1795, and the title as *Il finto medico per amore, intermezzo a 6. voci. Un atto, 16 scene, poesia di Domenico Somigli, rappresentato Carnevale 1796 nell' Regio Teatro della Piazza di S. Maria Novella.*

[23] *Lo sposo per oracolo, farsa per musica, Due parti, 19 scene.* Weaver and Weaver, *Chronology*, 733 (based on the *Indice de' spettacoli teatrali*, 45), report only one performance during carnival at the Piazza Vecchia.

[24] *La principessa pescatrice intermezzo di un solo atto Musica di Sig*[no]*re Ferdinando Rutini*. According to Weaver and Weaver, *Chronology*, 753, the score was copied by the same hand that copied Neri-Bondi's *Gli artigiani* (1798), and has identical watermarks. They further report common watermarks for the Rutini scores of *Il finto medico* and *Lo sposo per oracolo*.

Fig. 15.3. Title page of the libretto of *Le finte pazzie*
(Bologna, Biblioteca Civico Museo Bibliografico Musicale)

changes. The librettos were published separately by Pagani in Florence, though for these six scores only the librettos to *Le finte pazzie* (fig. 15.3) and *I tre desideri* have thus far been found. Stage directions are present only in the librettos.

Rutini's operas, like other Italian comic operas in this period, are remarkably similar in content and style. Five are intermezzos scored for five or six singers, with accompaniment by strings, pairs of oboes (or flutes) and horns, and continuo.[25] The continuo (basso line in the full score) is without figures. Both *La dama giardiniera* and *La principessa pescatrice* add chorus. Rutini's musical language is pale in comparison with Mozart's and Cherubini's, and, like that of his compatriots working in Italy, is generally conservative for the 1790s. The melodies are attractive. Rutini relies

---

[25] The usual instrumentation was 4 violins, 2 violas, 1 cello, 1 bass, 2 oboes (or flutes), 2 horns, and cembalo.

mainly on the strings (occasionally on oboes or flutes) for independent orchestral motives, supported by sustained chords in the oboes and horns. Introductory and closing ritornellos typically last a few measures, with striking obbligato parts present in key scenes. Between the voices there is little contrapuntal exchange, though in the introductions, central ensembles, and finales the voices work up to fugal discourse toward the end of the movement. In this, Rutini conforms to established theatrical practices, for, as the theorist Francesco Galeazzi remarked, " [in] the eccelesiastical [style] . . . it suffices to be an excellent contrapuntist . . . but in theatrical [style] the most able contrapuntist often . . . attracts the loudest whistles."[26] The manner of alternating solo and tutti material is also characteristic—soloists engaging in dialogue, to which the others, in homophony, react in tutti responses. Rutini's harmonic pallette is not colorful: his arias and ensemble numbers, like those of his contemporaries, are almost exclusively anchored in major keys, with the occasional exception of a cantabile lament of the heroine. Judging from the comments in the *Gazzetta toscana* and the *Osservatrice fiorentina*, Florentine audiences, like audiences throughout Italy, found the relatively unfluctuating diatonicism pleasing to their ears,[27] the critics labeling his a 'delicate harmony' ("una sensibile armonia") or an 'attractive' harmony ("gli intendenti non cessano di ammirare le armoniche bellezze").[28] A review written at the height of his popularity in 1797 pronounced his music more pleasurable to listen to than that of his contemporaries on three accounts: "an alluring harmony, a newness that is pleasing, and a liveliness (*brio*) that seduces" ("Quest'ultimo poi è stato superiormente agli altri sentito con piacere, poichè trovasi in esso un'armonia che alletta, una novità che piace, ed un brio che allegra").[29] The lively tone of the Rutini and Rutini/Somigli operas was also seized upon in reviews of his successful *Il matrimonio per industria* (1792) and after the opening performance of *Le finte pazzie*.[30] This quality of "brio che allegra" will receive our attention shortly, for it surely refers above all to that combination of dramatic and musical pacing, and varieties of comic invention by which these operas charm.

Le finte pazzie o sia La pupilla bizzarra

The full score manuscript copy of *Le finte pazzie* was acquired by the University of Louisville from Professor Antonello Palazzolo of Siena in 1993.[31] The history of the manuscript is not known. Palazzolo told Robert Weaver

---

[26] *Elementi teorico-pratici di musica*, vol. 2, no. 2 (Rome, 1796): "Lo stile Teatrale è quasi diametralmente opposto all'Ecclesiastico, in quanto che in questo basta esser eccellente Contrappuntista tutto è fatto, ma nel Teatrale il più valente Contrappuntista spesso non sa nulla, e si attrae dal Popolo le più sonore fischiate," as translated in Gregory W. Harwood, "Francesco Galeazzi's *Elementi teorico-pratico di musica*, Part Four, Section Two: An Annotated Translation and Commentary" (M.A. thesis, Brigham Young University, 1980), 140. Works by Cimarosa and Paisiello do not exhibit a greater degree of contrapuntal complexity: among other recent studies, see Friedrich Lippmann, "Il 'grande Finale' nell' opera buffa e nell' opera seria: Paisiello e Rossini," *Rivista italiana di musicologia* 27 (1992): 225-56; Lippmann, "Mozart und Cimarosa," *Die frühdeutsche Oper* (1981): 187-202; Francesco Blanchetti, "Tipologia musicale dei concertati nell'opera buffa di Giovanni Paisiello," *Rivista italiana di musicologia* 19 (1984): 234-60; Sabine Henze-Dohring, "La technica del concertato in Paisiello e Rossini," *Nuova rivista musicale italina* 1 (1988): 1-23; and Gordana Lazarevich, "Transformation of an Intermezzo: Cimarosa's *Il Pittor Parigiana* as a Reflection of 18th-Century Operatic Performance Practices," in *Napoli e il teatro musicale in europa tra sette e ottocento: Studi in onore di Friedrich Lippmann*, ed. Bianca Maria Antolini and Wolfgang Witzenmann, Quaderni della Rivista italiana di musicologia, 28 (Florence: Olschki, 1993), 175-89.

[27] André Grétry, for one, voiced criticism of his Italian opera contemporaries: "One finds little harmony since they do not know how to modulate." See "Reflections on Music (1789)," translated by Ulrich Weisstein from Grétry's *Mémoires ou Essais sur la musique* (Paris, 1812), in *The Essence of Opera*, ed. Weisstein (New York: Norton, 1964), 156.

[28] Writing about the premiere of *Il Matrimonio per industra* at the Pergola in 1792, the *Gazzetta universale* (February 1792), 367 (excerpt in Weaver and Weaver, *Chronology*, 668) states: "La musica tutta nuova è del nostro Concittadino Sig. Maestro Ferdinando Rutini, quale ha mostrato un brio, e buon gusto non comune, per cui riscosse un sincero universale gradimento, non tanto per la novità, quanto ancora per aver ritrovato in essa una sensibile armonia, e sodezza di contrappunto, specialmente nell'applaudito quintetto. . . ." About *Bellezza, ed onestà, ossia La villanella nobile*, the *Gazzetta toscana* (1794), 22 (excerpt in ibid., 698), noted: "il nuovo Intermezzo, posto in musica dall'abile Maestro Sig. Ferdinando Rutini, ha riscosso i più vivi applausi dagli affollati Spettatori e gl'Intendenti non cessano di ammirarvi le armoniche bellezze, ed il buon gusto del prelodato Sig. Rutini. . . ."

[29] The review was in regard to Rutini's *Il gazzetiere Olandese*: see *Gazzetta toscana* (1797), 13; excerpt transcribed in Weaver and Weaver, *Chronology*, 751.

[30] The comment is transcribed above in n. 28.

[31] The manuscript is housed with the collection of late eighteenth-early nineteenth century music that belonged to the private library of the Florentine family of Cavaliere Priore Pietro Leopoldo Ricasoli (1778-1850) and his wife, Lucrezia (1779-1827). The collection, comprising

he had received the score from a farmer, who had found it in his barn shortly after the end of World War II. The copyist is unknown, though the same hand prepared the full score of other Rutini buffa operas. The score is in two volumes (one for each act), of 134 and 139 folios, respectively. The folios measure 20 cm. x 27 cm., and comprise ten staves. A few folios are blank. Foliation in pencil has been added. Each volume is bound in cardboard covered with blue paper. As already mentioned, the libretto was published separately by Anton-Giuseppe Pagani of Florence, but without identification of the librettist. The texts in the full score and libretto are identical, but stage directions appear only in the libretto.

The opera premiered on 7 September 1794 at the Cocomero Theater. The five actor/singers in the cast were members of the resident company, the Compagnia Nazionale, directed by Pietro Andolfati, an actor and playwright, who also served as the theater's impresario between 1785 and 1795. During his years as impresario, Andolfati favored the performance of comic operas by Tuscan composers. He also translated French farces into Italian—many, it can be assumed, adapted for production at the Cocomero— others were for theaters in Milan and Venice. The orchestra probably consisted of four violins, two violas, two oboes, two horns, one cello, one double bass, and cembalo.[32] *Le finte pazzie* garnered unusually high praise from the *Gazzetta toscana* and the *Gazzetta universale*, which both reported:

> . . . with total pleasure was heard an intermezzo in two acts entitled *Le finte pazzie*, the poetry very entertaining and comical, and music entirely new by our young citizen Signor Ferdinando Rutini. Though this was not the first display of his by now recognized skill, that notwithstanding, this time, having composed a piece experts compliment for technique, attractive style, expression, and a harmony that invariably pleases, he has surpassed himself. The public, not failing to applaud with enthusiasm from the beginning to the end, delivered its due to the true worthiness [of the work]. The actors executed their respective parts with zeal and they received well-deserved applause for that. Let us hope to have frequent opportunities to hear other works of the aforesaid Signor Rutini, who brings honor to himself and his native land. . . .[33]

The plot of *Le finte pazzie,* in large measure typical of an intermezzo buffo, begins in the first act with Ernesto (tenor), a poor, young student, and his servant Carrucola (bass), who are looking for Lindora (soprano), the young beloved of Ernesto. She is being held prisoner at the secluded residence of her elderly guardian, the bachelor Don Fracastoro (bass), who, of course has firm intentions of marrying her himself. Also part of his household is the servant girl Lisetta (soprano), who is the beloved of Carrucola. Without revealing their identities, Ernesto and Carrucola gain entry to Don Fracastoro's residence and conspire with Lindora and Lisetta to help them escape. The young people prepare a diversion. Lindora will pretend to go insane, and the others will then insist that Don Fracastoro bring in a doctor. In act 2 Carrucola, disguised as the doctor and mouthing pidgeon Latin, arrives to cure Lindora,

---

450 manuscripts and prints, was saved from dispersal by Robert Weaver, and is 93% complete. A catalogue of the Ricasoli Collection and other manuscripts from the period acquired in the last few years by the University of Louisville Music Library, by Caterina Pampaloni and Robert Weaver, is in preparation.

[32] According to the libretto, the actors were Luisa Granati—Lindora; Giovacchino Bellandi—Ernesto; Filippo Fortunati—Don Fracastoro; Antonio Parlamagni— Carrucola; Maria Bellandi—Lisetta. The libretto does not name the complete roster of instrumentalists. On Andolfati, see Pietro Andolfati, in *Il Teatro moderno applaudito*, vol. 2 (Venice, 1796), cited in Gérard Peri, "'Nina, ossia la pazza per amore,' tra 'comédie Larmoyante' francese e opera romantica italiana," in *L'opera tra Venezia e Parigi*, ed. Maria Teresa Muraro, Studi di Musica Veneta, 14 (Florence: Olschki, 1988), 59-60; also see the *Dizionario biografico degli italiani* (Rome: Istituto della Enciclopedia Italiana, 1961), s.v. "Andolfati," by G. De Caro; and Weaver and Weaver, *Chronology*, 55.

[33] *Gazzetta toscana*, no. 37 (13 September 1794): 145: ". . . con universale piacere fu sentito un intermezzo in due Atti intitolato *Le Finte Pazzie*, Poesia molto piacevole e bizzarra, e Musica tutta nuova del nostro Giovine Concittadino Sig. Ferdinando Rutini. Quantunque questo non sia il primo Saggio della sua già conosciuta abilità, ciò non ostante questa volta ha superato se stesso, avendo composta una Musica, in cui i veri Intendenti ammirano Scienza, buon gusto, espressione, e un'armonia sempre dilettevole. Il Pubblico rese giustizia al vero merito non cessando d'applaudirlo con trasporto dal principio fino alla fine. Gli Attori tutti eseguirono con impegno le loro respettive parti, e ne riscossero i meritati applausi. Ci auguriamo avere spesso occasioni di poter sentire altre produzioni del suddetto Sig. Rutini, il quale fa onore a se e alla sua Patria, produttrice in ogni tempo di genj per le Bell'Arti." Transcription in Weaver and Weaver, *Chronology*, 708-09; the same review is partially given in the *Gazzetta universale*, 1794. Also see the *Gazzetta toscana*, no. 39 (27 September 1794): 153: "Parimene nel R. Teatro di via del Cocomero ottengono sempre un'favorevole incontro gl' Intermezzi del Sig. Maestro Ferdinando Rutini."

and after seeing her, tells Don Fracastoro that her case is very difficult and a magician should certainly be consulted. The group has a seance, convincing Don Fracastoro that the magician is present among them, then Lindora pretends to return to her senses. Don Fracastoro summons his courage and asks her for her hand in marriage; she is not in the least interested, but he is not someone to be dissuaded. Thus the young people must without delay come up with a plan. Ernesto and Carrucola tell Don Fracastoro that both he and Ernesto should marry in one ceremony, but should follow the ancient custom of the region which calls for the two women (Lindora and Lisetta) to be completely veiled. Thinking he will be marrying Lindora, Don Fracastoro agrees, but after the vows have been taken and the veils removed, he has of course been tricked: it is Ernesto who has married Lindora. Don Fracastoro wants to have their marriage annulled, but the others convince him it is by then too late. The intermezzo ends with all five characters singing praises to the newlyweds.

In formal structure *Le finte pazzie* adheres to the conventions of the period. The *introduzione* and the séance scene (act 2, scene 3) are composed for quartet. Portions of Lindora's first insanity scene (act 1, scene 8) utilize four voices as well. There are three duets, one for the lovers (act 1, scene 4), one for the young men (act 1, scene 11) and one for Lindora and her guardian (act 2, scene 8). And both finales are quintets (see table 15.1).[34]

Table 15.1.
Inventory of Scenes in Rutini's *Le finte pazzie o sia la pupilla bizzarra*

Characters: Lindora — S; Lisetta — S; Ernesto — T; Carrucola — B; Don Fracastoro — B
Orchestra: vl 1-2, ob 1-2, fl 1-2, hn 1-2, vla 1-2, b

Act 1

Overture (Largo-Allegro, 4/4, C Major)

scene 1	*Introduzione* "Che luogo solitario" (Largo, 3/4, F major — Allegro vivace, 4/4 — Largo, 3/4, E♭ major — Allegro, 4/4 — Allegro molto, 2/4, F major) — Ernesto, Carrucola, Don Fracastoro, Lindora
	Recitative — Ernesto, Don Fracastoro, Carrucola, Lisetta
	Aria "Sognai che un cacciatore vecchiaccio" (Andante grazioso, 2/4, A major) — Lisetta
scene 2	Recitative "Ma senta in questo sogno" — Don Fracastoro, Carrucola, Ernesto
scene 3	Recitative "Eppur Signor Tutore" — Ernesto, Carrucola
scene 4	Recitative "Ma che miro! Vien quà l'idolo amato" — Ernesto
	Duet "Nel rivederti o cara" (Larghetto, 4/4, B♭ major) — Ernesto and Lindora
scene 5	Recitative "Voi siete uno sguaiato" — Don Fracastoro, Ernesto, Lindora
scene 6	Recitative "Evviva finalmente ho trovato l'alloggio" — Carrucola, Don Fracastoro
scene 7	Recitative "Oh che terrore!" — Lisetta, Carrucola, Don Fracastoro, Ernesto
scene 8	Recitative "Olà fermate" — Lindora, Don Fracastoro, Ernesto, Carrucola
	Obbligato recitative "Numi che sento!" (Allegro, 4/4) — Lindora
	Cavatina "Ombra tremenda, e cara" (Largo, 4/4, E♭ major) — Lindora
	Aria "Superba di me stessa" (Maestoso, 4/4, C major — Larghetto, 3/4, E♭ major — Allegretto, 6/8, C major) — Lindora
scene 9	Recitative "Vedesti! Oh donne" — Ernesto, Carrucola, Lisetta
	°Cavatina "Sul più bello del mio sposalizio" (Andante, 6/8, G major) — Don Fracastoro
scene 10	Recitative "Ma venga Signorina" — Don Fracastoro, Lisetta, Ernesto

° = in libretto part of next scene

---

[34] In Rutini's later comic operas the number of ensemble scenes and the degree of concerted writing do not increase, though the operas are mainly scored for six voices. The majority of the later operas are also in only one act. Thus *Il finto medico per amore* of 1796 has a sextet for the finale, there is one quartet, a trio for the introduzione, and only one duet, that for the lovers. The chorus plays a substantial role in

Table 15.1—*Continued*

scene 11	Recitative "Carrucola in te spero" — Ernesto, Carrucola
	Duet "All'armi con donne?" (Andante maestoso, 2/4, E major) — Carrucola and Ernesto
scene 12	Recitative "Ma propriamente quì non v'è criterio!" — Don Fracastoro, Lindora, Carrucola, Ernesto, Lisetta
	Finale "Prendo Oresto" (Maestoso, 3/4, D major — Allegro molto, 2/4, A major — [Allegro molto] 6/8, F major — Andante sostenuto, 4/4, D major — Allegro assai, 2/4, D major) — Lindora, Lisetta, Ernesto, Carrucola, Don Fracastoro

Act 2

scene 1	Recitative "Se l'idea di Carrucola" — Ernesto, Don Fracastoro
scene 2	Recitative "Salvete Dominorum" — Carrucola as doctor, Don Fracastoro, Ernesto, Lisetta
scene 3	Recitative "A che riduce Amore" — Lindora, Don Fracastoro, Carrucola, Ernesto
	Quartet "Vieni, vieni, o gran Sabino" (Larghetto, 6/8, F major — Allegro, 4/4 — Largo 4/4 — Andante assai, 4/4 — Allegro molto, 2/4) — Don Fracastoro, Carrucola, Ernesto, Lindora
scene 4	Recitative "Non si può ritrovare in verità — Lisetta
	Aria "Quando, quando è d'accordo amore" (Andante, 2/4, G major) — Lisetta
scene 5	Recitative "Oh questa veramente è stata bella" — Lindora, Lisetta, Carrucola
	Aria "E la donna in singolare una cosa deliziosa" (Allegro moderato, 4/4, D major — Larghetto, 3/4, G major — Allegro assai, 4/4, D major) — Carrucola
scene 6	Recitative "Evviva il mio Carrucola" — Lisetta, Lindora, Don Fracastoro
scene 7	Recitative "Devotissimo" — Carrucola, Don Fracastoro, Lindora, Ernesto
	Obbligato Recitative "Oh Dio! Da quale orrore" (Agitato, 4/4 — Lento — Adagio) — Ernesto
	Aria "Finor da tetro orrore" (Maestoso, 4/4, E♭ major — Allegro molto, 4/4) — Ernesto
scene 8	Recitative "Ma che ti par' guarito?" — Don Fracastoro, Lindora
	Duet "Per te mi apri nel cuore" (Andante, 2/4, F major — Largo, 3/4 — Allegro, 2/4 — Allegro, 6/8) — Don Fracastoro and Lindora
scene 9	Recitative "In somma questi amanti" — Lisetta, Carrucola
scene 10**	Recitative "Oh forte ria" — Lindora, Carrucola, Lisetta
scene 11**	Recitative "Eppur il gran Tutore sarà burlato" — Lisetta, Carrucola, Ernesto, Don Fracastoro
scene 12**	Recitative "Lisetta non v'è più!" — Lindora, Don Fracastoro, Carrucola, Ernesto
	Obbligato Recitative "Vi scuso" (Andante, 4/4 — Allegro, 4/4 — Adagio, 4/4) — Lindora
	Rondò "Sia fedele il mio diletto" (Larghetto, 2/4, A major — Allegro vivace, 2/4) — Lindora
scene 13**	Recitative "Ordisco un altra frode" — Ernesto, Carrucola
scene 14**	Recitative "Oh questa se la crede l'è badiale!" — Don Fracastoro, Ernesto, Carrucola
scene 15**	Recitative "Dei matti n'avrò visti" — Carrucola, Ernesto
	Finale "Già l'ora è vicina dei nostri contenti" (Andante grazioso, 3/4, C major — Andante molto, 4/4, F major — Sostenuto, 3/4, F major — Allegro, 6/8, C major — Allegro moderato, 2/4, G major — Andante grazioso, C major — Allegro, 2/4 — Allegro molto, 6/8 — Più stretto) — Lindora, Lisetta, Ernesto, Carrucola, Don Fracastoro

** = in libretto part of preceding scene

La principessa pescatrice (probably 1797): the finale is a septet with chorus, the introduzione is a quartet with chorus, and the aria for the heroine adds chorus. There is also a second quartet, and a second duet. Cimarosa's popular *Il matrimonio segreto*, performed in Florence in 1793, 1794, and again in 1797, utilizes more ensembles: four duets, three trios, one quartet, one quintet, and sextets in each of the finales.

Allusions in *Le finte pazzie*

Le finte pazzie at times exhibits a sophistication that moves the opera beyond the level of merely delivering farcical banter in stereotypical musical numbers. Two scenes in particular—Lindora's two scenes of pretended insanity—are notable for their molding of language rich in imagery to music and dramatic action. In these, opera seria texts and classical allusions are introduced, undoubtedly with the intention of piquing the memories of the spectators, a large number of whom would have known the original texts and have taken pleasure in their parodistic recurrence. Lorenzo da Ponte was impressed by the literary inclinations of the Florentines he met when he visited the city in 1798: "What struck me above all was the manner of 'conversation' practiced," he recalled in his memoirs. "The principal topic [in the *salon*] was literature. Every evening there were readings of poetry, learned papers, essays in light vein, and two or three times a week, comedies, or tragedies, the parts for men and women being assigned by lot." The readings were from works by classical and living authors, and included Vittorio Alfieri's *Saul*, whose readers on that occasion, he noted, had all been Alfieri's pupils.[35] That upper-class Florentines in the 1790s would have recognized the allusions to opera seria in opera buffa is also extremely likely. As a French official wrote: "They get up at midday, usually have lunch at two o'clock, then take a siesta until six when they dress in order to drive out in their carriages to the Cascine Park. Then to the theater from nine o'clock till eleven and so home to supper and bed. This is what they do invariably from the first day of the year to the last."[36] If he is taken at his word, these indulgent Florentines saw every seria (and buffa) opera that played. The remainder of the essay will consider the context and use of such references and allusions in Lindora's scenes of pretended insanity (act 1 scene 8 and act 1 finale), as well as the opera's denouement (act 2 finale), with attention also to Rutini's adherence to convention, or his license, as well as his buffa techniques, including parody.

A large number of operas of the second half of the eighteenth century introduce at least one scene in which a character, for one reason or another, pretends to be someone else. Florence in these years saw the premieres of thirty-two operas with titles beginning "il finto" or "la finto": the feigned baronessa, contessa, cavaliere, servant, astronomer, doctor, chemist, singer, soldier, gardener, and so on.[37] Of special importance to our discussion are scenes involving feigned insanity. As is by now well documented, insanity scenes in opera seria dwelled on portrayals of the dementia, confusion, and even on the disorderly appearance, of the afflicted person. The most sensational opera of this type in the 1790s, playing to full houses in major cities throughout Europe, was the sentimental drama *La Nina o sia la pazzia per amore* (Nina, or the Love-Distressed Maid) in the reworked 1789 setting by Paisiello of the 1786 French creation of Benoit-Joseph Marsollier and Nicolas Delayrac. Paisiello's work, the Italian librettist Giuseppe Carpani claimed, had had all of Paris weeping. Its impact was such that, reportedly, at one performance in Naples in 1790 some viewers were so absorbed in Nina's circumstances they cried out to her on stage, attempting to give her comfort. When the opera opened in Florence in 1791 the *Osservatrice fiorentina* praised the choice of subject and the sensitivity and artistry involved in the handling of the material: "*La Nina, o La Pazza per Amore* at the Cocomero is a piece that will not fail to please anyone who knows the painful sensations that troubles of the heart cause the

---

[35] The passage in full is: "What struck me above all was the manner of 'conversation' practised by many of the most illustrious ladies in Florence. I was invited one evening to the *conversazione* of one of the leading matrons. To nobility of birth this lady coupled all the graces of a cultivated and natively superior mind. She was a widow, rich, young, beautiful. Her house was always open to foreigners of distinction, but along with these, and with princes, dukes and peers from all parts of the world, she received, feasted, and honored all people of talent, particularly poets, painters, sculptors, historians, physicians, lawyers and so on. There was music only once a week, saving special occasion, such as the first reception to some eminent musician. Dancing was permitted only once a month. Politics were rarely discussed; and cards were entirely banished. The principal topic of that assembly was literature. Every evening there were readings of poetry, learned papers, essays in light vein, and, two or three times a week, comedies, or tragedies, the parts for men and women being assigned by lot. Not being able to upset established custom, I was obliged to allow my name to be placed with the others in the urn, and it fell to me to read the part of Aristodemus in Monti's beautiful tragedy of that name. The second evening, I was invited to read some poetry of my own, and I delivered my dithyramb 'On Odors,' which seemed to be applauded. The third evening I listened with infinite delight to a reading of Alfieri's *Saul*. I was amazed. Yet there was nothing to be wondered at. All those who took part had been pupils of that great poet in declamation." *Memoirs of Lorenzo da Ponte*, trans. Elisabeth Abbott, ed. Arthur Livingston, rev. ed. (New York: Dover, 1959), 302-03.

[36] As translated in Christopher Hibbert, *Florence: The Biography of a City* (New York: Viking, 1993), 228.

[37] See the index of opera titles in Weaver and Weaver, *Chronology*, 951-52.

human psyche. The style is tender and charming, and the author's inventiveness is meritorious in knowing how to make the unhappy maid, the supposed death of whose lover made her lose her mind, return to sanity." In Venice the subject was so popular in 1793-94 that, in addition to Paisiello's opera—which had brought crowds streaming to the theater to applaud Angela Bruni in the title role—a play written by none other than Pietro Andolfati, the impresario of the Cocomero Theater in Florence, had managed without musical numbers, reportedly to move the audience to "an abundance of tears and very hearty applause" at every performance.[38]

The subject matter in *Nina* and other serious operas gave librettists and composers of comic opera, including Rutini, ample opportunity to parody the very disturbing elements that so fascinated the public. From a notice in the *Gazzetta toscana* we learn that Rutini made overt use of the technique. About a benefit concert in January 1795 for Antonio Parlamagni, one of the primo buffos of the Cocomero Theater, comes the comment that "a new duet that parodies the duet of *Elfrida*, executed by the said singer [Parlamagni] and the able prima buffa Sig[nora] Giacinta Big[g]i, expressly composed by Signor Ferdinando Rutini, was highly applauded."[39] Though the version of the Greek drama Rutini parodied is not identified, he was perhaps referring to the forthcoming Florentine staging of Paisiello's three-act tragic opera *L'Elfrida* (Naples, 1792), probably on Calzabigi's libretto. *L'Elfrida* opened at the Santa Maria Theater in August 1795. Several Paisiello operas, including his serious drama, *La Didone*, based on Metastasio's libretto, which opened in the month preceding *L'Elfrida*, and the extremely popular *Nina*, played in Florence in these years. Besides the performance in 1791, *Nina* was seen in 1793 and 1796, and was the subject of a ballet by Gaetano Gioja in 1798.[40]

First Scene of Pretended Insanity (act 1, scene 8): Lindora as Alcestis, Semiramis, and Pyrrhus

Lindora's first extended episode of insanity forms the central scene in the first act. In length the scene encompasses 212 measures. It serves to fool Don Fracastoro, bring the public to laughter at the absurdity of the happenings, and display the acting skill of the principal female singer, Luisa Granati. Although the scene is scored mainly for Lindora, it constitutes an ensemble of major dimensions on two accounts. The three male characters (Don Fracastoro, Ernesto, and Carrucola) are present; they contribute to the dialogue and stage action, and interject at one point in concerted tutti passages. In terms of the musical and the dramatic pacing, the scene produces an action chain, the momentum increasing with each new section until reaching its apex in the bravura final number. The buffa elements are central components in the success of the action chain. Scene 8 opens with this stage direction in the libretto:

> Lindora comes in bizarrely dressed as a prima donna, holding two sheets of music; behind her are her claque—that is, her servants holding her little dog (*suo cagnolino*), her little parasol (*suo ombrellino*), her parrot (*suo pappagallo*), and holding her train (*suo lungo strascico*).[41]

---

[38] For general discussion of types of parody, see Mary Hunter, "Some Representations of *opera seria* in *opera buffa*," *Cambridge Opera Journal* 3 (1993): 89-108. On the fascination with Paisiello's *La Nina* in these years, see Peri, 57-66, esp. 59-60, on the reaction of the Paris and Venetian audiences; and Stefano Castelvecchio, "From *Nina* to *Nina*: Psychodrama, Absorption and Sentiment in the 1780s," *Cambridge Opera Journal* 8 (1996): 91-112, esp. 101, for the report about the Naples performance in 1790. The comment in the *Osservatrice fiorentina* (1791): 122 (transcribed in Weaver and Weaver, *Chronology*, 636) is: "La *Nina*, o la Pazza per Amore del Cocomero è una Farsa ce piacerà sempre a chiunque conosce gli effetti dolorosi che producono sullo spirito umano i mali del core. Lo stile è tenero, e grazioso, ed è mirabile l'arte con cui l'autore à saputo fare ritorate [*sic*] alla ragione quell'infelice a cui la supposta morte dell'amante avea fatto perdere il cervello." On the Andolfati play, see *Il Teatro moderno applaudito*, vol. 2 (Venice, 1796): "Ma ben più celebre ancora rimarrà nella storia del teatro comico questa drammatica composizione, perché senza veruno degli accennati preziosi abbigliamenti musicali, colla sola veste della semplice natura, ogni qualvolta si rappresenta, sa strappare copiosissime lagrime e vivissimi applausi." Cited in Peri, 59-60.

[39] *Gazzetta toscana* (1795), 9; excerpt in Weaver and Weaver, *Chronology*, 713.

[40] The operas are listed as 1791[4], 1793[2], 1796[14], and the ballet as 1798[22], in Weaver and Weaver, *Chronology*. The ballet was complimented for its integration of chorus and dance; see the reviews of 17 and 24 November 1798 (in *Gazzetta toscana*, 181f., *Gazzetta universale*, 743f.; transcribed in Weaver and Weaver, *Chronology*, 788).

[41] "Lindora vestita bizzarramente da Cantatrice ec. con due carte di Musica in mano: dietro alcuni Servi con Canino, Ombrellino, Pappagallo ec. Un servo ridicolo che sempre li tien lo strascico, e detti"; see the libretto, p. 8.

The entire scene caricatures—in a delicious manner—the world of opera seria. It begins in recitative as Lindora first pretends to be Alcestis. It will be recalled that in Euripides' play King Admetus is dying when the oracle decrees he will be cured if someone will die in his place. To show her conjugal devotion, his wife Alcestis offers herself as the sacrifice. Gluck's tragic setting, *Alceste* was in fact mounted in Florence in 1786.[42] But in Rutini's comic scene, Lindora pretending to be Alcestis does not propose to die herself, but rather to kill her son. The dialogue is absurd and comical: Lindora: "S'ha da morir? Si, mora. Eccovi il figlio. Mangiatevelo in due . . . Numi consiglio" (There has to be a death? There will be a death. Here is my son. You eat him in two pieces. The gods advise it), to which Don Fracastoro responds "Il boccone è indigesto" (That morsel is indigestible). There are verbal allusions to music throughout the scene, a link with opera seria mad scenes in which such allusions are a not uncommon occurrence.[43] The stage directions call for Lindora to give one sheet of music to Don Fracastoro and the other (which hides a letter) to Ernesto. She speaks of making music, and at the moment of proclaiming "la, sol, fa, mi, re," spits on Don Fracastoro, making the excuse that a flat note was caught in her throat. The vocal line climbs to a B♮—not a flatted B—for the word "*bimmolle*" [*sic*] (flat), then rises to a (reiterated) C♯ and a D before falling to A, the last pitch further emphasized by the bass line an octave lower. The stage direction to "spit" is made clear by the libretto. Lindora's bawdy gesture gives way to two double entendres. First comes the response from Carrucola that her *music* (undoubtedly the action and sound of her spitting) is pleasing indeed. Then a little later in the recitative Carrucola proposes that they do a *fuga*, which Lindora, pretending to be a musician, claims is her "forte." But *fuga* seems also to be a double entendre, since the young people by their actions are preparing to take flight (*darsi alla fuga*) from Don Fracastoro's secluded estate.

In the obbligato recitative of twelve measures, allegro, that follows, "Numi che sento" ("Gods what do I hear"), the violins introduce agitated repeated sixteenth-note tremolos beginning with the exposition of tonic-dominant harmonies in the "grave and serious" E♭ major, followed by chromatic scalar motives and a brief excursion to C minor, Galeazzi's key for expressing ominous and lugubrious actions.[44] Experiencing "thunder, lightning, and darkness," Lindora utters "I see the ghost (*ombra*) of the irate Nino in nightdress." Here Rutini and his librettist seem to be making a pointed reference to the popular tragic melodrama of Alessio Prati, *La vendetta di Nino, ossia la morte di Semiramide*, to a libretto by Pietro Giovanini, staged in Florence in 1786, 1787, and 1791, and the source of a ballet in 1795; the libretto also returned in 1799 in a setting by Sebastiano Nasolini.

In the Giovanini/Prati setting of the Semiramis legend, Semiramis's murder of her husband Nino is bloodily avenged by their son Arsace, to whom she had planned an (unknowingly) incestuous marriage. Arsace's revenge is shown on stage in full view of the spectators. His action is guided by Nino's ghost. The subject was ripe for exploitation. By the mid 1780s the movement to stage violent murders and deaths had gained momentum, aided, as Marita McClymonds has shown, by the stance of the playwright Vittorio Alfieri, who renounced the contrived *liete fine* and called for murderous and suicidal actions to be seen. Alfieri resided in Florence between 1792 and his death in 1803. In Florence alone some sixteen ballets and operas mounted in the last two decades of the century begin with the fashionable title "morte"; several more works with other titles also featured violent on-stage death scenes. The Semiramis legend was singularly in vogue throughout Italy, used in twenty-seven settings between 1784 and 1800.[45]

---

[42] On Gluck's setting of the opera, see Daniel Heartz, *Haydn, Mozart, and the Viennese School, 1740-1780* (New York: Norton, 1995), 217-30. A ballet by Monari, entitled *La discesa d'Ercole nei campi elisi, o sia Admeto e Alceste*, was staged in Florence in 1783.

[43] See Paolo Fabbri, "On the Origins of an Operatic Topos: The Mad-Scene," in *Con che soavità: Studies in Italian Opera, Song, and Dance, 1580-1740*, ed. Iain Fenlon and Tim Carter (Oxford: Clarendon Press, 1995), 172-74, 179. On Salieri's use of musical references in *La finta scema*, see John A. Rice, "Comedy and Pathos in Salieri's *La finta scema*," in this volume.

[44] Galeazzi, *Elementi teorico-pratici di musica* [Rome, 1791-1796], ed. Harwood, 136-37: "E♭ è un tono eroico, maestoso all'estremo, grave, e serio"; "C . . . Il suo minore è un tono tragico, ed atto ad esprimere grandi disavventure, morti di Eroi, ed asioni grandi, ma luttose, funeste, e lugubri." On key symbolism for other composers, see Rita K. Steblin, *A History of Key Characteristics in the Eighteenth and Early Nineteenth Centuries* (Ann Arbor: UMI Research Press, 1983).

[45] Marita P. McClymonds, "'La morte di Semiramide ossia La vendetta di Nino' and the Restoration of Death and Tragedy to the Italian Operatic Stage in the 1780s and 90s," *Atti del XIV Congresso della Società Internazionale di Musicologia, Bologna 27 agosto-1 settembre 1990*, ed. Angelo Pompilio et al. (Turin: EDT, 1990), 285-92. For a recent contribution on Alfieri by McClymonds, see ch. 14 in the present volume. The ballets and operas staged in Florence beginning with death titles are: *La morte d'Agamenone* (1793), . . . *d'Attalia* (1783), *Oreste o sia la morte d'Egisto*

In Rutini's comic scene, at the point where Lindora pretends to see Nino's *ombra*, the stage directions instruct Carrucola to make an *ombra*, a shadow—another *double entendre*—in front of Don Fracastoro to allow the lovers to exchange notes (see fig. 15.4). The obbligato recitative gives way to declamatory recitative as Lindora continues, playing half the prima donna, half the comedienne: "He is beating his feet (she is instructed to cry). Ah, he makes a mess of it" ("Batte i piedi [piange]. Ah! S'è fatta la frittata.")

Fig. 15.4. Obbligato recitative "Numi che sento ecco tuona," from *Le finte pazzie* (ff. 62v-63v)

d'Egisto e Clitennestra (1793), . . . *D'Oloferne* (1795), . . . *Britannico* (1795), . . . *di Cesare* (1790), . . . *di Cleopatra* (1795 as an opera, 1797 as a ballet), . . . *di Clitemnestra* (1798), . . . *di Coriolano* (1781), . . . *di Mitridate* (1799), . . . *di Sansone* (1789, 1791), . . . *di emiramide* (1799), . . . *di Stenone* (1795). Others portraying murder and violence on stage include *Agamennone vendicato* (1780), *Giasone e Medea* (1785, 1800), *Il ratto delle Sabine* (1780), *Admeto e Alceste* (1782), *Vendetta di Nino* (1786 opera, 1795 ballet), *Vendetta di Medea* (1787, 1791). Weaver and Weaver, *Chronology*, 48-49, discuss earlier ballets of the 1770s by Antoine Pitrot treating themes of parricide and violence. On the history of the Semiramis legend, and comparison of the versions in the various librettos from 1593 to 1910, see Cesare Questa, *Semiramide Redenta* (Urbino: Edizioni Quattro Venti, 1989); on the libretto for the Prati version, see esp. pp. 47, 50, 156.

Fig. 15.5. Cavatina "Ombra tremenda, e cara del sopradetto Nino," from *Le finte pazzie* (score, ff. 64-67)

Lindora begins the ensuing cavatina of nineteen measures, "Ombra tremenda, e cara del sopradetto Nino" (Appalling and dear ghost of the aforesaid Nino), in E♭ major, largo, quoting verbatim two lines from the apparition scene in act 1, scene 11 of the Giovanini/Prati melodrama. In the melodrama it is Arsace who speaks the words "Ombra tremenda e cara, placa la smania amara; se il mio dolor non basta, dimmi che vuoi da me" ("Appalling and dear ghost, calm the bitter frenzy; if my suffering is not enough, tell me what you want from me"). And it is the ghost that throws him a message explaining Semiramis is his mother, who had his father, Nino, poisoned. In a later apparition scene Arsace is told to avenge his father's death and is given his father's sword to carry out the deed.

In Rutini's comic scene Lindora manages to get out the second line of the Giovanini/Prati text, "Placa la smania amara e . . .," when she is interrrupted by Ernesto and Carrucola in homorhythmic syllabic patter, who tell her to pass the note. Extending over four measures, the patter condenses the material through a not-uncommon buffa technique. Beginning in eighth notes in the tenor, the initial statement of the phrase "Lascia il bigliettino che poi si leggerà" ("Pass the note so that it can be read") takes up two measures. The second statement, the note values

Fig. 15.5.—Continued

having been halved to sixteenth notes shortly after the bass enters, is reduced to one measure. The third statement, primarily in dotted sixteenth and thirty-second notes whose chatter swells to *forte* as the orchestra also joins, also fills only one measure, as does the final statement, which emphatically repeats the second half of the instruction "che poi si leggerà, che poi si leggerà." The energetic patter effectively throws into relief the stage action of exchanging the note (see fig. 15.5, m. 6-10). The momentary interruption gives way to a contrasting allegro section (actually the second half of the cavatina), which returns the attention to Lindora's feigned madness. The fluctuation in the mood of her character is dramatized by the declamatory recitative and the striking harmonic movement away from the E♭ of the largo, with its connotations of night, to C major by way of B♭ (m. 8), G (m. 13), and C (m. 15), abandoned for F, in turn asserted as a dominant of C (m. 17) and then cadencing in that key via an auxillary diminished seventh. In the nine measures (m. 11-19) Semiramis's horror dissipates, and in her dream, while calling out to her maid servants, she progresses through a series of emotional states in rapid succession: from vile to love for Nino despite what she has done, to brief rumination on her resolve in removing him from the throne for her personal gain, to a

Table 15.2
Structural Outline of Lindora's aria "Superba di me stessa" (act 1, scene 8) of *Le finte pazzie*

Introduction		*Expository Section*					
tempo	maestoso ritornello					larghetto 3/4	
meter	C						
melodic material		1st group A	B			2nd group C	recit.
tonality	C (I)	C	G		modulatory	E♭	modulatory
text		"Superba di me stessa"	"Mia cara principessa"	"Io canto il me re do"		"Cara negli occhi tuoi"	"Ma chi s' avanza?"
meas.	1-19	20-31	32-45	46-60	61-63	64-69	70-73

final exultation of her action, the last coinciding with the close of the recitative passage within the cavatina in C major, in preparation for the bravura aria in the same key (fig. 15.5: "Tacete: già mi pare D'essere in soglio. Olà turchine Ancelle. Quell'empio, io l'amo ancora: Ma lo voglio vedere appiè del trono. Del Regno, e di quel cor l'arbitra io sono"; the aria begins "Superba di me stessa Andrò portando in fronte...," libretto, p. 10).

In Rutini's elongated scene other aspects of an opera seria ghost aria are parodied. Already in the obbligato recitative and the cavatina, Lindora, playing Semiramis, initially expresses horror, and a little grief, through some of the conventional devices—hesitation in the delivery of phrases, chromaticism, and trailing off into recitative at the end of both numbers. The interjections by the other characters would also be commonplace in such *seria* pieces. But the double entendres in the Rutini opera intensify the caricature: Lindora is not merely playing the part of the queen, she is also poking fun at old Don Fracastoro, and Ernesto and Carrucola are not in their interjections bemoaning her fate; rather, they are passing notes between the lovers.

Lindora begins the mock heroic aria "Superba di me stessa" (I am proud of myself) in a maestoso C major, Galeazzi's key for "expounding great events,"[46] though she loses her train of thought after completing the first two lines (see table 15.2). The long-held notes and wide leaps present in the melodic line are two further stereotypical traits of ghost arias. Rutini's masterful stroke at this highly dramatic point in the scene is to juxtapose dramatic with comic traits, within an expansive structural plan, creating an aria that is partly in opera seria bravura style, partly in buffa style. He retains the conventional buffa aria structure in two parts. The expository section (m. 1-73) relates the action; it comprises all lines of text except the last three, and undergoes modulation to a second key area. The second section (m. 74-134) is initiated with the reprise of the main key; in a faster tempo, it reintroduces text from the first part of the aria without the return of melodic ideas, and emphasizes the envoi of the final stanza (see table 15.2).

The aria begins with a ritornello of nineteen measures—long for Rutini—in which independent motives are introduced for two oboes and two horns. The second motive is a trumpet fanfare whose symbolism becomes apparent with the entrance of the voice. Lindora presents herself as the queen, boasting of the action that she herself will herald. Her entrance brings laughter despite the *maestoso* tempo, the voice jumping up a seventh with immediate dynamic contrast of *forte*, then *piano*, and with tremolos in the low strings (letter A in table 15.2, m. 20-31). After roulades for four measures ascending two octaves, and a fermata pause on the dominant—probably incorporating a short improvised cadenza—phrases in *parlato* follow (letter B, m. 32-45). As Lindora in her distraction thinks about her appearance ("My dear princess, what will I wear?"), her staccato phrases are short, two measures in length, separated by pauses—typical stock figures of the opera buffa style. Continuing in her role as queen in G major— for Galeazzi, a "cold and indifferent key"[47]—she instructs Don Fracastoro to carry one of her objects and Carrucola to adjust her train, and Ernesto to kiss her hand. Although she articulates the words "Addio Signor Soprano, I sing

---

[46] "C è tono grandioso, militare, atto ad esporre grandi avvenimenti, serio, maestoso, e di strepito"; in Harwood, ed., Galeazzi, *Elementi teorico-pratici*, 136.

[47] "G è tono innocente, semplice, freddo, indifferente, e di poco effetto"; ibid., 137.

Table 15.2—Continued

Section of Tonal Return							
allegretto	allegro				allegretto	(stretta)	final ritornello
6/8	C				6/8		
D	E				D	F	
C (I)					C (I)		C Major
"Ah non temete"	"Superba di me stessa"	"Cara principessa"	"Cara negli occhi tuoi"	"Ma chi s' avanza"	"Ah non temete"	"Burlarlo e mio piacere"	
(triumphant aside)		← repeats earlier text →				(restates envoi)	
74-80	81	85	91	99	102-09	110-23	123-34

the *mi re do*," she is not about to exit. The cadential motive "addio, addio, addio" (m. 43-45) is thrice repeated, another staple of *buffa* writing.

Again Rutini effectively expands and compresses musical and textual material, suitably varied. A melisma of chromatic sixteenth notes, ascending an octave, occurs on the first syllable of "canto," the entire phrase "canto il mi, re, do" filling up four measures. The same phrase is repeated with the coloratura on the first syllable lasting eight measures and encompassing the expanse from *b* to *a ́ ́*—one note short of two octaves. The third repetition of the phrase is given a third presentation: syllabic delivery that lasts but two measures (fig. 15.6, m. 46-64).

Since opera seria bravura arias usually present a contrasting section exhibiting a character's change in sentiment, Rutini's parody aria follows suit. He introduces the new section in E♭ (triple meter, *larghetto*), "Cara negli occhi tuoi" (Dear in your eyes), which, from the point of the dramatic structure, allows Lindora to address Ernesto: "With you I know how to flee" (letter C in table 15.2). She has, in fact, changed character and is now King Pyrrhus, the ruler of the Greek kingdom of Epirus. Her first two lines quote verbatim the text from Pyrrhus's rondò in Giovanni De Gamerra's seria libretto *Il Pirrò, re d'Epiro*, which was in fact mounted at the Pergola Theater in settings by Paisiello in 1791 and 1793, and by Zingarelli in 1792. The Zingarelli rondò was widely known through composer Václav Pichl's 1792 publication of variant ornamented versions sung by the renowned interpreter of the role, the castrato Luigi Marchesi. In Euripides's account in *Hecuba*, marriage between Pyrrhus and Polyxena of Troy is thwarted by a plot, and the oracle's decree that he avenge his father's murder with Trojan blood, though the oracle is reversed, just as Polyxena is about to die, so that her life is spared.[48] Rutini, after only three phrases of Pyrrhus's charming melody, with its triplet sixteenth-note accompaniment, writes fermata pauses to initiate a return to a modulatory passage whose shorter phrases, delivered in syllabic declamation, are punctuated during the pauses by orchestral motives (m. 69-73): "Ma chi s'avvanza? Quel vecchi?" (Who is coming? The old man?).

The acceleration of tension, both dramatically and musically, is evident in the tonal return section, which dovetails directly with the preceding expository section. This long subdivision of sixty measures, essentially in C major, has a conventional buffa aria profile, including a faster tempo. First is an *allegretto* in 6/8 comprising only seven measures (letter D in table 15.2, m. 74-80). The action has been completed, and Lindora emphasizes in an aside the message of the first half of the final stanza, "Ah non temete, burlerò è mio piacere" (Oh do not fear, ridiculing him is my pleasure). For the larger *allegro* segment in common time (letter E in table 15.2), Rutini adopts a loose return structure for the text, bringing back central thoughts without their melodic components, a conventional approach in *buffa* aria writing of the 1780s and 1790s.[49] The line of the opening quatrain, "Superba di me stessa," is heard, accompanied by pulsating tremolos in the strings and sustained chords in the oboes and horns (m. 81-87). After

---

[48] The Paisiello *Pirrò* had first been performed in Naples in 1787; on its Florentine performances, see Weaver and Weaver, *Chronology*, 651-53, 687-88. On the Zingarelli setting (Milan, 1791), see Will Crutchfield, "The Classical Era: Strings," in *Performance Practice: Music After 1600*, ed. Howard Mayer Brown and Stanley Sadie (New York: Norton, 1989), 304, and, for Florence, see Weaver and Weaver, *Chronology*, 666-67.

[49] On the opera buffa of the 1780s and 1790s, see John Platoff, "The Buffa Aria in Mozart's Vienna," *Cambridge Opera Journal* 2 (1990): 99-120.

Fig. 15.6. Aria "Superba di me stessa," meas. 46-64, from *Le finte pazzie* (score, ff. 73-75)

the buffa device of a fermata pause, Lindora begins the second quatrain, instructing Carrucola to adjust her train. But before continuing her instructions to the other two, she digresses instead to the opening line of the ensuing seven-line stanza "Cara negli occhi tuoi," which also receives a varied presentation (m. 91-93). Heightening the farcical element, earlier text phrases are now juxtaposed in short succession. The procedure does not build to *buffa* patter here, but to antiphonal alternation of vocal phrases and string motives: "Cara negl'occhi tuoi" (Dear in your eyes), then "Baciatemi la mano" (Kiss my hand), followed by "Con te saprò fuggire"(With you I know how to flee), then "Addio signor Soprano" (Goodbye signor Soprano), and finally, to halting dissonant recitative: "Ma chi s'avanza? Quel vecchio" (Who is coming? The old man)—(see fig. 15.7, m. 91-101).

The cheerful Allegretto in 6/8, anchored solidly in C major, returns, poking fun at Don Fracastoro, "Ah non temete" (Oh do not fear—letter D, m. 102-09), its first melodic phrase exactly as it appeared earlier in measures 74-80. The final portion (letter F, m. 110-23) appears not to initiate an acceleration in tempo, as might have happened

Fig. 15.7. Aria "Superba di me stessa," meas. 91-102, from *Le finte pazzie* (score, ff. 78v-79v)

Table 15.3
Structural Outline of the Act 1 Finale of *Le finte pazzie*

Recitative	FINALE Maestoso				Allegro molto				
	ritornello 3/4 D Major	solo entries L: "Prendo Oreste è qui lo metto"	solo- duet- trio tutti "Larà, larà"	solo DF: Guadate che spaventò"	2/4 A Major	solo DF: "Non posso"	trio- quintet tutti "Larà, larà" includes patter	Solo 6/8 F Major L: "Se questo finto errore"	Duet L & E: "Fuggite"
"Fate largo al ballo serio"									
Larà, larà" chassé"		DF: "Come un oca poveretto"			C: "Larà, larà"				
"Sor impre- sario mio la paga anticipato"		Lis: "Che stravaganza è questa?"			Lis" Lo fara poi straccar"				
"Son le furie d'Oreste"		(put DF on bed)	(dance around DF)		(DF pushed off bed; dancing intensifies)				
42 meas.	1-19	20-48	49-69	70-76	77-92	93-96	97-117	118-130	131-137

had Rutini written a stretta. Nonetheless, the momentum continues to build as the focus shifts to "Burlarlo è il mio piacere, e certo il burlerò" (Ridiculing him is my pleasure, and certainly I will poke fun at him). Both phrases are restated, with the repetitions coming in rapid succession, ending with the stock device of the triple repetition of the rhythmic-melodic cadential figure "il burlerò, il burlerò, il burlerò," the last statement *forte*, with full instrumentation.

Second Scene of Pretended Insanity (act 1 finale): Orestes' Furies

The finale to act 1, scene 12 continues the allusions to classical themes involving parricide, and also parodies aspects of opera seria, within a clearly laid out structural plan. Here (the libretto states) Lindora is dressed "as a ballerina with a pistol in her hand which she uses to menace Don Fracastoro, who is dressed as a ballerino from opera seria" (libretto, p. 13).[50] The stage directions reveal the dramatic action: Lindora insists he dance a *ballo serio*, threatening him with the pistol. In the recitative directly preceding the finale, she indicates she wishes to be paid in advance by her "impresario," to which Ernesto and Carrucola agree, and she continues bullying Don Fracastoro with the pistol until he gives up his purse. The purse is tossed to Carrucola, despite Fracastoro's feeble protests. Meanwhile Ernesto reminds them that they had been about to dance. Suddenly Lindora pretends to see Orestes's furies. Following the long opening ritornello of the finale, Lindora picks up old Don Fracastoro and throws him onto the bed, claiming she is taking Orestes and putting him to bed. To this Fracastoro complains that he is reduced to being the simpleton (literally, a poor goose), while the others dance around him so as not to awake Orestes. The possibility exists here that Rutini and his librettist were making a pointed reference to the five-act tragic ballet *Oreste o sia la morte d'Egisto e Clinnestra* [sic], composed and directed by the Florentine Francesco Clerici, which had been mounted at the Pergola Theater a few months earlier in the carnival season of 1793-94. In Euripides' play *Orestes*, it will be recalled, Orestes is pursued by the Furies, having gone mad after murdering his mother Clytemnestra, who had been haunted by the ghost of her husband Agamemnon, whose murder she had carried out with Aegisthus.[51]

---

[50] "Lindora da Ballerina con pistola in mano tenendo D. Fracastoro vestito in abito di Ballerino serio con cimiero ec. poi Ernesto, e Carrucola, indì Lisetta"; libretto, p. 13.

[51] The ballet was performed with the *dramma per musica*, *Margherita di Valdemar regina di Danimarca*, to music by various composers, during carnival in 1793-94; see Weaver and Weaver, *Chronology*, 693. In 1798 Moneta's opera *Oreste* played at the Pergola; see ibid., 787.

Table 15.3—Continued

	Andante sostenuto		Allegro assai						
Quintet tutti		Quintet tutti	ritornello	Quintet tutti	ritornello	tutti	ritornello	tutti	final ritornello
	4/4		2/4						
	D Major	"A che	D Major	"Che lieta	(same as	"Che lieta		"Che strana	D Major
"Larà, larà"	ritornello	delizia è		bizzarria"	opening of	bizzarria"		frenesia"	
		questa"+		+	allegro assai)	+		+	
					[stretta]				
		"Che confusione		"Che strano		"Che strana		"Il colpo è	
		è questa"		frenesia"		bizzarria"		fatto"	
				"Il colpo è					
				fatto"					
		"Larà, larà"		"Che torbida					
		(different		pazzia"+					
		texts)		"Che chiasso					
				che allegria"					
		(Ernesto gives		(repetition of					
		letter to Lindora)		texts)					
138-147	148-152	153-173	174-178	179-217	218-222	223-226	226-230	231-242	243-249

In outline the finales of both acts follow the procedures prescribed by Lorenzo da Ponte: the finale should be a comedy in itself; have no recitative, but various species of melody; present all singers in the cast in combinations of solos, duets, trios, quartets, quintets, and so on; have several tempo changes; and have an ending in a section of *strepitoso* and then *arcistrepitoso* with much noise and in an uproar with instruments, where, as Giambattista Lorenzi said, "all the actors sing the same words whether these are suitable to their characters or not," and Mozart said, that "the more noise the better, and the shorter the better, so that the audience may not have time to cool down with their applause."[52]

Despite a movement toward longer finales in comic opera, particularly for more elaborate *drammi giocosi*, the finales in Rutini's extant intermezzos remain in the realm of 200-300 measures. Music-making, specifically dancing, continues to be a subject at the end of the first act. In the recitative preceding the finale, the reference is to a *chassé*, a hunting dance. Here a double entendre is undoubtedly intended since the young people are pursuing Don Fracastoro in a vicious manner as if he were "a poor goose." In the finale proper the vaudeville principle is adopted, and thus the *ballo serio* becomes a recurring motive linking the various sections, forming part of all *tutti* responses that follow narrative or expressive solo and duet passages (see table 15.3). While Rutini does not give the horns or oboes a hunting motive, or even a prominent place in the scene, he does ensure that the *ballo*'s tempo accelerates by measure 77 to match the increase in the pace of the dramatic action. It is at this point, after Don Fracastoro sings alone of his fright ("Guardate lo spavento"), that Rutini abandons the tip-toe dancing in triple meter (D major, *maestoso*) for a brusque *allegro molto*. The modulation to "playful" A major coincides with the eye-catching stage action of Don Fracastoro being thrown off the bed and the dancing becoming animated.[53]

The general criticism of dances in Italian opera advanced by André Grétry, who called the tunes "usually pitiable, for they are neither dance tunes, nor singing tunes, nor harmonious"[54] is on the mark here. The scene relies essentially

---

[52] Lorenzo da Ponte, *An Extract from the Life of Lorenzo Da Ponte, with the History of Several Dramas Written by Him and Among Others, Il Figaro, Il Don Giovanni e La Scuola degli Amanti, Set to Music by Mozart* (New York, 1819), quoted in Daniel Heartz, "Constructing *Le nozze di Figaro*," *Journal of the Royal Musical Association* 112 (1987), 77-78, reprinted in his *Mozart's Operas* (Berkeley: University of California Press, 1990), 133-34; *Memoirs of Lorenzo Da Ponte* [1823], 59-60, preface to 1813 Naples edition of librettos of Giambattista Lorenzi, quoted in Michael Robinson, *Naples and Neapolitan Opera* (London: Clarendon Press, 1972), 203; letter of Mozart to Leopold Mozart, 26 September 1781 in *The Letters of Mozart and His Family*, trans. Emily Anderson, 3rd ed. (London: Macmillan, 1985), 770.

[53] Libretto, 14-15: "Ballano intorno a D. Fra.; fa saltare D. Fra." Galeazzi, *Elementi teorico-pratici di musica*, ed. Harwood, 137: "A è sommamente armonioso, espressivo, affettuoso, scherzevole, ridente, ed allegro."

[54] "Reflections on Music (1789)," in *The Essence of Opera*, ed. Weisstein, 156.

on slapstick for its momentum. While Rutini does not further increase the tempo, he extends the banal dancing with the unmelodious tune for forty measures, moving the last segment into continuous eighth-note patter by Carrucola in the bass against quarter notes from Lisetta and Don Fracastoro, and *forte-piano* swelled tremolos in the violins, giving way to all five voices in dotted-eighth and sixteenth-note patter, joined by the instruments.

Modulating to a key a third apart rather than continuing by the circle of fifths is a not infrequent procedure for underscoring the importance of a particular moment. Here in an expressive aside ("Se questo finto error," "If this feigned miscarriage of justice," m. 118), in a segment lacking tempo designation (F major, 6/8), Lindora reacts to the developments in the plot, communicating two thoughts: that the jesting of Don Fracastoro is making everyone laugh, and that women in love should flee before returning to their senses. Her legato line, with its graceful appoggiaturas, contrasts markedly with the preceding patter. The solo gives way to an equally brief duet with Ernesto about fleeing ("fuggite"), again followed by the dance motive "la, la, la larà" in all five voices.

An abrupt modulation to D major in measure 148, for Galeazzi "the most gay key music may have"[55] (*andante sostenuto*, common time), highlights the stage action of Ernesto passing a letter to Lindora. In a brief contrapuntal passage the young people sing contentedly while in the bass Carrucola continues the "larà larà" motive, and Don Fracastoro sings about how his own heart, from all the exertion, is beating "tarapatà, tarapatà." The addition of instruments and the *forte* dynamics over tonic-dominant and then dominant harmony accentuate the arrival of the closing section (m. 174), which, surprisingly, is not a stretta in a fast tempo, but an *allegro assai* initiated with a violin motive. The voices and instruments resound together "che liete bizzarria" (what happy wildness), except for Don Fracastoro, whose reaction is "che strana frenesia" (what a strange frenzy). The string motive is then brought back and the vocal parts break into varying combinations—from solo to duet, to solo, trio, solo, and on to contrapuntal quintet. No further stage action is called for in the libretto, or implied by the vocal utterances, a prescription for a stagnant ending. It is curious that Rutini does not heed Mozart's advice to make the ending short. Instead he repeats a large segment of the *allegro assai*, beginning with the opening string motive (m. 218-43), then closes rather lamely with a ritornello.

The Denouement (Act 2 Finale)

The second act finale is considerably more successful in dramatic and musical variety and pacing. Earlier in the act Lindora, appearing as an Amazon warrior, continues her intimidation of Don Fracastoro, this time with a sword, giving occasion for more buffoonery. Carrucola, disguised as a doctor, convinces Don Fracastoro that Lindora's insanity can only be cured by a magician. After the seance quintet involving the imaginary Sabino, in which Don Fracastoro is frightened and further menaced (essentially pushed while his eyes are closed), Lindora returns to her senses. With Don Fracastoro resolved to marry her, the young people put in place the plan to trick him during the marriage ceremony. The wedding scenario, with its materials for laughter and suspense, constitutes the sequence of events for the finale. There are no allusions to classical or seria texts.

The libretto gives only a few stage indications: the scene takes place outdoors, where two woodsheds (*capanni praticabili*) are situated, and into which Lindora and Lisetta enter.[56] From the dialogue it is clear Don Fracastoro is distracted—made to march like a sentry with Ernesto and Carrucola—and that the women change places. There is some jockeying, with adroit movements by Ernesto to mislead Don Fracastoro, as both men position themselves next to the women they think they will be marrying. The notary arrives and quickly conducts the ceremony. Although neither libretto nor score provides confirmation that only Lindora's and Ernesto's marriage has been notarized, it is a stock in trade of comic opera plots in this period that the old man ultimately remains the odd man out. Thus, the shock tutti of the discovery scene constitutes a reaction to the removal of the veils, and, presumably, to Don Fracastoro's realization that Ernesto has married Lindora, not Lisetta. Don Fracastoro's weak protests for annulment

---

[55] Galeazzi, *Elementi teorico-pratici di musica*, ed. Harwood, 137: "D è il Tono più allegro, e gajo che abbia la Musica: egli è strepitoso in sommo grado, atto ad esprimer feste, nozze, allegrie, giubili, esultazioni, encomj ec."

[56] Libretto, 30: "Scena ultima. Boschetto con due Capanni praticabili, e un' Albero in mezzo."

of the marriage are squashed, and everyone sings the refrain "Long live the newlyweds, long live love." Lisetta and Carrucola must also come together, though the libretto is ambiguous on this point, and the opera ends without the exchange of their vows.

Rutini effectively captures the fluctuating moods and the escalating intensity of the dramatic action, most noticeably through several tempo changes—nine in all (see table 15.4). The ending this time is a clear *stretta* whose tempo is reached through increasing increments, the last building up from *allegro* to *allegro molto*, and finally, to *più stretto*. This finale, with 332 measures, is longer than the first finale, but seems shorter: no sections are repeated, nor do instrumental ritornellos appear between vocal segments—devices largely responsible for impeding the forward motion in the earlier finale. Rutini also varies the combination of voices here (moving from trio to solo, to trio, quintet, solo, duet, solo, and finally to quintet) but he does not resort to a vaudeville refrain like the "la, la larà" *tutti* that further held the dramatic motion at bay in the first finale.

Table 15.4
Structural Outline of the Act 2 Finale of *Le finte pazzie*

Andante grazioso		Andante molto		Sostenuto	Allegro	Allegro moderato	Andante grazioso	Allegro	Allegro molto	Più stretto
3/4		4/4		3/4	6/8	2/4	3/4	2/4	6/8	6/8
trio	duet	solo	duet	trio	quintet	solo. duet	duet	solo. quintet	quintet	quintet
C Major		F Major		F Major	C Major	G Major	C Major	C Major	C Major	C Major
"Gia l'ora è vicina del nostro contento"	"In questo boschetto"	"A me non lo fanno"	"Son servo al gran soldato"	"Andiano unito il passo"	"E viva gli sposi e viva l'amor"	"La mia probabilmente"	"La destra vi dono"	"Scopra ha ha"	"E viva gli sposi e viva l'amor"	"E viva gli sposi e viva l'amor"
	(women hide in opposite locations)					(women change places: DF is unaware notary arrives)		(marriage vows taken)		
meas. 1-30	31-44	46-66	70-83	87-111	112-148	149-183	184-196	197-236	237-308	309-332

While Rutini continues to operate within major tonalities, his modulations, when these do occur, potently highlight conflicting emotions of characters or noteworthy dramatic action. Thus, following the lengthy C-major opening "Già l'ora è vicina dei nostri contenti" (The hour of our happiness is near), the arrival in F major in measure 46 draws attention to Don Fracastoro's solo debate whether the others might be trying to trick him, and his resolution to stand guard, "Ah me non me la fanno, Vuò stare in sentinella" (Ah, they wouldn't do it to me, I'll be the sentry). And the section in G major beginning in measure 149, "La mia probabilmente" (This one is probably mine), throws into relief the action of jockeying for positions, piquing the audience's curiosity as to whether, between the veils and the moving around, Ernesto might not be mistaken after all. But he indeed locates Lindora, and the return to C major in measure 184, "La destra vi dono, Vi dono il mio cuor" (I give you my hand, I give you my heart), marks the young couple's contentment as they sing of their union. For the remainder of the scene, from the shock tutti, "Scopra, ah, ah" (Unveiled, ah ah), to the *più stretto* "E viva gli sposi e viva l'amor" (Long live the newlyweds and love live love) there is no waivering from the central tonality.

From the point of view of the libretto, the resolution of the drama in *Le finte pazzie* is as expeditious as it is predictable. Devoid of any emotional depth, intellectual sharpness, or parodistic allusion, the story line comes across as uncultivated, and at times cloddishly provincial. To a conservative like Galeazzi, its scenario exhibits elements that by the mid-1790s made "modern comic dramas . . . truly the disgrace of the modern theater." In buffa drama, "not only are dramatic rules not observed," he comments in a footnote to part 4 of his *Elementi teorico-pratici di musica*, "but what is worse, neither good sense nor the purity of language itself. The subjects are usually extremely trivial, full of absurdities, the plot unnatural. . . ." The after effect has been that "for twenty and more years here, nothing but the *Scuola de' gelosi* and *Cosa rara* have been seen, in which little good sense shines through." To his way of thinking, *buffa* style deserved to be reformed, with "sensible comedies of Goldoni, many of Chiari, and of other good authors" set in the genre of *dramma giocoso*. For Galeazzi and others in his camp, the *dramma giocoso* was able "to give a more instructive [and] more sensible performance." Furthermore (in contrast, he clearly intends, to the farce or intermezzo), the *dramma giocoso* was also best able "to furnish more brilliant and more varied ideas to the maestro of music, therefore making his talents stand out."[57]

Galeazzi's points are, of course, well taken. Yet, leaving aside banalities of dramatic action and verse, *Le finte pazzie*'s lighthearted conclusion brings satisfaction, especially when its stirring musical tone is considered. Toward the end of the opera it is the music that rescues the drama from an uninteresting, humdrum close. In contrast to the solution of the first finale, the accelerating tempo and *stretta* principle serve exceedingly well, beginning in measure 197 of the second act finale, to energize the sonorous melee, fueling kinetic motion on a spiraling course that gains momentum as it surges to the act's conclusion. Despite the repetition of the phrase "E viva gli sposi e viva l'amor," its setting in sections of (to borrow Da Ponte's terminology) "strepitoso" (m. 237) and then "arcistrepitoso" (m. 309), averts ennui and perpetuates a sense of forward movement that is maintained until the end. All in all, in the larger sense the outcome for Rutini—at least as glowingly flaunted by the reviewer in the *Gazzetta toscana*—was indeed that in this intermezzo "he has surpassed himself." But, more to the point, the verdict was favorable for *Le finte pazzie*, resting audibly on the reactions of the audience. This intermezzo may not have "instructed," but the approbation that was heard—"not failing to applaud with enthusiasm from the beginning to the end"—is surely a telltale sign that, in its collective experience, the public had, as the reviewer phrased it, "delivered its due to the true worthiness [of the work]."[58]

---

[57] Galeazzi, *Elementi teorico-pratici di musica*, ed. Harwood, 190-91: "I Drammi buffi moderni sono veramente l'obbrobrio del moderno Teatro; non si osservano in essi non solo le drammatiche regole, ma quel che è peggio nè la stessa purità di lingua; gli argomenti sono per lo più trivialissimi, pieni di assurdi, l'intreccio fuor del naturale; non si da in somma cosa più detestabile che i drammi buffi, che vediamo in oggi sul Teatro: da venti e più anni in quà, non si è veduto, che la *Scuola de'gelosi* e la *Cosa rara*, in cui traluce qualche poco di buon senso; e perchè ridur non si potrebbero a drammi giocosi, le sensatissime Commedie del Goldoni, molte del Chiari, e di altri buoni Autori, e dare così uno spettacolo più istruttivo più sensato, e che fornirebbe al Maestro di Musica idee più sensato, e che fornirebbe al Maestro di Musica idee più sublimi, e più varie, onde fare spiccare i suoi talenti?" Galeazzi's comment appears as a footnote to his general statement in the text urging reform of opera buffa: "Buffo egli è cosi vario, come bizzarre sono le parole e siccome queste pure sono al presente insulse, e per lo più prive di alcun senso, così non saprei quì che regola dare, fino a tanto che sorga qualche bel genio, e riformi il Teatro Buffo, come il gran Metastasio, ed il suo antecessore Apostolo Zeno riformarono il serio"; in Harwood, ed., 145.

[58] As quoted in full above, n. 33.

16

The Magical Moment in Mozart's *Zauberflöte*, and a Note on the Production of the Opera at the Teatro di S. Maria in Florence in 1818

MARCELLO DE ANGELIS

In the nineteenth century, the name of Mozart as theatrical author appeared in Florence for the first time only in the spring of 1817. The opera that can in fact be traced to this date was *Don Giovanni*, with Antonio Gordigiani in the leading role. There was such success that in the following year the playbills advertised two re-makes of this masterpiece, sponsored by both the Teatro Nuovo (the old Pallacorda of the Accademia degli Intrepidi) and the Pergola Theater, which at that time was managed by the choreographer Gaetano Gioia. But despite justifiable expectations, Mozart failed to take the city by storm. With no less than six theaters open year round, under the patronage of Duke Pietro Leopoldo, Florence had acquired a position of theatrical pre-eminence in Italy. But the Italian innovation that came with the mounting of *Le nozze di Figaro* at the Pergola in the spring of 1788 was destined to remain an isolated event. The relationship between Mozart and the Tuscan capital, in fact, did not transcend even then the warm welcome he had received in his previous visit, which had been during the first week of April 1770. It was also during that first visit that the *enfant prodige*, who had improvised at the *cembalo* in the presence of Pietro Leopoldo, had met the ten-year-old Luigi Cherubini, an apprentice of great promise.

The Florentine undertaking of *The Magic Flute* was met with indifference. The opera was born and died after one single performance in the Teatro di S. Maria on 23 August 1818. The scant importance given to the event is also reflected in the choice of the performance date. The summer season was, in fact, a time when the aristocracy resided in their country villas. Certainly the summer season promoted traveling, and, therefore it could be argued, the opportunity existed for music-loving travelers to attend the opera, but there is no solid evidence for this. Also surprising is the theater's failure to publish the libretto, even though a fine translation by the Livornese Giovanni de Gamerra was readily available. De Gamerra's libretto had been used for the production of the opera presented in Italian in Dresden on 2 April 1794. De Gamerra had produced an excellent work in regard both to the musical rhythm and the transformation of the *parlato* into lines of eleven and seven syllables, thereby making it suitable for *secco* recitative.

The performance would have gone unnoticed were it not for the presence of an anonymous observer from the *Gazzetta di Firenze*, who, fortunately, jotted down a few impressions. As with the performance of *Don Giovanni* in the previous year, the *Flauto*, too, was interpolated with those *arie di bravura* which, at that time, were not particularly astonishing. Strangely, however, these seemed to have irritated the sensibility of the critic. "That renown Specter," one reads, "came close to dying a second time, were it not that in the posters and advertisements one could read in large characters the adjective immortal." Scanning the few but pivotal lines of the article, typical of the journalistic style of the period, it is clear that the general lines of the set design were based on an appreciation of the comic, and on expedients likely to stimulate the public's sense of curiosity. To the critic, these choices not only seemed to debase the work, but to render it downright unbecoming since, in his view, it was totally inadequate "to dismiss

---

This contribution appears as it was received, except for translation into English and concurrent clarification of one or two phrases. The Editor felt it best not to subject a critical essay of this type to further editorial intervention.

the affair of the *Flauto* with simple adjectives such as pretty, clear, and judicious." His evident visual dissatisfaction is underscored in the following passage: "The manner in which these various reptiles, quadruped and winged creatures, contributed to the general laughter was deemed satisfying—that is, they induced an indulgent public to laughter." In essence, he was annoyed by the overly decorative and bold setting, which he deemed too fake. In his view, this had defiled the most profound significance of the text. The question raised here is an interesting one because it points in the direction of the kind of confoundment that had brewed in Masonic circles following the Viennese premiere on 30 September 1791. But, at this point, it will suffice to note that the *Flauto magico* elicited much laughter by the public of the Teatro di S. Maria.

This was the result Mozart had in fact hoped to achieve, to convey with lightness and simplicity of means, a lofty message filled with love and hope. This reflected the reality of the last year of his life when he was engaged in a duel with death devoid of any element of terror. In a touching letter to his father on 4 April 1797, he had defined death as "the key to bliss." He wrote "In the last couple of years I have become so accustomed to this wonderful friend of mankind, that its shadow no longer holds anything frightening for me. Rather, it fills me with peace and comfort! I never go to sleep without first thinking (young though I am) that the next day I may no longer exist—and yet no one among the many who know me could say that, among men, I am brooding or sad—and for this happiness I give thanks to the Lord every day and I heartily wish it upon my fellow man."

Ferruccio Busoni, delineating an aphoristic portrait of the musician, aptly summarized the core of this emotional statement made by Wolfgang when he had just turned thirty-one: "He is as young as a youthful boy, and as wise as an old man, neither dated nor modern, even from the tomb he is still alive. His so-humane smile still shines forth, irradiating us all."

Mozart's prolific output was based on a dialectic of life and death, of love and redemption, of fidelity and certitude. As I shall try to demonstrate at the end of my essay, Mozart's output proceeded simultaneously on different, but not opposing, tracks. In the meantime let us look at the genesis of the work.

Emanuel Schikaneder, the author of the libretto, was fond of experimenting with new solutions of set design, rekindling the fascination of the Baroque wonder-struck theater: exotic animals, extravagant masks, scenographical changes, and sudden reversal of situations. He had met Mozart in Salzburg in 1780, but their friendship, however, had intensified only since 5 November 1784 with *Die Entführung aus dem Serail*. Having been disgraced at the court of Emperor Joseph II, who had seized on some gossip about libertine practices within the company, Schikaneder had been compelled to close shop. His wife Eleanor, accused of complicity in such practices, found nothing better to do than choose a new companion for herself in the person of the actor Johann Friedel. He had just opened the Freihaus Theater in the Viennese suburb of Wieden which, because of the particular location, was also known as "Auf der Wieden." In the spring of 1789 Friedel passed on to a better life, giving Schikaneder, who had reconciled with Eleanor, the opportunity to succeed him in its management. This was the *coup de chance* that allowed him to demonstrate the best of his indisputable ability to prepare shows designed with great displays of machines and scenographic effects.

To the first 1789 production of *Oberon*, on a libretto by Karl Ludwig Gieseke and music by Pavel Vranicky, a pupil of Haydn, there followed a second with a heroic-comic subject, *Der Stein der Weisen, oder die Zauberinsel*, on a libretto by the same Schikaneder and music by various authors, including Mozart, who had orchestrated the duet between Schikaneder and Mrs. Gerl, in a clear anticipation of Papageno and Papagena created by the same interpreters. The bass Franz Xaver Gerl, the teacher of the above-mentioned lady and future Sarastro, contributed to the production.

All, or almost all, of the components of *The Magic Flute* already existed when Mozart was asked to compose the music for a singspiel based on the novel *Lulu, oder die Zauberflöte* by August Jacob Liebeskind, which, in turn, had had its origins in a collection of fables published by Wieland in 1785-89. In addition, there was *Thamos, König von in Aegypten* of Baron Tobias Phillip von Gebler, already considered by Mozart, who had composed its choruses and intermezzos in 1779-80, and *Sethos*, a novel by the Frenchman Terrasson, that had been published in France in 1731 and is justly considered the closest relative to Schikaneder's future plot. Here we note the same Egyptian ambiance, the purification of the initiates through the four elements, their subdivision into two categories (the second initiate is allowed a romantic liaison just like the future Papageno and Papagena), the verses in the chorus of Sarastrus, which correspond to the "O Isis und Osiris," and the inscription the warriors read on the pyramid before their last exploit, which will appear paraphrased in Schikaneder's production. The story of this incredible dramaturgical collage ends with Lulu's conjuring up of the homogenous prince who, in turn, is saved by Astrifiammante. The latter hands him a flute, the magic flute with which he will be able to free the daughter who has been kept prisoner by an ogre. But here the unforeseen happens: the singspiel *Der Fagottist, oder die Zauberziter* had been staged at the Leopoldstadt Theater with music by Wenzel Muller that Joachim Peret had gotten from him. In order to avoid accusations of plagiarism it appeared sufficient to reverse the roles—that is, one might say, to transform the characters from positive to negative. The ogre (Lulu's magician) thus became a benevolent Magus who donned the robes of the chief of priests, and the Queen of the Night became the embodiment of malevolence. The Prince was carried down from the sky by three providential genies. It should be enough to go over the work *Thamos*, where in essence the figures of the malevolent Queen and the Magus priest are well delineated.

Let us leave aside for the moment other questions of a more musical character, over which streams of ink have been poured. The essential coordinates of the music had already been defined in the characterization of Sarastro's good kingdom, announced by the trombones at the entrance of the three pages at the beginning of the first finale, and by the "negative" portrayal of the Queen of the Night, suggested by the deeply ingrained diffidence toward women avowed by the venerable Prince Ignaz von Born of the Masonic lodge of the Vera Concordia in Vienna, to which Mozart also belonged. The overture was finished late, just a few hours before the beginning of the performance. The priests' march, on the other hand, seems to be an elaboration of a similar piece in Vranicky's *Oberon*.

After the final arrangement of the various pieces and the subdivision into fifteen scenes, the singspiel glides on without deviating from the fairy tale tapestry through which the triumph of good over evil, and of truth over obscure and negative forces advances. This is the ultimate moral of the work, conveyed by the music in *Thamos*, so profoundly different from the spirit of the *Zauberoper*, which was limited to furnishing a framework, a simplified atmosphere for the fantastic tapestry. Mozart succeeded in accomplishing the miracle of combining the expectations of an educated public with childish dreams, by blending the esoteric content to the essence of the fable. Not by chance the content of the *Flauto* harmonized so well, not only with puppet shows, but also in satisfying the demands of an exacting director such as Ingmar Bergman. The enchantment of joy and the initial self-consciousness find a perfect fusion in the music. The exemplary vocal and instrumental interpretation moves from a paradoxical irony to hieratic solutions underscored by heavy and solemn cadences. In this opera Mozart utilized all of the principles expressed in the preexisting models, theatrical and other. The true novelty consisted in the nature of the subject, considered much different from the "Turkishness" of the *Entführung* and from the humorous details of *Don Giovanni* as well. The composer broke decisively from the lines of contemporary dramaturgical tradition by inserting the ambiguity and myriad nuances of the fantastic content. Mozart's ability to work on a multitude of scores at once is surprising. He was, in fact, working on both *Titus* and the *Requiem* at the same time. The latter is strongly connected to the idea of death, which he seems to have focused on during the last year of his life, in addition to *Ave verum*, the Concerto in A major for clarinet and the Masonic cantata *Laut Verkunde unsre Freude*.

Every apparent contradiction of either an aesthetic or stylistic nature was recombined during that dramatic autumn and winter of 1791. If we were to use the analogy of a pyramid, it would be as if Mozart could climb from its base, where conflicting and pre-romantic elements are found, to its apex, where such elements converge into a fugue. These elements assume either an expressive stylization (see *Titus*), a sublimation of the sacred, or a search for an original purity *à la Rousseau*, which only the mainspring of a fable could provide.

The common objective can be individuated in the reconquest of a theatrical archetype, as had been reasserted in Gluck's reform. The idea of a myth expressed through music is thus crystallized. And if opera, likewise, participates in myth, we may be able to maintain that Mozart's score participates, perhaps more than any other in the Enlightenment, as a full-scale social movement. Sarastro's sphere, with its ambivalent swinging between just and unjust, is unaware of spitefulness, a quality from which Nietzsche, the enlightened mythologist, tried in a supreme effort to free humankind. The process of osmosis between myth and Enlightenment, between the concept of a blind system and the idea of freedom that can derive from it, in Mozart is ultimately realized in a contradiction-free profession of faith. Overcoming even Rousseau's assertions, which had risen from the conceptually-naive metaphor of the "noble savage," the boundaries with the metaphysical are reached. The profound meaning of the *Flauto magico*, and perhaps its secret, should be understood as a completely modern surge with which the composer approached the estranged world of surrealism.

17

Historicism in Nineteenth-Century German Oratorio

HOWARD E. SMITHER

The two most active geographical areas for oratorio in the nineteenth century were Germany and Britain.[1] Probably more performances of oratorios took place in Britain, though mostly heard were Handel's oratorios rather than new works. While Handel was also a favorite with audiences in Germany, German choral societies placed greater emphasis than did their British counterparts on singing contemporary oratorios. The present study focuses on German oratorio both because of the greater number of new oratorios produced in Germany and the greater variety of historicist phenomena exhibited in the works. Any explanation of why German oratorio took the course—indeed the courses— that it did must explore several important strands in the fabric of German political, social, and intellectual life in the nineteenth century. Particularly significant were escalating manifestations of cultural nationalism during and after the French occupation: romanticism, which had begun as a literary movement in the later eighteenth century and became essential to the prevailing view of music in the nineteenth century; historicism, an attitude that led to revivals of earlier music; Enlightenment and post-Enlightenment views of religion; and the cultural tendencies of the new middle class that gave rise to the amateur choral movement, exemplified in the formation of singing societies and the mounting of choral festivals for which occasions oratorios were often composed.

The present study focuses on only one of these strands: historicism. As this term has been used with various meanings,[2] it is important to clarify its use in this article. As understood here, historicism refers to an attitude which considers reflection on history—and use of history—essential, and may lead to the revival of conceptions, forms, styles, and musical works of the past.[3] In the nineteenth century particularly clear expressions in architecture are the extensive uses of early forms in neoclassic and Gothic-revival buildings throughout Europe and America.[4] The roots of historicism in Germany reach back to the second half of the eighteenth century. The writings of 1755-67 by Johann Joachim Winckelmann on classical archaeology and the arts of antiquity played an important role in shaping the neoclassical movement in architecture and the visual arts. He praised the "noble simplicity and calm grandeur" of ancient Greek art and asserted "There is but one way for the moderns to become great, and perhaps unequalled;

---

[1] The present article is based on research done for a book in press on the oratorio in the nineteenth and twentieth centuries, which is volume 4 of my *A History of the Oratorio* (Chapel Hill: University of North Carolina Press, 1977-).

[2] *Die Musik in Geschichte und Gegenwart* (hereafter *MGG*), 16 (1979), s.v. "Historismus," by Carl Dahlhaus.

[3] This is a modification of the definition found in Nikolaus Pevsner, "Möglichkeiten und Aspekte des Historismus: Versuch einer Frühgeschichte und Typologie des Historismus," in *Historismus und die bildende Kunst: Vorträge und Diskussion im Oktober 1963 in München und Schloss Anif*, ed. Ludwig Grote, Studien zur Kunst des neunzehnten Jahrhunderts, 1 (Munich: Prestel, 1965), 13-24. Pevsner's definition is adopted in Erich Doflein, "Historismus in der Musik," in *Die Ausbreitung des Historismus über die Musik*, ed. Walter Wiora, Studien zur Musikgeschichte des 19. Jahrhunderts, 14 (Regensburg: Gustav Bosse Verlag, 1969), 9-39. The numerous papers in *Die Ausbreitung des Historismus über die Musik* are important writings on historicism.

[4] For useful summaries of the histories of these architectural styles, see *The New Encyclopedia Britannica* (1994), s.v. "Classicism, 1750-1830" (anon.); and "Gothic Revival, c. 1730 - c. 1930," by Robin David Middleton and David John Watkin.

I mean, by imitating the ancients."[5] Goethe discovered beauty in the Gothic style of the Strasbourg cathedral, and in 1772 wrote glowingly of that magnificent structure.[6] By their reflections on art of the past, Winckelmann, Goethe, and their contemporaries were unconsciously laying the groundwork for nineteenth-century historicism in the visual arts and architecture. Likewise, and in the same period, such figures as Baron Gottfried van Swieten and Johann Friedrich Reichardt were initiating the beginnings of musical historicism, which would exert a strong influence on oratorio.

It is important to understand that the subject of historicism is inseparable from the subject of romanticism. Carl Dahlhaus, noting the disparate ideas embodied in the concept of romanticism as applied in literature and in the arts, cautioned against seeking a common root from which all derive. Yet he asserted that "disinhibition," or the removal of barriers, is an important motivating factor:

> . . . only within certain limits is it possible to reduce romanticism to a single essence without narrowing the subject or doing it methodological violence. Nevertheless, there is no overlooking the close connection between exoticism, historicism, and folklorism—all features as characteristic of nineteenth-century music as they are of the literature and painting of the time. . . . Whether the bourgeois educated classes—the "carrier strata" of musical romanticism—chose to overstep social bounds to folk music, historical bounds to early music, or geographical and ethnic bounds to oriental music, the motivation was always the same: an urge to "disinhibit," to remove the barriers posed by classical rules of style. There was an irresistible attraction to what seemed different or remote. . . .[7]

Attraction to "what seemed different or remote" contributed to the historicist fervor that led to the revivals of Bach and Handel, to the introduction of Handelian qualities in Haydn's *Creation*, to the clear echoes of Bach and Handel in Mendelssohn's *St. Paul* and *Elijah*, and to the emphasis on Gregorian chant in Liszt's *Die Legende von der heiligen Elisabeth* and *Christus*.[8] But as important as the Handel and Bach revivals were to oratorio in the nineteenth century, other historicist tendencies also played a prominent role, among them, the restoration of chorales from the time of Luther (a concomitant of the return to the Lutheran liturgy), the restoration of plainchant, and the Palestrina revival with its romantic enshrinement of *a cappella* singing as the ideal for worship.[9] Each of these will be dealt with in the present treatment of historicism as reflected in German oratorio.

* * * * *

With reference to Handel's English oratorios in Germany, the notion of their "revival" conventionally comes to mind, but more to the point is their "discovery." Handel's oratorios were virtually unknown in Germany until the 1770s, and they remained little known there until well into the nineteenth century. Among the early German performances of Handel's oratorios are the sporadic hearings of *Messiah* (beginning in Hamburg, 1772) and *Judas Maccabaeus* (Berlin,

---

[5] David Irwin, ed., *Winckelmann: Writings on Art* (London: Phaidon Press, 1972), 48 (from Irwin's introduction to Winckelmann's writings), and 61 (from Winckelmann's *Gedanken über die Nachahmung der griechischen Werke in der Mahlerey und Bildhauer-Kunst*, Dresden, 1755).

[6] Johann Wolfgang von Goethe, "Von deutscher Baukunst," in *Gedenkausgabe der Werke, Briefe und Gespräche [Goethes]*, ed. Christian Beutler, 25 vols. (Zurich: Artemis-Verlag 1949), 3:16-26.

[7] Carl Dahlhaus, *Nineteenth-Century Music*, trans. Bradford J. Robinson, California Studies in 19th-Century Music, 5 (Berkeley: University of California Press, 1989), 25.

[8] I group Liszt's oratorios with those of German authors, even though he was born in Hungary. He conceived *Die Legende von der heiligen Elisabeth* in Weimar, and intended it to premiere at a festival at Wartburg Castle in Eisenach. The festival was delayed, and the first performances took place in Pest. His *Christus*, composed in Rome, was first performed in Weimar. Thus both his oratorios fit well within a German context.

[9] For a turn-of-the-century survey of the relation of the nineteenth-century oratorio to the revival of earlier music, see Richard Hohenemser, *Welche Einflüsse hatte die Wiederbelebung der älteren Musik im 19. Jahrhundert auf die deutschen Komponisten?*, Breitkopf & Härtels Sammlung musikwissenschaftlicher Arbeiten von deutschen Hochschulen, 4 (Leipzig: Breitkopf & Härtel, 1900), 93-113.

1774),[10] Baron van Swieten's patronage of Handel's oratorios in Vienna of the 1780s and 90s (including commissions to Mozart for arrangements of *Messiah, Alexander's Feast*, and other works), and the grandiose renditions of *Messiah* directed by Johann Adam Hiller in Berlin and Leipzig (1786), and in Breslau (1788).[11] Playing a role in the Handel revival by emulating elements of his oratorio style are Haydn's *Creation* and *Seasons*, composed after Haydn's visits to London, where monumental Handel performances in Westminster Abbey had inspired him. According to Giuseppe Carpani, who knew Haydn, ". . . when he heard the music of Hendl [*sic*] in London, he was struck as if he had been put back to the beginning of his studies and had known nothing up to that moment. He meditated on every note and drew from those most learned scores the essence of true musical grandeur."[12]

The nineteenth century saw ever increasing performances, publications, and published praise of Handel's oratorios. The oratorios were heard mostly in music festivals. Few were given complete, however; cuts to adapt them to current concert life were common. In the first two decades of the century, *Messiah*, nearly always performed in the arrangement by Mozart, was the most frequently heard of Handel's oratorios and continued to be for the rest of the century. *Alexander's Feast, Judas Maccabaeus*, and *Samson* were occasionally given in those early decades, but later came *Saul* (first heard in 1820), *Jephtha* (1824), *Solomon* (1825), *Israel in Egypt* and *Joshua* (both by 1827), *Belshazzar* (1834), and *Athalia* (1837). Virtually all were performed not in the original scoring, but in new editions introducing added instruments and "improved" orchestration. In addition to *Messiah* and *Alexander's Feast* edited by Mozart, *Judas Maccabaeus* was given in an edition occasionally attributed in the time to Mozart, but which was probably by Joseph Starzer; *Samson, Israel in Egypt*, and *Jephtha* in editions by the Viennese Ignaz Franz von Mosel; and *Athalia, Joshua*, and *Judas Maccabaeus* in editions by the Hamburger Johann Heinrich Clasing. In 1856 the Deutsche Händel-Gesellschaft was founded for the publication of a complete, critical edition of the composer's music, with Friedrich Chrysander as the sole editor. Some critics heaped praise on Handel's *Messiah* as the ideal model for an oratorio, while others looked to his dramatic oratorios as models. Most oratorios in the nineteenth century, particularly from the third decade on, reflect Handelian procedures—above all in their choruses. It is not surprising that Gustav Schilling, in his *Geschichte der heutigen oder modernen Musik* (1841), devotes a section to "The Victory of Oratorio, Especially through Handel's Influence," in which he claims for Handel's oratorios a decisive role in shaping the direction of oratorio in his own time.[13]

But while the revival of Handel's oratorios made rapid progress in the early nineteenth century, the same cannot be said of Bach's choral works. When Mendelssohn conducted the Berlin Singakademie in a performance of Bach's recently discovered *St. Matthew Passion* in 1829, then thought to be the 100th anniversary of its first performance, the event became a landmark in both the Bach revival and the history of oratorio. Strangely enough from today's perspective, where Bach's cantatas, Passions, and oratorios loom large in the composer's work, the early phase of the Bach revival focused mainly on his instrumental music. In 1782, Johann Friedrich Reichardt expressed the same wonderment of Bach and Handel that Goethe had felt on contemplating the Strasbourg Cathedral (and he quoted Goethe extensively); however, the "Gothic" art of Bach that Reichardt admired was the instrumental fugue.[14] Through Swieten, Mozart came to know Bach's fugues, some of which he arranged for strings; he also took part in the

---

[10] On German performances of *Messiah* and other oratorios by Handel from the late eighteenth and the early nineteenth centuries, see Smither, *The Oratorio in the Classical Era*, A History of the Oratorio, 3 (1987), 229-31, 344-46, 353-55.

[11] On Hiller's performances, which were modeled on performances at the Handel Commemoration of 1784 in Westminster Abbey, see ibid., 229-31.

[12] Giuseppe Carpani, *Le Haydine* (Milan: C. Buccinelli, 1812), 162-63, as translated in H. C. Robbins Landon, *Haydn: Chronicle and Works*, vol. 3 (Bloomington: Indiana University Press, 1976-80), 84. Concerning Handel's influence on these oratorios by Haydn, see Smither, *The Oratorio in the Classical Era*, 448-90, 493, and 509-10.

[13] Gustav Schilling, *Geschichte der heutigen oder modernen Musik in ihrem zusammenhange mit der allgemeinen Welt- und Völkergeschichte* (Karlsruhe: Christian Theodor Groos, 1841), 554.

[14] Reichardt, in *Musikalisches Kunstmagazin* 1 (1782):196-97, reprinted in *Dokumente zum Nachwirken Johann Sebastian Bachs, 1750-1800*, ed. Hans-Joachim Schulze, Bach-Dokumente, 3 (Kassel: Bärenreiter, 1972), 357-60. The comparison of Bach's music to Gothic architecture became a recurring theme in the early nineteenth century. For a few examples, see Doflein, 12, and Martin Geck, *Die Wiederentdeckung der Matthäuspassion im 19. Jahrhundert: Die zeitgenössischen Dokumente und ihre ideengeschichtliche Deutung*, Studien zur Musikgeschichte des 19. Jahrhunderts, 9 (Regensburg: Gustav Bosse Verlag, 1967), 51, 58, 61.

Sunday performances at Swieten's apartment in the Court Library in Vienna, where one heard "nothing but Handel and Bach."[15]

Only after 1800 did new publications of Bach's music begin—in the first two decades of the century, the keyboard music (first, *Das wohltemperirte Clavier* in 1801) and the sonatas and suites for strings. The only vocal works published in that period were the motets (1802-03) and the Magnificat (1811). In the 1830s, however, the *St. John Passion*, *St. Matthew Passion*, and *B-Minor Mass* appeared, and in 1850, the centenary of Bach's death, the Bach-Gesellschaft was formed to publish a complete critical edition of his works. Influential in founding the society were Robert Schumann, Otto Jahn, Carl Ferdinand Becker, and Moritz Hauptmann. The first volume, which included ten cantatas, appeared in 1851.

The role of the Berlin Singakademie was paramount in the revival of Bach's vocal works. In 1800 Carl Friedrich Zelter succeeded Carl Friedrich Christian Fasch as director of this choral society and actively began cultivating music of the past. To some extent Zelter was following Fasch's lead, for, as early as 1794 Fasch had conducted his first Bach rehearsal in the Singakademie, with the motet *Komm, Jesu, komm*.[16] In the first three decades under Zelter, the Singakademie sang several Handel oratorios in public and rehearsed Bach's motets, the *B-Minor Mass*, and some numbers from the Passions in private. Zelter in this period considered the large-scale works by Bach inappropriate for public performance.[17]

As a composition student of Zelter's (since 1819) and a member of the Singakademie (since 1820), Felix Mendelssohn became acquainted with the score of the *St. Matthew Passion* in 1823, at the age of fourteen, when he received a manuscript copy as a Christmas gift.[18] About four years later he and his friend, the Zelter student and singer Eduard Devrient, proposed a public performance of the work as a centennial celebration. Zelter agreed and even allowed his twenty-year-old student to conduct the first performance in the hall of the Singakademie, which occurred—after two years of weekly rehearsals—on 11 March 1829.[19] The concert was viewed as a highly significant event. The audience numbered about 900 (the hall was filled to capacity) and included King Friedrich Wilhelm III and his court, and such other notable figures as Friedrich Schleiermacher, Friedrich Hegel, Gustav Droysen, and Heinrich Heine.[20] Two more performances were given to full houses, the second also conducted by Mendelssohn, the third by Zelter.[21] All performances were enthusiastically received. News of the work's overwhelming impact traveled fast, and subsequent performances were sung by choral societies in Frankfurt am Main (1829), Breslau (1830), Stettin (1831), Königsberg (1832), and Kassel (1832), and by the royal chapel in Dresden (1833).[22]

The importance of the rediscovery of the *St. Matthew Passion* for the Bach revival and for the history of oratorio cannot be overestimated. Bach was now viewed as a composer of monumental choral works, works comparable to those becoming known by Handel. He was acclaimed in this period of liturgical reform as a champion of German Protestantism, and his usefulness to German nationalists as a symbol of the cultural superiority of German music was greatly enhanced. For his *St. Paul* (1836) Mendelssohn relied heavily upon the procedures Bach had employed in the *St. Matthew Passion*. Countless other composers of oratorio followed suit, whether inspired directly by Bach's music or by way of Mendelssohn's *St. Paul*, itself an extremely influential model.

---

[15] Letter from W. A. Mozart to Leopold Mozart, 10 April 1782, in Wolfgang Amadeus Mozart, *Briefe und Aufzeichnungen, Gesamtausgabe*, ed. Wilhelm A. Bauer and Otto Erich Deutsch, vol. 3 (Kassel: Bärenreiter, 1962-75), 201. On Mozart's arrangements of fugues for Swieten, see Warren Kirkendale, "More Slow Introductions by Mozart to Fugues of J. S. Bach?," *Journal of the American Musicological Society* 17 (1964): 44.

[16] Georg Schünemann, *Carl Friedrich Zelter: Der Mensch und sein Werk* (Berlin: Berliner Bibliophilen-Abend, 1937), 20.

[17] Geck, 15.

[18] Ibid., 17. Geck cites Eduard Devrient, *Meine Erinnerungen an Felix Mendelssohn Bartholdy und seine Briefe an mich*, 2nd ed. (Leipzig, 1872), 19f.

[19] In the version performed, many recitatives, arias, and chorales were cut and numerous modifications introduced. For details, see Geck, 35-41.

[20] Ibid., 34.

[21] Mendelssohn was to have conducted all three performances, but his plans to leave for England, which could not be changed, prevented his conducting the third; see William A. Little, "Mendelssohn and the Berlin Singakademie: The Composer at the Crossroads," in *Mendelssohn and His World*, ed. R. Larry Todd (Princeton: Princeton University Press, 1991), 65-85.

[22] Geck includes a chapter on each performance.

In the Restoration period following the end of the wars of liberation from French domination and the conclusion of the Congress of Vienna, leaders in Germany sought to revive older values and to reverse the aftereffects of the French Revolution. Their search nourished the historicist movement by encouraging a return to religious thought, liturgy, and music of earlier times, which in turn had an effect on the oratorio.[23] Reacting against the liturgical freedom that had been largely embraced during the period of the Enlightenment (which some in the Restoration now perceived as one concrete sign of moral deterioration), and seeing in religion a source of moral regeneration, the Prussian King Friedrich Wilhelm III and Prussian church authorities effected important changes in the structure of public worship. In 1817, the tercentenary of the Lutheran Reformation, the king unified the Lutheran and Reformed (Calvinist) churches. In 1822 he introduced a new order of worship, the *Agende*, for the court and cathedral churches of Berlin, basing it on Luther's service. He also tried to impose the reform elsewhere, but with mixed results.[24]

Since the late eighteenth century, literary and musical figures—including Klopstock, Reichardt, Goethe, and Hoffmann—had lamented a decline in the quality of chorales sung in church and had urged a return to the chorales from the Reformation.[25] The new *Agende* addressed this problem by returning to the texts of Reformation chorales. These had been largely discarded in the course of the eighteenth century in favor of new *emfindsam* texts, which reflected a continuing Pietistic influence. (Attempts to restore the chorale melodies, with their original rhythms and modal qualities, would come later.) In the ensuing years following adoption of the *Agende*, numerous new collections of chorales appeared in which the editors purported to offer early, pre-Enlightenment chorales, and oratorio composers increasingly turned to early chorales—as Mendelssohn did for his *St. Paul*.[26]

The choral music favored by the new Prussian *Agende* was an *a cappella* style based on the Russian Orthodox music of Dmitri Bortnianskij, the director of the Imperial chapel in St. Petersburg. The style is essentially syllabic, homophonic, and activated by minimal counterpoint.[27] Although the king found his ideal for religious music in the Russian Orthodox Church—from which services instruments have always been banned—romantic historicists had already espoused a return to the *a cappella* style of the Renaissance.

Unlike the Catholic Church, which had maintained an *a cappella* tradition since the Renaissance,[28] German Protestants had long ago abandoned it. In the late eighteenth and the early nineteenth century historicists called for its restoration. One was Reichardt, who was deeply impressed by this tradition during visits to Italy (1783 and 1790). In 1791 he wrote reverently of Palestrina's "noble art," of his "exalted, solemn church style, of which the principal character consists of vigorous and often daring series of chords that are mostly consonant,"[29] and he compared modern church music unfavorably with the *a cappella* art of the Italian master. Having been introduced to Palestrina's music as a student under Fasch, Zelter shared in the Palestrina revival by performing his works with

---

[23] According to ibid., 70-71, the Neo-Pietist movement—a "movement of awakening" (*Erweckungsbewegung*)—that arose during the period of the Restoration, seems to have had virtually no effect on oratorio and in fact was antithetical to both opera and oratorio. Yet it may be that the continuation of the *emfindsam* oratorio libretto in the first half of the nineteenth century is related to this movement.

[24] On the new *Agende*, see Ulrich Leupold, *Die liturgischen Gesänge der evangelischen Kirche im Zeitalter der Auflärung und der Romantik* (Kassel: Bärenreiter, 1933), 118-44; see also *MGG* 1 (1949-51), s.v. "Agende," by Christhard Mahrenholz.

[25] On the chorale from the mid-eighteenth to the late nineteenth century, see *MGG* 4 (1955), s.v. "Gemeindegesang," by Walter Blankenburg; and Georg Feder, "Decline and Restoration," trans. Reinhard G. Pauly, in *Protestant Church Music: A History*, ed. Friedrich Blume et al. (New York: Norton, 1974), 336-47, 378-82.

[26] For a full discussion of the chorale in German oratorios of the early nineteenth century, see Glenn Stanley, "Bach's Erbe: The Chorale in the German Oratorio of the Early Nineteenth Century," *19th-Century Music* 11 (1987): 121-49.

[27] Friedrich Wilhelm III first heard Russian choral music when he met Tsar Alexander I in Bartenstein in 1807. As is known from correspondence, the king was overwhelmed with the sound of the imperial chapel at the Russian Orthodox Good Friday service; see Leupold, 120-21; see also his *Beilage* III-IV in the same work for an exchange of letters in 1824 between the king and the tsar on the subject of church music.

[28] The Sistine Chapel had retained this tradition, and other Catholic churches, both in Italy and north of the Alps, typically sang *a cappella* works in *stile antico* during Lent.

[29] See Reichardt in *Musikalisches Kunstmagazin* 2 (1791): 55; also see pp. 16-17 for other of his comments on Palestrina. For a discussion of Reichardt's position as the initiator of the Palestrina renaissance and the more generalized *a cappella* renaissance, see Walter Salmen, *Johann Friedrich Reichardt: Komponist, Schriftsteller, Kapellmeister und Verwaltungsbeamter der Goethezeit* (Freiburg i. Br.: Atlantis, 1963), 285-87.

the Singakademie.[30] Early nineteenth-century writings increasingly championed *a cappella* church music.[31] E. T. A. Hoffmann wrote in 1814 "Palestrina, following the practice of the time, wrote only for voices, with no instrumental accompaniment. Praise of the highest and holiest should flow straight from the human breast, without any foreign admixture or intermediary."[32] And even Beethoven, in a letter to Zelter in 1823, declared that the *a cappella* style "might be especially designated, the one true Church style."[33] By the time of Beethoven's letter, Palestrina's music had been heard in Vienna in Swieten's concerts of the 1790s, in the historical concerts of Raphael Georg Kiesewetter that had been initiated in 1816, and, of course, during Lent in the local churches.[34]

The view expressed by Hoffmann, Beethoven, and others was widely disseminated in a small book, *Über Reinheit der Tonkunst*, by Anton Friedrich Justus Thibaut.[35] A professor of Roman law at the University of Heidelberg, Thibaut was well known as a leader of an amateur chorus that performed early music. Such figures as Goethe, Tieck, Mendelssohn, and Schumann paid visits to his weekly rehearsals. Thibaut's book emphasized a return to the Palestrina style and to *a cappella* performance: "When human voices in church keep the tone fine, delicate, and floating, then the addition of instruments is almost an insult to the ear."[36] For Thibaut, "The true, 'holy' art of church music presupposes 'a deep, calm, introspective and pure cast of mind.' It is music that encapsulates itself from the outside world."[37] Thibaut's widely shared view was fundamental both to the Cecilian movement for the reform of Catholic church music and to music in the Protestant church.[38] Contributing significantly to the interest in *a cappella* performance in Protestant Germany were Carl von Winterfeld's writings between 1834 and 1852.[39] For Winterfeld, the music of Johannes Eccard (1553-1611) represented the ideal Protestant *a cappella* style—indeed, he raised Eccard "to the stature of a Protestant Palestrina."[40]

---

[30] Carl Friedrich Zelter, *Karl Friedrich Christian Fasch* (Berlin: Johann Friedrich Unger, 1801), 18, 55.

[31] See Leupold, 66-70.

[32] E. T. A. Hoffmann, "Alte und neue Kirchenmusik," *Allgemeine musikalische Zeitung* 16 (1814), column 582, as translated in *E. T. A. Hoffman's Musical Writings: "Kreisleriana," "The Poet and the Composer," Music Criticism*, ed. David Charlton, trans. Martyn Clarke (Cambridge: Cambridge University Press, 1989), 358.

[33] Beethoven to Zelter, Vienna, 25 March 1823, in *Beethoven's Letters*, explanatory notes by A. C. Kalischer, trans. with preface by J. S. Shedlock (1926; reprint, New York: Dover, 1972), 298.

[34] Herfrid Kier, "Musikalischer Historismus im vormärzlichen Wien," in *Die Ausbreitung des Historismus*, 56.

[35] 3rd ed. (Heidelberg: Akademische Verlagshandlung von J. C. B. Mohr, 1825). This extremely popular work went through seven editions, the last in 1907.

[36] Thibaut, 125.

[37] Dahlhaus, 181.

[38] On the reform of Catholic church music, which proceeded from essentially the same impulses as the reform of Protestant church music, see Walter Wiora, "Restauration und Historismus," in *Geschichte der Katolischen Kirchenmusik*, ed. Gustav Fellerer, vol. 2 (Kassel: Bärenreiter, 1976), 219-25; and, in the same volume, Johannes Schwermer, "Der Cäcilianismus," 226-36.

[39] Carl von Winterfeld, *Johannes Gabrieli und sein Zeitalter*, 3 vols. (Berlin: Im Verlage der Schlesinger'schen Buch- und Musikhandlung, 1834); *Zur Geschichte heiliger Tonkunst*, 2 vols. (1850-52; reprint, Hildesheim: Georg Olms, 1966); *Der evangelische Kirchengesang und sein Verhältnis zur Kunst des Tonsatzes*, 3 vols. (1843; reprint, Hildesheim: Georg Olms, 1966).

[40] Feder, 390. For Winterfeld's account of Eccard's music, see his *Kirchengesang*, 2:433-97. For a consideration of the background to Winterfeld's choice of Eccard for this role, see Adolf Nowak, "Johannes Eccards Ernennung zum preußischen Palestrina durch Obertribunalrat von Winterfeld," in *Studien zur Musikgeschichte Berlins im frühen 19. Jahrhundert*, ed. Carl Dahlhaus, Studien zur Musikgeschichte des 19. Jahrhunderts (Regensburg: Gustav Bosse, 1980), 293-300.

Although the present article focuses on Germany, it should be noted that the Palestrina revival and the *a cappella* movement were by no means purely German phenomena. In Paris, Alexandre Choron, who publicly performed Palestrina in his Institution royale de musique classique et religieuse, is alleged to have rhapsodized, "Palestrina c'est le Racine, c'est le Raphael, c'est le Jésus-Christ de la musique." See Willi Kahl, "Zur musikalischen Renaissancebewegung in Frankreich während der ersten Hälfte des 19. Jahrhunderts," in *Festschrift Joseph Schmidt-Görg zum 60. Geburtstag*, ed. Dagmar Weise (Bonn: Beethovenhaus, 1957), 165; Kahl's source for the quotation is Abbé Daniel, *Rapport sur le concours ouvert pour l'éloge de Choron* [1845], 2f. In Paris, François-Joseph Fétis performed works by Palestrina and other sixteenth-century composers in his historical concerts; see Robert Wangermée, "Les Premiere Concerts historiques à Paris," in *Mélanges Ernest Closson: Recueil d'articles musicologiques offert à Ernest Closson à l'occasion de son 65ᵉ anniversaire* (Brussels: Société Belge de Musicologie, 1948), 189.

The revival of *a cappella* singing and the Palestrina style had a significant effect on both church music and oratorio For many, *a cappella* singing became not only the ideal sound for worship, but a musical symbol of holiness, purity, and piety. A composer of an oratorio could draw upon this symbol when setting portions of texts reflecting those very qualities and simultaneously provide an effective change of sonority within an orchestrally accompanied work. Strictly speaking, of course, the term *a cappella* was interpreted in the nineteenth century as completely unaccompanied singing. Nevertheless, an approximation of an *a cappella* sound that was often used in oratorios, and that would evoke an audience response similar to pure *a cappella*, is a chorus supported by instruments either softly doubling the voices or playing an unobtrusive accompaniment. (For an amateur chorus this is a prudent device and one that oratorio composers often chose.) In fact, Koch's *Lexicon* of 1802, written before the height of the *a cappella* revival, assumes *colle parte* instrumentation: "with this expression [*a cappella*] is indicated, mainly in church music, that the instruments should go along in unison with the voices."[41]

Significant among historicist activities in nineteenth-century church music, and of some importance to oratorio, was the restoration of Gregorian chant in the Catholic church and, with the return to the Lutheran liturgy, the reintroduction of plainchant in Protestant churches as well. Early in the century a call to restore Gregorian chant within the Catholic Church of the French Empire (including Germany at that time) is found in Alexandre Choron's *Considération sur la nécessité de rétablir le chant de l'Eglise de Rome dans toutes les églises de l'Empire française* (Paris, 1811). In France the work of restoration began in the 1840s, and in Germany as part of the Cecilian movement in the 1860s.[42] From the mid century on, publication about plainchant rapidly increased and came to significantly affect the view of church music and oratorio.

* * * * *

Turning now to examples of historicism in nineteenth-century oratorio, a particularly obvious example is the revival of the French overture. Handel had used it to open *Messiah* and other oratorios, but it had long been obsolete in both opera and oratorio. In 1806, the French overture appears at the beginning of Johann Gottfried Schicht's *Das Ende des Gerechten*. Schicht participated in the Bach revival and edited some of Bach's music. He begins his French overture with an Adagio maestoso that incorporates the traditional dotted rhythms, and he follows it with a fugal Vivace. Numerous other oratorios, from throughout the century, begin with French overtures that either retain the traditional characteristics or slightly modify them.[43]

Choral styles, too, reflect the historicist trend. In most German oratorios of the late eighteenth century choruses are largely homophonic, and fugal writing is reserved for the final chorus.[44] It is therefore a striking change to find that many oratorios of the nineteenth century offer a balance of homophonic and contrapuntal choruses, as Handel's oratorios do. Fugue and fugato are common, and many fugues adopt some of the characteristics of *stile antico*, such as half-note motion (either marked *alla breve* or in 3/2 time), a severe subject, and *colla parte* orchestration. Such a fugue is shown in ex. 17.1, which forms the ending of the most widely performed oratorio in Germany of the 1820s, Friedrich Schneider's *Das Weltgericht* (1819). Fugue is basic to most of Schneider's fifteen oratorios, and his fugues seem to have been modeled mainly on Handel's. For instance, the beginning of a double-fugue from no. 9 in *Das Weltgericht*, illustrated in ex. 17.2, suggests in its first two measures Handel's setting of the text "For the Lord God

---

[41] Heinrich Christoph Koch, *Musikalisches Lexikon*, 2 vols. (1802; reprint, Hildesheim: Georg Olms, 1964), 47.

[42] For a useful survey, see *The New Grove Dictionary of Music and Musicians* (1980), s.v. "Plainchant II, 10: 19th-Century Restoration Attempts," by John A. Emerson.

[43] A few examples are Louis Spohr's *Die letzten Dinge* (1826), Friedrich Schneider's *Christus das Kind* (1829), Carl Loewe's *Die Zerstörung von Jerusalem* (1829; begins with a considerably modified French overture), Heinrich Elkamp's *Paulus* (1835), Ernst Reiter's *Das neue Paradies* (1845), Friedrich Kühmstedt's *Verklärung des Herrn* (1850), Julius Emil Leonhard's *Johannes der Täufer* (1856), Johann Vogt's *Die Auferweckung des Lazarus* (1858), Josef Gabriel von Rheinberger's *Christoforus* (1880), and Constanz Berneker's *Christi Himmelfahrt* (1888).

[44] On choral style in German oratorios of the later eighteenth century, see Smither, *The Oratorio in the Classical Era*, 372-73, 375. Haydn's oratorios are exceptional in their time for their numerous contrapuntal choruses, but his oratorios were strongly influenced by Handel and in that sense are early historicist works.

Example 17.1. Friedrich Schneider, *Das Weltgericht* (1819), ending.

Example 17.2. Schneider, *Das Weltgericht*, beginning of no. 9, "Sein Wort ist Wahrheit."

omnipotent reigneth" in the "Hallelujah" chorus of *Messiah*. The Handelian suggestion would probably have been obvious to members of the audience who were familiar with *Messiah*; on the other hand, this type of melody is also a generic example of a Baroque fugue. More clearly modeled throughout on the Handelian oratorio, however, are Johann Heinrich Clasing's *Belsazar* (1825) and *Die Tochter Jephtas* (1828), and Bernhard Klein's *Jephta* (1828) and *David* (1830). One of several oratorios by Carl Loewe in which the choruses show a strong link to Baroque style is his *Die Festzeiten* (1825-36).[45]

Lest one assume that the use of Baroque fugal style as a model met with universal approval, it is worth considering Wagner's point of view. In his treatise *Die deutsche Oper* of 1834, Wagner spoke out against historicism in oratorio, and indeed against oratorio itself. He singled out Friedrich Schneider in particular, no doubt because his oratorios were so popular at choral festivals then in vogue:

> Is it not an obvious misjudgement of the present day when one now writes oratorios, in whose content and form no one any longer believes? Who believes in the untruthful stiffness of a Schneider

---

[45] On Loewe's historicism in this work, see Feder, 357-62, and Reinhold Dusella, *Die Oratorien Carl Loewes*, Deutsche Musik im Osten, 1 (Bonn: Gudrun Schröder Verlag, 1991), 37-51, passim.

fugue, precisely because it is now composed by Friedrich Schneider? That which appears to us venerable on account of its truthfulness in Bach and Handel must necessarily be laughable to us in Friedrich Schneider, for, again be it said, one does not believe it with him, since it is by no means his own conviction.[46]

Wagner's view was gradually taken up by his vociferous admirers. Still, oratorio retained its popularity with choral societies and at festivals, and the historicist trend continued unabated.

Not only fugues, but also canons—virtually absent from oratorios of the late eighteenth century—appear from time to time in German oratorios of the nineteenth century. Perhaps the earliest canon in German oratorio in the century occurs in Schicht's *Das Ende des Gerechten*, which includes a section marked "canone alla quinta sotto," within the finale of part 1. Loewe reaches earlier than the Baroque period for a model in his oratorio *Johann Huss* (1841), based on the life of the fifteenth-century religious reformer. In that work he includes a "Missa canonica," a setting of the Kyrie of the Mass in a four-voice canon intended to evoke Huss's period.[47] Among other oratorios that include canons are Sigismund Neukomm's *Das Gesetz des alten Bundes, oder die Gesetzgebung auf Sinai* and Schneider's *Gideon* (1829).[48] The canon in the duet of false witnesses in Bach's *St. Matthew Passion* was clearly the model for the duet of false witnesses in Mendelssohn's *St. Paul* and in the chorus of false witnesses in Loewe's Passion oratorio *Das Sühnopfer des neuen Bundes* (1847).[49] Surely the greatest concentration of rigorously contrapuntal music in nineteenth-century oratorio comes at the end of the century in Friedrich Draeseke's monumental cycle *Christus: Ein Mysterium in einem Vorspiele und drei Oratorien* (1899).[50] In the four oratorios that make up the cycle (the *Vorspiel* is itself an oratorio), a large majority of the choruses are fugal,[51] and canonic writing appears as well.

The revival of Renaissance polyphony, particularly the polyphony of Palestrina, and the enshrinement of *a cappella* singing as a symbol of holiness in church music, had their effect on oratorio. In this period groups of holy personages and texts particularly important for their religious significance began to be characterized by the *a cappella* sound. Among the myriad instances that might be mentioned are Schneider's settings of angelic voices and occasionally of texts sung by other spiritual figures in *Das Weltgericht* (1819), *Pharao* (1828), and *Christus das Kind* (1829).[52] Mendelssohn followed the same procedure for the well-known *a cappella* trio in his *Elijah* (1846) "Hebe deine Augen auf" (Lift thine eyes), sung by the Angels watching over Elijah. Several times in *St. Paul* and *Elijah*, Mendelssohn makes effective use of *a cappella* settings to emphasize texts of religious importance, as does Spohr in *Die letzten Dinge* (1826).

Loewe makes abundant use of *a cappella* settings to highlight the spiritual quality of certain texts or personages. In his *Die Zerstörung von Jerusalem* (1829), for example, the Voices of Spirits sing a grave, homophonic, *a cappella* chorus, strongly contrasting with its dramatically active context. In *Johann Huss*, Loewe has the great reformer intone the incipit of a chorale, and his congregation joins in, all without accompaniment. Loewe provides an *a cappella* setting in *falsobordone* style for the *Improperia*—clearly suggesting Palestrina's *Improperia*—in his *Die Festzeiten* (in part 2, beginning of the Lenten section). And in Loewe's oratorio *Palestrina* (1841), its very subject a reflection of the period's

---

[46] Richard Wagner, *Sämtliche Schriften und Dichtungen*, Volks-Ausgabe, 6th ed., vol. 12 (Leipzig: Breitkopf & Härtel, [1912]), 4.

[47] The entire *Missa canonica* is reproduced in Dusella, *Die Oratorien Carl Loewes*, 133-38.

[48] In Neukomm's work, no. 15, "Es ist kein Gott," includes a canon at the lower fourth between soprano and bass solos followed after a choral episode by one at the octave between the tenor and soprano. In Schneider's oratorio, no. 4, labeled "Terzett. (Canone a due all'ottava)," is a prayer in canon between Sulamith (S) and Gideon (T), during which Joas (B) enters singing a free part in longer notes, while the canon continues.

[49] See Mendelssohn's *St. Paul*, no. 5; and Loewe's *Sühnopfer*, no. 16. But neither example is as strict a canon as Bach's.

[50] The most extensive writing on this work is Erich Roeder, *Felix Draeseke: Der Lebens- und Leidensweg eines deutschen Meister*, 2 vols. (Dresden and Berlin: Wilhelm Limpert-Verlag, 1932-37), 321-457.

[51] One of the most impressive choruses of the entire cycle is a massive double fugue in the second oratorio, *Christus der Prophet* (no. 4, the final chorus of part 2). Draeseke considered it his greatest contrapuntal achievement and printed it as a model in his textbook on counterpoint; see Roeder, *Felix Draeseke*, 350. Draeseke's textbook is *Der gebundene Styl: Lehrbuch für Kontrapunkt und Fuge* (Hanover: Oertel, 1902).

[52] In *Weltgericht* the *a cappella* quartet of four archangels returns several times as a reminiscence; in *Pharao*, again an *a cappella* setting is used for archangels. Cf. Helmut Lomnitzer, *Das musikalische Werk Friedrich Schneiders (1786-1853) insbesondere die Oratorien* (Marburg: Erich Mauersberger, 1961), 193; and in *Christus das Kind* the same type of setting is used for an ensemble of the Three Wise Men (cf. Lomnitzer, 200-01).

historicism, he quotes from an Ave Maria by Palestrina and from the Sanctus, Benedictus, and Agnus Dei of the *Missa Papae Marcelli*. In Loewe's *Sühnopfer*, *a cappella* singing is reserved for two reflective chorales, sung by a quartet of soloists, during the institution of the Eucharist (no. 11): one after Jesus offers the Apostles bread, the other after he offers them wine.[53]

In Ferdinand Ries's *Die Könige in Israël* (1837), at the end of part 1, an antiphonal chorus of Israelites and Philistines represents the God-fearing Israelites by an *a cappella* setting in serene, long-note values and the heathen Philistines by an agitated, orchestrally accompanied chorus. In Liszt's *Christus* (1868), the "Stabat mater speciosa" (no. 3) is set largely for *a cappella* chorus in a style suggestive of *falsobordone* (except for the harmony), as shown in ex. 17.3. In the same work the choruses in "The Beatitudes" and "The Lord's Prayer" are set in part *a cappella* and in part with unobtrusive accompaniment for the organ, presumably to insure the choral pitch while creating the impression

Example 17.3. Liszt, *Christus* (1868), beginning of no. 3, "Stabat mater speciosa."

---

[53] At several other points in the work, however, reflective chorales are sung by the chorus doubled by strings.

of an *a cappella* sound. At the end of the century, August Friedrich Klughardt, in *Die Zerstörung Jerusalems* (1899), follows the tradition established early in the century by setting Angelic Voices (no. 9, "Wandle getrost und fürchte dich nicht") for *a cappella* chorus (SSA).

The mere presence of a chorale in a nineteenth-century German oratorio is not necessarily a historicist element or evidence of a revival. In the later eighteenth century chorales were frequently heard in oratorios, but they were typically presented in a simple, homophonic setting; in that period elaborations associated with the Baroque had been virtually abandoned. In the nineteenth century, however, composers revived Baroque treatments of the chorale—thus it is the treatment, rather than the chorale's presence *per se*, that is the historicist element. Loewe's *Festzeiten*, for instance, includes chorale elaborations derived from the Baroque chorale-prelude tradition in part 1 (Advent section, "Wachet auf, ruft uns die Stimme") and part 3 (Pentecost section, "Ein feste Burg ist unser Gott").[54] Some of the chorales in Mendelssohn's *St. Paul* follow procedures of Baroque chorale elaboration: in no. 15, "Wachet auf!" the chorale is presented with interpolated brass fanfares between phrases; in no. 28, at the Adagio "O Jesu Christe, wahres Licht," orchestral interpolations separate the first five chorale phrases, which are sung *a cappella*;[55] in no. 35 the chorale "Wir glauben all' an einen Gott" is treated as a *cantus firmus* in long notes (see ex. 17.4). The chorus is given *colla parte* orchestration: the chorale tune is sung by the second soprano and doubled by two oboes, two horns, and an alto trombone, while other vocal lines are doubled by strings. In the same work, near the end of the overture the tune "Wachet auf!" is given a similar treatment. Chorales continue to appear occasionally as *cantus firmi* for the remainder of the century.[56]

Example 17.4. Mendelssohn, *St. Paul* (1836), chorale "Wir glauben all' an einen Gott."

Continued

---

[54] These and other chorale treatments in this work are summarized in Dusella, 39.

[55] The character of the interpolations in nos. 15 and 28, however, is typically Romantic, rather than Baroque. On this point, see Stanley, 129-31.

[56] Among the works that include *cantus firmus* treatment of chorales are: Ludwig Meinardus, *Simon Petrus* (1857), no. 17, "Schaff' in mir, Gott"; Johann Vogt, *Die Auferweckung des Lazarus* (1858), no. 19, double chorus; Martin Blumner, *Der Fall Jerusalems* (1874), no. 9, "Wenn meine Zeit vorüber," and in the same work, no. 25. Meinardus, *Luther in Worms* (1874), includes several: no. 2, "Pilgerlied," a "Choral mit Chor"; no. 12, the chorale "Gott wende alle Trübsal schwer" to the tune of "Ich heb' mein Augen sehnlich auf"; no. 14, a double chorus of Adherents of Rome and Adherents of Luther, plus a boy choir, singing the text "Der römisch Götz ist ausgethan" to the chorale tune "Vom Himmel hoch da komm'ich her" as *cantus firmus*; and later Luther sings "Ein feste Burg," while other voices weave counterpoints to it and that tune becomes a *cantus firmus*. In Heinrich von Herzogenberg's *Die Geburt Christi* (1895), no. 3, the chorus "Hier leiden wir die grösse Noth" employs a *cantus firmus* in soprano 1 on the tune "O Heiland reiss' die Himmel auf"; in Draeseke's *Christus* (1899), second oratorio, *Christus der Prophet*, no. 2, the chorale-paraphrase chorus on "Vom himmel hoch da komm ich her" includes a *cantus firmus* in the wind instruments.

Example 17.4.—*Continued*

As noted above, concern with restoring plainchant began in the first half of the century and gained momentum around the mid century, the period in which Liszt, who was himself interested in the restoration of Gregorian chant,[57] conceived his oratorios. Liszt's extensive use of Gregorian chant in *Die Legende von der heiligen Elisabeth* (1862) and *Christus* (1868) no doubt resulted from the historicism prevalent in his time, as well as his personal commitment to Catholicism. In *Elisabeth*, the motive that identifies the saint is based on a chant. The chant is shown in ex. 17.5a as it is given in the appendix to the score, where Liszt identifies it as an antiphon for the feast of St. Elizabeth.[58] It is the only recurring motive of the oratorio that is heard in every number, and it appears in more transformations than any other. Not only is it found in vocal lines and orchestral accompaniments, but purely orchestral passages are also based on it (exx. 17.5b-d show some of the many transformations). Liszt's *Christus* is even more strongly conditioned by chant than *Elisabeth*. Of the oratorio's fourteen numbers, nine begin with chant melodies.[59]

---

[57] See Merrick, 91-95.

[58] In the *Liber usualis*, no. 801 (Tournai: Desclée, 1934), p. 1553, a slightly different version of the chant, with the text "Elisabeth, pacis et patriae mater," is given as the antiphon for St. Elizabeth, Queen of Portugal, Widow, at the second Vespers on 8 July. Whether it may also have been used for St. Elizabeth of Hungary, the subject of Liszt's oratorio, is an open question, but it was apparently given to Liszt as a chant for her feast.

[59] Nos. 1, 2, 5-7, 10, 12-14.

Example 17.5. Liszt, *Die Legende von der heiligen Elisabeth* (1862):

a. Antiphon for the feast of St. Elizabeth, as given by Liszt in the appendix.

b. From the "Einleitung."

c. From no. 1, scene A.

d. From no. 2, scene D.

Plainchant did not become a prominent feature of German oratorio, yet composers other than Liszt occasionally made use of chant or chantlike melody. In Loewe's brief oratorios composed in 1860 for either organ or piano accompaniment—*Die Heilung des Blindgeborenen, Johannes der Täufer,* and *Die Auferweckung des Lazarus*—the recitatives are quite simple and sometimes based on a chantlike recitation tone. *Alarich* (1881) by Georg Vierling would appear to be influenced by chant in no. 2, the chorus "Agnus Dei," sung before St. Peter's Basilica in Rome during a procession of the Roman people and the clergy. And in the Draeseke cycle *Christus* (1899), the beginning of the first oratorio, *Christi Weihe*, extensively paraphrases the chant "Elisabeth Zachariae magnum virum genuit."[60]

The oratorio seems to have been more strongly influenced than all other major musical genres by the historical consciousness prevalent in the nineteenth century. Given that it was such a historically conscious era, why would other major genres not have equally reflected the historicist tendencies? For some genres there was of course little or nothing by way of significant precedent from the Baroque period or earlier to reflect—the symphony, the string quartet, the art song, and the piano sonata, for example, come readily to mind. In these we occasionally find references to the techniques and procedures of earlier times, but such references are not defining hallmarks of the genres. Then there is the case of opera. Opera was a quintessentially Baroque genre, and yet composers of opera in the nineteenth century moved increasingly away from—indeed actively rejected—the principles of Baroque opera. Handel was clearly not the model for composers of opera in this period that he was for composers of oratorio.

But oratorio is a religious genre, and this may be one key to answering the question. On the one hand, the nineteenth century, which had witnessed widespread industrialization, was an age of increasing secularization. On the other hand, religious values continued to be important, even though attendance in churches declined radically. Was the comfort of continuity with the past needed by the men and women who created the market for oratorio, as well as by the singers who sang in the many amateur choruses and festivals, and by their audiences? For the time being the question remains without a definitive answer; however, close scrutiny of the directions taken by church music over the course of the entire century may well affirm that hypothesis.

---

[60] The antiphon for second Vespers on June 24, the Feast of the Nativity of St. John the Baptist, printed in the *Liber usualis*, 1503.

18

Wanda Landowska and the Revival of the Harpsichord

ALICE HUDNALL CASH

Wanda Landowska—today the name evokes images of harpsichords and velvet dresses, brocade upholstery, and flocked wallpaper. To those of us who grew up with her recordings of the *Goldberg Variations* and the *Well-Tempered Clavier*, her name is synonymous with Bach on the harpsichord. But what do we really know about her struggle to revive the harpsichord?

From her earliest years in Warsaw, Landowska felt a deep affinity with the music of the Baroque. She had not yet heard a harpsichord, and did not know that the idea of a woman choosing a career in music might not be universally well received. Because her own family supported her intentions to perform and compose, and because her teachers recognized her exceptional talent, she never considered that there could be barriers in her future. When she entered the Hochschule für Musik in Berlin in 1896, at the age of seventeen, women were just beginning to be admitted to such institutions of higher learning, and, even then, they were often forced to attend classes that were segregated by gender. Fortunately, that was not Landowska's experience; in fact, during most of her life she enjoyed "male privilege." Her story is unusual, and it must be told. The major role that she played in restoring the harpsichord to the concert stage cannot be denied, though, as I have discussed elsewhere, there were attempts to denigrate her contributions for a wide variety of reasons.[1]

Twenty-five years ago harpsichordist and author Howard Schott wrote this tribute to all the pioneers of the early instrument and early music revival:

> Harpsichord playing, just as much as instrument building, has been undergoing change as a result of this revolution ever since. Indeed the revolution [harpsichord revival] can be said still to be in progress so that the time to assess its effects has not yet arrived. However, it is appropriate that we should not look back over the phase which has come to an end and review the course taken by the harpsichord revival. It is really quite unjust to decry the hard-won accomplishments of the pioneers in that movement. The harpsichord was the first of the early instruments to be brought back to a place of honour in musical life. The lutes and viols followed not long after, but the woodwinds and brasses had to wait far longer for their resurrections. We are only now coming to recognize the need to revive earlier forms of the violin family and their respective forms of bow. The contribution of the harpsichord revival to the renaissance of early music as a whole can hardly be overestimated.[2]

---

[1] Alice Hudnall Cash, "Wanda Landowska and the Revival of the Harpsichord: A Reassessment" (Ph.D. diss., University of Kentucky, in cooperation with the University of Louisville, 1990), where there is also discussion of Landowska's previously unknown compositions, her teaching, and recordings. See also the videotape produced by Attic, Goldwater, Pontius Productions, which draws on the dissertation (VAI International, 109 Wheeler Avenue, Pleasantville, NY 10570).

[2] "The Harpsichord Revival," *Early Music* 2, no. 2 (April 1974): 95.

Wanda Landowska's role in the revival of the harpsichord and early music can hardly be overestimated. In reviewing her life, one can believe she did not realize either the difficulty of the task she set for herself, or the extent of the impact the work she did during the eighty years of her life would have on future generations of musicians and music lovers.

The earliest mention of Landowska in Paris musical journals comes from *Le Ménéstral* of 15 December 1901. It is brief, and merely lists her name in conjunction with the first concert given by "La Société populaire de musique" at L'Hotel des Sociétés Savantes.[3] By the following February 16, she was beginning to accumulate positive reviews for her performances on the piano, particularly the Mozart Piano Concerto in E♭, K.271. The reviewer, Amadée Boutarel, wrote: "Madame Wanda Landowska has assured herself a pretty success and a loyal following with her elegant performance of Mozart's charming Piano Concerto in E-Flat, K.271."[4] Landowska performed and recorded this concerto many times throughout her career, always on the piano, and it is one of the many works that became closely associated with her.

On 15 February 1903, *Le Ménéstral*, which at that time kept the public informed, among other things, of the progress of women, announced, "a great victory for feminism from the artistic point of view and for the young artists of the weaker sex." The great victory, which was a total reversal of past policy, was a decision to make the Grand Prix du Rome open to women and men. This was indeed a victory for young women composers who were in most competitions considered to be in a separate category.[5] Because Landowska was no longer concentrating on composition, and was increasingly turning her attention to performing, these matters appear not to have had much impact on her. If Landowska was at all aware that being a woman was in any way a handicap, or that many of her female contemporaries did not enjoy the same degree of success and acceptance that she did, she never mentioned or wrote about it.[6]

By 1906 Landowska's reputation was well-established in Paris and was spreading to other countries. A notice in *Le Ménéstral* for 18 February 1906 mentions a concert Landowska played in Cologne. The next week she performed the Mozart Concerto K.271 at the same time that Eugène Enesco played the Bach Chaconne at another location. On February 25, a writer for *Le Ménéstral* informs us that:

> Two soloists were competing for the public's favor: both have had it equally. If only M. Enesco had known all the approbations with his lively and personal interpretation of Bach's *Chaconne* for solo violin. Mme. Landowska has not been less acclaimed after the graceful and spiritual Concerto in E-flat by Mozart, which she interpreted with a very correct feeling, a simple, unaffected style and a remarkable clarity.[7]

The writer obviously felt that Landowska and Enesco were musical equals, though they had played different instruments and had different interpretive gifts. In March of the same year Landowska published the sixteen-page booklet *Sur*

---

[3] *Le Ménéstral*, 15 December 1901, 399.

[4] "Madame Wanda Landowska s'est assurée un jolie succès auprès d'une assistance sympathique; elle a joué avec une certaine élégance le charmante concerto pour piano en mi bémol de Mozart"; *Le Ménéstral*, 16 February 1902. On the same program a "Concertstück" by Diémer was performed. Although the Mozart concerto K.271 was written for a French pianist, Mlle. Jeunehomme, her name cannot be found in the biographical dictionaries by Fétis, Grove, or Baker. As Alfred Einstein, *Mozart: His Character, His Work*, trans. Arthur Mendel and Nathan Broder (New York: Norton, 1968), 294-95, observed, this concerto was one of Mozart's boldest and most monumental works; yet, ironically, the woman who inspired it remains a legendary figure.

[5] "... une grande victoire du féminisme au point de vue artistique, et les jeunes artistes du sexe faible ...." *Le Ménéstral*, 15 February 1903.

[6] Landowska's diaries were willed to Denise Restout, who edited *Landowska on Music* (New York: Stein and Day, 1965), and have not been made available to researchers. It is thus not known at this time whether information in them may shed a different light on the effect traditional attitudes about a woman's place in music may have had upon decisions Landowska made or views she had of herself.

[7] "Deux soloistes se disputaient la faveur du publique: tous les deux l'ont eu à parts égales. Si M. Enesco a su conquérir tous les suffrage avec son exécution très personnelle de la *Chaconne* de Bach pour violon seul, Mme. Wanda Landowska n'a pas été moins acclamée après le spirituel et gracieux concerto pour piano en mi bémol de Mozart, qu'elle a interprété avec un sentiment très juste, un style simple sans affectation, une netteté remarquable." *Le Ménéstral*, 25 February 1906, 53.

l'interpretation des oeuvres de clavecin de J. S. Bach. One of her early important writings on music, it met with critical acclaim from colleagues and the press, including from *Le Ménéstral* on March 18.[8]

The book that she and her husband, Henri Lew, diligently researched and wrote, *Musique ancienne* was published in 1909. It, too, was well-received by her peers. A wide variety of topics were dealt with, ranging from her arguments against the notion of "progress" in music, which was a very wide-spread and accepted belief at the turn of the century, to chapters on the history of the harpsichord, as well as one on virtuosi, emphasizing the fact that virtuosi are by no means a new phenomenon. Today the book seems rather antagonistic in tone, but it is worth reading because it shows the depth of Landowska's research and understanding. She quotes seventy-four authors and composers in the course of the eighteen chapters, and cites works that were of great significance during the Baroque era, but which in her day had long since fallen into oblivion.[9]

Women's issues in the arts were being discussed in Paris and other European and American cities at this time. For centuries women had been thought to be incapable of sustained creative effort or too frail physically to meet the unceasing demands of composing, conducting, or concertizing. Their greatest contributions had been thought to be in producing the men who would accomplish these tasks and in providing a cheerful atmosphere and families for these men.[10] And yet, the belief had persisted that music was an ideal profession for women. Teaching children was regarded as "women's work" because women were believed to have been child-like themselves, and therefore more attuned to childhood ideals. Havelock Ellis (1859-1939), the well-known psychologist, wrote: "There is certainly no art in which women have shown themselves more helpless." Ellis interpreted the lack of achievement in music as an indication of the biological inferiority of women.[11] He, like others, failed to take into account the lack of opportunities women had. That they were excluded from participation in major symphony orchestras, were not allowed to play certain "masculine" instruments, or even in some cases to have access to higher education, was overlooked.

The so-called "women-composer question" occupied much space in the press on both sides of the Atlantic in the first decade of the twentieth century. Many writers felt that women were constitutionally and emotionally unsuited to the rigors of composition, and especially to large-scale works. Underlying this belief was a strong moral undercurrent that translated the "could not" into "ought not." Women who wrote in certain genres, such as operas or symphonies, ran the risk of being called "unfeminine" or worse, "unnatural." Many of the same writers also thought that this unsuitability applied to playing in orchestras composed primarily of men, and certainly to conducting orchestras. In his book *Woman's Work in Music* (1903), Arthur Elson wrote:

> The time has gone by when men need fear that they will have to do the sewing if their wives devote themselves to higher pursuits.... Whether women are in any way handicapped by the constitution of their sex is a point that is still undecided. It would seem that composition demanded no great physical strength and no one will deny that women often possess the requisite mental breadth. The average sweet girl graduate of the conservatories, who is made up chiefly of sentiment, and hates mathematics, will hardly make a very deep mark in any art.[12]

---

[8] This booklet was later incorporated in a slightly different version into her book with collaboration of Henri Lew-Landowski, *Musique ancienne* (Paris: Mercure de France, 1909).

[9] A bibliography of the sources quoted in *Musique ancienne*, and the complete table of contents, are given in Cash, appendix 2.

[10] See, for example, George Upton, *Woman in Music* (Boston: J. R. Osgood, 1880), 21-28; also see Carol Neuls-Bates, ed., *Women in Music: An Anthology of Source Readings from the Middle Ages to the Present* (New York: Harper and Row, 1982), xiv.

[11] Ellis's statement of 1894 is cited in Jane Bowers and Judith Tick, eds., *Women Making Music: The Western Art Tradition, 1150-1950* (Urbana: University of Illinois Press, 1986), 8-9.

[12] George Upton, a Chicago music critic, was one of the most adamant authors on this subject. His *Woman in Music* (1880) was quoted and cited for the next half century as documentation for why women were constitutionally incapable of becoming great composers. There is a growing literature on this topic: see Marcia Citron, "Gender, Professionalism and the Musical Canon," *Journal of Musicology* 8 (1990): 102-16; also see Cei Tullix, *Women in Music Newsletter* 7 (London: Battersea Arts Centre, Old Town Hall, Lavender Hill, 1989): 5; Carol Neuls-Bates, "Women's Orchestras in the United States, 1925-45," in *Women Making Music*, 349-69; also see Fredrique Petrides, "Women in Orchestras," *Etude* 16, no. 7 (1938): 429. Because the history of music was then recorded primarily by men, women's roles and abilities were inadequately explored. Consequently, why certain women born in the nineteenth century—and earlier—succeeded and others did not continues to be difficult to determine. To assume that those who succeeded did not encounter difficulties, however, would be a fallacy.

Although he goes on to cite Augusta Holmes as a woman who succeeded in music, throughout the book Elson perpetuates the myth that music is a social skill for women and that serious musical endeavors, such as composing, will probably never be something that women can do. Elson was an advocate of the idea that one of the greatest things a woman could do was be a patron of the arts and to encourage talented men to fulfill their gifts in music.[13]

Is it possible that this sort of thinking deterred Landowska from continuing in composition? Her compositions show that she was a gifted composer, but she must have believed that her greatest gifts were in the areas of performing and scholarship. Though we do not know in her case, some women of potential were likely discouraged from pursuing careers in composition or did not have the financial or personal freedom to pursue this goal independently. In the period she lived, a woman was still financially dependent on her father or husband and, if either man did not support her goals, she was greatly handicapped. Landowska, however, had the support of first her father, then her husband.

Le Ménéstral of 11 September 1909 announced verification that women musicians now numbered among the faculty at the Berlin Academy of Music: "Ten women teach there. In the voice department, mainly, six classes are taught by women. The head of the theory/composition section, M. Max Bruch has a woman substitute, Mme. Elisabeth Kuyper."[14] Landowska had left Berlin for Paris specifically because she had felt the atmosphere in Berlin to have been traditional with respect to the "proper place" for women in music. But the progress that had been made in Berlin came to affect Landowska, for, in 1913, the year her "Landowska Pleyel" was completed, and barely more than a decade since she had brought the harpsichord to public awareness, she was invited to begin the first harpsichord class at the Hochschule für Musik, her alma mater.[15]

At the conclusion of World War I Landowska returned alone to Paris, and once again started over (Lew had been killed mysteriously in Berlin, and rumors abounded that he had been a double agent). When the École Normale opened its doors in the fall of 1919, Landowska was one of its most famous and important teachers. Even though Nadia Boulanger also taught there, and despite her considerable influence in helping to get the school started, Boulanger was not mentioned in the initial publicity. By fall 1920 Landowska was on a concert tour in Spain; a review by Adolfo Salazar in the Madrid *El Sol* of July 20 is full of accolades for her performance of works by Handel, Rameau, and Bach on the harpsichord. From other Spanish reviews it is clear she was then quite popular in Spain, being referred to there as "the most famous harpsichordist in the world," and "the one who has succeeded in reviving the harpsichord and the music of the great masters." Three years later she made her first tour in the United States. The earliest review found of a performance by Landowska in this country comes from the *New York Herald* of 12 October 1923. It is relatively brief, but demonstrates the variety of repertoire that she played on her first tour here:

> Ancients and moderns vied with one another on the program of the New York Symphony Orchestra in Aeolian Hall yesterday afternoon. But the oldest conservative could have sat side by side with his modern brother without shuddering. The important event of the afternoon was the appearance of Mme. Wanda Landowska, assisted by Gustave Tinlot, violinist, and Georges Barrère, flutist. Mme. Landowska played Bach's fifth "Brandenburg" concerto for harpsichord, violin, flute and orchestra. The concerto was played Saturday afternoon in Carnegie Hall. Its intimate spirit and genial warmth were displayed to greater advantage in the smaller confines of Aeolian Hall. This famous old concerto, admirably revealed the essential polyphonic texture of the early instrumental forms, received a delightful interpretation. In Mme. Landowska's soli, Handel's "The Harmonious Blacksmith," Purcell's "Ground" and Scarlatti's "Sonata for Crossed Keyboards," the noble roughness of the harpsichord's

---

[13] Arthur Elson, *Woman's Work in Music* (Boston: L. C. Page and Co., 1903), 234-35.

[14] Holmes held degrees in composition, but found it necessary to adopt a male pseudonym in order to see her works published. She submitted two pieces with a male pseudonym and both were accepted, but when she later ceased practicing the subterfuge on principle, claimed she "virtually relinquished any chance for significant activity as a composer until the late 60's when attitudes began to change." See Edith Borroff, "Women Composers: Reminiscence and History," *College Music Symposium* 15 (1975): 27.

[15] "Dix femmes y enseignent. Dans les classes de chant, notamment, six cours ont été confiés à des musiciennes. Le titulaire du cours de théorie et de composition, M. Max Bruch, a pour suppléant une femme, Mme. Elisabeth Kuyper." *Le Ménéstral*, 11 September 1909, 293. See "Conversation with Harpsichordist Denise Restout," *Harpsichord* 7 (1974): 18, for a description of the early twentieth-century harpsichord Landowska played.

tones was wholly at home. The new music was "Ein Tanzspiel," by Franz Schrecker, at present director of the Berlin Hochschule and composer of several operas and orchestral works seldom heard in America.

There is evidence that Landowska succeeded in gaining entry into the "network" of active performers in this time, a strategy for advancing one's career usually not open to women, though she appears to have been welcomed because of her talent and intelligence, and through her determination. The concert that brought her world-wide attention was her debut with the Philadelphia Orchestra under Leopold Stokowski, with whom she shared a Polish heritage. Stokowski and Landowska also maintained a strong mutual admiration.[16]

While in the early days of her career in Paris much attention had been paid to the fact that she was a woman and that the instrument she played was such an "interesting curiosity." In the positive reviews of the 1920s the commentary moved to a higher level. This review, from the *Philadelphia Public Ledger*, was the real beginning of her reputation in the United States. Under the banner headline "WANDA LANDOWSKA WITH ORCHESTRA," and the smaller headline, "Polish Harpsichordist and Pianist, in American Debut, Plays Three Concertos," comes this sensitive critique:

> Yesterday's program of the Philadelphia Orchestra was one of tempered dynamics and the twilight mood. Its outstanding feature in creating an atmosphere and reviving the tradition of the music of a bygone day, was the American debut of the Polish harpsichordist and pianist, Wanda Landowska. To the great majority of those present she was introducing an unfamiliar instrument, and to listen properly it was necessary to put aside much of the cumbersome apparatus of modern life, together with the imposing scale and the magnificent dimensions of the modern concert hall, and remember the miniature pattern of intimacy, delicacy and fastidious grace that distinguished the chamber music of old.
>
> Stokowski had built his program carefully about its central objective. He began with the "Alceste" overture of Gluck, which laid for all that followed a foundation of large, spacious, organ-like chords in the simplicity of the "grand manner" of the patriarchs. He closed the program with the most profound and withal the tenderest reading of Schubert's "Unfinished Symphony" that our orchestra has given. The golden links, three in number, between the sweeping stateliness of Gluck and the eternal passion of Schubert were supplied by the performance of Madame Landowska. She played first the Handel concerto in B-flat for harpsichord and orchestra, then the Bach concerto in Italian style for harpsichord unsupported, and finally the Mozart concerto in E-flat for piano and orchestra. It was a heroic undertaking for one afternoon. And Madame Landowska is not an Amazon, not a "puma of the pianoforte," as a sister-pianist has been styled. She is a rarely sensitive and susceptible spirit, or she could not minister with such poetic refinement and quick intelligence as high priestess of the ancient instrument.
>
> The Handel music at once disclosed the infallable technician whose fingers at the fleetest pace seemed incapable of missing a single one of the notes that ran on in a dazzling chain, a whirling arabesque, a fountain shower from the plucked strings of that jewel case of curly maple and taut silvery wires. The Larghetto gave the welcome opportunity to hear the tones of a more delicate and pensive utterance. The Bach concerto brought the similar breathing interval of the Andante between the rapid percussion of the Allegro and the Presto. With the Mozart concerto the versatile performer went to the piano, and carried to its keyboard the harpsichord technique. She was not attempting to unleash the reverberatory thunders that are imprisoned beneath the lid of the modern piano. Perfectly in sympathy with her entourage, her mind and that of Stokowski communicative at all points, she left the stronger accents and violent stresses to the greater voices of the orchestra, disclosing for her part that facile fluency and miraculous assurance which reached a climax of melting eloquence in the Andante, rightly called by Madame Landowska one of the most beautiful to be found in any Mozart concerto.
>
> The spellbound silence all the while she played, quite as convincingly as the long applause that followed and brought four recalls, gave evidence of a conquest made by the sincerity of womanhood, and the soul of a true musician, revealed through the medium of an instrument that is more than an

---

[16] Oliver Daniel, *Stokowski: A Counterpoint of View* (New York: Dodd, Mead & Co., 1982), 246.

archaic survival, for it is the voice of an epoch of mannered courtliness and patrician refinement to
our crowded hours of febrile haste and confusion.[17]

The reviewer, identified only as "F.L.W.," displays an unusually sympathetic and perceptive understanding of both the instrument and the task at hand. It is typically sentimental and flowery but accurately reflects music criticism in the early twenties. H. C. Colles, a critic from the *New York Times*, was also in the audience that night. Colles was an active scholar with a more astute historical sense than most. He was able to put the music in context and to do some actual teaching in addition to judging. Under a column entitled simply "MUSIC" is this review:

The third of the Philadelphia's concerts at Carnegie Hall last night created an atmosphere very different from the steamheated air of the conventional symphony program. It consisted of pre-Beethoven music, for Schubert's unfinished symphony, played after the intermission, though chronologically later than Beethoven, seems in its clarity and simplicity of outline to belong more to the era from which Beethoven sprang than to that toward which he led; and all the first part of the program was chosen from purely eighteenth century work, Gluck, Handel, Bach and Mozart.
. . . But the eighteenth century composers lived in a freer air; they breathed it naturally without gasping and struggling or suffering from the palpitations in the effort. It was that which was realized in this concert in which Mr. Stokowski and his orchestra introduced Mme. Landowska with a harpsichord and a piano to the New York public. Everyone is aware today that the harpsichord was not, as used to be said, merely the precursor of the pianoforte, but an instrument producing a wholly different tone in a way of its own. Indeed, the harpsichord and the piano may be themselves taken as examples of the essential difference just alluded to between eighteenth and nineteenth century music, for the former is as incapable of the tonal climax as the latter is dependent upon it.[18]

After her successful world tours in the 1920s, she returned to the Paris environs and purchased a house in the village of Saint Leu-la-Forêt. During the period she lived and taught at her École de Musique Ancienne at St. Leu, 1927-38, she did not return to the United States. Her popularity increased enormously, but she preferred to tour in Europe, South America, and Africa, and to let North Americans come to her at St. Leu. This was, perhaps, an idiosyncracy of hers. She began to write again on a wide variety of topics; many of her writings were published, many others were not. Landowska always had an opinion and could invariably back it up with scholarly documentation. Her knowledge of Baroque treatises was encyclopedic, and her understanding of the history of the harpsichord and its construction was thorough and well-documented.[19] However, Landowska was ultimately a pragmatist and knowingly chose to play an instrument that had modern advantages, such as a metal frame, steel strings, foot-pedals for changing registration, and keys that were the same size as piano keys. She did not apologize for these things.

While at St. Leu she continued to collect keyboard instruments, the forerunners of the piano, and scores, thus amassing quite a valuable group of instruments and library. She was free to teach, practice, and write whenever she wanted because her two friends, Elsa Schunicke and Denise Restout took care of all secretarial and domestic duties. The devotion and commitment these two women, from different generations and countries, demonstrated toward Landowska is striking. Elsa had been with Landowska and Lew in Berlin, serving as domestic help to Wanda and domestic companion to Henri, and she had been as grief-striken as Landowska by his untimely death. Denise came to Landowska in 1933 as a girl of thirteen looking for an organ teacher, and, after playing for her, had been persuaded to switch to the harpsichord. By the age of sixteen Denise Restout became Landowska's teaching assistant and personal secretary, and it was she who later made all the arrangements for them to flee to the United States.

On 7 December 1941—Pearl Harbor Day—Wanda Landowska and Denise Restout arrived safely in New York City with $1300 and one Pleyel harpsichord. Because of their alien status they were initially held on Ellis Island.

---

[17] *Philadelphia Public Ledger*, 17 November 1923.

[18] H. C. Colles (1879-1943) was an English music critic, educated at the Royal College of Music and Worcester College, Oxford. He edited the third edition of *Grove's Dictionary* and was guest critic of the *New York Times* in the 1923-24 season.

[19] See appendix 2 in Cash for a list of theoretical works cited in *Musique ancienne*.

Landowska spoke some English, but at this time Restout neither spoke nor understood the language. Thanks to the efforts of Doda Conrad, a singer and the son of one of Landowska's schoolmates in Berlin, a petition was circulated among the most outstanding musicians in New York verifying that Wanda Landowska was indeed one of the greatest living musicians and should be released immediately on her own recognizance. The effort was successful and they were released shortly thereafter, but only after Landowska and Restout each paid a bond of $500. That left them alone in New York with a total of $300 and their Pleyel harpsichord.[20]

During their first winter in New York, both women gave some private lessons, but Landowska's real desire was to record again. That, she knew, would be her most secure source of income. Unfortunately, the recording industry was on strike in 1942-45, and recording was not possible. Her next idea was to give a recital in Town Hall, where she had been so successful in the twenties. The work she wanted to perform was Bach's *Goldberg Variations*, the work she had premiered at St. Leu eight years earlier to such international acclaim. Her manager in New York, whom she had re-engaged after returning to the United States, strongly discouraged the idea, maintaining that no one in New York knew the piece and that the recital would be a disaster. She was, apparently, typically calm in her reply, in essence saying "I am going to play the Goldberg Variations." The concert proved to be such a success that people had to be turned away. The decision to play the *Goldberg* was a pivotal one to her success in the United States. After that time the piece became almost a trademark of hers. Though hundreds of people have subsequently played the *Goldberg Variations*, Landowska is the one who premiered it in the twentieth century, first recorded it, and who reestablished her North American reputation with it.

Throughout her life, Landowska seemed to have an uncanny sense of what was best for her. Her strong beliefs enabled her to take risks that might have ruined a less stoic musician, but usually succeeded for Landowska. Once she determined to undertake a task, no one could deter or dissuade her from it. Denise Restout reports that the night Landowska played the *Goldberg* in Town Hall is indelibly emblazoned in her mind. The sight of Landowska coming out on the stage that night, however, was a shock for many in the audience:

> When she appeared on the stage that time she was so tiny and so frail-looking. Remember that she had gone through almost starvation in France and she was so thin that people in the hall did not think she would be able to play much of anything. Then she started to play. When she finished she looked like a young girl.[21]

Seventeen years later, journalist Robert Sabin wrote of that historic evening in an obituary for Landowska: "Landowska's return to the United States was unforgettably signalized by her recital in Town Hall, New York, on 21 February 1942, when she played the Bach *Goldberg Variations* before one of the most distinguished audiences ever assembled there."[22] But it is Virgil Thomson's review of that historic night which has become a classic in the annals of music criticism. His review amply demonstrates that only two months after her arrival in this country, following a fourteen-year absence, she was not only accepted as the foremost harpsichordist and authority on the harpsichord in her lifetime, but was revered as the individual who had restored the harpsichord to its proper place. Certainly Thomson needed no further persuasion. In the essay, he goes to the essence of why Landowska's playing was at that time more compelling than that of anyone else who had attempted to play the harpsichord in the twentieth century.[23]

In the mid-1950s, by the end of her career, her niche was carved. Her recordings of the *Goldberg Variations* and *The Well-Tempered Clavier* have established themselves as classic recordings of great artists of the past, and her writings and her students speak for themselves. Undoubtedly she will be remembered as eccentric, but not in a negative sense. Artists of her stature are allowed eccentricity. During the nineteenth century it was, of course, actively cultivated. Harold Schonberg of the *New York Times* frequently wrote about her, and in his obituary of her, noted:

---

[20] *Landowska on Music*, and Restout, "Mamusia—Vignettes of Wanda Landowska," *High Fidelity*, October 1960, 42-47. New information about Landowska's recording career at the end of her life is in Cash.

[21] *Landowska on Music*, 21.

[22] Robert Sabin, obituary for Wanda Landowska, *Musical America*, September 1959, 12.

[23] Virgil Thomson, *The Musical Scene* (New York: Knopf, 1947), 201-02.

> ... the learned little lady was no mean showman either. She knew how to hold an audience in the palm of her hand, and when she gave a concert it was to the accompaniment that all great artists receive—deathlike silence and attention. Her stage entrances were unforgettable. When she gave her 1948 series in Town Hall devoted to Bach's *Well-Tempered Clavier*, she had the stage fixed up as if it were a living room: the harpsichord dominating; a studio lamp to the left of the keyboard; the stage nearly darkened. Fifteen minutes before the start of the programs the audience was firmly in place. Mme. Landowska made her listeners wait a good while before she appeared. Then the stage door opened and The Presence appeared.[24]

The obituary describes the famous entrances that Landowska made; the slow "levitation" to the keyboard, eyes cast heavenward, hands folded as if in prayer, black velvet ballet slippers. He was obviously mesmerized by the woman and her public seemed to be too. But she was not just an actress:

> Her playing was on an equally romantic level. As an executant, she had a miraculous equality of touch, with a left hand that seemed to have a brain of its own. No artist in this generation (and, one is confident, in any generation) could, with equal deftness, clarify the polyphonic writing of the Baroque masters. And none could make the music so spring to life.[25]

Then Schonberg explains why her playing was so convincing and, despite its personal liberties, was well-accepted and appreciated by the musical public.

> Her secret was a lifetime of scholarship combined with a knowledge of when *not* to hold the printed page sacrosanct. (Of course that alone demands a lifetime of knowledge.) She was a genius at underlining the dramatic and emotional content of a piece. When she held on to a fermata, worlds tottered and breathing stopped until she continued the next phrase. Everything she did had emotional significance. She took liberties, all kinds of liberties, but like all great artists she could get away with them. In short, her entire musical approach was romantic: intensely personal, full of light and shade, never (despite her enormous scholarship) pedantic.[26]

Because of the sheer force of her personality and the brilliance of her talent, critics and public alike responded favorably, putting aside questions of gender. But the model that she left for other women musicians is significant: despite cultural proscriptions against women having careers in music, except as teachers of children, Landowska proceeded with her goals and aspirations. She will be remembered as a musician who persevered despite great personal tragedy—a woman who could have given up any number of times, but chose to continue on her path. Landowska was a musician of courage, conviction, and integrity who performed an invaluable service in restoring to us an almost-forgotten instrument, rich in history and repertory. She will be remembered as a musician whose childhood dream endowed us with a treasury of recordings, as a writer on music, and as a role model for young women who aspire to be musical pioneers. In his book *Virtuoso*, Harvey Sachs writes of her contributions: "Even without Landowska, the twentieth century would have rediscovered the music of the past. We were ripe for that consolation. But she brought it to us with conviction, zeal and charm—rare qualities in any age."[27]

---

[24] Harold C. Schonberg, "Landowska (1879-1959): Romantic Scholar," *New York Times*, 23 August 1959.

[25] Ibid.

[26] Ibid.

[27] Harvey Sachs, *Virtuoso* (New York: Thames and Hudson, 1982), 164. The bulk of Landowska's private archival material—letters, journals, and diaries—and all of her annotated scores and original compositions are held by Denise Restout, who has been writing a biography of Landowska and is unwilling to allow access to the material. She has stated Landowska was constantly writing her thoughts on music, topics ranging from how to teach and interpret music, to philosophical discourses on the meaning of music and how it relates to other arts. When the material becomes available it will be possible to evaluate other of her musicological writings and compositions, as well as the way she registered her music on the Pleyel harpsichord. An edition of the *Goldberg Variations*, *Well-Tempered Clavier*, *Two- and Three-Part Inventions*, and the works of the French clavecinistes that she recorded and taught, as fingered, phrased, and registered by Landowska, would be a further valuable addition to current editions of those works.

19

Stravinsky's *Scènes de Ballet* and Billy Rose's *The Seven Lively Arts*: The Abravanel Account

JOHN SCHUSTER-CRAIG

The earliest choreographed performances of Stravinsky's *Scènes de ballet* in 1944 as a part of the Broadway revue *The Seven Lively Arts* have left us with one of the most endearing anecdotes concerning Stravinsky. To quote from Roman Vlad's account:

> After the preview in Philadelphia the organizers sent Stravinsky a telegram which read: YOUR MUSIC GREAT SUCCESS STOP COULD BE SENSATIONAL SUCCESS IF YOU WOULD AUTHORIZE ROBERT RUSSELL BENNETT RETOUCH INSTRUMENTATION STOP BENNETT ORCHESTRATES EVEN THE WORKS OF COLE PORTER STOP. Stravinsky wired back: SATISFIED WITH GREAT SUCCESS.[1]

Vlad's account is taken almost verbatim from Eric Walter White's *Stravinsky*. White's account, which clearly implies that he is quoting the actual text of the telegram, was in turn an elaboration of the account in Alexandre Tansman's *Igor Stravinsky*, published in 1949.[2]

It is, of course, a touching, not to mention entertaining, story, showing Stravinsky confidently standing his ground, and insisting on the presentation of his work as he conceived it, without regard for the crass opinions of his producers more accustomed to the ways of Broadway. Unfortunately, it simply is not true in many respects, nor did the actual telegram sent by Anton Dolin read as White implied. Robert Craft and Vera Stravinsky included a portion of the actual text of the telegram sent to Stravinsky by Dolin, choreographer and dancer in *Scènes de ballet*, prior to the New York opening:

> BALLET GREAT SUCCESS.... CAN THE PAS DE DEUX BE ORCHESTRATED WITH THE STRINGS CARRYING THE MELODY THIS IS MOST IMPORTANT TO INSURE GREATER SUCCESS[3]

Craft and Vera Stravinsky also gave a fuller account of the ballet's genesis, and noted the circumstances surrounding the reduction in orchestra size a month into the New York run. This led Stephen Walsh to suggest that this "well-known story" of Stravinsky's refusal to rescore or allow the work to be rescored by another hand, had been "corrected, presumably for the last time, in *SPD* [*Stravinsky in Pictures and Documents*]."[4]

An earlier version of this essay was read at the annual meeting of the South-Central Chapter of the American Musicological Society, University of Louisville, March 1996.

[1] Roman Vlad, *Stravinsky*, 3rd ed. (New York: Oxford University Press, 1978), 127.

[2] Alexandre Tansman, *Igor Stravinsky: The Man and His Music*, trans. T. and C. Bleefield (New York: Putnam, 1949), 256; Eric Walter White, *Stravinsky: The Composer and His Works*, 2nd ed. (London: Faber, 1979), 421.

[3] Vera Stravinsky and Robert Craft, *Stravinsky in Pictures and Documents* (New York: Simon and Schuster, 1978), 375.

[4] Stephen Walsh, *The Music of Stravinsky* (Oxford: Clarendon Press, 1993), 182. In an endnote (p. 287), Walsh notes that "Since writing this chapter I have read the correspondence with Rose and Anton Dolin. The story as commonly told confuses Dolin's request for more effective scoring with Rose's later demand for a reduced version on economic grounds."

However, in any attempt to reconstruct an image of the past, there are usually things that resist being "corrected . . . for the last time." In June 1995, while working in the Eric Walter White Archives, I came across correspondence from Maurice Abravanel, the conductor of the first performances of the *Scènes de ballet*, to White, written shortly after the publication of the second edition of White's book in 1979. The correspondence offers yet another perspective on this premiere, although it leaves even still a number of questions unanswered.

Before summarizing Abravanel's reminiscence, it might be of interest to take a look at the principal players in this drama: Billy Rose, producer of the revue; Alicia Markova, prima ballerina in Stravinsky's work; Anton Dolin, choreographer and lead male dancer; and Abravanel, conductor of the Philadelphia run prior to the Broadway premiere, as well as for the first four weeks of the New York run.

Billy Rose, *né* William Samuel Rosenberg, was born in 1899 in Bronx, N.Y. During World War I he served as chief stenographer for the financier Bernard Baruch, head of the War Industries Board. In the 1920s he began to write songs, eventually composing some 400, including "Me and My Shadow," "That Old Gang of Mine," and "It's Only a Paper Moon." He was a frequent producer on Broadway, counting among his successes *Crazy Quilt*, the extravagant circus-musical *Jumbo*, and *Carmen Jones*, a musical comedy version of Bizet's *Carmen* featuring an all-black cast. He also produced, first near Cleveland on Lake Erie, and then in New York for the World's Fair of 1939, *Aquacades*, out-of-door productions that were a combination of swim meet and musical comedy, performed by a host of attractive young women in what were, for the time, fairly revealing examples of the swim suit. Rose owned several nightclubs, invested in real estate and the stock market, collected fine art (his collection, including original works of Titian, El Greco, and Rubens, was valued by *Time* magazine at $500,000 in 1944),[5] and was a highly-publicized philanthropist. One of his several wives was Fanny Brice, the comedienne of the *Ziegfeld Follies*; their relationship served as the basis for the film *Funny Lady* starring Barbra Streisand. He died in Jamaica in 1966.

Alicia Markova, *née* Lilian Alicia Marks, was born in London in 1910. She studied with Enrico Ceccheti, the respected St. Petersburg teacher who, with so many other Russian dancers, emigrated to London after the First World War. She made her debut at the age of fourteen with the Diaghilev Ballet and worked with Diaghilev until his death in 1929. She was the first English dancer to dance the lead role in Adolphe Adam's *Giselle*, which eventually became her signature role; she entitled her autobiography *Giselle and I*. She danced not only the classical repertory, but also excelled in early jazz ballets and other contemporary scores, including a Diaghilev production of Stravinsky's *Le Rossignol*. She retired from the stage in 1963, at which time she was named director of the Metropolitan Ballet in New York.

Anton Dolin, *né* Sydney Francis Patrick Chippendall Healey-Kay, was born in England in 1904 and received his dance training from Russian teachers, including Bronislava Nijinska. He began his career in the corps de ballet of Diaghilev's Ballets Russes. Dolin was considered one of the finest partners of his time. He danced leading roles in numerous classical ballets, but was also noted for creating such roles as the title role in Fokine's *Bluebeard*; the Cocteau/Milhaud *Le Train bleu* was conceived with Dolin in mind. Dolin was actively involved in creating the Camargo Society and with Markova formed both the Markova-Dolin Company and London's Festival Ballet. He authored numerous books on dance and in 1980 played the part of Cecchetti (Markova's teacher) in the motion picture *Nijinsky*.

Maurice Abravanel was born in 1903, and upon the recommendation of Bruno Walter became the conductor of the Metropolitan Opera in 1936. This position lasted only briefly, and from 1938 to 1948 he conducted frequently on Broadway, especially for the works of Kurt Weill, with whom he had studied in Europe. In 1947 he became music director of the Utah Symphony, an organization he nurtured into a world-class ensemble.

Billy Rose's *The Seven Lively Arts* was a Broadway revue intended to highlight all of the visual and performing arts. It was by anyone's standards a lavishly conceived evening. It generated $550,000 in advance ticket sales (with individual tickets going for as much as $24), and was reported to have cost $1,350,000 (including the expenditures for the purchase and renovation of the Ziegfeld Theater, which Rose acquired in January of 1944), a considerable sum of money in war-time America.[6] In addition to the Stravinsky ballet, the revue featured the comedian Bert

---

[5] *Time*, 18 December 1944, 75.

[6] *Time*, 18 December 1944, 72.

Lahr, Beatrice Lillie singing songs of Cole Porter, and Benny Goodman and his combo, as well as a large singing chorus, a line of showgirls, a corps de ballet, and an orchestra numbering forty. Salvador Dali was commissioned to paint seven paintings, described by Rose biographer Stephen Nelson as ". . . surreal anatomical interpretations of seven decidedly lively arts."[7] These were appropriately displayed in the lounge between the men's and women's restrooms.

As for the ballet score, Billy Rose first approached Kurt Weill. Weill preferred to write a symphonic work and declined to write the score for the ballet. Weill's symphonic score never materialized, and was replaced by William Schuman's *Circus Overture: Side Show*, which was dropped from the revue before the New York opening. After Weill declined to compose the ballet for the review, Stravinsky was approached. The scenario for the score is a series of scenes with no overall plot. Each scene is based dramatically on a scene from a classical ballet: the Pas de deux on a scene from *Swan Lake*, the Pantomime on a scene from *Coppelia*, and the remainder of the scenes from Markova's beloved *Giselle*.

What, then, was the nature of the controversy surrounding the premiere? There are two separate issues: Dolin's and Billy Rose's demand for cuts in the score and Dolin's request to alter the orchestration in the Pas de deux (Dolin also desired additional changes in the orchestration, at the end of Markova's solo and in the final apotheosis).[8] Abravanel addresses both issues. First, what changes were made in the orchestration, when were they made, and why?

The telegram of Dolin mentioned earlier dealt only with one passage: the central Pas de deux. Here Stravinsky's reply to Dolin was not different in substance from that reported by White. In a telegram to Abravanel (photocopy in the White archives along with Abravanel's correspondence), Stravinsky wrote:

> REFUSED TO CONSIDER DOLIN. EXTREMELY SHOCKING SUGGESTION OF CRIPPLING MY MUSIC BY CUTS AND THE ORCHESTRATION ONLY TO OBTAIN WHAT HE CALLS TREMENDOUS SUCCESS BEING ENTIRELY SATISFIED WITH MERELY GREAT SUCCESS MENTIONED IN HIS WIRE TODAY. REGARDS.

Abravanel's letter to White describes the attitudes of Billy Rose and Anton Dolin toward their commissioned ballet:

> When I played the score for Billy Rose he wanted to cut everything that was not Markova. With her and Dolin we stood fast against cuts and retouching(!) the orchestration, which of course was totally out of place in a Broadway show (1944!) with music by Cole Porter.[9]
>
> After the 3rd performance (matinee) in Philadelphia B. R. summoned Dolin, Markova and myself and told the dancers: "I have watched the show 3 times. For the Stravinsky you do wonderful things and never get any applause until the curtain falls. You do exactly the same things in the Pas de deux on Cole Porter's 'Easy to Love.' There at each performance you had 13 big 'hands.' *The applause is in the pit*. You must get Stravinsky['s] permission for changing the orchestration and for small cuts." Having refused to consider his request, I refused again and left with Markova, and, I believe, Dolin.
>
> Next morning I received the enclosed telegram.[10] When I showed it to Dolin, far from being ashamed of his double cross, he rushed to a Broadway columnist (Leonard Lyons) and gave his version which, with variations, found its way in every chronicle.[11]

The orchestration, however, was "retouched," but at a later date, four weeks into the show's New York run. Abravanel wrote:

---

[7] Stephen Nelson, *"Only A Paper Moon": The Theater of Billy Rose* (Ann Arbor: UMI Research Press, 1987), 135.

[8] Personal communication from Stephen Walsh, 20 February 1997.

[9] Letter of Maurice Abravanel to Eric Walter White, 28 February 1981, Eric Walter White Archives, Harry Ransom Humanities Research Center, University of Texas at Austin. I wish to thank the Ransom Center and Mrs. Maurice Abravanel for permission to publish excerpts from this letter. The statement is directly contradicted by Dolin in his autobiography *Last Words: A Final Autobiography* (London: Century, 1985), 133: "After the first performance in Philadelphia, both the conductor Abravenel [*sic*] and I agreed that the orchestration could indeed be improved upon."

[10] The telegram from Stravinsky quoted above.

[11] Abravanel to White, 28 February 1981, pp. 2-3.

> Later when he [Billy Rose] decided that he had to cut the orchestra from 45 to 32 he asked me to phone Stravinsky.[12] He would not do it himself. The phone conversation was quite funny. Stravinsky in Beverly Hills: "How is Seven Lively Arts going?"—Quite well. (I knew that his contract was for a weekly royalty of $200 with a guaranty of 25 weeks). "How long will it play?"—Oh! I think it might play through the summer.—(Here a little pause on I.S. part during which he assured himself mentally that this would mean an addition to the guaranteed $5000), then "Do you think the orchestration could be reduced?"—I answered that it could be done without too much harm and that Billy Rose otherwise would drop the *Scènes de ballet*, and that it was better to expose thousands of people to a reduced I.S. than to no I.S. at all.—At that he agreed, but only if I and no one else did the reduction.[13]

And what of the cuts Billy Rose wanted? Although he did not get his wish to cut "all that was not Markova," cuts were made. Abravanel wrote:

> The cuts? In wartime America there were no male ballet dancers. We had excellent "hoofers," Broadway-Hollywood tap dancers who were fine as directed by a very good honest Hollywood craftsman, but abominable and embarrassing as trained by Dolin and totally out of their element. I called Stravinsky and assured him that his orchestration would not be touched,[14] but recommended cutting most of the "corps de ballet" (!) or a total of about *3* minutes (out of 16-17 minutes). His calling that "Excerpts" made it possible to announce the N. Y. Philharmonic concert performance as a "world premiere."[15]

It is not at all difficult to see how, for example, the second movement, "Danses," with its shifting meters from 5/8 to 3/8, and with a frequent absence of a downbeat in the 5/8 measures, would have presented more than a few problems for the type of dancer Abravanel describes.

The cuts led Stravinsky to draw up a written agreement, sent to Abravanel on 4 December 1944, three days prior to the New York opening. The agreement required that the Stravinsky be advertised as *"Excerpts" from the Scènes de ballet*, or as *Scènes de ballet ("Excerpts")*. Stravinsky indicated that he preferred the first phrasing.

Abravanel later attended the New York Philharmonic concert première, with Alicia Markova; Stravinsky conducted. Abravanel's account of the first performance with the composer conducting is of interest:

> When I received the score and played it for Markova and Dolin, both asked whether the Adagio [the Pas de deux] could go faster. I refused not only because of I.S. indicated marking, but also because, played Adagio it had a neoclassical dignity and beauty, while in a faster tempo it took on a barrel organ smell. Weeks later Markova and I attended the Stravinsky concert where he took the Adagio almost Allegretto. Markova turned to me. We went backstage after the concert and I asked I.S. whether he had changed the tempo. "O that? Balanchine timed the length and we were afraid we would be taken off the air, so I took it a little faster" (it was Sunday afternoon and C.B.S. stopped the broadcasts after 1½ hours).[16]

The problems attending Stravinsky's portion of *The Seven Lively Arts* were not the only ones faced by Billy Rose. As Earl Conrad has noted in his biography of Billy Rose:

> ... the entire experience was a nightmare.... Virtually all of the stars were in a competition for each other's jugular, and for special favor. Bert Lahr and Beatrice Lillie were chosen for comedy; Benny Goodman for jazz; but Billy's main labors were with Cole Porter for the songs.... Lahr did not

---

[12] Robert Craft, in *Stravinsky in Pictures and Documents*, 376, states that the reduction in the number of players was from forty to twenty-eight. Based on his work with materials in the Paul Sacher Stiftung in Basle, Stephen Walsh has confirmed that the original number of players was forty, not forty-five; personal communication, 20 February 1997.

[13] Abravanel to White, 28 February 1981, pp. 4-5.

[14] This telephone call occurred prior to the call referred to in the previous excerpt.

[15] Abravanel to White, 28 February 1981, p. 3.

[16] Abravanel to White, 28 February 1981, p. 6.

like any of the skits and he presented numerous rehearsal problems. Lahr was ... always unhappy, always sure nothing was funny enough.... Beatrice Lillie arrived from London just before the show went into rehearsal, and she hated the songs Porter had written for her. Porter's contract stated that he was the sole composer, with the exception of the ballet music by Stravinsky and a ... number by William Schuman [which, as noted earlier, was dropped prior to the New York opening]. Porter would not listen to Miss Lillie's pleas to insert a couple of songs that she had brought from London. When the show opened in Philadelphia none of the costumes were ready.... As a result the first performance found most of the actors with partial costumes. There was more scenery in the alleys back of the theater than on stage.[17]

Rose boasted in pre-show publicity that the revue contained no social significance, and was intended as wartime escapism. On another occasion, he stated that by opening the show on the third anniversary of Pearl Harbor, he was paying tribute to the nation's strength and stability, a notion many found offensive. The show lasted only for 183 performances—that is, basically as long as it was sustained by advance ticket sales. Critic George Freedley wrote that "the production in all its parts simply does not create the perfect whole which is essential to a really good revue. The songs are mediocre, though pleasing; the lyrics ... are twisting, if not really witty. The sketches ... have many good lines, but not a single one is a smash. The dances ... are occasionally effective pictorially, but they lack the extra quality which comes from greatness."[18] *Time* magazine's reviewer summarized the revue similarly: "Stripped of its fancy wrappings, *The Seven Lively Arts* is oversized and overstuffed. At times the whole thing seems less like the seven lively arts (which presumably include dressmaking and sex) than like seven luxury hotels."[19]

It is, then, perhaps little surprising that Abravanel wrote in his letter to White that "It took me 37 years to put down and write all this, very reluctantly.... Now that I have finished, I feel like after vomiting. At the time, I felt that the people from the higher regions, in particular Dolin, had behaved like Hollywood and Broadway are reported to behave." Abravanel had clearly nursed for nearly four decades his resentment of Dolin's behavior, and wrote: "... Please leave Dolin (Sir Anton) alone. Though he deserves the worst, I wish him the best."[20]

Interestingly, Abravanel's recollections of Billy Rose were much more nuanced: "All in all, Billy Rose was true to form and was heaped with ridicule (which he probably did not mind as that was 'publicity').... But I always felt that Billy Rose, much as I resented his low taste, brashness, and vulgarity, had a touching respect and longing for the better things in life. He had beautiful paintings (a Renoir was still a work of art in 1940, not mostly a sound investment)."[21]

Abravanel's correspondence offers a fascinating perspective on the premiere of one of Stravinsky's less successful scores.[22] Abravanel's recollections, thirty-eight years after the fact, cannot be presumed to be perfectly accurate, as his recollection that there were forty-five players in the orchestra demonstrates. They nonetheless provide insight into an event that has been misrepresented in an extraordinary number and variety of sources. One question remains, however, unanswered by Abravanel's correspondence: how did Robert Russell Bennett become a part of the mythology of the *Scènes de ballet* premiere? Presumably Dolin, when he "rushed to a Broadway columnist," included Bennett as a part of his story, as Cole Porter's arranger. Stephen Walsh has concluded that "It was never suggested that he [Bennett] rescore Stravinsky."[23] This makes one of Abravanel's final comments all the more intriguing: "I could tell much more, like the night in Philadelphia where a copyist took all the parts out of the pit and Russell Bennett (the orchestrator) was rumored to be in the theater."[24] Dolin's story has had an incredibly long life; it is perhaps too much to expect at this date that we will ever know all of the details of this most troubled premiere.

---

[17] Earl Conrad, *Billy Rose: Manhattan Primitive* (Cleveland and New York: World Publishing Co., 1968), 169-70.

[18] Quoted in Samuel L. Leiter, *The Encyclopedia of the New York Stage, 1940-1950* (Westport, Conn.: Greenwood, 1992), 554.

[19] *Time*, 18 December 1944, 72.

[20] Abravanel to White, 28 February 1981, pp. 7-8.

[21] Abravanel to White, 28 February 1981, pp. 3-4.

[22] "... the Stravinsky score most often accused of vulgarity." Walsh, *The Music of Stravinsky* (Oxford: Oxford University Press, 1993), 182.

[23] Personal communication, 20 February 1997.

[24] Abravanel to White, 28 February 1981, p. 7.

20

Henry Wolking's Ballet
Forever Yesterday

JEANNE MARIE BELFY

Fifty years ago the Louisville Orchestra under conductor Robert Whitney embarked on a path of commissioning compositions by contemporary composers with civic and foundation support. One principal offshoot of the endeavor resulted in a historic recording project for new music, funded in part by a ground-breaking grant from the Rockefeller Foundation. Ten years and over two hundred compositions later, the Louisville Orchestra had established both the basic framework for orchestral commissioning projects and a model for the collaboration of orchestras and private foundations in support of serious new music.[1] By the 1990s, such activities are an assumed part of our American musical culture.

The music written for the Louisville Orchestra fifty years ago, though representative of the work of a broad spectrum of American and European composers, was by and large playable and not difficult to listen to, unlike much contemporary music often taught in universities in the 1960s, 70s, and 80s. At the end of our century, a new interest in championing an American art music that may reach a broader audience is again emerging. Some of this music today is being called "neo-romantic," "eclectic," or, more recently, "postmodern." Perhaps it is not too far in spirit from the neoclassical and nationalist works of the mainstream composers between the World Wars, although its aesthetics are colored by its self-conscious knowledge of the past. More than any previous "art" music, it is positioned to draw from an overwhelming array of sources—different styles of popular, commercial, ethnic, and historical musics (there are, after all, a lot of people on the planet these days). This essay looks at one recently commissioned work for the stage, a postmodern ballet score for a small chamber orchestra by Henry Wolking called *Forever Yesterday*, whose initial conception was inspired by the Louisville Orchestra's example.

Native American Dreams and African American Realities

On 17 April 1992, *Forever Yesterday* took its place in a historical chain of responses, conscious or not, to Antonin Dvořák's advice that American composers should use the music of the Negro and the Indian to create a truly American art music. Dubbed "a collaborative performing arts event with an artistic and environmental message,"[2] the production combined Henry Wolking's score for chamber orchestra with dance by the Idaho Dance Theater to choreography by co-artistic director Marla Hansen. A further collaborative gesture brought five huge metal totem poles to the

---

[1] On the Louisville Orchestra commissions of these years, see Jeanne Marie Belfy, "The Commissioning Project of the Louisville Orchestra 1948-58: A Study of the History and Music" (Ph.D. diss., University of Kentucky, in cooperation with the University of Louisville, 1986); also see Belfy, *The Louisville Orchestra New Music Project, An American Experiment in the Patronage of International Contemporary Music: Selected Composers' Letters to the Louisville Orchestra* (New York: Pendragon, 1983); Belfy, "Judith and the Louisville Orchestra: The Rest of the Story," *College Music Symposium* 31 (1991): 36-48; and Gerhard Herz, "Current Chronicle," *Musical Quarterly* 41 (1955): 76-85.

[2] Program cover, *Forever Yesterday* (Boise, Idaho), 17-18 April 1992.

set, the work of sculptor Rod Kagan of Ketchum (Sun Valley), Idaho. The work was commissioned by the Barlow Endowment for Music Composition at Brigham Young University, with additional funding from a Boise State University Faculty Research Grant.[3]

The performance was recorded and broadcast in the United States on National Public Radio's program *Performance Today*. The music was played by the Boise Chamber Orchestra, conducted by Michael Samball, who had conceived the project.[4] Samball revived the ballet for the Boise and McCall SummerFest '95, an outdoor festival, envisioning a sort of *Gesamtkunstwerk* with song and narration. Wolking, joined by writer Laura DeBeque, chose and reworked texts from George Cronyn's historic collection *American Indian Poetry*,[5] to be sung by soprano as introductions to each of the ballet's three movements. DeBeque also wrote narrative prose, inspired by her own study of Native American literature, which was read by alternating male and female actors between the songs and ballet music in the first and third movements. Her words became a sort of melodrama, underscored by Wolking's additional orchestral music. Idaho Dance Theater revived the original choreography, and Rod Kagan's sculptures were trucked back to Boise. The expanded *Forever Yesterday* was presented three times in an outdoor amphitheater in Boise, and once at the bottom of a ski resort in McCall, Idaho, in the summer of 1995.

For over 300 years Europeans, and later Americans, have made sporadic attempts to draw upon the images and indigenous sounds of Native American musics in the creation of Western art music for the concert and theatrical stage. In the last one hundred years, such attempts have often reflected the desire to create an "American" music, with the nationalist, folk-inspired examples of Dvořák and of other Europeans in mind. In rare instances, Native American composers trained in Western concert music have used Native American themes in what was intended to be a truly syncretic product.[6] New in the latter part of this century, particularly in the 1980s and 90s, has been a movement on the part of classically-trained composers to associate Native American culture with environmental concerns (mirroring a general inclination in contemporary American society toward such concerns); some have also ridden a wave of "New Age" trendiness.[7] In January 1996, *Opera News* writer Peter Wynne cited Utah Opera's centennial commission *Dreamkeepers* by David Carlson, along with the Opera Theatre of St. Louis's 1995 premiere of Stephen Paulus's *The Woman at Otowi Crossing*, and Cary John Franklin's *The Thunder of Horses,* as signs that "Perhaps these . . . will mark the beginning of a new Indianist movement in opera."[8] Another example that might be cited is the new choreography in a score by composer Eric Lundborg entitled *Skinwalkers*, premiered in the Eugene Ballet/Ballet Idaho's 1994-95 season, a ballet billed as a mystical evocation of the "Anasazi Indian myths and works of art," in which "the ancient ones come to life."[9]

One hundred years ago Dvořák's often-cited comments regarding the proper materials for use in creating an American nationalist music offered two American folk sources: Native American and African American.[10] With or

---

[3] Wolking, *Forever Yesterday* (Salt Lake City, Utah: Wolking Music Publications, 1992), cover of score.

[4] *Performance Today*, National Public Radio, broadcast 28 April 1992. At this writing, this broadcast remains the first and only musical performance from Boise, Idaho, to receive this type of recognition.

[5] George W. Cronyn, ed., *American Indian Poetry: An Anthology of Songs and Chants* (New York: Ballantine Books, 1991); originally published as *The Path on the Rainbow: An Anthology of Songs and Chants from the Indians of North America* (Liveright Publishing, 1934).

[6] The most notable example has been Louis Ballard.

[7] Tara C. Browner, "Transposing Cultures: the Appropriation of Native North American Musics 1890-1990" (Ph.D. diss., University of Michigan, 1995), makes a trenchant connection between the "white shamanism" of the late 1960s and 70s and the current so-called "New Age" movement. For an outline of the history of fashionable imitations of Native American religion, literature, and art, see pp. 133-47.

[8] Peter Wynne, "Return of the Native: David Carlson's *Dreamkeepers* Revives a Once-Popular American Opera Theme," *Opera News* 60 (6 January 1996): 29.

[9] Promotional materials, Ballet Idaho's 1994-95 season.

[10] Dvořák's involvement with the music (or perceived music) of both racial groups can be examined through the documents, published, among other sources, in John C. Tibbetts, ed., *Dvořák in America, 1892-1895* (Portland: Amadeus Press, 1993), especially in appendix A, pp. 355-84. Speaking to a reporter from the *New York Herald* in May 1893 (Tibbetts, 355), Dvořák made his first statement that "the future music of this country must be founded upon *what are called* [italics mine] the negro melodies." An article in *Harper's New Monthly Magazine*, February 1895 (Tibbetts, 377), makes clear his recognition that plantation songs performed by white actors in blackface minstrel shows were not the legitimate

without Dvořák's guidance, there seems to be little argument that the Africans who were forced to this continent had widespread and profound effects on the history of music in general and on nearly all music of the United States. The composer whose music is at the center of this essay, Henry Wolking, provides but one example of this influence, both in his musical background and in his compositional tendencies. African-American music has become synonymous with American popular music and, due principally to the development of jazz and jazz-related styles, exerts a major influence over most of the successful (defined here as music that more than a handful of specialists want to listen to) art music of the past seventy years.

Imagine compiling a list of American works that derive some harmonic, rhythmic, or melodic impetus from the culture of African Americans—its unwieldiness would be staggering. Few composers from the 1920s to the present have not paid attention to the rhythmic characteristics of jazz music. Nor has the impact of the whole ambit of African-American musical culture been confined to the U.S. or to North American borders; as is well known, modernists as far-removed from American popular culture as Igor Stravinsky and Karlheinz Stockhausen have paid homage to the pervasive power of African-American music.

While African Americans found many aspects of European-based musical structures and functions entirely adaptable to their own indigenous traditions, Native American musicians seem to have had little or nothing in common with the musical habits of their invaders. The influence of Native American music on the Western concert repertory has been slight and hardly long-lasting. Despite a catalog of interesting works showing "Indian" influence, most prominently occupied by the "Indianist" composers and their immediate peers, Edward MacDowell, Amy Beach, and others of their time, identifiably authentic Indian musical traits have not entered the basic vocabulary of composers of the Western art tradition. The mere fact that it is possible to "catalog" works that show Native American influence points to the relative obscurity of the phenomenon.

As it was in Dvořák's day, so it is now: Native American music has so little in common with Euro-American art or traditional music that efforts to blend the two are relatively isolated and contrived. In the words of Bruno Nettl, "The fact that North American Indian and European musical styles have not merged is probably . . . due in part to the great difference between them, a difference verging on incompatibility (in contrast, for instance, to the greater compatibility between European and African musics)."[11] When asked about the difficulties he encountered in purposefully setting about to compose a ballet based on "Native American themes," Wolking noted that Native American music has completely different functions in Native American cultures, and thus is, by nature, awkward to use for Euro-American purposes.[12] Before accepting the commission to write a Native American-inspired score, Wolking had spent time studying Native American literature and writing other pieces reflective of the environmental concerns that shape *Forever Yesterday*.

In a larger sense, the presence of folk, nationalist, ethnic, or multicultural elements in a considerable amount of non-commercial music of the late twentieth century (certainly in the example under examination) figures in the phenomenon of postmodernism in music. *Forever Yesterday*, with its reliance on several common Native American song/dances, some Native American song texts, and the unique timbres of several Native American instruments such as the Sioux flute and a variety of percussion, and with its expressed programmatic connection both to themes of the

---

folk music of black America. Still, as is well known, he argued for the inherent interconnectedness of the black American musical experience with the minstrel repertory. "Many of the negro melodies—most of them, I believe—are the creations of negroes born and reared in America. That is the peculiar aspect of the problem. The negro does not produce music of that kind elsewhere. I have heard black singers in Hayti [sic] for hours, and, as a rule, their songs are not unlike the monotonous and crude chantings of the Sioux tribes" (Tibbetts, 357). Dvořák's formal acceptance of both racial sources seems to have occurred in a December 1893 *New York Herald* article: "Since I have been in this country I have been deeply interested in the national music of the Negroes and the Indians. The character, the very nature of a race, is contained in its national music" (Tibbetts, 362). Dvořák's contact with actual Native American music of course remained limited. On its impact on his own composition, see John Clapham, "Dvořák and the American Indian," in Tibbetts, 113-22. It may be argued that the programmatic lore of Longfellow's *Hiawatha*, as in its documented connection to the *New World Symphony*, had more musical impact on Dvořák himself than any technical assimilation of Indian melodic or rhythmic characteristics. Clapham, in *Dvořák* (New York: Norton, 1979), 201-02, asserts that Dvořák's overriding interest was African-American music (black spirituals in particular), and that his deference to Native American resources was largely for its publicity value.

[11] Bruno Nettl, *Folk and Traditional Music of the Western Continents*, 3rd ed. (Englewood Cliffs, N.J.: Prentice-Hall, 1990), 178.

[12] Wolking, telephone interview with the writer, 7 July 1997.

environment and of Native American cultures, is above all a postmodern work. It is concerned with expressiveness and accessibility, and freely uses an eclectic gamut of techniques to realize its aim. A syncretic Native American/Euro-American art music may not yet have been achieved, but the combination of jazz-related harmonic practice with Native American sources has produced an effective, compelling score.

Henry Wolking

Wolking was born in Orlando, Florida. He completed a degree in music education at the University of Florida, Gainesville, in 1970. Primarily a jazz musician (trombone is his major instrument), Wolking spent part of his college years as one of two whites in a soul band that toured the "juke joints" of the black backwaters of northern Florida. He began his teaching career at the University of Utah in 1971, after completing a Master of Music degree in jazz at the University of North Texas. Two years later he won second prize in the International Trombone Composition Contest. Wolking's early classical works tend to feature brass instruments; among numerous jazz compositions for big band, several have been performed and recorded by the North Texas One O'Clock Jazz Band. Since the early 1980s Wolking has completed several commissions, including Symphony no. 1 "Lydian Horizons," which was premiered by the Utah Symphony in 1982 and became a semi-finalist in the Kennedy Center Friedheim Awards.

Wolking's music is available on several compact discs. In the past five years two single-movement works for symphony orchestra, *Methenyology*, and *A Luta Continua*, have appeared on the "Music of Six Continents" series. *Forests* (1993), in a performance by the Slovak Radio Symphony Orchestra under the direction of Robert Black on the Bratislava series, was reviewed in *Fanfare* by William Zagorsky, who described it as:

> An immediately accessible work—fine rhythmic impetus, effective orchestral colors, and a quite traditional harmonic palette until halfway through.... It includes several almost film-score (not a pejorative) perorations that always quickly resort back to the denser harmonies posited at the halfway mark.[13]

Pangaea for symphony orchestra, nominated for a 1994 Grammy Award, is recorded on CRS. It consists of the programmatic representation of continental drift. *Reaching* was commissioned by the Chilean chamber group Ensemble Bartók, and has been recorded by Canyon Lands Chamber Ensemble for release on the Centaur label. It was Wolking's trip to the premiere of *Reaching* at the third annual International Music Festival in Santiago, Chile, in 1991 that yielded the title "Forever Yesterday." It is the translation of "El Ayer, Siempre," the title of a fantasy picture and story book about the land of Chile seen through the imaginary eyes of its indigenous people, the Mapuche Indians.[14] Presented with this book at his departure from Santiago, Wolking found it inspirational, and began to think about the connection between its environmental ideas and the commission he had received for a Native American ballet. Most recently (1996), Wolking has been in London for the London Symphony recording of *Powell Canyons* for release on MMC, and in Warsaw (fall 1997) for the Warsaw Philharmonic recording of a double concerto featuring the Duehlmeier/Gritton Duo, also on MMC. The Modern Art Sextet in Berlin performed his chamber music piece *House of Sky* in 1996.

Wolking's orchestral compositions have received more than fifty public performances since 1992. The Louisville Orchestra programmed two of his compositions, *Methenyology* and *Blues Fantasy*, both dubbed "orchestral jazz" works, on the Night Light series in October 1995, and the Cincinnati Symphony performed *Methenyology*, *Blues Fantasy*, and *Black Dragon Canyon* in 1996. As their titles suggest, many of Wolking's orchestral works carry associations with the landscapes of Utah and the surrounding area: *Goblin Valley* (1988), commissioned by Christopher Wilkins for the Utah Symphony, is a reference to a state park in southern Utah on the eastern edge of the San Rafael desert; *Bear Songs* (1993) was for the Bear Lake Music Festival on the border of southeastern Idaho and northeastern Utah. Other works

---

[13] William Zagorsky, "On the Building of Pipelines: William Thomas McKinley and the Master Musicians Collective," *Fanfare* 17, no. 2 (November/December 1993): 129. The present discography of Wolking's music is: *Forest* (Slovak Radio Symphony Orchestra, cond. Robert Black, MMC Bratislava Series MMC2002, 1993); *House of Sky* (Contemporary Music Consortium of Utah, cond. Madeline F. Schatz, Crystal Records CRS 8947, 1989); *Pangaea* (Fairbanks Symphony Orchestra, cond. Madeline F. Schatz, CRS Artists 9459, 1994); *Super Frank* (Ashley Alexander Big Band, AMCD 302, 1987).

[14] George Munro, ed., *El Ayer, Siempre* (Santiago, Chile: Ediciones y Publicidad S.A., 1990).

reflect the jazz and big band heritage that informs most of what he writes: *"Lyric" for a Jazzman* (1988) and *Methenyology* (a reference to contemporary jazz guitarist Pat Metheny) were both commissioned by Christopher Wilkins for the Utah Symphony; *Blues Fantasy* was commissioned by the same conductor for the Colorado Springs Symphony. Wolking presents himself as a person deeply inspired by the outdoors and the natural environment, as well as someone obviously immersed in a huge, practical jazz tradition. His original jazz charts number over fifty publications; they represent a functional body of work which is used in educational or esoteric settings devoted to the contemporary jazz "big band." He has also published articles on jazz theory and arranging in *Educator*.

The Music

The full version of *Forever Yesterday* consists of three movements, "Earth," "Water," and "Sky," each preceded by a soprano solo which amplifies that movement's theme.[15] "Earth" and "Sky" are further introduced by narration with orchestral accompaniment in a type of melodrama, providing a transition between song and ballet. The song/narration sections are called "Prologue" and "Interludes"; they function by giving the dancers time to regroup between acts while involving the audience's attention. The whole work is about forty minutes in duration.[16] The general tempo of "Earth" is *moderato* to *allegro*, with occasional breaks in the tempo. "Water" begins in a rather rapid tempo and with an active texture, but this is juxtaposed against a graceful, lyric chant of relatively long note values, much in the manner of a Bach or a Hindemith chorale; in two distinct parts, the second section of "Water" is consistently very slow. "Sky" has the fastest tempo of all, ending without *ritardando*. Thus, in outline and character, *Forever Yesterday* can be viewed as following traditional classical four-movement form: first movement, "Earth," moderate to fast with several strong melodic themes and clear sections; second and third movements, "Water," with the fast, scherzo-like A section, followed by the very slow, quiet and lyrical B section; and fourth movement, "Sky," in a very fast ABA form, thematically less weighty and shorter in span than the preceding movements. But the classical structure becomes obscured by the presence of the additional, text-based materials, whose moods vary according to their placement in the acts.

Forever Yesterday begins with an unaccompanied soprano voice intoning a paraphrase of the Navajo "Beauty Way Chant" on a high A: "'Beauty before me, beauty behind me . . .'" This well-known chant of the *Dineh* (the "people" in Navajo) is summarized in their common greeting, "Walk in Beauty" ("Ho jo na sha"). The strings enter, quietly foreshadowing the soprano's next melody, which begins with the words "with it [beauty] I walk / with it I wander and return" and continues with an excerpt of "First Daylight Song" from a collection called "Mountain Chant of the Navajo," taken from George Cronyn's *American Indian Poetry: An Anthology of Songs and Chants*: "The curtain of daybreak is hanging . . . from the land of day."[17] The images of walking and wandering in beauty and the land of day are repeated by the soprano before the song concludes and the narration begins. In this and all subsequent settings of actual Indian texts, Wolking uses only melodies he composed, being careful not to paraphrase Native tunes that might carry their own textual implications.[18]

The text for the narration represents a collaboration between Wolking and Laura DeBeque, a teacher of English and a writer with a strong interest in Native American literature.[19] Two actors, female and male, exchange brief descriptive statements concerning the beginning of day in what is probably a western, wilderness setting.[20] Only the initial

---

[15] This and subsequent references to the score of *Forever Yesterday* are taken from manuscript copies used for the Idaho productions in 1992 and 1995. All musical examples are printed by permission of the composer.

[16] The Idaho audiences elected to interrupt this experience with applause following each act and even after the song "Flowing Water/Running Water," identifying the production as more of a ballet/theatrical event than a *Gesamtkunstwerk*.

[17] Cronyn, 70.

[18] Though this was a concern for Wolking, it bears remembering that issues having to do with the relationship between text and tone in Native American song are quite different from those affecting the same relationship in Western art music. On the not uncommon phenomenon that a number of Native American peoples downplay the importance of words in song, finding Western music "far too much associated with words," see Bruno Nettl, *Blackfoot Musical Thought: Comparative Perspectives* (Kent, Ohio: Kent State University Press, 1989), 50.

[19] The original narration was shortened by DeBeque to match the length of musical backdrop provided by Wolking.

[20] The probability of the Western setting is due to the repeated use of the character of "Elk," an animal no longer associated with the East.

statement makes direct reference to any human image, to the "group" which has "gathered beneath Deer Cliff" (an imaginary place in the wilderness). In keeping with the thematic content of "Earth," the narration makes reference to dawn, the beauty of nature, giving thanks for "the gifts of the earth," and the participation of the archetypal animals, the elk and the bear, in the celebration of the renewal of life through the coming of spring and of a new day. The narrative also suggests the use of dance as a vehicle for celebration, for giving thanks, and to portray the community.

Three Native American songs are present in the first ballet movement, "Act One: Earth," and are designated in the score as "Hopi Harvest Song," "Bear Dance," and "Elk Song." The music carries the additional Native American sound of several authentic instruments. The original dance score includes orchestration for an economical chamber orchestra: flute 1, flute 2 (doubling on piccolo), oboe (doubling on English horn), clarinet, bass clarinet, bassoon, horn, trumpet (doubling on fluegelhorn), trombone, timpani, two additional percussionists, piano, and a minimum string quintet (double strings except for bass were used in the first performance). Wolking also integrates several Native American instruments among the orchestra, most notably the Sioux flute on which the principal flutist must double. The unique timbre of this popularized Native American flute is enhanced by its discrepancies in pitch. Sioux flutes are not traditionally built to a standard pitch; Wolking's is significantly sharp and could not be lowered to concert pitch, certainly not without tremendous loss of volume, which was also problematic. Because the Sioux, or "courting" flute, occupies a prominent symbolic position in *Forever Yesterday*, reappearing at significant structural points, its projection is essential to the overall direction of the work. Over time, its gamey tuning came to connote the "Other," a true wildness or exoticism, one might say, whose emotional impact is not unlike that produced by the juxtaposed musical strata in a composition by Charles Ives or Gustav Mahler. Interestingly, the flutist, a woman, was initially discouraged from her task of adapting her technique to this instrument, as a Native American source questioned her use of what is traditionally an instrument for men only. The age-old cross-cultural symbolism of the flute as a male tool of seduction is invoked in this implied spring setting of "Earth."

"Earth" is divided into three clear sections. The first contains a frame of Sioux flute solos around a central orchestral episode which is developed on the same melodic material, but set in a contrasting rhythm and in a fast tempo. The narrow range of the Native American flute places most of its rhapsodic opening solo within a fifth—c'' to g'', with occasional dips to g' and rises to a''. The opening frame incorporates some extended techniques of bent pitches, alternate fingerings on the same pitch for timbral variation, and percussive articulations, and ends with an ornamented half-step trill. Wolking spent several months playing the Sioux flute himself, developing this section's melodic ideas on the instrument.[21] The melodic material, though original with Wolking, shows his impressions of the Native American flute music in which he immersed himself: short, descending melodic patterns move obsessively with small variations and ornaments, often set in sixteenth-note triplets. While the marimba maintains a steady sixteenth-note vamp in a moderate 4/4 time, with the quarter note equaling 64, the strings sustain tremolos which often change harmony on the beat or in staggered fashion, while the claves begin sharp accents squarely on, or on the division of, the beat. The Sioux flute intones a quasi-improvisatory melody in a combination of the Dorian and Mixolydian modes, with hints of a blues-note motive to follow. Juxtaposed flatted and raised thirds and sevenths set the mood for the central episode involving the full orchestra. The melodic and harmonic motion, together with the square meter in double time, project a lively rhythm and a blues style with a loose back-beat, an impression easily explained by Wolking's big-band and pop-music background. Example 20.1 shows the Sioux flute's third entrance, exposing most of the motivic ideas later developed in this section of "Earth." When the opening tempo returns (meas. 58), the Sioux flute's improvisatory rhythmic character no longer involves triplets, the strings replace tremolos with harmonics, and the marimba's regular pattern is absent. One percussionist is instructed to "improvise with the Indian flute" using the rattle, while the others supply atmospheric effects on bell tree and rubbed wine glass. The section concludes in a G tonality built on the cello and bass up through a hovering eleventh chord minus the third, with the flute solo emphasizing the minor (albeit sharped) seventh.

An abrupt key change to A♭ begins in the clarinet's presentation of the first actual Native American melody in the work, identified in the score as "Hopi Harvest Song," but appearing in the transcription by Louis Ballard as

---

[21] Wolking, telephone interview, 20 July 1997.

Example 20.1. Wolking, *Forever Yesterday*, flute 1, meas. 5-7.

"Tewa Entrance Song."[22] Wolking uses three measures of 7/8 time to simulate the a-metrical feel of the first three phrases of the original song. The resulting eighth-note pulse is probably more regular than in an authentic Native American rendition, but there is at least a similar sensation of unsteady time to the non-Native ear. The phrases mentioned—the second a literal repeat and the third a sequence down a third—are shown in ex. 20.2, which also includes the following measure in 3/4. The song is repeated in unison and octaves by the high woodwind choir once, preceding the entrance of the horn which sounds the second Native American melody, the "Bear Dance Song."[23]

Example 20.2. Wolking, *Forever Yesterday*, clarinet, ♩ = 98, meas. 67-70.

Highlighted by a characteristic roaring of the bone scraper, notched stick, or rasp in a pattern of ♩ ♩ ♫ ♫, the "Bear Dance Song" melody has a particularly triumphant, celebratory quality. Traditionally associated with the coming of spring and the awakening of the bear from hibernation, it is a powerful symbol of the seasonal rebirth of life on earth. Wolking visited a Northern Ute Indian celebration in which the Bear Dance Song was used. Because the dance is done in male/female pairs and there was a shortage of males, he was invited to participate. He reported that all the dancers were very old people, and unhesitating in their acceptance of his participation in this social dance.[24] Wolking situates the song in A♭ major, and has the first section of the melody with its repeated descending lines cadence on the tonic. The further extension of the tune by downward sequence takes it to the dominant, where the original ends. In this manner the melody develops a circular quality, for Western ears, always carrying some impetus of a return to the beginning. The Bear Dance Song as it occurs in the horn is shown in ex. 20.3.

After the full statement of the Bear Dance Song, the horn is joined by trumpet in octaves for a restatement, while the clarinet and first violin play the previously heard Hopi Harvest Song, beginning with synchronized anacruses against it. The Hopi Harvest Song, pitched in E♭, retains its durational values, but is notated throughout in 4/4 meter, throwing its accents off the beat. When the Hopi Harvest Song has run its course, as the Bear Dance Song continues, this melody is immediately restated in A♭ with fuller orchestration, colliding with the dominant-sounding final phrases of the Bear Dance Song (then centered in E♭). Later, both tunes are heard in the key of E♭, this time with the metrical needs of the Hopi Harvest Song taking precedence, in 7/8 meter. The Bear Dance Song loses time on its fifth and twelfth notes to accommodate the irregular meter of the other tune. Their similar downward motion, resting on E♭ in the second measure (meas. 109), provides a strong sense of coherence. The coherence, however, quickly splits apart because the first tune is constructed in one-measure repeated phrases and the second

---

[22] Louis W. Ballard, *American Indian Music for the Classroom* (Phoenix: Canyon Records, 1973), 21. Wolking states that he heard the melody on a field recording, where it was titled a "Hopi Harvest Song." In the latter half of the twentieth century it is not unusual to find Native American melodies or entire songs transferred from tribe to tribe. Songs may be given, sold, or simply imitated, especially with the advent of powwows and Pan-Indianism.

[23] A version of the Ute Bear Dance Song sung by Henry Williams can be heard on *Folk Music of the United States from the Archive of Folk Song* series, recorded and edited by Willard Rhodes and issued by the Library of Congress on *Great Basin: Paiute, Washo, Ute, Bannock, Shoshone* (LP AAFS L38).

[24] Wolking, telephone interview, 7 July 1997.

Example 20.3. Wolking, *Forever Yesterday*, horn, meas. 82-94.

travels by two-measure phrases. The submediant (C minor) harmony plays a role in supporting the latter part of the Bear Dance Song. A transition in C major using part of the first section's strongest rhythm-and-blues-style theme leads to the slow, quiet introduction of the final Native American melody, the "Elk Song."

In a key signature of C but with G as tonic, the second flute foreshadows the Elk Song with two improvisatory-sounding fragments, and is answered by the Sioux flute with a chromatically-altered version of the same phrase, pitched in C. After the joyous revelry of the previous two songs, the evocative, distant quality of the Sioux flute transforms the atmosphere into a mood of dignified, mystical anticipation for the Elk, who walks on top of the people, bringing them songs.[25] The trombone presents the full melody of the Elk Song in G, though the consequent phrases of the first four measures are always harmonized by the flatted seventh, a F major chord. The repetitive bass movement, heard again in the middle movement, is reminiscent of Mixolydian rock-and-roll harmonies. The F# of the major dominant chord is not heard until the twelfth measure of the song, though a strong dominant function is expressed during the song's second melodic phrase. In Wolking's metrical setting, thirteen measures, not counting a da capo specified in Ballard's transcription,[26] are required to complete the first eight measures (which are completely reorchestrated) of the Elk Song. Its long, sequential phrase structure is passed among various solo and doubled instruments, while other instruments simultaneously play complementing variations. The original melody, as heard from trombone through trumpet, is shown in ex. 20.4. Wolking makes the melody circular, as in the Bear Dance Song: the dominant harmony supports the last phrase, which leads to another tonic vamp that serves as a return to the opening of the Elk Song. The strong rhythmic propulsion associated with the 2/4 meter (seen in ex. 20.4, meas. 145 and 147) is exaggerated by a heavy accent on each measure's second beat, not a feature of the original song.

The momentum of the final section of "Earth" builds through repetition of the nostalgically harmonized Elk Song in increasingly dense orchestration, complex chords, and a long, gradual crescendo. The motion is briefly interrupted by a variation in quartal harmony for the strings. The climax is reached when a majestic, though bare, counterpoint of solo trombone, trumpet, and later horn, dissolves the thick texture with open arpeggiation, preserving the simple rhythmic patterns established in the song. The orchestra is gradually woven back into the dialogue. After quickly changing tonalities, the motion culminates strongly in C major with a return of phrases from the Elk Song. The movement concludes gracefully, without losing its momentum as a processional, on a tonic C, harmonized in open fifths.

The Interlude, "Flowing Water/Running Water," preceding "Act Two: Water," contains two song texts from Native American sources. The first continues the imagery of the "Mountain Chant of the Navajo" with an original musical setting of "Song of the Prophet."[27] The five syllables of the words "That flowing water" are heard in a descending

---

[25] Ballard, 49.

[26] Ibid., 51.

[27] Cronyn, 71.

Example 20.4. Wolking, *Forever Yesterday*, various winds, meas. 140-52.

pentatonic scale, a pattern ethnographically identified with many Native American cultures. The motive identified in ex. 20.5 is repeated and developed throughout the use of "Song of the Prophet."

Example 20.5. Wolking, *Forever Yesterday*, "Flowing Water/Running Water," horn, meas. 1.

The second song text, titled "As He Was Borne Along by the Flood He Sang," from the "Pima Ritual Song Cycle the Flood," is representative of various Southwestern Indian groups. It was originally part of a sequence of songs describing an ancient story of natural disaster and the rebirth of the earth through water. Wolking uses the text almost verbatim, changing the structure only slightly through phrase repetition. The repeating words "Running water, running water" are first presented in a rhythmical "sing/speak, breathy, whispering" (as indicated in the score) in rapid eighth notes. A sixteenth-note ostinato in the bass supports the repetitions of this part of the text, while pizzicato and staccato notes off the beat in the upper parts punctuate the excited, breathless quality of the music. The entire text is as follows:

> AS HE WAS BORNE ALONG BY THE FLOOD HE SANG
> Running water, running water, herein resounding,
> As on the clouds I am carried to the sky,
> Running water, running water, herein roaring,
> As on the clouds I am carried to the sky.[28]

The duple eighth notes come to symbolize the English word "water," and end the song with a last utterance in the double bass and timpani, ♪♪, instrumentally invoking the word which describes and titles the second movement of the ballet.

---

[28] Ibid., 84.

"Water" begins with an extended passage for percussion featuring the ten-keyed, tuned, hardwood drum. Although listed in the score as "Native American," the hardwood drum is a derivative of an indigenous African instrument. It is being manufactured in the American Southwest as modeled after the African log drum, which has similar pitch configurations. The drum contains a scale of ten pitches, essentially in D major with a skip from B to the second D (omitting any C). The xylophone-like "drum" part requires significant technical preparation on the part of the timpanist, as it moves in rapid sixteenth notes through the entire first half of the movement. Its use determines the key signature of D major for this section. By the fifth measure the marimba loosely imitates the hardwood drum, using only pitches available on the latter. Irregular fragments in the high register are interjected by the xylophone and woodwinds, and these increase in length, frequency, and volume. According to Wolking, this passage suggests the repetitious motion within the apparently stationary water of a waterfall.[29] The woodwind accents portray the first sporadic raindrops of a storm, then rapidly transform into a deluge. Maximum density is achieved by measure 236. Then the hardwood drum starts the pattern over again, soon joined by the Chilean rain sticks[30] and the Native American elk skin drum.

Over the second hardwood drum pattern, similar to the first, the horn intones the "Navajo Rain Chant" (see ex. 20.6). Wolking's countermelody in the trumpet completes the thematic material (see ex. 20.7). Note in measures 243 and 245 how the trumpet part amplifies the Navajo Rain Chant's motivic motion of a descending fourth ornamented by a descending minor third. During his research, Wolking was drawn to the simple two-measure rain chant, but at this writing could no longer recollect precisely where he had heard it.[31] A similar dialogue is developed between clarinet and oboe, as the texture thickens and begins to include the sharply accented staccato interjections by flutes and violins (raindrops). The rain dwindles via decrescendo and a thinning of the texture, down to a final repetition of the rain chant's last motive, the "do do do te do" of the second measure of the horn solo in ex. 20.6.

Example 20.6. Wolking, *Forever Yesterday*, horn, meas. 239-40.

Example 20.7. Wolking, *Forever Yesterday*, trumpet, meas. 242-46.

The rest of "Water," in the words of the composer, depicts a "crystal clear high mountain meadow lake."[32] The solo bassoon quietly introduces a legato melody which will be repeated, extended, and varied in a heterophonic or contrapuntal texture to conclude the movement. The signature interval in the melody is the ascending minor third with which it begins, *la-do*. It is perceived ambiguously, hovering between A minor and C major, and later, A♭ minor and C♭ major. The pentatonic absence of leading tone is conspicious; neither seventh nor fourth scale degrees complicate the harmony. When the melody is more thickly orchestrated for the A♭/C♭ variation, a heavy A♭ pedal point emerges

---

[29] Wolking, interview with correspondent Jyl Hoyt, *Performance Today*, National Public Radio, 28 April 1992.

[30] Chilean rain sticks utilized by the Mapuche Indians of South America have been widely marketed and imitated in the past ten years. The sticks are made by hammering the spines of a cactus inward to the hollow trunk, placing dried beans inside, and sealing both ends of the stalk. The motion of the beans falling through the spines from end to end as the stalk is slowly tilted produces the sonic effect of hundreds of splashing droplets.

[31] Wolking, telephone interview, 20 July 1997.

[32] Wolking, *Forever Yesterday*, manuscript score.

in the low strings and timpani, pulling the tonality to natural A♭ minor where it remains for the final flat VII to I cadence in the bassoon. The original melody has four additive phrases, each beginning with the ascending minor third, as seen in ex. 20.8. The predominant use of this motive is reminiscent of the cadence in Edward MacDowell's "To a Wild Rose," which has been discussed as an example of his successful integration of compatible Indian motives into his own "compositional technique and intention."[33]

Example 20.8. Wolking, *Forever Yesterday*, bassoon, meas. 265-69.

The final interlude, "The Wind Is Wandering," contains two parts, the first dealing with wind and cloud imagery. The opening line, "The wind is wandering, the wind is wandering, wandering," is the entire text of a song called "When the Spirit Wind Approached," from the Yuma tribe's "Songs of Kumastamxo."[34] Wolking mirrors the rhythmic implications of this text with alternating measures of 2/4, 3/8, 2/4, and 6/8 meter, setting the word "wandering" in the measures of 3/8 meter. A measure of 5/8 accompaniment separates this text from the next line, "see how the winds run their course," which is actually two short excerpts from the "Butterfly Song" of one Southwest group,[35] set in 7/8 and 3/4 meters. After one repetition of this segment, the words "Blossoming clouds in the sky / Like unto shimmering flowers / . . . Onward, lo, they come," from the Zuni "Song of the Blue-Corn Dance"[36] continue the irregular meters 7/8, 5/8, 3/8, 3/4, 6/8, and so forth. Throughout, the metrical accent emphasizes the natural rhythm of the spoken word; ex. 20.9 shows how this is accomplished in the first four measures. The orchestra plays a staccato downbeat, and continues to punctuate the soprano's line with short gestures that clarify the irregular meter and, sometimes, the beat. This rhythmic treatment can be viewed as a symbolic connection with the irregular meter and beat of much Native American song. Though classically-trained musicians are able to go only as far as changing meters and adjusting to new beat values which are directly proportionate to the old ones, there is still, as in the Hopi Harvest Song of "Earth," a rhythmic similarity between Wolking's composition and authentic Indian music. Nonetheless, there is still stronger similarity between Wolking's composition and much of what has become standard rhythmic practice in Western art music in this century, beginning, perhaps, with Stravinsky.

Example 20.9. Wolking, *Forever Yesterday*, "The Wind Is Wandering," soprano, meas. 1-4.

A sudden key change marks the transition to the second text, an excerpt from "Song of the Earth/Navajo," which is a translation by Natalie Curtis Burton, originally printed in *The Indians' Book*.[37] The lines "Now the Mother Earth/ And the Father Sky,/Meeting, joining one another,/Helpmates ever, they" are presented simply in duple meter. Word painting is reflected in tessitura; the recurring refrain, "All is beautiful, / All is beautiful, / All is beautiful, indeed," takes its rhythmic impetus from the triplet implication of the syllables of "beautiful." "The Wind Is Wandering" text returns with its irregular meter and beat. A *subito* piano and key change reprise the melodic material and next portion

---

[33] Francis Brancaleone, "Edward MacDowell and Indian Motives," *American Music* 7, no. 4 (winter 1989): 363.

[34] Cronyn, 130.

[35] Ibid., 108.

[36] Ibid., 82.

[37] Ibid., 118-19.

of the "Song of the Earth" to be used, "And the night of darkness / And the dawn of light / Meeting, helping one another. . . ." Subtle variations in the rhythm and melody reflect the new text, such as the ascending, prolonged major third to a high A on "light." The wandering wind music, now akin to a rondo theme, returns to finish the song portion.

The final narrative is underscored by piano, staccato orchestral music entirely in 4/4 time, eighth-note patterns, with occasional sections of duple sixteenth-note afterbeats, in the key of E minor. The actors describe first Elk, then Bear, in a kind of poetic shape-shifting exercise, rising from the earth and taking on elemental forms as the Elk becomes Eagle rising into the sky, and the Bear becomes earth, wind and water all at once. The male actor makes a comment about the ultimate mystery of spirituality—"There seems always a depth somewhere unexplored . . . "—and the female actor concludes the narration with a description of a dancer "with the quiet agility of Deer." The dancer leaves "hoofprints in the cushion of earth," while the "tiny white violets" on the ground change into butterfly wings "in the great exchange of life yesterday, forever."[38] The stage is set for the third movement.

The final movement, "Act 3: Sky," is a tapestry of ostinatos suggesting spiraling vapors and air currents, interrupted by just one section of traditional melodic material. Beginning in E major,[39] the strong tonality of "Sky" is emphasized within seconds by hammered tonic/dominant relationships in the timpani and low strings. This is super-imposed over rapid, sixteenth-note open fifths in the violins, a pattern which continues until the first climax, twenty-seven measures later. Single notes *tenuto* in the woodwinds and short, irregular scale figures rise and fall, growing in dynamics and frequency. The composer refers to this texture as "friendly chaos" in his program notes, suggesting the random, but benignly natural, movement of clouds and breezes. The insistent $d\sharp''$ in the flutes against the constant E-major tonic harmony results in a sort of unemotional urgency. At the climax, F is also emphasized, bringing into focus a dissonant cluster around the tonic E.

The next section begins *forte* without pause in D♭ major, the sixteenth-note ostinato now taken by violas and cellos, reinforced by relentless eighth notes on the large elk skin drum. The rapid, irregular figurations in the woodwinds take the shape of ascending scale fragments, while a sustained, descending semitone gesture surfaces in the flute, $b\flat''$ to a'', and is reinforced by other instruments. This motive, also played by the trumpet in this section, pervades "Sky." The following E-major episode, with its slightly relaxed momentum, serves to introduce a full-blown melody in the trumpet. Heard in C♯ minor at this occurrence, this melody will reappear near the end of "Sky," bringing it to an emotional conclusion.

Each episode in "Sky" tends to pull back the gathering excitement of the previous one. At measure 360, the sound of the Sioux flute returns, playing the trumpet's melody, but in the parallel C major. The other high woodwinds join as the legato melody continues, accompanied by a pedal on A, and parts of the major C7 chord. A powerful harmonic shift to the subdominant (F major) harmony accompanies the beginning of the second statement of this melody, highlighted by the return of the rasp or notched stick in a quarter-note ostinato. This symbolic return of the Bear recapitulates the spirit of the "Earth" movement, providing a moving sense of unity, further enhanced by the woodwinds' redevelopment of the opening Sioux flute motive used at the outset of "Earth," as shown in ex. 20.10. At measure 396, elements of the Elk Song from "Earth" are imbedded in the homophony of woodwind and string choir, played by the clarinet and first violin, as in ex. 20.11. A synthetic tune in the solo violin interrupts the unified character of the rest of "Sky," which, even with its echoes of "Earth," otherwise maintains its driven, minimalist affect. This folksy violin melody puzzled the composer in retrospect, who at first believed it to be an authentic Native American song. Yet he had not indicated it as such in the score, and when no source could be found, Wolking decided that he himself must have written the tune.[40] That seems very likely for, though I am no expert, the square, symmetrical *aba´b* phrasing is unlike any Native American melody I have encountered. The tune, in E♭ natural minor, does display some of the modal features typical of other melodies in the ballet. Accompanied by a light back-beat, this material is restated in E minor, then developed by the first violins in D minor as the rest of the orchestra works the

---

[38] Laura DeBeque and Henry Wolking, narrative text for *Forever Yesterday*, manuscript score, 1995 version.

[39] The G♯ third of the E-major chord is heard first in the low woodwinds and strings, functioning as a pivot with the final tonic A♭ in the bassoon in "Water," but this relationship was lost upon the insertion of the second song and narration.

[40] Wolking, telephone interview, 20 July 1997.

Example 20.10. Wolking, *Forever Yesterday*, clarinet, meas. 373-76.

Example 20.11. Wolking, *Forever Yesterday*, clarinet, meas. 396-97.

texture back into rapid ostinatos. Suddenly the trumpet breaks what has been 116 measures of consistent 4/4 meter for two measures of a 7/8 solo, a nod to the rhythmic idea though not the actual melody, of the Hopi Harvest Song. Now all three authentic Native American songs featured in the first movement have, in some way, been recapitulated, along with the essence of the composer's original Sioux flute melody (as well as its timbre). All that remains is to rebuild the ostinatos in density and dynamics, as they push to a screaming finish, an unrelenting pedal on B♭ providing the foundation for a quintal harmony consisting of the first five pitches of the F-major scale. The strength of the bass B♭ must force the listener to interpret the final sonority as a B♭ chord with missing third and added second, sixth, and seventh, an unapologetically ambiguous jazz chord.

Much of "Sky" (though not the final cadence) is lifted from the first and third movements of Wolking's earlier composition *House of Sky* and scored for "Pierrot" chamber ensemble (five instrumentalists as prescribed for Arnold Schoenberg's most well-known work). *House of Sky*[41] (1986) begins as a frankly post-minimalist composition, with all of the complex layers of conflicting ostinatos and other compelling, repetitious patterns one might expect from a committed minimalist. In adapting and expanding this material for *Forever Yesterday*'s "Sky," the composer orchestrated several of the basic episodes as they originally occurred, and eliminated the neo-expressionist, slow second movement, replacing it with the symmetrically phrased violin solo. By keeping most of the forward-moving harmony and adding clear solo melodic lines over the top, Wolking transformed *House of Sky* from a fairly abstract piece of chamber music into an accessible orchestral work.

Additional Compositional Concerns

The score was prepared without input from the choreographer, who began her work by listening to the composer's synthesized realization. When asked if issues of dance influenced his approach to composition beyond the prescribed programmatic themes, Henry Wolking noted that he had been obliged to use repetition and extend the length of his score beyond what he would have found necessary for a purely musical statement. As for models of dance composition that were on his mind as he developed this work, he replied *Rite of Spring*.[42] I asked about his compositional method as he planned large-scale tonal movement: why were certain modulations chosen, and how did he determine the overall harmonic movement of the work, which sounded natural and inevitable? Wolking indicated he began with melodic themes he either composed or quoted, then decided on the instrument that would carry the initial statement. Having chosen the most appropriate timbre for the melody, he moved to the range and key in which he wanted the instrument to play. In this way, choices regarding orchestration made early in the process, and which in a fashion were only tangentially relative to key, determined the tonal movement.[43]

---

[41] So titled after Ivan Doig's memoirs of childhood in Montana, *This House of Sky: Landscapes of a Western Mind* (Orlando, Fla.: Harcourt Brace & Co., 1978).

[42] Wolking, telephone interview, 7 July 1997.

[43] Ibid.

Of course, much of *Forever Yesterday* utilizes modal elements and extended harmonies derived from the jazz harmonic practice with which Wolking is so familiar. But surprising is the degree to which pentatonic and special motivic—including rhythmical motivic—qualities of Native American song are integrated beyond the areas of actual quotation. Added to the hierarchical importance of orchestration in determining key structure is the influence of the unique timbral qualities of Native American instruments. These extend the expressive range of the music in new directions, not merely producing interesting sound for its own sake, but for the sake of its deep emotional and programmatic connections.

The most meaningful "Native American Themes" are these programmatic connections, as it turns out. Eric Salzman described postmodernist music (in contrast to modernist music) in his *Twentieth-Century Music* thus: "Postmodern music looks outside to the culture. Context becomes an essential part of the work and the act of performance."[44] In part the anxiety of the late twentieth century about the degradation of the natural world, in part the genuinely-held belief by many Americans that Native Americans have a mystically superior approach to living with nature, provide the thematic basis for *Forever Yesterday*. Preoccupations of our culture today find assuagement in the perceived solutions of the Other, whom we have injured. The musics of Native Americans, their purposes different in their own cultures from the purposes of our musics in our cultures, transfuse part of their spiritual powers when quoted. Native American music does not exist for music's sake, in either context, but for the sake of ritual and spiritual communication, from human to human and from human to the supernatural. These elements surface in *Forever Yesterday* by means of melody, instrumentation, and text.

Wolking has chosen to address a wide audience by avoiding the modernist systems of serialism, atonality, and indeterminacy. He has also refused to subscribe solely to any particular method. He not-very-jokingly has attributed whatever compositional success he has achieved to the fact that he did not enter a doctoral program in composition; his stylistic tendencies are quite naturally guided by his practical work in the jazz world. But Wolking has acquired a much broader language by studying the contemporary scene, and manipulating minimalist techniques, avant-garde extended techniques, and, with *Forever Yesterday*, integrating non-European-based musical ideas into an extended orchestral score for dance theater. His music does not exist in the abstract or pure world of sound, but is always linked to extra-musical meaning. In a lecture he gave on "A Perspective of New Music in the Nineties," he summarized his own predilections:

> As there is no common language for music in this last decade of the century, a composer must "dig deeply" for truth in his or her expression. A composer's most powerful gift is imagination, and as true novelty is rare, what we offer are different ways of perceiving the similar materials. I have always been attracted to the vernacular sounds of jazz. There is a certain honesty of expression in a skilled jazz improvisor's approach to the creation of melody that I find refreshing; I believe in melodies.[45]

And in assessing postmodernism, he stated:

> Post-modern music cares less about labels and more about the three-way communication between audience, composer and performer. It is a reaction against Milton Babbitt's "Who cares if you listen" philosophy, it is anti-elitist as it doesn't attempt to speak exclusively to specialists.[46]

His assessment of postmodernism is not far removed from the view of the movement articulated ten years ago by Salzman, that "The language of tonality, and the associated uses of rhythmic and phrase repetition as well as recollection, come out of or relate to a broadly shared, culturally determined, and commonly understood basic vocabulary."[47]

---

[44] Eric Salzman, *Twentieth-Century Music: An Introduction*, 3rd ed. (Englewood Cliffs, N.J.: Prentice-Hall, 1988), 194.

[45] Wolking, "A Perspective of New Music of the Nineties," lecture, University of Utah, 1994.

[46] Ibid.

[47] Salzman, 194. Among other recent studies of postmodernism, see also Ingeborg Hoestery, ed., *Zeitgeist in Babel: The Post Modernist Controversy* (Bloomington: Indiana University Press, 1991), and Timothy Dean Taylor, "The Voracious Muse: Contemporary Cross-Cultural Musical Borrowings, Culture, and Postmodernism" (Ph.D. diss., University of Michigan, 1993).

Wolking uses tonality according to his own idiosyncratic methods, and tends toward the use of extended jazz harmonies. He understands the value of repetition to the vast majority of informed and uninformed listeners, and in this ballet score he integrates the element of repetition that is both inherent and highly valued in Native American musical cultures. Though the African American musical vocabulary has undoubtedly become the more "broadly shared, culturally determined and commonly understood" element in Wolking's compositions (as well as in the works of most contemporary composers), the Native American themes in *Forever Yesterday* accord that work a degree of meaning beyond the sphere of sound.

Appendix

Publications of Robert Lamar Weaver

COMPILED BY RICHARD GRISCOM

Books and Articles

"Florentine Comic Operas of the Seventeenth Century." Ph.D. diss., University of North Carolina at Chapel Hill, 1958.

"Sixteenth-Century Instrumentation." *Musical Quarterly* 47, no. 3 (July 1961): 363-78.

"The Orchestra in Early Italian Opera." *Journal of the American Musicological Society* 17, no. 1 (spring 1964): 83-89.

"Opera in Florence: 1646-1731." In *Studies in Musicology: Essays in the History, Style, and Bibliography of Music in Memory of Glen Haydon,* ed. James W. Pruett, 60-71. Chapel Hill: University of North Carolina Press, 1969.

"*Il Girello*, a 17th Century Burlesque Opera." *Quadrivium* 12, no. 2 (1971): 141-64. *Memorie e contributi alla musica dal medioevo all'eta moderna: Offerti a Federico Ghisi nel settantesimo compleanno (1901-71),* ed. Giuseppe Vecchi. Bologna: Istituto di Filologia Latina e Medioevale; Università degli Studi di Bologna, 1971.

Alessandro Melani (1639-1703). Wellesley Edition Cantata Index Series, fasc. 8. Wellesley, Mass.: Wellesley College, 1972.

Atto Melani (1626-1714). Wellesley Edition Cantata Index Series, fasc. 9. Wellesley, Mass.: Wellesley College, 1972.

"Materiali per le biografie dei fratelli Melani." *Rivista italiana di musicologia* 12, no. 2 (1977): 252-95.

(With Norma Wright Weaver.) *A Chronology of Music in the Florentine Theater, 1590-1750: Operas, Prologues, Farces, Intermezzos, and Plays with Incidental Music.* Detroit Studies in Music Bibliography, 38. Detroit: Information Coordinators, 1978.

The New Grove Dictionary of Music and Musicians. Edited by Stanley Sadie. London: Macmillan, 1980. S.v. "Melani, Jacopo; Melani, Atto; Melani, Alessandro"; "Rospigliosi, Giulio"; "Salvi, Antonio"; and "Villifranchi, Giovanni Cosimo."

(Editor.) *Essays on the Music of J. S. Bach and Other Divers Subjects: A Tribute to Gerhard Herz.* Louisville: University of Louisville; New York: distributed by Pendragon Press, 1981.

"Gerhard Herz." In *Essays on the Music of J. S. Bach,* 1-7.

"The Conflict of Religion and Aesthetics in Schoenberg's *Moses und Aron.*" In *Essays on the Music of J. S. Bach,* 291-303.

"The State of Research in Italian Baroque Opera." *Journal of Musicology* 1, no. 1 (January 1982): 44-49.

(General editor.) Jeanne Belfy, *The Louisville Orchestra New Music Project.* Louisville: University of Louisville, 1983.

"The Consolidation of the Main Elements of the Orchestra, 1470-1768." In *The Orchestra: Origins and Transformations,* ed. Joan Peyser, 1-35. New York: Scribners, 1986.

"Metastasio a Firenze." In *Metastasio e il mondo musicale,* ed. Maria Teresa Muraro, 199-206. Studi di musica veneta, 9. Firenze: Leo S. Olschki, 1986.

Inaugural Conference for the Ricasoli Collection: Patrons, Politics, Music and Art in Italy, 1738-1859, March 14-18, 1989. University of Louisville Publications in Musicology, no. 3. Louisville: University of Louisville, 1989.

"Finding and Preserving a Rare Music Library from Florence." *Chronicle of Higher Education*, 19 June 1989, B2.

"Report on the Ricasoli Collection." In *Atti del XIV congresso della Società internazionale di Musicologia, Bologna: Trasmissione e recezione delle forme di cultura musicale*, vol. 3: *Free Papers*, 315-28. Torino: Edizioni di Torino, 1990.

The New Grove Dictionary of Opera. Edited by Stanley Sadie. London: Macmillan, 1992. S.v. "Andolfati, Pietro"; "*Cascina, La*"; "Casori, Ferdinando"; "Florence"; "Fusai, Ippolito"; "Giotti, Cosimo"; "*Girello, Il*"; "Medici" (with Tim Carter); "Melani, Jacopo; Melani, Atto; Melani, Alessandro"; "Moneta, Giuseppe"; "Moniglia, Giovanni Andrea"; "Neri Bondi, Michele"; "*Podestà di Colognole, Il*"; "Rutini, Ferdinando"; "Rutini, Giovanni Marco"; "Somigli, Domenico"; "Tassi, Niccolò"; "Vanneschi, Francesco"; "Veroli, Giacomo"; and "Villifranchi, Giovanni Cosimo."

(With Norma Wright Weaver.) *A Chronology of Music in the Florentine Theater, 1751–1800: Operas, Prologues, Farces, Intermezzos, Concerts, and Plays with Incidental Music*. Detroit Studies in Music Bibliography, 70. Warren, Mich.: Harmonie Park Press, 1993.

"The Making of the President [of the University of Louisville] Campaign, 1995." *Leo* 5, no. 15 (22 February 1995): 1.

"The Ricasoli Collection." *Library Review* (University of Louisville) 45 (1995): 17-22.

"Uses for a U of L Campus in Italy." *Louisville Courier-Journal*, 14 February 1998, 9A.

"Bartók's Sixth String Quartet: A Programmatic Interpretation." In *Res musicae: Essays in Honor of James Pruett*, ed. Craig H. Russell and Paul R. Laird. Harmonie Park Press, forthcoming.

The New Grove Dictionary of Music and Musicians. 7th ed. London: Macmillan, forthcoming. S.v. "Felici, Alessandro; Felici, Bartolomeo"; "Melani, Jacopo; Melani, Atto; Melani, Alessandro"; "Moneta, Giuseppe"; "Moniglia, Giovanni Andrea"; "Neri Bondi, Michele"; "Vanneschi, Francesco"; and "Villifranchi, Giovanni Cosimo."

(With Marian C. Green.) *Patrons, Politics, Music, and Art in Italy, 1738–1859: Proceedings of the Inaugural Conference for the Ricasoli Collection*. Harmonie Park Press, forthcoming.

"Introduction: A History of the Preservation of the Ricasoli Collection." In ibid.

Reviews

William W. Austin, ed., *New Looks at Italian Opera: Essays in Honor of Donald J. Grout*. *Notes* 25, no. 4 (June 1969): 718-19.

Michael F. Robinson, *Opera before Mozart*. *Journal of Research in Music Education* 18, no. 3 (fall 1970): 302-03.

Egon Wellesz, *Zwei Studien für Klavier*, op. 29, and *Triptychon für Klavier*, op. 98. *Notes* 26, no. 3 (March 1970): 616-17.

Diether de la Motte, *10 Fantasien am Klavier*. *Notes* 26, no. 3 (March 1970): 617.

Gregory Woolf, *Mass with Electronic Tape*. *Notes* 27, no. 2 (December 1970): 340-42.

"Current Chronicle: Nashville, Tennessee." *Musical Quarterly* 57, no. 2 (April 1971): 317-22.

Irène Mamczarz, *Les intermèdes comiques italiens au XVIIIe siècle en France et en Italie*. *Notes* 31, no. 1 (September 1974): 51-53.

Dan Welcher, *Concerto da camera*. *Notes* 34, no. 3 (March 1978): 723.

The Music Criticism of Hugo Wolf, translated, edited, and annotated by Henry Pleasants. *Journal of the American Liszt Society* 10 (December 1981): 104-05.

The Letters of Claudio Monteverdi, introduced and translated by Denis Stevens. *American Recorder* 23, no. 4 (November 1982): 161.

Robin Holloway, *Debussy and Wagner*. *Journal of the American Liszt Society* 12 (December 1982): 101-03.

John D. Drummond, *Opera in Perspective*. *Journal of the American Liszt Society* 14 (December 1983): 100-09.

Lorenzo Bianconi, *Storia della musica*, vol. 4: *Il seicento*; and Flavio Testi, *La musica italiana nel seicento*. *Notes* 41, no. 1 (September 1984): 53-56.

Gary Tomlinson, *Monteverdi and the End of the Renaissance*. *American Recorder* 29, no. 4 (November 1988): 151.

Gabriella Biagi Ravenni, *Diva panthera: Musica e musicisti al servizio dello stato lucchese*. *Music & Letters* 76, no. 1 (February 1995): 105-07.

Music Editions

Cantatas by Alessandro Melani (1639-1703), Atto Melani (1626-1714). The Italian Cantata in the Seventeenth Century, ed. Carolyn Gianturco, vol. 11. New York: Garland, 1986.

Coordinator and historical commentator for publications of music in the Ricasoli Collection (various editors): Tommaso Giordani, *Quintetto in mi bemolle maggiore*; Buonaventure Terreni, *Sonata a quattro*; Alessandro Rolla, *Duetto no. 1 e no. 2*; Anonymous, *Duetto no. 4*; *Raccolta di duetti.* Gaiole in Chianti: Materiali Sonori, 1994-95.

Program and Record Liner Notes

Josquin des Prez, *Missa Pange Lingua.* Catawba College Choir, directed by Robert Weaver. Music Library Recordings 7085, [1959].

Nashville Symphony Orchestra, Nashville, Tenn., 1963-68.

Kentucky Center Chamber Players, Louisville, Ky., 1992-present.

Louisville Chamber Music Society, Louisville, Ky., various programs.

A Bassoonist's Voice: Matthew Karr, Bassoon. Centaur Records 2330, 1997.

Theses and Dissertations Supervised by Robert Lamar Weaver

GEORGE PEABODY COLLEGE, NASHVILLE

Calvin M. Bower. "Four Medieval Musical Texts Found in an Eleventh-Century Collectaneum." M.M., 1963.

Cynthia Belcher Drennan. "An Analysis and Comparison of Representative Thirteenth- and Sixteenth-Century Motets." M.M., 1965.

Ortrun Engehausen Gilbert. "The Evolution of the Passion Text and Its Musical Settings before J. S. Bach." M.M., 1965.

Ernest Charles Harriss. "A Translation of Sections of *Der volkommene Capellmeister* (Johann Mattheson)." M.M., 1965.

Calvin M. Bower. "Boethius' 'The Principles of Music': An Introduction, Translation, and Commentary." Ph.D., 1966. Published as *Fundamentals of Music Anicius Manlius Severinus Boethius.* Music Theory Translation Series. New Haven: Yale University Press, 1989.

Otto Frederick Becker. "The Maîtrise in Northern France and Burgundy during the Fifteenth Century." Ph.D., 1967.

Emily Harriet Amos. "The Cantus Firmus Organ Works of Hermann Schroeder." M.M., 1968.

Ruth Landes Pitts. "Don Juan Hidalgo, Seventeenth-Century Spanish Composer." Ph.D., 1968.

Ernest Charles Harriss. "Johann Mattheson's 'Der vollkommene Capellmeister': A Translation and Commentary." Ph.D., 1969. Published as *Johann Mattheson's Der vollkommene Capellmeister: A Revised Translation with Critical Commentary.* Studies in Musicology, ed. George Buelow. Ann Arbor: UMI Research Press, 1981.

Jeanne Ellison Shaffer. "The Cantus Firmus in Alessandro Scarlatti's Motets." Ph.D., 1970.

Franklin Parker Poole. "The Moravian Musical Heritage: Johann Christian Geisler's Music in America." Ph.D., 1971.

Bruce R. Smedley. "A Study of Ralph Vaughan Williams' *Hodie.*" M.M., 1971.

Darwin Gayle White. "Woodwind Scoring Practices in the Symphonies of Beethoven, Schubert, Mendelssohn, and Berlioz from 1800 to 1840." Ph.D., 1971.

David Merrell Bridges. "An Analysis of Selected Seventeenth-Century Italian Part-Songs." M.M., 1972.

Stephen L. Glover. "The Three Trumpet Concertos of Johann Melchior Molter (1696-1765)." M.A., 1972.

Michael A. Hernon. "Perugia Ms. 431 (G20): A Study of the Secular Italian Pieces." Ph.D., 1972.

James H. Laster. "Christian Hymnody in Iran." Ph.D., 1973.

George Louis Mabry. "The Vocal and Choral Works of Ernst von Dohnanyi." Ph.D., 1973.

Schuman Chuo Yang. "Twentieth-Century Chinese Solo Songs: A Historical and Analytical Study of Selected Chinese Solo Songs Composed or Arranged by Chinese Composers from the 1920's to the Present." Ph.D., 1973.

Samuel Battie Owens. "The Organ Mass and Girolamo Frescobaldi's *Fiore Musicali* of 1635; Music for Two Organs; Four Lenten Motets of Alessandro Scarlatti." D.M.A., 1974.

Judith Lorene Brown. "Form and Harmonic Motion of the First Movements of Five Piano Sonatas from Haydn to Schumann." M.M., 1975.

Nena Louise Frazier, a.k.a. Nena Couch. "A Study of the Ballets in *Il pastor fido*, *Ariodante*, and *Alcina* by George Frederic Handel, and *Les Indes galantes* by Jean-Philippe Rameau." M.M., 1975.

Paul Thomas Hebda. "Characteristics of Selected Twentieth-Century Dance Suites." M.M., 1975.

David Merrell Bridges. "The Social Setting of 'Musica da Camera' in Rome, 1667-1700." Ph.D., 1976.

Bruce Robert Smedley. "Contemporary Sacred Chamber Opera: A Medieval Form in the Twentieth Century." Ph.D., 1977.

Michael Stanley Hime. "Comparative Analysis of Selected Interpretations of *Till Eulenspiegel*, op. 28, by Richard Strauss: A Conductor's Viewpoint." M.M., 1977.

George Peabody College of Vanderbilt University

William James Dorroh. "A Study of Plainsong in the Organ Compositions of Eight Twentieth-Century French Composers." Ph.D., 1978.

Charles Edward Barret, Jr. "A Critical Edition of the Dijon Chansonnier: Dijon, Bibliothèque de la Ville, Ms. 512 (Ancienne 295)." Ph.D., 1981.

University of Louisville–University of Kentucky

Carole C. Birkhead. "The History of the Orchestra in Louisville." M.A., 1977.

Mary Sharp. "A Survey of Musical Quotation from 1940 to 1975." M.M., 1985.

Jeanne Marie Belfy. "The Commissioning Project of the Louisville Orchestra." Ph.D., 1986.

Deborah Carlton Loftis. "Big Singing Day in Benton, Kentucky: A Study of the Historical, Ethnic Identity and Musical Style of 'Southern Harmony Singers.'" Ph.D., 1987.

John William Schuster-Craig. "Compositional Procedures in Selected Works of Clermont Pepin (1926-)." Ph.D., 1987.

Alice Hudnall Cash. "Wanda Landowska and the Revival of the Harpsichord: A Reassessment." Ph.D., 1990.

Alexander Thomas Simpson. "Opera on Film: A Study of the History and the Aesthetic Principles and Conflicts of a Hybrid Genre." Ph.D., 1990.

Articles about the Weavers

F. W. Woolsey. "The Music Sleuths: Meet Robert & Norma Weaver, Tracers of Lost Librettos." *Louisville Courier-Journal Magazine*, 23 October 1983, 14-18.

"Southerners, Beyond the Walls of Academe: Dr. Robert L. Weaver." *Southern Living* 25 (March 1990): 130.

Index

Abravanel, Maurice, 286-89
academies
    Accademia degl'Elevati (Florence), 90-91
    Accademia degl'Immobili (Florence), 159-60
    Accademia degl'Imperturbabili (Venice), 138-40
    Accademia degl'Incogniti (Venice), 138
    Accademia dei Rinnovati (Ferrara), 69
    Accademia di Santa Cecilia (Rome), 69
    Accademia Filarmonica (Verona), 69
Addison, Charles, 149, 156
Adonis (Ferdinando Gonzaga), 91, 103
Adriani, Francesco, 71n
Affektenlehre, 191
Agee, Richard, 73
Agostini, Pier Simon, 139
Agricola, Johann Friedrich, 192n, 193
    Anleitung zur Singkunst (transl. of Tosi), 193
Agrippina (Handel), 147
Albinoni, Antonio, 136n
Albinoni, Tomaso, 136n
Albizzi, Luca Casimiro degli, 159-61
Albizzi, Luca degli, 159-61
Albrecht V of Bavaria, 68-69, 75
Alceste (Gluck), 246
Alcestis (Euripides), 246
Alessandri, Felice, 231
    Virginia (Pepoli), 231
Alexander's Feast (Handel), 265
Alfieri, Vittorio, 227-31, 244, 246
    reforms of libretto, 227-28
    operatic adaptation of *Virginia*, 229-31
    Saul, 244
    staging tragic endings, 228
    version of *Il Merope*, 228
Alma fugens (sequence), 42, 48
Altdorf, Benedictine convent, 51
Amadino, Ricciardo, 76-77, 79
Amalarius (Amalar)
    Liber officialis, 4
Ancona, 235
    Biblioteca Comunale Ms. Mus. 83, 235, 235n

Andolfati, Pietro, 245
    Il teatro moderno applaudito, 241n, 245n
Anerio, Felice, 69, 77, 79
Anfossi, Pasquale, 205, 213, 215, 222
Angelica e Medoro (Metastasio/Porpora), 117
Angerer, Joachim, O. P., 52n
Anne, Queen of England, 147, 157
Anonymous XI (CS III), 52, 62, 62n, 63
Anonymous *secundum* Johannem Valendrinum, 64
Antico, Andrea
    Liber quindecim missarum, 65n
Antigone (Traetta), 230
Antioco (Cavalli), 139
Antiquis, Giovanni Angelo, 76
Antonelli, Cornelio da Rimini (*detto il Turturino*), 76
Apollo und Hyacinth (Mozart), 195-96
Apolloni, Giovanni Filippo
    La Circe (Stradella), 119, 129
Aquitanian plainchant manuscript sources, 3, 9, 12-14, 24
Arcadelt, Jacques, 65n, 66, 72
Arcadian classicism, 187, 194
    neoclassical dramaturgy, 227, 230-31
Archilei, Vittoria, 71
Arcimboldi, Giovanni Angelo, 77
Arigone, Cardinal, 79
Ariosto, Ludovico, 69
Armida abbandonata (Jommelli), 205
Armidoro (Castoreo), 135
Ascanio in Alba (Mozart), 195-212
Athalia (Handel), 265
Atkinson, Charles, 13n, 30
Attaingnant, Pierre, 65
Die Auferweckung des Lazarus (Loewe), 276
Aureli, Aurelio
    Erismena (Cavalli), 137
    Le fortune di Rodope e Damira (Ziani), 137

Baccusi, Hippolito, 70, 79
Bach, C. P. E., 192n, 193
    Essay on the True Art of Playing Keyboard Instruments, 193n

Bach, J. C., xvi, 205
Bach, J. S., 193, 264-65
    Brandenburg Concerto No. 5, 280
    Chaconne, 278
    Goldberg Variations, 277, 283, 284n
    Magnificat, 266
    Mass in B minor, 266
    St. John Passion, 266
    St. Matthew Passion, 266, 271
Bach Gesellschaft, 266
Bach revival, 265, 269
Baglioni, Donato, 76
Baldini, Vittorio, 71n, 78
Ballard, Louis, 297n, 298n
Bamberg, Staatsbibliothek Ms. lit. 5, 35, 37
Bandini, Ottavio, 76
Barbieri, Luigi, 233
Bardi, Giovanni de', 71n, 78
Barrett, Charles Edward, Jr., xv, 310
Bartha, Dénes von, 52n, 61n, 62n, 63n, 64n
Bartók, Béla, 48, 308
Basile, Adriana, 93, 107
Basle, Paul Sacher Stiftung, 288n
Bastien und Bastienne (Mozart), 196
Bati, Luca, 94
Bazin, Germain, 114
Becker, Carl Ferdinand, 266
Beethoven, Ludwig van, xvi, 268
Beggar's Opera (Gay), 158
Belfy, Jeanne, xv, 291-305, 291n, 307, 310
Bellasio, Paolo, 77
Bellavere, Vincenzo (Bell'haver), 79
Bellù, Adele, 91n
Belsazar (Clasing), 270
Belshazzar (Handel), 265
Bembo, Pietro, 93
Benary, Peter, 190n, 193n
Benci, Antonio Francesco, 90, 111
Beneventan manuscripts, 4n
Berchem, Jacquet de, 74n
Berg, Adam, 71, 78
Berlin, 18, 192-93, 195, 265, 277, 280, 282
    Hochschule für Musik, 277, 281
    Singakademie, 265-66, 268
Bernardi, Francesco (Senesino), 154, 164
Bertani, Lelio, 70, 72n, 79
Bertoldo, Sperindio, 74
Besseler, Heinrich, 190n
Betterton, Thomas, 149, 155
La Betulia liberata (Mozart), 196
Bevilacqua, Mario, 69n, 76-77
Bianciardi, Vincenzio, 233
Bianconi, Lorenzo, 133n, 139n
Blenheim Palace, 145-48, 150, 152, 154, 156-58
Blessi, Manoli. *See* Molino
Boba, Marcantonio, 71n
Boccherini, Giovanni, 215
Boetticher, Wolfgang, 69n

Bologna, Biblioteca Civico Museo Bibliografico Musicale, 233n, 239
Bonagiunta, Giulio, 71
Bonduca (Purcell), 155-56
Boni, Girolamo, 77
Borchling, Conrad, 51n
Bordoni, Faustina, 154, 164
Borghese, Eleanora Boncompagni, funeral of, 113, 113n, 114n
Borghese, Don Giovanni Battista, 113-14
Bortnianskij, Dmitri, 267
Borusso, Guglielmo Adorno, 77
Bottegari, Cosimo, 69, 75
Boulanger, Nadia, 280
Bower, Calvin M., xiii, xv, xviii, xix, 3-32, 9n, 309
Bozza, Francesco, 70, 79
Bragard, Roger, 63n
Braun, Werner, 189, 193
Broschi, Carlo (Farinelli), 117, 165
Brown, Howard Mayer, 67n
Bruch, M. Max, 280
Brunner, Lance W., 33-49
Budapest, Hungarian National Archive, 213-14
Buelow, George, 188n, 190-91, 192n
Buonarroti, Michelangelo, 90
Busenello, Giovanni Francesco, 138
Bunaldi, Francesco, 78
Bursfeld, Benedictine abbey, 51
Busoni, Ferruccio, 260

Cahn, Peter, 61n
Calzabigi, Ranieri de', 118, 127, 215, 228-29, 231
    L'Elfrida (Paisiello), 245
    Il sogno d'Olimpia (de Majo), 118, 127-28
Cambio, Donato, 73
Cambio, Perissone, 73-74
Cannon, Beekman, 188
cantus (hexachord), 54, 56, 58, 62n, 63, 63n, 64
    in genere, 54, 62, 62n
    in specie, 54, 62, 62n, 63
Capello, Bianca, 67-68, 70
Caracciolo, Prince, 117
Carò, Anibal, 71, 71n
Caro, G. B., 71
Carpani, Giuseppe, 244-45, 265
Cash, Alice, xv, 277-84, 277n, 310
Castelvecchio, Stefano, 245n
Castoreo, Bortolo, 135
    Armidoro, 135
Castoreo, Giacomo, 135, 139
    Eurimene, 135
    Il pazzo politico, 135n
    Il prencipe corsaro, 135n
Cavaccio, Giovanni, 70
Cavalieri, Emilio de', 76
Cavalli, Francesco, 133, 133n, 135-37, 139
    Antioco, 139
    Erismena (Aureli), 137
    Giasone, 135
Cecilian movement, 268

Centurione, Daniello, 76
Cesti, Antonio, 134
Chartres, Bibliothèque Municipale Ms. 47, 12
Chailley, Jacques, 3n, 30
Chater, James, 72n
Cherubini, Luigi, xvi, 233, 239, 259
choral societies, 19th century, 263, 265-66
Choron, Alexandre
    Considération sur la nécessité de rétablir le chant de l'Eglise de Rome, 269
Cristiana de Lorena (de' Medici), 76
Christus (Liszt), 264, 272, 274
Christus das Kind (Schneider), 271
Christus: Ein Mysterium in einem Vorspiele und drei Oratorien (Draeseke), 271, 276
Chuang-tzu, 34
Church
    Catholic, 267, 269, 274
        Paschal Vigil *alleluia*, *sequentia*, and *prosae*, 10th-11th centuries, 3-32
        sequences, 10th-12th centuries, 33-49
        treatise from Ebstorf, 15th century, 51-64
    Protestant, 268-69
        Calvinist, 267
        Lutheran, 267-68
churches
    Imperial Chapel (St. Petersburg), 267
    St. Vitus Cathedral (Prague), 81-88
    San Lorenzo (Florence), 98
    San Lorenzo (Naples), 114, 122
    Santa Lucia dei Ginnasi (Rome), 113
    Santa Maria del Fiore Cathedral (Florence), 95
    Santa Maria dell'Orazione e Morte Archconfraternity (Rome), 115
Churchill, John, 147
Churchill, Sarah (Duchess of Marlborough), 146, 148
Cibber, Colley, 145, 146n, 149, 152, 154, 156
    The Fool in Fashion, 152
    Love's Last Shift, 145, 155
    The Provok'd Husband, 154n, 158
Cicognini, Giacinto Andrea, 141, 143
Cigna-Santi, Vittorio Amadeo, 196, 205
Cimarosa, Domenico, xvi
    L'italiana in Londra, 234
    Il matrimonio segreto, 243n
Cinthia & Endimion (D. Purcell), 155
La Circe (Apolloni/Stradella), 119, 129
Cisilino, Siro, 79
Clare, Earl of (later, Duke of Newcastle), 148
Claremont, 148, 157
Clasing, Johann Heinrich, 265
    Belsazar, 270
    Die Tochter Jephtas, 270
clavis, 54, 56, 61, 61n, 63, 63n, 64
    duplex, 54, 63
    mutabilis, 54, 63
    non mutabilis, 54, 63
    secundum artem, 54, 63, 63n
    secundum usum, 54, 63, 63n
    triplex, 54, 63
    unica, 54, 63
Clementi, Muzio, xvi
Clerici, Francesco, 233
    Oreste o sia la morte d'Egisto e Clinnestra, 254
Cochrane, Eric, 235n
Coke, Thomas, 146, 148, 150
    theatrical papers, 146n, 149n
comédie larmoyante, 205, 215
Componimento sacro per la festività dell' S.S. Natale (Metastasio/Costanzi), 116, 125
Compstoff, Ermanno, 166
Confederacy (Vanbrugh), 156
Confitemini Domino (alleluia), 3-32
Congaudent angelorum chori (sequence), 35-37
Congreve, William, 145, 149-50, 155-56
Conrad, Doda, 283
Conradus de Zabernia, 51, 52n
Conti, Gioacchino (Egiziello), 218-19
Contino, Giovanni, 74, 74n
corona, 65, 68, 70-74, 74n, 76, 78
Corsini, Bartolomeo, 166
Corteccia, Francesco, 66, 67n
Corti, Gino, 159, 161
Costanzi, Giovanni Battista
    Componimento sacro per la festività dell S.S. Natale (Metastasio), 116, 125
Cotellini, Marco, 196, 215, 230
Country Home (Vanbrugh), 155
Covent Garden House. *See* Theatre Royal at Drury Lane
Crakow, Biblioteka Jagiellonska
    autograph score, Mozart, *Lucio Silla*, 202-03
Craft, Robert, 285, 288n
Crescimbeni, Giovanni Maria
    L'istoria della volgar poesia, 118
Crocker, Richard, 3, 11n, 12, 14n, 30, 34, 41-42
Cronyn, George
    American Indian Poetry, 292, 298-99, 301
Cserba, Simon, O.P., 62n
Cummings, Anthony, 66n
Currezo, Claudio da, 78
Cuzzoni Sandoni, Francesca, 154, 167

La Dafne (Gagliano), 91-92, 104
Dahlhaus, Carl, 264, 268n
Dalla Casa, Girolamo, 79
Da Ponte, Lorenzo, 213, 244, 255, 258
    Memoirs, 244n, 255n
Daux, Camille, 23-24, 30
Davari, Stefano, 89n
David (Klein), 270
De Angelis, Marcello, 233, 233n, 234n, 237, 259-60
De Beque, Laura, 292, 295, 302
De Gamerra, Giovanni, 196, 205, 209, 215-20, 222-24, 259
    La finta scema (Salieri), 213-26
    Il Pirrò re d'Epiro (set by Paisiello and Zingarelli), 251
    translation of *Die Zauberflöte* (Schikaneder/Mozart), 259
De Goede, Nicholas, 3n, 31

Delayrac, Nicolas
    Nina (Marsollier), 244
Devrient, Eduard, 266
Dic nobis (sequence) 42-44
Diderot, Denis, 228
Didone (Metastasio/Paisiello), 245
Dobree, Bonomy, 146n, 153n, 154n
Dobszay, László, 34, 48-49
Dolan, Anton, 285-89
Donato, Baldissera, 74
Don Giovanni (Mozart), 259, 261
Draeseke, Friedrich
    Christus: Ein Mysterium in einem Vorspiele und drei Oratorien, 271, 276
dramma giocoso, 195, 234, 238, 255, 258
Dreves, Guido Maria, 3n, 19-20, 22-23, 30
Droysen, Gustav, 266
Drury Lane (Theatre Royal in Drury Lane/Covent Garden House/Dorset Garden Theatre), 146, 149-52, 154
Dryden, John, 153, 155
    Indian Queen (Purcell), 155
    Secular Masque, 155
Dubrovnik
    Samostan Mala Braca, Glazbeni Arhiv Ms. 45/1261, 236n; Ms. 45/1262, 235n
Dvořák, Antonin, 292

Easter Vigil, 3-32
Eberth, Georg (Jörg), 83
Ebstorf, 51
    Benedictine convent, 51
        reforms, 51n
    Klosterarchiv, Ms. V,3, 51-64
        edition and commentary, 53-54
        Guidonian hand, 54
        physical description, 52
        tonal system, 56
        vocal exercises in, 58-61
Ecce vicit (sequence) 41-44
Eccles, John, 152
Egiziello. *See under* Conti, Gioacchino
Einsiedeln, Stiftsbibliothek, Ms. 366, 35, 38
Einstein, Alfred, 68n
Einstein-Vogel, 69n, 74n, 75-79
Eleanora of Toledo (de' Medici), 62, 67
L'Elfrida (Paisiello), 245
Elijah (Mendelssohn), 264, 271
Elizabeth of Austria (wife of Philip IV of Spain), 114, 123
Ellis, Haverlock, 279-80
Elson, Arthur, 280n
Das Ende des Gerechten (Schicht), 269, 271
Enesco, Eugène, 278
Enlightenment, 187-88, 261, 263, 267
Enno, Sebastian, 141-42, 143n
Die Entführung aus dem Serail (Mozart), 260-61
Epiphaniam Domino (sequence), 41
Epithalamia in honorem . . . D. Nicolai Leopardi, 66n
Erismena (Cavalli), 137

Este, Alfonso d', 73
Este, Alfonso II d', 77, 96
Este, Ercole II d', 73
Este, Maria Beatrice d', 200, 204
Etherege, George, 145
Eupatra (G. Faustini/Ziani), 136
Eurimene (G. Castoreo), 135
Euripides
    Alcestis, 246
    Hecuba, 251
    Orestes, 254
Exultate Deo (alleluia), 46-47

Fabbri, Mario, 66n, 98n, 233n, 234n
Fabbri, Paolo, 246n
False Friend (Vanbrugh), 155
farce, 234, 237-38, 241, 258
Farinelli. *See* Broschi, Carlo
Farquhar, George, 145, 152
Fasch, Carl Friedrich Christian, 266-67
Faust, Ulrich, O.S.B., 51n
Faustina. *See* Bordoni, Faustina
Faustini, Giovanni, 132-36, 138-41
    Eupatra (Ziani), 136
Faustini, Marco, 133-40, 142, 143n
Feldman, Fritz, 64n
Feldman, Martha, 71n, 73, 73n
Felici, Alessandro, 233
Felici, Bartolomeo, xvi
Feliciani, Andrea, 71n, 78
Fellerer, Karl G., 192n
Fenaruolo, Girolamo, 71n
Fenlon, Iain, 76
Ferdinand, Archduke, Governor of Milan, 200, 204, 211
Ferdinand I, King of Bohemia and Hungary, Holy Roman Emperor, 81-82, 84
Ferdinand II, Archduke, Governor of Bohemia, then Holy Roman Emperor, 81, 84, 86-88
Ferdinando III of Habsburg-Lorraine, xx
Ferrara, 68-69, 73, 76-78
    Accademia degli Rinnovati, 69
Ferretti, Giovanni, 71n
Ferretti, Jacopo, 236
    La Polissena (Rutini), 237n
    Pulcinella (Rutini), 237n
Ferro, Giovanni, 71
Festa, Costanzo, 66
festa teatrale, 195, 200, 204, 205
Die Festzeiten (Loewe), 270, 273
Finger, Godfrey, 147, 152
La finta giardiniera (Mozart), 197
La finta scema (De Gamerra/Salieri), 213-24
La finta semplice (Mozart), 195-96
Le finte pazzie o sia la pupilla bizzarra (Rutini), 233-58
fireworks structures, 123-24
Firmian, Count Karl Joseph von, 200-01, 204
Flacconio, Giovanni Pietro, 79
Flaherty, Gloria, 188, 193n

Flöss, Johannes, 61n
Florence, xv-xx, 66-69, 71, 73, 89-91, 93, 95-96, 98, 100-11, 200, 228-30, 233-35, 237n, 239-41, 244-46, 251n, 254, 310
    Accademia degl'Elevati, 90-91
    Accademia degl'Immobili, 159
    Armonici (concert society), 234
    Biblioteca Medicea-Laurenziana, 90, 111
    Cocomero Theater, 159, 180, 234-35, 241, 245
    Compagnia dell'Arcangelo Raffaello, 91
    Compagnia Nazionale, 241
    French occupation of, 235
    Gazzetta di Firenze, 259
    Gazzetta Toscana, 234-35, 240-41, 245, 258
    Gazzetta universale, 234, 240n, 241, 245n
    Intrepidi Theater, 234
    L'Observatrice fiorentina, 234, 240
    Palazzo Guicciardini, 159
    Palazzo Pitti, 98, 106
    Pergola Theater, 159-60, 199n, 251, 254n, 259
    Porta Rossa Theater, 234
    production of Mozart, *Die Zauberflöte* in 1818, 259-61
    S. Maria del Fiore Cathedral, 95
    San Lorenzo Church, 98
    Teatro di S. Maria, 234, 245, 259-60
    Teatro Nuovo, 259
Florentine comic opera. *See under* Tuscan composers/repertory
Forever Yesterday (Wolking), 291-305
Formellis, Wilhelm, 86
Le fortune di Rodope e Damira (Aureli/Ziani), 137
France, xx, 220, 227-28, 235, 241, 260, 263, 266, 269
French Revolution, 266
Francesco I of Lorraine, xx
La frascatana (Paisiello), 213, 215, 222
Frascati, 72, 79, 119, 129
    Villa Aldobrandini, 129
    Villa Belvedere, 119
Frederick the Great, King, 192-93
Friedrich Wilhelm III, King of Prussia, 266-67
Fruchtman, Caroline, 145-158
Fuller, Sarah, 3n, 31
Funcke, Frau von, 52n
funeral catafalques. *See under* Borghese, Miraballo, Philip V

Gabrieli, Andrea, 68, 68n, 71n, 74
Gabrieli, Giovanni, 68, 69n, 70, 74
Gagliano, Giovanni Battista da, 98
Gagliano, Marco da, 89-111
    and S. Maria del Fiori, 95
    and Ferdinando Gonzaga, 95-98
    La Dafne, 91-92, 104
    Madrigali a cinque voci, book 5, 93
    Il Medoro, 98-100
    Musica a una, dua, e tre voci, 93
Galanti, Giovanni Battista, 72n, 78
Galeazzi, Francesco, 210
    Elementi teorico-pratici di musica, 240, 240n, 246, 246n, 250, 253n, 256-57
Galilei, Vincenzo, 67, 67n

Gardano, Angelo, 66-67, 70, 73, 75-79
Garlington, Aubrey, 233n
Gaspari, Gaetano, 68n, 78
Gasparini, Quirino, 205
Gay, John, 158
    Beggar's Opera, 158
George II, Prince Elector, later King of England, 150, 154, 156
Gerbert, Martin, O.S.B., 62n
Germany, oratorio in, 263-76
Gerusalemme liberata (Tasso), 66n
Gervasoni, Carlo, 234
    Nuova teoria di musica, 234-35
Ghisi, Federico, 67n, 68n
Gialdroni, Giuliana, 77
Giambullari, Pierfrancesco, 67
Gianturco, Carolyn, 113-29, 113n
Giasone (Cavalli), 135
Giazotto, Remo, 69n
Gideon (Schneider), 271
Gieburowski, Waclav, 52n, 61n, 62n; 63n, 64n
Giermann, Renate, 52, 52n
Gigli da Imola, Giulio, 72n, 78
Gioja, Gaetano
    Nina, 246
Giovanelli, Ruggiero, 79
Giovanini, Pietro
    La vendetta di Nino ossia la morte di Semiramis (set by Prati and Nasolini), 228, 246, 248
Giovanni of Austria, 67
Gisberti, Domencio, 139
    La pazzia in trono, 139
Giuliani, Francesco, xvi, 233, 235
Giuliani, Marco, 65, 69n, 74, 76
Gli amori d'Alessandro Magno e di Rossane (Lucio), 135n, 141
Glixon, Beth, 131-144, 133n, 136n, 137n, 138n
Glixon, Jonathan, 131-144, 133n, 136n, 137n, 138n
Glover, Jane, 133n, 137n
Gluck, Christoph Willibald, 212, 228-29
    Alceste, 246
Goethe, Johann Wolfgang von, 264-65, 267-68
Goldoni, Carlo, 196, 215, 220, 257, 258n
Goldschmidt, Hugo, 188-91, 193n, 194n
Goltzig, Achatzius, 88
Gonzaga, Caterina de' Medici, 89, 89n, 100
Gonzaga, Eleanora, 100
Gonzaga, Eleonora de' Medici, 89
Gonzaga, Ferdinando, 89-111
    Adonis, 91, 103
    compositions in *La Dafne*, 91n
    poetry of, 91-92
Gonzaga, Francesco, 89n, 95
Gonzaga, Vincenzo, 89, 95
Gottsched, Johann Christoph, 187, 189-90, 193n
    Critische Dichtkunst, 191n
Granjon, Robert, 73n
Graun, Karl Heinrich, 192
Graupner, Christoph, 190n
Green, Marian, xiii, xvi, xix-xx, 308

Grétry, André
    Mémoires ou essais sur la musique, 240n, 255
Grimaldi, Niccolino (Nicolini), 151, 169
Griscom, Richard, xiii, 233n, 307-10
Grove, or Love's Paradice (D. Purcell), 147n
Guarini, Giovanni Battista, 71
    Il Pastor Fido, 66n
Gümpel, Karl Werner, xv, 51-64, 52n, 61n, 63n
La guerriera spartana (Ziani), 135
Guglielmi, Pietro Alessandro, 209
Guido of Arezzo, 62, 62n
Guidonian hand, 52, 54-55

Haar, James, xiii, xv-xviii, 65-79, 68n
Haberl, F. X., 75n
Haec dies (gradual), 3
Hahn-Woernle, Birgit, 52n
Halifax, Earl of. *See* Montague
Hamburg, 190n, 193
Handel, George Frideric, xvi, 115, 147, 151, 154, 157, 160, 263-66, 269, 276, 281
    Agrippina, 147
    Alexander's Feast, 265
    Athalia, 265
    Belshazzar, 265
    Harmonious Blacksmith, 280
    Israel in Egypt, 265
    Jephtha, 265
    Joshua, 265
    Judas Maccabaeus, 264
    Messiah, 264-65, 269
    Rinaldo, 151, 157
    La Resurrezione, 115
    Samson, 265
    Solomon, 265
    Deutsche Händel-Gesellschaft, 265
Handschin, Jacques, 40n
Hansell, Kathleen, 195-212, 198n, 199n, 209n, 220n
harpsichord, 277-84
Harrán, Don, 74nn
Harriss, Ernest, xiii, xv, xvii, 187-194, 187n, 191n, 193n, 194n, 309
Härtel, Helmar, 52, 52n
Harwood, Gregory, 240n
Hasse, Johann Adolf, 118, 193n, 199n, 204
    Il Ruggiero, 204
    Siroe, 118
Hauptmann, Moritz, 266
Hawksmoor, Nicholas, 147-48, 154, 155, 157-58
Haydn, Franz Joseph, xvi, 217
    Creation, 264-65
    Seasons, 265
Heartz, Daniel, 65n, 246n, 255n
Hecuba (Euripides), 251
Hegel, Friedrich, 266
Die Heilung des Blindgeborenen (Loewe), 276
Heine, Heinrich, 266
Helm, Eugene, 192n, 194n
Herz, Gerhard, xiii, xv, xix, 307

Hieronymus de Moravia, 62, 62n
Hiley, David, 3, 11n, 12, 32
historicism, late 18th-19th centuries, 263, 266, 269, 272, 274
Hitchcock, H. Wiley, 96n
Hoc pium recitat, 23, 28
Høeg, Peter, 49
Hoffmann, E. T. A., 267
Holmes, Augusta, 280
Holmes, William C., 159-185, 159n
Holschneider, Andreas, 40n
Hosler, Bellamy Hamilton, 188, 193n
Howard, Charles, third Earl of Carlisle, 145-48
Howard Castle (Yorkshire), 145-48, 152, 154-58
Huglo, Michel, 64n
Hugo Spechtshart von Reutlingen, 61n, 63n
Humboldt Stiftung, 187
Hume, Robert, 145n, 148n, 150n, 151n
Hunter, Mary, 222n, 245n
Huseboe, Arthur, 145, 146n, 152n
Husmann, Heinrich, 3n, 9n, 10n, 11n, 32, 40n

Iam turma caelica, 22, 23, 27
Idomeneo (Mozart), 195, 197
Indian Queen (Dryden/Purcell), 155-56
Ingegneri, Angelo
    Della poesia rappresentativa & del modo di rappresentare le favole sceniche, 118
Ingegneri, Marc'Antonio, 72n, 79
Innocent XII (pope), 114
instrument building, 93-94, 104
    organ in S. Vitus Cathedral, Prague, 81-88
intermedi
    Medici wedding (1589), 67
intermezzo, 234, 237-38, 255, 258
Israel in Egypt (Handel), 265
L'Italiana in Londra (Cimarosa), 234
Iubilate Deo omnis arva, 20-22, 25

Jacobus Leodiensis (Jacques de Liège), 63, 63n
Jahn, Otto, 266
Jaitner, Klaus, 51n
Jammers, Ewald, 40n
Jephta (Klein), 270
Jephtha (Handel), 265
Johannes der Täufer (Loewe), 276
Johann Huss (Loewe), 271
Jommelli, Nicolò, 209
    Armida abbandonata, 205
Joseph II, Emperor, 213, 222-23, 260
Joshua (Handel), 265
Journey to London (Vanbrugh), 158
Judas Maccabaeus (Handel), 264

Kagan, Rod, 292
Kaufman, Henry W., 66n, 67n
Keck, Michael, 85-86
Keglevich, Count Johann, 213, 215, 223
Kenton, Egon, 69n

Kerman, Joseph, 70n
Khevenhüller, Prince Johann, 213, 222-23
Kiesewetter, Raphael Georg, 268
Kimbolton Castle, Cambridgeshire, 147-48, 152, 156
King Arthur (Purcell), 156
Kirkendale, Ursula, 115n
Kirkendale, Warren, 71n
Kit-Cat Club, 145n, 147-49
Klein, Bernhard
    David, 269
    Jephta, 269
Klopstock, Friedrich Gottlieb, 267
Klughardt, August Friedrich
    Die Zerstörung Jerusalems, 273
Kneller, Godfrey, 148
Koch, Heinrich Christoph
    Lexicon, 269
Die Könige in Israel (Ries), 272
Kohrs, Klaus Heinrich, 4n, 20n, 32
Kodály, Zoltan, 48
Kretzschmar, Hermann, 188, 194n

Ladislaus de Zalka, 52, 61-63
Laete mente (sequence), 42, 46-47
Landi, Antonio, 67
Landmann, Ortrun, 192n
Landowska, Wanda, 277-84
    in Berlin, 277, 280
    in Paris, 278-80, 282
    in U.S., 280-83
    obituary, 283-84
Lasso, Ferdinand, 72
Lasso, Orlando, 68-69, 72, 72n, 74, 79
Lasso, Rudolf, 72
Lee, Douglas A., 193n
Die Legende von der heiligen Elisabeth (Liszt), 264, 274-75
Legrenzi, Giovanni, 160
Leipzig, 188-91, 265
Lesure, François, 75
Leuchtmann, Horst, 68n, 69n, 71n, 75
Levy, Kenneth, 4n, 31
Lewis, Mary, 66n, 67n, 75-76
I lieti amanti (ed. M. Giuliani), 65n, 76
Lincoln, Harry, 72n, 78
Lincoln's Inn Fields Theatre. *See under* London
Lindgren, Lowell, 146n
Lippmann, Friedrich, 240n
Liszt, Franz
    Christus, 264, 272, 274
    Die Legende von der heiligen Elisabeth, 264, 274-75
Loewe, Carl
    Die Auferweckung des Lazarus, 276
    Die Festzeiten, 270, 273
    Die Heilung des Blindgeborenen, 276
    Johannes der Täufer, 276
    Johann Huss, 271
    Palestrina, 271
    Das Sühnopfer des neuen Bundes, 271
    Die Zerstörung von Jerusalem, 271

London, 145-46, 148-49, 151-52, 154-56, 158, 160, 265
    British Library, Ms. Harley 4951, 3, 4n, 5-8, 10, 12
    Drury Lane/Dorset Garden Theater (Theatre Royal in Drury Lane, Covent Garden Theatre), 146, 149-50, 152, 154-57
    Lincoln's Inn Fields Theatre, 146, 149-50, 155-56
    Queen's Theatre in the Haymarket, 145-47, 149n, 150-52, 154-57
    Royal Academy of Music, 151, 154
Loredano, Giovanni Francesco, 138
Lorenzi, Giambattista, 255
Louisville
    Dwight D. Anderson Music Library, University of Louisville, 233n, 235-38, 240
        Ricasoli Collection, xvi, xix-xx, 240, 307-08
        Rutini, *Le finte pazzie o sia la pupilla bizzarra* score, 233-58; motets, 235-36
    Louisville Orchestra, 291, 294
        commissioning project, 291
Love's Last Shift (Cibber), 145, 155
Lucio, Francesco, 134-35
    Gli amori d'Alessandro Magno e di Rossane, 135n, 141
    L'Orontea, 135n
    Pericle effeminato, 135
Lucio Silla (Mozart), 195-212
Lumley Castle, 148, 157
Luython, Carl, 87-88

MacClintock, Carol, 71n
Macerata, 236
madrigal collections, 16th century
    defined by place, 76-77
    for dynastic celebration, 75-76
    for a single occasion or person, 78
    on a poetic conceit, 78-79
    on a single poetic text, 78
    "thematic" anthologies, 65-79
Madrigali a cinque voci, book 5 (Gagliano), 93
Maessenus, Petrus, 81, 86
Maffei, Scipione, 171, 227-28
Majo, Giuseppe de, 118
    Il sogno d'Olimpia (Calzabigi), 118, 127
Malipiero, Ottaviano, 70, 79
Malvezzi, Cristofano, 76
Manara, Francesco, 76
Mancini, Franco, 131n, 144n
Manrique, 69
Mantua, 68-69, 89-111, 91n
    Archivio di Stato, Archivio Gonzaga, 89-111
manuscripts (music)
    Ancona, Biblioteca Comunale Ms. Mus. 83, 235
    Bamberg, Staatsbibliothek Ms. lit. 5, 35, 37
    Chartres, Bibliothèque Municipale, Ms. 47, 12
    Crakow, Biblioteka Jagiellonska, autograph score, Mozart, *Lucio Silla*, 202-03
    Dubrovnik, Samostan Mala Braca, Glazbeni Arhiv Ms. 45/1261, 236n; Ms. 45/1262, 235n
    Einsiedeln, Stiftsbibliothek Ms. 366, 35, 38
    Ebstorf, Klosterarchiv Ms. V,3, 51-64
    London, British Library Ms. Harley 4951, 3

Louisville, Dwight D. Anderson Music Library, University of Louisville, score, Rutini, *Le finte pazzie o sia la pupilla bizzarra*, 233-58, and motets, 235-36
Munich, Bayerische Staatsbibliothek Ms. Clm. 14083, 35-36
Paris, Bibliothèque Nationale Mss. lat. 776, 903, 1084, 1118, 1121, 1138 and 1338, nouv. acq. Lat. 1871, 3n, 4n, 5-8, 10, 10n, 11n, 12, 14-21, 21n, 23, 23n, 30, 32, 35, 40
Rome, Biblioteca Casanatense Ms Mus.1741, 42-47; Ms. Mus. 5902, 235n; Ms. Mus 6079, 236n
St. Gall, Stiftsbibliothek Ms. 484, 35, 39
Turin, Accademia Filarmonica, copy of score, Mozart, *Lucio Silla*, 204
Vienna, Österreichische Nationalbibliothek Ms. Mus. 16608, 216, 225-26; and Ms. Mus.17842, 215n

Manzuoli, Giovanni, 200-01, 204
Marchetti, Baldassare, 213, 215-16
Marefoschi, Countess Girolama Campagnoni, 236
Marenzio, Luca, 66n, 67n, 68, 68n, 70, 70n, 72, 74, 79
Maria Teresa, Empress, 200, 204
Marini, Lino, 71n
Markova, Alicia, 286-88
Marlborough, Duchess of (Sarah Churchill), 146, 148, 157-58
Marlborough, Duke of, 148, 151, 155, 157
Marpurg, 188
Martello, Pier Jacopo, 118
   Della tragedia antica e moderna, 118
Martinengo, Marc'Antonio, 72, 78
Masera, Maria Giovanna, 90n, 101-02
masque, 153-54
Massaino, Tiburtio, 75
Mathias von dem Knesebeck, 51
Il matrimonio segreto (Cimarosa), 243n
Mattheson, Johann, 187-94
   Grosse General-Bass-Schule, 193
   Grundlage einer Ehren-Pforte, 192
   Kleine General-Bass-Schule, 193
   Matthesonii Plus Ultra, 192n
   Mithridat wider den Gift einer welschen Satyre, genannt: La Musica, 192n
   Das neu-eröffnete Orchestre, 190n, 191
   Die neueste Untersuchung der Singspiele, 192n
   Der volkommene Capellmeister, 188-93
Maximilian II, Emperor, 84-87
Mayr, Simon, xvi
McClymonds, Marita, 227-31, 228n, 233n, 246n
McKinnon, James, 3, 9n, 31
Meckseper, Cord, 52n
Medici, Alessandro de', 63
Medici, Catherine de', 69n
Medici, Cosimo I de', 66-68, 75
Medici, Cosimo II de', 90
Medici, Ferdinando de', 68, 76
Medici, Francesco I de', 67
Medici, Gian Gastone de', xx
Medici, Giovanna de', 67
Medici, Leopoldo de', 119-20
Medici, Lorenzino de', 67
Medici, Maria Magdalena de', 90, 98

Medici court, 66-67, 91, 95, 100
Medici villa at Pratolino, 160-61
Il Medoro (Gagliano), 98-100, 103n
Melk
   Benedictine abbey, 52, 52n
     reform, 52, 52n
   manuscript nos. 662, 949, 985, 988, 1094, 1835, 52n
   manuscript nos. 873, 950, 1099, 63-64
Mendelssohn-Bartholody, Felix, 268
   and the Bach revival, 265-66
   Elijah, 264, 271
   St. Paul, 264, 266-67, 273-74
Le Ménéstrel, 278, 280
Mengozzi, Bernardo, 233
Il Merope (Alfieri), 228
Merritt, A. Tillman, 71n
Merulo, Claudio, 79
Messiah (Handel), 264-65, 269
Metastasio, Pietro, 116-17, 187, 196-97, 199, 201, 204-05, 209, 219, 258n, 307
   Angelica e Medoro (Porpora), 117
   Componimento sacro per la festività dell S.S. Natale (Costanzi), 116, 125
   La Dafne (Paisiello), 245
   Didone (Paisiello), 245
Milan, 196, 199-201, 204-05, 210, 212, 241
   La Scala Theater, 209
   Regio Ducal Theater, 195-97, 199, 205
   Teatro Re, 237
Milhous, Judith, 148n, 150n, 151n
Minor, Andrew C., 67n, 75
Minturno, Antonio, 69, 75
Miraballo, Don Antonio, funeral of, 114, 121
Missarum diversorum authorum, 65n
Mistake (Vanbrugh), 156
Mitchell, Bonner, 67n, 75
Mitchell, William, 193n
Mitridate (Mozart), 195-212
Mizler, Lorenz Christoph, 188, 190n, 191-93
   Musikalische Bibliothek, 192n
Modena, Teatro Ducale, 197n
Molino, Antonio (Manoli, Blessi), 78
Montague, Charles, Earl of Halifax, 147-48, 150-51
Montague, Charles, fourth Earl (later Duke) of Manchester, 147-48, 151, 156
Moneta, Giuseppe, xvi, 233, 235
Monte, Cardinal Francesco Maria de, 79
Monte, Philippe de, 68, 70, 74-75, 79, 86, 88
Monteverdi, Claudio, xv, 66n, 74, 89
Morelli, Giovanni, 133n
Morley, Thomas, 70
Morosini, Giulio, 79
Morsolino, Antonio, 72, 78
Mortellari, Michele, 205
Mosel, Ignaz Franz von, 265
Mozart, Leopold, 195-96, 201, 209, 211
Mozart, Wolfgang Amadeus, xvi, 195-212, 219, 222, 239, 255-56, 259-261, 278
   and Masonic circles in Vienna, 260-61

Apollo und Hyacinth, 195-96
arrangements of Handel's *Alexander's Feast* and *Messiah*, 265
Ascanio in Alba, 195-212
Bastien und Bastienne, 196
La Betulia liberata, 196
collaboration with Emanuel Schikaneder, 260-61
Don Giovanni, 259, 261
Die Entführung aus dem Serail, 260-61
La finta giardiniera, 197
La finta semplice, 195-96
Idomeneo, 195, 197
Lucio Silla, 195-212
Mitridate, 195-212
Le nozze di Figaro, 259
Piano Concerto in E♭, K.271, 278, 281
Il re pastore, 197
Die Schuldigkeit des ersten Gebots, 195-96
Il sogno di Scipione, 196-97
Thamos, 197, 260
Zaide, 197
Die Zauberflöte, 234n, 259-61
    Florence production in 1818, 259
    De Gamerra translation of libretto, 259
Munich, 68-69, 72, 78, 195, 197
    Bayerische Staatsbibliothek, Ms. Clm. 14083, 35-36
Murano, Maria Teresa, 131n, 144n
Muratori, Ludovico Antonio
    Della perfetta poesia italiana, 118
Musica de meser Bernardo pisano sopra le canzone del petrarcha, 61
Musica et Scolica enchiriadis, 10n
Musiche a una, dua, e tre voci (Gagliano), 93
mutation (*mutatio*), 56, 61n, 63, 63n, 64, 64n
Mutini, Claudio, 71n

Nagler, Alois, 67n
Naich, Hubert, 74n
Nanino, Giovanni Bernardino, 68, 72, 76, 79
Naples, 114, 117-18, 121-23, 126-28, 210, 244
    Piazza di Casandrino, 114, 114n
    San Carlo Theater, 118, 127-28, 197n, 199n, 209
    San Lorenzo Church, 114, 122
Nasco, Jan, 69n, 74n
Nasolini, Sebastiano, 246
Neri-Bondi, Michele, 233, 235, 238n
Netherlands, 96-97
Nettl, Bruno, 293n
Nettuno (near Rome), 114, 114n
    Pamphili Palace, 114
Neukomm, Sigismund
    Das Gesetz des alten Bundes, 271
neumatic notation, 13
Newcomb, Anthony, 69n
New York, 282-83
    New York Herald, 280
    New York Times, 282-84
Nichelmann, Christoph, 192, 193n
    Die Melodie nach ihrem Wesen sowohl als nach ihren Eigenschaften, 193

Nicoletti, Filippo, 77
Nietzsche, Friedrich, 261
Nina
    ballet by Gioja, 246
    opera by Paisiello and Carpani, 245-46
    play by Marsollier and Delayrac, 245-46
Nonantolan sequences, 33-49
    performance practice issues, 35-41
    Schola Hungarica performances, 41-49
Notker
    Liber ymnorum, 13, 14n, 21
Le nozze di Figaro (Mozart), 259

Oliva, Giovan Paolo, 77
Olivero, Pietro Domenico, 211
Omnes iubilate, 19, 21, 26
opera, 113, 118, 120
    Alfieri and opera seria, 227-31
    at the S. Aponal Theater, Venice, 131-44
    chorus in late 18th century, 238-39, 242n, 243n
    ghost arias in, 209, 220
    in London, 149-51, 154-56
    moral, 113
    mounted by Casimiro degli Albizzi, 159-86
    Mozart's *Die Zauberflöte* in Florence in 1818, 259-61
    Mozart's theatrical works for Milan, 195-212
    opera buffa, 213-26, 233-58
    opera seria, 195, 197-98, 200, 205, 209, 228-31, 244, 250-51, 276
    Rutini's *Le finte pazzie* and other operas, 233-58
    sacred, 113
    Salieri's *La finta scema*, 213-26
Opera of the Nobility, 154
oratorio, 113-16, 118, 120, 195
    chorale in, 267, 277, 273
    chorus in, 265
    in Germany, 263-76
    plainchant in, 274
    sacred, 113-15
Oreste o sia la morte d'Egisto e Clinnestra (Clerici), 254
Orestes (Euripides), 254
Orlandini, Giuseppe, 175, 184
L'Orontea (Lucio), 135n
Orsino, Pietro, 77
Osborne, Peregrine, 147
Osseda, Viceroy Duca d', 117
Ottoboni, Cardinal Pietro, 114, 116
Owens, Jessie Ann, 66, 73

Paer, Ferdinando, xvi
Pagani, Anton-Giuseppe, 234
Pagliardi, Giovanni Maria, 160
Paisiello, Giovanni, xvi, 209n, 244
    Didone (Metastasio), 245
    L'Elfrida (Calzabigi), 245
    La frascatana, 213, 215, 222
    Nina o sia la pazzia per amore (Carpani), 244-45
    Il Pirró re d'Epiro (De Gamerra), 251

Palazzolo, Antonello, 240-41
Palermo, 114
    fireworks structure in, 124
    Royal Palace, 114
Palestrina (Loewe), 271
Palestrina, Giovanni Pierluigi da, 68, 71n, 72, 74-75, 75n, 79, 267-68, 271-72
    revival, 268n
Palestrina, Ridolfo, 72
Pallavicino, Benedetto, 66n, 79
Palmer, Parker, 34
Pampaloni, Caterina, 241n
Pamphili, Prince, 114
Pamphili, Princess Olimpia, 119
Pangamus Carmina, 24, 29
Parini, Giuseppe, 196, 204-05
Paris, 203, 278-82
    Bibliothèque Nationale, Mss. lat. 776, 903, 1084, 118, 1121, 1138 and 1338, nouv. acq. lat.1871, 3n, 4n, 6-8, 10n, 11n, 12, 14-21, 23, 23n, 24, 30
    Ecole Normale de Musique, 280
Parisi, Susan, xiii, xv- xvi, 90n, 95n, 96n, 100n, 233-58, 234n
Paschal Vigil. *See under* Easter
Il Pastor Fido (Guarini), 66n, 71
La pazzia in trono (Gisberti), 139
Il pazzo politico, 135
Pecorina, Polissena, 73
Pellegrini, Giovan Francesco, 115n
Pentecost, 3, 23
Pepoli, Carlo, 231
    Virginia (Alessandri), 231
Pepusch, Johann Christoph, 158
Pergola Theater. *See under* Florence
Pergolesi, Giovanni Battista, xvi
Peri, Jacopo, 89-90, 111
Pericle effeminato (Lucio), 135
Perissone, Cambio, 74
Petrozzi, Fabio, 79
Petrucci, Ottaviano dei, 65
    Fragmenta missarum, 65n
    Missarum diversorum authorum, 65n
    Musica de meser Bernardo pisano sopra le canzone del Petrarcha, 65
Peverara, Laura, 69, 78
Pfanmüller, Friedrich (Phanmüller), 81-84
Pharao (Schneider), 271
Philadelphia
    Philadelphia Orchestra, 281
    Philadelphia Public Ledger, 281
Philip IV, King of Spain, 114
Philip V, King of Spain, 114, 116-17, 122
Philip, Prince (son of King Charles of Sicily), 118
Pietro Leopoldo of Austria, Grand Duke of Tuscany, xx, 213, 229, 234n, 259
Pignatta, Gaspare, 76
Pilgrim (Vanbrugh), 155
Piperno, Franco, 65, 65n, 66, 69n, 72n, 75n, 77
Piramo e Tisbe (Alfieri), 229
Il Pirrò re d'Epiro (De Gamerra, set by Paisiello and Zingarelli), 251

Pirrotta, Nino, 76
Pisa, 91, 98
Planchart, Alejandro, 30, 32, 41
Planetti, Antonio
    Dell'opera in musica, 118
Platoff, John, 216n, 251n
Pleyel, Ignace Joseph, xvi
Pogue, Samuel, 73n
Ponzi, Niccolo, 77
Pope, Alexander, 146
Porpora, Nicola, 117, 177
    Angelica e Medoro (Metastasio), 117
Porta, Costanzo, 68, 79
Povoledo, Elena, 131n, 144n
Powley, E. H., 70n, 78
Pozzo, Domenico, 83
Prague, 81-88
    Hradčanski Archív, 81n-88n
    St. Vitus Cathedral organ building project, 81-88
    Statní Ústřední Archív, 82n, 83n
Pratolino
    Medici theater and villa, 160-61
Prati, Alessio
    La vendetta di Nino ossia la morte di Semiramide (Giovanini), 228, 246
Il prencipe corsaro, 135
Preti, Alfonso, 77
Pretiosa solemnitas, 42, 48
Price, Curtis, 146n, 149n, 152n, 153n, 154n
Provok'd Husband (Cibbey), 154n, 158
Provok'd Wife (Vanbrugh), 155
Pruett, Lilian P., 81-88
Purcell, Daniel, 147, 152, 154
    Cinthia & Endimion, 155
    The Grove, or Love's Paradice, 147n
    The Rival Queens, or the Death of Alexander the Great, 147
Purcell, Henry, 149n, 152
    Bonduca, 155-56
    Indian Queen, 155-56
    King Arthur, 156
    Tempest, 156

Quadrio, Francesco Saverio
    Della storia e della ragione d'ogni poesia, 118
Quantz, Johann Joachim, 188, 192-93
    Versuch, 192-93
Queen's Theatre in the Haymarket. *See under* London

Raaff, Anton, 218
Rainero, Don, 95, 106
Il re pastore (Mozart), 197
Recordati, Aurelio, 96
Il regno di Maria Assunta in cielo (A. Scarlatti), 114
Reichardt, Johann Friedrich, 264-65, 267
Reilly, Edward, 193n
Relapse (Vanbrugh), 155
Renzi, Anna, 136, 137
Restout, Denise, 278n, 280n, 282, 283, 284n

La Resurrezione (Handel), 115
Ricasoli, Cavaliere Priore Pietro Leopoldo, 240n
Ricasoli, Lucrezia, 240n
Ricasoli Collection, University of Louisville, xvi, xix- xx, 240, 307-08
Riccardi, Marquis Francesco, 119n
Riccio, Scipione, 77
Riccomini, Antonio, 233, 235
Rice, John A., 213-26, 213n, 233n
Rich, Christopher, 149-50
Rich, John 154, 156
Ries, Ferdinand
    Die Könige in Israel, 272
Righini, Pietro, 178
Rinaldo (Handel), 151, 157
Rinuccini, Ottavio, 89, 95
Ritter, Gerhard, 193n
Rival Queens (D. Purcell), 147
Robletti, Giovanni Battista, 79
Rome, 69, 71-74, 76-77, 79, 90, 95-96, 113, 115-116, 119, 230
    Alibert Theater, 180
    Apollo Theater, 236
    Argentina Theater, 180, 197n, 236
    Biblioteca Casanatense, Ms. 1741, 43- 47; Ms. Mus. 5902, 235n; Ms. Mus. 6079, 236n
    Biblioteca Nazionale, 121-24, 126, 238n
    Biblioteca Vaticana, 125, 127-29
    Capranica Theater, 180
    Ottoboni Palace, 114, 125
    Piazza di Spagna,116
    Ruspoli Palace, 115
    Santa Lucia dei Ginnasi Church, 113
    Santa Maria dell'Orazione e Morte Archconfraternity, 115
    Valle Theater, 234
Rore, Cipriano, 76
Rosand, Ellen, 133n, 138n
Rose, Billy, 285-89
Rossini, Gioachino, xvi
Rostirolla, Giancarlo, 236n
Rousseau, Jean Jacques, 261
Royal Academy of Music. *See under* London
Rubens, Peter Paul, 89
Rudner, Albrecht, 86-88
Rudner, Joachim, 83-87
Rudolf II, Holy Roman Emperor, 87-88
Il Ruggiero (Hasse), 204
Ruspoli, Francesco Maria, 115
Rutini, Ferdinando, xvi, 233-58
    career, 234-37
    collaboration with Ferretti, 236-37, 237n
    Le finte pazzie o sia la pupilla bizzarra, 233-58
        finales, 254-58
        scenes of pretended insanity, 245-56
    motets, 235
    operas with Somigli, 237-39, 242, 242n-43n

Sachs, Harvey, 284
St. Gall
    Stiftsbibliothek, Ms. 484, 35, 39

St. Paul (Mendelssohn), 264, 266-67, 273-74
St. Petersburg, 160
    Imperial Chapel, 267
Salieri, Antonio
    La finta scema, 213-26
    parody of opera seria, 218-21
    Salieri on performers in *La finta scema*, 222-23
    Salieri's annotations to autograph score, 225-26
    serious scenes, 220-22
Salvadori, Andrea, 100
Salvadori, Giuseppe Gaetano
    Poetica toscana all'uso, 118
    Lo Sposalizio di Medoro ed Angelica, 117
Salzburg, 195-97
    Palace of Archbishop, 196
    University, 196
Samson (Handel), 265
Sanctae crucis celebremus (sequence), 42, 47
Santini (singer), 151, 179
Sanudo, Leonardo, 70, 78
Sarro, Domenico, 117, 179
    Scherno festivo tra le ninfe di partenope, 117, 126
Sartorio, Gasparo, 134-35
Saul (Alfieri), 244
Sborgi, Gaetano, xvi
Scarborough, Lord and Earl of, 148
Scarlatti, Alessandro, 114, 160
    Il regno di Maria Assunta in cielo, 114
Scarlatti, Domenico, 179
Scènes de ballet (Stravinsky), 285-89
Schäfke, Rudolf, 188n, 193n
Scheibe, Johann Adolph, 189-91, 193-94
    Compendium musices, 189, 190n
    Der critische Musikus, 190
Scherer, Jonas, 83-84
Schering, Arnold, 188, 194n
Scherno festivo tra le ninfe di Partenope (Sarro), 117, 126
Schicht, Johann Gottfried
    Das Ende des Gerechten, 269, 271
Schikaneder, Emanuel, 260
Schilling, Gustav, 265
    Geschichte der heutigen oder Modernen Musik, 265
Schlager, Karl-Heinz, 4n, 9n, 10n, 13n, 32
Schneider, Friedrich, 271
    Christus das Kind, 271
    Gideon, 271
    Pharao, 271
    Das Weltgericht, 269-71
Schola Hungarica, 33-49
Schonberg, Harold C., 283-84
Schott, Howard, 277
Schrade, Leo, 67n
Schrattenbach, Archbishop of Salzburg, 197
Schrattenbach, Wolfgang Annibale von, 117
Schuetze, George, 71, 78
Die Schuldigkeit des ersten Gebots (Mozart), 195-96
Schumann, Robert, 266, 268
Schunicke, Elsa, 282

Schuster-Craig, John, xv, 285-89, 310
Scotto, Girolamo, 71, 75-76, 78
Seay, Albert, 63n
Secular Masque (Dryden), 155
Semiramis legend, 246
    parodied in Rutini, *Le finte pazzie*, 246
sequences, 33-50
serenata, 113, 117-18, 196-97
    Angelica e Medoro (Metastasio/Porpora), 117
    Scherno festivo tra le ninfe di Partenope (Sarro), 117, 126
    Il sogno d'Olimpia (Calzabigi/de Majo), 118, 126-27
    Lo sposalizio di Medoro ed Angelica (Salvadori), 117
Senesino. *See* Bernardi, Francesco
Settesoldi, Enzo, 98n
Seven Lively Arts (Rose), 285-89
Siroe (Hasse), 118
Shakespeare, William, 228
Sheerin, Daniel, 22n
Smijers, Albert, 88
Smither, Howard, 115n, 263-76, 263n, 265n, 269n
Smits van Waesberghe, Joseph, 40n, 43, 62n
Soddemann, Fritz, 52n
Il sogno di Scipione (Mozart), 196-97
Il sogno d'Olimpia (Calzabigi/de Majo), 118, 127
Solerti, Angelo, 91n, 98n
solmization, 63-64
Solomon (Handel), 265
Somigli, Domencio, 235, 237-40, 242n
Sonneck, Oscar, 67n
Spohr, Louis/Ludwig
    Die letzten Dinge, 271
Spontone, 79
Lo Sposalizio di Medoro ed Angelica (Salvadori), 117
Stabile, Annibale, 79
stage sets, 125-28
Stäblein, Bruno, 32, 43n
Stans a longe (sequence), 42-43, 45
Starzer, Joseph, 265
Steele, Richard, 149, 152
Steiner, Ruth, 3n, 4n, 32
Stella, Vincenzo, 77
Stokowski, Leopold, 281-82
Stradella, Alessandro, 119
    La Circe (Apolloni), 119-20, 129
Strainchamps, Edmond, 89-111, 90n, 91n, 95n
Stravinsky, Igor, 285-89
    and Maurice Abravanel, 288-89,
    and Billy Rose, 286-89
    Scènes de ballet, 285-89
    Seven Lively Arts, 286-87
    Eric Walter White Archives, 286, 287n
    Paul Sacher Stiftung, Basle, 288n
Striggio, Alessandro, 67-68, 71, 71n, 72n, 76
Strozzi, Giulio, 138
Strozzi, Roberto, 76
Das Sühnopfer des neuen Bundes (Loewe), 271
Summi triumphum, 41-43, 45
Swieten, Baron Gottfried van, 264-65, 268
Swift, Jonathan, 147

Swiney, Owen, 150, 156
Sycamber de Venray, Rutgerus, 52n
Szendrei, Janka, 48-49
Szydlovita, Magister, 52, 61-63, 63n

Talman, William, 147
Tao Teching, 49
Tarchi, Angelo, 230-231
Tasso, Torquato, 71, 78
    Gerusalemme liberata, 66n
Tempest (Purcell), 156
Tertiis, Francesco de, 83
Thamos (Mozart), 197, 260
theaters
    Accademia Filarmonica (Verona), 197n
    Alibert (Rome), 180
    Apollo (Rome), 236
    Argentina (Rome), 180, 197n, 236
    Burgtheater (Vienna), 213
    Capranica (Rome), 180
    Cocomero (Florence), 159, 180, 234-35, 241, 245
    de' Fiorentini (Naples), 180
    de' Tintori (Florence), 234n
    di S. Maria (Florence), 234, 245, 259
    Drury Lane/Dorset Garden/Covent Garden (London), 146, 149-50, 152, 154-57
    Ducale (Modena), 199n
    Grimani (Venice), 180
    Intrepidi (Florence), 234
    Kärntnertortheater (Vienna), 213
    La Fenice (Venice), 131, 231
    La Scala (Milan), 195-97, 199, 205
    Nuovo (Florence), 259
    Pergola (Florence), 159-60, 192n, 251, 254, 259
    Porta Rossa (Florence), 234
    Queen's Theatre in the Haymarket (London), 145-47, 149n, 150-52, 154-57
    Re (Milan), 237
    Regio (Turin), 197n, 205, 210-11
    Regio Ducale (Milan), 195-97, 199, 205
    S. Aponal (Venice), 131-44
    S. Luca (Venice), 141
    San Bartolomeo (Naples), 180
    San Benedetto (Venice), 193n, 197n
    San Carlo (Naples), 118, 127-28, 197n, 199n, 209
    San Cassiano (Venice), 133-35, 138-39, 180
    San Giovanni/Grisostomo (Venice), 181
    San Moisè (Venice), 133-34, 181
    San Samuele (Venice), 181
    Sant'Angelo (Venice), 181
    Sant'Apollinare. *See* S. Aponal
    SS. Apostoli (Venice), 134, 141
    SS. Giovanni e Paolo (Venice), 133-34
    Valle (Rome), 234
thesis, 53, 62
Thibaut, Anton Friedrich Justus
    Über Reinheit der Tonkunst, 268
Thomson, Virgil, 283

Tieck, Ludwig, 268
Tinctoris, Johannes, 63, 63n
Tini, Simone, 77
Die Tochter Jephtas (Clasing), 270
tonal letters, 52, 54, 61, 63
tonal system, 52, 56-57, 62-64
Tonson, Jacob, 149
Toscanella, Orazio, 73n
Tosi, Pier Francesco, 193
Traetta, Tommaso
    Antigone, 230
Trefler, Wolfgang, 52n
Trivulci, Teodoro, 71n, 78
Troiano, Massimo, 68-69, 75
Turin
    Accademia Filharmonica, 197n
        copy of Mozart, *Lucio Silla* score, 204
    Teatro Regio, 197n, 205, 210-11
Tuscan composers/repertory, xv, xviii, 241
    Barbieri, Luifi, 233
    Bianciardi, Vincenzo, 233
    Clerici, Francesco, 233, 254
    Cherubini, Luigi xvi, 233
    Felici, Alessandro, xvi, 233
    Felici, Bartolomeo, xvi
    Giuliani, Francesco, xvi, 233, 235
    Mengozzi, Bernardo, 233
    Moneta, Giuseppe, xvi, 233, 235
    Neri-Bondi, Michele, 233, 235, 238n
    Riccomini, Antonio, 233, 235
    Rutini, Giovanni Marco, xvi, 234
    Rutini, Ferdinando, 233-58
    Sborgi, Gaetano, xvi

Uhde-Stahl, Brigitte, 52n
Urbani, Valentino, 151
Urbano, Pietro
    Astrilla, 135
Ut queant laxis, 54, 63

Vaiano, Geronimo, 71n, 78
Vanbrugh, John, 135-58
    Aesop, 155
    Country Home, 155
    Confederacy, 156
    False Friend, 155
    Journey to London, 158
    Mistake, 156
    Pilgrim, 155
    Provok'd Wife, 155
    Relapse, 155
Vecchi, Orazio, 68, 70, 72
La vendetta di Nino ossia la morte di Semiramide (Giovannini/Prati), 228, 246, 248
    parodied by Rutini, 245-54
Venice, 67, 69-71, 73, 74n, 75-79, 131-44
    Accademia degl'Imperturbabili, 138-39
    Archivio di Stato, 131-44
    Grimani Theater, 180
    La Fenice Theater, 131, 231
    S. Aponal Theater, 131-44
    S. Benedetto Theater, 197n
    S. Cassiano Theater, 133-35, 138-39, 180
    S. Giovanni/Grisostomo, 181
    S. Luca Theater, 141
    S. Moisè Theater, 133-34, 181
    S. Samuele, 181
    SS. Apostoli Theater, 134, 141
    SS. Giovanni e Paolo Theater, 133-34
    Sant'Angelo, 181
    Sant'Apollinare Theater. *See* S. Aponal
Venier, Domencio, 71n
Verdelot, Philippe, 65n
Vergeli, Paulo, 78
Verona, 69, 93
    Accademia Filarmonica, 69, 197n
Verovio, Simone, 73n, 77
Vico, Enea, 73n
Victimae paschali laudes (sequence), 35, 38
Vienna, xv, 81-83, 88, 195-97, 205, 213, 215-16, 220, 222, 228-29, 260-61, 264-65, 267
    Burgtheater, 213, 223
    Kärntnertortheater, 213, 223
    Nationaltheater, 223
    Österreichische Nationalbibliothek, Mus. Ms. 17842, 215n; Mus. Ms. 16608, 216, 225-26
    Tonkünstler-Societät, 197
Vierling, Georg
    Alarich, 276
villas
    Aldobrandini (Frascati), 129
    Archbishop's Palace (Salzburg), 196
    Belvedere (Frascati), 119
    Blenheim Palace (Woodstock), 145-48, 150, 152, 154, 156-58
    Guicciardini Palace (Florence), 159
    Howard Castle (Yorkshire), 145-48, 152, 154-58
    Kimbolton Castle (Cambridgeshire), 147-48, 152, 156
    Lumley Castle, 148, 157
    Medici Villa (Pratolino), 160-61
    Ottoboni Palace (Rome), 114, 125
    Pamphili Palace (Nettuno), 114
    Pitti Palace (Florence), 98, 106
    Prague Castle, 81-82, 86
    Royal Manor (Woodstock), 147-48
    Royal Palace (Palermo), 114
    Ruspoli Palace (Rome), 115
    Vincennes Château, 147n
Vincenti, Giacomo, 70n, 76-79
Viola, Francesco, 73-74, 76
Virginia (Pepoli/Alessandri), 231; (Alfieri), 229, 231
Vivaldi, Antonio, 175, 182
Vlad, Roman, 285
Vogel, Emil, 89-90, 91n, 92, 95, 100-02
Voltaire, 187, 227, 228
vox (solmization syllable), 53-54, 56, 58, 61, 61n, 63, 63n

Wagner, Peter, 3n
Wagner, Richard
  Die deutsche Oper, 270-71
Waldeck, Burian, 82
Waldeck, Ciprian, 82
Walker, D. P., 67n, 76
Walker, Thomas, 133n, 139n
Walsh, Stephen, 285, 289
Weaver, Robert Lamar, xiii, xv-xx, 159, 187, 233, 233n, 234n, 235n, 237, 237n, 238n, 240, 241n, 244n, 245n, 247n, 251n, 254n, 307-10
Weaver, Norma Wright, xiii, xv-xx, 159, 233, 233n, 235n, 237, 237n, 238n, 241n, 244n, 245n, 247n, 251n, 254n, 307, 308
Webb, Geoffrey, 146n, 147n, 148n, 149n, 151n, 157n, 158n
Weinberg, Bernard, 69n
Das Weltgericht (Schneider), 269-71
Wert, Giaches, 66n, 71, 74
White, Eric Walter, 285
  Archives, University of Texas, Austin, 286, 287n
Wichmann, Kurt, 193
Wilhelm of Bavaria, 68
Willaert, Adrian, 73-74
Willheim, Imanuel, 189, 190, 191n, 193
Winckelmann, Johann Joachim, 263-64
Winde, Paul von, 88
Wingell, Richard Joseph, 52n, 63n, 64n
Winterfeld, Carl von, 268
Wiora, Walter, 268n
Wöhlke, Franz, 191n, 192n

Wohlmut, Bonifacius, 84
Wolking, Henry, 291-305
  career, 294-95
  Forever Yesterday, 295-305
  orchestral compositions, 294-95
Woodstock
  Royal Manor, 147-48, 156
Wotquenne, Alfred, 77
Wren, Christopher, 147, 149
wu wei, 34
Wycherley, William, 145, 152

Zaide (Mozart), 197
Zanluca, Hippolito, 76
Zantani, Antonio, 73-74, 79
Die Zauberflöte (Mozart), 259-61
Zelter, Carl Friedrich, 266-67
Zeno, Apostolo, 227, 258n
Die Zerstörung von Jerusalem (Loewe), 271
Ziani, Pietro Andrea, 135-36
  Eupatra (G. Faustini), 136
  Le fortune di Rodope e Damira (Aureli), 137
  La guerriera spartana, 135
Zingarelli, Niccolò Antonio
  Il Pirrò re d'Epiro (De Gamerra), 251
Zinzendorff, Prince, 117n
Zorzi, Zuan Iacomo da, 73-74, 79
Zuccarini, Giovan Battista, 68, 68n, 70-71, 76
Zustinian, Elisabetta, 70

Contributors

Jeanne Marie Belfy is professor of music at Boise State University, where she teaches music history and oboe. Her dissertation, on the commissioning project of the Louisville Orchestra, 1948-58, was directed by Robert Weaver. She is the author of *The Louisville Orchestra New Music Project: An American Experiment in the Patronage of International Contemporary Music. Selected Composers' Letters to the Louisville Orchestra* (Pendragon, 1983) and "Judith and the Louisville Orchestra: The Rest of the Story" (*College Music Symposium*, 1991). She also serves as oboe recordings critic for the *Journal of the International Double Reed Society*.

Calvin M. Bower is professor of music and a Fellow in the Medieval Institute at the University of Notre Dame. His published work centers on the history of music theory during the Middle Ages. He is the author of *Fundamentals of Music Anicius Manlius Severinus Boethius* (Yale University Press, 1989). He recently edited the *Glossa maior* in *Institutionem musicam Boethii*, 4 volumes, with Michael Bernhard (Munich: Bavarian Academy of Sciences, 1993-), and is responsible for English text and definitions in the *Lexicon musicum latinum*. His dissertation, under the direction of Robert Weaver, was a translation of Boethius's *De institutione musica*.

Lance W. Brunner is associate professor of music at the University of Kentucky, and former director of the Commonwealth Fellowship Program for Appalachian community leaders. Winner of the Einstein Prize of the American Medieval Academy, he has done extensive work on medieval sequences. His research has been supported by awards from the National Endowment for the Humanities, German Academic Exchange (DAAD), American Council of Learned Societies, American Philosophical Society, and the Kellogg Foundation. His edition of the Nonantolan sequences was recently published by A-R Editions.

Alice Hudnall Cash completed the doctorate in musicology at the University of Kentucky in cooperation with the University of Louisville in 1990, with a dissertation on Wanda Landowska, supervised by Robert Weaver. A licensed clinical social worker, she is currently an adjunct professor in the Kent School of Social Work, University of Louisville. Her papers on "Toning and Chanting: Accessing the Non-Verbal" and "Toning and Chanting with Dissociative and Depressed Patients" have been presented in workshops at the last two annual meetings of the American Psychiatric Association.

Marcello de Angelis is professor of music history at the Facoltà di Magistero, Florence, Italy. Among other publications, he has authored *La musica del Granduca: Vita musicale e correnti critiche a Firenze, 1800-1855* (1978), *Le carte dell'impresario, Melodramma e costume teatrale nell'Ottocento* (1982), *L'archivio inedito dell'Impresario Alessandro Lanari nella Biblioteca Nazionale Centrale di Firenze, 1815-1870* (1982), *Leopardi e la musica* (1987), *Melodramma, spettacolo, musica nella Firenze dei Lorena, 1750-1800* (1990), and *La Felicità in Etruria. Melodramma, impresari, musica, virtuosi: Lo spettacolo nella Firenze dei Lorena* (Florence, 1990).

Caroline Sites Fruchtman is professor emerita of music at the University of Memphis. Her work on Italian vocal chamber music of the late Baroque, and music in comedies of the English Restoration, has been supported by Fulbright grants for research in Italy, and for lecturing in New Zealand. She was named a Fellow in the Memphis State Center for the Humanities in 1987. Her *Checklist of Vocal Chamber Works by Benedetto Marcello* is published in the series Detroit Studies in Music Bibliography. Also a harpsichordist, she has concertized with viola da gambist Efrim Fruchtman.

Carolyn Gianturco is associate professor of music history at the Università di Pisa, and the current president of the Italian Musicological Society. A founding member of the Associazione Toscana per la Ricerca delle Fonti Musicali, she directs the series Studi Musicali Toscani. Her book *The Life and Work of Alessandro Stradella (1639-1682)* was published by Oxford University Press in 1994. She has also edited Stradella cantatas (Garland and Laaber-Verlag), and produced, with Eleanor McCrickard, a thematic catalogue of Stradella's music (Pendragon, 1991). Among other topics, her essays have dealt with Monteverdi, Handel, the relationship of text and music, and distinguishing Baroque genres.

Beth L. Glixon teaches music history at the University of Kentucky. She has conducted extensive archival research on operas, singers, and musical life in Venice in the seventeenth century, supported by grants from the National Endowment for the Humanities and the Gladys Krieble Delmas Foundation. Her articles have appeared in *Early Music History*, *Journal of Musicology*, *Music & Letters*, and other journals. She is currently completing a book (with Jonathan Glixon) on Marco Faustini and opera production in *seicento* Venice.

Jonathan E. Glixon is associate professor of music at the University of Kentucky. Recipient of grants from the Gladys Krieble Delmas Foundation, National Endowment for the Humanities, and the American Philosophical Society, he is currently working on two books: nearing completion is a monograph on musical activities in Venetian confraternities from the thirteenth through the eighteenth centuries, and in preparation (with Beth L. Glixon) is a book about opera production in Venice in the seventeenth century. The results of his research are also published in the *Journal of the American Musicological Society*, *Journal of Musicology*, *Music & Letters*, and in other English, Italian, and Australian publications.

Marian C. Green is the founding editor of the *Journal of Musicology*. She has taught in recent years at New York University, Indiana University, and the University of Louisville. Wide-ranging in her interests, her research and writing have extended to topics in fifteenth-century studies, Mozart, and American popular music. She is the co-editor, with Robert L. Weaver, of the forthcoming *Patrons, Politics, Music, and Art in Italy 1738-1859: Proceedings of the Inaugural Conference for the Ricasoli Collection*, to be published by Harmonie Park Press.

Richard Griscom was head of the music library at the University of Louisville from 1988 to 1997, and is currently music librarian at the University of Illinois. He served as executive secretary of the Music Library Association from 1992 to 1996, and was appointed editor of *Notes* in 1997. He is the author of *The Recorder: A Guide to Writings About the Instrument* (Garland, 1994), and co-author, with A. Peter Brown, of *The French Music Publisher Guera of Lyon*, in Detroit Studies in Music Bibliography (this publisher, 1987).

Karl-Werner Gümpel came in 1969 from the Albert-Ludwigs-Universität in Freiburg to the University of Louisville, where he taught music history until 1998. His work centers on music theory in the Middle Ages and early Renaissance. An elected member of the Institut d'Estudis Catalans (Musicology, 1979; Liturgy, 1992) and a corresponding member of the Reial Acadèmia Catalana de Belles Arts de Sant Jordi, Barcelona (1984), he was honored in 1998 by the University of Louisville with the title of Distinguished University Professor. His *Manuscripts from the Carolingian Era up to c. 1500 in Portugal and Spain* appears as volume 5 in the series Theory of Music in *RISM* (Henle, 1997).

James Haar is W. R. Kenan Jr. Professor Emeritus of Music at the University of North Carolina. A former fellow at Villa I Tatti, he is the author of *Essays on Italian Poetry and Music in the Renaissance, 1350-1600* (Berkeley, 1986), *The Science and Art of Renaissance Music* (Princeton, 1998), and co-author, with Iain Fenlon, of *The Italian Madrigal in the Early Sixteenth Century: Sources and Interpretation* (Cambridge, 1988). He has published widely on Renaissance music, with special emphasis on the Italian madrigal. Elected to the American Academy of Arts and Sciences, he is a former president of the American Musicological Society and former editor-in-chief of the *Journal of the American Musicological Society*.

Kathleen Kuzmick Hansell is music acquisitions editor at the University of Chicago Press, and managing editor of *The Works of Giuseppe Verdi*. Her work centers on eighteenth- and nineteenth-century Italian opera and ballet. She has prepared critical editions of Mozart's *Lucio Silla* (Bärenreiter, 1986), Rossini's *Zelmira* (Fondazione Rossini, forthcoming), and Verdi's *Stiffelio* (University of Chicago Press/Ricordi, forthcoming). Her chapter "Il ballo teatrale e l'opera italiana" in volume 5 of *Storia dell'opera italiana* (Turin, 1988) will appear in English in the University of Chicago Press edition of the series.

Ernest Harriss II, professor of music at the University of Tennessee, Martin, has been on its faculty since 1969. He has published on Bach, Mattheson, Agricola, Hasse, and Haydn, among other subjects, and has prepared performing editions of Hasse's *Alcide al bivio* and *Piramo e Tisbe* for recent productions by La Stagione Frankfurt, in Frankfurt and Halle, and for a production in 1999 by the London Baroque, in Stockholm. His book *Johann Mattheson's "Der vollkommene Capellmeister": A Revised Translation with Critical Commentary* (Ann Arbor, 1981), had its inception in his dissertation work, which was directed by Robert Weaver.

Gerhard Herz, the first chairman of the American chapter of the Neue Bach-Gesellschaft, is professor emeritus at the University of Louisville, where he has been a member of the faculty since 1938. He has edited Bach cantatas nos. 4 and 140 in the *Norton Critical Scores*, and authored *Johann Sebastian Bach im Zeitalter des Rationalismus und der Frühromantik* (1935; reprint, 1985), *Bach Sources in America* (1984), and *Essays on J. S. Bach* (UMI Research Press, 1985), as well as many articles and essays. Herz is an honorary member of the Neue Bach-Gesellschaft, the American Bach Society, and the Riemenschneider Bach Institute, and recipient of the Albert Schweitzer International Prize for Music.

William C. Holmes (1928-99) was professor of music emeritus at the University of California, Irvine. A principal authority in the field of Italian opera, he authored books on both seventeenth- and eighteenth-century opera: *Opera Observed: Views of a Florentine Impresario in the Early Eighteenth Century* (University of Chicago Press, 1993) and *La Statira by Pietro Ottoboni and Alessandro*

Scarlatti (Pendragon, 1983), and published extensively in the principal journals and Festschriften. Among his editions are Cesti's *Orontea* (Wellesley Cantata Series, 1973), Scarlatti's *La Statira* (Harvard University Press, 1985), and Verdi's *La forza del destino*. He also contributed essays on opera in England and the Americas.

Marita Petzoldt McClymonds is associate professor of music at the University of Viriginia. She authored *Niccolo Jommelli: The Last Years, 1769-1774* (Ann Arbor, 1980), and edited, with Thomas Bauman, *Opera in the Enlightenment* (Cambridge, 1995). Under the auspices of RISM, she received awards from the NEH and Department of Education for an on-line database of the Schatz Libretto Collection, Library of Congress. She served as a consulting editor of *New Grove Opera* and area advisor for *The New Grove Dictionary*. She has published numerous articles on the operas of Mozart, Haydn, and their Italian contemporaries, and presently is completing a monograph on innovation in eighteenth-century Italian opera.

Susan Parisi has taught at Millikin University and the Universities of Nevada, Reno and Louisville, and currently is a Graduate College Scholar at the University of Illinois. Her research in Italian archives has been supported by fellowships from the American Council of Learned Societies, Fulbright, and Martha Baird Rockefeller Foundation. She has published on seventeenth- and eighteenth-century topics, with special emphasis on opera and monody, and the composers Monteverdi and Frescobaldi. She is working on a book on festivities and music in Mantua, 1580-1630.

Lilian P. Pruett is professor of music at North Carolina Central University. She has published articles on music and musical sources at the Habsburg courts in the sixteenth century, and on keyboard music from other periods. A founding member of the Southeastern Historical Keyboard Society, she has served as general editor of *Early Keyboard Journal* since 1991. She edited the *Directory of Music Research Libraries* V: *Czechoslovakia, Hungary, Poland, Yugoslavia* for the *Répertoire International des Sources Musicales* (Bärenreiter, 1985).

John A. Rice has taught at the University of Washington, Colby College, and the University of Houston. He is the author of two books, *W. A. Mozart: La clemenza di Tito* (Cambridge University Press, 1991), and *Antonio Salieri and Viennese Opera* (University of Chicago Press, 1998), and he has written the chapter on Vienna in *The Classical Era: From the 1740s to the End of the 18th Century* in the Music & Society series (Prentice Hall, 1989). His research has focused on many aspects of eighteenth-century music, with particular attention to musical patronage in Florence and Vienna, opera, and keyboard music.

John Schuster-Craig is associate professor and head of the department of music at Clayton College and State University in Morrow, Georgia. His doctoral dissertation, on Canadian composer Clermont Pepin, was completed at the University of Louisville, where he was a student of Robert Weaver. He has been an Andrew W. Mellon Research Fellow at the Harry Ransom Humanities Research Center, University of Texas. His interests have focused on the twentieth century, with recent attention to Michael Tippett. His articles have appeared in *Journal of the American Liszt Society*, *Music Review*, *SONUS*, and *Theoretically Speaking*.

Howard E. Smither is J. G. Hanes Professor Emeritus of the Humanities in Music at the University of North Carolina, and a former president of the American Musicological Society. He has published widely on music in the seventeenth and eighteenth centuries in the principal American and European musicological journals. His book now in press, *Oratorio in the Nineteenth and Twentieth Centuries* (University of North Carolina Press) is the fourth and final volume of his *History of the Oratorio* (1: *The Oratorio in the Baroque Era: Italy, Vienna, Paris*, 1977; 2: *The Oratorio in the Baroque Era: Protestant Germany and England*, 1977; 3: *The Oratorio in the Classical Era*, 1987).

Edmond Strainchamps is professor of music at the State University of New York at Buffalo. A former fellow at Villa I Tatti, he is co-editor, with Maria Rika Maniates, of *Music and Civilization: Essays in Honor of Paul Henry Lang* (Norton, 1984), winner of the Deems Taylor Prize. His recent work, on music in the late Renaissance and early Baroque, with principal attention to Florence and the works of da Gagliano, has appeared in such publications as *Early Music History*, *Essays Presented to Myron P. Gilmore*, *Musical Quarterly*, and *Music Theory and the Exploration of the Past*. He is presently cataloging the music of the seventeenth through nineteenth centuries in the Florence Cathedral.